EMMA

JANE AUSTEN

EMMA

An Annotated Edition

EDITED BY BHARAT TANDON

The Belknap Press of Harvard University Press

Cambridge, Massachusetts

London, England

2012

Printed in the United States of America

Frontispiece: Arthur Rackham, illustration of Olivia Primrose singing "When lovely woman stoops to folly" from Goldsmith's novel *The Vicar of Wakefield* (London: G. Harrap, 1929), opp. p. 166. Courtesy of Houghton Library, Harvard University.

LIBRARY OF CONGRESS CATALOGING-IN-PUBLICATION DATA

Austen, Jane, 1775–1817.
Emma : an annotated edition / Jane Austen ; edited by Bharat Tandon.
p. cm.
Includes bibliographical references.
ISBN 978-0-674-04884-3 (alk. paper)
1. Young women—Fiction. 2. Fathers and daughters—Fiction.
3. Female friendship—Fiction. 4. Mate selection—Fiction.
5. England—Fiction. I. Tandon, Bharat. II. Title.
PR4034.E5 2012b
823′.7—dc23 2012011215

For Tassia, Marley, Elio, Bipin, and Felix

The world of *Emma.*

Contents

Note on the Text

The text of this edition is based on the first edition of *Emma,* published in three volumes by John Murray in December 1815, and dated 1816. Obvious errors have been corrected and are listed at the end of this volume. To do justice to the idiosyncrasies, and the gestural expressiveness, of late eighteenth- and early nineteenth-century punctuation, I have left punctuation unchanged, except in instances where collation of different copies of the first edition has clearly shown the marks to result from mechanical accident rather than from compositorial intention.

In the notes, the old long "S" has been modernized throughout. When works cited are available in accessible modern editions, references are by volume and chapter; otherwise, full publication details and page numbers are provided.

EMMA

Introduction

In the summer of 1816, Mary Wollstonecraft Godwin, Percy Shelley, Lord Byron, Claire Clairmont, and John Polidori spent a night telling one another scary stories at the Villa Diodati in Switzerland—a famous night in Romantic literary history, as it was eventually to result in the publication of *Frankenstein,* by Mary Shelley (as she was by then), in 1818. However, Jane Austen beat them all to it by a year. For *Emma* is one of the most searching treatments in nineteenth-century fiction of "artificial people"—both the simplified creatures that our wishful imaginations so often conjure up in everyday encounters and their stylized literary relatives, fictional characters. Having mastered the narrative techniques that she had been bringing to creative fruition in *Pride and Prejudice* (1813) and *Mansfield Park* (1814), Austen found in *Emma* the ideal style for a story about the world, individuals' interpretations of it, and the perpetual difficulty of distinguishing between them. Navigating with startling fluency between psychological interiority and the social bustle of provincial life, Austen's most technically masterful work manages to be at once an exercise in romantic wish-fulfillment *and* a critical study of romantic wishes, a supremely accomplished early nineteenth-century novel *and* a skeptical exploration of just how much novels can and cannot accomplish.

Following the publication of her first three novels, Austen was by 1815 at least beginning to carve out something of a niche for herself, even if the world at large still knew her only as the anonymous

"Author of 'Sense and Sensibility' and 'Pride and Prejudice'" (as she was billed on the title page of *Mansfield Park*'s first edition). As a result, by the time she had finished *Emma* in the spring of that year, she had decided that she was not being best served by Thomas Egerton, who had published her fiction thus far. The immediate cause of the problem was Egerton's reluctance to publish the second edition of *Mansfield Park:* "Thank you—," she wrote to her niece Fanny Knight on November 30, 1814, "but it is not settled yet whether I *do* hazard a 2d Edition. We are to see Egerton today, when it will probably be determined.—People are more ready to borrow & praise, than to buy—which I cannot wonder at;—but tho' I like praise as well as anybody, I like what Edward calls *Pewter* too." Therefore, by the time her brother Henry had started negotiating with the London publishing house of John Murray, she was clearly not going to be done out of that "Pewter," as witnessed by the letter she wrote to her sister Cassandra on October 17, 1815: "Mr Murray's Letter is come; he is a Rogue of course, but a civil one. He offers £450—but wants to have the Copyright of MP. & S&S included. It will end in my publishing for myself I dare say." Despite Austen's suspicions of Murray as a person, she could hardly have been unaware that to have her new novel appear under the Murray imprimatur would link together the "Author of 'Pride and Prejudice,' &c. &c.," with the publisher of Walter Scott and Lord Byron, and Murray duly published the first edition of *Emma,* after a few annoying delays, just before Christmas.[1]

If we are to go by the reactions Austen collected from her family, friends, and associates, then *Emma* did not appear to be a radical advance on its predecessors; indeed, it may even have seemed a step backward. Fanny Knight liked it "not so well as either P. & P. or M P.—could not bear *Emma* herself"; Austen's mother "thought it more entertaining than M P.—but not so interesting as P. & P."; and Mrs. Digweed of Alton "did not like it so well as the others, in fact if she had not known the Author, could hardly have got through it." On the public stage, however, the association with Murray, and the surprising circumstances of the book's dedication to the prince regent, combined with Austen's own burgeoning reputation to garner *Emma* at least a little more critical notice—notably Scott's own long, un-

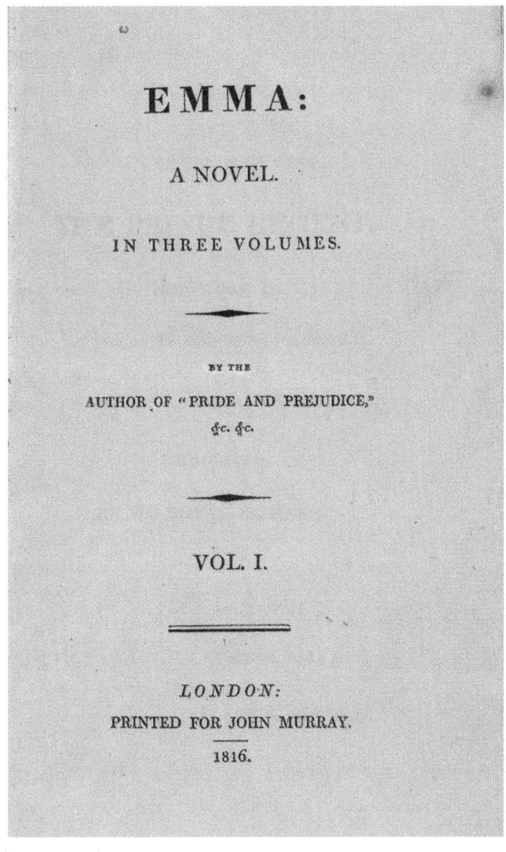
EMMA:

A NOVEL.

IN THREE VOLUMES.

BY THE

AUTHOR OF "PRIDE AND PREJUDICE,"

&c. &c.

VOL. I.

LONDON:

PRINTED FOR JOHN MURRAY.

1816.

Title page of the first edition of *Emma*, published in three volumes by John Murray in December 1815 (although it is dated 1816).

signed review (of which more later).[2] Austen's published work had needed from the beginning to be accountable to public taste, not least owing to the formal constraints and commercial expectations associated with the three-volume, circulating-library novel—conventions about "how a romance narrative goes" to which she adhered, while turning them to her advantage.[3] But *Emma* offers an especially intriguing conjunction—that of an anonymous, private author beginning to become identified as a public figure, someone whose works and style readers might recognize, even if they did not yet know her name.[4] Then again, that conjunction chimes felicitously with the novel's central imaginative questions: how far can an individual mind shape the world outside to its will, and when does one need to accede to, or resist, the force of others' interpretations? These questions are in turn given creative form in Austen's fullest development of that narrative technique for which she is so famous: free indirect style.

Free indirect style (or *style indirect libre*) embeds first-person thoughts within third-person grammar, a commingling of internal and external narrative viewpoints within the same sentence, with the result that there is always some uncertainty in a reader's mind as to whether certain judgments belong to a character's private consciousness or to the external perspective of a narrator. It is a technique that Austen uses only inconsistently in *Sense and Sensibility,* and then mainly in the latter parts of the novel; from *Pride and Prejudice* onward, though, free indirect style becomes an increasingly prevalent mode of telling, perhaps because it suits so well the double-consciousness that all her characters have to cultivate, the knowledge of private lives lived out in public. Take, for example, the sittings for Harriet's portrait in vol. I, chap. 6:

> The sitting began; and Harriet, smiling and blushing, and afraid of not keeping her attitude and countenance, presented a very sweet mixture of youthful expression to the steady eyes of the artist. But there was no doing anything, with Mr. Elton fidgetting behind her and watching every touch. She gave him credit for stationing himself where he might gaze and gaze again without offence; but was really obliged to put an end to it, and request him to place himself elsewhere.

Austen has great fun in this sequence, narrating Emma's acts of viewing largely from Emma's literal and metaphorical "point of view," while reminding a reader that "the eyes of the artist" are not the only eyes at work here, especially since subsequent events reveal that she, not Harriet, is the true object of Elton's desirous gaze. Given the direct emphasis on looking, this is a particularly overt example of the "perspectivism" that free indirect style can perform, but *Emma* abounds in other instances where juxtaposing and analyzing different points of view begin to shift from being a narrative technique to being the very subject of the novel (I discuss further implications of this technique in my notes to vol. I, chap. 3, and vol. I, chap. 8). At the heart of *Emma* is a brilliant interpretative game that Austen's comic style plays in deadly earnest: Austen challenges her readers to weigh the importance that one person might afford to an object or moment against the wholly different value that another might bring to it—and the possibility that they may well *both* be wrong.[5]

Austen's broader concerns with the meaning or meaninglessness of little objects and incidents came in turn to bear on how and why I annotated the text of *Emma*. After all, to provide notes for a novel that has imprinted itself so strongly on the popular consciousness without any such aids could be seen as unnecessary or, even worse, patronizing. Patricia Meyer Spacks has articulated this dilemma well in the introduction to her Harvard edition of *Pride and Prejudice* (2010):

> Fantasies don't demand notes. Why obstruct a novel so accessible as *Pride and Prejudice,* a novel of which readers have taken imaginative possession, with annotation that ties it down? If someone feels free to add zombies to a novel, the book's plot must seem to offer infinite opportunities for expansion. Writers apparently think it easy to elaborate Austen. After all, her novels are light on plot and on obvious kinds of detail . . . Yet few enthusiasts have found sequels or variations satisfactory in comparison with Austen's fiction. What seems simple in the reading turns out less simple in the writing. *Pride and Prejudice* provides, in fact, a lot of detail—just not the kind that we may expect. And that brings us back to notes, which thrive on detail, and which help readers realize how much richness details provide.[6]

This is finely put, and I agree entirely with Spacks's argument, in particular with her sense that a good literary annotation can provide something other than simple information (which may be too little) or interpretative coercion (which would be far too much), instead offering readers information in a way that is sympathetically attuned to the context of the novel itself.

"[A]ll works which describe manners," remarked Samuel Johnson, "require notes in sixty or seventy years"; therefore, following his arithmetic, *Emma* qualifies for annotation nearly three times over.[7] None of this, however, changes the fact that *Emma* does not "require" those notes in quite the same way as, say, Samuel Butler's *Hudibras* (1684) or Alexander Pope's *Dunciad* (1728 and 1743)—both works that oblige a modern reader to make some effort reconstructing a literary-historical context, in order to appreciate the precision with which the poems engage with and reconfigure that context. In contrast, a reader might get a pretty firm grasp on the central plot of *Emma* without necessarily knowing precisely what a barouche-landau or a Pembroke table were. That said, the contrast may not be as simple or as absolute as it first seems: what I discovered in my many readings of the novel over the years, and especially in the numerous rereadings that preceded my preparing this edition, was that while *Emma* still speaks fairly clearly to modern readers, Austen's choice of significant narrative details could often say more and other things to the novel's original readers, in ways that may no longer be so clear—and that was where annotation might be of help. As I reread the novel's fine detail more closely, the historical ambience surrounding Austen's words came to reveal, not some secret text that ran entirely against the grain of what I thought I knew—The Jane Austen Code, as it were—but resonances that only deepened my appreciation of those words, of the care with which Austen's relatively few details were chosen and pitched to be suggestive to readers less distant from them than we now are. The more I discovered of the often extraordinary, subtle ways in which *Emma* engages with its genre and its historical moment, the more I admired what my discoveries were telling me about Austen's talent; I didn't ever wish the genie back in the bottle, and it is my hope that other readers will share that feeling.

In addition, the fact that Austen's details articulate an oblique relationship to their circumstances (through what Irvin Ehrenpreis, in an important and underrated work, called "acts of implication") also offers a different light in which to consider the vexed question of what the novels' apparent silences about the great national and international events of the 1810s actually mean.[8] Tony Tanner's influential analysis of *Pride and Prejudice* provides a summary of the common image of Austen's apparent detachment from the grand stage of historical narrative, noting of the novel: "It is indeed possible to call its relevance to the society of the time into question, for, during a decade in which Napoleon was effectively engaging, if not transforming, Europe, Jane Austen wrote a novel in which the most important events are the fact that a man changes his manners and a young lady changes her mind."[9] Whether taken as a strength or a weakness, then, Austen's perceived distance from the grand historical stage has been an assumption underlying so many critical accounts of her art. Reviewing *Emma* in the *Quarterly Review* in 1816, Walter Scott (the pioneer of the modern notion of "historical fiction") generously noted Austen's own rather different strengths:

> [K]eeping close to common incidents, and to such characters as occupy the ordinary walks of life, she has produced sketches of such spirit and originality, that we never miss the excitation which depends upon a narrative of uncommon events, arising from the consideration of minds, manners, and sentiments, greatly above our own. In this class she stands almost alone; for the scenes of Miss Edgeworth are laid in higher life, varied by more romantic incident, and by her remarkable power of embodying and illustrating national character. But the author of *Emma* confines herself chiefly to the middling classes of society; her most distinguished characters do not rise greatly above well-bred country gentlemen and ladies; and those which are sketched with most

> originality and precision, belong to a class rather below that standard.[10]

Likewise, the American critic W. B. S. Clymer, writing in 1891, noted:,

> The scrutinizing criticism to which Jane Austen has for some time past been subjected omits explicit statement of a fundamental fact, which it yet fully establishes by implication, namely, that she is provincial . . . Balzac and George Eliot and Hawthorne all attempt to let the reader into a larger world of ideas than Jane Austen ever dreamed of. In so far as they succeed, they set astir "that vague hum, that indefinable echo, of the whole multitudinous life of man" which should, it has been said, be felt to pervade a great work of fiction. In so far as Jane Austen is incapable of attempting anything of the kind, she is in one sense provincial. That is her limitation. In the recognition of that limitation lies much of her strength and of her charm.[11]

The idea of Austen as naïve or ignorant about her times was significantly reassessed by critics such as Alistair M. Duckworth and Marilyn Butler in the 1970s; nevertheless, much criticism of the historically *referential* qualities of Austen's writing has not dissented from the fundamental image underpinning Scott's and Clymer's arguments—of her fiction as an art not unlike the British Navy at the very end of *Persuasion,* "more distinguished in its domestic virtues than in its national importance."[12]

And yet, may Austen's writing be, not so much an accidental or strategic avoidance of the historical, as the embodiment of a fundamentally different idea of what history feels like to its participants? The famous joke that Austen made to Cassandra about *Pride and Prejudice* may provide another way of approaching her. Writing on February 4, 1813, she joked: "The work is rather too light & bright & sparkling;—it wants shade;—it wants to be stretched out here & there with a long Chapter—of sense if it could be had, if not of solemn specious nonsense—about something unconnected with the story; an Essay on Writing, a critique on Walter Scott, or the history of Buonaparte—or anything that would form a contrast & bring the reader with increased delight to the playfulness & Epigrammatism of the general stile." On one level, Austen's letter satirizes the possible excesses of nit-picking reviewers ("rather too light & bright & sparkling"); on another, however, it homes in unerringly on the idea that a novel might be rendered worthier or weightier by the cosmetic addition of a few obviously "historical" flourishes ("a critique on Walter Scott, or the history of Buonaparte"). In the process, Austen highlights importantly the kinds of category-error that can be imposed on history by those with the benefit of hindsight. Those who know what the historical resonances of a moment turned out to be can then retro-fit their knowledge on to that moment, making it look more historically self-aware than it could possibly have been at the time. Take, for example, those films in which the "greatest hits" of a particular year are used as a form of musical shorthand to fix a viewer's imagination historically—when, in fact, those hits, in their original time, floated around among thousands of more ephemeral songs. And when this logic is applied to historical novels, the endpoint is something like the ghastly, anachronistic bodice-ripper *Eloise and Abelard,* of which Philip Roth gives us a hilarious glimpse in *I Married a Communist:* "How aroused he was, this man whose genius would revamp and revitalize the traditional teaching of Christian theology . . . her gut tightened as she thought, 'I am kissing the greatest writer and thinker of the twelfth century!'"[13]

In contrast, the historical "reticence" of *Emma* is anything but an omission or a tactical avoidance. If we place the novel at least partly back into the time of its original readings, then public history emerges as something other than the elephant in the room—something that the text cannot or will not mention. Rather, it's something that Austen didn't *need* to name directly—precisely because it was something that her readers were living through as a sober, unavoidable fact of daily existence. As a result, a modern reader may need to adjust his or her expectations in order to pick up on the more oblique allusions and in-jokes that so often pepper history before it gets retrospectively tidied up into "History." Even in *Emma,* it is not as if the world beyond Highbury were entirely invisible or inaudible; after all, the Surrey county militia, the slave trade, and the Abolitionist movement all make conspicuous appearances in the narrative, if not directly in the main action of the plot. Below this level of overtness, though, there exists a vast field of implication: clusters of social, cultural, and political resonances that Austen need only glance at in passing in order to set off in her readership. The generational divide between quadrille and whist players; the socioeconomic significance of owning a grand piano or a summer house; the aspirational social mobility that Mr. Cole displays by serving North Wiltshire and Stilton instead of a local Surrey cheese: these are details through which Austen could implicate whole complexes of social interaction, relying on the kind of shared knowledge and assumptions that no modern reader could reconstruct completely without some external recourse. It is here that I tried to take my cue for writing historical annotations; rather than telling readers how to interpret the novel (which would rob them of the whole fun of reading), I wanted only to shed enough light on Austen's details to enable individual readers to make their own informed decisions regarding exactly how the details connect with those contexts that time has rendered less manifest.

To take one notable example—all the more notable since it offers a signal challenge to ideas of *Emma* as being deliberately disengaged from the politics of the 1810s—consider that extraordinary, tart sketch of Mrs. Elton's family background in vol. II, chap. 4: "She brought no name, no blood, no alliance. Miss Hawkins was the youngest of the two daughters of a Bristol—merchant, of course, he must be called; but, as the whole of the profits of his mercantile life appeared so very moderate, it was not unfair to guess the dignity of his line of trade had been very moderate also." As is so often the case in Austen, this sentence, even while it appears to be dealing in statements, radiates any number of questions and uncertainties out into the textual and imaginative space surrounding it. For a start, there are the perennial questions of voice, perspective, and attribution: while this part of the narrative sounds as if it comes from somewhere apart from Emma's consciousness, it could hardly be mistaken for a detached and unbiased account; in which case, is the narrator "channelling" Emma's own distaste for Elton and his romantic presumptions in free indirect style, or does she or he simply have a completely separate set of prejudices about Mrs. Elton that just happen to be as hostile to her as Emma's? Likewise (and this is where a modern reader might find notes of use), Austen's comment "a Bristol—merchant, of course, he must be called" tips a significant wink to its contemporary readers, even if the precise import of that wink can never be settled absolutely. Even considered in isolation, simply to mention the word "Bristol" in polite company at the beginning of the nineteenth century was far from a neutral action. Bringing up this city (historically, one of the focal points of Britain's slave-trading economy) would have called up associations with some of the indignities in which the trading history of the empire was mired, and to which *Mansfield Park* had, also, hardly been blind or deaf. The embarrassment of the thought might well have produced an awkward flinch—which is exactly what Austen's text performs on the page, through the meaningfully silent long dash "—" next to "Bristol." Like Laurence Sterne's *Tristram Shandy* (1759–1767) before it, *Emma* can dangle a tantalizing innuendo before its readers, while decorously disclaiming responsibility for any inferences they may draw from it, trusting that, as Austen joked to Cassandra about *Pride and Prejudice,* "I do not write for such dull Elves/As have not a great deal of Ingenuity themselves." This is all well and good for an audience reading the novel in 1816, but a twenty-first-century reader might, not unreasonably, require a little bit more context from annotations, in order to exercise the "Ingenuity" that *Emma* invites, and so richly rewards.

Austen's fiction depicts a world so bound by ideas of what can and cannot be said, that it lives on gossip and implication, on hints and innuendoes; as I have been exploring here, the true historical life of an imaginative work can also consist as much in its oblique glances and feints as in "a critique on Walter Scott, or the history of Buonaparte." Viewed in this light, a novel such as *Emma* might be a fertile ground for a set of interpretative methods that have been influentially applied to later nineteenth-century fiction over the last decade: methods that come under the loose heading of "thing theory." Taking its lead from the critic Bill Brown, the modern incarnation of thing theory is particularly interested in how objects in the context of lived experience are invested with significance (including significance as parts of stories) over and above the simple fact of their material existence. "We begin to confront the thingness of objects," Brown observes, "when they stop working for us: when the drill breaks, when the car stalls, when the windows get filthy, when their flow within the circuits of production and distribution, consumption and exhibition, has been arrested, however momentarily. The story of objects asserting themselves as things, then, is the story of a changed relation to the human subject and thus the story of how the thing really names less an object than a particular subject-object relation."[14] It is that last phrase of Brown's that has had the greatest bearing on writing about realist fiction, for if "thingness" is not so much about objects in isolation as about a "subject-object relation," then the little objects that furnish and clutter so much nineteenth-century fiction may turn out to be haunted by the larger stories in which they participate.

One conventional line of thought about nineteenth-century fiction is that it accumulates lots of recognizable details from the real world, simply to further a reader's illusion that there's no meaningful difference between that world and the invented world of the novel (what the critic Roland Barthes so famously called the "reality effect").[15] But what if a novelist were to choose his or her details and things so that, even while they were furnishing the realist landscape of the novel, they were also telling, or at least hinting at, the other stories in which they figure—those larger social and political plots that I have been exploring? *Emma* certainly features some notable instances of things or names that bring with them larger stories of exchange and circulation: the references to Bristol, Clifton, and Kingston; Jane Fairfax's mysterious piano; Madeira wine; the horses at the Crown Inn, to name but a few. To this extent, it would lend itself to a retrospective extension of the kind of analysis conducted by Elaine Freedgood in the most accomplished work of thing-theorist novel criticism so far, her 2006 study *The Ideas in Things: Fugitive Meaning in the Victorian Novel:*

> The Victorian novel describes, catalogs, quantifies, and in general showers us with things . . . These things overwhelm us because we have learned to understand them as largely meaningless: the protocols for reading the realist novel have long focused us on subjects and plots; they have implicitly enjoined us *not* to interpret many or most of its objects. . . . What knowledge has remained unexplored and unexamined, safe in the words that have seemed to designate the most inconsequential and uninterpretable of things? . . . [C]ritical cultural archives have been preserved, unsuspected, in the things of realism that have been so little or so lightly read.[16]

Freedgood's analysis of the hidden stories that can blossom from the tiniest things within the frame of narrative sheds a valuable light on the field of cultural hints and implications that kept expanding every time I reread *Emma* for this edition, as does her implicit rejoinder to those who read fiction "little" or "lightly." Nevertheless, Austen's novels, *Emma* in particular, still feel as resistant to some aspects of thing theory as they are receptive to others. This is, in part, down to their specific position in the historical development of British fiction: Austen's social-psychological style sits somewhere between the high sentimentalist tradition of eighteenth-century writers like Samuel Richardson (in which, however detailed the descriptions may be, the true landscapes are those of the human heart and psyche) and the fully fledged, inventorial style more typical of Victorian realism, with the result that her novels establish basic material frames for their plots, without feeling the need to fill every square inch of those frames with physical "props." Moreover, these novels are less assured about the relations between ideas and things than Freedgood's repeated recourse to the preposition "in" would allow for. *Emma* dramatizes ideas in things, behind things, about things—and, perhaps most important, between things, and even detached completely from them. Following many commentators on *Emma,* I noted earlier that this is the novel in which Austen offers her most extended analysis of the parallels and differences between the imaginative agency of novelists, and the less professional acts of imagination that happen beyond the printed page; however, as the novel progresses, it ceases simply to be a witty analogy and becomes a challenging exploration of the will to *make* things and people meaningful, and the ways in which life so often thwarts that will, both inside and outside novels. We might all like lives and stories to work like endless medleys of arias; *Emma* educates its readers in the inevitability, and perhaps the necessity, of recitative.

One of the most touchingly absurd moments in *Emma* comes at the beginning of vol. III, chap. 4, when Harriet Smith solemnly and privately approaches Emma in order to stage a ritual burning of her *"Most precious treasures"* of Mr. Elton: "Within abundance of silver paper was a pretty little Tunbridge-ware box, which Harriet opened: it was well lined with the softest cotton; but, excepting the cotton, Emma saw only a small piece of court plaister." A scrap of sticking plaster and a pencil stub: how economically these two trivial items summarize the scatty artlessness of Harriet's mind; yet, at the same time, how keenly they suggest that even more substantial desires may still depend on investments of deep feeling in random objects and throwaway moments. After all, while Harriet is the character in the novel who is most comically moony about *"precious treasures,"* she is, crucially, far from being the only character to linger nostalgically over tiny things and happenings. In vol. I, chap. 11, Isabella Knightley cites as evidence of Mr. Weston's good nature "his flying Henry's kite for him that very windy day last Easter," and "his particular kindness last September twelvemonth in writing that note at twelve o'clock at night, on purpose to assure me that there was no scarlet fever at Cobham." Similarly, in vol. II, chap. 1, Miss Bates's esteem for Mr. Dixon (whom she has never met) is founded on the report of the day he saved Jane's life at Weymouth, "when they were out in that party on the water, and she, by the sudden whirling round of something or other among the sails, would have been dashed into the sea at once, and actually was all but gone, if he had not, with the greatest presence of mind, caught hold of her habit." Most surprisingly of all, though, the character in *Emma* who might initially be taken as Harriet's polar opposite, steadfast where she is flighty, turns out not to be immune to this impulse either. Knightley himself reveals his own weakness when discussing Emma's friendship with Harriet in vol. I, chap. 5:

> Emma has been meaning to read more ever since she was twelve years old. I have seen a great many lists of her drawing up at various times of books that she meant to read regularly through—and very good lists they were—very well chosen, and very neatly arranged—sometimes alphabetically, and sometimes by some other rule. The list she drew up when only fourteen—I remember thinking it did her judgment so much credit, that I preserved it some time; and I dare say she may have made out a very good list now. But I have done with expecting any course of steady reading from Emma.

He begins this complaint with an affectionate swipe at Emma's reading habits, and ends it with one ("But I have done with expecting any course of steady reading"); in between, though, he has given away more about his affection for Emma, and its nature, than he would care to admit. "The list she drew up," the one that he "preserved": what is this, if not just a more intellectually refined version of Harriet Smith and her *"Most precious treasures"?*

The truth, from which Austen draws much serious and comic energy, is that Harriet's emotional excess is not a complete aberration from the normal practice of the Highbury world, but the far end of a scale that seems to encompass most of the novel's inhabitants. On many occasions in *Emma,* characters, of whatever moral stamp, find themselves articulating their esteem, affection, or desire for others in terms of sentimental "souvenirs"—objects or recalled events that may be trivial or ephemeral in themselves, but that have become so freighted with emotional significance that they can stand for whole histories, or complexes of feeling. Harriet has only taken this to a ridiculous extreme, by turning the court plaster and pencil into something approaching the relics of a saint. One of the moments that marks out Amy Heckerling's hilarious movie *Clueless* (1995) as, to my mind, the best *Emma* adaptation to date, is the equivalent scene, in which the Harriet character Tai unburdens herself, with as much solemnity as in Austen's original, of her "relics" of Elton: a towel and a cassette tape of Coolio's "Rollin' with my Homies." Heckerling's choice of items recognizes at once the sheer disposability of pop-consumer items, and the fact that those items can seem like the most important things in the world when transfigured by teenage affection. Austen's time may not yet have witnessed the full rise of commodity culture (although the cachet afforded to Stilton cheese and Broadwood pianos implies that such a day is not far off); nevertheless, *Emma* is creatively alert to how desire, whether material or sexual, can profoundly change the practical functions of the most contingent things.

Indeed, desire is, at root, the fulcrum around which *Emma*'s treatment of wanting, things, and wanting things revolve. To come down to basics: despite what the protocols of modern dating might want to tell us, what people most value in others can rarely be encompassed in tick-boxes and balance sheets. Rather, the particularities of desire find their natural home among the contingent particularities of the world. Only a certain kind of person would reel off their beloved's qualities as an abstract list of virtues; in practice, people are more likely to cite the curve of a neck, the specific angle at which someone holds a glass, or a "charming" laugh that everyone else seems to find infuriating. (For this reason, one could make a case for Dickens as a more profound psychological realist than George Eliot.) Social fiction, with its distinctive scales of attention and depth of focus, is especially well equipped to notice such quirks, even while it makes them part of a larger and more deliberately shaped plot. *Emma,* though, illustrates pointedly that this can only be part of the truth about love; it is one thing to apprehend others' personalities in a convenient form of emotional shorthand, another thing altogether to behave as if that were all there was to them—which is exactly what Emma Woodhouse spends so much of the novel's first two volumes doing.

Time and again, Emma acts toward other characters in a way that reduces them to edited highlights of themselves, turning them into distorted, artificial people just as surely (if less horrifically) as any galvanic experiment in *Frankenstein.* Harriet, of course, is the most obvious recipient of Emma's simplifying attentions, an attitude that Austen's narrative skewers wonderfully by the mere addition of an indefinite article: "a Harriet Smith, therefore, one whom she could summon at any time to a walk, would be a valuable addition to her privileges." Emma's ability to think of "a Harriet Smith," as one might think of a new bonnet or a pug dog, shrinks her protégée into an interchangeable accessory rather than a human being, let alone a friend. If, then, Emma acts like a surrogate novelist, she's acting like a surrogate *bad* novelist, one content to sculpt characters out of formulaic traits and set them doing the same thing over and over again. Austen's narrative, though, has other ideas; even as Emma tries to reduce other people to easily legible ciphers, the novel works in the opposite direction, opening out the murky three-dimensionality of human character, and reminding us that there are limits to any reading, of a character or of a novel. The narrator's famous aphorism in vol. III, chap. 13, could thus stand as an epigraph for the whole novel: "Seldom, very seldom, does complete truth belong to any human disclosure; seldom can it happen that something is not a little disguised, or a little mistaken." One means by which Austen repeatedly reinforces this thought is by having characters reveal themselves, however subtly, as more or other than Emma (and, by association, a reader who often has no choice but to see through her eyes) conceives them to be. Much of the charm of the bait-and-switch trickery of vol. I, for example, springs from a reader's growing suspicions about the real object of Elton's affections, despite all the insistence to the contrary being filtered through Emma's willful consciousness. Similarly, the whole of Emma's married future almost goes down the drain, along with the novel's romance plot, owing to her persistent problems in divining exactly whom Harriet is after at any particular point, with the result that she ends up unwittingly encouraging her friend to think herself worthy of Knightley.

As the novel goes on, a reader is made ever more aware of the imaginative gymnastics that Austen's free indirect style is asking him or her to perform: the feat of seeing much of the plot through Emma's eyes, while trying at the same time to "see around" the limits of her perspective. From the tiniest detail to the largest subplot, we must attempt not to miss what Emma is missing, or at least misinterpreting. Take Miss Bates, for instance: is she not one character so worn down into her own mannerisms that Emma might safely take her for granted? Perhaps, but Austen stages one tiny, shocking moment on Box Hill in vol. III, chap. 7, in which Miss Bates flickers, for a split second, into three dimensions:

> "Oh! very well," exclaimed Miss Bates, "then I need not be uneasy. 'Three things very dull indeed.' That will just do for me, you know. I shall be sure to say three dull things as soon as ever I open my mouth, shan't I?—(looking round with the most good-humoured dependence on every body's assent)—Do not you all think I shall?"

Austen's parenthetical stage-direction suggests uncomfortably that Miss Bates is at least partly aware of the ridiculous figure she cuts, even if she is unable to do anything about it; this cannot help casting a different light on all her other appearances in the novel, even at the precise moment when Emma herself is being most insensitive to her.

Emma's third volume also features the novel's largest revelation: the fact that there has been a whole romance plot (indeed, a plot that a lesser writer would have placed at the very center of the novel) going on offstage, with Knightley the only character even to have suspected anything afoot between Jane and Frank Churchill. Here, too, the breaking of Jane and Frank's enforced silence obliges Emma, and her readers, to reassess their "readings" of character in the light of this new information, Emma admitting, as Jane's repressed back story and personality finally unfold, that her supposed Highbury rival might have made her a much better friend than Harriet Smith.

Emma, then, plays off different ways of reading personality against one another, exploring their relative strengths and weaknesses: if it might be right, in the moment, to see someone as a set of *"Most precious treasures,"* to do so over time might risk simplifying them damagingly, turning them into the distorted creatures of our imagination. Then again, nor is *Emma* a cautionary, didactic novel about the perils of the imagination, after the fashion of eighteenth-century tales like Charlotte Lennox's novel *The Female Quixote* (1752); over the course of the book, Emma Woodhouse learns, not to tame her imagination, but to come to a mature and imaginative understanding that other people's characters, viewed over time, are unpredictable and promiscuous minglings of light and shade, familiarity and mystery, aria and recitative. And, naturally, only someone with Emma's active imagination could come to that understanding in the first place.

Human character is not the only thing that needs to be understood as it unfolds over time; the same is true of fictional plots. Indeed, one of *Emma*'s most radical creative achievements lies in Austen's suggestion that there may be some important parallels between the general wish to make others' personalities hang together and the specialized expectations readers bring to their reading of stories: in both cases, the desire to create chains of "highlights" is measured up against the potential costs of doing so.

As a precociously brilliant teenage writer, Austen discovered herself as a novelist by showing up virtually every convention of late eighteenth-century fiction as potentially worn-out or ludicrous. Reading through the three slim volumes of Austen's juvenilia (surely one of the most valuable documents of a literary apprenticeship we possess), it is hard to ignore how often the nature of fictional plotting itself becomes the object of her unillusioned comic gaze. A recurring technique in the juvenilia is that of stuffing as much plot-business into as short a space as possible, as in "Edgar and Emma" ("Mr Willmot was the representative of a very ancient Family & possessed besides his paternal Estate, a considerable share in a Lead mine & a ticket in the Lottery"), or "The Beautifull Cassandra" ("She then proceeded to a Pastry-cooks where she devoured six ices, refused to pay for them, knocked down the Pastry Cook & walked away"). Compare these early skits with the "Plan of a Novel, according to hints from various quarters" that Austen composed after *Emma,* and it is clear that the possible absurdity of plotting remained a consistent spur to Austen's comedy throughout her career, even if it took a variety of forms:

> Heroine inconsolable for some time—but afterwards crawls back towards her former Country—having at least 20 narrow escapes of falling into the hands of Anti-hero—& at last in the very nick of time, turning a corner to avoid him, runs into the arms of the Hero himself, who having just shaken off the scruples which fetter'd him before, was at the very moment setting off in pursuit of her.—The Tenderest & completest Eclaircissment takes place, & they are happily united.

To hark back to my earlier analogy, Austen's parodies delight in presenting stories that are so relentlessly filled with arias that they might well leave a reader yearning for the breathing space of recitative—typifying the ambivalent attitude that runs throughout Austen's work, even if it rarely appears so blatantly in the mature novels. Plots have many strengths: they are the "hooks" that draw readers into novels and keep them going, the psychological motors of narrative desire; over and above this, they can provide the pleasure of an artistic shape that is rarely if ever perceptible in lived experience, even when a novel itself is cleaving faithfully to the knotty details of everyday life. By the same token, a plot that is too rigid or too obviously visible risks alienating its readers through what John Keats famously complained about as "palpable design."[17] Austen's style tries different ways of navigating between these extremes, reproducing any number of recognized conventions (such as the timing of the three-volume novel, and the marriage plot that would make a novel marketable in an early nineteenth-century circulating library), even as it picks away at the limits of any story's ability to order the messiness of existence.

If Austen's chosen method in the juvenilia was to crowd narrative events too closely together, her two great novels of the mid-1810s, *Mansfield Park* and *Emma,* explore what can be done by experimenting with the space between them. This is in part down to these novels' histories of composition; as is well known, Austen reworked *Sense and Sensibility* and *Pride and Prejudice* from lost prototypes, the first of which was almost certainly originally written in epistolary form. Moreover, they owe more than the later works do to the stage comedies of Richard Brinsley Sheridan (and, more distantly, to Shakespearean comedies like *Much Ado about Nothing*); thus, they draw on two forms that depend for much of their effect on scenes and tableaux. *Mansfield Park* is the first full-length, three-volume story that Austen conceived from the beginning as a third-person narrative; as such, it is much more steeped in notions of the unfolding, linear, chronological plot—with which it proceeds to play fast and loose. One aspect of this novel that sometimes mystifies readers is its seeming aversion to conventional ideas of "eventfulness": the plot of romance, setbacks, and eventual union is all there, but it hardly seems uppermost in the narrator's priorities. Rather, we are presented with anticipated events that either don't arrive or are barely narrated when they do, with far more space afforded in the text to all the bits in between (and while there have been many notable critical works on beginnings and endings, the world still awaits a major study of bits-in-between).[18] Viewed next to this experimental masterpiece of comic frustration, *Emma* might feel more reassuringly steady: the reliance of the novel's "free indirect" style on Emma's point of view immediately makes a reader more psychologically intimate with the heroine than he or she ever is with Fanny Price in *Mansfield Park,* and the various romance plots are much closer to the center of the story.

Even so, *Emma* is clearly a romance that has learned a lot from the example of *Mansfield Park,* as witnessed by its own delays (the first, much deferred arrival of Frank Churchill in Highbury, the ball at the Crown) and speculative predictions (the visit of the Sucklings and their barouche-landau, and Emma's failed attempts at matchmaking). So much in this novel is, like *Pride and Prejudice* before it, "light & bright & sparkling"; yet *Emma,* unlike the earlier work, invites its characters and readers to recognize how profoundly such elements are implicated in and surrounded by a world that is anything but.

In her excellent commentary on the "Hard Romance" of *Emma,* Barbara Everett pinpoints what this counterweight might imply for the novel's heroine, and for us; "Miss Bates," she notes, "reflects back to Emma something in her own life which she is coming to understand, and be horrified by: an inescapable mundanity, as of the experience of endlessly swimming through gruel."[19] Gruel is an especially fine analogy to bring to this novel; for one thing, as the favorite treat of both Mr. Woodhouse and his elder daughter, this thin concoction of oatmeal and water (with, perhaps, a little butter for luxury) prompts some of the most transcendentally banal conversation in the whole of Austen's fiction: "The gruel came and supplied a great deal to be said—much praise and many comments—undoubting decision of its wholesomeness for every constitution, and pretty severe Philippics upon the many houses where it was never met with tolerable;—but, unfortunately, among the failures which the daughter had to instance, the most recent, and therefore most prominent, was in her own cook at South End, a young woman hired for the time, who never had been able to understand what she meant by a basin of nice smooth gruel, thin, but not too thin." Even more daringly, though, there are times when navigating through the plot of *Emma,* with the unpredictable relations between its memorable events and its *longueurs,* can feel uncomfortably like swimming through gruel, too—after all, one never knows exactly when another morsel of proper narrative substance is going to emerge from the quotidian gloop that is so often the stuff of life in Highbury. One of the most fascinating qualities of *Emma* is its rereadability: the impression it can give that all its elements have somehow reconstellated themselves into a subtly new work on every reading; but it may be that this supreme achievement depends on the presence of the novel's recitatives, the in-between spaces that shed fresh light on the central set-pieces whenever we begin *Emma* again. For Emma Woodhouse and for us, they are the necessary cost of fulfilled romance.

Indeed, an aspect of Emma's story that emerges more clearly with every reading is how close it comes to happening very differently, or not happening at all; even once she and Knightley are betrothed, there seems to be no way forward for them during Mr. Woodhouse's lifetime, until they are rescued by one of the most unlikely *dei ex machina* in English fiction. If it were not for those turkey thieves and their felicitous timing, then Emma and Knightley would presumably have had to remain half-fulfilled indefinitely, looking on as Harriet and Robert Martin enjoyed married life, and hearing reports, via Miss Bates, of Jane and Frank's wedded bliss up in Yorkshire. As it turns out, *Emma* follows *Mansfield Park* in presenting a plot much concerned with matters of moral desert, only to make its ending crucially dependent on matters of sheer contingency. Austen furthers this effect by surrounding Emma with characters and situations that can be read as alternative or counterfactual versions of her own, as if to emphasize the precariousness of her happy position. Mr. Woodhouse, for example, embodies one aspect of his daughter's personality—her habit of imposing her own standards on everyone else—taken to a pathological extreme. More disturbingly, there are Jane Fairfax and Miss Bates. Jane is an exact contemporary of Emma's, beautiful and intelligent, and conspicuously more talented in her musical accomplishments—yet she is the one who, for so much of the novel, seems inexorably destined to a future of sexless wage-slavery as a governess ("When I am quite determined as to the time, I am not at all afraid of being long unemployed. There are places in town, offices, where inquiry would soon produce something—Offices for the sale—not quite of human flesh—but of human intellect"). And as regards Jane's aunt, Harriet naïvely stumbles upon an awkward possibility when she protests at her mentor's determination to remain unmarried:

> "But then, to be an old maid at last, like Miss Bates!"
>
> "That is as formidable an image as you could present, Harriet; and if I thought I should ever be like Miss Bates! so silly—so satisfied—so smiling—so prosing—so undistinguishing and unfastidious—and so apt to tell every thing relative to every body about me, I would marry to-morrow. But between *us,* I am convinced there never can be any likeness, except in being unmarried."
>
> "But still, you will be an old maid! and that's so dreadful!"

Only one kind of good luck—money—stands between Emma on the one hand and Miss Bates's present and Jane's possible future on the other, just as Emma and Knightley's romance is eventually saved by another kind of good luck: the benevolent agency of the novelist herself.

So it is that fictional plots prove just as recalcitrant in *Emma* as human characters, as neither plots nor characters will simply sit still and do what we want them to do—Austen's genius in *Emma* is to reward her readers for this recognition by (eventually) giving them what they were probably wishing for all along, pairing off Emma with Knightley, Jane with Frank, and Harriet with Robert Martin. But the precariousness of this achievement is all the more visible to the reader of a novel. In lived experience, every moment in time has its alternative possibilities; yet however momentous the consequences of any choice, all the alternatives disappear irreversibly into the ether as soon as that choice is made. Books, by contrast, preserve events in words that can be read and reread, with the result that everything that happens in a novel is surrounded by a more palpable cloud of counterfactual possibilities, of all the things that might have happened but didn't.

After all the trials and mistakes, Austen concludes her novel just at the point where Emma and Knightley's married life begins ("the perfect happiness of the union"), lending it a marvelous impunity—since we will never be able to know how things turned out in the long run, thus protecting the heroine and hero forever from the attritions of time. This novel, which, as I have discussed, glancingly and allusively includes so many of the pressures and anxieties of its time, has the audacity to end with something that could, quite literally, "only happen in a novel"; then again, it could only end in the way it does by existing in the light of those real anxieties that it precariously shuts out. At the end of Thomas Hardy's novel *The Mayor of Casterbridge* (1886), the narrator describes Elizabeth-Jane Farfrae as "she whose youth had seemed to teach that happiness was but the occasional episode in a general drama of pain." *Emma* is a far, far more optimistic work than Hardy's; and yet, what makes it indisputably one of the great nineteenth-century novels is its openness, even as this happiest of romances comes together, to the thought that the victories it finely and rightly celebrates may just be enchanted islands in a sea of gruel.

Notes

1 Kathryn Sutherland provides an in-depth analysis of Austen's commercial relationship with John Murray in her article "Jane Austen's Dealings with John Murray and His Firm," *Review of English Studies.* Advance access published March 31, 2012, doi:10.1093/res/hgs020. Print version forthcoming February 2013.

2 The novel's dedication reads, "To His Royal Highness the Prince Regent, This Work Is, By His Royal Highness's Permission Most Respectfully Dedicated, By His Royal Highness's Dutiful And Obedient Humble Servant, The Author." The back-story of this dedication shows that even a writer in Austen's situation could not wholly avoid the undesired consequences of literary "celebrity." On her visit to London at the end of 1815, during which she finalized the publishing arrangements for *Emma* with John Murray, Austen was invited to Carlton House, the prince regent's London residence, by its librarian, the former navy chaplain James Stanier Clarke. During the visit, she was informed of the regent's admiration for her work, and asked (with the expectation of her ready acceptance) if she might dedicate her new novel to her most illustrious reader. Austen was clearly unsure of the precise weight of the request, writing back to Clarke on November 15: "I Intreat you to have the goodness to inform me how such a Permission is to be understood, & whether it is incumbent on me to shew my sense of the Honour, by inscribing the Work now in the Press, to H. R. H.—I shd be equally concerned to appear either presumptuous or Ungrateful." In his reply the following day, Clarke clarified the terms of the offer: "It is certainly not *incumbent* on you to dedicate your work now in the Press to His Royal Highness: but if you wish to do the Regent that honour either now or at any future period, I am happy to send you that permission which need not require any more trouble or solicitation on your Part." He also offered Austen some comic fodder in his genteelly narcissistic suggestion that she might "delineate in some future Work the Habits of Life and Character and enthusiasm of a Clergyman—who would pass his time between the metropolis & the Country." Having arranged the dedication with Murray, Austen archly deflected Clarke's suggestions in her letter of December 11: "I am quite honoured by your thinking me capable of drawing such a Clergyman as you have the sketch of in your note of Nov: 16. But I assure you I am *not.* The comic part of the Character I might be equal to, but not the Good, the Enthusiastic, the Literary . . . And I think I may boast myself to be, with all possible Vanity, the most unlearned, & uninformed Female who ever dared to be an Authoress" (*Jane Austen's Letters,* ed. Deirdre Le Faye [Oxford: Oxford University Press, 1995], pp. 296, 306).

3 For more on Austen's fiction and the economics of the circulating libraries, see Lee Erickson, *The Economy of Literary Form: English Literature and the Industrialization of Publishing, 1800–1850* (Baltimore: Johns Hopkins University Press, 1996), pp. 125–141.

4 The confirmation of Austen's identity as a novelist appeared only after her death, in Henry Austen's "Biographical Notice," appended to the posthumous first edition of *Northanger Abbey* and *Persuasion* in 1818: "The following pages," he noted, "are the production of a pen which has also contributed in no small degree to the entertainment of the public. And when the public, which has not been insensible to the merits of 'Sense and Sensibility,' 'Pride and Prejudice,' 'Mansfield Park,' and 'Emma,' shall now be informed that the hand which guided that pen is now mouldering in the grave, perhaps a brief account of Jane Austen will be read with a kindlier sentiment than mere curiosity." However, even in her lifetime, Austen's authorship was an open secret among London's literary and social circles, especially after the events that resulted in *Emma*'s dedication to the prince regent. Even to those not in the know, however, the wording of her successive title pages conveyed an image of their author. Egerton's title page for *Sense and Sensibility* allowed Austen the relative anonymity of remaining "A Lady"; however, the title page of *Pride and Prejudice* identified her as "The Author of 'Sense and Sensibility,'" that of *Mansfield Park* as "The Author of 'Sense and Sensibility,' and 'Pride and Prejudice,'" and Murray's title page for *Emma* was comfortable enough with a reader's knowledge of Austen's oeuvre to rest easy with "By the Author of 'Pride and Prejudice,' *&c. &c.*" The downside of this identification was that Austen could be judged by the standard of her other works, as witnessed, for example, by the *Critical Review*'s equivocally positive notice of *Pride and Prejudice* ("The sentiments, which are dispersed over the work, do great credit to the *sense* and *sensibility* of the authoress"). For more examples of Austen's early reviews, see B. C. Southam, ed., *Jane Austen: The Critical Heritage,* 2 vols. (London: Routledge and Kegan Paul, 1968–1987); for more on title pages and other "marginal" parts of books, see E. A. Levenston, *The Stuff of Texts: Physical Aspects of Texts and Their Relation to Literary Meaning* (Albany: State University of New York Press, 1992), and Gérard Genette, *Paratexts: Thresholds of Meaning,* trans. J. E. Lewin (Cambridge: Cambridge University Press, 1997).

5 Excellent discussions of free indirect style include Dorrit Cohn, *Transparent Minds: Narrative Modes for Presenting Consciousness in Fiction* (Princeton: Princeton University Press, 1978); Geoffrey N. Leech and Michael H. Short, *Style in Fiction* (London: Longman, 1981); David Lodge, *Consciousness and the Novel: Connected Essays* (London: Secker & Warburg, 2002); and James Wood, "Jane Austen's Heroic Consciousness," in *The Broken Estate: Essays on Literature and Belief* (London: Jonathan Cape, 1999), pp. 17–28.

6 Introduction to *Pride and Prejudice: An Annotated Edition,* ed. Patricia Meyer Spacks (Cambridge, MA: The Belknap Press of Harvard University Press, 2010), p. 7.

7 Quoted in James Boswell, *The Life of Samuel Johnson* [1791], ed. R. W. Chapman (Oxford: Oxford University Press, 1904; rev. ed., 1970), p. 509.

8 Irvin Ehrenpreis, *Acts of Implication: Suggestion and Covert Meaning in the Works of Dryden, Swift, Pope, and Austen* (Berkeley: University of California Press, 1980).

9 Tony Tanner, *Jane Austen* (Cambridge, MA: Harvard University Press, 1986), p. 103.

10 *Quarterly Review,* March 1816, reprinted in B. C. Southam, ed., *Jane Austen: The Critical Heritage,* 2 vols. (London: Routledge & Kegan Paul, 1968–1987), vol. 1, pp. 63–64.

11 *Scribner's Magazine,* February 1891, reprinted in *Jane Austen: The Critical Heritage,* vol. 2, pp. 188–189.

12 See Alistair M. Duckworth, *The Improvement of the Estate* (Baltimore: Johns Hopkins University Press, 1971), and Marilyn Butler, *Jane Austen and the War of Ideas* (Oxford: Clarendon Press, 1975; 2nd ed., 1987). An important recent historical study is William H. Galperin, *The Historical Austen* (Philadelphia: University of Pennsylvania Press, 2003).

13 Philip Roth, *I Married a Communist* (Boston: Houghton Mifflin, 1998; repr. New York: Vintage International, 1998), p. 134.

14 Bill Brown, "Thing Theory," *Critical Inquiry,* 28:1 (Autumn 2001), p. 4.

15 Roland Barthes, "The Reality Effect," in Tzvetan Todorov, ed., *French Literary Theory Today,* trans. R. Carter (Cambridge: Cambridge University Press, 1982), pp. 11–17. Barthes also discusses his ideas on the mendacity of realist fiction in *S/Z,* trans. R. Miller (New York: Farrar, Strauss, and Giroux, 1974; repr. Oxford: Blackwell, 1990).

16 Elaine Freedgood, *The Ideas in Things: Fugitive Meaning in the Victorian Novel* (Chicago: University of Chicago Press, 2006), p. 1.

17 On February 3, 1818, Keats wrote to John Hamilton Reynolds: "We hate poetry that has a palpable design upon us—and if we do not agree, seems to put its hand in its breeches pocket." *The Letters of John Keats,* ed. M. Buxton Forman (Oxford: Oxford University Press, 1931; 4th ed., 1952), p. 95.

18 See, for example, Edward W. Said, *Beginnings: Intention and Method* (New York: Basic Books, 1975; repr. London: Granta Books, 1997); Frank Kermode, *The Sense of an Ending: Studies in the Theory of Fiction* (New York: Oxford University Press, 1967); D. A. Miller, *Narrative and Its Discontents: Problems of Closure in the Traditional Novel* (Princeton: Princeton University Press, 1981).

19 Barbara Everett, "Hard Romance," *London Review of Books,* February 8, 1996, p. 14.

VOLUME I

I

Emma Woodhouse, handsome, clever, and rich, with a comfortable home and happy disposition, seemed to unite some of the best blessings of existence; and had lived nearly twenty-one years in the world with very little to distress or vex her.

She was the youngest of the two daughters of a most affectionate, indulgent father, and had, in consequence of her sister's marriage, been mistress of his house from a very early period. Her mother had died too long ago for her to have more than an indistinct remembrance of her caresses, and her place had been supplied by an excellent woman as governess, who had fallen little short of a mother in affection.[1]

Sixteen years had Miss Taylor been in Mr. Woodhouse's family,[2] less as a governess than a friend, very fond of both daughters, but particularly of Emma. Between *them* it was more the intimacy of sisters. Even before Miss Taylor had ceased to hold the nominal office of governess, the mildness of her temper had hardly allowed her to impose any restraint; and the shadow of authority being now long passed away, they had been living together as friend and friend very mutually attached,[3] and Emma doing just what she liked; highly esteeming Miss Taylor's judgment, but directed chiefly by her own.

The real evils indeed of Emma's situation were the power of having rather too much her own way, and a disposition to think a little too well of herself; these were the disadvantages which threatened alloy[4] to her many enjoyments. The danger, however, was at present

1 Possibly a glance at Miranda's memory of her early life in Act I, Scene 2, of Shakespeare's play *The Tempest:*

> 'tis far off,
> And rather like a dream than an assurance
> That my remembrance warrants.

2 The chronology of Austen's exposition places Miss Taylor/Mrs. Weston at least in her middle thirties. By the standards of Austen's society, marriage at such an age, although not unheard of, might well have been considered unusual. Indeed, there are repeated hints in Austen's novels that twenty-seven is a representative age at which a woman might expect society to consider her no longer marriageable. Charlotte Lucas in *Pride and Prejudice* is twenty-seven when she settles for marriage to Mr. Collins (see vol. I, chap. 4), the pressures of time and economic want lurking behind her decision: "Mr. Collins to be sure was neither sensible nor agreeable . . . But still he would be her husband.—Without thinking highly either of men or of matrimony, marriage had always been her object; it was the only honourable provision for well-educated women of small fortune, and however uncertain of giving happiness, must be their pleasantest preservative from want. This preservative she had now obtained; and at the age of twenty-seven, without having ever been handsome, she felt all the good luck of it" (vol. I, chap. 22). Anne Elliot in *Persuasion* is treated as comparably obsolete by her own family, and as a reader finds out on the first

so unperceived, that they did not by any means rank as misfortunes with her.

Sorrow came—a gentle sorrow—but not at all in the shape of any disagreeable consciousness.—Miss Taylor married. It was Miss Taylor's loss which first brought grief. It was on the wedding-day of this beloved friend that Emma first sat in mournful thought of any continuance. The wedding over and the bride-people[5] gone, her father and herself were left to dine together, with no prospect of a third to cheer a long evening. Her father composed himself to sleep after dinner, as usual, and she had then only to sit and think of what she had lost.

The event had every promise of happiness for her friend. Mr. Weston was a man of unexceptionable character, easy fortune,[6] suitable age and pleasant manners; and there was some satisfaction in considering with what self-denying, generous friendship she had always wished and promoted the match; but it was a black morning's work for her. The want of Miss Taylor would be felt every hour of every day. She recalled her past kindness—the kindness, the affection of sixteen years—how she had taught and how she had played with her from five years old—how she had devoted all her powers to attach[7] and amuse her in health—and how nursed her through the various illnesses of childhood. A large debt of gratitude was owing here; but the intercourse of the last seven years, the equal footing and perfect unreserve which had soon followed Isabella's marriage on their being left to each other, was yet a dearer, tenderer recollection. It had been a friend and companion such as few possessed, intelligent, well-informed, useful, gentle, knowing all the ways of the family, interested in all its concerns, and peculiarly interested in herself, in every pleasure, every scheme of her's;—one to whom she could speak every thought as it arose, and who had such an affection for her as could never find fault.

How was she to bear the change?—It was true that her friend was going only half a mile from them; but Emma was aware that great must be the difference between a Mrs. Weston only half a mile from them, and a Miss Taylor in the house; and with all her advantages, natural and domestic, she was now in great danger of suffering from

page of the novel ("Anne, born August 9, 1787"), she too is twenty-seven by the time the main events of the plot are taking place. Austen's repeated use of twenty-seven in the novels may also be an oblique private reference, since she herself was just about to turn twenty-seven when she briefly accepted, and then rejected, Harris Bigg-Wither's marriage proposal in December 1802.

3 As Knightley points out later, this arrangement is beneficial for friendship but does not make for a particularly successful discharging of a governess's duties.

4 "Abatement, diminution" (Samuel Johnson, *A Dictionary of the English Language* [1755]; hereafter Johnson); "admixture of that which lowers the character or takes from the value" (*Oxford English Dictionary;* hereafter *OED).*

5 The wedding party in general, not just the bride's side of the family. In its original Old English usage, "bride" carried the force of "wedding," and this meaning survives in combinations such as "bride-people," "bride-cake," and "bride-night" (see, for example, Thomas Hardy's poem "The Bride-Night Fire," first published in *Wessex Poems* [1898]).

6 Independent means.

7 To attract her attention and sympathy, to interest her.

8 A habitual invalid. The term, deriving from the Latin *valetudo,* "health," originally denoted nothing more than a person of a sickly or delicate constitution (Johnson, for example, defined it as "weakly; sickly; infirm of health"), but by the end of the eighteenth century, it often also carried resonances of a pathological concern with health and illness, and even of hypochondria. In his essay on Walter Scott from *The Spirit of the Age* (1825), William Hazlitt describes the bracing effect of historical fiction: "Highland manners, characters, scenery, superstitions, Northern dialect and costume, the wars, the religion, and politics of the sixteenth and seventeenth centuries, give a charming and wholesome relief to the fastidious refinement and 'over-laboured lassitude' of modern readers, like the effect of plunging a nervous valetudinarian into a cold-bath" (*The*

intellectual solitude. She dearly loved her father, but he was no companion for her. He could not meet her in conversation, rational or playful.

The evil of the actual disparity in their ages (and Mr. Woodhouse had not married early) was much increased by his constitution and habits; for having been a valetudinarian[8] all his life, without activity of mind or body, he was a much older man in ways than in years; and though everywhere beloved for the friendliness of his heart and his amiable temper,[9] his talents could not have recommended him at any time.

Her sister, though comparatively but little removed by matrimony, being settled in London, only sixteen miles off,[10] was much beyond her daily reach; and many a long October and November evening must be struggled through at Hartfield, before Christmas brought the next visit from Isabella and her husband and their little children to fill the house and give her pleasant society again.

Highbury, the large and populous village almost amounting to a town, to which Hartfield, in spite of its separate lawn and shrubberies[11] and name, did really belong, afforded her no equals. The Woodhouses were first in consequence[12] there. All looked up to them. She had many acquaintance in the place, for her father was universally civil, but not one among them who could be accepted in lieu of Miss Taylor for even half a day. It was a melancholy change; and Emma could not but sigh over it and wish for impossible things, till her father awoke, and made it necessary to be cheerful. His spirits required support. He was a nervous man, easily depressed; fond of every body that he was used to, and hating to part with them; hating change of every kind. Matrimony, as the origin of change, was always disagreeable; and he was by no means yet reconciled to his own daughter's marrying, nor could ever speak of her but with compassion, though it had been entirely a match of affection, when he was now obliged to part with Miss Taylor too; and from his habits of gentle selfishness and of being never able to suppose that other people could feel differently from himself, he was very much disposed to think Miss Taylor had done as sad a thing for herself as for them, and would have been a great deal happier if she had spent all the rest of her life at

Complete Works of William Hazlitt, vol. 11, ed. P. P. Howe [London: J. M. Dent and Sons, 1932], p. 61).

9 The contrast between these two terms would have been stronger to Austen's readers than it might appear today, especially since "heart" and "temper" were both key terms in the moral vocabulary of much eighteenth-century British thought. Johnson, for instance, offers no fewer than twenty literal and metaphorical senses of "heart," including "affection, inclination," "disposition of mind," and "conscience; sense of good or ill." "Temper," by contrast, denoted something more like "habitual disposition," often as witnessed in social interactions.

10 This is the first element in the novel's precise triangulation of Highbury's geographically impossible nonlocation. Although Highbury is deliberately presented as a place that might exist, surrounded by places in Surrey that *do* exist, it is in fact as nonexistent as Prospero's magic island and the coast of Bohemia in the plays of Shakespeare. Austen keeps Highbury on the cusp between realism and romance, at once inviting a reader to map it onto and identify it with the real Surrey, and rendering any precise mapping impossible by providing illogical coordinates—since nowhere could be sixteen miles from London, nine miles from Richmond, *and* seven miles from Box Hill.

11 Ornamental plots of shrubs, which could often serve the purpose of demarcating smaller spaces within a large garden.

12 Social rank.

13 To harness the horses and attach them to a carriage.

Hartfield. Emma smiled and chatted as cheerfully as she could, to keep him from such thoughts; but when tea came, it was impossible for him not to say exactly as he had said at dinner,

"Poor Miss Taylor!—I wish she were here again. What a pity it is that Mr. Weston ever thought of her!"

"I cannot agree with you, papa; you know I cannot. Mr. Weston is such a good-humoured, pleasant, excellent man, that he thoroughly deserves a good wife;—and you would not have had Miss Taylor live with us for ever and bear all my odd humours, when she might have a house of her own?"

"A house of her own!—but where is the advantage of a house of her own? This is three times as large.—And you have never any odd humours, my dear."

"How often we shall be going to see them and they coming to see us!—We shall be always meeting! *We* must begin, we must go and pay our wedding-visit very soon."

"My dear, how am I to get so far? Randalls is such a distance. I could not walk half so far."

"No, papa, nobody thought of your walking. We must go in the carriage to be sure."

"The carriage! But James will not like to put the horses to[13] for such a little way;—and where are the poor horses to be while we are paying our visit?"

"They are to be put into Mr. Weston's stable, papa. You know we have settled all that already. We talked it all over with Mr. Weston last night. And as for James, you may be very sure he will always like going to Randalls, because of his daughter's being housemaid there. I only doubt whether he will ever take us anywhere else. That, was your doing, papa. You got Hannah that good place. Nobody thought of Hannah till you mentioned her—James is so obliged to you!"

"I am very glad I did think of her. It was very lucky, for I would not have had poor James think himself slighted upon any account; and I am sure she will make a very good servant; she is a civil, pretty-spoken girl; I have a great opinion of her. Whenever I see her, she always curtseys and asks me how I do, in a very pretty manner; and when you have had her here to do needlework, I observe she always

A brass-mounted rosewood and marquetry games table, in the manner of Seddon, c. 1820; courtesy of Thomas Colbourn & Sons. As can be seen here, the chessboard opens out to reveal the backgammon table beneath.

turns the lock of the door the right way and never bangs it. I am sure she will be an excellent servant; and it will be a great comfort to poor Miss Taylor to have somebody about her that she is used to see. Whenever James goes over to see his daughter you know, she will be hearing of us. He will be able to tell her how we all are."

Emma spared no exertions to maintain this happier flow of ideas, and hoped, by the help of backgammon,[14] to get her father tolerably through the evening, and be attacked by no regrets but her own. The backgammon-table was placed; but a visitor immediately afterwards walked in and made it unnecessary.

Mr. Knightley, a sensible man about seven or eight-and-thirty, was not only a very old and intimate friend of the family, but particularly connected with it as the elder brother of Isabella's husband. He lived about a mile from Highbury, was a frequent visitor and always welcome, and at this time more welcome than usual, as coming directly from their mutual connections in London. He had returned to a late dinner[15] after some days absence, and now walked up to

14 The board game's history goes back at least 5,000 years in the Middle East and Asia, but it was only in the seventeenth century that it gained popularity in England (the earliest *OED* citation for the word comes from 1645). It is a measure of the respectability that backgammon had accrued by the middle of the eighteenth century that Primrose, in chap. 2 of Oliver Goldsmith's novel *The Vicar of Wakefield* (1766), allows it to be his sole indulgence in gaming: "Walking out, drinking tea, country dances, and forfeits, shortened the rest of the day, without the assistance of cards, as I hated all manner of gaming, except backgammon, at which my old friend and I sometimes took a two-penny hit."

15 The differences between Regency and modern conventions of measuring time and mealtimes mean that some familiar words in Austen's fiction can have slightly unfamiliar denotations. Dinner in Austen's time was the first proper meal taken after breakfast, and the dinner hour varied from about four in the afternoon to around six-thirty in the evening.

Three very different visualizations of Mr. Knightley: Chris Hammond, "He stood up in tall indignation," from *Emma* (London: George Allen, 1898); Paul Rudd as "Josh" in Amy Heckerling's film *Clueless* (1995); and Jeremy Northam in Douglas McGrath's film *Emma* (1996).

Hartfield to say that all were well in Brunswick-square.[16] It was a happy circumstance and animated Mr. Woodhouse for some time. Mr. Knightley had a cheerful manner which always did him good; and his many inquiries after "poor Isabella" and her children were answered most satisfactorily. When this was over, Mr. Woodhouse gratefully observed, "It is very kind of you, Mr. Knightley, to come out at this late hour to call upon us. I am afraid you must have had a shocking walk."

"Not at all, sir. It is a beautiful, moonlight[17] night; and so mild that I must draw back from your great fire."

"But you must have found it very damp and dirty. I wish you may not catch cold."

16 A fashionable square in the Bloomsbury district of London, originally built as part of the grounds of Thomas Coram's Foundling Hospital in 1746–1752. Brunswick Square and Mecklenburgh Square were planned by S. P. Cockerell in 1790, and building work based on his design began in 1792. Even by 1814, Brunswick Square would have offered John and Isabella Knightley the advantage of proximity to the fashionable heart of London, while also being far enough north to preserve some open space, and access to the fresh air that Isabella's hypochondria craves (see her boast, "We are so very airy!" in vol. I, chap. 12).

17 A transferred, adjectival usage of "moonlight" for "moonlit." Shakespeare provides a famous example in

"Dirty, sir! Look at my shoes. Not a speck on them."

"Well! that is quite surprizing, for we have had a vast deal of rain here. It rained dreadfully hard for half an hour, while we were at breakfast. I wanted them to put off the wedding."

"By the bye—I have not wished you joy. Being pretty well aware of what sort of joy you must both be feeling, I have been in no hurry with my congratulations. But I hope it all went off tolerably well. How did you all behave? Who cried most?"

"Ah! poor Miss Taylor! 'tis a sad business."

"Poor Mr. and Miss Woodhouse, if you please; but I cannot possibly say 'poor Miss Taylor.' I have a great regard for you and Emma; but when it comes to the question of dependence or independence![18]—At any rate, it must be better to have only one to please, than two."

"Especially when *one* of those two is such a fanciful,[19] troublesome creature!" said Emma playfully. "That, is what you have in your head, I know—and what you would certainly say if my father were not by."

"I believe it is very true, my dear, indeed," said Mr. Woodhouse with a sigh. "I am afraid I am sometimes very fanciful and troublesome."

"My dearest papa! you do not think I could mean *you,* or suppose Mr. Knightley to mean *you.* What a horrible idea! Oh, no! I meant only myself. Mr. Knightley loves to find fault with me you know—in a joke—it is all a joke. We always say what we like to one another."

Mr. Knightley, in fact, was one of the few people who could see faults in Emma Woodhouse, and the only one who ever told her of them: and though this was not particularly agreeable to Emma herself, she knew it would be so much less so to her father, that she would not have him really suspect such a circumstance as her not being thought perfect by every body.

"Emma knows I never flatter her," said Mr. Knightley; "but I meant no reflection on any body. Miss Taylor has been used to have two persons to please; she will now have but one. The chances are that she must be a gainer."

"Well," said Emma, willing to let it pass—"you want to hear about the wedding, and I shall be happy to tell you, for we all behaved

A Midsummer Night's Dream, II.1, where Titania tells Oberon, "If you will patiently dance in our Round,/ And see our Moone-light reuels, goe with vs."

18 Knightley is not blind to the fact that Miss Taylor, however well Mr. Woodhouse may have been paying her, will now be a lot less "poor" in her new life as Mrs. Weston.

19 Capricious or whimsical.

The Foundling Hospital, London, from David Hughson, *Walks Through London* (London: Sherwood, Neely, and Jones, 1817). The land that was developed into Brunswick Square in the 1790s originally formed part of its grounds.

charmingly. Every body was punctual, every body in their best looks. Not a tear, and hardly a long face to be seen. Oh! no, we all felt that we were going to be only half a mile apart, and were sure of meeting every day."

"Dear Emma bears every thing so well," said her father. "But, Mr. Knightley, she is really very sorry to lose poor Miss Taylor, and I am sure she *will* miss her more than she thinks for."

Emma turned away her head, divided between tears and smiles.

"It is impossible that Emma should not miss such a companion," said Mr. Knightley. "We should not like her so well as we do, sir, if we could suppose it. But she knows how much the marriage is to Miss Taylor's advantage; she knows how very acceptable it must be at Miss Taylor's time of life to be settled in a home of her own, and how important to her to be secure of a comfortable provision, and therefore cannot allow herself to feel so much pain as pleasure. Every friend of Miss Taylor must be glad to have her so happily married."

"And you have forgotten one matter of joy to me," said Emma, "and a very considerable one—that I made the match myself. I made the match, you know, four years ago; and to have it take place, and be proved in the right, when so many people said Mr. Weston would never marry again, may comfort me for any thing."

Mr. Knightley shook his head at her. Her father fondly replied, "Ah! my dear, I wish you would not make matches and foretel things, for whatever you say always comes to pass. Pray do not make any more matches."

"I promise you to make none for myself, papa; but I must, indeed, for other people. It is the greatest amusement in the world! And after such success you know!—Every body said that Mr. Weston would never marry again. Oh dear, no! Mr. Weston, who had been a widower so long, and who seemed so perfectly comfortable without a wife, so constantly occupied either in his business in town or among his friends here, always acceptable wherever he went, always cheerful—Mr. Weston need not spend a single evening in the year alone if he did not like it. Oh, no! Mr. Weston certainly would never marry again. Some people even talked of a promise to his wife on her deathbed, and others of the son and the uncle not letting him. All manner of solemn nonsense was talked on the subject, but I believed none of it. Ever since the day (about four years ago) that Miss Taylor and I met with him in Broadway-lane, when, because it began to mizzle,[20] he darted away with so much gallantry, and borrowed two umbrellas for us from Farmer Mitchell's, I made up my mind on the subject. I planned the match from that hour; and when such success has blessed me in this instance, dear papa, you cannot think that I shall leave off match-making."

"I do not understand what you mean by 'success;'" said Mr. Knightley. "Success supposes endeavour. Your time has been properly and delicately spent, if you have been endeavouring for the last four years to bring about this marriage. A worthy employment for a young lady's mind! But if, which I rather imagine, your making the match, as you call it, means only your planning it, your saying to yourself one idle day, 'I think it would be a very good thing for Miss Taylor if Mr. Weston were to marry her,' and saying it again to yourself every now and then afterwards,—why do you talk of success? where is your merit?—what are you proud of?—you made a lucky guess; and *that* is all that can be said."

"And have you never known the pleasure and triumph of a lucky guess?—I pity you.—I thought you cleverer—for depend upon it, a lucky guess is never merely luck. There is always some talent in it. And as to my poor word 'success,' which you quarrel with, I do not know that I am so entirely without any claim to it. You have drawn two pretty pictures—but I think there may be a third—a something between the do-nothing and the do-all. If I had not promoted Mr. Weston's visits here, and given many little encouragements, and smoothed many little matters, it might not have come to any thing after all. I think you must know Hartfield enough to comprehend that."

"A straight-forward, open-hearted man, like Weston, and a rational unaffected woman, like Miss Taylor, may be safely left to manage their own concerns. You are more likely to have done harm to yourself, than good to them, by interference."

"Emma never thinks of herself, if she can do good to others;" rejoined Mr. Woodhouse, understanding but in part. "But, my dear,

20 To rain lightly or drizzle; compare vol. II, chap. 5, of *Northanger Abbey,* in which Catherine Morland's disappointment at the abbey is conveyed by the fact that "[t]he breeze had not seemed to waft the sighs of the murdered to her; it had wafted nothing worse than a thick mizzling rain." Emma clearly interprets the fact that Mr. Weston was so precipitate in fetching umbrellas at the first sign of rain as a token of his attraction to his future wife. This is also the first instance in the novel of a character's recalling a past event in loving, nostalgic detail (see Introduction).

pray do not make any more matches, they are silly things, and break up one's family circle grievously."

"Only one more, papa; only for Mr. Elton. Poor Mr. Elton! You like Mr. Elton, papa,—I must look about for a wife for him. There is nobody in Highbury who deserves him—and he has been here a whole year, and has fitted up his house so comfortably that it would be a shame to have him single any longer—and I thought when he was joining their hands to-day, he looked so very much as if he would like to have the same kind office done for him! I think very well of Mr. Elton, and this is the only way I have of doing him a service."

"Mr. Elton is a very pretty[21] young man to be sure, and a very good young man, and I have a great regard for him. But if you want to shew him any attention, my dear, ask him to come and dine with us some day. That will be a much better thing. I dare say Mr. Knightley will be so kind as to meet him."

"With a great deal of pleasure, sir, at any time," said Mr. Knightley laughing; "and I agree with you entirely that it will be a much better thing. Invite him to dinner, Emma, and help him to the best of the fish and the chicken, but leave him to chuse his own wife. Depend upon it, a man of six or seven-and-twenty can take care of himself."

21 Elegant; the term does not necessarily carry the associations of androgynous good looks that it now possesses. For example, in vol. I, book II, chap. 5, of Fanny Burney's *Cecilia* (1782), Mortimer Delvile is described as "a very pretty young man, and much admired," although when he appears in person two chapters later, Burney's narrative is at pains to point out that "his features, though not handsome, were full of expression, and a noble openness of manners and address spoke the elegance of his education, and the liberality of his mind." It may not be coincidental that Burney's description here prefigures some of the aspects outlined in Austen's presentations of her male leads.

2

Mr. Weston was a native of Highbury, and born of a respectable family, which for the last two or three generations had been rising into gentility and property. He had received a good education, but on succeeding early in life to a small independence, had become indisposed for any of the more homely[1] pursuits in which his brothers were engaged; and had satisfied an active cheerful mind and social temper by entering into the militia of his county, then embodied.[2]

Captain Weston was a general favourite; and when the chances of his military life had introduced him to Miss Churchill, of a great Yorkshire family, and Miss Churchill fell in love with him, nobody was surprized except her brother and his wife, who had never seen him, and who were full of pride and importance, which the connection would offend.

Miss Churchill, however, being of age, and with the full command of her fortune[3]—though her fortune bore no proportion to the family-estate—was not to be dissuaded from the marriage, and it took place to the infinite mortification of Mr. and Mrs. Churchill, who threw her off[4] with due decorum. It was an unsuitable connection, and did not produce much happiness. Mrs. Weston ought to have found more in it, for she had a husband whose warm heart and sweet temper made him think every thing due to her in return for the great goodness of being in love with him; but though she had one sort of spirit, she had not the best. She had resolution enough to pursue her own will in spite of her brother, but not enough to refrain

1 Plain, unglamorous.

2 The English county militias provided a supplement to the standing army, for the specific purpose of defending the "home front." After being substantially modernized by the Militia Act of 1757, the militias were frequently "embodied" (mobilized) at times of national crisis, in particular when an invasion was feared; as J. R. Western notes, "[t]he mobilisation of the militia began late in 1792, even before the declaration of war." Mr. Weston had been part of the Surrey militia, founded and first embodied in 1759; his having met and married Miss Churchill of Yorkshire as a result of "the chances of his military life" points to the fact that a militia would rarely be deployed in its home county, for fear of conflicts of interest. Presided over by the lords lieutenant, the principal officers of the Crown in their respective counties, the militias were designed (at least in theory) to protect the domestic "property" by giving officers ranks that rose on a scale linked to their own property qualifications. This did not always work in practice: as Western points out, although "militia officers afford some shining examples of devoted public service . . . even in the relatively respectable higher ranks there was much that was deplorable. Young men of the better class often proved unfit for responsible posts" (*The English Militia in the Eighteenth Century: The Story of a Political Issue, 1660–1802* [London: Routledge & Kegan Paul, 1965], pp. 219, 311). The absence of direct action abroad also meant that more of a militia officer's time could be spent socializing, as witnessed, for

example, by the activities of Wickham in *Pride and Prejudice.*

3 In unconditional control of her income.

4 Disowned her.

5 Mitigating factor.

"Uniform of the 2nd Surrey Militia, in 1814," from John Davis, *Historical Records of the Second Royal Surrey, or Eleventh Regiment of Militia* (London and Belfast: Marcus Ward & Co., 1877).

from unreasonable regrets at that brother's unreasonable anger, nor from missing the luxuries of her former home. They lived beyond their income, but still it was nothing in comparison of Enscombe: she did not cease to love her husband, but she wanted at once to be the wife of Captain Weston, and Miss Churchill of Enscombe.

Captain Weston, who had been considered, especially by the Churchills, as making such an amazing match, was proved to have much the worst of the bargain; for when his wife died after a three years' marriage, he was rather a poorer man than at first, and with a child to maintain. From the expense of the child, however, he was soon relieved. The boy had, with the additional softening claim[5] of a lingering illness of his mother's, been the means of a sort of reconciliation; and Mr. and Mrs. Churchill, having no children of their own, nor any other young creature of equal kindred to care for, offered to take the whole charge of the little Frank soon after her decease. Some scruples and some reluctance the widower-father may be supposed to have felt; but as they were overcome by other considerations, the child was given up to the care and the wealth of the Churchills, and he had only his own comfort to seek and his own situation to improve as he could.

A complete change of life became desirable. He quitted the militia and engaged in trade, having brothers already established in a good way in London, which afforded him a favourable opening. It was a concern which brought just employment enough. He had still a small house in Highbury, where most of his leisure days were spent; and between useful occupation and the pleasures of society, the next eighteen or twenty years of his life passed cheerfully away. He had, by that time, realized an easy competence[6]—enough to secure the purchase of a little estate adjoining Highbury, which he had always longed for—enough to marry a woman as portionless[7] even as Miss Taylor, and to live according to the wishes of his own friendly and social[8] disposition.

It was now some time since Miss Taylor had begun to influence his schemes; but as it was not the tyrannic influence of youth on youth, it had not shaken his determination of never settling till he could purchase Randalls, and the sale of Randalls was long looked forward to: but he had gone steadily on, with these objects in view, till they were accomplished. He had made his fortune, bought his house, and obtained his wife; and was beginning a new period of existence with every probability of greater happiness than in any yet passed through. He had never been an unhappy man; his own temper had secured him from that, even in his first marriage; but his second must shew him how delightful a well-judging and truly amiable woman could be, and must give him the pleasantest proof of its being a great deal better to chuse than to be chosen, to excite gratitude than to feel it.

He had only himself to please in his choice: his fortune was his

6 Secured a comfortable and sufficient living.

7 Without a "portion" or dowry of her own, without any money settled on her, and therefore less marriageable in economic terms.

8 Sociable.

own; for as to Frank, it was more than being tacitly brought up as his uncle's heir, it had become so avowed an adoption as to have him assume the name of Churchill on coming of age.[9] It was most unlikely, therefore, that he should ever want his father's assistance. His father had no apprehension[10] of it. The aunt was a capricious woman, and governed her husband entirely; but it was not in Mr. Weston's nature to imagine that any caprice could be strong enough to affect one so dear, and, as he believed, so deservedly dear. He saw his son every year in London, and was proud of him; and his fond report of him as a very fine young man had made Highbury feel a sort of pride in him too. He was looked on as sufficiently belonging to the place to make his merits and prospects a kind of common concern.[11]

Mr. Frank Churchill was one of the boasts of Highbury, and a lively curiosity to see him prevailed, though the compliment was so little returned that he had never been there in his life. His coming to visit his father had been often talked of but never achieved.

Now, upon his father's marriage, it was very generally proposed, as a most proper attention, that the visit should take place. There was not a dissentient voice on the subject, either when Mrs. Perry drank tea with Mrs. and Miss Bates, or when Mrs. and Miss Bates returned the visit. Now was the time for Mr. Frank Churchill to come among them; and the hope strengthened when it was understood that he had written to his new mother on the occasion. For a few days every morning visit in Highbury included some mention of the handsome[12] letter Mrs. Weston had received. "I suppose you have heard of the handsome letter Mr. Frank Churchill had written to Mrs. Weston? I understand it was a very handsome letter, indeed. Mr. Woodhouse told me of it. Mr. Woodhouse saw the letter, and he says he never saw such a handsome letter in his life."

It was, indeed, a highly-prized letter. Mrs. Weston had, of course, formed a very favourable idea of the young man; and such a pleasing attention was an irresistible proof of his great good sense, and a most welcome addition to every source and every expression of congratulation which her marriage had already secured. She felt herself a most fortunate woman; and she had lived long enough to know how

9 Such arrangements were by no means uncommon at the time; indeed, Austen's elder brother Edward (1767–1852) was adopted by her father's wealthy, childless second cousin Thomas Knight of Godmersham Park in Kent in 1783, and finally took the Knight surname in 1812. While it is always dangerous to link biographical detail too transparently to its fictional reworkings, it is hard not to detect in *Emma*'s portrayals some resentment toward the peremptory and economically driven nature of such adoptions. David Nokes also offers an excellent, suggestive interpretation of William Wellings's commemorative silhouette of the handing over of Edward: "As a composition, this silhouette is as much about power as about family feelings. By visually antedating the time of Edward's adoption, the Knights effectively reduce the role of the natural parents, while the game of chess, which occupies the centre of the picture, transforms the boy into a pawn in a game of dynastic manoeuvres" (*Jane Austen: A Life* [London: Fourth Estate, 1997], p. 75).

10 Fear.

11 A sly hint at Frank Churchill's future relations with Highbury at large: even though everyone seems to feel an interest in Frank, Austen's placing "sort of" and "kind of" so close together registers the fact that a community's relationship with a "favourite son" whom they haven't even met yet can only ever be a conjectural one.

12 Elegantly and articulately written, although there may also be a play on the more familiar sense of "comely" or "good-looking, since Frank's letters repeatedly have to stand as substitutes for his actual, physical presence.

fortunate she might well be thought, where the only regret was for a partial separation from friends, whose friendship for her had never cooled, and who could ill bear to part with her!

She knew that at times she must be missed; and could not think, without pain, of Emma's losing a single pleasure, or suffering an hour's ennui, from the want of her companionableness:[13] but dear Emma was of no feeble character; she was more equal to her situation than most girls would have been, and had sense and energy and spirits that might be hoped would bear her well and happily through its little difficulties and privations. And then there was such comfort in the very easy distance of Randalls from Hartfield, so convenient for even solitary female walking, and in Mr. Weston's disposition and

13 Sociability.

William Wellings, silhouette of Edward Austen (1767–1852) being adopted by the Knights of Godmersham, 1783. The iconography of the image seems designed to naturalize the boy's transplantation away from his biological parents.

circumstances, which would make the approaching season no hindrance to their spending half the evenings in the week together.

Her situation was altogether the subject of hours of gratitude to Mrs. Weston, and of moments only of regret; and her satisfaction—her more than satisfaction—her cheerful enjoyment was so just and so apparent, that Emma, well as she knew her father, was sometimes taken by surprize at his being still able to pity "poor Miss Taylor," when they left her at Randalls in the centre of every domestic comfort, or saw her go away in the evening attended by her pleasant husband to a carriage of her own. But never did she go without Mr. Woodhouse's giving a gentle sigh, and saying:

"Ah! poor Miss Taylor. She would be very glad to stay."

There was no recovering Miss Taylor—nor much likelihood of ceasing to pity her: but a few weeks brought some alleviation to Mr. Woodhouse. The compliments of his neighbours were over; he was no longer teased by being wished joy of so sorrowful an event; and the wedding-cake,[14] which had been a great distress to him, was all eat up. His own stomach could bear nothing rich, and he could never believe other people to be different from himself. What was unwholesome to him, he regarded as unfit for any body; and he had, therefore, earnestly tried to dissuade them from having any wedding-cake at all, and when that proved vain, as earnestly tried to prevent any body's eating it. He had been at the pains of consulting Mr. Perry, the apothecary,[15] on the subject. Mr. Perry was an intelligent, gentlemanlike man, whose frequent visits were one of the comforts of Mr. Woodhouse's life; and, upon being applied to, he could not but acknowledge, (though it seemed rather against the bias of inclination,) that wedding-cake might certainly disagree with many—perhaps with most people, unless taken moderately. With such an opinion, in confirmation of his own, Mr. Woodhouse hoped to influence every visitor of the new-married pair; but still the cake was eaten; and there was no rest for his benevolent nerves[16] till it was all gone.

There was a strange rumour in Highbury of all the little Perrys being seen with a slice of Mrs. Weston's wedding-cake in their hands: but Mr. Woodhouse would never believe it.

14 Eighteenth- and early nineteenth-century wedding cakes bore a recognizable relation to their modern versions in that they contained flour, eggs, sugar, spices, and dried fruit, and were covered in marzipan and sugar icing. However, the cake would usually be left undecorated.

15 Apothecaries were traditionally the lowest of the three grades of medical practitioner, ranking below physicians and surgeons; indeed, it was not until a year after the imagined action of *Emma* that the profession was officially licensed and regulated by Parliament, via "An Act for better regulating the Practice of Apothecaries throughout England and Wales" (1815), which stipulated: "And whereas much mischief and inconvenience has arisen from great numbers of persons in many parts of England and Wales exercising the functions of an apothecary, who are wholly ignorant and utterly incompetent to the exercise of such functions, whereby the health and lives of the community are greatly endangered, and it is become necessary that provision should be made for remedying such evils; be it therefore further enacted, That the said master, wardens, and Society of the art and mystery of Apothecaries of the city of London, incorporated by the said recited charter of His Majesty King James the First, and their successors, shall be and they are hereby appointed and constituted, directed and empowered for ever to superintend the execution of the provisions of this Act, and to enforce and carry the several regulations and provisions thereof, in relation to the several persons practising the art or mystery or profession of an apothecary throughout England and Wales, and all the other purposes of this Act, into full execution." Although in theory the apothecary's role was restricted to the compounding and preparation of remedies, apothecaries (especially those in rural areas) often served in a wider variety of capacities, anticipating many of the functions of the modern general practitioner. In *The Villager's Friend and Physician; or, A Familiar Address on the Preservation of Health, and the Removal of Disease, on it's first Appearance; Supposed to be delivered by a Village Apothecary* (1800), James Parkinson sketched the typical round of the village apothecary's existence: "Aware that the lives of his fellow-creatures depend upon the judgement he may form, and on the measures he may adopt, his mind is constantly harrassed with anxiously attending to the event of some distressfully interesting case . . . Nor is this all; recollect with how little consideration for his comfort, is the time, as well as the labour, of a village apothecary trifled with. Have you to consult your lawyer, or to employ any other man almost in the village, you will require his attendance, at that time which may best suit his convenience; but should a trifling rash on the skin, which has hardly excited your attention for a week or two, at last induce you to call for the attendance of your apothecary, the application will generally be deferred to the close of the day: nor will the roughest and most tempestuous weather excuse his attendance, which will, in general, be thought necessary to be insisted on *directly,* to give energy and effect to your message; not considering that he who calls wolf unnecessarily, may call in vain, when in real danger" ([London: C. Whittingham, 1800; 2nd ed., 1804], p. 6). Mr. Perry's persistent offstage presence in *Emma* likewise indicates the variety of roles, both medical and pastoral, that an apothecary might be expected to play within the community, as well as the importance of health, along with economics and religion, as a channel of social cohesion and comparison. John Wiltshire offers a suggestive exploration of the role of medicine in the novels in *Jane Austen and the Body* (Cambridge: Cambridge University Press, 1992); see also his chapter "Medicine, Illness and Disease," in Todd, ed., *Jane Austen in Context* (Cambridge: Cambridge University Press, 2005), pp. 306–316. For more on Keats as apothecary and poet, see Donald C. Goellnicht, *The Poet-Physician: Keats and Medical Science* (Pittsburgh: University of Pittsburgh Press, 1984), and Hermione de Almeida, *Romantic Medicine and John Keats* (New York: Oxford University Press, 1991).

16 Mr. Woodhouse's "nerves" are anything but "benevolent" here, since they can conceive of doing good to others only in terms of his own tastes.

left: M. Darly (after R. St. G. Mansergh), "Matthew Manna, a country apothecary outside his shop," 1783; top: unknown artist, *The Village Doctor Besieg'd,* c. 1800. The latter image conveys both the centrality of village apothecaries to their communities and the risks attendant upon disappointing patients.

3

Mr. Woodhouse was fond of society in his own way. He liked very much to have his friends come and see him;[1] and from various united causes, from his long residence at Hartfield, and his good nature, from his fortune, his house, and his daughter, he could command the visits of his own little circle, in a great measure as he liked. He had not much intercourse with any families beyond that circle; his horror of late hours[2] and large dinner-parties made him unfit for any acquaintance, but such as would visit him on his own terms. Fortunately for him, Highbury, including Randalls in the same parish, and Donwell Abbey in the parish adjoining, the seat of Mr. Knightley, comprehended many such. Not unfrequently, through Emma's persuasion, he had some of the chosen and the best to dine with him, but evening-parties were what he preferred, and, unless he fancied himself at any time unequal to company, there was scarcely an evening in the week in which Emma could not make up a card-table for him.

Real, long-standing regard brought the Westons and Mr. Knightley; and by Mr. Elton, a young man living alone without liking it, the privilege of exchanging any vacant evening of his own blank solitude for the elegancies and society of Mr. Woodhouse's drawing-room and the smiles of his lovely daughter,[3] was in no danger of being thrown away.

After these came a second set; among the most come-at-able[4] of whom were Mrs. and Miss Bates and Mrs. Goddard, three ladies almost always at the service of an invitation from Hartfield, and who

1 As subsequent events make clear, however, he is much more reluctant to make the effort to visit anyone else.

2 In vol. I, chap. 9, we find out that the regular dinner hour at Highbury is four o'clock.

3 One of the many puzzles set by Austen's employment of free indirect style: Is Emma's being "lovely" a general truth of Highbury society or a hint of Elton's opinion of her?

4 Easily accessible and obtainable.

Engraving after Francis Hayman—"Playing the Game at Quadrille, after an Original Painting in Vauxhall Gardens," c. 1750. By the time of *Emma,* quadrille was clearly established as the card game of an older generation.

were fetched and carried home so often that Mr. Woodhouse thought it no hardship for either James or the horses. Had it taken place only once a year, it would have been a grievance.

Mrs. Bates, the widow of a former vicar of Highbury, was a very old lady, almost past every thing but tea and quadrille.[5] She lived with her single daughter in a very small way,[6] and was considered with all the regard and respect which a harmless old lady, under such untoward circumstances, can excite. Her daughter enjoyed a most uncommon degree of popularity for a woman neither young, handsome, rich, nor married. Miss Bates stood in the very worst predicament in the world for having much of the public favour; and she had no intellectual superiority to make atonement to herself, or frighten those who might hate her, into outward respect. She had never boasted either beauty or cleverness. Her youth had passed without distinction, and her middle of life was devoted to the care of a failing mother, and the endeavour to make a small income go as far as possible. And yet she was a happy woman, and a woman whom no one named with-

5 Quadrille developed during the eighteenth century as a four-handed evolution of the three-handed game of hombre or ombre, which was introduced by Royalists returning from European exile after the Restoration. However, as David Parlett has noted, by 1800, the game had fallen out of fashion, owing to a complex of circumstances: "it remained popular with Englishwomen until the end of the century," he remarks, "when revolutionary Francophobia combined with Whist to drive it into limbo . . . Like so many once fashionable games, it lingered longer in the provinces than in the metropolis" (*A History of Card Games* [Oxford: Oxford University Press, 1991], p. 203). Hence Mr. Woodhouse's and Mrs. Bates's devotion to quadrille marks them out as late-Augustan remnants, both chronologically and geographically out of step with fashion. For further information on the eighteenth-century rules of quadrille, see, for example, Edmond Hoyle, *Mr Hoyle's Games of Whist, Quadrille, Piquet, Chess, and Back-Gammon, Complete. In which are contained, The Method of Playing and Betting at Those Games, upon equal, or advantageous Terms. Including The Laws of several Games. The Fourteenth Edition* (London: Thomas Osborne, Henry Woodfall, and Richard Baldwin, 1765), pp. 93–120.

6 Very modestly; in "tight" economic circumstances.

7 It was fashionable at the time for schools to advertise themselves, in (often unrealistically) elevated terms, as "seminaries" or "establishments." In particular, "Seminary for Young Ladies" and "Ladies' Seminary" became terms of choice for aspirational girls' schools in the early nineteenth century, as witnessed by an advertisement in the *Times* from March 18, 1814 (coeval with the imaginary timeline of vol. II of *Emma*): "Boarding School.—Wanted, in a small respectable Ladies' Seminary, near town, a young Lady, as Teacher; must be capable of teaching French and English grammatically; music and writing; and fully acquainted with the nature of a school: respectable references will be expected."

The reality of early nineteenth-century "seminaries" was often far less genteel than their aspirations. For example, in his satirical 1807 poem *Stultifera Navis* out good-will. It was her own universal good-will and contented temper which worked such wonders. She loved every body, was interested in every body's happiness, quick-sighted to every body's merits; thought herself a most fortunate creature, and surrounded with blessings in such an excellent mother and so many good neighbours and friends, and a home that wanted for nothing. The simplicity and cheerfulness of her nature, her contented and grateful spirit, were a recommendation to every body and a mine of felicity to herself. She was a great talker upon little matters, which exactly suited Mr. Woodhouse, full of trivial communications and harmless gossip.

Mrs. Goddard was the mistress of a School—not of a seminary, or an establishment, or any thing which professed, in long sentences of refined nonsense, to combine liberal acquirements with elegant morality upon new principles and new systems—and where young ladies for enormous pay might be screwed out of health and into vanity—but a real, honest, old-fashioned Boarding-school, where a reasonable quantity of accomplishments were sold at a reasonable price, and where girls might be sent to be out of the way and scramble themselves into a little education, without any danger of coming back prodigies.[7] Mrs. Goddard's school was in high repute—and very deservedly; for Highbury was reckoned a particularly healthy spot: she had an ample house and garden, gave the children plenty of wholesome food, let them run about a great deal in the summer, and in winter dressed their chilblains[8] with her own hands. It was no wonder that a train of twenty young couple[9] now walked after her to church. She was a plain, motherly kind of woman, who had worked hard in her youth, and now thought herself entitled to the occasional holiday of a tea-visit;[10] and having formerly owed much to Mr. Woodhouse's kindness, felt his particular claim on her to leave her neat parlour hung round with fancy-work[11] whenever she could, and win or lose a few sixpences[12] by his fireside.

These were the ladies whom Emma found herself very frequently able to collect; and happy was she, for her father's sake, in the power; though, as far as she was herself concerned, it was no remedy for the absence of Mrs. Weston. She was delighted to see her father

["Ship of Fools"], the infamous Shakespearean forger William Henry Ireland takes aim at the curriculum:

> Instead of mentally advancing,
> Your miss's first great object's dancing,
> By which one truth I must reveal is,
> Empty's the head, as light the heel is.

However, one of his footnotes tackles the economic actuality of the seminaries much more directly: "As to the idea of genius in the scholar, that is never taken into consideration; and I have literally seen *school drawings* that would have disgraced an Ouran Outang. And to speak truly of the persons employed to teach at seminaries, they are but the fag end, the tag rag and bobtail of proficients in those very arts they pretend to be so well schooled in; and I must confess that they very frequently reminded me of the old woman, who took infinite pains to teach her boy to milk a boar. But to the point: it is truly surprising to see how easily a school bill is whipped up, what with entrances of masters, or rather *labourers;* charges for books which were never had; usage of the globes and piano forte, whose tones might well vie with the clank that resounds from a cracked tin kettle; and the more genteel sum which is tacked to the account, for miss being a parlour boarder, who is honoured with slip slop tea and a bit of the brown off the meat. These are the wheels within wheels that set so many seminaries in motion" ([Philadelphia: C. and A. Conrad and Co., 1807], pp. 87, 89).

In contrast, Mrs. Goddard's insistence on the down-to-earth term "Boarding-school" indicates the no-nonsense education her boarders are to expect.

8 Sores caused by exposure to intense cold.

9 It was acceptable in early nineteenth-century usage for nouns denoting plural quantities, such as "couple" and "pair," to retain their singular form even when used plurally. The practice still survives in phrases such as "two brace of partridges" and "two dozen loaves."

10 Tea would be served some time after dinner, at around seven or eight.

11 Decorative needlework, embroidery.

look comfortable, and very much pleased with herself for contriving things so well; but the quiet prosings[13] of three such women made her feel that every evening so spent, was indeed one of the long evenings she had fearfully anticipated.

As she sat one morning, looking forward to exactly such a close of the present day, a note was brought from Mrs. Goddard, requesting, in most respectful terms, to be allowed to bring Miss Smith with her; a most welcome request: for Miss Smith was a girl of seventeen whom Emma knew very well by sight and had long felt an interest in, on account of her beauty. A very gracious invitation was returned, and the evening no longer dreaded by the fair mistress of the mansion.

Harriet Smith was the natural[14] daughter of somebody. Somebody had placed her, several years back, at Mrs. Goddard's school, and somebody had lately raised her from the condition of scholar to that of parlour-boarder.[15] This was all that was generally known of her history. She had no visible friends but what had been acquired at Highbury, and was now just returned from a long visit in the country to some young ladies who had been at school there with her.

She was a very pretty girl, and her beauty happened to be of a sort which Emma particularly admired. She was short, plump, and fair, with a fine bloom,[16] blue eyes,[17] light hair, regular features, and a look of great sweetness; and before the end of the evening, Emma was as much pleased with her manners as her person, and quite determined to continue the acquaintance.

She was not struck by any thing remarkably clever in Miss Smith's conversation, but she found her altogether very engaging—not inconveniently shy, not unwilling to talk—and yet so far from pushing,[18] shewing so proper and becoming a deference, seeming so pleasantly grateful for being admitted to Hartfield, and so artlessly impressed by the appearance of every thing in so superior a style to what she had been used to, that she must have good sense and deserve encouragement. Encouragement should be given. Those soft blue eyes and all those natural graces should not be wasted on the inferior society of Highbury and its connections. The acquaintance she had already formed were unworthy of her. The friends from

12 In predecimal currency, a sixpence was one-half of a shilling, and one-fortieth of a pound.

13 "Dull, prolix, or tedious writing or speech" *(OED).*

14 Illegitimate.

15 A scholar was a regular pupil who boarded in the school dormitory, whereas a parlor-boarder, upon payment of higher fees, lodged with the proprietor's family and enjoyed certain additional privileges. Parlor-boarders were often the children of rich absentees, which may be one of the factors that fuels Emma's speculations about Harriet's noble parentage here. In "Our School," his *Household Words* article from October 11, 1851, Charles Dickens recalled his education in the mid-1820s: "We remember an idiotic goggle-eyed boy, with a big head and half-crowns without end, who suddenly appeared as a parlour-boarder, and was rumoured to have come by sea from some mysterious part of the earth where his parents rolled in gold" *("Gone Astray" and Other Papers from "Household Words," 1851–59,* ed. Michael Slater [London: J. M. Dent, 1998], p. 38). Notable parlor-boarders in nineteenth-century fiction include James Steerforth in Dickens's *David Copperfield* (1849–1850) and Miss Swartz in William Makepeace Thackeray's *Vanity Fair* (1847–1848). See also Richard Cronin and Dorothy McMillan, "Emma, Harriet Martin, and Parlour Boarders," *Notes and Queries,* 52:1 (2005), pp. 19–22.

16 Specifically, color in the cheeks, rosiness of complexion. "Bloom" also works as a subtle index in *Persuasion.* Whereas in the novel's opening chapter "Anne Elliot had been a very pretty girl, but her bloom had vanished early," her return to the world of active importance, and her eventual reunion with Captain Wentworth, are signposted by the return of color to her cheeks, as in vol. I, chap. 12: "She was looking remarkably well; her very regular, very pretty features, having the bloom and freshness of youth restored by the fine wind which had been blowing on her complexion, and by the animation of eye which it had also produced."

17 This is the first explicit reference in the novel to the color of Harriet's eyes, a circumstance that comes to

whom she had just parted, though very good sort of people, must be doing her harm. They were a family of the name of Martin, whom Emma well knew by character, as renting a large farm of Mr. Knightley, and residing in the parish of Donwell—very creditably she believed—she knew Mr. Knightley thought highly of them—but they must be coarse and unpolished, and very unfit to be the intimates of a girl who wanted only a little more knowledge and elegance to be quite perfect. *She* would notice her; she would improve her; she would detach her from her bad acquaintance, and introduce her into good society; she would form her opinions and her manners. It would be an interesting, and certainly a very kind undertaking; highly becoming her own situation in life, her leisure, and powers.[19]

She was so busy in admiring those soft blue eyes, in talking and listening, and forming all these schemes in the in-betweens, that the evening flew away at a very unusual rate; and the supper-table,[20] which always closed such parties, and for which she had been used to sit and watch the due time, was all set out and ready, and moved forwards to the fire, before she was aware. With an alacrity beyond the common impulse of a spirit which yet was never indifferent to the credit of doing every thing well and attentively, with the real goodwill of a mind delighted with its own ideas, did she then do all the honours of the meal, and help and recommend the minced chicken and scalloped oysters[21] with an urgency which she knew would be acceptable to the early hours and civil scruples of their guests.

Upon such occasions poor Mr. Woodhouse's feelings were in sad warfare. He loved to have the cloth laid, because it had been the fashion of his youth;[22] but his conviction of suppers being very unwholesome made him rather sorry to see any thing put on it; and while his hospitality would have welcomed his visitors to every thing, his care for their health made him grieve that they would eat.

Such another small basin of thin gruel[23] as his own, was all that he could, with thorough self-approbation, recommend, though he might constrain himself, while the ladies were comfortably clearing the nicer things, to say:

"Mrs. Bates, let me propose your venturing on one of these eggs. An egg boiled very soft is not unwholesome. Serle understands boil-

carry particular importance later in the novel, notably in vol. III, chap. 7, when Frank Churchill jokingly stipulates that his putative bride must have "hazle eyes."

18 Excessively forward.

19 This is a particularly marked example of Austen's experimentation with the narrative technique of free indirect style (see Introduction), in which the third-person storytelling is focalized through an individual's point of view. The narration is insistently evaluative ("bad acquaintance," "good society," "interesting," "becoming"), but these are Emma's evaluations, not those of the nameless narrator nor of the flesh-and-blood Austen herself.

20 Especially in households that held to the early dinner hour, a lighter, late supper was often taken by those who had stayed up to play cards.

21 Oysters baked in the shell or in an equivalent dish with cream, butter, and breadcrumbs; variations on this recipe are still popular.

22 The fashion of early dinner hours and, consequently, more substantial suppers.

23 Maria Rundell's recipe for "Water Gruel" gives some indication of the "pleasures" of the dish: "Put a large spoonful of oatmeal by degrees into a pint of water, and when smooth boil it. *Another way.*—Rub smooth a large spoonful of oatmeal, with two of water, and pour it into a pint of water boiling on the fire; stir it well, and boil it quick; but take care it does not boil over. In a quarter of an hour strain it off; and add salt and a bit of butter when eaten. Stir until the butter be incorporated" (*A New System of Domestic Cookery; formed Upon Principles of Economy* [London: John Murray, 1807; rev. ed., 1808], p. 286).

ing an egg better than any body. I would not recommend an egg boiled by any body else—but you need not be afraid—they are very small, you see—one of our small eggs will not hurt you. Miss Bates, let Emma help you to a *little* bit of tart—a *very* little bit. Ours are all apple tarts. You need not be afraid of unwholesome preserves here. I do not advise the custard. Mrs. Goddard, what say you to *half* a glass of wine? A *small* half glass—put into a tumbler of water? I do not think it could disagree with you."

Emma allowed her father to talk—but supplied her visitors in a much more satisfactory style; and on the present evening had particular pleasure in sending them away happy. The happiness of Miss Smith was quite equal to her intentions. Miss Woodhouse was so great a personage in Highbury, that the prospect of the introduction had given as much panic as pleasure—but the humble, grateful, little girl went off with highly gratified feelings, delighted with the affability with which Miss Woodhouse had treated her all the evening, and actually shaken hands with her at last!

4

Harriet Smith's intimacy at Hartfield was soon a settled thing. Quick and decided in her ways, Emma lost no time in inviting, encouraging, and telling her to come very often; and as their acquaintance increased, so did their satisfaction in each other. As a walking companion, Emma had very early foreseen how useful she might find her. In that respect Mrs. Weston's loss had been important. Her father never went beyond the shrubbery, where two divisions of the grounds[1] sufficed him for his long walk, or his short, as the year varied; and since Mrs. Weston's marriage her exercise had been too much confined. She had ventured once alone to Randalls, but it was not pleasant; and a Harriet Smith, therefore, one whom she could summon at any time to a walk, would be a valuable addition to her privileges. But in every respect as she saw more of her, she approved her, and was confirmed in all her kind designs.

Harriet certainly was not clever, but she had a sweet, docile,[2] grateful disposition; was totally free from conceit; and only desiring to be guided by any one she looked up to. Her early attachment to herself was very amiable; and her inclination for good company, and power of appreciating what was elegant and clever, shewed that there was no want of taste, though strength of understanding must not be expected. Altogether she was quite convinced of Harriet Smith's being exactly the young friend she wanted—exactly the something which her home required.[3] Such a friend as Mrs. Weston was out of the question. Two such could never be granted. Two such she did not want.[4] It was quite a different sort of thing—a sentiment distinct

1 Two different lengths of walk, according to the season.

2 "Teachable; easily instructed; tractable" (Johnson).

3 As with "a Harriet Smith" above, Austen's phrasing suggests Harriet as a commodity or an accessory that Emma can own.

4 "Want" is employed here in its more conventional modern sense (dating only from the eighteenth century) of "desire."

and independent. Mrs. Weston was the object of a regard, which had its basis in gratitude and esteem. Harriet would be loved as one to whom she could be useful. For Mrs. Weston there was nothing to be done; for Harriet every thing.

Her first attempts at usefulness were in an endeavour to find out who were the parents; but Harriet could not tell. She was ready to tell every thing in her power, but on this subject questions were vain. Emma was obliged to fancy what she liked—but she could never believe that in the same situation *she* should not have discovered the truth. Harriet had no penetration.[5] She had been satisfied to hear and believe just what Mrs. Goddard chose to tell her; and looked no farther.

Mrs. Goddard, and the teachers, and the girls, and the affairs of the school in general, formed naturally a great part of her conversation—and but for her acquaintance with the Martins of Abbey-Mill Farm, it must have been the whole. But the Martins occupied her thoughts a good deal; she had spent two very happy months with them, and now loved to talk of the pleasures of her visit, and describe the many comforts and wonders of the place. Emma encouraged her talkativeness—amused by such a picture of another set of beings, and enjoying the youthful simplicity which could speak with so much exultation of Mrs. Martin's having "*two* parlours, two very good parlours indeed; one of them quite as large as Mrs. Goddard's drawing-room; and of her having an upper maid who had lived five-and-twenty years with her; and of their having eight cows, two of them Alderneys, and one a little Welch cow, a very pretty little Welch cow, indeed;[6] and of Mrs. Martin's saying, as she was so fond of it, it should be called *her* cow; and of their having a very handsome summer-house in their garden, where some day next year they were all to drink tea:—a very handsome summer-house,[7] large enough to hold a dozen people."

For some time she was amused, without thinking beyond the immediate cause; but as she came to understand the family better, other feelings arose. She had taken up a wrong idea, fancying it was a mother and daughter, a son and son's wife, who all lived together; but when it appeared that the Mr. Martin, who bore a part in the narra-

5 Sharpness of perception, insight.

6 The Alderney was a decorative, light-brown dairy cow from the Channel Islands, extremely popular in Austen's time both for its decorative qualities and for its high yield of rich milk; for example, in Tobias Smollett's 1771 novel *The Expedition of Humphry Clinker,* Tabitha Bramble bemoans the loss of an Alderney house cow that "gave four gallons a day." The appellation "Alderney" was often applied not only to cattle bred on the island of Alderney but also to those from other Channel Islands such as Guernsey, since Alderney was the last port of call for cattle boats before they reached the English mainland. The Austens themselves owned Alderneys at the family home in Steventon, as witnessed by a letter from Austen's mother, Cassandra, to her relative Mrs. Walter on August 26, 1770: "What Luck we shall have with those sort of Cows I can't say. My little Alderney one turns out tolerably well, and makes more Butter than we use, and I have just bought another of the same sort, but as her Calf is but just gone, can not say what she will be good for yet" (quoted in William Austen-Leigh and Richard Arthur Austen-Leigh, *Jane Austen: A Family Record* [1913], revised and enlarged by Deirdre Le Faye [London: The British Library, 1989], p. 21).

7 A small building or shed in a garden, for the purposes of shelter and entertainment on hot, sunny days. The fact that the Martins possess not only a summer-house but two Alderney cows (decorative as well as practical animals) suggests that the Martins, while they may not be a "genteel" family according to the socioeconomic standards of the time, have a greater level of social refinement and leisure than Emma's prejudice is willing to allow them at this point in the novel.

tive, and was always mentioned with approbation for his great good-nature in doing something or other, was a single man; that there was no young Mrs. Martin, no wife in the case; she did suspect danger to her poor little friend from all this hospitality and kindness—and that if she were not taken care of, she might be required to sink herself[8] for ever.

With this inspiriting[9] notion, her questions increased in number and meaning; and she particularly led Harriet to talk more of Mr. Martin,—and there was evidently no dislike to it. Harriet was very ready to speak of the share he had had in their moonlight walks and merry evening games; and dwelt a good deal upon his being so very good-humoured and obliging. "He had gone three miles round one day, in order to bring her some walnuts, because she had said how fond she was of them—and in every thing else he was so very obliging! He had his shepherd's son into the parlour one night on purpose to sing to her. She was very fond of singing. He could sing a little himself. She believed he was very clever, and understood every thing. He had a very fine flock; and while she was with them, he had been bid more for his wool than any body in the country.[10] She believed every body spoke well of him. His mother and sisters were very fond of him. Mrs. Martin had told her one day, (and there was a blush as she said it,) that it was impossible for any body to be a better son; and therefore she was sure whenever he married he would make a good husband. Not that she *wanted* him to marry. She was in no hurry at all."

"Well done, Mrs. Martin!" thought Emma. "You know what you are about."

"And when she had come away, Mrs. Martin was so very kind as to send Mrs. Goddard a beautiful goose: the finest goose Mrs. Goddard had ever seen. Mrs. Goddard had dressed it[11] on a Sunday, and asked all the three teachers, Miss Nash, and Miss Prince, and Miss Richardson, to sup with her."

"Mr. Martin, I suppose, is not a man of information beyond the line of his own business. He does not read?"

"Oh, yes!—that is, no—I do not know—but I believe he has read a good deal—but not what you would think any thing of. He reads the

8 Lower herself socially.

9 Animating.

10 Used in this context to mean "region" rather than the whole nation.

11 Had it prepared.

An Alderney cow, from George Vasey, *A Monograph of the Genus Bos* (London: J. R. Smith, 1857).

Agricultural Reports[12] and some other books, that lay in one of the window seats—but he reads all *them* to himself. But sometimes of an evening, before we went to cards, he would read something aloud out of the Elegant Extracts[13]—very entertaining. And I know he has read the Vicar of Wakefield.[14] He never read the Romance of the Forest,[15] nor the Children of the Abbey.[16] He had never heard of such books before I mentioned them, but he is determined to get them now as soon as ever he can."

The next question was:

"What sort of looking man is Mr. Martin?"

"Oh! not handsome—not at all handsome. I thought him very plain at first, but I do not think him so plain now.[17] One does not, you know, after a time. But, did you never see him? He is in Highbury every now and then, and he is sure to ride through every week in his way to Kingston.[18] He has passed you very often."

"That may be—and I may have seen him fifty times, but without having any idea of his name. A young farmer, whether on horseback or on foot, is the very last sort of person to raise my curiosity.

Portrait of Oliver Goldsmith (c. 1730–1774) after Joshua Reynolds, 1769–1770. Goldsmith's novel *The Vicar of Wakefield* (1766) is alluded to significantly on more than one occasion in *Emma.*

12 After the founding of the Board of Agriculture and Internal Improvement in 1793, one of the new body's first tasks was to take a broad survey of the state of the nation's farming. To this end, the board published reports on the various counties, on which farmers were invited to comment, prior to the publication of the revised versions, which took place over the first two decades of the new century. Being a capable, informed, modern farmer, Robert Martin would most likely be consulting the most recent version of William Stevenson's *General View of the Agriculture of the County of Surrey* (London: Sherwood, Neely, and Jones, 1813).

13 The influential anthologist Vicesimus Knox published *Elegant Extracts; or, Useful and Entertaining Passages in Prose* in 1770, and its companion volume, *Elegant Extracts; or, Useful and Entertaining Pieces of Poetry,* in 1784. In the late eighteenth century, anthologies, along with the growth of literary criticism into a self-conscious activity and genre, played a significant role in shaping both the idea of "English Literature" and the make-up of the literary canon. As Leah Price has argued, they "established not only the content of the canon to date, but also the rules by which future literature would be transmitted, notably the expectation that every anthology-piece bear a signature and that its signatory be dead" (*The Anthology and the Rise of the Novel: From Richardson to George Eliot* [Cambridge: Cambridge University Press, 2000], p. 67). However, for all their salutary influence on the spread of literacy and literature, some contemporary commentators also bemoaned the popularity of anthologies, often implying that they both inculcated and ministered to a "piecemeal" habit of learning; in particular, they came to be seen as part of the apparatus of female "accomplishment," a complaint that united writers of widely differing political stamps. Mary Wollstonecraft famously satirized female education in the introduction to her manifesto *Vindication of the Rights of Woman* (1792), noting that women "spend many of the first years of their lives in acquiring a smattering of accomplishments; meanwhile strength of body and mind are sacrificed to libertine notions of beauty." The conservative, evangelical Hannah More was just as caustic. In *Strictures on the*

Modern System of Female Education (2 vols.; London: T. Cadell & W. Davies, 1799), she condemned the role of anthologies as "an infallible receipt for a superficial mind," portraying a world dominated by "the hackney'd quotations of certain *accomplished* young ladies, who will be frequently found not to have come legitimately by any thing they know: I mean, not to have drawn it from its true spring, the original works of the author from which some *beauty-monger* has severed it" (vol. I, p. 174). Samuel Taylor Coleridge expressed a more generalized disgust with the contemporary state of reading practice when writing to Thomas Poole on January 28, 1810; he reminds his addressee "that these are Awe-ful Times!—that the love of Reading, as a refined pleasure weaning the mind from grosser enjoyments, which it was one of the Spectator's chief Objects to awaken, has by that work, & those that followed (Connoisseur, World, Mirror &c) but still more, by Newspapers, Magazines, and Novels, been carried into excess: and the Spectator itself has innocently contributed to the general taste for unconnected writing—just as if 'Reading made easy' should act to give men an aversion to words of more than two syllables, instead of drawing them *thro'* those words into the power of reading Books in general" (*Selected Letters,* ed. H. J. Jackson [Oxford: Oxford University Press, 1988], pp. 142–143). While Austen did not share Coleridge's grander cultural pessimism, her fictional and nonfictional portrayals of "female accomplishment" do have some affinities with Wollstonecraft's and More's reservations; as a result, the role of anthologies in forming the mind is treated equivocally. In a letter to her sister Cassandra of May 26, 1801, she remarks of Miss Holder of Ashe Park: "She has an idea of your being remarkably lively; therefore get ready the proper selection of adverbs, & due scraps of Italian & French" (*Letters,* p. 90). The most notable beneficiary of anthologies in the novels is Catherine Morland in vol. I, chap. 1, of *Northanger Abbey,* who "read all such works as heroines must read to supply their memories with those quotations which are so serviceable and so soothing in the vicissitudes of their eventful lives," but whose literary knowledge appears to consist largely of quotable "soundbites" from Pope, Gray, Thomson, and Shakespeare as a result. For more on Knox, see Price, *The Anthology and the Rise of the Novel,* pp. 67–77; for more on education and female accomplishments, see D. D. Devlin, *Jane Austen and Education* (London: Macmillan, 1975), and Gary Kelly, "Education and Accomplishments," in Janet Todd, ed., *Jane Austen in Context* (Cambridge: Cambridge University Press, 2005), pp. 252–261.

14 An extremely popular sentimental novel by Oliver Goldsmith, first published in 1766. Modern criticism is divided as to whether the story of Dr. Primrose and his family is the acme of the eighteenth-century "virtue in distress" narrative, or in fact an artful parody of sentimentalism; see Robert H. Hopkins, *The True Genius of Oliver Goldsmith* (Baltimore: Johns Hopkins University Press, 1969), and John Mullan, *Sentiment and Sociability: The Language of Feeling in the Eighteenth Century* (Oxford: Clarendon Press, 1988), pp. 136–146.

15 A Gothic novel by Ann Radcliffe, published in 1791.

16 A Gothic novel by Regina Maria Roche, published in 1798. Radcliffe and Roche are among the authors who are recommended to Catherine Morland in *Northanger Abbey* and come to work such unfortunate influence upon the imagination of the young heroine. Radcliffe's novel *The Mysteries of Udolpho* (1794) is the work whose plot shapes Catherine's lurid Gothic fantasies about General Tilney, and Roche's *Clermont: A Tale* (1798) is one of the list of "horrid" novels on Isabella Thorpe's list of recommended reading in vol. I, chap. 6: "Castle of Wolfenbach, Clermont, Mysterious Warnings, Necromancer of the Black Forest, Orphan of the Rhine, and Horrid Mysteries."

17 This suggests that Harriet is warming gradually to Robert Martin—a familiar pattern among Austen's female characters with regard to their eventual partners. Of course, thanks to Emma, this particular process is soon put in jeopardy.

18 A large market town in Surrey, some ten miles from London (and therefore about six miles from the imaginary location of Highbury), originally founded at the first crossing point on the Thames upstream from London Bridge, and subsequently the seat and coronation place of Saxon kings. Kingston's status as the larg-

The yeomanry[19] are precisely the order of people with whom I feel I can have nothing to do. A degree or two lower, and a creditable appearance might interest me; I might hope to be useful to their families in some way or other. But a farmer can need none of my help, and is therefore in one sense as much above my notice as in every other he is below it."

"To be sure. Oh! yes, it is not likely you should ever have observed him—but he knows you very well indeed—I mean by sight."

"I have no doubt of his being a very respectable young man. I know indeed that he is so; and as such wish him well. What do you imagine his age to be?"

"He was four-and-twenty the 8th of last June, and my birth-day is the 23d—just a fortnight and a day's difference! which is very odd!"

"Only four-and-twenty. That is too young to settle. His mother is perfectly right not to be in a hurry. They seem very comfortable as they are, and if she were to take any pains to marry him, she would probably repent it. Six years hence, if he could meet with a good sort of young woman in the same rank as his own, with a little money, it might be very desirable."

"Six years hence! dear Miss Woodhouse, he would be thirty years old!"

"Well, and that is as early as most men can afford to marry, who are not born to an independence. Mr. Martin, I imagine, has his fortune entirely to make—cannot be at all beforehand with the world.[20] Whatever money he might come into when his father died, whatever his share of the family property, it is, I dare say, all afloat,[21] all employed in his stock, and so forth; and though, with diligence and good luck, he may be rich in time, it is next to impossible that he should have realised[22] any thing yet."

"To be sure, so it is. But they live very comfortably. They have no in-doors man[23]—else they do not want for any thing; and Mrs. Martin talks of taking a boy[24] another year."

"I wish you may not get into a scrape,[25] Harriet, whenever he does marry;—I mean, as to being acquainted with his wife—for though his sisters, from a superior education, are not to be altogether objected to, it does not follow that he might marry any body at all fit

est and most important market town in the vicinity gives it a vital relation to the agricultural economy of Donwell and Highbury.

19 Yeomen were the order of tenant farmers who tended the land themselves. They lay lower in rank than landed gentlemen such as Knightley.

20 Cannot have ready money to spare. In vol. I, chap. 6, of *Sense and Sensibility,* Mrs. Dashwood's plans for improving Barton Cottage are shadowed by thoughts of the cost, and her recognition that she can spend only what she has: "I shall see how much I am beforehand with the world in the spring, and we will plan our improvements accordingly."

21 Invested, and therefore not available as a "liquid" asset.

22 Received a return on.

23 A house servant, as opposed to a gardener or ostler.

24 Any male domestic servant, not necessarily a young one.

25 An awkward or embarrassing situation. The *OED* dates this sense from the beginning of the eighteenth century.

for you to notice. The misfortune of your birth ought to make you particularly careful as to your associates. There can be no doubt of your being a gentleman's daughter, and you must support your claim to that station by every thing within your own power, or there will be plenty of people who would take pleasure in degrading you."

"Yes, to be sure—I suppose there are. But while I visit at Hartfield, and you are so kind to me, Miss Woodhouse, I am not afraid of what any body can do."

"You understand the force of influence pretty well, Harriet; but I would have you so firmly established in good society, as to be independent even of Hartfield and Miss Woodhouse. I want to see you permanently well connected—and to that end it will be advisable to have as few odd[26] acquaintance as may be; and, therefore, I say that if you should still be in this country when Mr. Martin marries, I wish you may not be drawn in, by your intimacy with the sisters, to be acquainted with the wife, who will probably be some mere farmer's daughter, without education."

"To be sure. Yes. Not that I think Mr. Martin would ever marry any body but what had had some education—and been very well brought up. However, I do not mean to set up my opinion against your's—and I am sure I shall not wish for the acquaintance of his wife. I shall always have a great regard for the Miss Martins, especially Elizabeth, and should be very sorry to give them up, for they are quite as well educated as me. But if he marries a very ignorant, vulgar woman, certainly I had better not visit her, if I can help it."

Emma watched her through the fluctuations of this speech, and saw no alarming symptoms of love. The young man had been the first admirer, but she trusted there was no other hold, and that there would be no serious difficulty on Harriet's side to oppose any friendly arrangement of her own.

They met Mr. Martin the very next day, as they were walking on the Donwell road. He was on foot, and after looking very respectfully at her, looked with most unfeigned satisfaction at her companion. Emma was not sorry to have such an opportunity of survey; and walking a few yards forward, while they talked together, soon made her quick[27] eye sufficiently acquainted with Mr. Robert Martin. His

26 "Odd" here carries the sense of "socially unacceptable" or "ungenteel."

27 Sharp, perceptive.

appearance was very neat, and he looked like a sensible[28] young man, but his person had no other advantage; and when he came to be contrasted with gentlemen, she thought he must lose all the ground he had gained in Harriet's inclination. Harriet was not insensible of manner;[29] she had voluntarily noticed her father's gentleness with admiration as well as wonder. Mr. Martin looked as if he did not know what manner was.

They remained but a few minutes together, as Miss Woodhouse must not be kept waiting; and Harriet then came running to her with a smiling face, and in a flutter of spirits, which Miss Woodhouse hoped very soon to compose.

"Only think of our happening to meet him!—How very odd! It was quite a chance, he said, that he had not gone round by Randalls. He did not think we ever walked this road. He thought we walked towards Randalls most days. He has not been able to get the Romance of the Forest yet. He was so busy the last time he was at Kingston that he quite forgot it, but he goes again to-morrow. So very odd we should happen to meet! Well, Miss Woodhouse, is he like what you expected? What do you think of him? Do you think him so very plain?"

"He is very plain, undoubtedly—remarkably plain:—but that is nothing, compared with his entire want of gentility. I had no right to expect much, and I did not expect much; but I had no idea that he could be so very clownish,[30] so totally without air.[31] I had imagined him, I confess, a degree or two nearer gentility."

"To be sure," said Harriet, in a mortified voice, "he is not so genteel as real gentlemen."

"I think, Harriet, since your acquaintance with us, you have been repeatedly in the company of some, such very real gentlemen, that you must yourself be struck with the difference in Mr. Martin. At Hartfield you have had very good specimens of well educated, well bred men. I should be surprized if, after seeing them, you could be in company with Mr. Martin again without perceiving him to be a very inferior creature—and rather wondering at yourself for having ever thought him at all agreeable before. Do not you begin to

28 Considering Emma's prejudicially low opinion of Robert Martin at this point, she or the narrator may be employing "sensible" in Johnson's last and least reputable sense: "In low conversation it has sometimes the sense of reasonable; judicious; wise."

29 Not insensitive to good and ill manners. "Manner," "manners," "mannered," and related terms took the temperature of, and participated in, much that was of importance in the ideological climate of the late eighteenth and early nineteenth centuries. After the Revolution of 1688 and the Protestant succession, manners and conversible sociability were seen by many as positive agents of social cohesion, typified in the early years of the eighteenth century by the periodical writings of Joseph Addison and Richard Steele in the *Tatler* and the *Spectator.* As Edward and Lillian Bloom have remarked: "In an age when conversation was regarded as a refinement of class, not divorced from the ethical, Addison and Steele more successfully than any preceding English writers translated the tone of civilized oral exchange into print. The easy flow of written speech became not only their literary signature but their avowal of communal identity" ("Joseph Addison: The Artist in the Mirror," in Edward A. Bloom, Lillian D. Bloom, and E. Leites, *Educating the Audience: Addison, Steele, and Eighteenth-Century Culture* [Los Angeles: William Andrews Clark Memorial Library, 1984], p. 6). However, by the end of the century, manners had become prime targets for writers and thinkers of radical sympathies, as witnessed by the emergence of "mannered" and "mannerism" as terms of disapproval: the *OED*'s first citation for the former comes from 1801, and for the latter, from 1803.

30 "Uncivil; ill-bred; ill-mannered" (Johnson); also with an imputation of rusticity.

31 "The mien, or manner, of the person" (Johnson).

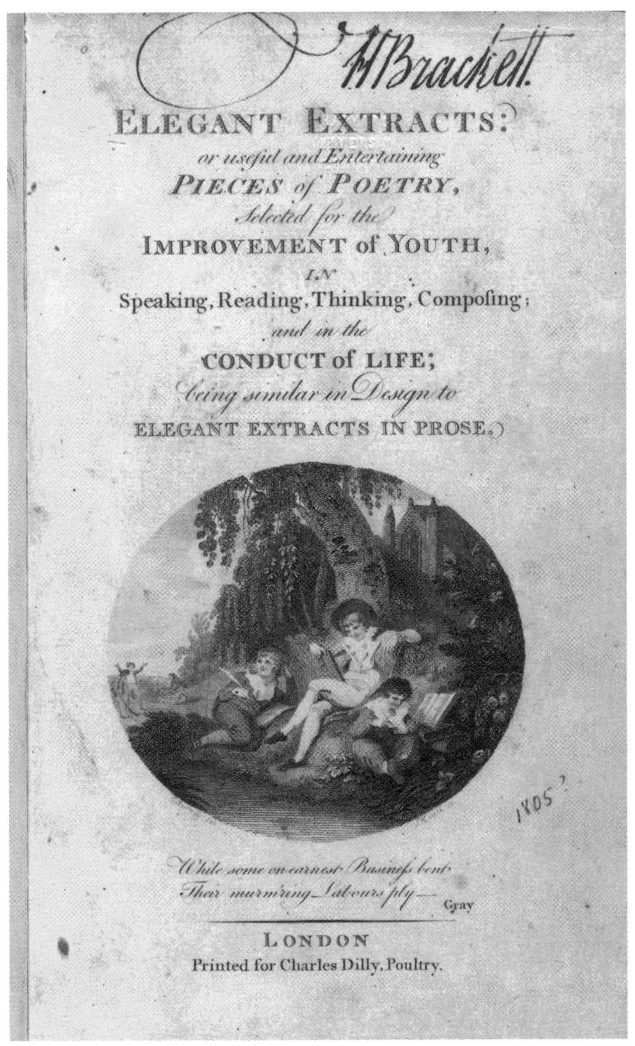

H Brackett.

ELEGANT EXTRACTS:
or useful and Entertaining
PIECES of POETRY,
Selected for the
IMPROVEMENT of YOUTH,
IN
Speaking, Reading, Thinking, Compoſing;
and in the
CONDUCT of LIFE;
being similar in Design to
ELEGANT EXTRACTS IN PROSE.

1805?

While some on earnest Busineſs bent
Their murm'ring Labours ply— Gray

LONDON
Printed for Charles Dilly, Poultry.

Title page of Vicesimus Knox, *Elegant Extracts; Or, Useful and Entertaining Pieces of Poetry* (London: C. Dilly, 1770). Knox's anthologies played a vital role in establishing a canon of "English Literature" in the late eighteenth century, as well as forming an essential part of Catherine Morland's reading in *Northanger Abbey.*

feel that now? Were not you struck? I am sure you must have been struck by his awkward look and abrupt manner—and the uncouthness of a voice, which I heard to be wholly unmodulated[32] as I stood here."

"Certainly, he is not like Mr. Knightley. He has not such a fine air and way of walking as Mr. Knightley. I see the difference plain enough. But Mr. Knightley is so very fine a man!"

"Mr. Knightley's air is so remarkably good, that it is not fair to compare Mr. Martin with *him*. You might not see one in a hundred, with *gentleman* so plainly written as in Mr. Knightley. But he is not the only gentleman you have been lately used to. What say you to Mr. Weston and Mr. Elton? Compare Mr. Martin with either of *them*. Compare their manner of carrying themselves; of walking; of speaking; of being silent. You must see the difference."

"Oh, yes!—there is a great difference. But Mr. Weston is almost an old man. Mr. Weston must be between forty and fifty."

"Which makes his good manners the more valuable. The older a person grows, Harriet, the more important it is that their manners should not be bad—the more glaring and disgusting any loudness, or coarseness, or awkwardness becomes. What is passable in youth, is detestable in later age. Mr. Martin is now awkward and abrupt; what will he be at Mr. Weston's time of life?"

"There is no saying, indeed!" replied Harriet, rather solemnly.

"But there may be pretty good guessing. He will be a completely gross,[33] vulgar farmer—totally inattentive to appearances, and thinking of nothing but profit and loss."

"Will he, indeed, that will be very bad."

"How much his business engrosses him already, is very plain from the circumstance of his forgetting to inquire for the book you recommended. He was a great deal too full of the market to think of any thing else—which is just as it should be, for a thriving man. What has he to do with books? And I have no doubt that he *will* thrive and be a very rich man in time—and his being illiterate[34] and coarse need not disturb *us*."

"I wonder he did not remember the book"—was all Harriet's answer, and spoken with a degree of grave displeasure which Emma

32 Not varying its pitch, volume, tone, and tempo according to context; Robert Martin may also have a more "countrified" accent.

33 "Intellectually coarse; palpable; impure; unrefined" (Johnson).

34 In this context, unacquainted with literature and *belles lettres,* rather than unable to read. (Robert Martin can, after all, read the Agricultural Reports.)

thought might be safely left to itself. She, therefore, said no more for some time. Her next beginning was,

"In one respect, perhaps, Mr. Elton's manners are superior to Mr. Knightley's or Mr. Weston's. They have more gentleness. They might be more safely held up as a pattern. There is an openness, a quickness, almost a bluntness in Mr. Weston, which every body likes in *him* because there is so much good humour with it—but that would not do to be copied. Neither would Mr. Knightley's downright,[35] decided, commanding sort of manner—though it suits *him* very well; his figure and look, and situation in life seem to allow it; but if any young man were to set about copying him, he would not be sufferable. On the contrary, I think a young man might be very safely recommended to take Mr. Elton as a model. Mr. Elton is good humoured, cheerful, obliging, and gentle. He seems to me, to be grown particularly gentle of late. I do not know whether he has any design of ingratiating himself with either of us, Harriet, by additional softness, but it strikes me that his manners are softer than they used to be. If he means anything, it must be to please you. Did not I tell you what he said of you the other day?"

She then repeated some warm personal praise which she had drawn from Mr. Elton, and now did full justice to; and Harriet blushed and smiled, and said she had always thought Mr. Elton very agreeable.

Mr. Elton was the very person fixed on by Emma for driving the young farmer out of Harriet's head. She thought it would be an excellent match; and only too palpably desirable, natural, and probable, for her to have much merit in planning it. She feared it was what every body else must think of and predict. It was not likely, however, that any body should have equalled her in the date of the plan, as it had entered her brain during the very first evening of Harriet's coming to Hartfield. The longer she considered it, the greater was her sense of its expediency.[36] Mr. Elton's situation was most suitable, quite the gentleman himself, and without low connections; at the same time not of any family that could fairly object to the doubtful birth of Harriet. He had a comfortable home for her, and Emma imagined a very sufficient income; for though the vicarage of High-

35 Plain and direct.

36 In this context, the primary sense is the neutral one of "aptness" or "suitability," but the word may also be haunted by its other (now more recognizable) usage, to denote self-serving convenience.

37 Overly choosy.

bury was not large, he was known to have some independent property; and she thought very highly of him as a good-humoured, well-meaning, respectable young man, without any deficiency of useful understanding or knowledge of the world.

She had already satisfied herself that he thought Harriet a beautiful girl, which she trusted, with such frequent meetings at Hartfield, was foundation enough on his side; and on Harriet's, there could be little doubt that the idea of being preferred by him would have all the usual weight and efficacy. And he was really a very pleasing young man, a young man whom any woman not fastidious[37] might like. He was reckoned very handsome; his person much admired in general, though not by her, there being a want of elegance of feature which she could not dispense with:—but the girl who could be gratified by a Robert Martin's riding about the country to get walnuts for her, might very well be conquered by Mr. Elton's admiration.

Watercolor and pencil portrait of Jane Austen by Cassandra Austen, c. 1810. Austen's nephew James Edward Austen-Leigh commissioned a much more soft-featured engraving based on this portrait for *A Memoir of Jane Austen* (1871), and this engraving remained the standard template for images of the author. Cassandra's portrait is still the only fully authenticated image of Jane Austen's face, although critics are currently debating the authenticity of a portrait drawing, dating from around 1815, which was discovered by Paula Byrne.

5

"I DO NOT KNOW WHAT YOUR OPINION MAY BE, Mrs. Weston," said Mr. Knightley, "of this great intimacy between Emma and Harriet Smith, but I think it a bad thing."

"A bad thing! Do you really think it a bad thing?—why so?"

"I think they will neither of them do the other any good."

"You surprize me! Emma must do Harriet good: and by supplying her with a new object of interest, Harriet may be said to do Emma good. I have been seeing their intimacy with the greatest pleasure. How very differently we feel!—Not think they will do each other any good! This will certainly be the beginning of one of our quarrels about Emma, Mr. Knightley."

"Perhaps you think I am come on purpose to quarrel with you, knowing Weston to be out, and that you must still fight your own battle."

"Mr. Weston would undoubtedly support me, if he were here, for he thinks exactly as I do on the subject. We were speaking of it only yesterday, and agreeing how fortunate it was for Emma, that there should be such a girl in Highbury for her to associate with. Mr. Knightley, I shall not allow you to be a fair judge in this case. You are so much used to live alone, that you do not know the value of a companion; and perhaps no man can be a good judge of the comfort a woman feels in the society of one of her own sex, after being used to it all her life. I can imagine your objection to Harriet Smith. She is not the superior young woman which Emma's friend ought to be. But on the other hand, as Emma wants to see her better informed, it will be an inducement to her to read more herself. They will read together. She means it, I know."

"Emma has been meaning to read more ever since she was twelve years old. I have seen a great many lists of her drawing up at various times of books that she meant to read regularly through—and very good lists they were—very well chosen, and very neatly arranged—sometimes alphabetically, and sometimes by some other rule. The list she drew up when only fourteen—I remember thinking it did her judgment so much credit, that I preserved it some time;[1] and I dare say she may have made out a very good list now. But I have done with[2] expecting any course of steady reading from Emma. She will never submit to any thing requiring industry and patience, and a subjection of the fancy to the understanding.[3] Where Miss Taylor failed to stimulate, I may safely affirm that Harriet Smith will do nothing. —You never could persuade her to read half so much as you wished.—You know you could not."

"I dare say," replied Mrs. Weston, smiling, "that I thought so *then;* —but since we have parted, I can never remember Emma's omitting to do any thing I wished."

"There is hardly any desiring to refresh such a memory as *that*"—said Mr. Knightley, feelingly; and for a moment or two he had done. "But I," he soon added, "who have had no such charm thrown over my senses,[4] must still see, hear, and remember. Emma is spoiled by being the cleverest of her family. At ten years old, she had the misfortune of being able to answer questions which puzzled her sister at seventeen. She was always quick and assured: Isabella slow and diffident. And ever since she was twelve, Emma has been mistress of the house and of you all. In her mother she lost the only person able to cope with her. She inherits her mother's talents, and must have been under subjection to her."

"I should have been sorry, Mr. Knightley, to be dependent on *your* recommendation, had I quitted Mr. Woodhouse's family and wanted another situation; I do not think you would have spoken a good word for me to any body. I am sure you always thought me unfit for the office I held."

1 The first hint that Harriet Smith is not the only character in the novel given to keeping sentimental souvenirs; see Introduction.

2 Given up.

3 Knightley here uses "fancy" to suggest a capricious and superficial employment of the imagination on Emma's part, contrasted with a rooted "understanding." The latter chimes with the Johnsonian definition of "fancy" to denote "imagination; the power by which the mind forms to itself images and representations of things, persons, or scenes of being," as opposed to "understanding," which denoted "Intellectual powers; faculties of the mind, especially those of knowledge and judgment." Austen's repeated recourse to "fancy" as a term for Emma's irresponsible, "imaginist" scheming shows that she still cleaves to the Johnsonian senses of the word. However, in the 1810s, "fancy" was also acquiring new valencies as part of the aesthetic vocabulary of Romantic poetry. For Coleridge, Fancy was the poor relative of Imagination, if indeed it was a relative at all. In the fourth chapter of *Biographia Literaria* (1817), he recalls how reading Wordsworth had led him to reflect "that fancy and imagination were two distinct and widely different faculties," a thought that gives rise to his famous attempt to define the two terms in the thirteenth chapter of his work:

> The IMAGINATION then I consider either as primary, or secondary. The primary IMAGINATION I hold to be the living Power and prime Agent of all human Perception, and as a repetition in the finite mind of the eternal act of creation in the infinite I AM. The secondary I consider as an echo of the former, co-existing with the conscious will, yet still as identical with the primary in the kind of its agency, and differing only in degree, and in the mode of its operation. It dissolves, diffuses, dissipates, in order to recreate; or where this process is rendered impossible, yet still at all events it struggles to idealize and to unify. It is essentially vital, even as all objects (as objects) are essentially fixed and dead.

Portrait of Samuel Taylor Coleridge (1772–1834) by Peter Vandyke, 1795. Even as Austen held to an older, Johnsonian understanding of the relations between "fancy" and "understanding," Coleridge was developing his own aesthetic distinctions between "fancy" and "imagination," as memorably discussed in his book *Biographia Literaria* (1817).

"Yes," said he, smiling. "You are better placed *here;* very fit for a wife, but not at all for a governess. But you were preparing yourself to be an excellent wife all the time you were at Hartfield. You might not give Emma such a complete education as your powers would seem to promise; but you were receiving a very good education from *her,* on the very material matrimonial point of submitting your own will, and doing as you were bid; and if Weston had asked me to recommend him a wife, I should certainly have named Miss Taylor."

"Thank you. There will be very little merit in making a good wife to such a man as Mr. Weston."

> FANCY, on the contrary, has no other counters to play with, but fixities and definites. The Fancy is indeed no other than a mode of Memory emancipated from the order of time and space; and blended with, and modified by that empirical phenomenon of the will, which we express by the word CHOICE.

The Collected Works of Samuel Taylor Coleridge, vol. 7: I, ed. J. Engell and W. J. Bate (Princeton: Princeton University Press, 1983), pp. 82, 304–305. For more on this and earlier theories, see R. L. Brett, *Fancy and Imagination* (London: Methuen, 1969).

4 In his article "Henry James and Charm" (*Essays in Criticism,* 61:2 [2011], pp. 115–136), Adrian Poole offers an incisive analysis of the range of "charm" and "charming" in nineteenth-century fiction, including *Emma.* "'Charming,'" he observes, "is a word you'd expect to find in the polite, leisured world of 'the novel of manners.' It is easily portable and limitlessly applicable . . . As words, 'charm' and 'charming' are as innocent and promiscuous as money" (p. 116).

"Why, to own the truth, I am afraid you are rather thrown away, and that with every disposition to bear, there will be nothing to be borne.[5] We will not despair, however. Weston may grow cross from the wantonness of comfort,[6] or his son may plague him."[7]

"I hope not *that.*—It is not likely. No, Mr. Knightley, do not foretel vexation from that quarter."

"Not I, indeed. I only name possibilities. I do not pretend to Emma's genius for foretelling and guessing. I hope, with all my heart, the young man may be a Weston in merit, and a Churchill in fortune.—But Harriet Smith—I have not half done about Harriet Smith. I think her the very worst sort of companion that Emma could possibly have. She knows nothing herself, and looks upon Emma as knowing every thing. She is a flatterer in all her ways; and so much the worse, because undesigned. Her ignorance is hourly flattery. How can Emma imagine she has any thing to learn herself, while Harriet is presenting such a delightful inferiority? And as for Harriet, I will venture to say that *she* cannot gain by the acquaintance. Hartfield will only put her out of conceit[8] with all the other places she belongs to. She will grow just refined enough to be uncomfortable with those among whom birth and circumstances have placed her home. I am much mistaken if Emma's doctrines give any strength of mind, or tend at all to make a girl adapt herself rationally to the varieties of her situation in life.—They only give a little polish."

"I either depend more upon Emma's good sense than you do, or am more anxious for her present comfort; for I cannot lament the acquaintance. How well she looked last night!"

"Oh! you would rather talk of her person than her mind, would you? Very well; I shall not attempt to deny Emma's being pretty."

"Pretty! say beautiful rather. Can you imagine any thing nearer perfect beauty[9] than Emma altogether—face and figure?"

"I do not know what I could imagine, but I confess that I have seldom seen a face or figure more pleasing to me than her's. But I am a partial[10] old friend."

"Such an eye!—the true hazle eye[11]—and so brilliant! regular features, open countenance, with a complexion! oh! what a bloom of full

5 That is, Mrs. Weston's "education" of Emma will be wasted, since Mr. Weston makes so few demands.

6 Grow peevish and arrogant in his leisure.

7 Become an embarrassment to him.

8 Make her dissatisfied.

9 An early instance in the novel of "perfect," a word that, along with "perfection," will come to have a significant role in the narrative texture of vol. III.

10 Biased.

11 Austen gives her heroine the same color eyes as her own: James Edward Austen-Leigh remembered that "she had full round cheeks, with mouth and nose small and well formed, bright hazel eyes, and brown hair forming natural curls close round her face," and Caroline Austen described her aunt as having "a *bright,* but not a *pink* colour—a clear brown complexion and very good hazle eyes" (*A Memoir of Jane Austen and Other Family Recollections,* ed. Kathryn Sutherland [Oxford: Oxford University Press, 2002], pp. 70, 169).

health, and such a pretty height and size; such a firm and upright figure. There is health, not merely in her bloom, but in her air, her head, her glance. One hears sometimes of a child being 'the picture of health;'[12] now Emma always gives me the idea of being the complete picture of grown-up health. She is loveliness itself. Mr. Knightley, is not she?"

"I have not a fault to find with her person," he replied. "I think her all you describe. I love to look at her; and I will add this praise, that I do not think her personally vain. Considering how very handsome she is, she appears to be little occupied with it; her vanity lies another way. Mrs. Weston, I am not to be talked out of my dislike of her intimacy with Harriet Smith, or my dread of its doing them both harm."

"And I, Mr. Knightley, am equally stout in my confidence of its not doing them any harm. With all dear Emma's little faults, she is an excellent creature. Where shall we see a better daughter, or a kinder sister, or a truer friend? No, no; she has qualities which may be trusted; she will never lead any one really wrong; she will make no lasting blunder; where Emma errs once, she is in the right a hundred times."

"Very well; I will not plague you any more. Emma shall be an angel, and I will keep my spleen to myself till Christmas brings John and Isabella. John loves Emma with a reasonable and therefore not a blind affection,[13] and Isabella always thinks as he does; except when he is not quite frightened enough about the children. I am sure of having their opinions with me."

"I know that you all love her really too well to be unjust or unkind; but excuse me, Mr. Knightley, if I take the liberty (I consider myself, you know, as having somewhat of the privilege of speech that Emma's mother might have had) the liberty of hinting that I do not think any possible good can arise from Harriet Smith's intimacy being made a matter of much discussion among you. Pray excuse me; but supposing any little inconvenience may be apprehended from the intimacy, it cannot be expected that Emma, accountable to nobody but her father, who perfectly approves the acquaintance, should

12 The phrase goes back at least as far as the eighteenth century; in book IX, chap. 3, of *Tom Jones* (1749), Fielding's narrator describes his hero's features thus: "His face, besides being the picture of health, had in it the most apparent marks of sweetness and good-nature."

13 That is, an affection in which the heart is not disconnected completely from the mind. The idea of rational affection is also an important recurring motif in *Pride and Prejudice,* as seen in the narrator's reflections, in vol. III, chap. 4, on Elizabeth's change of heart toward Darcy: "If gratitude and esteem are good foundations of affection, Elizabeth's change of sentiment will be neither improbable nor faulty."

put an end to it, so long as it is a source of pleasure to herself. It has been so many years my province to give advice, that you cannot be surprized, Mr. Knightley, at this little remains of office."

"Not at all," cried he; "I am much obliged to you for it. It is very good advice, and it shall have a better fate than your advice has often found; for it shall be attended to."

"Mrs. John Knightley is easily alarmed, and might be made unhappy about her sister."

"Be satisfied," said he, "I will not raise any outcry. I will keep my ill-humour to myself. I have a very sincere interest in Emma. Isabella does not seem more my sister; has never excited a greater interest; perhaps hardly so great. There is an anxiety, a curiosity in what one feels for Emma. I wonder what will become of her!"[14]

"So do I," said Mrs. Weston gently; "very much."

"She always declares she will never marry, which, of course, means just nothing at all. But I have no idea that she has yet ever seen a man she cared for. It would not be a bad thing for her to be very much in love with a proper object. I should like to see Emma in love, and in some doubt of a return; it would do her good. But there is nobody hereabouts to attach her;[15] and she goes so seldom from home."

"There does, indeed, seem as little to tempt her to break her resolution, at present," said Mrs. Weston, "as can well be; and while she is so happy at Hartfield, I cannot wish her to be forming any attachment which would be creating such difficulties, on poor Mr. Woodhouse's account. I do not recommend matrimony at present to Emma, though I mean no slight to the state I assure you."

Part of her meaning was to conceal some favourite thoughts of her own and Mr. Weston's on the subject, as much as possible. There were wishes at Randalls respecting Emma's destiny, but it was not desirable to have them suspected; and the quiet transition which Mr. Knightley soon afterwards made to "What does Weston think of the weather; shall we have rain?"[16] convinced her that he had nothing more to say or surmise about Hartfield.

14 Knightley's "curiosity" sounds oddly like that of a novel reader at this point.

15 To inspire her affections.

16 In the *Idler,* no. 11 (June 24, 1758), Johnson wryly notes "that when two Englishmen meet, their first talk is of the weather; they are in haste to tell each other, what each must already know, that it is hot or cold, bright or cloudy, windy or calm" (*The Works of Samuel Johnson,* vol. II, ed. W. J. Bate, John M. Bullitt, and L. F. Powell [New Haven: Yale University Press, 1963], p. 36).

6

Emma could not feel a doubt of having given Harriet's fancy a proper direction and raised the gratitude of her young vanity to a very good purpose, for she found her decidedly more sensible[1] than before of Mr. Elton's being a remarkably handsome man, with most agreeable manners; and as she had no hesitation in following up the assurance of his admiration, by agreeable hints, she was soon pretty confident of creating as much liking on Harriet's side, as there could be any occasion for. She was quite convinced of Mr. Elton's being in the fairest way of falling in love,[2] if not in love already. She had no scruple[3] with regard to him. He talked of Harriet, and praised her so warmly, that she could not suppose any thing wanting which a little time would not add. His perception of the striking improvement of Harriet's manner, since her introduction at Hartfield, was not one of the least agreeable proofs of his growing attachment.

"You have given Miss Smith all that she required," said he; "you have made her graceful and easy. She was a beautiful creature when she came to you, but, in my opinion, the attractions you have added are infinitely superior to what she received from nature."

"I am glad you think I have been useful to her; but Harriet only wanted drawing out, and receiving a few, very few hints. She had all the natural grace of sweetness of temper and artlessness in herself. I have done very little."

"If it were admissible to contradict a lady," said the gallant Mr. Elton—

1 Aware.

2 In an ideal situation for falling in love.

3 Doubt, hesitation.

"I have perhaps given her a little more decision of character, have taught her to think on points which had not fallen in her way before."

"Exactly so; that is what principally strikes me. So much superadded decision of character! Skilful has been the hand."[4]

"Great has been the pleasure, I am sure. I never met with a disposition more truly amiable."

"I have no doubt of it." And it was spoken with a sort of sighing animation, which had a vast deal of the lover. She was not less pleased another day with the manner in which he seconded a sudden wish of her's, to have Harriet's picture.

"Did you ever have your likeness taken, Harriet?" said she: "Did you ever sit for your picture?"

Harriet was on the point of leaving the room, and only stopt to say, with a very interesting naïveté,[5]

"Oh! dear, no, never."

No sooner was she out of sight, than Emma exclaimed,

"What an exquisite possession a good picture of her would be! I would give any money for it. I almost long to attempt her likeness myself. You do not know it I dare say, but two or three years ago I had a great passion for taking likenesses, and attempted several of my friends, and was thought to have a tolerable eye in general. But from one cause or another, I gave it up in disgust. But really, I could almost venture, if Harriet would sit to me. It would be such a delight to have her picture!"

"Let me entreat you," cried Mr. Elton; "it would indeed be a delight! Let me entreat you, Miss Woodhouse, to exercise so charming a talent in favour of your friend. I know what your drawings are. How could you suppose me ignorant? Is not this room rich in specimens of your landscapes and flowers; and has not Mrs. Weston some inimitable figure-pieces[6] in her drawing-room, at Randalls?"

Yes, good man!—thought Emma—but what has all that got to do with taking likenesses? You know nothing of drawing. Don't pretend to be in raptures about mine. Keep your raptures for Harriet's face. "Well, if you give me such kind encouragement, Mr. Elton, I believe I shall try what I can do. Harriet's features are very delicate, which

4 Emma fails to notice, here and elsewhere, that Elton expresses greater admiration for her influence over Harriet than for Harriet herself.

5 Affecting artlessness. The adjective "interesting" often carries a significant extra freight in this period. For example, Lady Davy, the wife of the eminent scientist Sir Humphry Davy, complained about a lack of "interest" in *Pride and Prejudice*, in a letter to Sarah Ponsonby (one of the famous female cohabitors, "The Ladies of Llangollen") on May 14, 1813: "'Pride and Prejudice' I do not very much like. Want of interest is the fault I can least excuse in works of mere amusement" (*The Hamwood Papers of the Ladies of Llangollen and Caroline Hamilton*, ed. Mrs. G. H. Bell [London: Macmillan and Co., 1930], p. 351). Brian Southam comments on this complaint: "This word had taken a rather specialized meaning from its use in sentimental literature, where 'interest' invariably meant romantic interest. The force of this meaning to the early nineteenth-century reader comes across clearly in Egerton's advertisement for *Sense and Sensibility,* styling it simply enough an 'Interesting Novel'" (Introduction to *Jane Austen: The Critical Heritage,* 2 vols. [London: Routledge & Kegan Paul, 1968–1987], vol. 1, p. 9).

6 Full-length studies of the human form, as distinct from partial portraits or "likenesses."

makes a likeness difficult; and yet there is a peculiarity in the shape of the eye and the lines about the mouth which one ought to catch."

"Exactly so—The shape of the eye and the lines about the mouth—I have not a doubt of your success. Pray, pray attempt it. As you will do it, it will indeed, to use your own words, be an exquisite possession."

"But I am afraid, Mr. Elton, Harriet will not like to sit. She thinks so little of her own beauty. Did not you observe her manner of answering me? How completely it meant, 'why should my picture be drawn?'"

"Oh! yes, I observed it, I assure you. It was not lost on me. But still I cannot imagine she would not be persuaded."

Harriet was soon back again, and the proposal almost immediately made; and she had no scruples which could stand many minutes against the earnest pressing of both the others. Emma wished to go to work directly, and therefore produced the portfolio containing her various attempts at portraits, for not one of them had ever been finished, that they might decide together on the best size for Harriet. Her many beginnings were displayed. Miniatures,[7] half-lengths, whole-lengths, pencil, crayon,[8] and water-colours had been all tried in turn. She had always wanted to do everything, and had made more progress both in drawing and music than many might have done with so little labour as she would ever submit to. She played and sang;—and drew in almost every style;[9] but steadiness had always been wanting; and in nothing had she approached the degree of excellence which she would have been glad to command, and ought not to have failed of. She was not much deceived as to her own skill either as an artist or a musician, but she was not unwilling to have others deceived, or sorry to know her reputation for accomplishment often higher than it deserved.

There was merit in every drawing—in the least finished, perhaps the most; her style was spirited;[10] but had there been much less, or had there been ten times more, the delight and admiration of her two companions would have been the same. They were both in extasies.[11] A likeness pleases every body; and Miss Woodhouse's performances must be capital.[12]

7 Miniatures are small but very detailed paintings. In a letter to James Edward Austen (later Austen-Leigh) of December 16–17, 1816, Austen compared her own art to that of the miniaturist in a way that later came to define her (whether for good or ill) as an artist of the minuscule: "the little bit (two Inches wide) of Ivory on which I work with so fine a Brush, as produces little effect after much labour" (*Letters,* p. 323). A representative example of the way Austen's readers and critics picked up on this analogy can be found in G. H. Lewes's famous article of 1859: "It is intelligible how the blaze of Scott should have thrown her into the shade, at first: beside his frescoes her works are but miniatures; exquisite as miniatures, yet incapable of ever filling that space in the public eye which was filled by his massive and masterly pictures" (*Jane Austen: The Critical Heritage,* vol. 1, p. 149).

8 Chalks.

9 A suggestion both of Emma's intellectual powers and of her inability to channel and direct them successfully.

10 Robust and energetic.

11 Raptures (in the ironic, pejorative sense defined by Johnson as "excessive joy").

12 The best of their kind.

"No great variety of faces for you," said Emma. "I had only my own family to study from. There is my father—another of my father—but the idea of sitting for his picture made him so nervous, that I could only take him by stealth; neither of them very like therefore. Mrs. Weston again, and again, and again, you see. Dear Mrs. Weston! always my kindest friend on every occasion. She would sit whenever I asked her. There is my sister; and really quite her own little elegant figure!—and the face not unlike. I should have made a good likeness of her, if she would have sat longer, but she was in such a hurry to have me draw her four children that she would not be quiet. Then, here come all my attempts at three of those four children;—there they are, Henry and John and Bella, from one end of the sheet to the other, and any one of them might do for any one of the rest.[13] She was so eager to have them drawn that I could not refuse; but there is no making children of three or four years old stand still you know; nor can it be very easy to take any likeness of them, beyond the air and complexion, unless they are coarser featured than any mama's children ever were. Here is my sketch of the fourth, who was a baby. I took him, as he was sleeping on the sofa, and it is as strong a likeness of his cockade[14] as you would wish to see. He had nestled down his head most conveniently. That's very like. I am rather proud of little George. The corner of the sofa is very good. Then here is my last"—unclosing a pretty sketch of a gentleman in small size, whole-length—"my last and my best—my brother, Mr. John Knightley.—This did not want much of being finished, when I put it away in a pet,[15] and vowed I would never take another likeness. I could not help being provoked; for after all my pains, and when I had really made a very

13 A minor, comic variation on a concern that takes much more serious forms elsewhere in *Emma* and across Austen's fiction: the uniqueness or interchangeability of human beings (see Introduction).

14 A rosette, or ornamental arrangement of ribbons, attached to an item of headgear. Soldiers, as well as babies, wore cockades, as witnessed by Mr. Edwardes's remark in *The Watsons,* Austen's unfinished fragment from 1805: "There is no resisting a Cockade my dear."

15 In a sulk, in a fit of pique.

Miniature of Jane Austen's vivacious paternal cousin Eliza Hancock, later de Feuillide and Austen (1761–1813), c. 1780; by kind permission of Tibbie Adams. Born in Calcutta, Eliza was the goddaughter of Warren Hastings, later governor-general of India, whose munificence to her has led some biographers to speculate (with little other evidence) that he was in fact her biological father. In 1781, Eliza married Jean-François Capot de Feuillide, who was guillotined by the French revolutionaries in 1794; she eventually married Austen's brother Henry in 1797.

good likeness of it—(Mrs. Weston and I were quite agreed in thinking it *very* like)—only too handsome—too flattering—but that was a fault on the right side—after all this, came poor dear Isabella's cold approbation of—'Yes, it was a little like—but to be sure it did not do him justice.' We had had a great deal of trouble in persuading him to sit at all. It was made a great favour of; and altogether it was more than I could bear; and so I never would finish it, to have it apologized over as an unfavourable likeness, to every morning visitor in Brunswick-square;—and, as I said, I did then forswear ever drawing anybody again. But for Harriet's sake, or rather for my own, and as there are no husbands and wives in the case at present, I will break my resolution now."

Mr. Elton seemed very properly struck and delighted by the idea, and was repeating, "No husbands and wives in the case *at present* indeed, as you observe. Exactly so. No husbands and wives," with so interesting[16] a consciousness,[17] that Emma began to consider whether she had not better leave them together at once. But as she wanted to be drawing, the declaration must wait a little longer.

She had soon fixed on the size and sort of portrait. It was to be a whole-length in water-colours, like Mr. John Knightley's, and was destined, if she could please herself, to hold a very honourable station over the mantle-piece.

The sitting began; and Harriet, smiling and blushing, and afraid of not keeping her attitude and countenance,[18] presented a very sweet mixture of youthful expression to the steady eyes of the artist. But there was no doing anything, with Mr. Elton fidgetting behind her and watching every touch.[19] She gave him credit for stationing himself where he might gaze and gaze again without offence; but was really obliged to put an end to it, and request him to place himself elsewhere. It then occurred to her to employ him in reading.

"If he would be so good as to read to them, it would be a kindness indeed! It would amuse away the difficulties of her part, and lessen the irksomeness of Miss Smith's."

Mr. Elton was only too happy. Harriet listened, and Emma drew in peace. She must allow him to be still frequently coming to look; anything less would certainly have been too little in a lover; and he was

16 See note 5 above.

17 Self-consciousness, deliberate emphasis.

18 Not being able to keep her body and face still.

19 Pencil-stroke.

ready at the smallest intermission of the pencil, to jump up and see the progress, and be charmed.—There was no being displeased with such an encourager, for his admiration made him discern a likeness almost before it was possible. She could not respect his eye, but his love and his complaisance[20] were unexceptionable.[21]

The sitting was altogether very satisfactory; she was quite enough pleased with the first day's sketch to wish to go on. There was no want of likeness, she had been fortunate in the attitude, and as she meant to throw in a little improvement to the figure, to give a little more height, and considerably more elegance, she had great confidence of its being in every way a pretty drawing at last, and of its filling its destined place with credit to them both—a standing[22] memorial of the beauty of one, the skill of the other, and the friendship of both; with as many other agreeable associations as Mr. Elton's very promising attachment was likely to add.

Harriet was to sit again the next day; and Mr. Elton, just as he ought, entreated for the permission of attending and reading to them again.

"By all means. We shall be most happy to consider you as one of the party."

The same civilities and courtesies, the same success and satisfaction, took place on the morrow, and accompanied the whole progress of the picture, which was rapid and happy. Every body who saw it was pleased, but Mr. Elton was in continual raptures, and defended it through every criticism.

"Miss Woodhouse has given her friend the only beauty she wanted,"—observed Mrs. Weston to him—not in the least suspecting that she was addressing a lover.—"The expression of the eye is most correct, but Miss Smith has not those eye-brows and eyelashes. It is the fault of her face that she has them not."

"Do you think so?" replied he. "I cannot agree with you. It appears to me a most perfect resemblance in every feature. I never saw such a likeness in my life. We must allow for the effect of shade, you know."

"You have made her too tall, Emma," said Mr. Knightley.[23]

20 Desire to please, but with a possible ironic undertow of servility.

21 Beyond reproach.

22 Lasting.

23 Knightley, as usual, does not mince his words when talking to Emma.

Emma knew that she had, but would not own it, and Mr. Elton warmly added,

"Oh, no! certainly not too tall; not in the least too tall. Consider, she is sitting down—which naturally presents a different—which in short gives exactly the idea—and the proportions must be preserved, you know. Proportions, fore-shortening.[24]—Oh, no! it gives one exactly the idea of such a height as Miss Smith's. Exactly so indeed!"

"It is very pretty," said Mr. Woodhouse. "So prettily done! Just as your drawings always are, my dear. I do not know any body who draws so well as you do. The only thing I do not thoroughly like is, that she seems to be sitting out of doors, with only a little shawl over her shoulders—and it makes one think she must catch cold."

"But, my dear papa, it is supposed to be summer; a warm day in summer. Look at the tree."

"But it is never safe to sit out of doors, my dear."

"You, sir, may say any thing," cried Mr. Elton; "but I must confess that I regard it as a most happy[25] thought, the placing of Miss Smith out of doors; and the tree is touched with such inimitable spirit! Any other situation would have been much less in character. The naïveté of Miss Smith's manners—and altogether—Oh, it is most admirable! I cannot keep my eyes from it. I never saw such a likeness."

The next thing wanted was to get the picture framed; and here were a few difficulties. It must be done directly;[26] it must be done in London; the order must go through the hands of some intelligent person whose taste could be depended on; and Isabella, the usual doer of all commissions, must not be applied to, because it was December, and Mr. Woodhouse could not bear the idea of her stirring out of her house in the fogs of December. But no sooner was the distress known to Mr. Elton, than it was removed. His gallantry was always on the alert. "Might he be trusted with the commission, what infinite pleasure should he have in executing it! he could ride to London at any time. It was impossible to say how much he should be gratified by being employed on such an errand."

"He was too good!—she could not endure the thought!—she would not give him such a troublesome office[27] for the world"—

24 Elton is attempting to impress Emma with his knowledge of painterly aesthetics but succeeds only in parading his ignorance: "proportions" alludes to the principle of geometrical perspective popularized by fifteenth-century Italian artists; however, the perspectival effect of foreshortening is famous for making objects appear shorter than they really are, not taller.

25 Appropriate.

26 As soon as possible.

27 Charge, errand.

28 An object placed in trust.

29 Reach around eagerly for compliments to bestow.

brought on the desired repetition of entreaties and assurances,—and a very few minutes settled the business.

Mr. Elton was to take the drawing to London, chuse the frame, and give the directions; and Emma thought she could so pack it as to ensure its safety without much incommoding him, while he seemed mostly fearful of not being incommoded enough.

"What a precious deposit!"[28] said he with a tender sigh, as he received it.

"This man is almost too gallant to be in love," thought Emma. "I should say so, but that I suppose there may be a hundred different ways of being in love. He is an excellent young man, and will suit Harriet exactly; it will be an 'Exactly so,' as he says himself; but he does sigh and languish, and study for compliments[29] rather more than I could endure as a principal. I come in for a pretty good share as a second. But it is his gratitude on Harriet's account."

7

The very day of Mr. Elton's going to London produced a fresh occasion for Emma's services towards her friend. Harriet had been at Hartfield, as usual, soon after breakfast; and after a time, had gone home to return again to dinner:[1] she returned, and sooner than had been talked of, and with an agitated, hurried look, announcing something extraordinary to have happened which she was longing to tell. Half a minute brought it all out. She had heard, as soon as she got back to Mrs. Goddard's, that Mr. Martin had been there an hour before, and finding she was not at home, nor particularly expected, had left a little parcel for her from one of his sisters, and gone away; and on opening this parcel, she had actually found, besides the two songs which she had lent Elizabeth to copy,[2] a letter to herself; and this letter was from him, from Mr. Martin, and contained a direct proposal of marriage. "Who could have thought it! She was so surprized she did not know what to do. Yes, quite a proposal of marriage; and a very good letter, at least she thought so. And he wrote as if he really loved her very much—but she did not know—and so, she was come as fast as she could to ask Miss Woodhouse what she should do."—Emma was half ashamed of her friend for seeming so pleased and so doubtful.

"Upon my word," she cried, "the young man is determined not to lose any thing for want of asking. He will connect himself well if he can."

"Will you read the letter?" cried Harriet. "Pray do. I'd rather you would."

1 Breakfast would often not be finished until the late morning, and considering the early dinner hour at Hartfield, this would not leave Harriet with a great deal of time in between. See note 15 to vol. I, chap. 1.

2 Some of Austen's own transcripts of musical scores still survive and are on display at Chawton Cottage, where Austen lived from 1809 until 1817, and where *Sense and Sensibility* and *Pride and Prejudice* were redrafted, and her other major works, including *Emma,* were written. For more on the context of musical scores in Austen's times, see Patrick Piggott, *The Innocent Diversion: A Study of Music in the Life and Writings of Jane Austen* (London: Douglas Cleverdon, 1979).

Emma was not sorry to be pressed. She read, and was surprized. The style of the letter was much above her expectation. There were not merely no grammatical errors, but as a composition it would not have disgraced a gentleman; the language, though plain, was strong and unaffected, and the sentiments it conveyed very much to the credit of the writer. It was short, but expressed good sense, warm attachment, liberality,[3] propriety,[4] even delicacy of feeling. She paused over it, while Harriet stood anxiously watching for her opinion, with a "Well, well," and was at last forced to add, "Is it a good letter? or is it too short?"

"Yes, indeed, a very good letter," replied Emma rather slowly—"so good a letter, Harriet, that every thing considered, I think one of his sisters must have helped him. I can hardly imagine the young man whom I saw talking with you the other day could express himself so well, if left quite to his own powers, and yet it is not the style of a woman; no, certainly, it is too strong and concise; not diffuse enough for a woman.[5] No doubt he is a sensible man, and I suppose may have a natural talent for—thinks strongly and clearly—and when he takes a pen in hand, his thoughts naturally find proper words. It is so with some men. Yes, I understand the sort of mind. Vigorous, decided, with sentiments to a certain point, not coarse. A better written letter, Harriet, (returning it,) than I had expected."

"Well," said the still waiting Harriet;—"well—and—and what shall I do?"

"What shall you do! In what respect? Do you mean with regard to this letter?"

"Yes."

"But what are you in doubt of? You must answer it of course—and speedily."

"Yes. But what shall I say? Dear Miss Woodhouse, do advise me."

"Oh, no, no! the letter had much better be all your own. You will express yourself very properly, I am sure. There is no danger of your not being intelligible, which is the first thing. Your meaning must be unequivocal; no doubts or demurs:[6] and such expressions of gratitude and concern for the pain you are inflicting as propriety requires, will present themselves unbidden to *your* mind, I am persuaded. *You*

3 Breadth or generosity of mind. This was a relatively recent usage of the word, which the *OED* dates to the early nineteenth century. In vol. I, chap. 5, of *Persuasion,* Admiral Croft's "liberality" is one of the qualities that wins over Sir Walter Elliot when making the arrangements for Kellynch Hall: "there was such a hearty good humour, such an open, trusting liberality on the Admiral's side, as could not but influence Sir Walter."

4 A proper sense of social decorum. Tony Tanner (acknowledging David Baddiel) has also drawn attention to the way in which the sense of "propriety" as "decorum" in the late eighteenth century bleeds into the sense of "propriety" as "economic possession": "To secure the proper relationship between property and propriety in her novels was . . . not the wish-fulfilment of a genteel spinster but a matter of vital social—and political—importance. That is why it is in many ways irrelevant to argue whether she was a relatively mindless reactionary or an incipient Marxist. She did believe in the values of her society; but she saw that those values had to be authentically embodied and enacted if that society was to survive—or deserve to survive" (*Jane Austen* [Basingstoke: Macmillan, 1986], p. 18).

5 The supposedly distinctive forms of feminine correspondence formed important points of discussion and debate in eighteenth- and nineteenth-century epistolary culture; however, critics have questioned how absolute the gendering of epistolary style actually was. As Mary A. Favret has argued, "[w]e accept too readily the notion that the letter allows us a window into the intimate, and usually feminine, self" (*Romantic Correspondence: Women, Politics and the Fiction of Letters* [Cambridge: Cambridge University Press, 1993], p. 10).

6 Hesitations.

need not be prompted to write with the appearance of sorrow for his disappointment."

"You think I ought to refuse him then," said Harriet, looking down.

"Ought to refuse him! My dear Harriet, what do you mean? Are you in any doubt as to that? I thought—but I beg your pardon, perhaps I have been under a mistake. I certainly have been misunderstanding you, if you feel in doubt as to the *purport* of your answer. I had imagined you were consulting me only as to the wording of it."

Harriet was silent. With a little reserve of manner, Emma continued:

"You mean to return a favourable answer, I collect."[7]

"No, I do not; that is, I do not mean—What shall I do? What would you advise me to do? Pray, dear Miss Woodhouse, tell me what I ought to do?"

"I shall not give you any advice, Harriet. I will have nothing to do with it. This is a point which you must settle with your own feelings."

"I had no notion that he liked me so very much," said Harriet, contemplating the letter. For a little while Emma persevered in her silence; but beginning to apprehend the bewitching flattery of that letter might be too powerful, she thought it best to say,

7 I gather.

A page from Austen's music manuscripts at Chawton Cottage. Austen not only was a keen performer of music but also transcribed a good deal. In addition, transcription was an economical way of circulating musical scores among family and friends.

"I lay it down as a general rule, Harriet, that if a woman *doubts* as to whether she should accept a man or not, she certainly ought to refuse him. If she can hesitate as to 'Yes,' she ought to say 'No' directly.[8] It is not a state to be safely entered into with doubtful feelings, with half a heart. I thought it my duty as a friend, and older than yourself, to say thus much to you. But do not imagine that I want to influence you."

"Oh! no, I am sure you are a great deal too kind to—but if you would just advise me what I had best do—No, no, I do not mean that—As you say, one's mind ought to be quite made up—One should not be hesitating—It is a very serious thing.—It will be safer to say 'No,' perhaps.—Do you think I had better say 'No?'"

"Not for the world," said Emma, smiling graciously, "would I advise you either way. You must be the best judge of your own happiness. If you prefer Mr. Martin to every other person; if you think him the most agreeable man you have ever been in company with, why should you hesitate? You blush, Harriet.—Does any body else occur to you at this moment under such a definition? Harriet, Harriet, do not deceive yourself; do not be run away with by gratitude and compassion. At this moment whom are you thinking of?"

The symptoms were favourable.—Instead of answering, Harriet turned away confused, and stood thoughtfully by the fire; and though the letter was still in her hand, it was now mechanically twisted about without regard. Emma waited the result with impatience, but not without strong hopes. At last, with some hesitation, Harriet said—

"Miss Woodhouse, as you will not give me your opinion, I must do as well as I can by myself; and I have now quite determined, and really almost made up my mind—to refuse Mr. Martin. Do you think I am right?"

"Perfectly, perfectly right, my dearest Harriet; you are doing just what you ought. While you were at all in suspense I kept my feelings to myself, but now that you are so completely decided I have no hesitation in approving. Dear Harriet, I give myself joy of this. It would have grieved me to lose your acquaintance, which must have been the consequence of your marrying Mr. Martin. While you were

8 Despite Emma's transparently dubious motives, the wording of her sentiment itself is not wholly removed from some of Austen's own recorded thoughts on the subject of marriage. Compare, for example, her letter to her niece Fanny Knight of November 30, 1814: "Your own feelings & none but your own, should determine such an important point.—So far however as answering your question, I have no scruple.—I am perfectly convinced that your present feelings, supposing you were to marry *now,* would be sufficient for his happiness;—but when I think how very, very far it is from a *Now,* & take everything that *may be,* into consideration, I dare not say, 'determine to accept him.' The risk is too great for *you,* unless your own Sentiments prompt it" (*Letters,* pp. 285–286).

in the smallest degree wavering, I said nothing about it, because I would not influence; but it would have been the loss of a friend to me. I could not have visited Mrs. Robert Martin, of Abbey-Mill Farm. Now I am secure of you[9] for ever."

Harriet had not surmised her own danger, but the idea of it struck her forcibly.

"You could not have visited me!" she cried, looking aghast. "No, to be sure you could not; but I never thought of that before. That would have been too dreadful!—What an escape!—Dear Miss Woodhouse, I would not give up the pleasure and honour of being intimate with you for any thing in the world."

"Indeed, Harriet, it would have been a severe pang to lose you; but it must have been. You would have thrown yourself out of all good society. I must have given you up."

"Dear me!—How should I ever have borne it! It would have killed me never to come to Hartfield any more!"

"Dear affectionate creature!—*You* banished to Abbey-Mill Farm!—*You* confined to the society of the illiterate[10] and vulgar all your life! I wonder how the young man could have the assurance to ask it. He must have a pretty good[11] opinion of himself."

"I do not think he is conceited either, in general," said Harriet, her conscience opposing such censure; "at least he is very good natured, and I shall always feel much obliged to him, and have a great regard for—but that is quite a different thing from—and you know, though he may like me, it does not follow that I should—and certainly I must confess that since my visiting here I have seen people—and if one comes to compare them, person and manners, there is no comparison at all, *one* is so very handsome and agreeable. However, I do really think Mr. Martin a very amiable young man, and have a great opinion of him; and his being so much attached to me—and his writing such a letter—but as to leaving you, it is what I would not do upon any consideration."

"Thank you, thank you, my own sweet little friend. We will not be parted. A woman is not to marry a man merely because she is asked, or because he is attached to her, and can write a tolerable letter."

"Oh! no;—and it is but a short letter too."

9 Assured of your acquaintance.

10 See note 34 to chap. 4 above.

11 Fairly high, although this may be an early instance of the more modern sense of "very high." There is a comparable ambiguity in John Keats's description of the composition of *Endymion,* in a letter to his sister Fanny of September 10, 1817: "proceeding at a pretty good rate with a Poem which I hope you will see early in the next year" (*The Letters of John Keats,* ed. M. Buxton Forman [London: Oxford University Press, 1931; 4th ed., 1952], p. 37).

12 Even Emma recognizes that Harriet is now back-tracking too far.

13 Act.

Emma felt the bad taste of her friend,[12] but let it pass with a "very true; and it would be a small consolation to her, for the clownish manner which might be offending her every hour of the day, to know that her husband could write a good letter."

"Oh! yes, very. Nobody cares for a letter; the thing is, to be always happy with pleasant companions. I am quite determined to refuse him. But how shall I do?[13] What shall I say?"

Emma assured her there would be no difficulty in the answer, and advised its being written directly, which was agreed to, in the hope of her assistance; and though Emma continued to protest against any assistance being wanted, it was in fact given in the formation of ev-

James Gillray, "High Change in Bond Street," 1796. Gillray's caricature captures the fact that Bond Street was one of the most fashionable streets in late eighteenth- and early nineteenth-century London; it still has strong connections with high-end fashion today.

ery sentence. The looking over his letter again, in replying to it, had such a softening tendency, that it was particularly necessary to brace her up[14] with a few decisive expressions; and she was so very much concerned at the idea of making him unhappy, and thought so much of what his mother and sisters would think and say, and was so anxious that they should not fancy her ungrateful, that Emma believed if the young man had come in her way at that moment, he would have been accepted after all.

This letter, however, was written, and sealed, and sent. The business was finished, and Harriet safe. She was rather low all the evening, but Emma could allow for her amiable regrets, and sometimes relieved them by speaking of her own affection, sometimes by bringing forward the idea of Mr. Elton.

"I shall never be invited to Abbey-Mill again," was said in rather a sorrowful tone.

"Nor if you were, could I ever bear to part with you, my Harriet. You are a great deal too necessary at Hartfield, to be spared to Abbey-Mill."

"And I am sure I should never want to go there; for I am never happy but at Hartfield."

Some time afterwards it was, "I think Mrs. Goddard would be very much surprized if she knew what had happened. I am sure Miss Nash would—for Miss Nash thinks her own sister very well married, and it is only a linen-draper."[15]

"One should be sorry to see greater pride or refinement in the teacher of a school, Harriet. I dare say Miss Nash would envy you such an opportunity as this of being married. Even this conquest would appear valuable in her eyes. As to anything superior for you, I suppose she is quite in the dark. The attentions of a certain person can hardly be among the tittle-tattle of Highbury yet. Hitherto I fancy you and I are the only people to whom his looks and manners have explained themselves."

Harriet blushed and smiled, and said something about wondering that people should like her so much. The idea of Mr. Elton was certainly cheering; but still, after a time, she was tender-hearted again towards the rejected Mr. Martin.

14 To firm up her resolve.

15 There was nothing intrinsically demeaning about being a linen-draper, other than the basic fact of its being a trade—which would in itself be far too low a station for someone of the birth that Emma attributes to Harriet. The most famous linen-draper in late eighteenth-century literature was probably the hero of William Cowper's popular comic poem from 1792, *The Diverting History of John Gilpin:*

> I am a linnen-draper bold,
>   As all the world doth know,
> And my good friend the Callender
>   Will lend his horse to go.

"Now he has got my letter," said she softly. "I wonder what they are all doing—whether his sisters know—if he is unhappy, they will be unhappy too. I hope he will not mind it so very much."

"Let us think of those among our absent friends who are more cheerfully employed," cried Emma. "At this moment, perhaps, Mr. Elton is shewing your picture to his mother and sisters, telling how much more beautiful is the original, and after being asked for it five or six times, allowing them to hear your name, your own dear name."

"My picture!—But he has left my picture in Bond-street."[16]

"Has he so!—Then I know nothing of Mr. Elton. No, my dear little modest Harriet, depend upon it the picture will not be in Bond-street till just before he mounts his horse to-morrow. It is his companion all this evening, his solace, his delight. It opens his designs to his family, it introduces you among them, it diffuses through the party those pleasantest feelings of our nature, eager curiosity and warm prepossession.[17] How cheerful, how animated, how suspicious, how busy their imaginations all are!"

Harriet smiled again, and her smiles grew stronger.

16 A long and very fashionable street in the West End of London, running from Piccadilly at the south end to Oxford Street at the north. Old Bond Street (at the south end) was built from 1684, partly funded by Sir Thomas Bond, and the construction of New Bond Street began at the turn of the eighteenth century. There are still some fine art merchants on and near the street today, although the predominant businesses are designer fashion boutiques.

17 Strong prejudice in favor.

8

HARRIET SLEPT AT HARTFIELD THAT NIGHT. For some weeks past she had been spending more than half her time there, and gradually getting to have a bed-room appropriated to herself; and Emma judged it best in every respect, safest and kindest, to keep her with them as much as possible just at present. She was obliged to go the next morning for an hour or two to Mrs. Goddard's, but it was then to be settled that she should return to Hartfield, to make a regular[1] visit of some days.

While she was gone, Mr. Knightley called, and sat some time with Mr. Woodhouse and Emma, till Mr. Woodhouse, who had previously made up his mind to walk out, was persuaded by his daughter not to defer it, and was induced by the entreaties of both, though against the scruples of his own civility, to leave Mr. Knightley for that purpose. Mr. Knightley, who had nothing of ceremony about him, was offering by his short, decided answers, an amusing contrast to the protracted apologies and civil hesitations of the other.

"Well, I believe, if you will excuse me, Mr. Knightley, if you will not consider me as doing a very rude thing, I shall take Emma's advice and go out for a quarter of an hour. As the sun is out, I believe I had better take my three turns[2] while I can. I treat you without ceremony, Mr. Knightley. We invalids think we are privileged people."

"My dear sir, do not make a stranger of me."

"I leave an excellent substitute in my daughter. Emma will be happy to entertain you. And therefore I think I will beg your excuse and take my three turns—my winter walk."[3]

1 Scheduled.

2 This would, presumably, be the shorter of the two "divisions" of Mr. Woodhouse's walk mentioned in vol. I, chap. 4.

3 Winter walks feature prominently in *The Task* (1785), the most famous work by one of Austen's favorite poets, William Cowper. They prompt the titles of the poem's last two books, "The Winter Morning Walk" and "The Winter Walk at Noon." Book VI, for example, offers this evocation of the scene:

> The night was winter in his roughest mood,
> The morning sharp and clear. But now at noon
> Upon the southern side of the slant hills,
> And where the woods fence off the northern blast,
> The season smiles resigning all its rage
> And has the warmth of May. The vault is blue
> Without a cloud, and white without a speck
> The dazzling splendour of the scene below.

However, as we find out in vol. I, chap. 15, Mr. Woodhouse himself would never have ventured out in such conditions.

"You cannot do better, sir."

"I would ask for the pleasure of your company, Mr. Knightley, but I am a very slow walker, and my pace would be tedious to you; and besides, you have another long walk before you, to Donwell Abbey."

"Thank you, sir, thank you; I am going this moment myself; and I think the sooner *you* go the better. I will fetch your great coat and open the garden door for you."

Mr. Woodhouse at last was off; but Mr. Knightley, instead of being immediately off likewise, sat down again, seemingly inclined for more chat. He began speaking of Harriet, and speaking of her with more voluntary praise than Emma had ever heard before.

"I cannot rate her beauty as you do," said he; "but she is a pretty little creature, and I am inclined to think very well of her disposition. Her character depends upon those she is with; but in good hands she will turn out a valuable woman."

"I am glad you think so; and the good hands, I hope, may not be wanting."

"Come," said he, "you are anxious for a compliment, so I will tell you that you have improved her. You have cured her of her schoolgirl's giggle; she really does you credit."

"Thank you. I should be mortified indeed if I did not believe I had been of some use; but it is not every body who will bestow praise where they may. *You* do not often overpower me with it."

"You are expecting her again, you say, this morning?"

"Almost every moment. She has been gone longer already than she intended."

"Something has happened to delay her; some visitors perhaps."

"Highbury gossips!—Tiresome wretches!"

"Harriet may not consider every body tiresome that you would."

Emma knew this was too true for contradiction, and therefore said nothing. He presently added, with a smile,

"I do not pretend to fix on times or places,[4] but I must tell you that I have good reason to believe your little friend will soon hear of something to her advantage."

"Indeed! how so? of what sort?"

4 Austen's characters and narrators are frequently skeptical or vague about the precise moments of transition and importance in romantic relationships. Compare Darcy's admission, in vol. III, chap. 18, of *Pride and Prejudice:* "I cannot fix on the hour, or the spot, or the look, or the words, which laid the foundation. It is too long ago. I was in the middle before I knew that I *had* begun"; and the narrator's principled abstention in the final chapter of *Mansfield Park:* "I purposely abstain from dates on this occasion, that every one may be at liberty to fix their own, aware that the cure of unconquerable passions, and the transfer of unchanging attachments, must vary much as to time in different people."

"A very serious sort, I assure you;" still smiling.

"Very serious! I can think of but one thing—Who is in love with her? Who makes you their confidant?"

Emma was more than half in hopes of Mr. Elton's having dropt a hint. Mr. Knightley was a sort of general friend and adviser, and she knew Mr. Elton looked up to him.

"I have reason to think," he replied, "that Harriet Smith will soon have an offer of marriage, and from a most unexceptionable quarter: —Robert Martin is the man. Her visit to Abbey-Mill, this summer, seems to have done his business. He is desperately in love and means to marry her."

"He is very obliging,"[5] said Emma; "but is he sure that Harriet means to marry him?"

"Well, well, means to make her an offer then. Will that do? He came to the Abbey two evenings ago, on purpose to consult me about it. He knows I have a thorough regard for him and all his family, and, I believe, considers me as one of his best friends. He came to ask me whether I thought it would be imprudent in him to settle so early; whether I thought her too young: in short, whether I approved his choice altogether; having some apprehension perhaps of her being considered (especially since *your* making so much of her) as in a line of society above him.[6] I was very much pleased with all that he said. I never hear better sense from any one than Robert Martin. He always speaks to the purpose; open, straight forward, and very well judging. He told me every thing; his circumstances and plans, and what they all proposed doing in the event of his marriage. He is an excellent young man, both as son and brother. I had no hesitation in advising him to marry. He proved to me that he could afford it; and that being the case, I was convinced he could not do better. I praised the fair lady too, and altogether sent him away very happy. If he had never esteemed my opinion before, he would have thought highly of me then; and, I dare say, left the house thinking me the best friend and counsellor man ever had. This happened the night before last. Now, as we may fairly suppose, he would not allow much time to pass before he spoke to the lady, and as he does not appear to have spoken

5 That is very courteous of him.

6 Robert Martin's class-anxiety has two possible sources: although there is no hard evidence either way at this stage, it is possible that, as Emma firmly believes, Harriet will prove to be of genteel stock, and therefore "above" a farmer like him; in addition, as Austen's narrative hints here, Harriet's association with the Woodhouses seems to be raising her social standing by itself. However, as Knightley points out, in the absence of any evidence of parentage, Harriet has no such natural ascendancy over the likes of Robert Martin.

yesterday, it is not unlikely that he should be at Mrs. Goddard's to day; and she may be detained by a visitor, without thinking him at all a tiresome wretch."

"Pray, Mr. Knightley," said Emma, who had been smiling to herself through a great part of this speech, "how do you know that Mr. Martin did not speak yesterday?"

"Certainly," replied he, surprized, "I do not absolutely know it; but it may be inferred. Was not she the whole day with you?"

"Come," said she, "I will tell you something, in return for what you have told me. He did speak yesterday—that is, he wrote, and was refused."

This was obliged to be repeated before it could be believed; and Mr. Knightley actually looked red with surprize and displeasure, as he stood up, in tall indignation,[7] and said,

"Then she is a greater simpleton than I ever believed her. What is the foolish girl about?"

"Oh! to be sure," cried Emma, "it is always incomprehensible to a man that a woman should ever refuse an offer of marriage. A man always imagines a woman to be ready for anybody who asks her."[8]

"Nonsense! a man does not imagine any such thing. But what is the meaning of this? Harriet Smith refuse Robert Martin? madness, if it is so; but I hope you are mistaken."

"I saw her answer, nothing could be clearer."

"You saw her answer! you wrote her answer too. Emma, this is your doing. You persuaded her to refuse him."

"And if I did, (which, however, I am far from allowing,) I should not feel that I had done wrong. Mr. Martin is a very respectable young man, but I cannot admit him to be Harriet's equal; and am rather surprized indeed that he should have ventured to address her. By your account, he does seem to have had some scruples. It is a pity that they were ever got over."

"Not Harriet's equal!" exclaimed Mr. Knightley loudly and warmly; and with calmer asperity, added, a few moments afterwards, "No, he is not her equal indeed, for he is as much her superior in sense as in situation. Emma, your infatuation about that girl blinds you. What are Harriet Smith's claims, either of birth, nature or education, to

7 Both in a state of lofty disapproval or "high dudgeon" and, presumably (since Knightley has just stood up), a punning transferred epithet based on his own physical height.

8 Austen takes this comic truism to a surreal extreme in *Pride and Prejudice* in her portrayal of Mr. Collins, whose unwillingness to countenance Elizabeth Bennet's refusal of him in vol. I, chap. 19, places the heroine in a seemingly impossible logical quandary: "If what I have hitherto said can appear to you in the form of encouragement, I know not how to express my refusal in such a way as may convince you of its being one."

9 No money settled on her as a regular annuity.

10 Limited intelligence.

11 A misalliance, a marriage down the social scale. This is the first instance in the novel where the precise gradations of Highbury's class system become serious matters of debate. Austen's fictions very rarely mention either the full aristocracy or the poor working class directly, focusing regularly on the landed country gentry and, more particularly, on the class from which the Austens themselves came: the ranks of professionals who, while not being hereditary landowners themselves, might raise themselves socially by their earnings and by their acquisition and display of commodities, the trappings of what we would now call "lifestyle." Among Austen's novels, *Emma* is especially attentive to the consumer commodities through which such social relations are mediated, such as carriages, foodstuffs, clothes, and musical instruments. (I discuss some of these significances in greater detail in the Introduction.)

Another aspect of contemporary economic and class relations (the two are not cleanly separable) that figures large in the novel is the increasing mobility in either direction around these social levels. If the Bateses have "sunk" from the station they once occupied when Miss Bates's late father held the relatively comfortable position of vicar, Mr. Weston has earned enough in "trade" to set himself up as a gentleman of leisure. And while the Coles may have no genteel history or ancestral relationship to the land, they are any connection higher than Robert Martin? She is the natural daughter of nobody knows whom, with probably no settled provision at all,[9] and certainly no respectable relations. She is known only as parlour-boarder at a common school. She is not a sensible girl, nor a girl of any information. She has been taught nothing useful, and is too young and too simple to have acquired any thing herself. At her age she can have no experience, and with her little wit,[10] is not very likely ever to have any that can avail her. She is pretty, and she is good tempered, and that is all. My only scruple in advising the match was on his account, as being beneath his deserts, and a bad connexion for him. I felt, that as to fortune, in all probability he might do much better; and that as to a rational companion or useful helpmate, he could not do worse. But I could not reason so to a man in love, and was willing to trust to there being no harm in her, to her having that sort of disposition, which, in good hands, like his, might be easily led aright and turn out very well. The advantage of the match I felt to be all on her side; and had not the smallest doubt (nor have I now) that there would be a general cry-out upon her extreme good luck. Even *your* satisfaction I made sure of. It crossed my mind immediately that you would not regret your friend's leaving Highbury, for the sake of her being settled so well. I remember saying to myself, 'Even Emma, with all her partiality for Harriet, will think this a good match.'"

"I cannot help wondering at your knowing so little of Emma as to say any such thing. What! think a farmer, (and with all his sense and all his merit Mr. Martin is nothing more,) a good match for my intimate friend! Not regret her leaving Highbury for the sake of marrying a man whom I could never admit as an acquaintance of my own! I wonder you should think it possible for me to have such feelings. I assure you mine are very different. I must think your statement by no means fair. You are not just to Harriet's claims. They would be estimated very differently by others as well as myself; Mr. Martin may be the richest of the two, but he is undoubtedly her inferior as to rank in society.—The sphere in which she moves is much above his.—It would be a degradation."[11]

"A degradation to illegitimacy and ignorance, to be married to a respectable, intelligent gentleman-farmer!"

catching up with the Woodhouses in terms of their disposable income. The novel's class politics are not easy to pin down; one might argue that the *dénouement* validates the old hierarchies, with Emma marrying the landed gentleman and Harriet marrying the tenant farmer. However, the overall movement of the plot emphasizes not only the irreversible influence of "new money" in the social economy of Highbury but also the entitlement of characters such as the Westons and the Coles to consideration alongside the more established families. Likewise, the ironic separation between character and narrator, on which free indirect style depends, should caution a reader against identifying Emma's often snobbish views of social distinction simplistically with those of her author. In this instance, for example, her sense of Harriet's social superiority to Robert Martin is based entirely on her own subjective opinion. For useful introductions to these issues, see Juliet McMaster's chapter "Class" in Edward Copeland and Juliet McMaster, eds., *The Cambridge Companion to Jane Austen* (Cambridge: Cambridge University Press, 1997), pp. 115–130, and Thomas Keymer's chapter "Rank" in Janet Todd, ed., *Jane Austen in Context* (Cambridge: Cambridge University Press, 2005), pp. 387–396.

"As to the circumstances of her birth, though in a legal sense she may be called Nobody,[12] it will not hold in common sense. She is not to pay for the offence of others, by being held below the level of those with whom she is brought up.—There can scarcely be a doubt that her father is a gentleman—and a gentleman of fortune.—Her allowance is very liberal; nothing has ever been grudged for her improvement or comfort.—That she is a gentleman's daughter, is indubitable to me; that she associates with gentlemen's daughters, no one, I apprehend, will deny.—She is superior to Mr. Robert Martin."

"Whoever might be her parents," said Mr. Knightley, "whoever may have had the charge of her, it does not appear to have been any part of their plan to introduce her into what you would call good society. After receiving a very indifferent education she is left in Mrs. Goddard's hands to shift[13] as she can;—to move, in short, in Mrs. Goddard's line, to have Mrs. Goddard's acquaintance. Her friends evidently thought this good enough for her; and it *was* good enough. She desired nothing better herself. Till you chose to turn her into a friend, her mind had no distaste for her own set, nor any ambition beyond it. She was as happy as possible with the Martins in the summer. She had no sense of superiority then. If she has it now, you have given it. You have been no friend to Harriet Smith, Emma. Robert Martin would never have proceeded so far, if he had not felt persuaded of her not being disinclined to him. I know him well. He has too much real feeling to address any woman on the hap-hazard of selfish passion.[14] And as to conceit, he is the farthest from it of any man I know. Depend upon it he had encouragement."

It was most convenient to Emma not to make a direct reply to this assertion; she chose rather to take up her own line of the subject again.

"You are a very warm friend to Mr. Martin; but, as I said before, are unjust to Harriet. Harriet's claims to marry well are not so contemptible as you represent them. She is not a clever girl, but she has better sense than you are aware of, and does not deserve to have her understanding spoken of so slightingly. Waving[15] that point, however, and supposing her to be, as you describe her, only pretty and good-natured, let me tell you, that in the degree she possesses them, they

12 Emma shows herself here to be aware of some of the details of English common law concerning illegitimacy, in particular, the fact that an illegitimate child was referred to as "filius nullius," or "Nobody's child."

13 "To find some expedient; to act or live through with difficulty" (Johnson).

14 Out of sudden and capricious self-interest.

15 Alternative spelling of "waiving," setting aside. See also vol. III, chap. 7.

are not trivial recommendations to the world in general, for she is, in fact, a beautiful girl, and must be thought so by ninety-nine people out of an hundred; and till it appears that men are much more philosophic on the subject of beauty[16] than they are generally supposed; till they do fall in love with well-informed minds instead of handsome faces, a girl, with such loveliness as Harriet, has a certainty of being admired and sought after, of having the power of choosing from among many, consequently a claim to be nice. Her good-nature, too, is not so very slight a claim, comprehending, as it does, real, thorough sweetness of temper and manner, a very humble opinion of herself, and a great readiness to be pleased with other people. I am very much mistaken if your sex in general would not think such beauty, and such temper, the highest claims a woman could possess."

"Upon my word, Emma, to hear you abusing the reason you have, is almost enough to make me think so too. Better be without sense, than misapply it as you do."

"To be sure!" cried she playfully. "I know *that* is the feeling of you all. I know that such a girl as Harriet is exactly what every man delights in—what at once bewitches his senses and satisfies his judgment. Oh! Harriet may pick and choose. Were you, yourself, ever to marry, she is the very woman for you. And is she, at seventeen, just entering into life, just beginning to be known, to be wondered at because she does not accept the first offer she receives? No—pray let her have time to look about her."

"I have always thought it a very foolish intimacy," said Mr. Knightley presently, "though I have kept my thoughts to myself; but I now perceive that it will be a very unfortunate one for Harriet. You will puff her up with such ideas of her own beauty, and of what she has a claim to, that, in a little while, nobody within her reach will be good enough for her. Vanity working on a weak head, produces every sort of mischief. Nothing so easy as for a young lady to raise her expectations too high. Miss Harriet Smith may not find offers of marriage flow in so fast, though she is a very pretty girl. Men of sense, whatever you may chuse to say, do not want silly wives. Men of family would not be very fond of connecting themselves with a girl of such obscurity—and most prudent men would be afraid of the inconve-

16 Cerebral, preferring brains to looks.

17 Arguing further about it.

18 A glancing allusion to Wollstonecraft's treatise *A Vindication of the Rights of Woman.*

nience and disgrace they might be involved in, when the mystery of her parentage came to be revealed. Let her marry Robert Martin, and she is safe, respectable, and happy for ever; but if you encourage her to expect to marry greatly, and teach her to be satisfied with nothing less than a man of consequence and large fortune, she may be a parlour-boarder at Mrs. Goddard's all the rest of her life—or at least, (for Harriet Smith is a girl who will marry somebody or other,) till she grow desperate, and is glad to catch at the old writing master's son."

"We think so very differently on this point, Mr. Knightley, that there can be no use in canvassing it.[17] We shall only be making each other more angry. But as to my *letting* her marry Robert Martin, it is impossible; she has refused him, and so decidedly, I think, as must prevent any second application. She must abide by the evil of having refused him, whatever it may be; and as to the refusal itself, I will not pretend to say that I might not influence her a little; but I assure you there was very little for me or for anybody to do. His appearance is so much against him, and his manner so bad, that if she ever were disposed to favour him, she is not now. I can imagine, that before she had seen anybody superior, she might tolerate him. He was the brother of her friends, and he took pains to please her; and altogether, having seen nobody better (that must have been his great assistant) she might not, while she was at Abbey-Mill, find him disagreeable. But the case is altered now. She knows now what gentlemen are; and nothing but a gentleman in education and manner has any chance with Harriet."

"Nonsense, errant nonsense, as ever was talked!" cried Mr. Knightley.—"Robert Martin's manners have sense, sincerity, and good-humour to recommend them; and his mind has more true gentility than Harriet Smith could understand."

Emma made no answer, and tried to look cheerfully unconcerned, but was really feeling uncomfortable and wanting him very much to be gone. She did not repent what she had done; she still thought herself a better judge of such a point of female right[18] and refinement than he could be; but yet she had a sort of habitual respect for his judgment in general, which made her dislike having it so loudly against her; and to have him sitting just opposite to her in angry state, was very disagreeable. Some minutes passed in this unpleasant silence, with only one attempt on Emma's side to talk of the weather, but he made no answer. He was thinking. The result of his thoughts appeared at last in these words.

"Robert Martin has no great loss—if he can but think so; and I hope it will not be long before he does. Your views for Harriet are best known to yourself; but as you make no secret of your love of match-making, it is fair to suppose that views, and plans, and proj-

Portrait of Mary Wollstonecraft (1759–1797) by John Opie, 1790–1791. The most significant figure in late eighteenth-century British feminist thought, as well as the mother of Mary Wollstonecraft Godwin (later Shelley), the author of *Frankenstein,* Wollstonecraft offers some significant points of comparison with Austen. Like Austen, she perceived with great clarity the stultifying effects of the culture of "female accomplishments" on young women; however, unlike Austen, she conceived large-scale alternatives to such a culture, as detailed in *A Vindication of the Rights of Woman* (1792).

ects you have;—and as a friend I shall just hint to you that if Elton is the man, I think it will be all labour in vain."

Emma laughed and disclaimed. He continued,

"Depend upon it, Elton will not do. Elton is a very good sort of man, and a very respectable vicar of Highbury, but not at all likely to make an imprudent match. He knows the value of a good income as well as anybody. Elton may talk sentimentally, but he will act rationally.[19] He is as well acquainted with his own claims, as you can be with Harriet's. He knows that he is a very handsome young man, and a great favourite wherever he goes; and from his general way of talking in unreserved moments, when there are only men present, I am convinced that he does not mean to throw himself away. I have heard him speak with great animation of a large family of young ladies that his sisters are intimate with, who have all twenty thousand pounds apiece."

"I am very much obliged to you," said Emma, laughing again. "If I had set my heart on Mr. Elton's marrying Harriet, it would have been very kind to open my eyes; but at present I only want to keep Harriet to myself. I have done with match-making indeed. I could never hope to equal my own doings at Randalls. I shall leave off while I am well."

"Good morning to you,"—said he, rising and walking off abruptly. He was very much vexed. He felt the disappointment of the young man, and was mortified to have been the means of promoting it, by the sanction[20] he had given; and the part which he was persuaded Emma had taken in the affair, was provoking him exceedingly.

Emma remained in a state of vexation too; but there was more indistinctness in the causes of her's, than in his. She did not always feel so absolutely satisfied with herself, so entirely convinced that her opinions were right and her adversary's wrong, as Mr. Knightley. He walked off in more complete self-approbation than he left for her. She was not so materially cast down, however, but that a little time and the return of Harriet were very adequate restoratives. Harriet's staying away so long was beginning to make her uneasy. The possibility of the young man's coming to Mrs. Goddard's that morning, and meeting with Harriet and pleading his own cause, gave alarming

19 Sentiment and rationality were the (apparent) polar opposites around which much of the ideological and aesthetic controversy of the 1790s circled. Both radical and conservative factions accused their opponents of being blinded and muddled by sentiment, regardless of the sentimental tactics they themselves employed. See Marilyn Butler, *Jane Austen and the War of Ideas* (Oxford: Clarendon Press, 1975; 2nd ed., 1987), pp. 8–56.

20 Approval.

James Gillray, "A pig in a poke. Whist, whist," 1788.

21 Thoughtless.

ideas. The dread of such a failure after all became the prominent uneasiness; and when Harriet appeared, and in very good spirits, and without having any such reason to give for her long absence, she felt a satisfaction which settled her with her own mind, and convinced her, that let Mr. Knightley think or say what he would, she had done nothing which woman's friendship and woman's feelings would not justify.

He had frightened her a little about Mr. Elton; but when she considered that Mr. Knightley could not have observed him as she had done, neither with the interest, nor (she must be allowed to tell herself, in spite of Mr. Knightley's pretensions) with the skill of such an observer on such a question as herself, that he had spoken it hastily and in anger, she was able to believe, that he had rather said what he wished resentfully to be true, than what he knew anything about. He certainly might have heard Mr. Elton speak with more unreserve than she had ever done, and Mr. Elton might not be of an imprudent, inconsiderate[21] disposition as to money-matters; he might naturally be rather attentive than otherwise to them; but then, Mr. Knightley did not make due allowance for the influence of a strong passion at war with all interested motives. Mr. Knightley saw no such passion, and of course thought nothing of its effects; but she saw too much of it, to feel a doubt of its overcoming any hesitations that a reasonable prudence might originally suggest; and more than a reasonable, becoming degree of prudence, she was very sure did not belong to Mr. Elton.

Harriet's cheerful look and manner established her's: she came back, not to think of Mr. Martin, but to talk of Mr. Elton. Miss Nash had been telling her something, which she repeated immediately with great delight. Mr. Perry had been to Mrs. Goddard's to attend a sick child, and Miss Nash had seen him, and he had told Miss Nash, that as he was coming back yesterday from Clayton Park, he had met Mr. Elton, and found to his great surprize that Mr. Elton was actually on his road to London, and not meaning to return till the morrow, though it was the whist-club night,[22] which he had been never known to miss before; and Mr. Perry had remonstrated with him about it, and told him how shabby[23] it was in him, their best player, to absent himself, and tried very much to persuade him to put off his journey only one day; but it would not do; Mr. Elton had been determined to go on, and had said in a *very particular* way indeed, that he was going on business which he would not put off for any inducement in the world; and something about a very enviable commission, and being the bearer of something exceedingly precious. Mr. Perry could not quite understand him, but he was very sure there must be a *lady* in the case,[24] and he told him so; and Mr. Elton only looked very conscious[25] and smiling, and rode off in great spirits. Miss Nash had told her all this, and had talked a great deal more about Mr. Elton; and said, looking so very significantly at her, "that she did not pretend to understand what his business might be, but she only knew that any woman whom Mr. Elton could prefer, she should think the luckiest woman in the world; for, beyond a doubt, Mr. Elton had not his equal for beauty or agreeableness."

22 If, in 1814, quadrille marked a character as decidedly out of fashion, playing whist was a way of indicating that one was, even in rural Surrey, in touch with the latest metropolitan activities, hence the fact that both Mr. Perry and Mr. Elton are active members of the Highbury gentlemen's whist club. However, as David Parlett notes, devotion to whist could also be a sign of an unthinking thralldom to fashion: "As often happens with classic games," he writes, "the recognition of Whist as a social accomplishment meant that many people who would really have been more at ease with something else felt morally obliged to subordinate their taste to that of the prevailing fashion, with unhappy and counter-productive results" (*A History of Card Games* [Oxford: Oxford University Press, 1991], p. 220).

23 Mean (in a jocular sense).

24 The first allusion in the novel to John Gay's poem "The Hare and Many Friends"; see note 7 to vol. III, chap. 16.

25 Self-conscious.

9

Mr. Knightley might quarrel with her, but Emma could not quarrel with herself. He was so much displeased, that it was longer than usual before he came to Hartfield again; and when they did meet, his grave looks shewed that she was not forgiven. She was sorry, but could not repent.[1] On the contrary, her plans and proceedings were more and more justified, and endeared to her by the general appearances of the next few days.

The Picture, elegantly framed, came safely to hand soon after Mr. Elton's return, and being hung over the mantle-piece of the common sitting-room,[2] he got up to look at it, and sighed out his half sentences of admiration just as he ought;[3] and as for Harriet's feelings, they were visibly forming themselves into as strong and steady an attachment as her youth and sort of mind admitted. Emma was soon perfectly satisfied of Mr. Martin's being no otherwise remembered, than as he furnished a contrast with Mr. Elton, of the utmost advantage to the latter.

Her views of improving her little friend's mind, by a great deal of useful reading and conversation, had never yet led to more than a few first chapters, and the intention of going on to-morrow. It was much easier to chat than to study; much pleasanter to let her imagination range and work at Harriet's fortune, than to be labouring to enlarge her comprehension or exercise it on sober facts; and the only literary pursuit which engaged Harriet at present, the only mental provision she was making for the evening of life, was the collecting and transcribing all the riddles of every sort that she could meet

1 This contrast would have carried a greater force for Austen's original readers than may be apparent now, as Johnson's definitions of the two terms suggest. His first sense of "sorry" is "grieved for something past. It is generally used of slight or casual miscarriages or vexations, but sometimes of greater things. It does not imply any long continuance of grief"; the third sense of "repent" is "to have such sorrow for sin, as produces amendment of life."

2 This would be the sitting-room used to receive visitors, as opposed to one for the family's use.

3 Compare Mary Bennet's "some new observations of thread-bare morality" in *Pride and Prejudice,* vol. I, chap. 12. Austen's free indirect style is teasingly ambiguous here, since it is in retrospect unclear whether Elton's "admiration" is more for the picture's sitter or its artist.

with, into a thin quarto[4] of hot-pressed paper,[5] made up by her friend, and ornamented with cyphers[6] and trophies.[7]

In this age of literature, such collections on a very grand scale are not uncommon.[8] Miss Nash, head-teacher at Mrs. Goddard's, had written out at least three hundred; and Harriet, who had taken the first hint of it from her, hoped, with Miss Woodhouse's help, to get a great many more. Emma assisted with her invention, memory and taste; and as Harriet wrote a very pretty hand, it was likely to be an arrangement of the first order, in form[9] as well as quantity.

Mr. Woodhouse was almost as much interested in the business as the girls, and tried very often to recollect something worth their putting in. "So many clever riddles as there used to be when he was young—he wondered he could not remember them! but he hoped he should in time." And it always ended in "Kitty, a fair but frozen maid."

His good friend Perry too, whom he had spoken to on the subject, did not at present recollect any thing of the riddle kind; but he had desired Perry to be upon the watch, and as he went about so much, something, he thought, might come from that quarter.

It was by no means his daughter's wish that the intellects of Highbury in general should be put under requisition.[10] Mr. Elton was the only one whose assistance she asked. He was invited to contribute any really good enigmas, charades, or conundrums[11] that he might recollect; and she had the pleasure of seeing him most intently at work with his recollections; and at the same time, as she could perceive, most earnestly careful that nothing ungallant, nothing that did not breathe a compliment to the sex should pass his lips. They owed to him their two or three politest puzzles; and the joy and exultation with which at last he recalled, and rather sentimentally recited, that well-known charade,

> My first doth affliction denote,
>   Which my second is destin'd to feel;
> And my whole is the best antidote
>   That affliction to soften and heal.—[12]

4 A book in which the pages are folded twice after printing, as opposed to a folio (folded once) and an octavo (folded three times).

5 Paper manufactured by being pressed between hot metal plates, and therefore smoother and more luxurious. In Lecture VIII of his *Lectures on the English Poets* (1818) William Hazlitt used the "upmarket" associations of hot-pressed paper to pass a glancing judgment on Thomas Campbell, author of the famous 1799 poem *The Pleasures of Hope:* "Mr. Campbell always seems to me to be thinking how his poetry will look when it comes to be hot-pressed on superfine wove paper, to have a disproportionate eye to points and commas, and dread of errors of the press. He is so afraid of doing wrong, of making the smallest mistake, that he does little or nothing" (*The Complete Works of William Hazlitt,* vol. 5, ed. P. P. Howe [London: J. M. Dent and Sons, 1930], p. 149).

6 Ornamental letters, monograms.

7 Ornamental symbols.

8 Examples include *A Choice Collection of Riddles, Charades, Rebusses, &c., Chiefly Original* (1792), *Master Sharpwit's Puzzle-Cap: Being a Choice Collection of Riddles & Charades* (1800), *The Vase of Fancy, or, Happy Association of Mirth and Ingenuity: Being an Excellent Collection of Riddles, Charades, &c.* (1806), and *The Whim Wham, or, Evening Amusement, for All Ages and Sizes: Being an Entire New Set of Riddles, Charades, Questions, and Transpositions* (1810). However, as the reference to Miss Nash indicates, the transcription and collection of riddles and ciphers into albums also formed part of a network of shared manuscript activity by women in the period. Samantha Matthews has commented on this practice: "Known as friendship albums in America, they are typically compilations of original and copied verse and prose, small portrait sketches and landscape watercolours, flower paintings, silhouettes, *decoupage,* pressed flowers and other mementoes, kept by young women with intellectual and artistic aspirations . . . Over time, the album accumulated personal texts and

made her quite sorry to acknowledge that they had transcribed it some pages ago already.

"Why will not you write one yourself for us, Mr. Elton?" said she; "that is the only security[13] for its freshness; and nothing could be easier to you."

"Oh, no! he had never written, hardly ever, any thing of the kind in his life. The stupidest fellow! He was afraid not even Miss Woodhouse"—he stopt a moment—"or Miss Smith could inspire him."[14]

The very next day however produced some proof of inspiration. He called for a few moments, just to leave a piece of paper on the table containing, as he said, a charade, which a friend of his had ad-

associations, becoming a unique record of the owner's relationships and community, an oblique and fallible individual and group biography" ("'O All Pervading Album!': Place and Displacement in Romantic Albums and Album Poetry," in Christoph Bode and Jacqueline Labbe, eds., *Romantic Localities: Europe Writes Place* [London, Pickering & Chatto, 2010], p. 100).

9 Presentation.

10 Pressed into service.

11 Enigmas are riddles that challenge their readers to interpret obscure metaphors; charades are specifically riddles in which clues provide the individual syllables of the key word (as in "My first doth affliction denote"); conundrums are question-and-answer riddles that depend on plays of sound and sense (such as Mr. Weston's "What two letters of the alphabet are there, that express perfection?" in vol. III, ch. 7).

12 The first syllable is "woe," the second "man," providing the solution "woman."

13 Guarantee.

14 This is a fine literary example of what later came to be known as a "Freudian slip." In *The Psychopathology of Everyday Life* (1901), Freud remarks that "[a] slip of the tongue can be amusing when it emerges in confirmation of something the speaker is denying" (trans. Anthea Bell [London: Penguin, 2002], p. 89).

A
CHOICE COLLECTION
OF
RIDDLES,
CHARADES, REBUSSES,
&c.
CHIEFLY ORIGINAL.
BY
PETER PUZZLEWELL, Esq.

LONDON:
PRINTED FOR E. NEWBERY, CORNER OF ST. PAUL'S CHURCH-YARD.
1792.

Title page of "Peter Puzzlewell," *A Choice Collection of Riddles, Charades, Rebusses, &c.* (London: E. Newbery, 1792). In addition to printed collections such as this one, handwritten collections of riddles, charades, and ciphers were circulated among female friends, as witnessed by Emma and Harriet's activity here.

dressed to a young lady, the object of his admiration, but which, from his manner, Emma was immediately convinced must be his own.

"I do not offer it for Miss Smith's collection," said he. "Being my friend's, I have no right to expose it in any degree to the public eye, but perhaps you may not dislike looking at it."

The speech was more to Emma than to Harriet, which Emma could understand. There was deep consciousness about him, and he found it easier to meet her eye than her friend's. He was gone the next moment:—after another moment's pause,

"Take it," said Emma, smiling, and pushing the paper towards Harriet—"it is for you. Take your own."

But Harriet was in a tremor, and could not touch it; and Emma, never loth to be first, was obliged to examine it herself.

To Miss ———.
CHARADE.

My first displays the wealth and pomp of kings,
  Lords of the earth! their luxury and ease.
Another view of man, my second brings,
  Behold him there, the monarch of the seas!

But ah! united, what reverse we have!
  Man's boasted power and freedom, all are flown;
Lord of the earth and sea, he bends a slave,
  And woman, lovely woman, reigns alone.

  Thy ready wit the word will soon supply,
  May its approval beam in that soft eye!

She cast her eye over it, pondered, caught the meaning, read it through again to be quite certain, and quite mistress of the lines, and then passing it to Harriet, sat happily smiling, and saying to herself, while Harriet was puzzling over the paper in all the confusion of hope and dulness, "Very well, Mr. Elton, very well, indeed. I have read worse charades. *Courtship*—a very good hint. I give you credit for it. This is feeling your way. This is saying very plainly—'Pray, Miss Smith, give me leave to pay my addresses to you. Approve my charade and my intentions in the same glance.'

May its approval beam in that soft eye!

Harriet exactly. Soft, is the very word for her eye—of all epithets, the justest that could be given.

Thy ready wit the word will soon supply.

Humph—Harriet's ready wit! All the better. A man must be very much in love indeed, to describe her so. Ah! Mr. Knightley, I wish you had the benefit of this; I think this would convince you. For once in your life you would be obliged to own yourself mistaken. An excellent charade indeed! and very much to the purpose. Things must come to a crisis[15] soon now."

She was obliged to break off from these very pleasant observations, which were otherwise of a sort to run into great length, by the eagerness of Harriet's wondering questions.

"What can it be, Miss Woodhouse?—what can it be? I have not an idea—I cannot guess it in the least. What can it possibly be? Do try to find it out, Miss Woodhouse. Do help me. I never saw any thing so hard. Is it kingdom? I wonder who the friend was—and who could be the young lady! Do you think it is a good one? Can it be woman?

And woman, lovely woman, reigns alone.

Can it be Neptune?

Behold him there, the monarch of the seas!

Or a trident? or a mermaid? or a shark? Oh, no! shark is only one syllable. It must be very clever, or he would not have brought it. Oh! Miss Woodhouse, do you think we shall ever find it out?"

"Mermaids and sharks! Nonsense! My dear Harriet, what are you thinking of? Where would be the use of his bringing us a charade made by a friend upon a mermaid or a shark? Give me the paper and listen.

15 Come to a head. "Crisis" in this context merely denotes a decisive moment rather than the sense, which became dominant in the latter part of the nineteenth century, of an emergency.

16 The best part, since cream rises to the top of milk.

"For Miss——, read Miss Smith.

My first displays the wealth and pomp of kings,
  Lords of the earth! their luxury and ease.

That is *court.*

Another view of man, my second brings;
  Behold him there, the monarch of the seas!

That is *ship;*—plain as can be.—Now for the cream.[16]

But ah! united, (*courtship,* you know,) what reverse we have!
  Man's boasted power and freedom, all are flown.
Lord of the earth and sea, he bends a slave,
  And woman, lovely woman, reigns alone.

A very proper compliment!—and then follows the application, which I think, my dear Harriet, you cannot find much difficulty in comprehending. Read it in comfort to yourself. There can be no doubt of its being written for you and to you."

Harriet could not long resist so delightful a persuasion. She read the concluding lines, and was all flutter and happiness. She could not speak. But she was not wanted to speak. It was enough for her to feel. Emma spoke for her.

"There is so pointed, and so particular a meaning in this compliment," said she, "that I cannot have a moment's doubt as to Mr. Elton's intentions. You are his object—and you will soon receive the completest proof of it. I thought it must be so. I thought I could not be so deceived; but now, it is clear; the state of his mind is as clear and decided, as my wishes on the subject have been ever since I knew you. Yes, Harriet, just so long have I been wanting the very circumstance to happen which has happened. I could never tell whether an attachment between you and Mr. Elton were most desirable or most natural. Its probability and its eligibility have really so equalled each other! I am very happy. I congratulate you, my dear Harriet, with all my heart. This is an attachment which a woman may well feel pride in creating. This is a connection which offers nothing but good. It will give you every thing that you want—consideration, independence, a proper home—it will fix you in the centre of all your real friends, close to Hartfield and to me, and confirm our intimacy for ever. This, Harriet, is an alliance which can never raise a blush in either of us."

"Dear Miss Woodhouse"—and "Dear Miss Woodhouse," was all that Harriet, with many tender embraces could articulate at first; but when they did arrive at something more like conversation, it was sufficiently clear to her friend that she saw, felt, anticipated, and remembered just as she ought. Mr. Elton's superiority had very ample acknowledgment.

"Whatever you say is always right," cried Harriet, "and therefore I suppose, and believe, and hope it must be so; but otherwise I could not have imagined it. It is so much beyond any thing I deserve. Mr. Elton, who might marry any body! There cannot be two opinions about *him*. He is so very superior. Only think of those sweet verses—'To Miss———.' Dear me, how clever!—Could it really be meant for me?"

"I cannot make a question, or listen to a question about that. It is a certainty. Receive it on my judgment. It is a sort of prologue to the play, a motto[17] to the chapter; and will be soon followed by matter-of-fact prose."

"It is a sort of thing which nobody could have expected. I am sure, a month ago, I had no more idea myself!—The strangest things do take place!"

—"When Miss Smiths and Mr. Eltons get acquainted—they do indeed—and really it is strange; it is out of the common course that what is so evidently, so palpably desirable—what courts the prearrangement of other people, should so immediately shape itself into the proper form. You and Mr. Elton are by situation called together; you belong to one another by every circumstance of your respective homes. Your marrying will be equal to the match at Randalls. There

17 Poetic epigraph; at the time Austen was writing, the most famous creative exponent of the chapter-epigraph in English was Walter Scott, who, by his own admission, invented many of the poetic "sources" he was purporting to cite. See Gérard Genette, *Paratexts: Thresholds of Meaning,* trans. J. E. Lewin (Cambridge: Cambridge University Press, 1997), pp. 144–160.

does seem to be a something in the air of Hartfield which gives love exactly the right direction, and sends it into the very channel where it ought to flow.

> The course of true love never did run smooth—[18]

A Hartfield edition of Shakespeare would have a long note on that passage."

"That Mr. Elton should really be in love with me,—me, of all people, who did not know him, to speak to him, at Michaelmas![19] And he, the very handsomest man that ever was, and a man that every body looks up to, quite like Mr. Knightley! His company so sought after, that every body says he need not eat a single meal by himself if he does not chuse it; that he has more invitations than there are days in the week. And so excellent in the Church! Miss Nash has put down all the texts he has ever preached from since he came to Highbury. Dear me! When I look back to the first time I saw him! How little did I think!—The two Abbotts and I ran into the front room and peeped through the blind when we heard he was going by, and Miss Nash came and scolded us away, and staid to look through herself; however, she called me back presently, and let me look too, which was very good-natured. And how beautiful we thought he looked! He was arm in arm with Mr. Cole."

"This is an alliance which, whoever—whatever your friends may be,[20] must be agreeable to them, provided at least they have common sense; and we are not to be addressing our conduct to fools. If they are anxious to see you *happily* married, here is a man whose amiable character gives every assurance of it;—if they wish to have you settled in the same country and circle which they have chosen to place you in, here it will be accomplished; and if their only object is that you should, in the common phrase, be *well* married, here is the comfortable fortune, the respectable establishment, the rise in the world which must satisfy them."

"Yes, very true. How nicely you talk; I love to hear you. You understand every thing. You and Mr. Elton are one as clever as the other. This charade!—If I had studied a twelvemonth, I could never have made any thing like it."

18 Lysander's words to Hermia in *A Midsummer Night's Dream,* Act I, Scene 1. *Emma* is not the only Austen novel to bear comparison to Shakespeare's play: the sequence in *Mansfield Park,* vol. I, chaps. 9–10, in which Fanny Price observes the shifting amatory relations in the grounds of Sotherton, also owes much to the Shakespearean comedy. Jocelyn Harris offers a brilliant reading of the depth of *Emma*'s intertextual relations to *A Midsummer Night's Dream* in *Jane Austen's Art of Memory* (Cambridge: Cambridge University Press, 1989), pp. 169–187.

19 The feast of St. Michael the Archangel, held on September 29.

20 Whoever your relations may be, and whatever their station in life.

"I thought he meant to try his skill, by his manner of declining it yesterday."

"I do think it is, without exception, the best charade I ever read."

"I never read one more to the purpose, certainly."

"It is as long again as almost all we have had before."

"I do not consider its length as particularly in its favour. Such things in general cannot be too short."

Harriet was too intent on the lines to hear. The most satisfactory comparisons were rising in her mind.

"It is one thing," said she, presently—her cheeks in a glow—"to have very good sense in a common way, like every body else, and if there is any thing to say, to sit down and write a letter, and say just what you must, in a short way; and another, to write verses and charades like this."

Emma could not have desired a more spirited rejection of Mr. Martin's prose.

"Such sweet lines!" continued Harriet—"these two last!—But how shall I ever be able to return the paper, or say I have found it out?—Oh! Miss Woodhouse, what can we do about that?"

"Leave it to me. You do nothing. He will be here this evening, I dare say, and then I will give it him back, and some nonsense or other will pass between us, and you shall not be committed.—Your soft eyes shall chuse their own time for beaming. Trust to me."

"Oh! Miss Woodhouse, what a pity that I must not write this beautiful charade into my book! I am sure I have not got one half so good."

"Leave out the two last lines, and there is no reason why you should not write it into your book."

"Oh! but those two lines are"——

——"The best of all. Granted;—for private enjoyment; and for private enjoyment keep them. They are not at all the less written you know, because you divide them. The couplet does not cease to be, nor does its meaning change. But take it away, and all *appropriation*[21] ceases, and a very pretty gallant charade remains, fit for any collection. Depend upon it, he would not like to have his charade slighted, much better than his passion. A poet in love must be encouraged in

21 Personal reference.

both capacities, or neither. Give me the book, I will write it down, and then there can be no possible reflection on you."

Harriet submitted, though her mind could hardly separate the parts, so as to feel quite sure that her friend were not writing down a declaration of love. It seemed too precious an offering for any degree of publicity.

"I shall never let that book go out of my own hands," said she.

"Very well," replied Emma, "a most natural feeling; and the longer it lasts, the better I shall be pleased. But here is my father coming: you will not object to my reading the charade to him. It will be giving him so much pleasure! He loves any thing of the sort, and especially any thing that pays woman a compliment. He has the tenderest spirit of gallantry towards us all!—You must let me read it to him."

Harriet looked grave.

"My dear Harriet, you must not refine[22] too much upon this charade.—You will betray your feelings improperly, if you are too conscious and too quick, and appear to affix more meaning, or even quite all the meaning which may be affixed to it. Do not be overpowered by such a little tribute of admiration. If he had been anxious for secrecy, he would not have left the paper while I was by; but he rather pushed it towards me than towards you. Do not let us be too solemn on the business. He has encouragement enough to proceed, without our sighing out our souls over this charade."

"Oh! no—I hope I shall not be ridiculous about it. Do as you please."

Mr. Woodhouse came in, and very soon led to the subject again, by the recurrence of his very frequent inquiry of "Well, my dears, how does your book go on?—Have you got any thing fresh?"

"Yes, papa, we have something to read you, something quite fresh. A piece of paper was found on the table this morning—(dropt, we suppose, by a fairy)—containing a very pretty charade, and we have just copied it in."

She read it to him, just as he liked to have any thing read, slowly and distinctly, and two or three times over, with explanations of every part as she proceeded—and he was very much pleased, and, as

22 Although the *OED* cites this usage as one of its examples for the meaning "to improve *on* or *upon* something by introducing refinements," this does not quite cover what Emma seems to be implying. Rather, she would appear to be advising Harriet not to interpret the charade too assiduously in front of other people, so as not to give herself away.

Arthur Rackham, illustration of Olivia Primrose singing "When lovely woman stoops to folly" from Goldsmith's novel *The Vicar of Wakefield* (London: G. Harrap, 1929), opp. p. 166. Austen alludes to this song more than once in *Emma.*

she had foreseen, especially struck with the complimentary conclusion.

"Aye, that's very just, indeed, that's very properly said. Very true. 'Woman, lovely woman.'[23] It is such a pretty charade, my dear, that I can easily guess what fairy brought it.—Nobody could have written so prettily, but you, Emma."

Emma only nodded, and smiled.—

After a little thinking, and a very tender sigh, he added,

"Ah! it is no difficulty to see who you take after! Your dear mother was so clever at all those things! If I had but her memory! But I can remember nothing;—not even that particular riddle which you have heard me mention; I can only recollect the first stanza; and there are several.

> Kitty, a fair but frozen maid,
> Kindled a flame I yet deplore,
> The hood-wink'd boy I called to aid,
> Though of his near approach afraid,
> So fatal to my suit before.[24]

And that is all that I can recollect of it—but it is very clever all the way through. But I think, my dear, you said you had got it."

"Yes, papa, it is written out in our second page. We copied it from the Elegant Extracts. It was Garrick's, you know."

"Aye, very true.—I wish I could recollect more of it.

> Kitty, a fair but frozen maid.

The name makes me think of poor Isabella; for she was very near being christened Catherine after her grandmama. I hope we shall have her here next week. Have you thought, my dear, where you shall put her—and what room there will be for the children?"

"Oh! yes—she will have her own room, of course; the room she always has;—and there is the nursery for the children,—just as usual, you know.—Why should there be any change?"

"I do not know, my dear—but it is so long since she was here!—not since last Easter, and then only for a few days.—Mr. John Knight-

23 Mr. Woodhouse may be particularly drawn to Elton's hackneyed phrase for its echo of the famous song from Goldsmith's novel *The Vicar of Wakefield.* "When Lovely Woman Stoops to Folly," one of the most popular sentimental songs of the later eighteenth century, comes originally from chap. 24, where it is sung by the ill-used Olivia Primrose:

> When lovely woman stoops to folly,
> And finds, too late, that men betray,
> What charm can soothe her melancholy,
> What art can wash her guilt away?
>
> The only art her guilt to cover,
> To hide her shame from every eye,
> To give repentance to her lover,
> And wring his bosom, is—to die.

The poetry of Mr. Woodhouse's youth seems to be the only literature with which he is familiar.

24 A riddle by the famous actor-manager and literary wit David Garrick (1717–1779), first published in 1757. The full version runs thus:

A Riddle

> Kitty, a fair, but frozen maid,
> Kindled a flame I still deplore;
> The hood-wink'd boy I call'd in aid,
> Much of his near approach afraid,
> So fatal to my suit before.
>
> At length, propitious to my pray'r,
> The little urchin came;
> At once he sought the midway air,
> And soon he clear'd, with dextrous care,
> The bitter relicks of my flame.
>
> To Kitty, Fanny now succeeds,
> She kindles slow, but lasting fires:
> With care my appetite she feeds;
> Each day some willing victim bleeds,
> To satisfy my strange desires.
>
> Say, by what title, or what name,
> Must I this youth address?

ley's being a lawyer is very inconvenient.—Poor Isabella!—she is sadly taken away from us all!—and how sorry she will be when she comes, not to see Miss Taylor here!"

"She will not be surprized, papa, at least."

"I do not know, my dear. I am sure I was very much surprized when I first heard she was going to be married."

"We must ask Mr. and Mrs. Weston to dine with us, while Isabella is here."

"Yes, my dear, if there is time.—But—(in a very depressed tone)—she is coming for only one week. There will not be time for any thing."

"It is unfortunate that they cannot stay longer—but it seems a case of necessity. Mr. John Knightley must be in town again on the 28th, and we ought to be thankful, papa, that we are to have the whole of the time they can give to the country, that two or three days are not to be taken out for the Abbey. Mr. Knightley promises to give up his claim this Christmas—though you know it is longer since they were with him, than with us."

"It would be very hard indeed, my dear, if poor Isabella were to be anywhere but at Hartfield."

Mr. Woodhouse could never allow for Mr. Knightley's claims on his brother, or any body's claims on Isabella, except his own. He sat musing a little while, and then said,

"But I do not see why poor Isabella should be obliged to go back so soon, though he does. I think, Emma, I shall try and persuade her to stay longer with us. She and the children might stay very well."

"Ah! papa—that is what you never have been able to accomplish, and I do not think you ever will. Isabella cannot bear to stay behind her husband."

This was too true for contradiction. Unwelcome as it was, Mr. Woodhouse could only give a submissive sigh; and as Emma saw his spirits affected by the idea of his daughter's attachment to her husband, she immediately led to such a branch of the subject as must raise them.

"Harriet must give us as much of her company as she can while my brother and sister are here. I am sure she will be pleased with the

Cupid and he are not the same,
Tho' both can raise, or quench a flame—
I'll kiss you if you guess.

The solution to the riddle is a chimney-sweep. In a novel thick with overt and covert riddles and charades, this is one of the most blatant, but also one of the most teasing. The fact that Mr. Woodhouse can only remember the first stanza may superficially recall his eighteenth-century literary antecedent, Uncle Toby in Sterne's *Tristram Shandy,* but his claim that "it is very clever all the way through" suggests tantalizingly unnarrated possibilities—especially since the riddle as a whole ("To Kitty, Fanny now succeeds") is far too salacious ever to have made it into *Elegant Extracts,* whence Emma claims to have copied it. In her influential article "Slipping into the Ha-Ha: Bawdy Humour and Body Politics in Jane Austen's Novels" (*Nineteenth-Century Literature,* 55:3 [2000], pp. 309–339), Jill Heydt-Stevenson comments cogently on some of the riddle's suggestions. Not only does she offer an extended reading of Garrick's sexual innuendos ("[t]he riddle addresses the plight of a man [the narrator] who has been infected with venereal disease" [p. 318]), but she also follows the lead that Austen's narrative offers in the direction of Mr. Woodhouse's possible back-story. "Through a series of covert associations," she argues, "Austen raises the ludicrous and hilarious possibility that the clearly asexual Mr. Woodhouse might have been a libertine in his youth and now suffers from tertiary syphilis. For example, Emma's father, a hypochondriac, cannot bear to be cold and so prefers a fire, even in midsummer; the riddle's narrator, ill with venereal disease, also longs for 'fire' to cure him. Both Mr. Woodhouse and the narrator despise marriage and want to surround themselves with young virgins, who will keep them 'well.' Further, it is also deliciously, though seditiously, funny that one of the reputed cures for venereal disease was a light diet, mostly consisting of a thin gruel—Mr. Woodhouse's favourite meal" (p. 320).

children. We are very proud of the children, are not we, papa? I wonder which she will think the handsomest, Henry or John?"

"Aye, I wonder which she will. Poor little dears, how glad they will be to come. They are very fond of being at Hartfield, Harriet."

"I dare say they are, sir. I am sure I do not know who is not."

"Henry is a fine boy, but John is very like his mamma. Henry is the eldest, he was named after me, not after his father.[25] John, the second, is named after his father. Some people are surprized, I believe, that the eldest was not, but Isabella would have him called Henry, which I thought very pretty of her. And he is a very clever boy, indeed. They are all remarkably clever; and they have so many pretty ways. They will come and stand by my chair, and say, 'Grandpapa, can you give me a bit of string?' and once Henry asked me for a knife, but I told him knives were only made for grandpapas. I think their father is too rough with them very often."

"He appears rough to you," said Emma, "because you are so very gentle yourself; but if you could compare him with other papas, you would not think him rough. He wishes his boys to be active and hardy; and if they misbehave, can give them a sharp word now and then; but he is an affectionate father—certainly Mr. John Knightley is an affectionate father. The children are all fond of him."

"And then their uncle comes in, and tosses them up to the ceiling in a very frightful way!"

"But they like it, papa; there is nothing they like so much. It is such enjoyment to them, that if their uncle did not lay down the rule of their taking turns, which ever began would never give way to the other."

"Well, I cannot understand it."

"That is the case with us all, papa. One half of the world cannot understand the pleasures of the other."

Later in the morning, and just as the girls were going to separate in preparation for the regular four o'clock dinner, the hero of this inimitable charade walked in again. Harriet turned away; but Emma could receive him with the usual smile, and her quick eye soon discerned in his the consciousness of having made a push[26]—of having thrown a die;[27] and she imagined he was come to see how it might

25 It was customary for a first son to be named after his father.

26 Made a decisive move.

27 An allusion to the famous phrase "iacta alea est" ("the die has been cast"), attributed by Suetonius to Julius Caesar on his crossing the Rubicon in 49 BC.

turn up. His ostensible reason, however, was to ask whether Mr. Woodhouse's party could be made up in the evening without him, or whether he should be in the smallest degree necessary at Hartfield. If he were, every thing else must give way, but otherwise his friend Cole had been saying so much about his dining with him—had made such a point of it, that he had promised him conditionally to come.

Emma thanked him, but could not allow of his disappointing his friend on their account; her father was sure of his rubber.[28] He reurged—she re-declined; and he seemed then about to make his bow, when taking the paper from the table, she returned it—

"Oh! here's the charade you were so obliging as to leave with us; thank you for the sight of it. We admired it so much, that I have ventured to write it into Miss Smith's collection. Your friend will not take it amiss I hope. Of course I have not transcribed beyond the eight first lines."

Mr. Elton certainly did not very well know what to say. He looked rather doubtingly—rather confused; said something about "honour;" —glanced at Emma and at Harriet, and then seeing the book open on the table, took it up, and examined it very attentively.[29] With the view of passing off an awkward moment, Emma smilingly said,

"You must make my apologies to your friend; but so good a charade must not be confined to one or two. He may be sure of every woman's approbation while he writes with such gallantry."

"I have no hesitation in saying," replied Mr. Elton, though hesitating a good deal while he spoke, "I have no hesitation in saying—at least if my friend feels at all as *I* do—I have not the smallest doubt that, could he see his little effusion honoured as *I* see it, (looking at the book again, and replacing it on the table,) he would consider it as the proudest moment of his life."

After this speech he was gone as soon as possible. Emma could not think it too soon; for with all his good and agreeable qualities, there was a sort of parade in his speeches which was very apt to incline her to laugh. She ran away to indulge the inclination, leaving the tender and the sublime[30] of pleasure to Harriet's share.

28 A set of three games of cards.

29 Given his intentions and priorities, Elton is confused that Emma has avowedly excised what are, to his mind, the two most important lines of the charade.

30 The fact that Austen can employ "sublime" ironically as a term of "novel slang" is a measure of how interest in the sublime had grown in Britain in the second half of the eighteenth century, following the publication of Edmund Burke's *Philosophical Enquiry into the Origin of our Ideas of the Sublime and Beautiful* (1757). See also Andrew Ashfield and Peter De Bolla, eds., *The Sublime: A Reader in British Eighteenth-Century Aesthetic Theory* (Cambridge: Cambridge University Press, 1996).

10

Though now the middle of December, there had yet been no weather to prevent the young ladies from tolerably regular exercise; and on the morrow, Emma had a charitable visit to pay to a poor sick family, who lived a little way out of Highbury.

Their road to this detached cottage was down Vicarage-lane, a lane leading at right-angles from the broad, though irregular, main street of the place; and, as may be inferred, containing the blessed abode of Mr. Elton. A few inferior dwellings were first to be passed, and then, about a quarter of a mile down the lane rose the Vicarage; an old and not very good house, almost as close to the road as it could be. It had no advantage of situation;[1] but had been very much smartened up by the present proprietor; and, such as it was, there could be no possibility of the two friends passing it without a slackened pace and observing eyes.—Emma's remark was—

"There it is. There go you and your riddle-book one of these days." —Harriet's was—

"Oh! what a sweet house!—How very beautiful!—There are the yellow curtains that Miss Nash admires so much."

"I do not often walk this way *now,*" said Emma, as they proceeded, "but *then* there will be an inducement, and I shall gradually get intimately acquainted with all the hedges, gates, pools, and pollards[2] of this part of Highbury."

Harriet, she found, had never in her life been within side the Vicarage, and her curiosity to see it was so extreme, that, considering

1 Then, as now, front garden space was highly prized in England, both for reasons of privacy and to minimize noise from passing traffic. James Edward Austen-Leigh notes that while Steventon Rectory, Austen's childhood home, was ideal in this respect ("North of the house, the road from Deane to Popham Lane ran at a sufficient distance from the front to allow a carriage drive, through turf and trees"), Chawton Cottage "was so close to the road that the front door opened upon it; while a very narrow enclosure, paled in on each side, protected the building from danger of collision with any runaway vehicle" (*A Memoir of Jane Austen and Other Family Recollections,* ed. Kathryn Sutherland [Oxford: Oxford University Press, 2002], pp. 23, 67).

2 Trees cut back above a certain height, to encourage growth and provide wood.

Engraving of Steventon Rectory, Hampshire, from J. E. Austen-Leigh, *A Memoir of Jane Austen* (London: R. Bentley, 1870). This illustration of Austen's first home, where she lived from her birth in 1775 until the family's removal to Bath in 1801, clearly shows the ample space in front of the house.

exteriors and probabilities, Emma could only class it, as a proof of love, with Mr. Elton's seeing ready wit in her.

"I wish we could contrive it," said she; "but I cannot think of any tolerable pretence for going in;—no servant that I want to inquire about of his housekeeper—no message from my father."

She pondered, but could think of nothing. After a mutual silence of some minutes, Harriet thus began again—

"I do so wonder, Miss Woodhouse, that you should not be married, or going to be married! so charming as you are!"—

Emma laughed, and replied,

"My being charming, Harriet, is not quite enough to induce me to marry; I must find other people charming—one other person at least. And I am not only, not going to be married, at present, but have very little intention of ever marrying at all."

"Ah! so you say; but I cannot believe it."

"I must see somebody very superior to any one I have seen yet, to be tempted; Mr. Elton, you know, (recollecting herself,) is out of the question: and I do *not* wish to see any such person. I would rather not be tempted. I cannot really change for the better. If I were to marry, I must expect to repent it."

"Dear me!—it is so odd to hear a woman talk so!"—

"I have none of the usual inducements of women to marry. Were I to fall in love, indeed, it would be a different thing! but I never have been in love; it is not my way, or my nature; and I do not think I ever shall. And, without love, I am sure I should be a fool to change such a situation as mine. Fortune I do not want; employment I do not want; consequence I do not want: I believe few married women are half as much mistress of their husband's house, as I am of Hartfield; and never, never could I expect to be so truly beloved and important; so always first and always right in any man's eyes as I am in my father's."

"But then, to be an old maid[3] at last, like Miss Bates!"

"That is as formidable an image as you could present, Harriet; and if I thought I should ever be like Miss Bates![4] so silly—so satisfied—so smiling—so prosing—so undistinguishing[5] and unfastidious—and so apt to tell every thing relative to every body about me, I would marry to-morrow. But between *us,* I am convinced there never can be any likeness, except in being unmarried."

"But still, you will be an old maid! and that's so dreadful!"

"Never mind, Harriet, I shall not be a poor old maid; and it is poverty only which makes celibacy contemptible to a generous public! A single woman, with a very narrow income, must be a ridiculous, disagreeable, old maid! the proper sport[6] of boys and girls; but a single woman, of good fortune, is always respectable, and may be as sensible and pleasant as anybody else. And the distinction is not quite so much against the candour[7] and common sense of the world as appears at first; for a very narrow income has a tendency to contract the mind, and sour the temper. Those who can barely live, and who live perforce in a very small, and generally very inferior, society, may well be illiberal[8] and cross. This does not apply, however, to Miss Bates; she is only too good natured and too silly to suit me; but, in general, she is very much to the taste of everybody, though single and though poor. Poverty certainly has not contracted her mind: I really believe, if she had only a shilling in the world, she would be very likely to give away sixpence of it;[9] and nobody is afraid of her: that is a great charm."

3 The (often insulting) expression dates back as far as the sixteenth century.

4 For all Emma's anxious disavowals of any similarity between Miss Bates and herself, the fact that a reader hears her impersonation of the older woman's speech habits before Miss Bates's first direct speech in the novel makes it sound uncannily as if Miss Bates were echoing Emma, rather than the other way around.

5 Lacking in discernment.

6 A fit target for ridicule.

7 Fair judgment.

8 Ungenerous, small-minded.

9 In the old, predecimal currency, sixpence was equal to half a shilling.

Photograph of Chawton Cottage, Hampshire. Compare this house's proximity to the main road with the ample front plot of the Steventon property.

"Dear me! but what shall you do? how shall you employ yourself when you grow old?"

"If I know myself, Harriet, mine is an active, busy mind, with a great many independent resources; and I do not perceive why I should be more in want of employment at forty or fifty than one-and-twenty. Woman's usual occupations of eye and hand and mind will be as open to me then, as they are now; or with no important variation. If I draw less, I shall read more; if I give up music, I shall take to carpet-work.[10] And as for objects of interest, objects for the affections, which is in truth the great point of inferiority, the want of which is really the great evil to be avoided in *not* marrying, I shall be very well off, with all the children of a sister I love so much, to care about. There will be enough of them, in all probability, to supply every sort of sensation that declining life can need. There will be enough for every hope and every fear; and though my attachment to none can equal that of a parent, it suits my ideas of comfort better than what is warmer and blinder. My nephews and nieces!—I shall often have a niece with me."

"Do you know Miss Bates's niece? That is, I know you must have seen her a hundred times—but are you acquainted?"

"Oh! yes; we are always forced to be acquainted whenever she comes to Highbury. By the bye, *that* is almost enough to put one out of conceit with a niece. Heaven forbid! at least, that I should ever bore people half so much about all the Knightleys together, as she does about Jane Fairfax. One is sick of the very name of Jane Fairfax. Every letter from her is read forty times over; her compliments to all friends go round and round again; and if she does but send her aunt the pattern of a stomacher,[11] or knit a pair of garters for her grandmother, one hears of nothing else for a month. I wish Jane Fairfax very well; but she tires me to death."

They were now approaching the cottage, and all idle topics were superseded. Emma was very compassionate; and the distresses of the poor were as sure of relief from her personal attention and kindness, her counsel and her patience, as from her purse. She understood their ways, could allow for their ignorance and their temptations, had no romantic expectations of extraordinary virtue from those,

10 Carpet work does appear to be identified in Austen's fiction with older women, such as Mrs. Jennings in vol. III, chap. 6, of *Sense and Sensibility,* and Lady Bertram in vol. II, chap. 1, of *Mansfield Park.*

11 A stomacher was a decorative piece of clothing worn under the laces of a woman's bodice.

for whom education had done so little;[12] entered into their troubles with ready sympathy, and always gave her assistance with as much intelligence as good-will. In the present instance, it was sickness and poverty together which she came to visit; and after remaining there as long as she could give comfort or advice, she quitted the cottage with such an impression of the scene as made her say to Harriet, as they walked away,

"These are the sights, Harriet, to do one good. How trifling they make every thing else appear!—I feel now as if I could think of nothing but these poor creatures all the rest of the day; and yet, who can say how soon it may all vanish from my mind?"

"Very true," said Harriet. "Poor creatures! one can think of nothing else."

"And really, I do not think the impression will soon be over," said Emma, as she crossed the low hedge, and tottering footstep[13] which ended the narrow, slippery path through the cottage garden, and brought them into the lane again. "I do not think it will," stopping to look once more at all the outward wretchedness of the place, and recal the still greater within.

"Oh! dear, no," said her companion.

They walked on. The lane made a slight bend; and when that bend was passed, Mr. Elton was immediately in sight; and so near as to give Emma time only to say farther,

"Ah! Harriet, here comes a very sudden trial of our stability in good thoughts. Well, (smiling,) I hope it may be allowed that if compassion has produced exertion and relief to the sufferers, it has done all that is truly important. If we feel for the wretched, enough to do all we can for them, the rest is empty sympathy, only distressing to ourselves."

Harriet could just answer, "Oh! dear, yes," before the gentleman joined them. The wants and sufferings of the poor family, however, were the first subject on meeting. He had been going to call on them. His visit he would now defer; but they had a very interesting parley about what could be done and should be done. Mr. Elton then turned back to accompany them.

12 Emma displays here an affinity with Cowper's *Task,* especially the demythologizing description of the "peasant's nest" in book 1:

> Here, I have said, at least I should possess
> The poet's treasure, silence, and indulge
> The dreams of fancy, tranquil and secure.
> Vain thought! the dweller in that still retreat
> Dearly obtains the refuge it affords.
> Its elevated scite forbids the wretch
> To drink sweet waters of the chrystal well;
> He dips his bowl into the weedy ditch,
> And heavy-laden brings his bev'rage home
> Far-fetch'd and little worth; nor seldom waits,
> Dependent on the baker's punctual call,
> To hear his creaking panniers at the door,
> Angry and sad and his last crust consumed.
> So farewel envy of the *peasant's nest.*

Austen's other favorite poet, George Crabbe (1754–1832), also casts doubt on fanciful poetic descriptions of poverty in *The Village* (1783):

> Ye gentle souls who dream of rural ease,
> Whom the smooth stream and smoother sonnet please,
> Go! if the peaceful cot your praises share,
> Go look within, and ask if peace be there:
> If peace be his—that drooping weary sire
> Or theirs, that offspring round the feeble fire,
> Or hers, that matron pale, whose trembling hand
> Turns on the wretched hearth the expiring brand.

13 A small stile, a wooden step to ease access.

"To fall in with each other on such an errand as this," thought Emma; "to meet in a charitable scheme; this will bring a great increase of love on each side. I should not wonder if it were to bring on the declaration. It must, if I were not here. I wish I were anywhere else."

Anxious to separate herself from them as far as she could, she soon afterwards took possession of a narrow footpath, a little raised on one side of the lane, leaving them together in the main road. But she had not been there two minutes when she found that Harriet's habits of dependence and imitation were bringing her up too, and that, in short, they would both be soon after her. This would not do; she immediately stopped, under pretence of having some alteration to make in the lacing of her half-boot,[14] and stooping down in complete occupation of the footpath, begged them to have the goodness to walk on, and she would follow in half a minute. They did as they were desired; and by the time she judged it reasonable to have done with her boot, she had the comfort of further delay in her power, being overtaken by a child from the cottage, setting out, according to orders, with her pitcher, to fetch broth from Hartfield.[15] To walk by the side of this child, and talk to and question her, was the most natural thing in the world, or would have been the most natural, had she been acting just then without design; and by this means the others were still able to keep ahead, without any obligation of waiting for her. She gained on them, however, involuntarily; the child's pace was quick, and theirs rather slow; and she was the more concerned at it, from their being evidently in a conversation which interested them. Mr. Elton was speaking with animation, Harriet listening with a very pleased attention; and Emma having sent the child on, was beginning to think how she might draw back a little more, when they both looked around, and she was obliged to join them.

Mr. Elton was still talking, still engaged in some interesting detail; and Emma experienced some disappointment when she found that he was only giving his fair companion an account of the yesterday's party at his friend Cole's, and that she was come in herself for the

14 A boot reaching some way up the calf, but not as far as the knee.

15 As Maggie Lane cogently points out, the relations of social interdependence in *Emma* are often articulated through the movements of food (compare Knightley's benevolent gift of apples, and the Woodhouses' gift of a hindquarter of pork, to the Bateses). "Thus," she argues, "for the purposes of teaching Emma how to live, Jane Austen creates the only organic community of her fiction, and the device she uses to show its interdependency is food. The cultivation, distribution, cookery and above all the sharing of food play an important part in both the physical and the moral life of Highbury." *Jane Austen and Food* (London: The Hambledon Press, 1995), p. 154.

Stilton cheese, the north Wiltshire,[16] the butter, the cellery, the beetroot[17] and all the dessert.

"This would soon have led to something better of course," was her consoling reflection; "any thing interests between those who love; and any thing will serve as introduction to what is near the heart. If I could but have kept longer away!"

They now walked on together quietly, till within view of the vicarage pales,[18] when a sudden resolution, of at least getting Harriet into the house, made her again find something very much amiss about her boot, and fall behind to arrange it once more. She then broke the lace off short, and dexterously throwing it into a ditch, was presently obliged to entreat them to stop, and acknowledge her inability to put herself to rights so as to be able to walk home in tolerable comfort.

"Part of my lace is gone," said she, "and I do not know how I am to contrive.[19] I really am a most troublesome companion to you both, but I hope I am not often so ill-equipped. Mr. Elton, I must beg leave to stop at your house, and ask your housekeeper for a bit of ribband or string, or any thing just to keep my boot on."

Mr. Elton looked all happiness at this proposition; and nothing could exceed his alertness and attention in conducting them into his house and endeavouring to make every thing appear to advantage. The room they were taken into was the one he chiefly occupied, and looking forwards; behind it was another with which it immediately communicated; the door between them was open, and Emma passed into it with the housekeeper to receive her assistance in the most comfortable manner. She was obliged to leave the door ajar as she found it; but she fully intended that Mr. Elton should close it. It was not closed however, it still remained ajar; but by engaging the housekeeper in incessant conversation, she hoped to make it practicable for him to chuse his own subject[20] in the adjoining room. For ten minutes she could hear nothing but herself. It could be protracted no longer. She was then obliged to be finished and make her appearance.

The lovers were standing together at one of the windows. It had a most favourable aspect; and, for half a minute, Emma felt the glory of having schemed successfully. But it would not do; he had not come

16 Another of Austen's subtle intimations of social relations through objects. Blue Stilton cheese first became popular in the early eighteenth century, when travelers on the main road from London to York would stop at the village of Stilton in Cambridgeshire (although the cheese itself was made in nearby Leicestershire, one of the three counties still permitted to produce true Stilton). Unlike Stilton, North Wiltshire cheese fell out of fashion over the course of the nineteenth century, although the modern Baydon Hill cheese is based on an original North Wiltshire recipe and technique. However, the cheese was massively popular at the end of the eighteenth century: as Val Cheke notes, by 1798 some 5,000 tons of North Wiltshire was being produced every year (*The Story of Cheese-Making in Britain* [London: Routledge & Kegan Paul, 1959], p. 118). As with the generational shift between quadrille and whist, the fact that the younger men of the neighborhood, such as Elton and Cole, serve Stilton and North Wiltshire marks them out as part of a more modern economy of commodity consumption. Lane notes: "By the early nineteenth century cheese, the reputation of which had formerly suffered from being thought labourers' food, was establishing the place at that stage in the meal which it has retained ever since. Only with the improved transport of the period could a variety of cheeses from different parts of the country be brought in their prime to the rich man's table, and begin to acquire their individual names after their places of origin" (*Jane Austen and Food,* p. 45). Thus to serve a named cheese from a relatively distant part of the country (Stilton is about seventy-four miles from Leatherhead in Surrey, Malmesbury in North Wiltshire about seventy-eight miles) would carry the exotic cachet of what are now known as "food miles," the assumption being that a commodity was more valuable the farther it had to travel to its point of consumption. A notable fictional depiction of this faddishness occurs in book VIII, chap. 9, of Fanny Burney's novel *Camilla: or A Picture of Youth* (1796), where the rakish young Clermont Lynmere is upbraided for having Stilton sent to him in Germany: "A boy to be sending over out of Germany into England for Stilton cheese!"

to the point. He had been most agreeable, most delightful; he had told Harriet that he had seen them go by, and had purposely followed them; other little gallantries and allusions had been dropt, but nothing serious.

"Cautious, very cautious," thought Emma; "he advances inch by inch, and will hazard nothing till he believes himself secure."

Still, however, though every thing had not been accomplished by her ingenious device, she could not but flatter herself that it had been the occasion of much present enjoyment to both, and must be leading them forward to the great event.

17 Celery is still often served with cheese at dessert in England, but beetroot has largely fallen out of fashion.

18 Wooden fencing.

19 Manage.

20 Emma hopes her enforced absence will allow Elton to declare himself to Harriet.

Vincent Van Gogh, *Small House on a Road with Pollard Willows,* 1881.

II

Mr. Elton must now be left to himself. It was no longer in Emma's power to superintend his happiness or quicken his measures.[1] The coming of her sister's family was so very near at hand, that first in anticipation and then in reality, it became henceforth her prime object of interest; and during the ten days of their stay at Hartfield it was not to be expected—she did not herself expect—that any thing beyond occasional, fortuitous assistance could be afforded by her to the lovers. They might advance rapidly if they would, however; they must advance somehow or other whether they would or no. She hardly wished to have more leisure for them. There are people, who the more you do for them, the less they will do for themselves. Mr. and Mrs. John Knightley, from having been longer than usual absent from Surry, were exciting of course rather more than the usual interest. Till this year, every long vacation[2] since their marriage had been divided between Hartfield and Donwell Abbey; but all the holidays of this autumn had been given to sea-bathing for the children,[3] and it was therefore many months since they had been seen in a regular way by their Surry connections, or seen at all by Mr. Woodhouse, who could not be induced to get so far as London, even for poor Isabella's sake; and who consequently was now most nervously and apprehensively happy in forestalling[4] this too short visit.

He thought much of the evils of the journey for her, and not a little of the fatigues of his own horses and coachman who were to bring some of the party the last half of the way; but his alarms were needless; the sixteen miles being happily accomplished, and Mr. and Mrs.

1 To make him move faster in his wooing of Harriet, as one might speed up a courtship dance.

2 The Long Vacation of the Inns of Court now runs from the end of July to the beginning of October. However, in the late eighteenth and early nineteenth centuries, the break was much longer and more flexible, often running from late June until early November. For example, the Long Vacation of 1813 ran from July 7 to November 6, and that of 1814 from June 29 to November 7.

3 The reputed medical benefits of sea-bathing were a growing concern in English culture after the middle of the eighteenth century and contributed significantly to the growth of seaside resorts. In *Practical Observations Concerning Sea Bathing* (London: T. Cadell & W. Davies, 1804), A. P. Buchan remarked that "[b]athing in the sea, by exposing the body for a time to a medium of a lower temperature than it is accustomed to, combined with the opportunity of breathing a pure air, appears . . . to restore to the constitution a portion of that irritability which had been previously exhausted, by the heat, the impure atmosphere, and, above all, by the enervating modes of life peculiar to great towns. The transition from languor and lassitude to vigorous and florid health, which is sometimes so rapid during even a short course of judiciously regulated sea-bathing, as to render it difficult to recognize the meagre invalid who, a few weeks before, had repaired to the sea-coast in search of health, seems to afford a

John Knightley, their five children, and a competent number of nursery-maids, all reaching Hartfield in safety. The bustle and joy of such an arrival, the many to be talked to, welcomed, encouraged, and variously dispersed and disposed of, produced a noise and confusion which his nerves could not have born under any other cause, nor have endured much longer even for this; but the ways of Hartfield and the feelings of her father were so respected by Mrs. John Knightley, that in spite of maternal solicitude for the immediate enjoyment of her little ones, and for their having instantly all the liberty and attendance,[5] all the eating and drinking, and sleeping and playing, which they could possibly wish for, without the smallest delay, the children were never allowed to be long a disturbance to him, either in themselves or in any restless attendance on them.

Mrs. John Knightley was a pretty, elegant little woman, of gentle, quiet manners, and a disposition remarkably amiable and affectionate; wrapt up in her family; a devoted wife, a doating mother, and so tenderly attached to her father and sister that, but for these higher ties, a warmer love might have seemed impossible. She could never see a fault in any of them. She was not a woman of strong understanding or any quickness; and with this resemblance of her father, she inherited also much of his constitution; was delicate in her own health, over-careful of that of her children, had many fears and many nerves,[6] and was as fond of her own Mr. Wingfield in town as her father could be of Mr. Perry. They were alike too, in a general benevolence[7] of temper, and a strong habit of regard for every old acquaintance.

Mr. John Knightley was a tall, gentleman-like, and very clever man; rising in his profession, domestic,[8] and respectable in his private character; but with reserved manners which prevented his being generally pleasing; and capable of being sometimes out of humour. He was not an ill-tempered man, not so often unreasonably cross as to deserve such a reproach; but his temper was not his great perfection; and, indeed, with such a worshipping wife, it was hardly possible that any natural defects in it should not be increased. The extreme sweetness of her temper must hurt his. He had all the clearness and quickness of mind which she wanted, and he could sometimes act an ungracious, or say a severe thing. He was not a great fa-

strong confirmation of this opinion" (pp. 47–48). He also observed that "[a]utumn is the season of the year generally made choice of in this country as most proper for the purpose of bathing in the sea" (p. 1).

4 Anticipating.

5 Attention.

6 Nervous conditions, anxieties. Mrs. Bennet in *Pride and Prejudice* is similarly prey to a great variety of "nerves" throughout the novel.

7 This is the first occurrence in the novel of a phrase that will become more prominent in vol. III.

8 Devoted to his home (hence his reluctance to leave London).

vourite with his fair sister-in-law. Nothing wrong in him escaped her. She was quick in feeling the little injuries to Isabella, which Isabella never felt herself. Perhaps she might have passed over more had his manners been flattering to Isabella's sister, but they were only those of a calmly kind brother and friend, without praise and without blindness;[9] but hardly any degree of personal compliment could have made her regardless of that greatest fault of all in her eyes which he sometimes fell into, the want of respectful forbearance towards her father. There he had not always the patience that could have been wished. Mr. Woodhouse's peculiarities and fidgettiness were sometimes provoking him to a rational remonstrance or sharp retort equally ill bestowed. It did not often happen; for Mr. John Knightley had really a great regard for his father-in-law, and generally a strong sense of what was due to him; but it was too often for Emma's charity, especially as there was all the pain of apprehension[10] frequently to be endured, though the offence came not. The beginning, however, of every visit displayed none but the properest feelings, and this being of necessity so short might be hoped to pass away in unsullied cordiality. They had not been long seated and composed when Mr. Woodhouse, with a melancholy shake of the head and a sigh, called his daughter's attention to the sad change at Hartfield since she had been there last.

"Ah! my dear," said he, "poor Miss Taylor—It is a grievous business!"

"Oh! yes, sir," cried she with ready sympathy, "how you must miss her! And dear Emma too!—what a dreadful loss to you both!—I have been so grieved for you.—I could not imagine how you could possibly do without her.—It is a sad change indeed.—But I hope she is pretty well, sir."

"Pretty well, my dear—I hope—pretty well.—I do not know but that the place agrees with her tolerably."

Mr. John Knightley here asked Emma quietly whether there were any doubts of the air of Randalls.

"Oh, no—none in the least. I never saw Mrs. Weston better in my life—never looking so well. Papa is only speaking his own regret."

"Very much to the honour of both," was the handsome reply.

9 John Knightley clearly shares his brother's straight-talking habits.

10 Anticipation.

"And do you see her, sir, tolerably often?" asked Isabella in the plaintive tone which just suited her father.

Mr. Woodhouse hesitated.—"Not near so often, my dear, as I could wish."

"Oh! papa, we have missed seeing them but one entire day since they married. Either in the morning or evening of every day, excepting one, have we seen either Mr. Weston or Mrs. Weston, and generally both, either at Randalls or here—and as you may suppose, Isabella, most frequently here. They are very, very kind in their visits. Mr. Weston is really as kind as herself. Papa, if you speak in that melancholy way, you will be giving Isabella a false idea of us all. Every body must be aware that Miss Taylor must be missed, but every body ought also to be assured that Mr. and Mrs. Weston do really prevent our missing her by any means to the extent we ourselves anticipated—which is the exact truth."

"Just as it should be," said Mr. John Knightley, "and just as I hoped it was from your letters. Her wish of shewing you attention could not be doubted, and his being a disengaged[11] and social man makes it all easy. I have been always telling you, my love, that I had no idea of the change being so very material to Hartfield as you apprehended; and now you have Emma's account, I hope you will be satisfied."

"Why to be sure," said Mr. Woodhouse—"yes, certainly—I cannot deny that Mrs. Weston, poor Mrs. Weston, does come and see us pretty often—but then—she is always obliged to go away again."

"It would be very hard upon Mr. Weston if she did not, papa.—You quite forget poor Mr. Weston."

"I think, indeed," said John Knightley pleasantly, "that Mr. Weston has some little claim. You and I, Emma, will venture to take the part of the poor husband. I, being a husband, and you not being a wife, the claims of the man may very likely strike us with equal force. As for Isabella, she has been married long enough to see the convenience of putting all the Mr. Westons aside as much as she can."

"Me, my love," cried his wife, hearing and understanding only in part.—"Are you talking about me?—I am sure nobody ought to be, or can be, a greater advocate for matrimony than I am; and if it had not been for the misery of her leaving Hartfield, I should never have

11 Not tied up in day-to-day business.

John Hassell, "Payne's Hill [Painshill, Cobham], the seat of Lady Carhampton," 1822.

thought of Miss Taylor but as the most fortunate woman in the world; and as to slighting Mr. Weston, that excellent Mr. Weston, I think there is nothing he does not deserve. I believe he is one of the very best tempered men that ever existed. Excepting yourself and your brother, I do not know his equal for temper. I shall never forget his flying Henry's kite for him that very windy day last Easter—and ever since his particular kindness last September twelvemonth in writing that note at twelve o'clock at night,[12] on purpose to assure me that there was no scarlet fever[13] at Cobham,[14] I have been convinced there could not be a more feeling heart nor a better man in existence.—If any body can deserve him, it must be Miss Taylor."

"Where is the young man?" said John Knightley. "Has he been here on this occasion—or has he not?"

"He has not been here yet," replied Emma. "There was a strong expectation of his coming soon after the marriage, but it ended in nothing; and I have not heard him mentioned lately."

"But you should tell them of the letter, my dear," said her father. "He wrote a letter to poor Mrs. Weston, to congratulate her, and a very proper handsome letter it was. She shewed it to me. I thought it very well done of him indeed. Whether it was his own idea you know, one cannot tell. He is but young, and his uncle perhaps—"

"My dear papa, he is three-and-twenty.—You forget how time passes."

"Three-and-twenty!—is he indeed?—Well, I could not have thought it—and he was but two years old when he lost his poor mother! Well, time does fly indeed!—and my memory is very bad. However, it was an exceeding good, pretty letter, and gave Mr. and Mrs. Weston a great deal of pleasure. I remember it was written from Weymouth, and dated Sept. 28th—and began, 'My dear Madam,' but I forget how it went on; and it was signed 'F. C. Weston Churchill.'—I remember that perfectly."

"How very pleasing and proper of him!" cried the good-hearted Mrs. John Knightley. "I have no doubt of his being a most amiable young man. But how sad it is that he should not live at home with his father! There is something so shocking in a child's being taken away from his parents and natural home! I never can comprehend how Mr.

12 Isabella here joins the number of characters who linger nostalgically on particular moments from the past (see Introduction).

13 John Clark gives a vivid description of the symptoms of the bacterial disease known as scarlet fever: "The disease in general began with sickness, lassitude, chillness, or shivering. The patient soon complained of head-ach, and pain and soreness of the throat. The skin became hot, the pulse very quick, often full and firm; but sometimes it was small and feeble, though generally hard. At night the fever ran high, and the patients were restless, and often delirious" (*Observations on Fevers, Especially Those of the Continued Type; and on the Scarlet Fever Attended with Ulcerated Sore-Throat* [London: T. Cadell, 1778], pp. 206–207). There were several serious outbreaks of scarlet fever in England around the turn of the nineteenth century.

14 A town in Surrey, five miles north of Leatherhead.

Weston could part with him. To give up one's child! I really never could think well of any body who proposed such a thing to any body else."

"Nobody ever did think well of the Churchills, I fancy," observed Mr. John Knightley coolly. "But you need not imagine Mr. Weston to have felt what you would feel in giving up Henry or John. Mr. Weston is rather an easy, cheerful tempered man, than a man of strong feelings; he takes things as he finds them, and makes enjoyment of them somehow or other, depending, I suspect, much more upon what is called *society* for his comforts, that is, upon the power of eating and drinking, and playing whist with his neighbours five times a-week, than upon family affection, or any thing that home affords."

Emma could not like what bordered on a reflection on Mr. Weston, and had half a mind to take it up; but she struggled, and let it pass. She would keep the peace if possible;[15] and there was something honourable and valuable in the strong domestic habits, the all-sufficiency of home to himself, whence resulted her brother's disposition to look down on the common rate[16] of social intercourse, and those to whom it was important.—It had a high claim to forbearance.

15 An indication of Emma's genuine (if sometimes misguided) investment in social decorum, and a hint that she can look beyond social surfaces.

16 Standard form.

12

Mr. Knightley was to dine with them—rather against the inclination of Mr. Woodhouse, who did not like that any one should share with him in Isabella's first day. Emma's sense of right however had decided it; and besides the consideration of what was due to each brother, she had particular pleasure, from the circumstance of the late disagreement between Mr. Knightley and herself, in procuring him the proper invitation.

She hoped they might now become friends again. She thought it was time to make up. Making-up indeed would not do. *She* certainly had not been in the wrong, and *he* would never own that he had. Concession must be out of the question; but it was time to appear to forget that they had ever quarrelled; and she hoped it might rather assist the restoration of friendship, that when he came into the room she had one of the children with her[1]—the youngest, a nice little girl about eight months old, who was now making her first visit to Hartfield, and very happy to be danced about in her aunt's arms. It did assist; for though he began with grave looks and short questions, he was soon led on to talk of them all in the usual way, and to take the child out of her arms with all the unceremoniousness of perfect amity. Emma felt they were friends again; and the conviction giving her at first great satisfaction, and then a little sauciness,[2] she could not help saying, as he was admiring the baby,

"What a comfort it is that we think alike about our nephews and nieces. As to men and women, our opinions are sometimes very dif-

1 Emma is not the first character in Austen's fiction to employ a child as a means of emotional manipulation; compare the protagonist's plot in Letter 5 of *Lady Susan* (c. 1795): "I mean to win my Sister in law's heart through her Children; I know all their names already, & am going to attach myself with the greatest sensibility to one in particular, a young Frederic, whom I take on my lap & sigh over for his dear Uncle's sake."

2 Cheekiness.

ferent; but with regard to these children, I observe we never disagree."

"If you were as much guided by nature in your estimate of men and women, and as little under the power of fancy and whim in your dealings with them, as you are where these children are concerned, we might always think alike."

"To be sure—our discordancies must always arise from my being in the wrong."

"Yes," said he, smiling—"and reason good.[3] I was sixteen years old when you were born."

"A material difference then," she replied—"and no doubt you were much my superior in judgment at that period of our lives; but does not the lapse of one-and-twenty years bring our understandings a good deal nearer?"

"Yes—a good deal *nearer.*"

"But still, not near enough to give me a chance of being right, if we think differently."

"I have still the advantage of you by sixteen years' experience, and by not being a pretty young woman and a spoiled child. Come, my dear Emma, let us be friends and say no more about it. Tell your aunt, little Emma, that she ought to set you a better example than to be renewing old grievances, and that if she were not wrong before, she is now."

"That's true," she cried—"very true. Little Emma, grow up a better woman than your aunt. Be infinitely cleverer and not half so conceited. Now, Mr. Knightley, a word or two more, and I have done. As far as good intentions went, we were *both* right, and I must say that no effects on my side of the argument have yet proved wrong. I only want to know that Mr. Martin is not very, very bitterly disappointed."

"A man cannot be more so," was his short, full answer.

"Ah!—Indeed I am very sorry.—Come, shake hands with me."

This had just taken place and with great cordiality, when John Knightley made his appearance, and "How d'ye do, George?" and "John, how are you?" succeeded in the true English style,[4] burying under a calmness that seemed all but indifference, the real attach-

3 With good reason.

4 Compare Knightley's later disapproval of Frank Churchill's "un-English" manners and mannerisms in vol. I, chap. 18: "No, Emma, your amiable young man can be amiable only in French, not in English. He may be very 'aimable,' have very good manners, and be very agreeable; but he can have no English delicacy towards the feelings of other people: nothing really amiable about him." Of course, to be identified as, or accused of being, too "French" in 1814 might also carry additional connotations of being unpatriotic; Linda Colley remarks that "[u]nder Napoleon, the French reverted in the British imagination to what they had so often seemed in the past: spiritless victims of over-powerful government at home and ferocious exponents of military aggression abroad" (*Britons: Forging the Nation, 1707–1837* [New Haven: Yale University Press, 1992; repr. London: Vintage, 1996], p. 330).

5 Marked by both conversational ease and overall sociability. Throughout the eighteenth century and on into the early nineteenth, "conversation" denoted not only the practices of social talk but also a person's whole bearing and mode of being in the world, as witnessed by early eighteenth-century accounts of polite conversation as a civilizing force. For instance, Shaftesbury argued in "Sensus Communis" (1709) for the classical dialogue as a model for modern ease: "It is not to be imagined what advantage the reader has when he can thus cope with his author, who is willing to come on a fair stage with him and exchange the tragic buskin for an easier and more natural gait and habit" (*Characteristics of Men, Manners, Opinions, Times,* ed. L. E. Klein [Cambridge: Cambridge University Press, 1999], p. 35). For further discussion of the idea of "conversability" see also Peter Burke, *The Art of Conversation* (Cambridge: Polity Press, 1993), Brian Vickers and Nancy S. Struever, *Rhetoric and the Pursuit of Truth: Language Change in the Seventeenth and Eighteenth Centuries* (Los Angeles: William Andrews Clark Memorial Library, 1985), and Bharat Tandon, *Jane Austen and the Morality of Conversation* (London: Anthem Press, 2003), pp. 1–54.

ment which would have led either of them, if requisite, to do every thing for the good of the other.

The evening was quiet and conversible,[5] as Mr. Woodhouse declined cards entirely for the sake of comfortable talk with his dear Isabella, and the little party made two natural divisions; on one side he and his daughter; on the other the two Mr. Knightleys; their subjects totally distinct, or very rarely mixing—and Emma only occasionally joining in one or the other.

The brothers talked of their own concerns and pursuits, but principally of those of the elder, whose temper was by much the most communicative, and who was always the greater talker. As a magistrate,[6] he had generally some point of law to consult John about, or, at least, some curious anecdote to give; and as a farmer, as keeping in hand the home-farm[7] at Donwell, he had to tell what every field was to bear next year,[8] and to give all such local information as could not fail of being interesting to a brother whose home it had equally been the longest part of his life, and whose attachments were strong. The plan of a drain,[9] the change of a fence, the felling of a tree, and the destination of every acre for wheat, turnips, or spring corn, was entered into with as much equality of interest by John, as his cooler manners rendered possible; and if his willing brother ever left him any thing to inquire about,[10] his inquiries even approached a tone of eagerness.

While they were thus comfortably occupied, Mr. Woodhouse was enjoying a full flow of happy regrets and fearful affection with his daughter.

"My poor dear Isabella," said he, fondly taking her hand, and interrupting, for a few moments, her busy labours for some one of her five children—"How long it is, how terribly long since you were here! And how tired you must be after your journey! You must go to bed early, my dear—and I recommend a little gruel to you before you go.—You and I will have a nice basin of gruel[11] together. My dear Emma, suppose we all have a little gruel."

Emma could not suppose any such thing, knowing, as she did, that both the Mr. Knightleys were as unpersuadable on that article as herself;—and two basins only were ordered. After a little more dis-

6 Lay magistrates, operating under the jurisdiction of the lords lieutenant of their respective counties, were responsible for a variety of local administrative and legal duties, including hearing and enforcing noncriminal judgments.

7 That part of an estate farmed by the landowner for his own benefit, rather than by tenant farmers such as Robert Martin.

8 Knightley has to inform his brother of the contents of each field because he is, as a responsible farmer, practicing the four-field system of crop rotation, designed to maximize yields and minimize disease. The four-field system (usually involving wheat, barley, turnips, and clover) was originally devised by farmers in Flanders, and its introduction to Britain in the 1730s is generally attributed to the Whig statesman Charles Townshend (1674–1738), who gained the popular nickname of "Turnip Townshend" as a result. John Scott's "Eclogue II: Rural Business, or The Agriculturists," extols the virtues of the system:

> Would ye from tillage ample gains receive,
> With change of crops th'exhausted soil relieve;
> Next purple clover let brown wheat be seen,
> And bearded barley after turnips green.

(*The Poetical Works of John Scott Esq.* [London: J. Buckland, 1782], p. 111)

9 As a landowner whose estate includes the floodplain of a river, and the owner of a house whose grounds slope markedly (see vol. III, chap. 6), Knightley would need to pay attention to the drainage of low-lying fields.

10 The first hint in the novel that Knightley is capable of discoursing at length on the minutiae of farming practice—not a particularly fashionable topic of conversation, even in Highbury. Emma alludes to this habit much later on, when she jokes about Knightley's discussing "business, shows of cattle, or new drills" with Robert Martin in vol. III, chap. 18.

11 See Introduction.

course in praise of gruel, with some wondering at its not being taken every evening by every body, he proceeded to say, with an air of grave reflection,

"It was an awkward business, my dear, your spending the autumn at South End[12] instead of coming here. I never had much opinion of the sea air."

"Mr. Wingfield most strenuously recommended it, sir—or we should not have gone. He recommended it for all the children, but particularly for the weakness in little Bella's throat,—both sea air and bathing."

"Ah! my dear, but Perry had many doubts about the sea doing her any good; and as to myself, I have been long perfectly convinced, though perhaps I never told you so before, that the sea is very rarely of use to any body. I am sure it almost killed me once."

C. C. Coventry, *Royal Terrace from the Sea, 1807.* Southend's aspirations toward becoming a fashionable watering-place were advanced significantly by "Royal" visits in 1801 and 1803.

12 South End (now known as Southend-on-Sea) is a seaside resort on the Essex coast, to the north of the Thames estuary. Originally simply part of the "south end" of Prittlewell, it was developed as a town in its own right from the late eighteenth century onward; a plan was made in 1768 to promote the town as a sea-bathing resort, with the development having grown to some fifty houses by 1780. Thomas Archer commended the town's virtues in *A Poetical Description of New South-End, in the County of Essex, and its Vicinity* (1793):

> If in the cooling tide you wish to lave,
> A guide conducts you to the briny wave:
> Veil'd by the awning of the close machine,
> You bathe securely, decent, and unseen.
> If bent for exercise you mount your horse,
> The level Beach presents a spacious course.
> . . . If pleasant prospect, and romantic scene,
> Salubrious air, and atmosphere serene,
> Sweet rural walks, and company polite,
> And courteous entertainment can invite;
> This Bathing-Place shall gain a mighty name,
> And stand conspicuous in the lists of Fame;
> Tho' no Marine Pavilion it can boast,
> Nor Royal Guests have visited the Coast.

(London: William Lane, 1793), pp. 11–12, 15–16. However, this want of "Royal Guests" was supplied by the visits of Princess Charlotte of Wales in 1801 (on the advice of the royal doctors) and of her mother, Princess Caroline, in 1803.

"Come, come," cried Emma, feeling this to be an unsafe subject, "I must beg you not to talk of the sea. It makes me envious and miserable;—I who have never seen it![13] South End is prohibited, if you please. My dear Isabella, I have not heard you make one inquiry after Mr. Perry yet; and he never forgets you."

"Oh! good Mr. Perry—how is he, sir?"

"Why, pretty well; but not quite well. Poor Perry is bilious,[14] and he has not time to take care of himself—he tells me he has not time to take care of himself—which is very sad—but he is always wanted all round the country. I suppose there is not a man in such practice any where. But then, there is not so clever a man any where."

"And Mrs. Perry and the children, how are they? do the children grow?—I have a great regard for Mr. Perry. I hope he will be calling soon. He will be so pleased to see my little ones."

"I hope he will be here to-morrow, for I have a question or two to ask him about myself of some consequence. And, my dear, whenever he comes, you had better let him look at little Bella's throat."

"Oh! my dear sir, her throat is so much better that I have hardly any uneasiness about it. Either bathing has been of the greatest service to her, or else it is to be attributed to an excellent embrocation[15] of Mr. Wingfield's, which we have been applying at times ever since August."[16]

"It is not very likely, my dear, that bathing should have been of use to her—and if I had known you were wanting an embrocation, I would have spoken to—"

"You seem to me to have forgotten Mrs. and Miss Bates," said Emma, "I have not heard one inquiry after them."

"Oh! the good Bateses—I am quite ashamed of myself—but you mention them in most of your letters. I hope they are quite well. Good old Mrs. Bates—I will call upon her to-morrow, and take my children.—They are always so pleased to see my children.—And that excellent Miss Bates!—such thorough worthy people!—How are they, sir?"

"Why, pretty well, my dear, upon the whole. But poor Mrs. Bates had a bad cold about a month ago."

13 A measure of the isolation of Emma's existence, since Brighton, for example, is only some forty miles away from Highbury.

14 The term "bilious" at the beginning of the nineteenth century could denote a range of disorders, some medically specific, others still carrying some of the metaphorical associations of the older vocabulary of the four "humours" (blood, phlegm, black bile, and yellow bile). It is likely here that Mr. Woodhouse simply means that Perry is prone to some kind of upset stomach or gastric problem.

15 "A liquid used for bathing or moistening any diseased part; now usually restricted to those applied by rubbing; a liniment" *(OED)*.

16 Given that it is now December, this is not a great endorsement of Mr. Wingfield's medication. Austen contrives an even more surreal joke about the efficacy of medical treatments (in particular, the time they take to have effects) in chap. 5 of *Sanditon* (1817), where Diana Parker's letter relates the following emergency: "Two years ago I happened to be calling on Mrs Sheldon when her Coachman sprained his foot as he was cleaning the Carriage & cd hardly limp into the House—but by the immediate use of Friction alone steadily persevered in, (& I rubbed his Ancle with my own hand for six Hours without Intermission)—he was well in three days."

"How sorry I am! But colds were never so prevalent as they have been this autumn. Mr. Wingfield told me that he had never known them more general or heavy—except when it has been quite an influenza."[17]

"That has been a good deal the case, my dear; but not to the degree you mention. Perry says that colds have been very general, but not so heavy as he has very often known them in November. Perry does not call it altogether a sickly season."

"No, I do not know that Mr. Wingfield considers it *very* sickly except—"

"Ah! my poor dear child, the truth is, that in London it is always a sickly season. Nobody is healthy in London,[18] nobody can be. It is a dreadful thing to have you forced to live there!—so far off!—and the air so bad!"

"No, indeed—*we* are not at all in a bad air. Our part of London is so very superior to most others!—You must not confound us with London in general, my dear sir. The neighbourhood of Brunswick Square is very different from almost all the rest. We are so very airy! I should be unwilling, I own, to live in any other part of the town;—there is hardly any other that I could be satisfied to have my children in:—but *we* are so remarkably airy!—Mr. Wingfield thinks the vicinity of Brunswick Square decidedly the most favourable as to air."

"Ah! my dear, it is not like Hartfield. You make the best of it—but after you have been a week at Hartfield, you are all of you different creatures; you do not look like the same. Now I cannot say, that I think you are any of you looking well at present."

"I am sorry to hear you say so, sir; but I assure you, excepting those little nervous head-aches and palpitations which I am never entirely free from any where, I am quite well myself; and if the children were rather pale before they went to bed, it was only because they were a little more tired than usual, from their journey and the happiness of coming. I hope you will think better of their looks to-morrow; for I assure you Mr. Wingfield told me, that he did not believe he had ever sent us off altogether, in such good case.[19] I trust, at least, that you do not think Mr. Knightley looking ill,"—turning her eyes with affectionate anxiety towards her husband.

17 The term "influenza" had only been in use in its strict medical sense, to denote "a specific febrile zymotic disorder" *(OED),* since the eighteenth century (the *OED*'s first citation comes from 1743). There were epidemics in 1762, 1775, 1782, and 1803. In March 1803, from amid the latest outbreak, Richard Pearson's work *Some Observations on the Present Epidemic Catarrhal Fever, or Influenza* offered an account of the most common symptoms. "After some alternations of chillness and heat," he noted, "the patient is seized with a heaviness or pain of the head, with sneezing, wateriness of the eyes, hoarseness and cough. These symptoms come on in the order here stated. In the course of a few hours the headach increases, the skin becomes hot, with a pain in the back and limbs, or transitory stitches across the chest. The tongue is white, the pulse quick or frequent, and for the most part soft. There is more or less of sickness at the stomach, and sometimes vomiting. The bowels are generally costive; and considerable uneasiness, often amounting to great pain, is felt in some part of the abdomen" ([London: C. & R. Baldwin, 1803], p. 4).

In addition, however, the term had been used metaphorically since at least 1774 to describe "a prevalent craze" *(OED);* therefore, for Austen to give Isabella the phrase "quite an influenza" may also carry the satirical implication that she has (here as elsewhere in the chapter) inherited her father's hypochondriac relish for fashionable diseases. From her juvenilia to her final manuscripts, Austen presents characters comically making distinctions between afflictions: in Letter the 14th of *Love and Freindship* (1790), Laura recalls the dying words of her friend Sophia: "beware of fainting-fits . . . Though at the time they may be refreshing & Agreable yet beleive me they will in the end, if too often repeated & at improper seasons, prove destructive to your Constitution. . . . My fate will teach you this . . . I die a Martyr to my greif for the loss of Augustus. . . . One fatal swoon has cost me my Life. . . . Beware of swoons Dear Laura . . . a frenzy fit is not one quarter so pernicious; it is an exercise to the Body & if not too violent, is I dare say conducive to Health in its consequences—Run mad as often as you chuse; but do not faint—."

"Middling, my dear; I cannot compliment you. I think Mr. John Knightley very far from looking well."

"What is the matter, sir?—Did you speak to me?" cried Mr. John Knightley, hearing his own name.

"I am sorry to find, my love, that my father does not think you looking well—but I hope it is only from being a little fatigued. I could have wished, however, as you know, that you had seen Mr. Wingfield before you left home."

"My dear Isabella,"—exclaimed he hastily—"pray do not concern yourself about my looks. Be satisfied with doctoring and coddling[20] yourself and the children, and let me look as I chuse."

"I did not thoroughly understand what you were telling your brother," cried Emma,[21] "about your friend Mr. Graham's intending to have a bailiff from Scotland, to look after his new estate. But will it answer? Will not the old prejudice[22] be too strong?"

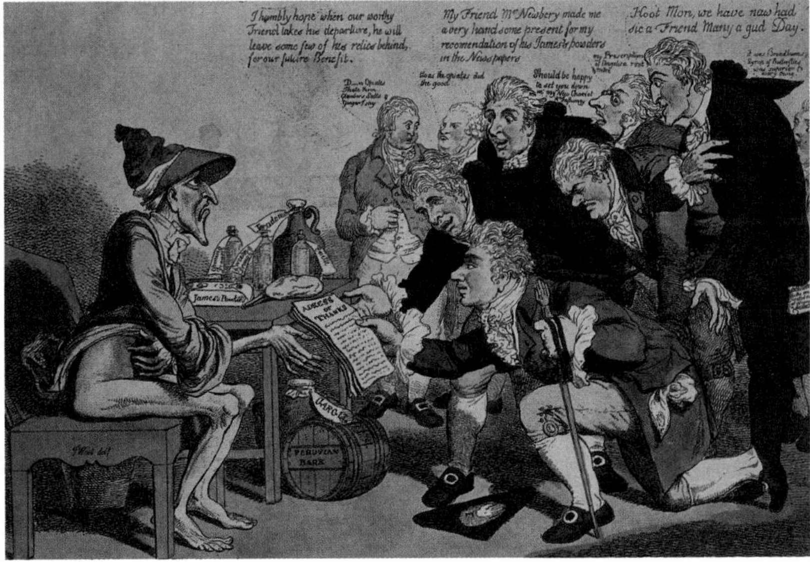

Temple West, "An address of thanks from the faculty to the Right Hon. Mr Influenzy for his kind visit to the country," 1803. There were epidemics of influenza in 1762, 1775, 1782, and 1803, which brought no one any good—except, perhaps, the doctors, as this cartoon implies.

18 The association of the metropolis with physical (and often moral) ill health was nothing new; however, Austen would also have been familiar with this disapproval as a sophisticated, recurring literary trope in the work of Cowper; in book I of *The Task,* the speaker utters the famous sentiment:

> God made the country, and man made the town.
> What wonder then, that health and virtue, gifts
> That can alone make sweet the bitter draught
> That life holds out to all, should most abound
> And least be threatened in the fields and groves?

19 In such good physical condition.

20 Treating as an invalid.

21 The narrator's unusually intensive choice of verb here suggests how willfully Emma is trying to wrench the conversation away from Mr. Woodhouse and Isabella's favorite topic, ill health.

22 In reality, "the old prejudice" against Scotland and the Scots denoted a cluster of attitudes. After the 1715 and 1745 Rebellions, there remained, in some quarters of English society, a suspicious association of Scots with the possession of Jacobite sympathies; in addition, readers of *Emma* would have been freshly alerted to "the old prejudice" by the appearance in 1814 of the most famous Romantic treatment of Jacobite history, Scott's *Waverley.*

23 Weight, importance.

24 Speeches of denunciation. Austen is applying ironically a term deriving from the vehement speeches against Philip of Macedon made by the Athenian orator Demosthenes (384–322 BC).

And she talked in this way so long and successfully that, when forced to give her attention again to her father and sister, she had nothing worse to hear than Isabella's kind inquiry after Jane Fairfax;—and Jane Fairfax, though no great favourite with her in general, she was at that moment very happy to assist in praising.

"That sweet, amiable Jane Fairfax!" said Mrs. John Knightley—"It is so long since I have seen her, except now and then for a moment accidentally in town! What happiness it must be to her good old grandmother and excellent aunt, when she comes to visit them! I always regret excessively on dear Emma's account that she cannot be more at Highbury; but now their daughter is married, I suppose Colonel and Mrs. Campbell will not be able to part with her at all. She would be such a delightful companion for Emma."

Mr. Woodhouse agreed to it all, but added,

"Our little friend Harriet Smith, however, is just such another pretty kind of young person. You will like Harriet. Emma could not have a better companion than Harriet."

"I am most happy to hear it—but only Jane Fairfax one knows to be so very accomplished and superior!—and exactly Emma's age."

This topic was discussed very happily, and others succeeded of similar moment,[23] and passed away with similar harmony; but the evening did not close without a little return of agitation. The gruel came and supplied a great deal to be said—much praise and many comments—undoubting decision of its wholesomeness for every constitution, and pretty severe Philippics[24] upon the many houses where it was never met with tolerable;—but, unfortunately, among the failures which the daughter had to instance, the most recent, and therefore most prominent, was in her own cook at South End, a young woman hired for the time, who never had been able to understand what she meant by a basin of nice smooth gruel, thin, but not too thin. Often as she had wished for and ordered it, she had never been able to get any thing tolerable. Here was a dangerous opening.

"Ah!" said Mr. Woodhouse, shaking his head and fixing his eyes on her with tender concern.—The ejaculation in Emma's ear expressed, "Ah! there is no end of the sad consequences of your going to South

End. It does not bear talking of." And for a little while she hoped he would not talk of it, and that a silent rumination might suffice to restore him to the relish of his own smooth gruel. After an interval of some minutes, however, he began with,

"I shall always be very sorry that you went to the sea this autumn, instead of coming here."

"But why should you be sorry, sir?—I assure you, it did the children a great deal of good."

"And, moreover, if you must go to the sea, it had better not have been to South End. South End is an unhealthy place. Perry was surprized to hear you had fixed upon South End."

"I know there is such an idea with many people, but indeed it is quite a mistake, sir.—We all had our health perfectly well there, never found the least inconvenience from the mud;[25] and Mr. Wingfield says it is entirely a mistake to suppose the place unhealthy; and I am sure he may be depended on, for he thoroughly understands the nature of the air, and his own brother and family have been there repeatedly."

25 Being near the mouth of the estuary, Southend has always produced significant amounts of coastal mud, much of it refuse from the capital city upstream. The inhabitants of Highbury—especially, but not exclusively, Mr. Woodhouse—are more widely cautious about possible mud, as witnessed by Mrs. Elton's misplaced fastidiousness in vol. III, chap. 6: "let a woman have ever so many resources, it is not possible for her to be always shut up at home;—and very long walks, you know—in summer there is dust, and in winter there is dirt." Indeed, one of the historical advantages of the Surrey and Berkshire stretches of the Thames as places of residence was that they were upstream of the polluting city itself. However, the reality of dirt in *Emma* rarely lives up to expectations; it is significant that *Persuasion* and *Sanditon,* with their greater focus on seaside locations, are correspondingly more attentive to the forms of dirt that those locations generate.

"View of Cromer from the West Cliff in the very early 1800s; ships in the offing, lighthouse and signal station on the hill and characters in the foreground," from Edmund Bartell, *Cromer Considered as a Watering Place* (1806). On Mr. Perry's recommendation, Mr. Woodhouse holds Cromer to be a much healthier resort than Southend—conveniently ignoring its much greater distance from London.

"You should have gone to Cromer,[26] my dear, if you went any where.—Perry was a week at Cromer once, and he holds it to be the best of all the sea-bathing places. A fine open sea, he says, and very pure air. And, by what I understand, you might have had lodgings there quite away from the sea—a quarter of a mile off—very comfortable. You should have consulted Perry."

"But, my dear sir, the difference of the journey;—only consider how great it would have been.—A hundred miles, perhaps, instead of forty."[27]

"Ah! my dear, as Perry says, where health is at stake, nothing else should be considered; and if one is to travel, there is not much to chuse between forty miles and an hundred.—Better not move at all, better stay in London altogether than travel forty miles to get into a worse air. This is just what Perry said. It seemed to him a very ill-judged measure."

Emma's attempts to stop her father had been vain; and when he had reached such a point as this, she could not wonder at her brother-in-law's breaking out.

"Mr. Perry," said he, in a voice of very strong displeasure, "would do as well to keep his opinion till it is asked for. Why does he make it any business of his, to wonder at what I do?—at my taking my family to one part of the coast or another?—I may be allowed, I hope, the use of my judgment as well as Mr. Perry.—I want his directions no more than his drugs." He paused—and growing cooler in a moment, added, with only sarcastic dryness, "If Mr. Perry can tell me how to convey a wife and five children a distance of an hundred and thirty miles with no greater expense or inconvenience than a distance of forty, I should be as willing to prefer Cromer to South End as he could himself."

"True, true," cried Mr. Knightley,[28] with most ready interposition—"very true. That's a consideration indeed.—But John, as to what I was telling you of my idea of moving the path to Langham, of turning it more to the right that it may not cut through the home meadows, I cannot conceive any difficulty. I should not attempt it, if it were to be the means of inconvenience to the Highbury people, but if you call to mind exactly the present line of the path. . . . The only way of

26 A seaside resort on the north Norfolk coast, still famous for its crabs. Like Southend, it became a fashionable location in the late eighteenth and early nineteenth centuries, being particularly popular with local business families.

27 Cromer is some 115 miles from London, Southend around 36 miles.

28 Knightley, like Emma before him, is trying to wrest the conversation back from matters of illness and health, and the narrator gives him the same verb.

proving it, however, will be to turn to our maps. I shall see you at the Abbey to-morrow morning I hope, and then we will look them over, and you shall give me your opinion."

Mr. Woodhouse was rather agitated by such harsh reflections on his friend Perry, to whom he had, in fact, though unconsciously, been attributing many of his own feelings and expressions;—but the soothing attentions of his daughters gradually removed the present evil, and the immediate alertness of one brother, and better recollections of the other, prevented any renewal of it.

Watercolor of Jane Austen by Cassandra Austen, c. 1802. The fact that Austen is facing away from the viewer, her features hidden by her bonnet, has lent itself readily to the mythology of the "secretive" author.

13

1 Son-in-law.

2 See note 15 to vol. I, chap. 1.

There could hardly be an happier creature in the world, than Mrs. John Knightley, in this short visit to Hartfield, going about every morning among her old acquaintance with her five children, and talking over what she had done every evening with her father and sister. She had nothing to wish otherwise, but that the days did not pass so swiftly. It was a delightful visit;—perfect, in being much too short.

In general their evenings were less engaged with friends than their mornings: but one complete dinner engagement, and out of the house too, there was no avoiding, though at Christmas. Mr. Weston would take no denial; they must all dine at Randalls one day;—even Mr. Woodhouse was persuaded to think it a possible thing in preference to a division of the party.

How they were all to be conveyed, he would have made a difficulty if he could, but as his son[1] and daughter's carriage and horses were actually at Hartfield, he was not able to make more than a simple question on that head; it hardly amounted to a doubt; nor did it occupy Emma long to convince him that they might in one of the carriages find room for Harriet also.

Harriet, Mr. Elton, and Mr. Knightley, their own especial set, were the only persons invited to meet them;—the hours were to be early,[2] as well as the numbers few; Mr. Woodhouse's habits and inclination being consulted in every thing.

The evening before this great event (for it was a very great event that Mr. Woodhouse should dine out, on the 24th of December) had been spent by Harriet at Hartfield, and she had gone home so much indisposed with a cold, that, but for her own earnest wish of being nursed by Mrs. Goddard, Emma could not have allowed her to leave the house. Emma called on her the next day, and found her doom already signed with regard to Randalls. She was very feverish and had a bad sore-throat: Mrs. Goddard was full of care and affection, Mr. Perry was talked of, and Harriet herself was too ill and low to resist the authority which excluded her from this delightful engagement, though she could not speak of her loss without many tears.

Emma sat with her as long as she could, to attend her in Mrs. Goddard's unavoidable absences, and raise her spirits by representing how much Mr. Elton's would be depressed when he knew her state; and left her at last tolerably comfortable, in the sweet dependence[3] of his having a most comfortless visit, and of their all missing her very much. She had not advanced many yards from Mrs. Goddard's door, when she was met by Mr. Elton himself, evidently coming towards it, and as they walked on slowly together in conversation about the invalid—of whom he, on the rumour of considerable illness, had been going to inquire, that he might carry some report of her to Hartfield—they were overtaken by Mr. John Knightley returning from the daily visit to Donwell, with his two eldest boys, whose healthy, glowing faces shewed all the benefit of a country run, and seemed to ensure a quick dispatch of the roast mutton and rice pudding[4] they were hastening home for. They joined company and proceeded together. Emma was just describing the nature of her friend's complaint;—"a throat very much inflamed, with a great deal of heat about her, a quick low pulse, &c. and she was sorry to find from Mrs. Goddard that Harriet was liable to very bad sore-throats, and had often alarmed her with them."—Mr. Elton looked all alarm on the occasion, as he exclaimed,

"A sore-throat!—I hope not infectious. I hope not of a putrid infectious sort.[5] Has Perry seen her? Indeed you should take care of yourself as well as of your friend. Let me entreat you to run no risks. Why does not Perry see her?"

Emma, who was not really at all frightened herself, tranquillized this excess of apprehension by assurances of Mrs. Goddard's experi-

3 Assurance.

4 Given that roast mutton and rice pudding are both rich dishes, one might surmise that John Knightley's tastes are having some influence over Mr. Woodhouse's while the young Knightleys are at Hartfield. That said, it seems unlikely that the rice pudding would have been identical to the "Rich Rice Pudding" detailed by Maria Rundell: "Boil half a pound of rice in water, with a little bit of salt, till quite tender; drain it dry; mix it with the yolks and whites of four eggs, a quarter of a pint of cream, with two ounces of fresh butter melted in the latter four ounces of beef-suet or marrow, or veal-suet taken from a fillet of veal, finely shred, three quarters of a pound of currants, two spoonfuls of brandy, one of peach-water, or ratafia, nutmeg, and grated lemon-peel. When well mixed, put a paste round the edge, and fill the dish. Slices of candied orange, lemon, and citron if approved. Bake in a moderate oven" *(A New System of Domestic Cookery; formed Upon Principles of Economy* [London: John Murray, 1807; rev. ed., 1808], p. 143).

5 "Putrid sore throat" often denoted streptococcal pharyngitis, diphtheria, or typhus. In vol. III, chap. 17, of *Sense and Sensibility,* the characters' fears for Marianne's life are actuated by the apothecary's "pronouncing her disorder to have a putrid tendency."

6 The effort of conducting the Christmas Day church services.

7 Brother-in-law.

ence and care; but as there must still remain a degree of uneasiness which she could not wish to reason away, which she would rather feed and assist than not, she added soon afterwards—as if quite another subject,

"It is so cold, so very cold—and looks and feels so very much like snow, that if it were to any other place or with any other party, I should really try not to go out to-day—and dissuade my father from venturing; but as he has made up his mind, and does not seem to feel the cold himself, I do not like to interfere, as I know it would be so great a disappointment to Mr. and Mrs. Weston. But, upon my word, Mr. Elton, in your case, I should certainly excuse myself. You appear to me a little hoarse already, and when you consider what demand of voice and what fatigues to-morrow will bring,[6] I think it would be no more than common prudence to stay at home and take care of yourself to-night."

Mr. Elton looked as if he did not very well know what answer to make; which was exactly the case; for though very much gratified by the kind care of such a fair lady, and not liking to resist any advice of her's, he had not really the least inclination to give up the visit;—but Emma, too eager and busy in her own previous conceptions and views to hear him impartially, or see him with clear vision, was very well satisfied with his muttering acknowledgment of its being "very cold, certainly very cold," and walked on, rejoicing in having extricated him from Randalls, and secured him the power of sending to inquire after Harriet every hour of the evening.

"You do quite right," said she;—"We will make your apologies to Mr. and Mrs. Weston."

But hardly had she so spoken, when she found her brother[7] was civilly offering a seat in his carriage, if the weather were Mr. Elton's only objection, and Mr. Elton actually accepting the offer with much prompt satisfaction. It was a done thing; Mr. Elton was to go, and never had his broad handsome face expressed more pleasure than at this moment; never had his smile been stronger, nor his eyes more exulting than when he next looked at her.

"Well," said she to herself, "this is most strange!—After I had got him off so well, to chuse to go into company, and leave Harriet ill behind!—Most strange indeed!—But there is, I believe, in many men, especially single men, such an inclination—such a passion for dining out—a dinner engagement is so high in the class of their pleasures, their employments, their dignities, almost their duties, that any thing gives way to it—and this must be the case with Mr. Elton; a most valuable, amiable, pleasing young man undoubtedly, and very much in love with Harriet; but still, he cannot refuse an invitation, he must dine out wherever he is asked. What a strange thing love is! he can see ready wit in Harriet, but will not dine alone for her."

Soon afterwards Mr. Elton quitted them, and she could not but do him the justice of feeling that there was a great deal of sentiment in his manner of naming Harriet at parting; in the tone of his voice while assuring her that he should call at Mrs. Goddard's for news of her fair friend, the last thing before he prepared for the happiness of meeting her again, when he hoped to be able to give a better report; and he sighed and smiled himself off in a way that left the balance of approbation much in his favour.

After a few minutes of entire silence between them, John Knightley began with—

"I never in my life saw a man more intent on being agreeable than Mr. Elton. It is downright labour to him where ladies are concerned. With men he can be rational and unaffected, but when he has ladies to please every feature works."

"Mr. Elton's manners are not perfect," replied Emma; "but where there is a wish to please, one ought to overlook, and one does overlook a great deal. Where a man does his best with only moderate powers, he will have the advantage over negligent superiority. There is such perfect good temper and good will in Mr. Elton as one cannot but value."

"Yes," said Mr. John Knightley presently, with some slyness, "he seems to have a great deal of good-will towards *you*."

"Me!" she replied with a smile of astonishment, "are you imagining me to be Mr. Elton's object?"

"Such an imagination has crossed me, I own, Emma; and if it never occurred to you before, you may as well take it into consideration now."

8 Moderate.

9 Inconveniences.

"Mr. Elton in love with me!—What an idea!"

"I do not say it is so; but you will do well to consider whether it is so or not, and to regulate[8] your behaviour accordingly. I think your manners to him encouraging. I speak as a friend, Emma. You had better look about you, and ascertain what you do, and what you mean to do."

"I thank you; but I assure you you are quite mistaken. Mr. Elton and I are very good friends, and nothing more;" and she walked on, amusing herself in the consideration of the blunders which often arise from a partial knowledge of circumstances, of the mistakes which people of high pretensions to judgment are for ever falling into; and not very well pleased with her brother for imagining her blind and ignorant, and in want of counsel. He said no more.

Mr. Woodhouse had so completely made up his mind to the visit, that in spite of the increasing coldness, he seemed to have no idea of shrinking from it, and set forward at last most punctually with his eldest daughter in his own carriage, with less apparent consciousness of the weather than either of the others; too full of the wonder of his own going, and the pleasure it was to afford at Randalls to see that it was cold, and too well wrapt up to feel it. The cold, however, was severe; and by the time the second carriage was in motion, a few flakes of snow were finding their way down, and the sky had the appearance of being so overcharged as to want only a milder air to produce a very white world in a very short time.

Emma soon saw that her companion was not in the happiest humour. The preparing and the going abroad in such weather, with the sacrifice of his children after dinner, were evils, were disagreeables[9] at least, which Mr. John Knightley did not by any means like; he anticipated nothing in the visit that could be at all worth the purchase; and the whole of their drive to the Vicarage was spent by him in expressing his discontent.

"A man," said he, "must have a very good opinion of himself when he asks people to leave their own fireside, and encounter such a day as this, for the sake of coming to see him. He must think himself a most agreeable fellow; I could not do such a thing. It is the greatest absurdity—Actually snowing at this moment!—The folly of not allowing people to be comfortable at home—and the folly of people's not staying comfortably at home when they can! If we were obliged to go out such an evening as this, by any call of duty or business, what a hardship we should deem it;—and here are we, probably with rather thinner clothing than usual,[10] setting forward voluntarily, without excuse, in defiance of the voice of nature, which tells man, in every thing given to his view or his feelings, to stay at home himself, and keep all under shelter that he can;—here are we setting forward to spend five dull hours in another man's house, with nothing to say or to hear that was not said and heard yesterday, and may not be said and heard again to-morrow. Going in dismal weather, to return probably in worse;—four horses and four servants taken out for nothing but to convey five idle, shivering creatures into colder rooms and worse company than they might have had at home."

Emma did not find herself equal to give the pleased assent, which no doubt he was in the habit of receiving, to emulate the "Very true, my love," which must have been usually administered by his travelling companion; but she had resolution enough to refrain from making any answer at all. She could not be complying, she dreaded being quarrelsome; her heroism reached only to silence. She allowed him to talk, and arranged the glasses,[11] and wrapped herself up, without opening her lips.

They arrived, the carriage turned, the step was let down, and Mr. Elton, spruce, black, and smiling, was with them instantly. Emma thought with pleasure of some change of subject. Mr. Elton was all obligation and cheerfulness; he was so very cheerful in his civilities indeed, that she began to think he must have received a different account of Harriet from what had reached her. She had sent[12] while dressing, and the answer had been, "Much the same—not better."

"*My* report from Mrs. Goddard's," said she presently, "was not so pleasant as I had hoped—'Not better,' was *my* answer."

His face lengthened immediately; and his voice was the voice of sentiment as he answered.

"Oh! no—I am grieved to find—I was on the point of telling you that when I called at Mrs. Goddard's door, which I did the very last thing before I returned to dress, I was told that Miss Smith was not

10 Thinner because of the fashions of evening dress.

11 Closed the windows of the carriage.

12 Absolute form of the verb "to send," meaning "sent a message."

better, by no means better, rather worse. Very much grieved and concerned—I had flattered myself that she must be better after such a cordial as I knew had been given in the morning."

Emma smiled and answered—"My visit was of use to the nervous part of her complaint, I hope; but not even I can charm[13] away a sore throat; it is a most severe cold indeed. Mr. Perry has been with her, as you probably heard."

"Yes—I imagined—that is—I did not"—

"He has been used to her in these complaints, and I hope to-morrow morning will bring us both a more comfortable report. But it is impossible not to feel uneasiness. Such a sad loss to our party to-day!"

"Dreadful!—Exactly so, indeed.—She will be missed every moment."

This was very proper; the sigh which accompanied it was really estimable; but it should have lasted longer. Emma was rather in dismay when only half a minute afterwards[14] he began to speak of other things, and in a voice of the greatest alacrity and enjoyment.

"What an excellent device,"[15] said he, "the use of a sheep-skin for carriages. How very comfortable they make it;—impossible to feel cold with such precautions. The contrivances of modern days indeed have rendered a gentleman's carriage perfectly complete. One is so fenced and guarded from the weather, that not a breath of air can find its way unpermitted. Weather becomes absolutely of no consequence. It is a very cold afternoon—but in this carriage we know nothing of the matter.—Ha! snows a little I see."

"Yes," said John Knightley, "and I think we shall have a good deal of it."

"Christmas weather," observed Mr. Elton. "Quite seasonable; and extremely fortunate we may think ourselves that it did not begin yesterday, and prevent this day's party, which it might very possibly have done, for Mr. Woodhouse would hardly have ventured had there been much snow on the ground; but now it is of no consequence. This is quite the season indeed for friendly meetings. At Christmas every body invites their friends about them,[16] and people think little of even the worst weather. I was snowed up at a friend's house once

13 See note 4 to vol. I, chap. 5.

14 Throughout her fiction, Austen is comically and acutely sensitive to the proprieties of time and duration, and her narrators and characters frequently joke about events' happening too soon or too late, too quickly or too slowly. Compare, for example, Mr. Bennet's quip about Darcy's taciturn nature in vol. I, chap. 4, of *Pride and Prejudice:* "Mrs. Long told me last night that he sat close to her for half an hour without once opening his lips." In both these instances, Austen's joke derives from the unspoken assumption that "half a minute" and "half an hour" are disproportionate to their contexts, the first too short a time, the second too long. Emma, though, does not interpret this impropriety as suggesting that Harriet may not be Elton's true object.

15 Invention, innovation.

16 Although it is true that the recognizable modern Christmas was invented (or revived, depending on one's perspective) by the Victorians, Elton's observation shows that the convivial associations of Christmas had not declined completely after the seventeenth-century Puritan reaction against it. See J. A. R. Pimlott, *The Englishman's Christmas: A Social History* (Hassocks and Atlantic Highlands, NJ: The Harvester Press, 1978).

for a week. Nothing could be pleasanter. I went for only one night, and could not get away till that very day se'nnight."[17]

Mr. John Knightley looked as if he did not comprehend the pleasure, but said only, coolly,

"I cannot wish to be snowed up a week at Randalls."

At another time Emma might have been amused, but she was too much astonished now at Mr. Elton's spirits for other feelings. Harriet seemed quite forgotten in the expectation of a pleasant party.

"We are sure of excellent fires," continued he, "and every thing in the greatest comfort. Charming people, Mr. and Mrs. Weston;—Mrs. Weston indeed is much beyond praise, and he is exactly what one values, so hospitable, and so fond of society;—it will be a small party, but where small parties are select, they are perhaps the most agreeable of any. Mr. Weston's dining-room does not accommodate more than ten comfortably; and for my part, I would rather, under such circumstances, fall short by two than exceed by two. I think you will agree with me, (turning with a soft air to Emma,) I think I shall certainly have your approbation, though Mr. Knightley perhaps, from being used to the large parties of London, may not quite enter into our feelings."

"I know nothing of the large parties of London, sir—I never dine with any body."

"Indeed! (in a tone of wonder and pity,) I had no idea that the law had been so great a slavery. Well, sir, the time must come when you will be paid for all this, when you will have little labour and great enjoyment."

"My first enjoyment," replied John Knightley, as they passed through the sweep-gate,[18] "will be to find myself safe at Hartfield again."

17 Exactly a week later.

18 The gate of a curved front drive.

14

1 Welcome.

Some change of countenance was necessary for each gentleman as they walked into Mrs. Weston's drawing-room;—Mr. Elton must compose his joyous looks, and Mr. John Knightley disperse his ill-humour. Mr. Elton must smile less, and Mr. John Knightley more, to fit them for the place.—Emma only might be as nature prompted, and shew herself just as happy as she was. To her, it was real enjoyment to be with the Westons. Mr. Weston was a great favourite, and there was not a creature in the world to whom she spoke with such unreserve, as to his wife; not any one, to whom she related with such conviction of being listened to and understood, of being always interesting and always intelligible, the little affairs, arrangements, perplexities and pleasures of her father and herself. She could tell nothing of Hartfield, in which Mrs. Weston had not a lively concern; and half an hour's uninterrupted communication of all those little matters on which the daily happiness of private life depends, was one of the first gratifications of each.

This was a pleasure which perhaps the whole day's visit might not afford, which certainly did not belong to the present half hour; but the very sight of Mrs. Weston, her smile, her touch, her voice was grateful[1] to Emma, and she determined to think as little as possible of Mr. Elton's oddities, or of any thing else unpleasant, and enjoy all that was enjoyable to the utmost.

The misfortune of Harriet's cold had been pretty well gone through before her arrival. Mr. Woodhouse had been safely seated long enough to give the history of it, besides all the history of his own and Isabella's coming, and of Emma's being to follow, and had in deed just got to the end of his satisfaction that James should come and see his daughter, when the others appeared, and Mrs. Weston, who had been almost wholly engrossed by her attentions to him, was able to turn away and welcome her dear Emma.

Emma's project of forgetting Mr. Elton for a while, made her rather sorry to find, when they had all taken their places, that he was close to her. The difficulty was great of driving his strange insensibility towards Harriet, from her mind, while he not only sat at her elbow, but was continually obtruding his happy countenance on her notice, and solicitously addressing her upon every occasion. Instead of forgetting him, his behaviour was such that she could not avoid the internal suggestion of "Can it really be as my brother imagined? can it be possible for this man to be beginning to transfer his affections from Harriet to me?—Absurd and insufferable!"—Yet he would be so anxious for her being perfectly warm, would be so interested about her father, and so delighted with Mrs. Weston; and at last would begin admiring her drawings with so much zeal and so little knowledge as seemed terribly like a would-be lover, and made it some effort with her to preserve her good manners. For her own sake she could not be rude; and for Harriet's, in the hope that all would yet turn out right, she was even positively civil; but it was an effort; especially as something was going on amongst the others, in the most overpowering period of Mr. Elton's nonsense, which she particularly wished to listen to. She heard enough to know that Mr. Weston was giving some information about his son; she heard the words "my son," and "Frank," and "my son," repeated several times over; and from a few other half-syllables very much suspected that he was announcing an early visit from his son; but before she could quiet Mr. Elton, the subject was so completely past that any reviving question from her would have been awkward.

Now, it so happened that in spite of Emma's resolution of never marrying, there was something in the name, in the idea of Mr. Frank Churchill, which always interested her. She had frequently thought—especially since his father's marriage with Miss Taylor—that if she *were* to marry, he was the very person to suit her in age, character and condition. He seemed by this connection between the families, quite to belong to her. She could not but suppose it to be a match that every body who knew them must think of. That Mr. and Mrs. Weston did think of it, she was very strongly persuaded; and though not meaning to be induced by him, or by any body else, to give up a situation which she believed more replete with good than any she could change it for, she had a great curiosity to see him, a decided intention of finding him pleasant, of being liked by him to a certain degree, and a sort of pleasure in the idea of their being coupled in their friends' imaginations.

With such sensations, Mr. Elton's civilities were dreadfully ill-timed; but she had the comfort of appearing very polite, while feeling very cross—and of thinking that the rest of the visit could not possibly pass without bringing forward the same information again, or the substance of it, from the open-hearted Mr. Weston.—So it proved;—for when happily released from Mr. Elton, and seated by Mr. Weston, at dinner, he made use of the very first interval in the cares of hospitality, the very first leisure from the saddle of mutton, to say to her,

"We want[2] only two more to be just the right number. I should like to see two more here,—your pretty little friend, Miss Smith, and my son—and then I should say we were quite complete. I believe you did not hear me telling the others in the drawing room that we are expecting Frank? I had a letter from him this morning, and he will be with us within a fortnight."

Emma spoke with a very proper degree of pleasure; and fully assented to his proposition of Mr. Frank Churchill and Miss Smith making their party quite complete.

"He has been wanting to come to us," continued Mr. Weston, "ever since September: every letter has been full of it; but he cannot command his own time. He has those to please who must be pleased, and who (between ourselves)[3] are sometimes to be pleased only by a good many sacrifices. But now I have no doubt of seeing him here about the second week in January."

"What a very great pleasure it will be to you! and Mrs. Weston is

2 Are missing.

3 Mr. Weston's habit of repeatedly voicing his resentment of Mrs. Churchill in apparent confidences becomes a running joke as the novel goes on.

so anxious to be acquainted with him, that she must be almost as happy as yourself."

"Yes, she would be, but that she thinks there will be another put-off.[4] She does not depend upon his coming so much as I do: but she does not know the parties so well as I do. The case, you see, is—(but this is quite between ourselves: I did not mention a syllable of it in the other room. There are secrets in all families, you know)—The case is, that a party of friends are invited to pay a visit at Enscombe in January; and that Frank's coming depends upon their being put off. If they are not put off, he cannot stir. But I know they will, because it is a family that a certain lady,[5] of some consequence, at Enscombe, has a particular dislike to: and though it is thought necessary to invite them once in two or three years, they always are put off when it comes to the point. I have not the smallest doubt of the issue. I am as confident of seeing Frank here before the middle of January, as I am of being here myself; but your good friend there

The three volumes of *Emma,* published in December 1815. After Austen had published her first three novels with Thomas Egerton, her brother Henry negotiated a new deal with John Murray, publisher of Byron and Walter Scott.

4 Postponement.

5 In sentimental fiction, the circumlocution "certain lady" frequently carried connotations of social disgrace or scandal.

6 Caprices.

7 "Drawing-room," and its original, unelided version, "withdrawing-room," originally denoted simply a private room adjoining a more public one. However, by Austen's time, it was customary for women to withdraw to the drawing-room after the main part of dinner, while the men took wine.

8 Optimistic.

(nodding towards the upper end of the table) has so few vagaries[6] herself, and has been so little used to them at Hartfield, that she cannot calculate on their effects, as I have been long in the practice of doing."

"I am sorry there should be any thing like doubt in the case," replied Emma; "but am disposed to side with you, Mr. Weston. If you think he will come, I shall think so too; for you know Enscombe."

"Yes—I have some right to that knowledge; though I have never been at the place in my life.—She is an odd woman!—But I never allow myself to speak ill of her, on Frank's account; for I do believe her to be very fond of him. I used to think she was not capable of being fond of any body, except herself: but she has always been kind to him (in her way—allowing for little whims and caprices, and expecting every thing to be as she likes). And it is no small credit, in my opinion, to him, that he should excite such an affection; for, though I would not say it to any body else, she has no more heart than a stone to people in general; and the devil of a temper."

Emma liked the subject so well, that she began upon it, to Mrs. Weston, very soon after their moving into the drawing-room:[7] wishing her joy—yet observing, that she knew the first meeting must be rather alarming.—Mrs. Weston agreed to it; but added, that she should be very glad to be secure of undergoing the anxiety of a first meeting at the time talked of: "for I cannot depend upon his coming, I cannot be so sanguine[8] as Mr. Weston. I am very much afraid that it will all end in nothing. Mr. Weston, I dare say, has been telling you exactly how the matter stands."

"Yes—it seems to depend upon nothing but the ill-humour of Mrs. Churchill, which I imagine to be the most certain thing in the world."

"My Emma!" replied Mrs. Weston, smiling, "what is the certainty of caprice?" Then turning to Isabella, who had not been attending before—"You must know, my dear Mrs. Knightley, that we are by no means so sure of seeing Mr. Frank Churchill, in my opinion, as his father thinks. It depends entirely upon his aunt's spirits and pleasure; in short, upon her temper. To you—to my two daughters, I may venture on the truth. Mrs. Churchill rules at Enscombe, and is a very odd-tempered woman; and his coming now, depends upon her being willing to spare him."

"Oh, Mrs. Churchill; every body knows Mrs. Churchill," replied Isabella: "and I am sure I never think of that poor young man without the greatest compassion. To be constantly living with an ill-tempered person, must be dreadful.[9] It is what we happily have never known any thing of; but it must be a life of misery. What a blessing, that she never had any children! Poor little creatures, how unhappy she would have made them!"

Emma wished she had been alone with Mrs. Weston. She should then have heard more: Mrs. Weston would speak to her, with a degree of unreserve which she would not hazard with Isabella; and, she really believed, would scarcely try to conceal any thing relative to the Churchills from her, excepting those views on the young man, of which her own imagination had already given her such instinctive knowledge. But at present there was nothing more to be said. Mr. Woodhouse very soon followed them into the drawing-room. To be sitting long after dinner, was a confinement that he could not endure. Neither wine nor conversation was any thing to him; and gladly did he move to those with whom he was always comfortable.

While he talked to Isabella, however, Emma found an opportunity of saying,

"And so you do not consider this visit from your son as by any means certain. I am sorry for it. The introduction must be unpleasant, whenever it takes place; and the sooner it could be over, the better."

"Yes; and every delay makes one more apprehensive[10] of other delays. Even if this family, the Braithwaites, are put off, I am still afraid that some excuse may be found for disappointing us. I cannot bear to imagine any reluctance on his side; but I am sure there is a great wish on the Churchills' to keep him to themselves. There is jealousy. They are jealous even of his regard for his father. In short, I can feel no dependence on his coming, and I wish Mr. Weston were less sanguine."

"He ought to come," said Emma. "If he could stay only a couple of days, he ought to come; and one can hardly conceive a young man's

9 From what we see of John Knightley's temper in the novel, Isabella may have more in common with Frank than she admits here.

10 Fearful.

11 Persistently frustrated.

not having it in his power to do as much as that. A young *woman,* if she fall into bad hands, may be teazed,[11] and kept at a distance from those she wants to be with; but one cannot comprehend a young *man*'s being under such restraint, as not to be able to spend a week with his father, if he likes it."

"One ought to be at Enscombe, and know the ways of the family, before one decides upon what he can do," replied Mrs. Weston. "One ought to use the same caution, perhaps, in judging of the conduct of any one individual of any one family; but Enscombe, I believe, certainly must not be judged by general rules: *she* is so very unreasonable; and every thing gives way to her."

"But she is so fond of the nephew: he is so very great a favourite. Now, according to my idea of Mrs. Churchill, it would be most natural, that while she makes no sacrifice for the comfort of the husband, to whom she owes every thing, while she exercises incessant caprice towards *him,* she should frequently be governed by the nephew, to whom she owes nothing at all."

"My dearest Emma, do not pretend, with your sweet temper, to understand a bad one, or to lay down rules for it: you must let it go its own way. I have no doubt of his having, at times, considerable influence; but it may be perfectly impossible for him to know beforehand *when* it will be."

Emma listened, and then coolly said, "I shall not be satisfied, unless he comes."

"He may have a great deal of influence on some points," continued Mrs. Weston, "and on others, very little: and among those, on which she is beyond his reach, it is but too likely, may be this very circumstance of his coming away from them to visit us."

15

Mr. Woodhouse was soon ready for his tea; and when he had drank his tea he was quite ready to go home; and it was as much as his three companions could do, to entertain away his notice of the lateness of the hour, before the other gentlemen appeared. Mr. Weston was chatty and convivial, and no friend to early separations of any sort; but at last the drawing-room party did receive an augmentation. Mr. Elton, in very good spirits,[1] was one of the first to walk in. Mrs. Weston and Emma were sitting together on a sopha. He joined them immediately, and with scarcely an invitation, seated himself between them.

Emma, in good spirits too, from the amusement afforded her mind by the expectation of Mr. Frank Churchill, was willing to forget his late[2] improprieties, and be as well satisfied with him as before, and on his making Harriet his very first subject, was ready to listen with most friendly smiles.

He professed himself extremely anxious about her fair friend—her fair, lovely, amiable friend. "Did she know?—had she heard any thing about her, since their being at Randalls?—he felt much anxiety—he must confess that the nature of her complaint alarmed him considerably." And in this style he talked on for some time very properly, not much attending to any answer, but altogether sufficiently awake to the terror of a bad sore throat; and Emma was quite in charity with him.[3]

But at last there seemed a perverse turn; it seemed all at once as if he were more afraid of its being a bad sore throat on her account,

1 The first punning hint of Elton's intoxicated state.

2 Recent.

3 Kindly disposed toward him once more.

than on Harriet's—more anxious that she should escape the infection, than that there should be no infection in the complaint. He began with great earnestness to entreat her to refrain from visiting the sick chamber again, for the present—to entreat her to *promise him* not to venture into such hazard till he had seen Mr. Perry and learnt his opinion; and though she tried to laugh it off and bring the subject back into its proper course, there was no putting an end to his extreme solicitude about her. She was vexed. It did appear—there was no concealing it—exactly like the pretence of being in love with her, instead of Harriet; an inconstancy, if real, the most contemptible and abominable! and she had difficulty in behaving with temper.[4] He turned to Mrs. Weston to implore her assistance, "Would not she give him her support?—would not she add her persuasions to his, to induce Miss Woodhouse not to go to Mrs. Goddard's, till it were certain that Miss Smith's disorder had no infection? He could not be satisfied without a promise—would not she give him her influence in procuring it?"

"So scrupulous for others," he continued, "and yet so careless for herself! She wanted me to nurse my cold by staying at home to-day, and yet will not promise to avoid the danger of catching an ulcerated sore throat[5] herself! Is this fair, Mrs. Weston?—Judge between us. Have not I some right to complain? I am sure of your kind support and aid."

Emma saw Mrs. Weston's surprize, and felt that it must be great, at an address which, in words and manner, was assuming to himself the right of first interest in her; and as for herself, she was too much provoked and offended to have the power of directly saying any thing to the purpose. She could only give him a look; but it was such a look as she thought must restore him to his senses; and then left the sopha, removing to a seat by her sister, and giving her all her attention.

She had not time to know how Mr. Elton took the reproof, so rapidly did another subject succeed; for Mr. John Knightley now came into the room from examining the weather, and opened on them all with the information of the ground being covered with snow, and of

4 Equanimity, composure.

5 Commonly associated with scarlet fever in contemporary medical accounts. For example, John Clark remarked: "No epidemic, the small pox excepted, was ever observed to vary so much, in different patients exposed to the same contagion, as the Scarlet Fever attended with Ulcerated Sore-Throat. In some it was so mild, as to require little aid from medicine . . . whilst in others it was so malignant, as to yield to no plan of treatment" (*Observations on Fevers, Especially Those of the Continued Type; and on the Scarlet Fever Attended with Ulcerated Sore-Throat* [London: T. Cadell, 1780], p. 206).

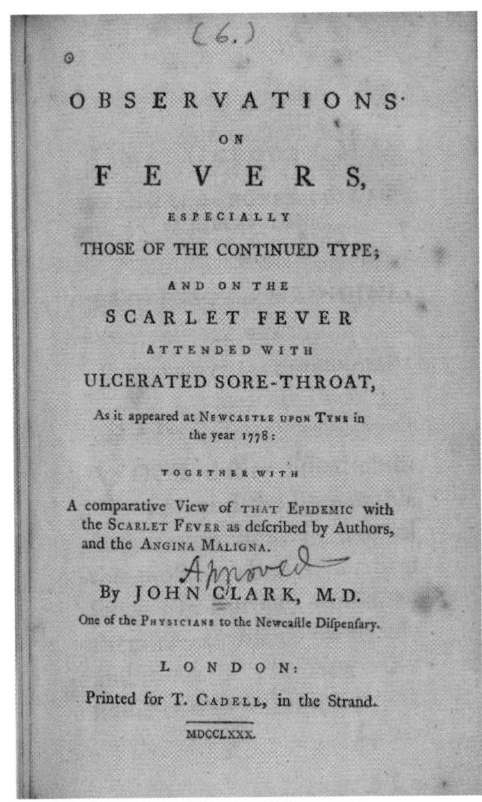

(6.)

OBSERVATIONS
ON
FEVERS,
ESPECIALLY
THOSE OF THE CONTINUED TYPE;
AND ON THE
SCARLET FEVER
ATTENDED WITH
ULCERATED SORE-THROAT,
As it appeared at NEWCASTLE UPON TYNE in the year 1778:
TOGETHER WITH
A comparative View of THAT EPIDEMIC with the SCARLET FEVER as deſcribed by Authors, and the ANGINA MALIGNA.

Approved

By JOHN CLARK, M.D.
One of the PHYSICIANS to the Newcaſtle Diſpenſary.

LONDON:
Printed for T. CADELL, in the Strand.
MDCCLXXX.

Title page of John Clark, *Observations on Fevers, Especially Those of the Continued Type; and on the Scarlet Fever Attended with Ulcerated Sore-Throat* (London: T. Cadell, 1780). "Ulcerated" or "putrid" sore throats were causes of great concern in the period, as they often indicated potentially fatal conditions.

its still snowing fast, with a strong drifting wind; concluding with these words to Mr. Woodhouse:

"This will prove a spirited beginning of your winter engagements, sir. Something new for your coachman and horses to be making their way through a storm of snow."

Poor Mr. Woodhouse was silent from consternation; but every body else had something to say; every body was either surprized or not surprized, and had some question to ask, or some comfort to offer. Mrs. Weston and Emma tried earnestly to cheer him and turn his attention from his son-in-law, who was pursuing his triumph rather unfeelingly.

"I admired your resolution very much, sir," said he, "in venturing out in such weather, for of course you saw there would be snow very soon. Every body must have seen the snow coming on. I admired your spirit; and I dare say we shall get home very well. Another hour or two's snow can hardly make the road impassable; and we are two carriages; if *one* is blown over in the bleak part of the common field there will be the other at hand. I dare say we shall be all safe at Hartfield before midnight."

Mr. Weston, with triumph of a different sort, was confessing that he had known it to be snowing some time, but had not said a word, lest it should make Mr. Woodhouse uncomfortable, and be an excuse for his hurrying away. As to there being any quantity of snow fallen or likely to fall to impede their return, that was a mere joke; he was afraid they would find no difficulty. He wished the road might be impassable, that he might be able to keep them all at Randalls; and with the utmost good-will was sure that accommodation might be found for every body, calling on his wife to agree with him, that, with a little contrivance, every body might be lodged, which she hardly knew how to do, from the consciousness of there being but two spare rooms in the house.

"What is to be done, my dear Emma?—what is to be done?" was Mr. Woodhouse's first exclamation, and all that he could say for some time. To her he looked for comfort; and her assurances of safety, her representation of the excellence of the horses, and of James, and of their having so many friends about them, revived him a little.

His eldest daughter's alarm was equal to his own. The horror of being blocked up at Randalls, while her children were at Hartfield, was full in her imagination; and fancying the road to be now just passable for adventurous people, but in a state that admitted no delay, she was eager to have it settled, that her father and Emma should remain at Randalls, while she and her husband set forward instantly through all the possible accumulations of drifted snow that might impede them.

"You had better order the carriage directly, my love," said she; "I dare say we shall be able to get along, if we set off directly; and if we do come to any thing very bad, I can get out and walk. I am not at all afraid. I should not mind walking half the way. I could change my shoes, you know, the moment I got home; and it is not the sort of thing that gives me cold."

"Indeed!" replied he. "Then, my dear Isabella, it is the most extraordinary sort of thing in the world, for in general every thing does give you cold. Walk home!—you are prettily shod for walking home, I dare say.[6] It will be bad enough for the horses."

Isabella turned to Mrs. Weston for her approbation of the plan. Mrs. Weston could only approve. Isabella then went to Emma; but Emma could not so entirely give up the hope of their being all able to get away; and they were still discussing the point, when Mr. Knightley, who had left the room immediately after his brother's first report of the snow, came back again, and told them that he had been out of doors to examine, and could answer for there not being the smallest difficulty in their getting home, whenever they liked it, either now or an hour hence. He had gone beyond the sweep[7]—some way along the Highbury road—the snow was no where above half an inch deep—in many places hardly enough to whiten the ground; a very few flakes were falling at present, but the clouds were parting, and there was every appearance of its being soon over. He had seen the coachmen, and they both agreed with him in there being nothing to apprehend.

To Isabella, the relief of such tidings was very great, and they were scarcely less acceptable to Emma on her father's account, who was immediately set as much at ease on the subject as his nervous constitution allowed; but the alarm that had been raised could not be appeased so as to admit of any comfort for him while he continued at Randalls. He was satisfied of there being no present danger in returning home, but no assurances could convince him that it was safe to stay; and while the others were variously urging and recommending, Mr. Knightley and Emma settled it in a few brief sentences: thus—

"Your father will not be easy; why do not you go?"

6 On those occasions when a woman of the time did brave a wet or snowy road, she would probably have worn pattens—strap-on overshoes that raised the sole above the level of the ground—rather than the delicate shoes that John Knightley implies his wife is wearing here. As James Edward Austen-Leigh remarks of Jane and Cassandra Austen, "when the roads were dirty, the sisters took long walks in pattens" (*A Memoir of Jane Austen and Other Family Recollections,* ed. Kathryn Sutherland [Oxford: Oxford University Press, 2002], p. 36).

7 Curved driveway.

"I am ready, if the others are."

"Shall I ring the bell?"

"Yes, do."

And the bell was rung, and the carriages spoken for. A few minutes more, and Emma hoped to see one troublesome companion deposited in his own house, to get sober and cool, and the other recover his temper and happiness when this visit of hardship were over.

The carriage came: and Mr. Woodhouse, always the first object on such occasions, was carefully attended to his own by Mr. Knightley and Mr. Weston; but not all that either could say could prevent some renewal of alarm at the sight of the snow which had actually fallen, and the discovery of a much darker night than he had been prepared for. "He was afraid they should have a very bad drive. He was afraid poor Isabella would not like it. And there would be poor Emma in the carriage behind. He did not know what they had best do. They must keep as much together as they could;" and James was talked to, and given a charge to go very slow and wait for the other carriage.

Isabella stept in after her father; John Knightley, forgetting that he did not belong to their party, stept in after his wife very naturally; so that Emma found, on being escorted and followed into the second carriage by Mr. Elton, that the door was to be lawfully shut on them, and that they were to have a tête-à-tête drive.[8] It would not have been the awkwardness of a moment, it would have been rather a pleasure, previous to the suspicions of this very day; she could have talked to him of Harriet, and the three-quarters of a mile would have seemed but one. But now, she would rather it had not happened. She believed he had been drinking too much of Mr. Weston's good wine, and felt sure that he would want to be talking nonsense.

To restrain him as much as might be, by her own manners, she was immediately preparing to speak with exquisite calmness and gravity of the weather and the night; but scarcely had she begun, scarcely had they passed the sweep-gate and joined the other carriage, than she found her subject cut up[9]—her hand seized—her attention demanded, and Mr. Elton actually making violent love to her:[10] availing himself of the precious opportunity, declaring sentiments which

8 A private drive with only Mr. Elton and herself in the carriage. The term "tête-à-tête" often (although not exclusively) carried the added connotation of intrigue, or at least intimacy: for example, in vol. II, chap. 16, of Mary Brunton's *Self-Control* (1810), which Austen described as "an excellently-meant, elegantly-written Work, without anything of Nature or Probability in it" (to Cassandra Austen, October 11–12, 1813, *Letters,* p. 234), Laura is worried about the propriety of meeting Colonel Hargrave again so soon, since "to offer him another tête à tête seemed so like soliciting a renewal of his ardours."

9 Rudely interrupted.

10 Professing his affections vehemently. The modern sense of the verb "make love" to denote sexual intercourse is a much later application of the phrase, dating from the early twentieth century; up to that time, it was used solely to refer to the more chaste activities of courtship and wooing—making it one of those curious phrases whose meaning has been almost completely transformed by semantic change. Likewise, "violent" in this context denotes vehemence rather than the almost exclusively physical connotations that the word carries nowadays. Compare Mr. Collins's attempted proposal to Elizabeth Bennet in vol. I, chap. 19, of *Pride and Prejudice* (which this scene resembles in several ways): "And now nothing remains for me but to assure you in the most animated language of the violence of my affection."

must be already well known, hoping—fearing—adoring—ready to die if she refused him; but flattering himself that his ardent attachment and unequalled love and unexampled[11] passion could not fail of having some effect, and in short, very much resolved on being seriously accepted as soon as possible. It really was so. Without scruple[12]—without apology—without much apparent diffidence, Mr. Elton, the lover of Harriet, was professing himself *her* lover. She tried to stop him; but vainly; he would go on, and say it all. Angry as she was, the thought of the moment made her resolve to restrain herself when she did speak. She felt that half this folly must be drunkenness, and therefore could hope that it might belong only to the passing hour. Accordingly, with a mixture of the serious and the playful, which she hoped would best suit his half and half[13] state, she replied,

"I am very much astonished, Mr. Elton. This to *me!* you forget yourself—you take me for my friend—any message to Miss Smith I shall be happy to deliver; but no more of this to *me,* if you please."

"Miss Smith!—Message to Miss Smith!—What could she possibly mean!"—And he repeated her words with such assurance of accent, such boastful pretence of amazement, that she could not help replying with quickness,

"Mr. Elton, this is the most extraordinary conduct! and I can account for it only in one way; you are not yourself, or you could not speak either to me, or of Harriet, in such a manner. Command yourself enough to say no more, and I will endeavour to forget it."

But Mr. Elton had only drunk wine enough to elevate his spirits, not at all to confuse his intellects.[14] He perfectly knew his own meaning; and having warmly protested against her suspicion as most injurious, and slightly[15] touched upon his respect for Miss Smith as her friend,—but acknowledging his wonder that Miss Smith should be mentioned at all,—he resumed the subject of his own passion, and was very urgent for a favourable answer.

As she thought less of his inebriety, she thought more of his inconstancy and presumption; and with fewer struggles for politeness, replied,

11 Unprecedented, peerless.

12 Hesitation.

13 Half-drunk, comparable to the modern idiom "half-cut."

14 "Intellectual powers; mental faculties; 'wits,' 'senses'" *(OED).*

15 Carelessly, dismissively.

16 Given Mr. Elton's condition, there may be a play here—as with "in very good spirits" earlier in the chapter—on the idea of his being ruddy-faced with drunkenness (the word derives from the Latin *sanguineus*, "bloody"), as well as optimistic about his matrimonial prospects.

"It is impossible for me to doubt any longer. You have made yourself too clear. Mr. Elton, my astonishment is much beyond any thing I can express. After such behaviour, as I have witnessed during the last month, to Miss Smith—such attentions as I have been in the daily habit of observing—to be addressing me in this manner—this is an unsteadiness of character, indeed, which I had not supposed possible! Believe me, sir, I am far, very far, from gratified in being the object of such professions."

"Good heaven!" cried Mr. Elton, "what can be the meaning of this?—Miss Smith!—I never thought of Miss Smith in the whole course of my existence—never paid her any attentions, but as your friend: never cared whether she were dead or alive, but as your friend. If she has fancied otherwise, her own wishes have misled her, and I am very sorry—extremely sorry—But, Miss Smith, indeed!—Oh! Miss Woodhouse! who can think of Miss Smith, when Miss Woodhouse is near! No, upon my honour, there is no unsteadiness of character. I have thought only of you. I protest against having paid the smallest attention to any one else. Every thing that I have said or done, for many weeks past, has been with the sole view of marking my adoration of yourself. You cannot really, seriously, doubt it. No!—(in an accent meant to be insinuating)—I am sure you have seen and understood me."

It would be impossible to say what Emma felt, on hearing this—which of all her unpleasant sensations was uppermost. She was too completely overpowered to be immediately able to reply: and two moments of silence being ample encouragement for Mr. Elton's sanguine[16] state of mind, he tried to take her hand again, as he joyously exclaimed—

"Charming Miss Woodhouse! allow me to interpret this interesting silence. It confesses that you have long understood me."

"No, sir," cried Emma, "it confesses no such thing. So far from having long understood you, I have been in a most complete error with respect to your views, till this moment. As to myself, I am very sorry that you should have been giving way to any feelings——Nothing could be farther from my wishes—your attachment to my friend

Harriet—your pursuit of her, (pursuit, it appeared,) gave me great pleasure, and I have been very earnestly wishing you success: but had I supposed that she were not your attraction to Hartfield, I should certainly have thought you judged ill in making your visits so frequent. Am I to believe that you have never sought to recommend yourself particularly to Miss Smith?—that you have never thought seriously of her?"

"Never, madam," cried he, affronted, in his turn: "never, I assure you. *I* think seriously of Miss Smith!—Miss Smith is a very good sort of girl; and I should be happy to see her respectably settled. I wish her extremely well: and, no doubt, there are men who might not object to—Every body has their level: but as for myself, I am not, I think, quite so much at a loss.[17] I need not so totally despair of an equal alliance,[18] as to be addressing myself to Miss Smith!—No, madam, my visits to Hartfield have been for yourself only; and the encouragement I received"—

"Encouragement!—I give you encouragement!—sir, you have been entirely mistaken in supposing it. I have seen you only as the admirer of my friend. In no other light could you have been more to me than a common acquaintance. I am exceedingly sorry: but it is well that the mistake ends where it does. Had the same behaviour continued, Miss Smith might have been led into a misconception of your views; not being aware, probably, any more than myself, of the very great inequality which you are so sensible of. But, as it is, the disappointment is single, and, I trust, will not be lasting. I have no thoughts of matrimony at present."

He was too angry to say another word; her manner too decided to invite supplication; and in this state of swelling resentment, and mutually deep mortification, they had to continue together a few minutes longer, for the fears of Mr. Woodhouse had confined them to a foot pace.[19] If there had not been so much anger, there would have been desperate awkwardness; but their straight-forward emotions left no room for the little zigzags of embarrassment. Without knowing when the carriage turned into Vicarage-lane, or when it stopped, they found themselves, all at once, at the door of his house; and

17 Quite so desperate.

18 This is Elton's valuation, but he would, strictly speaking, have been marrying "above himself" had he secured Emma's affections—something that Emma feels acutely.

19 A walking pace, and given Mr. Woodhouse's demands, possibly a human rather than an equine one.

he was out before another syllable passed.—Emma then felt it indispensable to wish him a good night. The compliment was just returned, coldly and proudly; and, under indescribable irritation of spirits, she was then conveyed to Hartfield.

There she was welcomed, with the utmost delight, by her father, who had been trembling for the dangers of a solitary drive from Vicarage-lane—turning a corner which he could never bear to think of—and in strange hands—a mere common coachman—no James; and there it seemed as if her return only were wanted to make every thing go well: for Mr. John Knightley, ashamed of his ill-humour, was now all kindness and attention; and so particularly solicitous for the comfort of her father, as to seem—if not quite ready to join him in a basin of gruel—perfectly sensible[20] of its being exceedingly wholesome; and the day was concluding in peace and comfort to all their little party, except herself.—But her mind had never been in such perturbation, and it needed a very strong effort to appear attentive and cheerful till the usual hour of separating allowed her the relief of quiet reflection.

20 Willing to admit.

16

The hair was curled, and the maid sent away, and Emma sat down to think and be miserable.—It was a wretched business, indeed!—Such an overthrow of every thing she had been wishing for!—Such a development of every thing most unwelcome!—Such a blow for Harriet!—That was the worst of all. Every part of it brought pain and humiliation, of some sort or other; but, compared with the evil to Harriet, all was light; and she would gladly have submitted to feel yet more mistaken—more in error—more disgraced by misjudgment, than she actually was, could the effects of her blunders have been confined to herself.

"If I had not persuaded Harriet into liking the man, I could have born any thing. He might have doubled his presumption to me—But poor Harriet!"

How she could have been so deceived!—He protested that he had never thought seriously of Harriet—never! She looked back as well as she could; but it was all confusion. She had taken up the idea, she supposed, and made every thing bend to it. His manners, however, must have been unmarked,[1] wavering, dubious,[2] or she could not have been so misled.

The picture!—How eager he had been about the picture!—and the charade!—and an hundred other circumstances;—how clearly they had seemed to point at Harriet. To be sure, the charade, with its "ready wit"—but then, the "soft eyes"—in fact it suited neither; it

1 Noncommittal.

2 Ambiguous.

3 Dull, obtuse.

4 Gentility.

5 Imprudently.

6 Sure of his own deserts.

7 Raise himself up the social scale.

was a jumble without taste or truth. Who could have seen through such thick-headed[3] nonsense?

Certainly she had often, especially of late, thought his manners to herself unnecessarily gallant; but it had passed as his way, as a mere error of judgment, of knowledge, of taste, as one proof among others that he had not always lived in the best society, that with all the gentleness[4] of his address, true elegance was sometimes wanting; but, till this very day, she had never, for an instant, suspected it to mean any thing but grateful respect to her as Harriet's friend.

To Mr. John Knightley was she indebted for her first idea on the subject, for the first start of its possibility. There was no denying that those brothers had penetration. She remembered what Mr. Knightley had once said to her about Mr. Elton, the caution he had given, the conviction he had professed that Mr. Elton would never marry indiscreetly;[5] and blushed to think how much truer a knowledge of his character had been there shewn than any she had reached herself. It was dreadfully mortifying; but Mr. Elton was proving himself, in many respects, the very reverse of what she had meant and believed him; proud, assuming,[6] conceited; very full of his own claims, and little concerned about the feelings of others.

Contrary to the usual course of things, Mr. Elton's wanting to pay his addresses to her had sunk him in her opinion. His professions and his proposals did him no service. She thought nothing of his attachment, and was insulted by his hopes. He wanted to marry well, and having the arrogance to raise his eyes to her, pretended to be in love; but she was perfectly easy as to his not suffering any disappointment that need be cared for. There had been no real affection either in his language or manners. Sighs and fine words had been given in abundance; but she could hardly devise any set of expressions, or fancy any tone of voice, less allied with real love. She need not trouble herself to pity him. He only wanted to aggrandize[7] and enrich himself; and if Miss Woodhouse of Hartfield, the heiress of thirty thousand pounds, were not quite so easily obtained as he had fancied, he would soon try for Miss Somebody else with twenty, or with ten.

But—that he should talk of encouragement, should consider her as aware of his views, accepting his attentions, meaning (in short), to marry him!—should suppose himself her equal in connection or mind!—look down upon her friend, so well understanding the gradations of rank below him, and be so blind to what rose above, as to fancy himself shewing no presumption in addressing her!—It was most provoking.

Perhaps it was not fair to expect him to feel how very much he was her inferior in talent, and all the elegancies of mind. The very want of such equality might prevent his perception of it; but he must know that in fortune and consequence she was greatly his superior. He must know that the Woodhouses had been settled for several generations at Hartfield, the younger branch of a very ancient family—and that the Eltons were nobody. The landed property of Hartfield certainly was inconsiderable, being but a sort of notch in the Donwell Abbey estate,[8] to which all the rest of Highbury belonged; but their fortune, from other sources, was such as to make them scarcely secondary to Donwell Abbey itself, in every other kind of consequence; and the Woodhouses had long held a high place in the consideration of the neighbourhood which Mr. Elton had first entered not two years ago, to make his way as he could, without any alliances but in trade, or any thing to recommend him to notice but his situation and his civility.—But he had fancied her in love with him; that evidently must have been his dependence;[9] and after raving a little about the seeming incongruity of gentle manners and a conceited head, Emma was obliged in common honesty to stop and admit that her own behaviour to him had been so complaisant[10] and obliging, so full of courtesy and attention, as (supposing her real motive unperceived) might warrant a man of ordinary observation and delicacy, like Mr. Elton, in fancying himself a very decided favourite. If *she* had so misinterpreted his feelings, she had little right to wonder that *he,* with self-interest to blind him, should have mistaken her's.

The first error and the worst lay at her door. It was foolish, it was wrong, to take so active a part in bringing any two people together. It

8 A small pocket of land surrounded by Knightley's holdings.

9 Conviction.

10 In this context, compliant or accommodating.

was adventuring too far, assuming too much, making light of what ought to be serious, a trick[11] of what ought to be simple. She was quite concerned and ashamed, and resolved to do such things no more.

"Here have I," said she, "actually talked poor Harriet into being very much attached to this man. She might never have thought of him but for me; and certainly never would have thought of him with hope, if I had not assured her of his attachment, for she is as modest and humble as I used to think him. Oh! that I had been satisfied with persuading her not to accept young Martin. There I was quite right. That was well done of me; but there I should have stopped, and left the rest to time and chance. I was introducing her into good company, and giving her the opportunity of pleasing some one worth having; I ought not to have attempted more. But now, poor girl, her peace is cut up for some time. I have been but half a friend[12] to her; and if she were *not* to feel this disappointment so very much, I am sure I have not an idea of any body else who would be at all desirable for her;—William Coxe—Oh! no, I could not endure William Coxe—a pert[13] young lawyer."

She stopt to blush and laugh at her own relapse, and then resumed a more serious, more dispiriting cogitation upon what had been, and might be, and must be. The distressing explanation she had to make to Harriet, and all that poor Harriet would be suffering, with the awkwardness of future meetings, the difficulties of continuing or discontinuing the acquaintance, of subduing feelings, concealing resentment, and avoiding eclat,[14] were enough to occupy her in most unmirthful reflections some time longer, and she went to bed at last with nothing settled but the conviction of her having blundered most dreadfully.

To youth and natural cheerfulness like Emma's, though under temporary gloom at night, the return of day will hardly fail to bring return of spirits. The youth and cheerfulness of morning are in happy analogy, and of powerful operation; and if the distress be not poignant enough to keep the eyes unclosed, they will be sure to open to sensations of softened pain and brighter hope.

11 Complex artifice.

12 Emma is still being too kind to herself, given that Knightley has already accused her of being "no friend to Harriet Smith" in vol. I, chap. 8.

13 Cheeky, impudent.

14 In this context, the word carries the sense of a distasteful or embarrassing public exposure. Elizabeth Bennet famously uses the term in a more conventional sense, that of conversational brilliance, in vol. I, chap. 17, of *Pride and Prejudice:* "We are each of an unsocial, taciturn disposition, unwilling to speak, unless we expect to say something that will amaze the whole room, and be handed down to posterity with all the eclat of a proverb."

Emma got up on the morrow more disposed for comfort than she had gone to bed, more ready to see alleviations of the evil before her, and to depend on getting tolerably out of it.

It was a great consolation that Mr. Elton should not be really in love with her, or so particularly amiable as to make it shocking to disappoint him—that Harriet's nature should not be of that superior sort in which the feelings are most acute and retentive—and that there could be no necessity for any body's knowing what had passed except the three principals, and especially for her father's being given a moment's uneasiness about it.

These were very cheering thoughts; and the sight of a great deal of snow on the ground did her further service, for any thing was welcome that might justify their all three being quite asunder at present.

The weather was most favourable for her; though Christmas-day, she could not go to church. Mr. Woodhouse would have been miserable had his daughter attempted it, and she was therefore safe from either exciting or receiving unpleasant and most unsuitable ideas. The ground covered with snow, and the atmosphere in that unsettled state between frost and thaw, which is of all others the most unfriendly for exercise, every morning beginning in rain or snow, and every evening setting in to freeze, she was for many days a most honourable prisoner. No intercourse with Harriet possible but by note; no church for her on Sunday any more than on Christmas-day; and no need to find excuses for Mr. Elton's absenting himself.

It was weather which might fairly confine every body at home; and though she hoped and believed him to be really taking comfort in some society or other, it was very pleasant to have her father so well satisfied with his being all alone in his own house, too wise to stir out; and to hear him say to Mr. Knightley, whom no weather could keep entirely from them,—

"Ah! Mr. Knightley, why do not you stay at home like poor Mr. Elton?"

These days of confinement would have been, but for her private perplexities, remarkably comfortable, as such seclusion exactly suited her brother, whose feelings must always be of great importance to his companions; and he had, besides, so thoroughly cleared off his ill-humour[15] at Randalls, that his amiableness never failed him during the rest of his stay at Hartfield. He was always agreeable and obliging, and speaking pleasantly of every body. But with all the hopes of cheerfulness, and all the present comfort of delay, there was still such an evil hanging over her in the hour of explanation with Harriet, as made it impossible for Emma to be ever perfectly at ease.

15 Purged himself of his ill temper.

17

Mr. and Mrs. John Knightley were not detained long at Hartfield. The weather soon improved enough for those to move who must move; and Mr. Woodhouse having, as usual, tried to persuade his daughter to stay behind with all her children, was obliged to see the whole party set off, and return to his lamentations over the destiny of poor Isabella;—which poor Isabella, passing her life with those she doated on, full of their merits, blind to their faults, and always innocently busy, might have been a model of right[1] feminine happiness.

The evening of the very day on which they went, brought a note from Mr. Elton to Mr. Woodhouse, a long, civil, ceremonious[2] note, to say, with Mr. Elton's best compliments, "that he was proposing to leave Highbury the following morning in his way to Bath, where, in compliance with the pressing entreaties of some friends, he had engaged to spend a few weeks, and very much regretted the impossibility he was under, from various circumstances of weather and business, of taking a personal leave of Mr. Woodhouse, of whose friendly civilities he should ever retain a grateful sense—and had Mr. Woodhouse any commands, should be happy to attend to them."

Emma was most agreeably surprized.—Mr. Elton's absence just at this time was the very thing to be desired. She admired him for contriving it, though not able to give him much credit for the manner in which it was announced. Resentment could not have been more plainly spoken than in a civility to her father, from which she was so pointedly excluded. She had not even a share in his opening compli-

1 True, authentic.

2 Ornately overformal.

3 Attractive, alluring.

4 Interested.

ments.—Her name was not mentioned;—and there was so striking a change in all this, and such an ill-judged solemnity of leave-taking in his grateful acknowledgments, as she thought, at first, could not escape her father's suspicion.

It did however.—Her father was quite taken up with the surprize of so sudden a journey, and his fears that Mr. Elton might never get safely to the end of it, and saw nothing extraordinary in his language. It was a very useful note, for it supplied them with fresh matter for thought and conversation during the rest of their lonely evening. Mr. Woodhouse talked over his alarms, and Emma was in spirits to persuade them away with all her usual promptitude.

She now resolved to keep Harriet no longer in the dark. She had reason to believe her nearly recovered from her cold, and it was desirable that she should have as much time as possible for getting the better of her other complaint before the gentleman's return. She went to Mrs. Goddard's accordingly the very next day, to undergo the necessary penance of communication; and a severe one it was.—She had to destroy all the hopes which she had been so industriously feeding—to appear in the ungracious character of the one preferred—and acknowledge herself grossly mistaken and mis-judging in all her ideas on one subject, all her observations, all her convictions, all her prophesies for the last six weeks.

The confession completely renewed her first shame—and the sight of Harriet's tears made her think that she should never be in charity with herself again.

Harriet bore the intelligence very well—blaming nobody—and in every thing testifying such an ingenuousness of disposition and lowly opinion of herself, as must appear with particular advantage at that moment to her friend.

Emma was in the humour to value simplicity and modesty to the utmost; and all that was amiable, all that ought to be attaching,[3] seemed on Harriet's side, not her own. Harriet did not consider herself as having any thing to complain of. The affection of such a man as Mr. Elton would have been too great a distinction.—She never could have deserved him—and nobody but so partial[4] and kind a friend as Miss Woodhouse would have thought it possible.

Her tears fell abundantly—but her grief was so truly artless, that no dignity could have made it more respectable in Emma's eyes—and she listened to her and tried to console her with all her heart and understanding—really for the time convinced that Harriet was the superior creature of the two—and that to resemble her would be more for her own welfare and happiness than all that genius or intelligence could do.

It was rather too late in the day to set about being simple-minded and ignorant; but she left her with every previous resolution confirmed of being humble and discreet, and repressing imagination all the rest of her life. Her second duty now, inferior only to her father's claims, was to promote Harriet's comfort, and endeavour to prove her own affection in some better method than by match-making. She got her to Hartfield, and shewed her the most unvarying kindness, striving to occupy and amuse her, and by books and conversation, to drive Mr. Elton from her thoughts.

Time, she knew, must be allowed for this being thoroughly done; and she could suppose herself but an indifferent judge of such matters in general, and very inadequate to sympathize in an attachment to Mr. Elton in particular; but it seemed to her reasonable that at Harriet's age, and with the entire extinction of all hope, such a progress might be made towards a state of composure by the time of Mr. Elton's return, as to allow them all to meet again in the common routine of acquaintance, without any danger of betraying sentiments or increasing them.

Harriet did think him all perfection, and maintain the non-existence of any body equal to him in person or goodness—and did, in truth, prove herself more resolutely in love than Emma had foreseen; but yet it appeared to her so natural, so inevitable to strive against an inclination of that sort *unrequited,* that she could not comprehend its continuing very long in equal force.

If Mr. Elton, on his return, made his own indifference as evident and indubitable as she could not doubt he would anxiously do, she could not imagine Harriet's persisting to place her happiness in the sight or the recollection of him.

Their being fixed, so absolutely fixed, in the same place, was bad for each, for all three. Not one of them had the power of removal, or of effecting any material change of society. They must encounter each other, and make the best of it.

Harriet was further unfortunate in the tone of her companions at Mrs. Goddard's; Mr. Elton being the adoration of all the teachers and great girls[5] in the school; and it must be at Hartfield only that she could have any chance of hearing him spoken of with cooling moderation or repellant truth.[6] Where the wound had been given, there must the cure be found if anywhere; and Emma felt that, till she saw her in the way of cure,[7] there could be no true peace for herself.

5 Senior pupils.

6 Given the extended medical metaphor in this paragraph ("wound . . . cure . . . cure"), and Harriet's recent fever, it is apt that both "cooling" and "repellant" have specific medical applications. The *OED* lists one sense of the adjective "cooling" as "that makes cool or cooler; *esp.* (of medicine, etc.) that lowers the temperature of the blood, body, etc.," and the original sense of "repellent," dating from 1643, is "of medicines or medical applications: Having the effect of repelling morbid humours, etc."

7 On the road to recovery.

18

Mr. Frank Churchill did not come. When the time proposed drew near, Mrs. Weston's fears were justified in the arrival of a letter of excuse. For the present, he could not be spared, to his "very great mortification and regret; but still he looked forward with the hope of coming to Randalls at no distant period."

Mrs. Weston was exceedingly disappointed—much more disappointed, in fact, than her husband, though her dependence on seeing the young man had been so much more sober:[1] but a sanguine temper, though for ever expecting more good than occurs, does not always pay for its hopes by any proportionate depression. It soon flies over the present failure, and begins to hope again. For half an hour Mr. Weston was surprized and sorry; but then he began to perceive that Frank's coming two or three months later would be a much better plan; better time of year; better weather; and that he would be able, without any doubt, to stay considerably longer with them than if he had come sooner.

These feelings rapidly restored his comfort, while Mrs. Weston, of a more apprehensive disposition, foresaw nothing but a repetition of excuses and delays; and after all her concern for what her husband was to suffer, suffered a great deal more herself.

Emma was not at this time in a state of spirits to care really about Mr. Frank Churchill's not coming, except as a disappointment at Randalls. The acquaintance at present had no charm for her. She wanted, rather, to be quiet, and out of temptation; but still, as it was desirable that she should appear, in general, like her usual self, she

1 Measured, qualified.

2 Day of rejoicing and celebration, public holiday.

3 Insisted upon it.

4 To look down on his origins.

took care to express as much interest in the circumstance, and enter as warmly into Mr. and Mrs. Weston's disappointment, as might naturally belong to their friendship.

She was the first to announce it to Mr. Knightley; and exclaimed quite as much as was necessary, (or, being acting a part, perhaps rather more,) at the conduct of the Churchills, in keeping him away. She then proceeded to say a good deal more than she felt, of the advantage of such an addition to their confined society in Surry; the pleasure of looking at some body new; the gala-day[2] to Highbury entire, which the sight of him would have made; and ending with reflections on the Churchills again, found herself directly involved in a disagreement with Mr. Knightley; and, to her great amusement, perceived that she was taking the other side of the question from her real opinion, and making use of Mrs. Weston's arguments against herself.

"The Churchills are very likely in fault," said Mr. Knightley, coolly; "but I dare say he might come if he would."

"I do not know why you should say so. He wishes exceedingly to come; but his uncle and aunt will not spare him."

"I cannot believe that he has not the power of coming, if he made a point of it.[3] It is too unlikely, for me to believe it without proof."

"How odd you are! What has Mr. Frank Churchill done, to make you suppose him such an unnatural creature?"

"I am not supposing him at all an unnatural creature, in suspecting that he may have learnt to be above his connections,[4] and to care very little for any thing but his own pleasure, from living with those who have always set him the example of it. It is a great deal more natural than one could wish, that a young man, brought up by those who are proud, luxurious, and selfish, should be proud, luxurious, and selfish too. If Frank Churchill had wanted to see his father, he would have contrived it between September and January. A man at his age—what is he?—three or four-and-twenty—cannot be without the means of doing as much as that. It is impossible."

"That's easily said, and easily felt by you, who have always been your own master. You are the worst judge in the world, Mr. Knightley,

View of Weymouth from the Look-out, taken May 1812, published June 25, 1813, by I. W. Upham, Weymouth.

of the difficulties of dependence. You do not know what it is to have tempers to manage."

"It is not to be conceived that a man of three or four-and-twenty should not have liberty of mind or limb to that amount. He cannot want money—he cannot want leisure. We know, on the contrary, that he has so much of both that he is glad to get rid of them at the idlest[5] haunts in the kingdom. We hear of him for ever at some watering-place or other. A little while ago, he was at Weymouth.[6] This proves that he can leave the Churchills."

"Yes, sometimes he can."

"And those times are, whenever he thinks it worth his while; whenever there is any temptation of pleasure."

"It is very unfair to judge of any body's conduct, without an intimate knowledge of their situation. Nobody, who has not been in the interior of a family, can say what the difficulties of any individual of that family may be. We ought to be acquainted with Enscombe, and with Mrs. Churchill's temper, before we pretend to decide upon what her nephew can do. He may, at times, be able to do a great deal more than he can at others."

"There is one thing, Emma, which a man can always do, if he chuses, and that is his duty; not by manoeuvring and finessing,[7] but by vigour and resolution. It is Frank Churchill's duty to pay this attention to his father. He knows it to be so, by his promises and messages; but if he wished to do it, it might be done. A man who felt rightly would say at once, simply and resolutely, to Mrs. Churchill—'Every sacrifice of mere pleasure you will always find me ready to make to your convenience; but I must go and see my father immediately. I know he would be hurt by my failing in such a mark of respect to him on the present occasion. I shall, therefore, set off to-morrow.'—If he would say so to her at once, in the tone of decision becoming a man, there would be no opposition made to his going."

"No," said Emma, laughing; "but perhaps there might be some made to his coming back again. Such language for a young man entirely dependent, to use!—Nobody but you, Mr. Knightley, would imagine it possible. But you have not an idea of what is requisite

5 Most trivially fashionable.

6 A resort in southwest England, on the Dorset coast, important in the development of seaside locations as tourist destinations. It became particularly fashionable at the end of the eighteenth century, not least owing to its popularity with George III, who spent fourteen summers there between 1789 and 1805. However, precisely because of its association with the old king rather than with the prince regent, it did not have quite the fashionable cachet of a resort like Brighton, although it is clearly chic enough for Frank Churchill. In vol. I, chap. 13, of *Mansfield Park*, it is revealed that Tom Bertram first met John Yates at Weymouth.

7 Using cunning.

in situations directly opposite to your own. Mr. Frank Churchill to be making such a speech as that to the uncle and aunt, who have brought him up, and are to provide for him!—Standing up in the middle of the room, I suppose, and speaking as loud as he could!—How can you imagine such conduct practicable?"

"Depend upon it, Emma, a sensible man would find no difficulty in it. He would feel himself in the right; and the declaration—made, of course, as a man of sense would make it, in a proper manner—would do him more good, raise him higher, fix his interest stronger[8] with the people he depended on, than all that a line of shifts[9] and expedients can ever do. Respect would be added to affection. They would feel that they could trust him; that the nephew, who had done rightly by his father, would do rightly by them; for they know, as well as he does, as well as all the world must know, that he ought to pay this visit to his father; and while meanly exerting their power to delay it, are in their hearts not thinking the better of him for submitting to their whims. Respect for right conduct is felt by every body. If he would act in this sort of manner, on principle, consistently, regularly, their little[10] minds would bend to his."

"I rather doubt that. You are very fond of bending little minds; but where little minds belong to rich people in authority, I think they have a knack of swelling out, till they are quite as unmanageable as great ones. I can imagine, that if you, as you are, Mr. Knightley, were to be transported and placed all at once in Mr. Frank Churchill's situation, you would be able to say and do just what you have been recommending for him; and it might have a very good effect. The Churchills might not have a word to say in return; but then, you would have no habits of early obedience and long observance[11] to break through. To him who has, it might not be so easy to burst forth at once into perfect independence, and set all their claims on his gratitude and regard at nought. He may have as strong a sense of what would be right, as you can have, without being so equal under particular circumstances to act up to it."

"Then, it would not be so strong a sense. If it failed to produce equal exertion, it could not be an equal conviction."

8 Do his cause more good.

9 Evasions.

10 Petty, mean.

11 Ingrained custom.

12 Declarations, with a strong undertow of insincerity. In Letter III of *Lady Susan,* likewise, Catherine Vernon writes suspiciously of Lady Susan's "professions of regret, & general resolutions of prudence."

13 Of high birth, and therefore with greater social "consequence."

14 Slow in having such ideas occur to her.

"Oh! the difference of situation and habit! I wish you would try to understand what an amiable young man may be likely to feel in directly opposing those, whom as child and boy he has been looking up to all his life."

"Your amiable young man is a very weak young man, if this be the first occasion of his carrying through a resolution to do right against the will of others. It ought to have been an habit with him by this time, of following his duty, instead of consulting expediency. I can allow for the fears of the child, but not of the man. As he became rational, he ought to have roused himself and shaken off all that was unworthy in their authority. He ought to have opposed the first attempt on their side to make him slight his father. Had he begun as he ought, there would have been no difficulty now."

"We shall never agree about him," cried Emma; "but that is nothing extraordinary. I have not the least idea of his being a weak young man: I feel sure that he is not. Mr. Weston would not be blind to folly, though in his own son; but he is very likely to have a more yielding, complying, mild disposition than would suit your notions of man's perfection. I dare say he has; and though it may cut him off from some advantages, it will secure him many others."

"Yes; all the advantages of sitting still when he ought to move, and of leading a life of mere idle pleasure, and fancying himself extremely expert in finding excuses for it. He can sit down and write a fine flourishing letter, full of professions[12] and falsehoods, and persuade himself that he has hit upon the very best method in the world of preserving peace at home and preventing his father's having any right to complain. His letters disgust me."

"Your feelings are singular. They seem to satisfy every body else."

"I suspect they do not satisfy Mrs. Weston. They hardly can satisfy a woman of her good sense and quick feelings: standing in a mother's place, but without a mother's affection to blind her. It is on her account that attention to Randalls is doubly due, and she must doubly feel the omission. Had she been a person of consequence[13] herself, he would have come I dare say; and it would not have signified whether he did or no. Can you think your friend behind-hand in these sort of considerations?[14] Do you suppose she does not often say all this to herself? No, Emma, your amiable young man can be amiable only in French, not in English. He may be very 'aimable,' have very good manners, and be very agreeable; but he can have no English delicacy towards the feelings of other people: nothing really amiable about him."[15]

"You seem determined to think ill of him."

"Me!—not at all," replied Mr. Knightley, rather displeased; "I do not want to think ill of him. I should be as ready to acknowledge his merits as any other man; but I hear of none, except what are merely personal; that he is well grown and good-looking, with smooth, plausible[16] manners."

"Well, if he have nothing else to recommend him, he will be a treasure at Highbury. We do not often look upon fine young men, well-bred and agreeable. We must not be nice[17] and ask for all the virtues into the bargain. Cannot you imagine, Mr. Knightley, what a *sensa-*

Robert Cruikshank, "Comparative Anatomy or The Dandy Tribe," 1818. One of a series of savage attacks on the fashionable excesses of dandyism that Cruikshank published between 1818 and 1819, this caricature figures the dandies as a tribe or species of hybrid human/animal grotesques.

15 See note 4 to vol. I, chap. 12.

16 Pleasant, but with a strong connotation of ingratiation or insincerity. For example, in Robert Bage's famous radical novel *Hermsprong; or Man As He Is Not,* 3 vols. (London: William Lane, 1796), Doctor Blick interprets the protagonist's general popularity as a cause for suspicion: "no man would give himself the trouble to please every body, without great and uncommon motives. In proportion as he was plausible, he must be the more dangerous" (vol. III, p. 180).

17 Too particular.

tion[18] his coming will produce? There will be but one subject throughout the parishes of Donwell and Highbury; but one interest—one object of curiosity; it will be all Mr. Frank Churchill; we shall think and speak of nobody else."

"You will excuse my being so much overpowered. If I find him conversible, I shall be glad of his acquaintance; but if he is only a chattering coxcomb,[19] he will not occupy much of my time or thoughts."

"My idea of him is, that he can adapt his conversation to the taste of every body, and has the power as well as the wish of being universally agreeable. To you, he will talk of farming; to me, of drawing or music; and so on to every body, having that general information on all subjects which will enable him to follow the lead, or take the lead, just as propriety may require, and to speak extremely well on each; that is my idea of him."

"And mine," said Mr. Knightley warmly,[20] "is, that if he turn out any thing like it, he will be the most insufferable fellow breathing! What! at three-and-twenty to be the king of his company—the great man—the practised politician, who is to read every body's character, and make every body's talents conduce to the display of his own superiority; to be dispensing his flatteries around, that he may make all appear like fools compared with himself! My dear Emma, your own good sense could not endure such a puppy[21] when it came to the point."

"I will say no more about him," cried Emma, "you turn every thing to evil. We are both prejudiced; you against, I for him; and we have no chance of agreeing till he is really here."

"Prejudiced! I am not prejudiced."

"But I am very much, and without being at all ashamed of it. My love for Mr. and Mrs. Weston gives me a decided prejudice in his favour."

"He is a person I never think of from one month's end to another," said Mr. Knightley, with a degree of vexation, which made Emma immediately talk of something else, though she could not comprehend why he should be angry.

18 This use of "sensation" to denote a strong, sudden collective reaction to an event was a relatively new one, the *OED* dating it only from 1779; even by Austen's time, by far the most widespread sense of the term was the traditional one, of a sensory feeling or intuition (this is, indeed, almost always the sense in which it occurs in Austen's fiction). One indication of the social milieux in which the newer, looser sense was gaining ground can be seen in Thomas Haynes Bayly's 1820 poem "The Dandies of the Present, and the Macaronies of the Past"; as the poem offers a partial defense of the modern "coxcombs" of Bath ("Can ye, oh! damsels, injure those, whose pride/Is to be seen gallanting at your side?"), a footnote suggests: "Could a youth in the full costume of the present day have suddenly appeared before our ancestors, and sported a waltz or a quadrille, he would have caused no small sensation." The modern sense was, however, to rise into extraordinary prominence by the middle of the nineteenth century, with the growing interest in public "sensations" in both popular journalism and fiction. See Thomas Boyle, *Black Swine in the Sewers of Hampstead: Beneath the Surface of Victorian Sensationalism* (London: Hodder & Stoughton, 1990), and Michael Diamond, *Victorian Sensation; or, The Spectacular, the Shocking, and the Scandalous in Nineteenth-Century Britain* (London: Anthem Press, 2003).

19 "A foolish, conceited, showy person, vain of his accomplishments, appearance, or dress" *(OED)*. In vol. II, chap. 2, of *Sense and Sensibility,* Lucy Steele describes Robert Ferrars to Elinor Dashwood as "silly and a great coxcomb"; and in vol. I, chap. 12, of *Northanger Abbey,* Isabella Thorpe calls Captain Tilney "the greatest coxcomb I ever saw."

20 Angrily.

21 Conceited young man.

To take a dislike to a young man, only because he appeared to be of a different disposition from himself, was unworthy the real liberality of mind which she was always used to acknowledge in him; for with all the high opinion of himself, which she had often laid to his charge, she had never before for a moment supposed it could make him unjust to the merit of another.[22]

22 It is only much later in the novel that the reader finds out what motivates Knightley's dislike.

Volume II

I

Emma and Harriet had been walking together one morning, and, in Emma's opinion, been talking enough of Mr. Elton for that day. She could not think that Harriet's solace or her own sins required more; and she was therefore industriously getting rid of the subject as they returned;—but it burst out again when she thought she had succeeded, and after speaking some time of what the poor must suffer in winter, and receiving no other answer than a very plaintive—"Mr. Elton is so good to the poor!" she found something else must be done.

They were just approaching the house where lived Mrs. and Miss Bates. She determined to call upon them and seek safety in numbers. There was always sufficient reason for such an attention; Mrs. and Miss Bates loved to be called on, and she knew she was considered by the very few who presumed ever to see imperfection in her, as rather negligent in that respect, and as not contributing what she ought to the stock of their scanty comforts.

She had had many a hint from Mr. Knightley and some from her own heart, as to her deficiency—but none were equal to counteract the persuasion of its being very disagreeable,—a waste of time—tiresome women—and all the horror of being in danger of falling in with the second rate and third rate of Highbury, who were calling on them for ever, and therefore she seldom went near them. But now she made the sudden resolution of not passing their door without going in—observing, as she proposed it to Harriet, that, as well as she could calculate, they were just now quite safe from any letter from Jane Fairfax.

The house belonged to people in business. Mrs. and Miss Bates occupied the drawing-room floor;[1] and there, in the very moderate sized apartment, which was every thing to them, the visitors were most cordially and even gratefully welcomed; the quiet neat old lady, who with her knitting was seated in the warmest corner, wanting even to give up her place to Miss Woodhouse, and her more active, talking[2] daughter, almost ready to overpower them with care and kindness, thanks for their visit, solicitude for their shoes, anxious inquiries after Mr. Woodhouse's health, cheerful communications about her mother's, and sweet-cake[3] from the beaufet[4]—"Mrs. Cole had just been there, just called in for ten minutes, and had been so good as to sit an hour with them, and *she* had taken a piece of cake and been so kind as to say she liked it very much; and therefore she hoped Miss Woodhouse and Miss Smith would do them the favour to eat a piece too."

The mention of the Coles was sure to be followed by that of Mr. Elton. There was intimacy between them, and Mr. Cole had heard from Mr. Elton since his going away. Emma knew what was coming; they must have the letter over again, and settle how long he had been gone, and how much he was engaged in company, and what a favourite he was wherever he went, and how full the Master of the Ceremonies' ball[5] had been; and she went through it very well, with all the interest and all the commendation that could be requisite, and always putting forward to prevent Harriet's being obliged to say a word.

This she had been prepared for when she entered the house; but meant, having once talked him handsomely over, to be no farther incommoded[6] by any troublesome topic, and to wander at large amongst all the Mistresses and Misses of Highbury and their card-parties. She had not been prepared to have Jane Fairfax succeed Mr. Elton; but he was actually hurried off by Miss Bates, she jumped away from him at last abruptly to the Coles, to usher in a letter from her niece.

1 The floor above the ground floor.

2 Loquacious, talkative; however, there also is a grammatical awkwardness in Austen's placement of the adjective, and her pitching it between transitivity and intransitivity, that may suggest the prodigious nature of Miss Bates's speech. Compare the description of the malodorous landlady Miss Carridge in chapter 5 of Samuel Beckett's novel *Murphy* (1938): "She stood there, smelling, ravished in contemplation of her tea being taken."

3 As the name implies, cake made with a particularly high proportion of sugar.

4 Sideboard, side table.

5 A highlight of the social season in Bath, at which men and women were introduced by the Master of Ceremonies; it was, of course, popular with those seeking a matrimonial partner in the long term, something that Elton is clearly doing. Catherine Morland is introduced to Henry Tilney by the Master of Ceremonies in vol. I, chap. 3, of *Northanger Abbey*.

6 Inconvenienced.

Thomas Rowlandson, *The Comforts of Bath,* plate 10: "The Ball" (London, 1798). The Master of Ceremonies' Ball was one of the social highlights of the Bath calendar, an event at which many people met their future partners. Rowlandson views Bath somewhat less admiringly than its fashionable promoters would have done.

"Oh! yes—Mr. Elton, I understood—certainly as to dancing—Mrs. Cole was telling me that dancing at the rooms at Bath was—— Mrs. Cole was so kind as to sit some time with us, talking of Jane; for as soon as she came in, she began inquiring after her, Jane is so very great a favourite there. Whenever she is with us, Mrs. Cole does not know how to shew her kindness enough; and I must say that Jane deserves it as much as anybody can. And so she began inquiring after her directly, saying, 'I know you cannot have heard from Jane lately, because it is not her time for writing;' and when I immediately said, 'But indeed we have, we had a letter this very morning,' I do not know that I ever saw anybody more surprized. 'Have you, upon your honour!' said she; 'well, that is quite unexpected. Do let me hear what she says.'"

Emma's politeness was at hand directly,[7] to say, with smiling interest—

7 Austen's phrasing slyly suggests that "Emma's politeness" is something extraneous to her at this point—aptly, considering how annoying she finds any talk of Jane Fairfax.

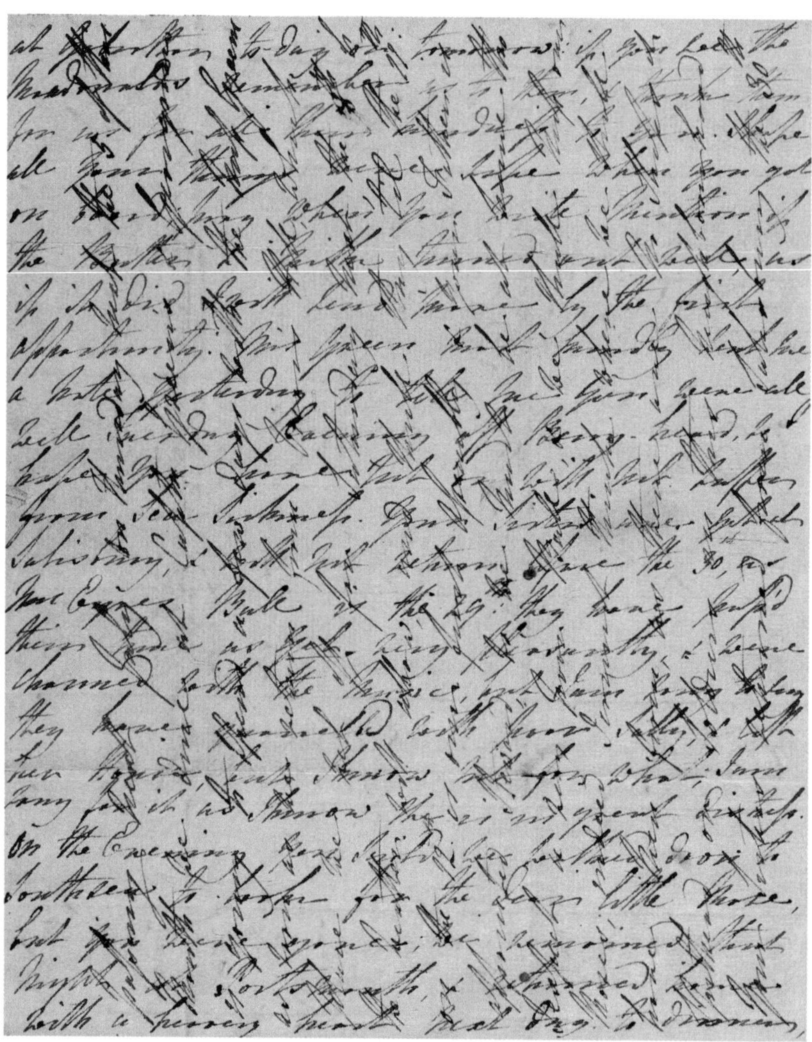

An Austen family letter, clearly showing the technique of crossing: from George Purvis, Esq., to his son George Thomas Maitland Purvis, December 20, 1821. George Thomas Purvis married Austen's niece Mary-Jane in 1828.

"Have you heard from Miss Fairfax so lately? I am extremely happy. I hope she is well?"

"Thank you. You are so kind!" replied the happily deceived aunt, while eagerly hunting for the letter.—"Oh! here it is. I was sure it could not be far off; but I had put my huswife[8] upon it, you see, without being aware, and so it was quite hid, but I had it in my hand so very lately that I was almost sure it must be on the table. I was reading it to Mrs. Cole, and since she went away, I was reading it again to my mother, for it is such a pleasure to her—a letter from Jane—that she can never hear it often enough; so I knew it could not be far off, and here it is, only just under my huswife—and since you are so kind as to wish to hear what she says;—but first of all, I really must, in justice to Jane, apologise for her writing so short a letter—only two pages you see—hardly two—and in general she fills the whole paper and crosses half.[9] My mother often wonders that I can make it out so well. She often says, when the letter is first opened, 'Well, Hetty, now I think you will be put to it to make out all that chequer-work.'[10]—don't you, ma'am?—And then I tell her, I am sure she would contrive to make it out herself, if she had nobody to do it for her—every word of it—I am sure she would pore over it till she had made out every word. And, indeed, though my mother's eyes are not so good as they were, she can see amazingly well still, thank God! with the help of spectacles. It is such a blessing! My mother's are really very good indeed. Jane often says, when she is here, 'I am sure, grandmama, you must have had very strong eyes to see as you do—and so much fine work[11] as you have done too!—I only wish my eyes may last me as well.'"

All this spoken extremely fast obliged Miss Bates to stop for breath; and Emma said something very civil about the excellence of Miss Fairfax's handwriting.

"You are extremely kind," replied Miss Bates highly gratified; "you who are such a judge, and write so beautifully yourself. I am sure there is nobody's praise that could give us so much pleasure as Miss Woodhouse's. My mother does not hear; she is a little deaf you know. Ma'am," addressing her, "do you hear what Miss Woodhouse is so obliging to say about Jane's handwriting?"

8 A small case for storing sewing equipment and materials.

9 Letters were originally folded and sealed, rather than being posted in separate envelopes. However, for reasons of economy, those who could not afford to send letters of many pages, such as Jane Fairfax (and, indeed, Austen herself), would often fill the page, then continue writing at right angles to the original script. See Jo Modert, ed., *Jane Austen's Manuscript Letters in Facsimile* (Carbondale: Southern Illinois University Press, 1990).

10 Cross-hatching.

11 Delicate needlework.

And Emma had the advantage of hearing her own silly compliment repeated twice over before the good old lady could comprehend it. She was pondering, in the mean while, upon the possibility, without seeming very rude, of making her escape from Jane Fairfax's letter, and had almost resolved on hurrying away directly under some slight excuse, when Miss Bates turned to her again and seized her attention.

"My mother's deafness is very trifling you see—just nothing at all. By only raising my voice, and saying anything two or three times over, she is sure to hear; but then she is used to my voice. But it is very remarkable that she should always hear Jane better than she does me.[12] Jane speaks so distinct! However, she will not find her grandmama at all deafer than she was two years ago; which is saying a great deal at my mother's time of life—and it really is full two years, you know, since she was here. We never were so long without seeing her before, and as I was telling Mrs. Cole, we shall hardly know how to make enough of her now."

"Are you expecting Miss Fairfax here soon?"

"Oh, yes; next week."

"Indeed!—That must be a very great pleasure."

"Thank you. You are very kind. Yes, next week. Every body is so surprized; and every body says the same obliging things. I am sure she will be as happy to see her friends at Highbury, as they can be to see her. Yes, Friday or Saturday; she cannot say which, because Colonel Campbell will be wanting the carriage himself one of those days. So very good of them to send her the whole way! But they always do, you know. Oh, yes, Friday or Saturday next. That is what she writes about. That is the reason of her writing out of rule,[13] as we call it; for in the common course, we should not have heard from her before next Tuesday or Wednesday."

"Yes, so I imagined. I was afraid there could be little chance of my hearing any thing of Miss Fairfax to-day."

"So obliging of you! No, we should not have heard, if it had not been for this particular circumstance, of her being to come here so soon. My mother is so delighted!—for she is to be three months with us at least. Three months, she says so, positively, as I am going to

12 This may be less a comment on Mrs. Bates's deafness than on the skill with which she selectively employs it.

13 Contrary to custom, especially when referring to social habits and rules. In *The Watsons,* Mr. Musgrave remarks: "And as to Mrs Edwardes' carriage being used the day after a Ball, it is a thing quite out of rule I assure you."

have the pleasure of reading to you. The case is, you see, that the Campbells are going to Ireland. Mrs. Dixon has persuaded her father and mother to come over and see her directly. They had not intended to go over till the summer, but she is so impatient to see them again —for till she married, last October, she was never away from them so much as a week, which must make it very strange to be in different kingdoms, I was going to say, but however different countries,[14] and so she wrote a very urgent letter to her mother—or her father, I declare I do not know which it was, but we shall see presently in Jane's letter—wrote in Mr. Dixon's name as well as her own, to press their coming over directly, and they would give them the meeting in Dublin, and take them back to their country-seat, Baly-craig, a beautiful place, I fancy. Jane has heard a great deal of its beauty; from Mr. Dixon I mean—I do not know that she ever heard about it from any body else; but it was very natural, you know, that he should like to speak of his own place while he was paying his addresses—and as Jane used to be very often walking out with them—for Colonel and Mrs. Campbell were very particular about their daughter's not walking out often with only Mr. Dixon, for which I do not at all blame them; of course she heard everything he might be telling Miss Campbell about his own home in Ireland. And I think she wrote us word that he had shewn them some drawings of the place, views that he had taken himself. He is a most amiable, charming[15] young man, I believe. Jane was quite longing to go to Ireland, from his account of things."

At this moment, an ingenious and animating suspicion entering Emma's brain with regard to Jane Fairfax, this charming Mr. Dixon, and the not going to Ireland, she said, with the insidious design of further discovery,

"You must feel it very fortunate that Miss Fairfax should be allowed to come to you at such a time. Considering the very particular friendship between her and Mrs. Dixon, you could hardly have expected her to be excused from accompanying Colonel and Mrs. Campbell."

"Very true, very true, indeed. The very thing that we have always been rather afraid of; for we should not have liked to have her at such

14 Although Scotland had been joined to England and Wales by the 1707 Acts of Union, Ireland became the final element of the United Kingdom of Great Britain and Ireland only after the 1800 Acts of Union, which came into effect on New Year's Day, 1801; so Miss Bates's slip is understandable.

15 See note 4 to vol. I, chap. 5.

a distance from us, for months together—not able to come if any-thing was to happen. But you see, every thing turns out for the best. They want her (Mr. and Mrs. Dixon) excessively to come over with Colonel and Mrs. Campbell; quite depend upon it; nothing can be more kind or pressing than their *joint* invitation, Jane says, as you will hear presently; Mr. Dixon does not seem in the least backward in any attention. He is a most charming young man. Ever since the service he rendered Jane at Weymouth,[16] when they were out in that party on the water, and she, by the sudden whirling round of something or other among the sails, would have been dashed into the sea at once, and actually was all but gone, if he had not, with the greatest presence of mind, caught hold of her habit[17]—(I can never think of it without trembling!)—But ever since we had the history of that day, I have been so fond of Mr. Dixon!"

"But, in spite of all her friend's urgency, and her own wish of seeing Ireland, Miss Fairfax prefers devoting the time to you and Mrs. Bates?"

"Yes—entirely her own doing, entirely her own choice; and Colonel and Mrs. Campbell think she does quite right, just what they should recommend; and indeed they particularly ***wish*** her to try her native air,[18] as she has not been quite so well as usual[19] lately."

"I am concerned to hear of it. I think they judge wisely. But Mrs. Dixon must be very much disappointed. Mrs. Dixon, I understand, has no remarkable degree of personal beauty; is not, by any means, to be compared with Miss Fairfax."

"Oh! no. You are very obliging to say such things—but certainly not. There is no comparison between them. Miss Campbell always was absolutely plain—but extremely elegant and amiable."

"Yes, that of course."

"Jane caught a bad cold, poor thing! so long ago as the 7th of November, (as I am going to read to you,) and has never been well since. A long time, is not it, for a cold to hang upon her? She never mentioned it before, because she would not alarm us. Just like her! so considerate!—But however, she is so far from well, that her kind friends the Campbells think she had better come home, and try an

16 Another of the novel's precise, nostalgic memories of past moments (see Introduction).

17 Clothing.

18 It was a common belief in late eighteenth- and early nineteenth-century culture that people's "native air" would be more effective than any other in restoring their delicate constitutions to health. For example, vol. IV, chap. 9, of Thomas Holcroft's novel *The Adventures of Hugh Trevor* (1794–1797) describes the character of Mr. Evelyn thus: "his frame was delicate, a too long abode in London always occasioned pulmonary symptoms, and experience taught him that his native air was more healthful and animating than any other." That said—especially considering the intimations of mortality that Austen musters around Jane Fairfax—"native air" was also often sought by, and recommended for, the dying; there is a disquietingly prescient instance of such a wish in book IV of John Keats's *Endymion: A Poetic Romance* (1818), when the goddess Cynthia, disguised as the Indian Maid, declares, "Yet I would have, great gods, but one short hour/Of native air—let me but die at home."

19 The first of many references in the novel to Jane Fairfax's delicate state of health. Remarking upon Austen's "custom of following her creations outside the printed page," William Austen-Leigh and Richard Arthur Austen-Leigh record the family anecdote that "Jane Fairfax survived her elevation only nine or ten years" (*Jane Austen: Her Life and Letters* [London: Smith, Elder & Co., 1913], p. 307).

air that always agrees with her; and they have no doubt that three or four months at Highbury will entirely cure her—and it is certainly a great deal better that she should come here, than go to Ireland, if she is unwell. Nobody could nurse her, as we should do."

"It appears to me the most desirable arrangement in the world."

"And so she is to come to us next Friday or Saturday, and the Campbells leave town in their way to Holyhead[20] the Monday following—as you will find from Jane's letter. So sudden!—You may guess, dear Miss Woodhouse, what a flurry it has thrown me in! If it was not for the drawback of her illness—but I am afraid we must expect to see her grown thin, and looking very poorly. I must tell you what an unlucky thing happened to me, as to that. I always make a point of reading Jane's letters through to myself first, before I read them aloud to my mother, you know, for fear of there being any thing in them to distress her. Jane desired me to do it, so I always do: and so I began to-day with my usual caution; but no sooner did I come to the mention of her being unwell, than I burst out quite frightened with, 'Bless me! poor Jane is ill!'—which my mother, being on the watch,

20 A port town in northwest Wales, just beyond the west coast of the island of Anglesey, which has been a major point of embarkation to Ireland for some 4,000 years; ferries still run from Holyhead to Dublin and the nearby seaport of Dún Laoghaire.

William Daniell, *The Harbour Lighthouse at Holyhead Port,* 1813.

heard distinctly, and was sadly alarmed at. However, when I read on, I found it was not near so bad as I fancied at first; and I make so light of it now to her, that she does not think much about it. But I cannot imagine how I could be so off my guard! If Jane does not get well soon, we will call in Mr. Perry. The expense shall not be thought of; and though he is so liberal, and so fond of Jane that I dare say he would not mean to charge anything for attendance, we could not suffer it to be so, you know. He has a wife and family to maintain, and is not to be giving away his time. Well, now I have just given you a hint of what Jane writes about, we will turn to her letter, and I am sure she tells her own story a great deal better than I can tell it for her."

"I am afraid we must be running away," said Emma, glancing at Harriet, and beginning to rise—"My father will be expecting us. I had no intention, I thought I had no power of staying more than five minutes, when I first entered the house. I merely called, because I would not pass the door without inquiring after Mrs. Bates; but I have been so pleasantly detained! Now, however, we must wish you and Mrs. Bates good morning."

And not all that could be urged to detain her succeeded. She regained the street—happy in this, that though much had been forced on her against her will, though she had in fact heard the whole substance of Jane Fairfax's letter, she had been able to escape the letter itself.

2

JANE FAIRFAX WAS AN ORPHAN, the only child of Mrs. Bates's youngest daughter.

The marriage of Lieut. Fairfax, of the —— regiment of infantry, and Miss Jane Bates, had had its day of fame and pleasure, hope and interest; but nothing now remained of it, save the melancholy remembrance of him dying in action abroad—of his widow sinking under consumption and grief soon afterwards—and this girl.

By birth she belonged to Highbury: and when at three years old, on losing her mother, she became the property, the charge, the consolation, the fondling[1] of her grandmother and aunt, there had seemed every probability of her being permanently fixed there; of her being taught only what very limited means could command, and growing up with no advantages of connection or improvement to be engrafted on what nature had given her in a pleasing person, good understanding, and warm-hearted, well meaning relations.

But the compassionate feelings of a friend of her father gave a change to her destiny. This was Colonel Campbell, who had very highly regarded Fairfax, as an excellent officer and most deserving young man; and farther, had been indebted to him for such attentions, during a severe camp-fever,[2] as he believed had saved his life. These were claims which he did not learn to overlook, though some years passed away from the death of poor Fairfax, before his own return to England put any thing in his power. When he did return, he sought out the child and took notice of her. He was a married man, with only one living child, a girl, about Jane's age: and Jane became

1 Beloved favorite.

2 An outbreak of contagious disease (usually typhus) in a military encampment.

3 Allowances, annuities.

4 The more traditional "female accomplishments," such as drawing and music.

5 These "masters" would have been specialists, hired by the well-off Campbells to instruct Jane in the individual accomplishments.

6 Capable of.

7 Talents.

their guest, paying them long visits and growing a favourite with all; and before she was nine years old, his daughter's great fondness for her, and his own wish of being a real friend, united to produce an offer from Colonel Campbell of undertaking the whole charge of her education. It was accepted; and from that period Jane had belonged to Colonel Campbell's family, and had lived with them entirely, only visiting her grandmother from time to time.

The plan was that she should be brought up for educating others; the very few hundred pounds which she inherited from her father making independence impossible. To provide for her otherwise was out of Colonel Campbell's power; for though his income, by pay and appointments,[3] was handsome, his fortune was moderate and must be all his daughter's; but, by giving her an education, he hoped to be supplying the means of respectable subsistance hereafter.

Such was Jane Fairfax's history. She had fallen into good hands, known nothing but kindness from the Campbells, and been given an excellent education. Living constantly with right-minded and well-informed people, her heart and understanding had received every advantage of discipline and culture; and Col. Campbell's residence being in London, every lighter talent[4] had been done full justice to, by the attendance of first-rate masters.[5] Her disposition and abilities were equally worthy of all that friendship could do; and at eighteen or nineteen she was, as far as such an early age can be qualified for the care of children, fully competent to[6] the office of instruction herself; but she was too much beloved to be parted with. Neither father nor mother could promote, and the daughter could not endure it. The evil day was put off. It was easy to decide that she was still too young; and Jane remained with them, sharing, as another daughter, in all the rational pleasures of an elegant society, and a judicious mixture of home and amusement, with only the drawback of the future, the sobering suggestions of her own good understanding to remind her that all this might soon be over.

The affection of the whole family, the warm attachment of Miss Campbell in particular, was the more honourable to each party from the circumstance of Jane's decided superiority both in beauty and acquirements.[7] That nature had given it in feature could not be unseen by the young woman, nor could her higher powers of mind be unfelt by the parents. They continued together with unabated regard however, till the marriage of Miss Campbell, who by that chance, that luck which so often defies anticipation in matrimonial affairs, giving attraction to what is moderate rather than to what is superior, engaged the affections of Mr. Dixon, a young man, rich and agreeable, almost as soon as they were acquainted; and was eligibly and happily settled, while Jane Fairfax had yet her bread to earn.

This event had very lately taken place; too lately for any thing to be yet attempted by her less fortunate friend towards entering on her path of duty; though she had now reached the age which her own judgment had fixed on for beginning. She had long resolved that one-and-twenty should be the period.[8] With the fortitude of a devoted noviciate, she had resolved at one-and-twenty to complete the sacrifice, and retire from all the pleasures of life, of rational intercourse, equal society, peace and hope, to penance and mortification for ever.[9]

The good sense of Colonel and Mrs. Campbell could not oppose such a resolution, though their feelings did. As long as they lived, no exertions would be necessary, their home might be her's for ever; and for their own comfort they would have retained her wholly; but this would be selfishness:—what must be at last, had better be soon. Perhaps they began to feel it might have been kinder and wiser to have resisted the temptation of any delay, and spared her from a taste of such enjoyments of ease and leisure as must now be relinquished. Still, however, affection was glad to catch at any reasonable excuse for not hurrying on the wretched moment. She had never been quite well since the time of their daughter's marriage;[10] and till she should have completely recovered her usual strength, they must forbid her engaging in duties, which, so far from being compatible with a weakened frame and varying spirits, seemed, under the most favourable circumstances, to require something more than human perfection of body and mind to be discharged with tolerable comfort.

With regard to her not accompanying them to Ireland, her account to her aunt contained nothing but truth, though there might be some truths not told. It was her own choice to give the time of

8 Deadline, cut-off point.

9 A novitiate (or noviciate) is a novice in a religious order. Along with this term, the other vocabulary in this sentence suggests a parallel between entering the governess trade and "taking the veil" in a convent. This analogy is oddly appropriate, since becoming a governess was often tantamount to resigning any matrimonial prospects—and it points up some of the unpalatable links between biology, gender, and economics in Austen's time. Whereas a woman with a degree of economic comfort could be considered marriageable until her late twenties (see note 2 to vol. I, chap. 1), Jane is choosing to resign any chance at twenty-one—unless, of course, someone comes to rescue her before she commits herself. The enforcedly desexualized status of governesses in the nineteenth century also made them (like nuns in late eighteenth-century gothic writing) figures of forbidden or transgressive sexual desire, as witnessed by Charlotte Brontë's *Jane Eyre* (1847) and Henry James's *Turn of the Screw* (1898). For a comprehensive overview of the governess trade, see Alice Renton, *Tyrant or Victim?: A History of the British Governess* (London: Weidenfeld and Nicolson, 1981).

10 Another ominous hint at Jane's possible mortality.

their absence to Highbury; to spend, perhaps, her last months of perfect liberty with those kind relations to whom she was so very dear: and the Campbells, whatever might be their motive or motives, whether single, or double, or treble, gave the arrangement their ready sanction, and said, that they depended more on a few months spent in her native air, for the recovery of her health, than on any thing else. Certain it was that she was to come; and that Highbury, instead of welcoming that perfect novelty which had been so long promised it—Mr. Frank Churchill—must put up for the present with Jane Fairfax, who could bring only the freshness of a two years absence.

Emma was sorry;—to have to pay civilities to a person she did not like through three long months!—to be always doing more than she wished, and less than she ought! Why she did not like Jane Fairfax might be a difficult question to answer; Mr. Knightley had once told her it was because she saw in her the really accomplished young woman,[11] which she wanted to be thought herself; and though the accusation had been eagerly refuted at the time, there were moments of self-examination in which her conscience could not quite acquit her. But "she could never get acquainted with her: she did not know how it was, but there was such coldness and reserve—such apparent indifference whether she pleased or not—and then, her aunt was such an eternal talker!—and she was made such a fuss with by every body!—and it had been always imagined that they were to be so intimate—because their ages were the same, every body had supposed they must be so fond of each other." These were her reasons—she had no better.

It was a dislike so little just—every imputed fault was so magnified by fancy, that she never saw Jane Fairfax the first time after any considerable absence, without feeling that she had injured her; and now, when the due visit was paid, on her arrival, after a two years' interval, she was particularly struck with the very appearance and manners, which for those two whole years she had been depreciating. Jane Fairfax was very elegant, remarkably elegant; and she had herself the highest value[12] for elegance. Her height was pretty, just such as almost everybody would think tall, and nobody could think very tall;

11 That is, someone who *inhabits* her accomplishments, rather than just aspiring toward them.

12 Regard.

her figure particularly graceful; her size a most becoming medium, between fat and thin, though a slight appearance of ill-health seemed to point out the likeliest evil of the two.[13] Emma could not but feel all this; and then, her face—her features—there was more beauty in them all together than she had remembered; it was not regular, but it was very pleasing beauty. Her eyes, a deep grey,[14] with dark eyelashes and eye-brows, had never been denied their praise; but the skin, which she had been used to cavil at,[15] as wanting colour, had a clearness and delicacy which really needed no fuller bloom. It was a style of beauty, of which elegance was the reigning character, and as such, she must, in honour, by all her principles, admire it:—elegance, which, whether of person or of mind, she saw so little in Highbury. There, not to be vulgar, was distinction, and merit.

In short, she sat, during the first visit, looking at Jane Fairfax with two-fold complacency;[16] the sense of pleasure and the sense of rendering justice, and was determining that she would dislike her no longer. When she took in her history, indeed, her situation, as well as her beauty; when she considered what all this elegance was destined to, what she was going to sink from, how she was going to live, it seemed impossible to feel any thing but compassion and respect;[17] especially, if to every well-known particular entitling her to interest, were added the highly probable circumstance of an attachment to Mr. Dixon, which she had so naturally started to herself.[18] In that case, nothing could be more pitiable or more honourable than the sacrifices she had resolved on. Emma was very willing now to acquit her of having seduced Mr. Dixon's affections from his wife, or of any thing mischievous which her imagination had suggested at first. If it were love, it might be simple, single, successless love on her side alone. She might have been unconsciously sucking in the sad poison, while a sharer of his conversation with her friend; and from the best, the purest of motives, might now be denying herself this visit to Ireland, and resolving to divide herself effectually[19] from him and his connections by soon beginning her career of laborious duty.

Upon the whole, Emma left her with such softened, charitable feelings, as made her look around in walking home, and lament that

13 Yet another mention of Jane's delicate health, with her tendency toward thinness possibly suggesting a susceptibility to consumption (tuberculosis). For more on cultural images of tuberculosis and their attendant ethical problems, see Susan Sontag's classic work *Illness as Metaphor* (New York: Farrar, Strauss, and Giroux, 1978), especially her argument that "[a]ccording to the mythology of TB, there is generally some passionate feeling which provokes, which expresses itself in, a bout of TB" (p. 22).

14 The first mention in the novel of the color of Jane's eyes, as distinct from the blue eyes of Harriet and the hazel eyes of Emma.

15 Quibble about.

16 "Pleasure; satisfaction; gratification" (Johnson).

17 Austen creates an ominous and uncanny textual link between Jane and Miss Bates, by having Knightley repeat or unconsciously adapt many of this sentence's key terms ("situation," "considered," "sink," "compassion") in his rebuke to Emma on Box Hill in vol. III, chap. 7: "Were she your equal in situation—but, Emma, consider how far this is from being the case. She is poor; she has sunk from the comforts she was born to; and, if she live to old age, must probably sink more. Her situation should secure your compassion."

18 Another telling employment of free indirect style by Austen.

19 Completely, absolutely.

Highbury afforded no young man worthy of giving her independence; nobody that she could wish to scheme about for her.

These were charming feelings—but not lasting. Before she had committed herself by any public profession of eternal friendship for Jane Fairfax, or done more towards a recantation of past prejudices and errors, than saying to Mr. Knightley, "She certainly is handsome; she is better than handsome!" Jane had spent an evening at Hartfield with her grandmother and aunt, and every thing was relapsing much into its usual state. Former provocations re-appeared. The aunt was as tiresome as ever; more tiresome, because anxiety for her health was now added to admiration of her powers; and they had to listen to the description of exactly how little bread and butter she ate for breakfast, and how small a slice of mutton for dinner, as well as to see exhibitions of new caps and new work-bags[20] for her mother and herself; and Jane's offences rose again. They had music; Emma was obliged to play; and the thanks and praise which necessarily followed appeared to her an affectation of candour, an air of greatness,[21] meaning only to shew off in higher style her own very superior performance. She was, besides, which was the worst of all, so cold, so cautious! There was no getting at her real opinion. Wrapt up in a cloak of politeness, she seemed determined to hazard nothing. She was disgustingly, was suspiciously reserved.

If any thing could be more, where all was most, she was more reserved on the subject of Weymouth and the Dixons than any thing. She seemed bent on giving no real insight into Mr. Dixon's character, or her own value for his company, or opinion of the suitableness of the match. It was all general approbation and smoothness; nothing delineated[22] or distinguished. It did her no service however. Her caution was thrown away.[23] Emma saw its artifice, and returned to her first surmises. There probably *was* something more to conceal than her own preference; Mr. Dixon, perhaps, had been very near changing one friend for the other, or been fixed only to Miss Campbell, for the sake of the future twelve thousand pounds.[24]

The like reserve prevailed on other topics. She and Mr. Frank Churchill had been at Weymouth at the same time. It was known that they were a little acquainted; but not a syllable of real informa-

20 Bags for storing sewing kits, presumably made as gifts by Jane herself.

21 A pretense of generosity.

22 Described in detail.

23 Wasted.

24 Much less than Emma's own portion, but nevertheless a considerable amount.

tion could Emma procure as to what he truly was. "Was he handsome?"—"She believed he was reckoned a very fine young man." "Was he agreeable?"—"He was generally thought so." "Did he appear a sensible young man; a young man of information?"—"At a watering-place, or in a common London acquaintance, it was difficult to decide on such points. Manners were all that could be safely judged of, under a much longer knowledge than they had yet had of Mr. Churchill. She believed every body found his manners pleasing." Emma could not forgive her.

William Redmore Bigg, *The Romps,* 1796. The painting suggests the kind of daily disorder with which a governess would be expected to deal, for very little remuneration.

3

Emma could not forgive her;—but as neither provocation nor resentment were discerned by Mr. Knightley, who had been of the party, and had seen only proper attention and pleasing behaviour on each side, he was expressing the next morning, being at Hartfield again on business with Mr. Woodhouse, his approbation of the whole; not so openly as he might have done had her father been out of the room, but speaking plain enough to be very intelligible to Emma. He had been used to think her unjust to Jane, and had now great pleasure in marking an improvement.

"A very pleasant evening," he began, as soon as Mr. Woodhouse had been talked into what was necessary, told that he understood, and the papers swept away;—"particularly pleasant. You and Miss Fairfax gave us some very good music. I do not know a more luxurious state, sir, than sitting at one's ease to be entertained a whole evening by two such young women; sometimes with music and sometimes with conversation. I am sure Miss Fairfax must have found the evening pleasant, Emma. You left nothing undone. I was glad you made her play so much, for having no instrument at her grandmother's, it must have been a real indulgence."[1]

"I am happy you approved," said Emma, smiling; "but I hope I am not often deficient in what is due to guests at Hartfield."

"No, my dear," said her father instantly; "*that* I am sure you are not. There is nobody half so attentive and civil as you are. If any thing, you are too attentive. The muffin[2] last night—if it had been handed round once, I think it would have been enough."

1 Favor.

2 These would be the traditional yeasted cakes, cooked on a griddle, that are now known as "English muffins" in the United States; the sweet, cake-like American muffin was a later nineteenth-century development.

"No," said Mr. Knightley, nearly at the same time; "you are not often deficient; not often deficient either in manner or comprehension. I think you understand me, therefore."

An arch look expressed—"I understand you well enough;" but she said only, "Miss Fairfax is reserved."

"I always told you she was—a little; but you will soon overcome all that part of her reserve which ought to be overcome, all that has its foundation in diffidence. What arises from discretion must be honoured."

"You think her diffident. I do not see it."

"My dear Emma," said he, moving from his chair into one close by her, "you are not going to tell me, I hope, that you had not a pleasant evening."

"Oh! no; I was pleased with my own perseverance in asking questions, and amused to think how little information I obtained."

"I am disappointed," was his only answer.

"I hope every body had a pleasant evening," said Mr. Woodhouse, in his quiet way. "I had. Once, I felt the fire rather too much; but then I moved back my chair a little, a very little, and it did not disturb me. Miss Bates was very chatty and good-humoured, as she always is, though she speaks rather too quick. However, she is very agreeable, and Mrs. Bates too, in a different way. I like old friends; and Miss Jane Fairfax is a very pretty sort of young lady, a very pretty and a very well-behaved young lady indeed. She must have found the evening agreeable, Mr. Knightley, because she had Emma."

"True, sir; and Emma, because she had Miss Fairfax."

Emma saw his anxiety, and wishing to appease it, at least for the present, said, and with a sincerity which no one could question—

"She is a sort of elegant creature that one cannot keep one's eyes from. I am always watching her to admire; and I do pity her from my heart."

Mr. Knightley looked as if he were more gratified than he cared to express; and before he could make any reply, Mr. Woodhouse, whose thoughts were on the Bates's, said—

"It is a great pity that their circumstances should be so confined! a great pity indeed! and I have often wished—but it is so little one can venture to do—small, trifling presents, of any thing uncommon—Now we have killed a porker, and Emma thinks of sending them a loin or a leg; it is very small and delicate—Hartfield pork is not like any other pork—but still it is pork—and, my dear Emma, unless one could be sure of their making it into steaks, nicely fried, as our's are fried, without the smallest grease, and not roast it, for no stomach can bear roast pork[3]—I think we had better send the leg—do not you think so, my dear?"

"My dear papa, I sent the whole hind-quarter. I knew you would wish it. There will be the leg to be salted, you know, which is so very nice, and the loin to be dressed directly[4] in any manner they like."

"That's right, my dear, very right. I had not thought of it before, but that was the best way. They must not over-salt the leg; and then, if it is not over-salted, and if it is very thoroughly boiled, just as Serle[5] boils our's, and eaten very moderately of, with a boiled turnip, and a little carrot or parsnip, I do not consider it unwholesome."

"Emma," said Mr. Knightley presently, "I have a piece of news for you. You like news—and I heard an article in my way hither that I think will interest you."

"News! Oh! yes, I always like news. What is it?—why do you smile so?—where did you hear it?—at Randalls?"

He had time only to say,

"No, not at Randalls; I have not been near Randalls,"

When the door was thrown open, and Miss Bates and Miss Fairfax walked into the room. Full of thanks, and full of news, Miss Bates knew not which to give quickest. Mr. Knightley soon saw that he had lost his moment, and that not another syllable of communication could rest with him.

"Oh! my dear sir, how are you this morning? My dear Miss Woodhouse—I come quite overpowered. Such a beautiful hind-quarter of pork! You are too bountiful! Have you heard the news? Mr. Elton is going to be married."

Emma had not had time even to think of Mr. Elton, and she was so completely surprized that she could not avoid a little start, and a little blush, at the sound.

3 Mr. Woodhouse's reservations about roast pork are by no means representative of a time that witnessed, among other works, Charles Lamb's legendary 1822 essay "A Dissertation Upon Roast Pig." Lamb is much more convinced about the healthful qualities of pork ("[t]he strong man may batten on him, and the weakling refuseth not his mild juices"), being inspired to one of the great rhapsodies in nineteenth-century writing about food:

> There is no flavour comparable, I will contend, to that of the crisp, tawny, well-watched, not over-roasted, *crackling,* as it is well called—the very teeth are invited to their share of pleasure at this banquet in overcoming the coy, brittle resistance—with the adhesive oleaginous—O call it not fat—but an indefinable sweetness growing up to it—the tender blossoming of fat—fat cropped in the bud—taken in the shoot—in the first innocence—the cream and quintessence of the child-pig's yet pure food—the lean, no lean, but a kind of animal manna—or, rather, fat and lean (if it must be so) so blended and running into each other, that both together make but one ambrosian result, or common substance.

Selected Prose, ed. A. Phillips (Harmondsworth: Penguin, 1985), pp. 166, 165. Denise Gigante offers a fine reading of Lamb's essay as a critique of various standards of contemporary aesthetic and culinary "taste" in her book *Taste: A Literary History* (New Haven, CT: Yale University Press, 2005), pp. 89–116.

4 Prepared immediately.

5 The cook at Hartfield.

"There is my news:—I thought it would interest you," said Mr. Knightley, with a smile which implied a conviction of some part of what had passed between them.

"But where could *you* hear it?" cried Miss Bates. "Where could you possibly hear it, Mr. Knightley? For it is not five minutes since I received Mrs. Cole's note—no, it cannot be more than five—or at least ten—for I had got my bonnet and spencer[6] on, just ready to come out—I was only gone down to speak to Patty again about the pork—Jane was standing in the passage—were not you, Jane?—for my mother was so afraid that we had not any salting-pan[7] large enough. So I said I would go down and see, and Jane said, 'Shall I go down instead? for I think you have a little cold, and Patty has been washing the kitchen.' Oh! my dear, said I—well, and just then came the note.

6 A close-fitting, bodice-like jacket worn by women.

7 Hannah Glasse gives the following instructions for making ham:

> You must take a fat hind-quarter of pork, and cut off a fine ham; take two ounces of salt-petre, a pound of coarse sugar, a pound of common salt, and two ounces of sal-prunella, mix all together, and rub it well; let it lie a month in this pickle, turning and basting it every day, then hang it in wood-smoke as you do beef, in a dry place, so as no heat comes to it; and if you keep them long, hang them a month or two in a damp place, and it will make them cut fine and short. Never lay these hams in water till you boil them, and then boil them in a copper, (if you have one,) or the biggest pot you have.

The Art of Cookery, Made Plain and Easy (London: 1748; rev. ed., London: T. Longman, B. Law, et al., 1796), p. 296.

Portrait of Charles Lamb (1775–1834) by William Hazlitt, 1804. Lamb's praise of the joys of pork fat and crisp crackling in "A Dissertation Upon Roast Pig" (1822) would have horrified Mr. Woodhouse.

8 Overwhelm.

Dress and spencer; green taffeta trimmed with darker green silk pom-poms, c. 1807.

A Miss Hawkins—that's all I know. A Miss Hawkins of Bath. But, Mr. Knightley, how could you possibly have heard it? for the very moment Mr. Cole told Mrs. Cole of it, she sat down and wrote to me. A Miss Hawkins"—

"I was with Mr. Cole on business an hour and half ago. He had just read Elton's letter as I was shewn in, and handed it to me directly."

"Well! that is quite——I suppose there never was a piece of news more generally interesting. My dear sir, you really are too bountiful. My mother desires her very best compliments and regards, and a thousand thanks, and says you really quite oppress[8] her."

"We consider our Hartfield pork," replied Mr. Woodhouse—"indeed it certainly is, so very superior to all other pork, that Emma and I cannot have a greater pleasure than"—

"Oh! my dear sir, as my mother says, our friends are only too good to us. If ever there were people who, without having great wealth themselves, had every thing they could wish for, I am sure it is us. We may well say that 'our lot is cast in a goodly heritage.'[9] Well, Mr. Knightley, and so you actually saw the letter; well"—

"It was short, merely to announce—but cheerful, exulting, of course."—Here was a sly glance at Emma. "He had been so fortunate as to—I forget the precise words—one has no business to remember them. The information was, as you state, that he was going to be married to a Miss Hawkins. By his style, I should imagine it just settled."

"Mr. Elton going to be married!" said Emma, as soon as she could speak. "He will have everybody's wishes for his happiness."

"He is very young to settle," was Mr. Woodhouse's observation. "He had better not be in a hurry. He seemed to me very well off as he was. We were always glad to see him at Hartfield."

"A new neighbour for us all, Miss Woodhouse!" said Miss Bates, joyfully; "my mother is so pleased!—she says she cannot bear to have the poor old Vicarage without a mistress. This is great news, indeed. Jane, you have never seen Mr. Elton!—no wonder that you have such a curiosity to see him."

Jane's curiosity did not appear of that absorbing nature as wholly to occupy her.

"No—I have never seen Mr. Elton," she replied, starting on this appeal; "is he—is he a tall man?"

"Who shall answer that question?" cried Emma. "My father would say 'yes,' Mr. Knightley 'no;' and Miss Bates and I that he is just the happy medium. When you have been here a little longer, Miss Fairfax, you will understand that Mr. Elton is the standard of perfection in Highbury, both in person and mind."

"Very true, Miss Woodhouse, so she will. He is the very best young man—But, my dear Jane, if you remember, I told you yesterday he was precisely the height of Mr. Perry. Miss Hawkins,—I dare say, an excellent young woman. His extreme attention to my mother—wanting her to sit in the vicarage-pew,[10] that she might hear the better, for my mother is a little deaf, you know—it is not much, but she does not hear quite quick.[11] Jane says that Colonel Campbell is a little deaf. He fancied bathing might be good for it—the warm bath[12]—but she says it did him no lasting benefit. Colonel Campbell, you

9 Miss Bates is eliding phrases from Psalm 16, verses 5–6. The precise wording in the 1611 Authorized Version runs as follows: "The LORD *is* the portion of mine inheritance, and of my cup: thou maintainest my lot . . . The lines are fallen vnto mee in pleasant places; yea, I have a goodly heritage."

10 A pew in the front row of the nave, reserved for the use of the vicar's family and friends.

11 Absolutely clearly.

12 Warm baths were recommended by many contemporary writers for their health-giving properties. For example, in *The Code of Health and Longevity; or, a General View of the Rules and Principles Calculated for the Preservation of Health, and the Attainment of Long Life* (Edinburgh: A. Constable & Co., 1807; 3rd ed., London: 1816), John Sinclair claims: "The Warm Bath may be considered as one of the most powerful and universal restoratives with which we are acquainted. Instead of heating the body, it has a cooling effect. It diminishes, under a proper system, the quickness of the pulse. It is of eminent service when the body is overheated, either after fatigue from travelling, or severe bodily exercise; or after violent exertion and perturbation of mind. Warm baths, by their softening powers, are likewise, very beneficial to the young. Their advantage to the old cannot be doubted" (p. 483). However, among the numerous diseases that warm baths supposedly cure, Sinclair does not specifically mention deafness.

13 She may not be "quick," but this remark suggests that even Miss Bates (albeit with some prompting from Mrs. Cole) had suspicions regarding Elton's designs on Emma, before Emma noticed them herself.

know, is quite our angel. And Mr. Dixon seems a very charming young man, quite worthy of him. It is such a happiness when good people get together—and they always do. Now, here will be Mr. Elton and Miss Hawkins; and there are the Coles, such very good people; and the Perrys—I suppose there never was a happier or a better couple than Mr. and Mrs. Perry. I say, sir," turning to Mr. Woodhouse, "I think there are few places with such society as Highbury. I always say, we are quite blessed in our neighbours.—My dear sir, if there is one thing my mother loves better than another, it is pork—a roast loin of pork"—

"As to who, or what Miss Hawkins is, or how long he has been acquainted with her," said Emma, "nothing I suppose can be known. One feels that it cannot be a very long acquaintance. He has been gone only four weeks."

Nobody had any information to give; and, after a few more wonderings, Emma said,

"You are silent, Miss Fairfax—but I hope you mean to take an interest in this news. You, who have been hearing and seeing so much of late on these subjects, who must have been so deep in the business on Miss Campbell's account—we shall not excuse your being indifferent about Mr. Elton and Miss Hawkins."

"When I have seen Mr. Elton," replied Jane, "I dare say I shall be interested—but I believe it requires *that* with me. And as it is some months since Miss Campbell married, the impression may be a little worn off."

"Yes, he has been gone just four weeks, as you observe, Miss Woodhouse," said Miss Bates, "four weeks yesterday.—A Miss Hawkins.—Well, I had always rather fancied it would be some young lady hereabouts; not that I ever——Mrs. Cole once whispered to me—but I immediately said, 'No, Mr. Elton is a most worthy young man——but'—In short, I do not think I am particularly quick at those sort of discoveries.[13] I do not pretend to it. What is before me, I see. At the same time, nobody could wonder if Mr. Elton should have aspired——Miss Woodhouse lets me chatter on, so good-humouredly. She knows I would not offend for the world. How does Miss Smith do? She seems quite recovered now. Have you heard from

Nineteenth-century photograph of "The Great Roman Bath, Bath." The healing powers of the waters of Bath, enshrined in the legend of the ancient King Bladud, were given official sanction when the Romans founded "Aquae Sulis" around AD 43.

Mrs. John Knightley lately? Oh! those dear little children. Jane, do you know I always fancy Mr. Dixon like Mr. John Knightley? I mean in person—tall, and with that sort of look—and not very talkative."

"Quite wrong, my dear aunt; there is no likeness at all."

"Very odd! but one never does form a just idea of any body beforehand. One takes up a notion, and runs away with it. Mr. Dixon, you say, is not, strictly speaking, handsome"

"Handsome! Oh! no—far from it—certainly plain. I told you he was plain."

"My dear, you said that Miss Campbell would not allow him to be plain, and that you yourself—"

"Oh! as for me, my judgment is worth nothing. Where I have a regard, I always think a person well-looking. But I gave what I believed the general opinion, when I called him plain."

"Well, my dear Jane, I believe we must be running away. The weather does not look well, and grandmamma will be uneasy. You are too obliging, my dear Miss Woodhouse; but we really must take leave. This has been a most agreeable piece of news indeed. I shall just go round by Mrs. Cole's; but I shall not stop three minutes: and, Jane, you had better go home directly—I would not have you out in a shower!—We think she is the better for Highbury already. Thank you, we do indeed. I shall not attempt calling on Mrs. Goddard, for I really do not think she cares for any thing but *boiled* pork:[14] when we dress the leg it will be another thing.[15] Good morning to you, my dear sir. Oh! Mr. Knightley is coming too. Well, that is so very!—I am sure if Jane is tired, you will be so kind as to give her your arm.—Mr. Elton and Miss Hawkins.—Good morning to you."

Emma, alone with her father, had half her attention wanted by him, while he lamented that young people would be in such a hurry to marry—and to marry strangers too—and the other half she could give to her own view of the subject. It was to herself an amusing and a very welcome piece of news, as proving that Mr. Elton could not have suffered long; but she was sorry for Harriet: Harriet must feel it—and all that she could hope was, by giving the first information herself, to save her from hearing it abruptly from others. It was now about the time that she was likely to call. If she were to meet Miss

14 Mrs. Goddard appears to share Mr. Woodhouse's tastes in food as well as in card games.

15 It will be "another thing" because the most popular method of cooking home-cured ham was by boiling. Hannah Glasse's instructions are as follows: "When you boil a ham, put it into your copper when the water is pretty warm, for cold water draws the colour out; when it boils, be careful it boils very slowly. A ham of twenty pounds takes four hours and a half, larger and smaller in proportion" (*The Art of Cookery*, p. 26).

Bates in her way!—and upon its beginning to rain, Emma was obliged to expect that the weather would be detaining her at Mrs. Goddard's, and that the intelligence would undoubtedly rush upon her without preparation.

The shower was heavy, but short; and it had not been over five minutes, when in came Harriet, with just the heated, agitated look which hurrying thither with a full heart was likely to give; and the "Oh! Miss Woodhouse, what do you think has happened!" which instantly burst forth, had all the evidence of corresponding perturbation. As the blow was given, Emma felt that she could not now shew greater kindness than in listening; and Harriet, unchecked, ran eagerly through what she had to tell. "She had set out from Mrs. Goddard's half an hour ago—she had been afraid it would rain—she had been afraid it would pour down every moment—but she thought she might get to Hartfield first—she had hurried on as fast as possible; but then, as she was passing by the house where a young woman was making up a gown for her, she thought she would just step in and see how it went on; and though she did not seem to stay half a moment there, soon after she came out it began to rain, and she did not know what to do; so she ran on directly, as fast as she could, and took shelter at Ford's."—Ford's was the principal woolen-draper, linen-draper, and haberdasher's shop united;[16] the shop first in size and fashion in the place.—"And so, there she had set, without an idea of any thing in the world, full ten minutes, perhaps—where, all of a sudden, who should come in—to be sure, it was so very odd!—but they always dealt at Ford's—who should come in, but Elizabeth Martin and her brother!—Dear Miss Woodhouse! only think. I thought I should have fainted. I did not know what to do. I was sitting near the door—Elizabeth saw me directly; but he did not; he was busy with the umbrella. I am sure she saw me, but she looked away directly, and took no notice; and they both went to quite the farther end of the shop; and I kept sitting near the door!—Oh! dear; I was so miserable! I am sure I must have been as white as my gown. I could not go away you know, because of the rain; but I did so wish myself any where in the world but there.—Oh! dear, Miss Woodhouse—well, at last, I fancy, he looked round and saw me; for instead of going on with their buy-

16 Shops such as Ford's often served as social focal points for provincial women, as they supplied all the necessary materials for those women to have clothes made up.

17 Flooded.

ings, they began whispering to one another. I am sure they were talking of me; and I could not help thinking that he was persuading her to speak to me—(do you think he was, Miss Woodhouse?)—for presently she came forward—came quite up to me, and asked me how I did, and seemed ready to shake hands, if I would. She did not do any of it in the same way that she used; I could see she was altered; but, however, she seemed to *try* to be very friendly, and we shook hands, and stood talking some time; but I know no more what I said—I was in such a tremble!—I remember she said she was sorry we never met now; which I thought almost too kind! Dear, Miss Woodhouse, I was absolutely miserable! By that time, it was beginning to hold up, and I was determined that nothing should stop me from getting away—and then—only think!—I found he was coming up towards me too—slowly you know, and as if he did not quite know what to do; and so he came and spoke, and I answered—and I stood for a minute, feeling dreadfully, you know, one can't tell how; and then I took courage, and said it did not rain, and I must go: and so off I set; and I had not got three yards from the door, when he came after me, only to say, if I was going to Hartfield, he thought I had much better go round by Mr. Cole's stables, for I should find the near way quite floated[17] by this rain. Oh! dear, I thought it would have been the death of me! So I said, I was very much obliged to him: you know I could not do less; and then he went back to Elizabeth, and I came round by the stables—I believe I did—but I hardly knew where I was, or any thing about it. Oh! Miss Woodhouse, I would rather done any thing than have had it happen: and yet, you know, there was a sort of satisfaction in seeing him behave so pleasantly and so kindly. And Elizabeth, too. Oh! Miss Woodhouse, do talk to me and make me comfortable again."

Very sincerely did Emma wish to do so; but it was not immediately in her power. She was obliged to stop and think. She was not thoroughly comfortable herself. The young man's conduct, and his sister's, seemed the result of real feeling, and she could not but pity them. As Harriet described it, there had been an interesting mixture of wounded affection and genuine delicacy in their behaviour. But she had believed them to be well meaning, worthy people before;

and what difference did this make in the evils of the connection? It was folly to be disturbed by it. Of course, he must be sorry to lose her—they must be all sorry. Ambition, as well as love, had probably been mortified. They might all have hoped to rise by Harriet's acquaintance: and besides, what was the value of Harriet's description? —so easily pleased—so little discerning;—what signified her praise?

She exerted herself; and did try to make her comfortable, by considering all that had passed as a mere trifle, and quite unworthy of being dwelt on.

"It might be distressing, for the moment," said she, "but you seem to have behaved extremely well; and it is over—and may never—can never, as a first meeting, occur again, and therefore you need not think about it."

Harriet said, "very true;" and she "would not think about it;" but still she talked of it—still she could talk of nothing else; and Emma, at last, in order to put the Martins out of her head, was obliged to hurry on the news, which she had meant to give with so much tender caution; hardly knowing herself whether to rejoice or be angry, ashamed or only amused, at such a state of mind in poor Harriet—such a conclusion of Mr. Elton's importance with her!

Mr. Elton's rights, however, gradually revived. Though she did not feel the first intelligence as she might have done the day before, or an hour before, its interest soon increased; and before their first conversation was over, she had talked herself into all the sensations of curiosity, wonder and regret, pain and pleasure, as to this fortunate Miss Hawkins, which could conduce to place the Martins under proper subordination in her fancy.

Emma learned to be rather glad that there had been such a meeting. It had been serviceable in deadening the first shock, without retaining any influence to alarm. As Harriet now lived, the Martins could not get at her, without seeking her, where hitherto they had wanted either the courage or the condescension to seek her; for since her refusal of the brother, the sisters had never been at Mrs. Goddard's; and a twelvemonth might pass without their being thrown together again, with any necessity, or even any power of speech.

"The Linen Draper" from *The Book of English Trades; and Library of the Useful Arts* (London: Richard Phillips, 1818). Linen drapers formed an important part of the social economy of Austen's world, as many women could afford only locally produced, bespoke imitations of fashionable London dress patterns.

4

Human nature is so well disposed towards those who are in interesting situations, that a young person, who either marries or dies, is sure of being kindly spoken of.

A week had not passed since Miss Hawkins's name was first mentioned in Highbury, before she was, by some means or other, discovered to have every recommendation of person and mind; to be handsome, elegant, highly accomplished, and perfectly amiable: and when Mr. Elton himself arrived to triumph in his happy prospects, and circulate the fame of her merits, there was very little more for him to do, than to tell her Christian name, and say whose music she principally played.

Mr. Elton returned, a very happy man. He had gone away rejected and mortified—disappointed in a very sanguine hope, after a series of what had appeared to him strong encouragement;[1] and not only losing the right lady, but finding himself debased to the level of a very wrong one. He had gone away deeply offended—he came back engaged to another—and to another as superior, of course, to the first, as under such circumstances what is gained always is to what is lost. He came back gay and self-satisfied, eager and busy, caring nothing for Miss Woodhouse, and defying Miss Smith.

The charming Augusta Hawkins, in addition to all the usual advantages of perfect beauty and merit, was in possession of an independent fortune, of so many thousands as would always be called ten; a point of some dignity, as well as some convenience: the story told well; he had not thrown himself away—he had gained a woman of

1 "Series" could govern a singular noun-ending in Austen's time; compare words like "pair" and "couple."

2 Chance meeting. The fashionably Gallic form, as opposed to "rencounter," may be Elton's own term for the event, reported indirectly.

3 While "Green" and "Brown" are perfectly standard English surnames, Austen's juxtaposition of them in a passage that relates Elton's courtship in such generic terms ("he had gained a woman," "the lady had been so easily impressed"), in addition to Emma's views in vol. I, chap. 16 ("if Miss Woodhouse of Hartfield, the heiress of thirty thousand pounds, were not quite so easily obtained as he had fancied, he would soon try for Miss Somebody else with twenty, or with ten"), suggests that Mr. Green and Mrs. Brown may be color-coded types or social ciphers, rather than the real names of characters—not unlike Professor Plum, Miss Scarlett, and Colonel Mustard in the popular twentieth-century board game *Cluedo* (*Clue!* in the United States), and Mr. White, Mr. Orange, Mr. Pink, and Mr. Blonde in Quentin Tarantino's film *Reservoir Dogs* (1992).

4 The contrast between "substance" and "shadow" may originally have more philosophically rigorous sources in English neo-Platonic thought, since Plato's theory of Forms posits the perceptible world as the "shadow" version of the true world of ideal forms. This is the contrast, for example, that lies behind the most famous analogy in the *Republic,* that of the cave: according to Socrates, limited human perceptions are

10,000*l.* or thereabouts; and he had gained her with such delightful rapidity—the first hour of introduction had been so very soon followed by distinguishing notice; the history which he had to give Mrs. Cole of the rise and progress of the affair was so glorious—the steps so quick, from the accidental rencontre,[2] to the dinner at Mr. Green's, and the party at Mrs. Brown's[3]—smiles and blushes rising in importance—with consciousness and agitation richly scattered—the lady had been so easily impressed—so sweetly disposed—had in short, to use a most intelligible phrase, been so very ready to have him, that vanity and prudence were equally contented.

He had caught both substance and shadow[4]—both fortune and affection, and was just the happy man he ought to be; talking only of himself and his own concerns—expecting to be congratulated—ready to be laughed at—and, with cordial, fearless smiles, now addressing all the young ladies of the place, to whom, a few weeks ago, he would have been more cautiously gallant.

The wedding was no distant event, as the parties had only themselves to please,[5] and nothing but the necessary preparations[6] to wait for; and when he set out for Bath again, there was a general expectation, which a certain glance of Mrs. Cole's did not seem to contradict, that when he next entered Highbury he would bring his bride.

During his present short stay, Emma had barely seen him; but just enough to feel that the first meeting was over, and to give her the impression of his not being improved by the mixture of pique[7] and pretension, now spread over his air.[8] She was, in fact, beginning very much to wonder that she had ever thought him pleasing at all; and his sight was so inseparably connected with some very disagreeable feelings, that except in a moral light, as a penance, a lesson, a source of profitable humiliation to her own mind, she would have been thankful to be assured of never seeing him again. She wished him very well; but he gave her pain, and his welfare twenty miles off would administer most satisfaction.

The pain of his continued residence in Highbury, however, must certainly be lessened by his marriage. Many vain solicitudes would be prevented—many awkwardnesses smoothed by it. A *Mrs. Elton* would be an excuse for any change of intercourse; former intimacy

analogous to prisoners who have been kept restrained in a cave all their lives, and who therefore mistake the shadows cast on the wall in front of them as the whole of their reality, rather than a secondary effect of movements that they don't perceive. However, the most likely source for Austen's employment of the phrase is probably Shakespeare: Sonnet 53 opens "What is your substance, whereof are you made,/That millions of strange shaddowes on you tend?," and in Act III, Scene 2, of *The Merchant of Venice,* Bassanio responds to his passing the test of the caskets, remarking:

> Yet looke how farre
> The substance of my praise doth wrong this
> shadow
> In vnderprizing it, so farre this shadow
> Doth limpe behinde the substance.

Jocelyn Harris has recently suggested that by "[t]ranslating precursors into other registers and contexts," Austen "usually improves on her originals" ("Jane Austen," in Adrian Poole, ed., *The Cambridge Companion to English Novelists* [Cambridge: Cambridge University Press, 2010], p. 99); if she is glancing at *The Merchant of Venice* here, there is a finely ironic contrast between Bassanio's original situation (where true love triumphs over materialism) and Elton's (where materialistic expediency is labeled as true love).

5 Elton is master of his own affairs, and his bride-to-be is an orphan.

6 Not only the organization of the service and celebration but also the public proclamation of the banns in church. Following the legislation by Lord Hardwicke in 1754, a marriage was not considered legal unless the banns had been read on three Sundays preceding the wedding, to allow for any potential objections to be raised.

7 Resentment.

8 "Air" was a significant part of the moral vocabulary of sociable behavior in the early eighteenth century, and it is significant that Johnson's own citation for this sense of the word comes from Joseph Addison (1672–1719), who did as much as any writer of the time to promote the virtues of "conversability."

9 High birth.

10 Advantageous social connection.

11 This moment offers a significant counter to the argument that Austen's novels studiously ignore contemporary politics. As with the social resonances that Austen derives in *Emma* from such items as foodstuffs and clothing, she relies on a shared body of background knowledge (frequently unsignposted) in her audience, off which she can then play knowingly by means of a significant word or phrase. In his seminal work "Logic and Conversation" (1967), the philosopher of language Paul Grice coined the term "implicature" to describe instances where speakers diverge from shared linguistic norms of expression—by saying more, less, or other than might be expected in that context—so as to adumbrate or "implicate" something that they do not actually state (see Grice, *Studies in the Way of Words* [Cambridge, MA: Harvard University Press, 1989], pp. 1–144). Seen this way, Austen's novels, which could be considered relatively light on direct political-historical *references* (see Introduction), are nevertheless brimming with social *implicatures,* which by their very nature work less directly.

The narrator's reference to Augusta Hawkins's father and his line of business is a particularly significant instance of such an effect: the performative typographical flinch of the long dash alerts a reader to the fact that *something* isn't being said, while remaining reticent as to what, precisely, that something is. However, the place-name itself is packed with potential historical and political resonances that are summoned up simply by mentioning it. Some British place-names have acquired such distinctive associations that they have subsequently become bywords or shorthands for certain ideas. For example, during the seventeenth century, the city of Birmingham (or, in its dialectal form, "Brummagem") was beginning to rival London as a center of metal production, but it also became tainted by its association with the manufacture of counterfeit coins, with the result that "brummagem" passed into the language as a general term for fakery: the Protestant supporters of the Exclusion Bill in 1680 were famously termed "brummagems" by their political opponents, and the damaging association of the adjective with shoddy, counterfeit goods lived on long into the nineteenth century. Likewise, although Bristol had a long history as the major sea-trading port of the British Empire by the end of the eighteenth century, Austen's readers would have also been alerted to its more nefarious implication in the slave trade, not least as a result of the efforts of William Wilberforce and other abolitionists that culminated in the Slave Trade Act of 1807. Anti-slavery literature often cemented the connection with Bristol: the working-class Bristol poet Ann Yearsley, for instance, wrote in "A Poem on the Inhumanity of the Slave-Trade" (London: G. G. J. & J. Robinson, 1788):

> Bristol, thine heart hath throbb'd to glory.—
> Slaves,
> E'en Christian slaves, have shook their chains,
> and gaz'd
> With wonder and amazement on thee.
> . . .
> I know the crafty merchant will oppose
> The plea of nature to my strain, and urge
> His toils are for his children: the soft plea
> Dissolves my soul—*but when I sell a son,*
> *Thou God of nature, let it be my own!*
>
> Behold that Christian! See what horrid joy
> Lights up his moody features, while he grasps
> The wish'd-for gold, purchase of human blood!
> (pp. 1, 6–7)

Thus, while scoring on one level off the small-time nature of Mr. Hawkins's business, Austen's sentence can, through the associations of "Bristol," make more nebulous suggestions about how that business may be mired in the economics of slavery; this would certainly be consistent with Mrs. Elton's later touchiness about the Sucklings and the slave trade in vol. II., chap. 17.

The presence of slavery in the narrative and economic "peripheral vision" of the novels has been one of the major areas of debate in Austen criticism since the early 1990s. The debate was largely inaugurated by Edward Said's hugely influential discussion of *Mansfield Park* in his work *Culture and Imperialism* (London:

might sink without remark. It would be almost beginning their life of civility again.

Of the lady, individually, Emma thought very little. She was good enough for Mr. Elton, no doubt; accomplished enough for Highbury—handsome enough—to look plain, probably, by Harriet's side. As to connection, there Emma was perfectly easy; persuaded, that after all his own vaunted claims and disdain of Harriet, he had done nothing. On that article, truth seemed attainable. *What* she was, must be uncertain; but *who* she was, might be found out; and setting aside the 10,000*l.* it did not appear that she was at all Harriet's superior. She brought no name, no blood,[9] no alliance.[10] Miss Hawkins was the youngest of the two daughters of a Bristol—merchant, of course, he must be called;[11] but, as the whole of the profits of his mercantile life appeared so very moderate, it was not unfair to guess the dignity of his line of trade had been very moderate also. Part of every winter she had been used to spend in Bath; but Bristol was her home, the very heart of Bristol; for though the father and mother had died some years ago, an uncle remained—in the law line—nothing more distinctly honourable was hazarded of him, than that he was in the law line; and with him the daughter had lived. Emma guessed him to be the drudge[12] of some attorney, and too stupid to rise. And all the grandeur of the connection seemed dependent on the elder sister, who was *very well married,* to a gentleman in a *great way,*[13] near Bristol, who kept two carriages![14] That was the wind-up[15] of the history; that was the glory of Miss Hawkins.

Could she but have given Harriet her feelings about it all! She had talked her into love; but alas! she was not so easily to be talked out of it. The charm of an object to occupy the many vacancies of Harriet's mind was not to be talked away. He might be superseded by another; he certainly would indeed; nothing could be clearer; even a Robert Martin would have been sufficient; but nothing else, she feared, would cure her. Harriet was one of those, who, having once begun, would be always in love. And now, poor girl! she was considerably worse from this re-appearance of Mr. Elton. She was always having a glimpse of him somewhere or other. Emma saw him only once; but two or three times every day Harriet was sure *just* to meet with

Chatto and Windus, 1993). "In *Mansfield Park,*" he argues, "which within Jane Austen's work carefully defines the moral and social values informing her other novels, references to Sir Thomas Bertram's overseas possessions are threaded through; they give him his wealth, occasion his absences, fix his social status at home and abroad, and make possible his values, to which Fanny Price (and Austen herself) finally subscribes" (p. 73). Said also goes on to claim that "by the very odd combination of casualness and stress, Austen reveals herself to be *assuming* . . . the importance of an empire to the situation at home. Let me go further. Since Austen refers to and uses Antigua as she does in *Mansfield Park,* there needs to be a commensurate effort on the part of her readers to understand concretely the historical valences in the reference" (pp. 106–107). The subsequent critical debate, conducted both in books and in periodicals, produced some valuable insights, notably Brian Southam's *TLS* piece "The Silence of the Bertrams" (February 17, 1995, pp. 13–14) and exchanges on the letters pages of March 3, March 10, March 17, and April 7 of that year. For some significant developments of questions raised by Said, see the essays in You-me Park and Rajeswari Sunder Rajan, eds., *The Postcolonial Jane Austen* (London and New York: Routledge, 2000), especially Jon Mee's "Austen's Treacherous Ivory: Female Patriotism, Domestic Ideology, and Empire" (pp. 74–92), and Clara Tuite's "Domestic Retrenchment and Imperial Expansion: The Property Plots of *Mansfield Park*" (pp. 93–115).

12 "One employed in mean labour" (Johnson).

13 Very well off.

14 As *Emma* shows, possession of a carriage was an important token of possessing disposable income, a sign that one was rising economically toward the level of the gentry.

15 Conclusion.

16 Even the angle at which he wore his hat.

him, or *just* to miss him, *just* to hear his voice, or see his shoulder, *just* to have something occur to preserve him in her fancy, in all the favouring warmth of surprize and conjecture. She was, moreover, perpetually hearing about him; for, excepting when at Hartfield, she was always among those who saw no fault in Mr. Elton, and found nothing so interesting as the discussion of his concerns; and every report, therefore, every guess—all that had already occurred, all that might occur in the arrangement of his affairs, comprehending income, servants, and furniture, was continually in agitation around her. Her regard was receiving strength by invariable praise of him, and her regrets kept alive, and feelings irritated by ceaseless repetitions of Miss Hawkins's happiness, and continual observation of, how much he seemed attached!—his air as he walked by the house—the very sitting of his hat,[16] being all in proof of how much he was in love!

Had it been allowable entertainment, had there been no pain to her friend, or reproach to herself, in the waverings of Harriet's mind, Emma would have been amused by its variations. Sometimes Mr. Elton predominated, sometimes the Martins; and each was occasionally useful as a check to the other. Mr. Elton's engagement had been the cure of the agitation of meeting Mr. Martin. The unhappiness produced by the knowledge of that engagement had been a little put aside by Elizabeth Martin's calling at Mrs. Goddard's a few days afterwards. Harriet had not been at home; but a note had been prepared and left for her, written in the very style to touch; a small mixture of reproach, with a great deal of kindness; and till Mr. Elton himself appeared, she had been much occupied by it, continually pondering over what could be done in return, and wishing to do more than she dared to confess. But Mr. Elton, in person, had driven away all such cares. While he staid, the Martins were forgotten; and on the very morning of his setting off for Bath again, Emma, to dissipate some of the distress it occasioned, judged it best for her to return Elizabeth Martin's visit.

How that visit was to be acknowledged—what would be necessary—and what might be safest, had been a point of some doubtful consideration. Absolute neglect of the mother and sisters, when invited to come, would be ingratitude. It must not be: and yet the danger of a renewal of the acquaintance!—

After much thinking, she could determine on nothing better, than Harriet's returning the visit; but in a way that, if they had understanding, should convince them that it was to be only a formal acquaintance. She meant to take her in the carriage, leave her at the Abbey Mill, while she drove a little farther, and call for her again so soon, as to allow no time for insidious applications[17] or dangerous recurrences to the past, and give the most decided proof of what degree of intimacy was chosen for the future.

She could think of nothing better: and though there was something in it which her own heart could not approve—something of ingratitude, merely glossed over—it must be done, or what would become of Harriet?

17 Artful references.

5

Small heart had Harriet for visiting. Only half an hour before her friend called for her at Mrs. Goddard's, her evil stars had led her to the very spot where, at that moment, a trunk, directed to *The Rev. Philip Elton, White-Hart, Bath,*[1] was to be seen under the operation of being lifted into the butcher's cart, which was to convey it to where the coaches past; and every thing in this world, excepting that trunk and the direction, was consequently a blank.

She went, however; and when they reached the farm, and she was to be put down, at the end of the broad, neat gravel-walk, which led between espalier apple-trees[2] to the front door, the sight of every thing which had given her so much pleasure the autumn before, was beginning to revive a little local agitation; and when they parted, Emma observed her to be looking around with a sort of fearful curiosity, which determined her not to allow the visit to exceed the proposed quarter of an hour.[3] She went on herself, to give that portion of time to an old servant who was married, and settled in Donwell.

The quarter of an hour brought her punctually to the white gate again; and Miss Smith receiving her summons, was with her without delay, and unattended by any alarming young man. She came solitarily down the gravel walk—a Miss Martin just appearing at the door, and parting with her seemingly with ceremonious civility.

Harriet could not very soon give an intelligible account. She was feeling too much; but at last Emma collected from her enough to understand the sort of meeting, and the sort of pain it was creating. She had seen only Mrs. Martin and the two girls. They had received her

1 The White Hart was a famous coaching inn on Stall Street in Bath, located very close to the Pump-Room. In his diary for June 28, 1793, James Woodforde calls the White Hart "a very noble Inn," although Austen also hints at its extraordinary bustle in her letter to Cassandra of September 15–16, 1813: "Poor F. Cage has suffered a good deal from her accident. The noise of the White Hart was terrible to her." In vol. II, chap. 10, of *Persuasion,* Charles and Mary Musgrove "were come to Bath for a few days with Mrs. Musgrove, and were at the White Hart." The original inn was demolished in 1869 to make way for the Grand Pump-Room Hotel.

2 Apple trees trained in rows across wooden trellises.

3 A fifteen-minute visit would be considered polite but not friendly; John Trusler remarks: "On paying visits of ceremony, care should be taken not to make them too long, nor too frequent; a quarter of an hour, or twenty minutes, is sufficient time to exchange compliments, or run over the topics of the day; but if the visiters become congenial to each other, and intimacy succeed, time and length of visits, need not be pointed out, they will direct themselves" (*A System of Etiquette* [Bath, 1804; 2nd ed., 1819], p. 27).

Chromo/litho of "The White Hart, Bath, in the Old Coaching Time," c. 1870.

doubtingly, if not coolly; and nothing beyond the merest commonplace had been talked almost all the time—till just at last, when Mrs. Martin's saying, all of a sudden, that she thought Miss Smith was grown, had brought on a more interesting subject, and a warmer manner. In that very room she had been measured last September, with her two friends. There were the pencilled marks and memorandums on the wainscot[4] by the window. *He* had done it. They all seemed to remember the day, the hour, the party, the occasion[5]—to feel the same consciousness, the same regrets—to be ready to return to the same good understanding; and they were just growing again like themselves, (Harriet, as Emma must suspect, as ready as the best of them to be cordial and happy,) when the carriage re-appeared, and all was over. The style of the visit, and the shortness of it, were then felt to be decisive. Fourteen minutes to be given to those with whom she had thankfully passed six weeks not six months ago![6]—Emma could not but picture it all, and feel how justly they might resent, how naturally Harriet must suffer. It was a bad business. She would have given a great deal, or endured a great deal, to have had the Martins in a higher rank of life. They were so deserving, that a *little* higher should have been enough: but as it was, how could she have done otherwise?—Impossible!—She could not repent. They must be separated; but there was a great deal of pain in the process—so much to herself at this time, that she soon felt the necessity of a little consolation, and resolved on going home by way of Randalls to procure it. Her mind was quite sick of Mr. Elton and the Martins. The refreshment of Randalls was absolutely necessary.

It was a good scheme; but on driving to the door they heard that neither "master nor mistress was at home;" they had both been out some time; the man believed they were gone to Hartfield.

"This is too bad," cried Emma, as they turned away. "And now we shall just miss them; too provoking!—I do not know when I have been so disappointed." And she leaned back in the corner, to indulge her murmurs, or to reason them away; probably a little of both—such being the commonest process of a not ill-disposed mind. Presently the carriage stopt; she looked up; it was stopt by Mr. and Mrs. Weston, who were standing to speak to her. There was

4 Wooden paneling.

5 The women here show themselves to be as prone to precise, nostalgic longing as many of the other characters.

6 Another example of Austen's care in narrating duration. Not only is Harriet's visit significantly curtailed one minute before the allotted time, but a reader is invited to infer a major emotional shift in her relations with the Martins, from the mathematical relation between "fourteen minutes," "six weeks," and "six months." Compare the joke in Letter the 4th of *Love and Friendship* (1790): "Isabel had seen the World. She had passed 2 Years at one of the first Boarding schools in London; had spent a fortnight in Bath & had supped one night in Southampton."

instant pleasure in the sight of them, and still greater pleasure was conveyed in sound—for Mr. Weston immediately accosted her with,

"How'd ye do?—how'd ye do?—We have been sitting with your father—glad to see him so well. Frank comes to-morrow—I had a letter this morning—we see him to-morrow by dinner time to a certainty—he is at Oxford to-day, and he comes for a whole fortnight; I knew it would be so. If he had come at Christmas he could not have staid three days; I was always glad he did not come at Christmas; now we are going to have just the right weather for him, fine, dry, settled weather. We shall enjoy him completely; every thing has turned out exactly as we could wish."

There was no resisting such news, no possibility of avoiding the influence of such a happy face as Mr. Weston's, confirmed as it all was by the words and the countenance of his wife, fewer and quieter, but not less to the purpose. To know that *she* thought his coming certain was enough to make Emma consider it so, and sincerely did she rejoice in their joy. It was a most delightful re-animation of exhausted spirits. The worn-out past was sunk in the freshness of what was coming; and in the rapidity of half a moment's thought, she hoped Mr. Elton would now be talked of no more.

Mr. Weston gave her the history of the engagements at Enscombe, which allowed his son to answer for having an entire fortnight at his command, as well as the route and the method of his journey; and she listened, and smiled, and congratulated.

"I shall soon bring him over to Hartfield," said he, at the conclusion.

Emma could imagine she saw a touch of the arm at this speech, from his wife.

"We had better move on, Mr. Weston," said she, "we are detaining the girls."

"Well, well, I am ready;"—and turning again to Emma, "but you must not be expecting such a *very* fine young man; you have only had *my* account you know; I dare say he is really nothing extraordinary:"—though his own sparkling eyes at the moment were speaking a very different conviction.

Photograph of espalier fruit trees at Temple Newsam Park, Yorkshire.

Emma could look perfectly unconscious and innocent, and answer in a manner that appropriated nothing.[7]

"Think of me to-morrow, my dear Emma, about four o'clock," was Mrs. Weston's parting injunction; spoken with some anxiety, and meant only for her.

"Four o'clock!—depend upon it he will be here by three," was Mr. Weston's quick amendment; and so ended a most satisfactory meeting. Emma's spirits were mounted quite up to happiness; every thing wore a different air; James and his horses seemed not half so sluggish as before. When she looked at the hedges, she thought the elder at least must soon be coming out;[8] and when she turned round to Harriet, she saw something like a look of spring, a tender smile even there.

"Will Mr. Frank Churchill pass through Bath as well as Oxford?"—was a question, however, which did not augur much.[9]

But neither geography nor tranquillity could come all at once, and Emma was now in a humour to resolve that they should both come in time.

The morning of the interesting[10] day arrived, and Mrs. Weston's faithful pupil did not forget either at ten, or eleven, or twelve o'clock, that she was to think of her at four.

"My dear, dear, anxious friend,"—said she, in mental soliloquy, while walking down stairs from her own room, "always over-careful for every body's comfort but your own; I see you now in all your little fidgets, going again and again into his room, to be sure that all is right." The clock struck twelve as she passed through the hall. "'Tis twelve, I shall not forget to think of you four hours hence; and by this time to-morrow, perhaps, or a little later, I may be thinking of the possibility of their all calling here. I am sure they will bring him soon."

She opened the parlour door, and saw two gentlemen sitting with her father—Mr. Weston and his son. They had been arrived only a few minutes, and Mr. Weston had scarcely finished his explanation of Frank's being a day before his time, and her father was yet in the midst of his very civil welcome and congratulations,

7 In a manner that betrayed no sense of a personal reference to her.

8 Given that this scene takes place in early February, "coming out" can only mean "coming into leaf," as elderflowers do not appear in Britain until late May and early June. The precise chronology of blossom is a major topic of critical debate regarding the Box Hill picnic (see vol. III, chap. 6).

9 In her eagerness to sneak an allusion to Elton into the conversation, Harriet imagines an unlikely route for Frank Churchill to travel on his way to Highbury, since Bath is some eighty-eight miles west of Leatherhead, and Oxford some forty-eight miles northwest of it.

10 Important.

when she appeared, to have her share of surprize, introduction, and pleasure.

The Frank Churchill so long talked of, so high in interest, was actually before her—he was presented to her, and she did not think too much had been said in his praise; he was a *very* good looking young man; height, air, address, all were unexceptionable, and his countenance had a great deal of the spirit and liveliness of his father's; he looked quick and sensible. She felt immediately that she should like him; and there was a well-bred ease of manner, and a readiness to talk, which convinced her that he came intending to be acquainted with her, and that acquainted they soon must be.

He had reached Randalls the evening before. She was pleased with the eagerness to arrive which had made him alter his plan, and travel earlier, later, and quicker, that he might gain half a day.

"I told you yesterday," cried Mr. Weston with exultation, "I told you all that he would be here before the time named. I remembered what I used to do myself. One cannot creep[11] upon a journey; one cannot help getting on faster than one has planned; and the pleasure of coming in upon one's friends before the look-out begins, is worth a great deal more than any little exertion it needs."

"It is a great pleasure where one can indulge in it," said the young man, "though there are not many houses that I should presume on so far; but in coming *home* I felt I might do any thing."

The word *home* made his father look on him with fresh complacency.[12] Emma was directly sure that he knew how to make himself agreeable; the conviction was strengthened by what followed. He was very much pleased with Randalls, thought it a most admirably arranged house, would hardly allow it even to be very small, admired the situation, the walk to Highbury, Highbury itself, Hartfield still more, and professed himself to have always felt the sort of interest in the country which none but one's *own* country gives, and the greatest curiosity to visit it. That he should never have been able to indulge so amiable a feeling before, passed suspiciously through Emma's brain; but still if it were a falsehood, it was a pleasant one, and pleasantly handled. His manner had no air of study or exaggera-

11 Tarry, dither.

12 "Civility; complaisance" (Johnson).

tion. He did really look and speak as if in a state of no common enjoyment.

Their subjects in general were such as belong to an opening acquaintance. On his side were the inquiries,—"Was she a horsewoman?—Pleasant rides?—Pleasant walks?—Had they a large neighbourhood?—Highbury, perhaps, afforded society enough?—There were several very pretty houses in and about it.—Balls—had they balls?—Was it a musical society?"

But when satisfied on all these points, and their acquaintance proportionably advanced, he contrived to find an opportunity, while their two fathers were engaged with each other, of introducing his mother-in-law,[13] and speaking of her with so much handsome praise, so much warm admiration, so much gratitude for the happiness she secured to his father, and her very kind reception of himself, as was an additional proof of his knowing how to please—and of his certainly thinking it worth while to try to please her. He did not advance a word of praise beyond what she knew to be thoroughly deserved by Mrs. Weston; but undoubtedly he could know very little of the matter. He understood what would be welcome; he could be sure of little else. "His father's marriage," he said, "had been the wisest measure, every friend must rejoice in it; and the family from whom he had received such a blessing must be ever considered as having conferred the highest obligation on him."

He got as near as he could to thanking her for Miss Taylor's merits, without seeming quite to forget that in the common course of things it was to be rather supposed that Miss Taylor had formed Miss Woodhouse's character, than Miss Woodhouse Miss Taylor's. And at last, as if resolved to qualify his opinion completely for travelling round to its object, he wound it all up with astonishment at the youth and beauty of her person.

"Elegant, agreeable manners, I was prepared for," said he; "but I confess that, considering every thing, I had not expected more than a very tolerably well-looking woman of a certain age;[14] I did not know that I was to find a pretty young woman in Mrs. Weston."

"You cannot see too much perfection in Mrs. Weston for my feelings," said Emma; "were you to guess her to be *eighteen,* I should lis-

13 Stepmother.

14 Darcy makes a similarly dismissive remark to Bingley when he first encounters Elizabeth Bennet in vol. I, chap. 3, of *Pride and Prejudice:* "She is tolerable; but not handsome enough to tempt *me;* and I am in no humour at present to give consequence to young ladies who are slighted by other men."

ten with pleasure; but *she* would be ready to quarrel with you for using such words. Don't let her imagine that you have spoken of her as a pretty young woman."

"I hope I should know better," he replied; "no, depend upon it, (with a gallant bow,) that in addressing Mrs. Weston I should understand whom I might praise without any danger of being thought extravagant in my terms."

Emma wondered whether the same suspicion of what might be expected from their knowing each other, which had taken strong possession of her mind, had ever crossed his; and whether his compliments were to be considered as marks of acquiescence, or proofs of defiance. She must see more of him to understand his ways; at present she only felt they were agreeable.

She had no doubt of what Mr. Weston was often thinking about. His quick eye she detected again and again glancing towards them with a happy expression; and even, when he might have determined not to look, she was confident that he was often listening.

Her own father's perfect exemption from any thought of the kind, the entire deficiency in him of all such sort of penetration or suspicion, was a most comfortable circumstance. Happily he was not farther from approving matrimony than from foreseeing it.—Though always objecting to every marriage that was arranged, he never suffered beforehand from the apprehension of any; it seemed as if he could not think so ill of any two persons' understanding as to suppose they meant to marry till it were proved against them. She blessed the favouring blindness. He could now, without the drawback of a single unpleasant surmise, without a glance forward at any possible treachery in his guest, give way to all his natural kind-hearted civility in solicitous inquiries after Mr. Frank Churchill's accommodation on his journey, through the sad evils of sleeping two nights on the road, and express very genuine unmixed anxiety to know that he had certainly escaped catching cold—which, however, he could not allow him to feel quite assured of himself till after another night.

A reasonable visit paid, Mr. Weston began to move.—"He must be going. He had business at the Crown about his hay, and a great many

15 Emma's uncertainty about the criteria employed in the "fashionable world" is a further indication of Highbury's social and geographical isolation from it.

errands for Mrs. Weston at Ford's; but he need not hurry any body else." His son, too well bred to hear the hint, rose immediately also, saying,

"As you are going farther on business, sir, I will take the opportunity of paying a visit, which must be paid some day or other, and therefore may as well be paid now. I have the honour of being acquainted with a neighbour of yours, (turning to Emma,) a lady residing in or near Highbury; a family of the name of Fairfax. I shall have no difficulty, I suppose, in finding the house; though Fairfax, I believe, is not the proper name—I should rather say Barnes, or Bates. Do you know any family of that name?"

"To be sure we do," cried his father; "Mrs. Bates—we passed her house—I saw Miss Bates at the window. True, true, you are acquainted with Miss Fairfax; I remember you knew her at Weymouth, and a fine girl she is. Call upon her, by all means."

"There is no necessity for my calling this morning," said the young man; "another day would do as well; but there was that degree of acquaintance at Weymouth which"—

"Oh! go to-day, go to-day. Do not defer it. What is right to be done cannot be done too soon. And besides, I must give you a hint, Frank; any want of attention to her *here* should be carefully avoided. You saw her with the Campbells when she was the equal of every body she mixed with, but here she is with a poor old grandmother, who has barely enough to live on. If you do not call early it will be a slight."

The son looked convinced.

"I have heard her speak of the acquaintance," said Emma, "she is a very elegant young woman."

He agreed to it, but with so quiet a "Yes," as inclined her almost to doubt his real concurrence; and yet there must be a very distinct sort of elegance for the fashionable world, if Jane Fairfax could be thought only ordinarily gifted with it.[15]

"If you were never particularly struck by her manners before," said she, "I think you will to-day. You will see her to advantage; see her and hear her—no, I am afraid you will not hear her at all, for she has an aunt who never holds her tongue."

"You are acquainted with Miss Jane Fairfax, sir, are you?" said Mr. Woodhouse, always the last to make his way in conversation; "then give me leave to assure you that you will find her a very agreeable young lady. She is staying here on a visit to her grandmamma and aunt, very worthy people; I have known them all my life. They will be extremely glad to see you, I am sure, and one of my servants shall go with you to shew you the way."

"My dear sir, upon no account in the world; my father can direct me."

"But your father is not going so far; he is only going to the Crown, quite on the other side of the street, and there are a great many houses; you might be very much at a loss, and it is a very dirty walk, unless you keep on the foot-path; but my coachman can tell you where you had best cross the street."

Mr. Frank Churchill still declined it, looking as serious as he could, and his father gave his hearty support by calling out, "My good friend, this is quite unnecessary; Frank knows a puddle of water when he sees it, and as to Mrs. Bates's, he may get there from the Crown in a hop, step, and jump."[16]

They were permitted to go alone; and with a cordial nod from one, and a graceful bow from the other, the two gentlemen took leave. Emma remained very well pleased with this beginning of the acquaintance, and could now engage to think of them all at Randalls any hour of the day, with full confidence in their comfort.

16 This precursor of the modern athletic discipline of the triple jump was already popular by the beginning of the eighteenth century, and the phrase was in wide colloquial usage to describe trifling distances or expeditious travel; in vol. I, chap. 8, of William Godwin's radical thriller *Things as They Are; or, The Adventures of Caleb Williams* (1794), the villain Falkland's henchman Grimes exclaims: "As I comed along to you, I saw Mun, coachey, pop along from the back-door to the stables. He was within a hop, step, and jump of me."

6

1 "Morning" in Austen's time denoted the entire period between breakfast and dinner; therefore, a morning could, in theory, last until as late as six-thirty or even seven o'clock. A "morning visit," however, would usually conclude before the hosts' dinner hour.

The next morning brought Mr. Frank Churchill again. He came with Mrs. Weston, to whom and to Highbury he seemed to take very cordially. He had been sitting with her, it appeared, most companionably at home, till her usual hour of exercise; and on being desired to chuse their walk, immediately fixed on Highbury.—"He did not doubt there being very pleasant walks in every direction, but if left to him, he should always chuse the same. Highbury, that airy, cheerful, happy-looking Highbury, would be his constant attraction."—Highbury, with Mrs. Weston, stood for Hartfield; and she trusted to its bearing the same construction with him. They walked thither directly.

Emma had hardly expected them: for Mr. Weston, who had called in for half a minute, in order to hear that his son was very handsome, knew nothing of their plans; and it was an agreeable surprize to her, therefore, to perceive them walking up to the house together, arm in arm. She was wanting to see him again, and especially to see him in company with Mrs. Weston, upon his behaviour to whom her opinion of him was to depend. If he were deficient there, nothing should make amends for it. But on seeing them together, she became perfectly satisfied. It was not merely in fine words or hyperbolical compliment that he paid his duty; nothing could be more proper or pleasing than his whole manner to her—nothing could more agreeably denote his wish of considering her as a friend and securing her affection. And there was time enough for Emma to form a reasonable judgment, as their visit included all the rest of the morning.[1] They were all three walking about together for an hour or two—first round the shrubberies of Hartfield, and afterwards in Highbury. He was delighted with every thing; admired Hartfield sufficiently for Mr. Woodhouse's ear; and when their going farther was resolved on, confessed his wish to be made acquainted with the whole village, and found matter of commendation and interest much oftener than Emma could have supposed.

Some of the objects of his curiosity spoke[2] very amiable feelings. He begged to be shewn the house which his father had lived in so long, and which had been the home of his father's father; and on recollecting that an old woman who had nursed him was still living, walked in quest of her cottage from one end of the street to the other; and though in some points of pursuit or observation there was no positive merit, they shewed, altogether, a good-will towards Highbury in general, which must be very like a merit to those he was with.

Emma watched and decided, that with such feelings as were now shewn, it could not be fairly supposed that he had been ever voluntarily absenting himself; that he had not been acting a part, or making a parade of insincere professions;[3] and that Mr. Knightley certainly had not done him justice.

Their first pause was at the Crown Inn, an inconsiderable house, though the principal one of the sort, where a couple of pair of post-horses were kept, more for the convenience of the neighbourhood than from any run[4] on the road; and his companions had not expected to be detained by any interest excited there; but in passing it they gave the history of the large room visibly added; it had been built many years ago for a ball-room, and while the neighbourhood had been in a particularly populous, dancing state, had been occasionally used as such;—but such brilliant days had long passed away,[5] and now the highest purpose for which it was ever wanted was to accommodate a whist club established among the gentlemen and half-gentlemen[6] of the place. He was immediately interested. Its character as a ball-room caught him; and instead of passing on, he stopt for several minutes at the two superior sashed windows[7] which were open, to look in and contemplate its capabilities, and lament that its

2 Bespoke, witnessed.

3 Compare Letter 19 of Austen's novel *Lady Susan,* in which Lady Susan complains cynically of "the parade of propriety which prevented Miss Summers from keeping the girl."

4 Any particular demand.

5 Post-horses would be kept at coaching inns, both for post-riders and as horses that private travelers could hire for the next stage of their journey. That the Crown has these post-horses at all, combined with the reference to the disused ballroom, suggests that Highbury may once have been better connected with the fashionable outside world than it is now.

6 Men who, while not gentlemen by birth, were qualified by economic standards to be considered alongside them.

7 The admiration of windows carries a particular force in writing of this time, since, between 1696 and 1851, households paid Window Tax according to the number of windows they possessed; therefore, the simple possession of numerous windows was in itself a visible (and transparent) symbol of wealth. Compare vol. II, chap. 6, of *Pride and Prejudice,* in which Mr. Collins conceitedly shows Elizabeth around the estate at Rosings: "Every park has its beauty and its prospects; and Elizabeth saw much to be pleased with, though she could not be in such raptures as Mr. Collins expected the scene to inspire, and was but slightly affected by his enumeration of the windows in front of the house, and his relation of what the glazing altogether had originally cost Sir Lewis De Bourgh."

original purpose should have ceased. He saw no fault in the room, he would acknowledge none which they suggested. No, it was long enough, broad enough, handsome enough. It would hold the very number for comfort. They ought to have balls there at least every fortnight through the winter. Why had not Miss Woodhouse revived the former good old days of the room?—She who could do any thing in Highbury! The want of proper[8] families in the place, and the conviction that none beyond the place and its immediate environs could be tempted to attend, were mentioned; but he was not satisfied. He could not be persuaded that so many good-looking houses as he saw around him, could not furnish numbers enough for such a meeting; and even when particulars were given and families described, he was

8 Suitably eminent (this is probably Emma's own evaluation).

Photograph of the Wheatsheaf, at the end of Popham Lane in North Waltham, Hampshire. In the days before regular mail delivery services, the coaching inns past which the mail-coaches drove would often act as *de facto* post offices, from which customers could collect their letters. The inn now known as the Wheatsheaf served this function for the Austen family when they lived at nearby Steventon; in a letter to Cassandra of February 11, 1801, Austen mentioned a letter from their brother Charles, which was "conveyed to Popham Lane by Captn Boyle in his way to Midgham."

still unwilling to admit that the inconvenience of such a mixture would be any thing, or that there would be the smallest difficulty in every body's returning into their proper place the next morning. He argued like a young man very much bent on dancing; and Emma was rather surprized to see the constitution of the Weston prevail so decidedly against the habits of the Churchills. He seemed to have all the life and spirit, cheerful feelings, and social inclinations of his father, and nothing of the pride or reserve of Enscombe. Of pride, indeed, there was, perhaps, scarcely enough; his indifference to a confusion of rank, bordered too much on inelegance of mind. He could be no judge, however, of the evil he was holding cheap. It was but an effusion of lively spirits.

At last he was persuaded to move on from the front of the Crown; and being now almost facing the house where the Bateses lodged, Emma recollected his intended visit the day before, and asked him if he had paid it.

"Yes, oh! yes—" he replied; "I was just going to mention it. A very successful visit:—I saw all the three ladies; and felt very much obliged to you for your preparatory hint. If the talking aunt had taken me quite by surprize, it must have been the death of me. As it was, I was only betrayed into paying a most unreasonable visit. Ten minutes would have been all that was necessary, perhaps all that was proper;[9] and I had told my father I should certainly be at home before him—but there was no getting away, no pause; and, to my utter astonishment, I found, when he (finding me no where else) joined me there at last, that I had been actually sitting with them very nearly three quarters of an hour. The good lady had not given me the possibility of escape before."

"And how did you think Miss Fairfax looking?"

"Ill, very ill—that is, if a young lady can ever be allowed to look ill. But the expression is hardly admissible, Mrs. Weston, is it? Ladies can never look ill. And, seriously, Miss Fairfax is naturally so pale, as almost always to give the appearance of ill health.—A most deplorable want of complexion."

Emma would not agree to this, and began a warm defence of Miss Fairfax's complexion. "It was certainly never brilliant, but she would

9 Frank is at pains here to point out that he considers Jane and the Bateses worthy only of an informal, fleeting visit, so as to acquit himself of any suspicion.

not allow it to have a sickly hue in general; and there was a softness and delicacy in her skin which gave peculiar elegance to the character of her face." He listened with all due deference; acknowledged that he had heard many people say the same—but yet he must confess, that to him nothing could make amends for the want of the fine glow of health. Where features were indifferent, a fine complexion gave beauty to them all; and where they were good, the effect was—fortunately he need not attempt to describe what the effect was.

"Well," said Emma, "there is no disputing about taste.—At least you admire her except her complexion."

He shook his head and laughed.—"I cannot separate Miss Fairfax and her complexion."

"Did you see her often at Weymouth? Were you often in the same society?"

At this moment they were approaching Ford's, and he hastily exclaimed, "Ha! this must be the very shop that every body attends every day of their lives, as my father informs me. He comes to Highbury himself, he says, six days out of the seven, and has always business at Ford's. If it be not inconvenient to you, pray let us go in, that I may prove myself to belong to the place, to be a true citizen of Highbury. I must buy something at Ford's. It will be taking out my freedom.[10]—I dare say they sell gloves."

"Oh! yes, gloves and every thing. I do admire your patriotism. You will be adored in Highbury. You were very popular before you came, because you were Mr. Weston's son—but lay out half-a-guinea at Ford's, and your popularity will stand upon your own virtues."

They went in; and while the sleek, well-tied parcels of "Men's Beavers"[11] and "York Tan"[12] were bringing down and displaying on the counter, he said—"But I beg your pardon, Miss Woodhouse, you were speaking to me, you were saying something at the very moment of this burst of my *amor patriæ*.[13] Do not let me lose it. I assure you the utmost stretch of public fame would not make me amends for the loss of any happiness in private life."

"I merely asked, whether you had known much of Miss Fairfax and her party at Weymouth."

10 Qualifying myself as a free citizen of Highbury.

11 Although Frank Churchill is looking for gloves here, "Men's Beavers" more usually referred to men's hats made from beaver fur.

12 Light-brown leather gloves, traditionally manufactured in the city of York.

13 Latin for "love of one's native country."

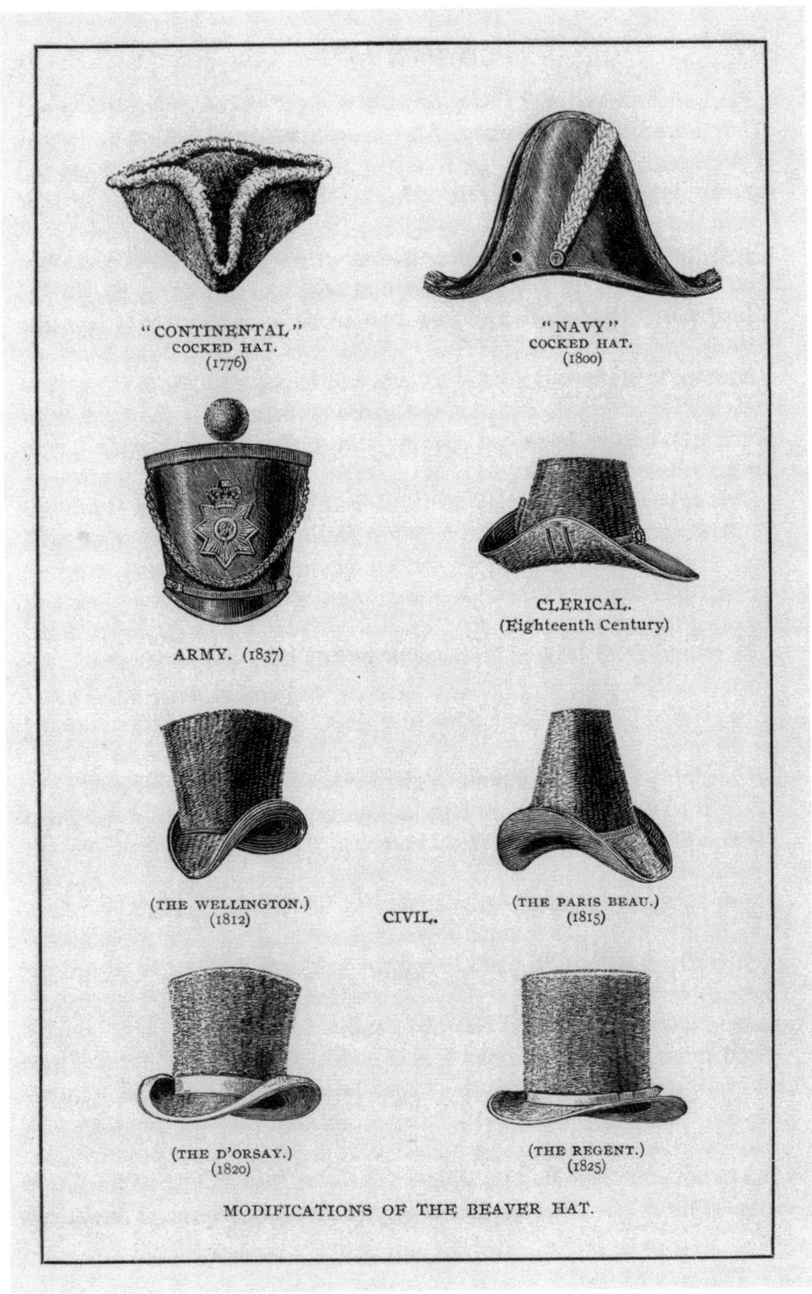

"Modifications of the Beaver Hat" from Horace T. Martin, *Castorologia, or the History and Traditions of the Canadian Beaver* (London: Edward Stanford, 1892). Beaver fur was used to manufacture both hats and gloves.

14 In the light of subsequent events, Frank's statement is duplicitously vague.

"And now that I understand your question, I must pronounce it to be a very unfair one. It is always the lady's right to decide on the degree of acquaintance. Miss Fairfax must already have given her account.—I shall not commit myself by claiming more than she may chuse to allow."

"Upon my word! you answer as discreetly as she could do herself. But her account of every thing leaves so much to be guessed, she is so very reserved, so very unwilling to give the least information about any body, that I really think you may say what you like of your acquaintance with her."

"May I indeed?—Then I will speak the truth, and nothing suits me so well. I met her frequently at Weymouth. I had known the Campbells a little in town; and at Weymouth we were very much in the same set. Col. Campbell is a very agreeable man, and Mrs. Campbell a friendly, warm-hearted woman. I like them all."

"You know Miss Fairfax's situation in life, I conclude; what she is destined to be."

"Yes—(rather hesitatingly)—I believe I do."[14]

"You get upon delicate subjects, Emma," said Mrs. Weston smiling, "remember that I am here.—Mr. Frank Churchill hardly knows what to say when you speak of Miss Fairfax's situation in life. I will move a little farther off."

"I certainly do forget to think of *her,*" said Emma, "as having ever been any thing but my friend and my dearest friend."

He looked as if he fully understood and honoured such a sentiment.

When the gloves were bought and they had quitted the shop again, "Did you ever hear the young lady we were speaking of, play?" said Frank Churchill.

"Ever hear her!" repeated Emma. "You forget how much she belongs to Highbury. I have heard her every year of our lives since we both began. She plays charmingly."

"You think so, do you?—I wanted the opinion of some one who could really judge. She appeared to me to play well, that is, with considerable taste, but I know nothing of the matter myself.—I am excessively fond of music, but without the smallest skill or right of judging of any body's performance.—I have been used to hear her's admired; and I remember one proof of her being thought to play well:—a man, a very musical man, and in love with another woman—engaged to her—on the point of marriage—would yet never ask that other woman to sit down to the instrument, if the lady in question could sit down instead—never seemed to like to hear one if he could hear the other. That I thought, in a man of known musical talent, was some proof."

"Proof, indeed!" said Emma, highly amused.[15]—"Mr. Dixon is very musical, is he? We shall know more about them all, in half an hour, from you, than Miss Fairfax would have vouchsafed in half a year."

"Yes, Mr. Dixon and Miss Campbell were the persons; and I thought it a very strong proof."

"Certainly—very strong it was; to own the truth, a great deal stronger than, if *I* had been Miss Campbell, would have been at all agreeable to me. I could not excuse a man's having more music than love—more ear than eye—a more acute sensibility to fine sounds than to my feelings. How did Miss Campbell appear to like it?"

"It was her very particular friend, you know."

"Poor comfort!" said Emma, laughing. "One would rather have a stranger preferred than one's very particular friend—with a stranger it might not recur again—but the misery of having a very particular friend always at hand, to do every thing better than one does oneself!—Poor Mrs. Dixon! Well, I am glad she is gone to settle in Ireland."

"You are right. It was not very flattering to Miss Campbell; but she really did not seem to feel it."

"So much the better—or so much the worse:—I do not know which. But, be it sweetness or be it stupidity in her—quickness of friendship, or dulness of feeling—there was one person, I think, who must have felt it: Miss Fairfax herself. *She* must have felt the improper and dangerous distinction."

"As to that—I do not——"

"Oh! do not imagine that I expect an account of Miss Fairfax's sensations from you, or from any body else. They are known to no human being, I guess, but herself. But if she continued to play whenever she was asked by Mr. Dixon, one may guess what one chuses."

15 Emma interprets this story as "proof" of an attachment between Jane and Mr. Dixon, not of her musical accomplishment.

"There appeared such a perfectly good understanding among them all—" he began rather quickly, but checking himself, added, "however, it is impossible for me to say on what terms they really were—how it might all be behind the scenes. I can only say that there was smoothness outwardly. But you, who have known Miss Fairfax from a child, must be a better judge of her character, and of how she is is likely to conduct herself in critical situations, than I can be."

"I have known her from a child, undoubtedly; we have been children and women together; and it is natural to suppose that we should be intimate,—that we should have taken to each other whenever she visited her friends. But we never did. I hardly know how it has happened; a little, perhaps, from that wickedness on my side which was prone to take disgust towards a girl so idolized and so cried up[16] as she always was, by her aunt and grandmother, and all their set. And then, her reserve—I never could attach myself to any one so completely reserved."

"It is a most repulsive quality, indeed," said he. "Oftentimes very convenient, no doubt, but never pleasing. There is safety in reserve, but no attraction. One cannot love a reserved person."

"Not till the reserve ceases towards oneself; and then the attraction may be the greater. But I must be more in want of a friend, or an agreeable companion, than I have yet been, to take the trouble of conquering any body's reserve to procure one. Intimacy between Miss Fairfax and me is quite out of the question. I have no reason to think ill of her—not the least—except that such extreme and perpetual cautiousness of word and manner, such a dread of giving a distinct idea about any body, is apt to suggest suspicions of there being something to conceal."

He perfectly agreed with her: and after walking together so long, and thinking so much alike, Emma felt herself so well acquainted with him, that she could hardly believe it to be only their second meeting. He was not exactly what she had expected; less of the man of the world in some of his notions, less of the spoiled child of fortune,[17] therefore better than she had expected. His ideas seemed more moderate—his feelings warmer. She was particularly struck by his manner of considering Mr. Elton's house, which, as well as the

16 Praised (with an undertow of hyperbole).

17 One of the great, unnarrated mysteries in *Emma*'s world of gossip and mishearing is the mystery of how this phrase makes its way (albeit in a distorted form) from Emma's internalized thoughts into Frank Churchill's knowledge in vol. III, chap. 14 ("Miss W. calls me the child of good fortune"). A reader never sees Emma voice or write this thought, yet it has clearly reached Frank by someone's agency.

church, he would go and look at, and would not join them in finding much fault with. No, he could not believe it a bad house; not such a house as a man was to be pitied for having. If it were to be shared with the woman he loved, he could not think any man to be pitied for having that house. There must be ample room in it for every real comfort. The man must be a blockhead who wanted more.

Mrs. Weston laughed, and said he did not know what he was talking about. Used only to a large house himself, and without ever thinking how many advantages and accommodations[18] were attached to its size, he could be no judge of the privations inevitably belonging to a small one. But Emma, in her own mind, determined that he *did* know what he was talking about, and that he shewed a very amiable inclination to settle early in life, and to marry, from worthy motives. He might not be aware of the inroads on domestic peace to be occasioned by no housekeeper's room, or a bad butler's pantry, but no doubt he did perfectly feel that Enscombe could not make him happy, and that whenever he were attached, he would willingly give up much of wealth to be allowed an early establishment.[19]

18 Conveniences.

19 To be able to set up an independent home and domestic staff as soon as possible.

7

1 As wigs fell out of fashion toward the end of the eighteenth century, it became consequently more important for men to keep their hair trimmed. Of course, it transpires that Frank is not "merely" in London "to have his hair cut," but also to order the musical instrument that will generate so much mystery and speculation later in the novel.

2 Whim.

3 A small carriage, holding up to three people.

4 Purpose.

Emma's very good opinion of Frank Churchill was a little shaken the following day, by hearing that he was gone off to London, merely to have his hair cut.[1] A sudden freak[2] seemed to have seized him at breakfast, and he had sent for a chaise[3] and set off, intending to return to dinner, but with no more important view[4] that appeared than having his hair cut. There was certainly no harm in his travelling sixteen miles twice over on such an errand; but there was an air of foppery and nonsense in it which she could not approve. It did not accord with the rationality of plan, the moderation in expense, or even the unselfish warmth of heart which she had believed herself to discern in him yesterday. Vanity, extravagance, love of change, restlessness of temper, which must be doing something, good or bad; heedlessness as to the pleasure of his father and Mrs. Weston, indifferent as to how his conduct might appear in general; he became liable to all these charges. His father only called him a coxcomb, and thought it a very good story; but that Mrs. Weston did not like it, was clear enough, by her passing it over as quickly as possible, and making no other comment than that "all young people would have their little whims."

With the exception of this little blot, Emma found that his visit hitherto had given her friend only good ideas of him. Mrs. Weston was very ready to say how attentive and pleasant a companion he made himself—how much she saw to like in his disposition altogether. He appeared to have a very open temper—certainly a very cheerful and lively one; she could observe nothing wrong in his notions, a great deal decidedly right; he spoke of his uncle with warm regard, was fond of talking of him—said he would be the best man in the world if he were left to himself; and though there was no being attached to the aunt, he acknowledged her kindness with gratitude, and seemed to mean always to speak of her with respect. This was all very promising; and, but for such an unfortunate fancy for having his hair cut, there was nothing to denote him unworthy of the distinguished honour which her imagination had given him; the honour, if not of being really in love with her, of being at least very near it, and saved only by her own indifference—(for still her resolution held of never marrying)—the honour, in short, of being marked out for her by all their joint acquaintance.

Mr. Weston, on his side, added a virtue to the account which must have some weight. He gave her to understand that Frank admired her extremely—thought her very beautiful and very charming; and with so much to be said for him altogether, she found she must not judge him harshly. As Mrs. Weston observed, "all young people would have their little whims."

There was one person among his new acquaintance in Surry, not so leniently disposed.[5] In general he was judged, throughout the parishes of Donwell and Highbury, with great candour;[6] liberal allowances were made for the little excesses of such a handsome young man—one who smiled so often and bowed so well; but there was one spirit among them not to be softened, from its power of censure, by bows or smiles—Mr. Knightley. The circumstance was told him at Hartfield; for the moment, he was silent; but Emma heard him almost immediately afterwards say to himself, over a newspaper he held in his hand, "Hum! just the trifling, silly fellow I took him for." She had half a mind to resent;[7] but an instant's observation convinced her that it was really said only to relieve his own feelings,[8] and not meant to provoke; and therefore she let it pass.

Although in one instance the bearers of not good tidings, Mr. and Mrs. Weston's visit this morning was in another respect particularly opportune. Something occurred while they were at Hartfield, to make Emma want their advice; and, which was still more lucky, she wanted exactly the advice they gave.

5 Forgiving.

6 Used here in the sense of "fairness" or "impartiality."

7 Protest.

8 Later events suggest that these "feelings" may be more complex than Emma allows for here.

9 Displaying only some of the gentry's refinements of behavior and speech.

10 The Coles's business house or firm in London.

11 Social ambitions.

12 It is notable here that Emma is far more rigidly class-conscious and anxious about the Coles's economic mobility than are most of her social peers in Highbury (see vol. I, chap. 8).

This was the occurrence:—The Coles had been settled some years in Highbury, and were very good sort of people—friendly, liberal, and unpretending; but, on the other hand, they were of low origin, in trade, and only moderately genteel.[9] On their first coming into the country, they had lived in proportion to their income, quietly, keeping little company, and that little unexpensively; but the last year or two had brought them a considerable increase of means—the house in town[10] had yielded greater profits, and fortune in general had smiled on them. With their wealth, their views[11] increased; their want of a larger house, their inclination for more company. They added to their house, to their number of servants, to their expenses of every sort; and by this time were, in fortune and style of living, second only to the family at Hartfield. Their love of society, and their new dining-room, prepared every body for their keeping dinner-company; and a few parties, chiefly among the single men, had already taken place. The regular and best families Emma could hardly suppose they would presume to invite—neither Donwell, nor Hartfield, nor Randalls. Nothing should tempt *her* to go, if they did; and she regretted that her father's known habits would be giving her refusal less meaning than she could wish. The Coles were very respectable in their way, but they ought to be taught that it was not for them to arrange the terms on which the superior families would visit them. This lesson, she very much feared, they would receive only from herself; she had little hope of Mr. Knightley, none of Mr. Weston.[12]

But she had made up her mind how to meet this presumption so many weeks before it appeared, that when the insult came at last, it found her very differently affected. Donwell and Randalls had received their invitation, and none had come for her father and herself; and Mrs. Weston's accounting for it with "I suppose they will not take the liberty with you; they know you do not dine out," was not quite sufficient. She felt that she should like to have had the power of refusal; and afterwards, as the idea of the party to be assembled there, consisting precisely of those whose society was dearest to her, occurred again and again, she did not know that she might not have been tempted to accept. Harriet was to be there in the evening, and the Bateses. They had been speaking of it as they walked about Highbury the day before, and Frank Churchill had most earnestly lamented her absence. Might not the evening end in a dance? had been a question of his. The bare possibility of it acted as a further irritation on her spirits; and her being left in solitary grandeur,[13] even supposing the omission to be intended as a compliment, was but poor comfort.

It was the arrival of this very invitation while the Westons were at Hartfield, which made their presence so acceptable; for though her first remark, on reading it, was that "of course it must be declined," she so very soon proceeded to ask them what they advised her to do, that their advice for her going was most prompt and successful.

She owned that, considering every thing, she was not absolutely without inclination for the party. The Coles expressed themselves so properly[14]—there was so much real attention in the manner of it—so much consideration for her father. "They would have solicited the honour earlier, but had been waiting[15] the arrival of a folding-screen from London, which they hoped might keep Mr. Woodhouse from any draught of air, and therefore induce him the more readily to give them the honour of his company." Upon the whole, she was very persuadable; and it being briefly settled among themselves how it might be done without neglecting his comfort—how certainly Mrs. Goddard, if not Mrs. Bates, might be depended on for bearing him company—Mr. Woodhouse was to be talked into an acquiescence of his daughter's going out to dinner on a day now near at hand, and spending the whole evening away from him. As for *his* going, Emma did not wish him to think it possible; the hours would be too late, and the party too numerous. He was soon pretty well resigned.

"I am not fond of dinner-visiting," said he—"I never was. No more is Emma. Late hours do not agree with us. I am sorry Mr. and Mrs. Cole should have done it. I think it would be much better if they would come in one afternoon next summer, and take their tea with us—take us in their afternoon walk; which they might do, as our hours are so reasonable, and yet get home without being out in the damp of the evening. The dews of a summer evening are what I would not expose any body to. However, as they are so very desirous to have dear Emma dine with them, and as you will both be there, and Mr.

13 Splendid isolation.

14 That is, according to the rules of epistolary etiquette.

15 Awaiting.

Regency mahogany four-fold screen with foliate cresting, c. 1815.

Knightley too, to take care of her, I cannot wish to prevent it, provided the weather be what it ought, neither damp, nor cold, nor windy." Then turning to Mrs. Weston, with a look of gentle reproach—"Ah! Miss Taylor, if you had not married, you would have staid at home with me."

"Well sir," cried Mr. Weston, "as I took Miss Taylor away, it is incumbent on me to supply her place, if I can; and I will step to Mrs. Goddard in a moment, if you wish it."

But the idea of any thing to be done in a *moment,* was increasing, not lessening Mr. Woodhouse's agitation. The ladies knew better how to allay it. Mr. Weston must be quiet, and every thing deliberately arranged.

With this treatment, Mr. Woodhouse was soon composed enough for talking as usual. "He should be happy to see Mrs. Goddard. He had a great regard for Mrs. Goddard; and Emma should write a line, and invite her. James could take the note. But first of all, there must be an answer written to Mrs. Cole."

"You will make my excuses, my dear, as civilly as possible. You will say that I am quite an invalid, and go no where, and therefore must decline their obliging invitation; beginning with my *compliments,* of course. But you will do every thing right. I need not tell you what is to be done. We must remember to let James know that the carriage will be wanted on Tuesday. I shall have no fears for you with him. We have never been there above once since the new approach was made; but still I have no doubt that James will take you very safely. And when you get there, you must tell him at what time you would have him come for you again; and you had better name an early hour. You will not like staying late. You will get very tired when tea is over."

"But you would not wish me to come away before I am tired, papa?"

"Oh! no, my love; but you will soon be tired. There will be a great many people talking at once. You will not like the noise."

"But, my dear sir," cried Mr. Weston, "if Emma comes away early, it will be breaking up the party."

"And no great harm if it does," said Mr. Woodhouse. "The sooner every party breaks up, the better."

"But you do not consider how it may appear to the Coles. Emma's going away directly after tea might be giving offence. They are good-natured people, and think little of their own claims; but still they must feel that any body's hurrying away is no great compliment; and Miss Woodhouse's doing it would be more thought of than any other person's in the room. You would not wish to disappoint and mortify the Coles, I am sure, sir; friendly, good sort of people as ever lived, and who have been your neighbours these *ten* years."

"No, upon no account in the world. Mr. Weston, I am much obliged to you for reminding me. I should be extremely sorry to be giving them any pain. I know what worthy people they are. Perry tells me that Mr. Cole never touches malt liquor.[16] You would not think it to look at him, but he is bilious—Mr. Cole is very bilious. No, I would not be the means of giving them any pain. My dear Emma, we must consider this. I am sure, rather than run the risk of hurting Mr. and Mrs. Cole, you would stay a little longer than you might wish. You will not regard being tired. You will be perfectly safe, you know, among your friends."

"Oh, yes, papa. I have no fears at all for myself; and I should have no scruples of staying as late as Mrs. Weston, but on your account. I am only afraid of your sitting up for me. I am not afraid of your not being exceedingly comfortable with Mrs. Goddard. She loves piquet,[17] you know; but when she is gone home, I am afraid you will be sitting up by yourself, instead of going to bed at your usual time—and the idea of that would entirely destroy my comfort. You must promise me not to sit up."

He did, on the condition of some promises on her side: such as that, if she came home cold, she would be sure to warm herself thoroughly; if hungry, that she would take something to eat; that her own maid should sit up for her; and that Serle and the butler should see that every thing were safe in the house, as usual.

16 Beer or ale.

17 A two-handed card game, almost certainly originating in fifteenth-century France. Rev. Primrose teaches his daughters to play piquet in vol. I, chap. 16, of *The Vicar of Wakefield*.

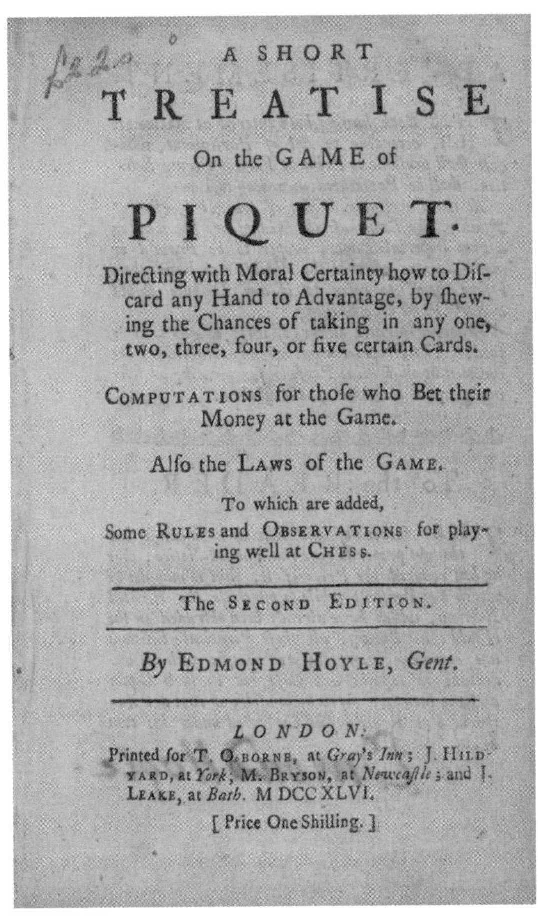

A SHORT
TREATISE
On the GAME of
PIQUET.
Directing with Moral Certainty how to Discard any Hand to Advantage, by shewing the Chances of taking in any one, two, three, four, or five certain Cards.
COMPUTATIONS for those who Bet their Money at the Game.
Also the LAWS of the GAME.
To which are added,
Some RULES and OBSERVATIONS for playing well at CHESS.

The SECOND EDITION.

By EDMOND HOYLE, *Gent.*

LONDON:
Printed for T. OSBORNE, at *Gray's Inn*; J. HILDYARD, at *York*; M. BRYSON, at *Newcastle*; and J. LEAKE, at *Bath*. M DCC XLVI.
[Price One Shilling.]

Title page of Edmund Hoyle, *A Short Treatise on the Game of Piquet* (London: F. Cogan, 1744; 2nd ed. 1746).

8

Frank Churchill came back again; and if he kept his father's dinner waiting, it was not known at Hartfield; for Mrs. Weston was too anxious for his being a favourite with Mr. Woodhouse, to betray any imperfection which could be concealed.

He came back, had had his hair cut, and laughed at himself with a very good grace, but without seeming really at all ashamed of what he had done. He had no reason to wish his hair longer, to conceal any confusion of face; no reason to wish the money unspent, to improve his spirits. He was quite as undaunted and as lively as ever; and after seeing him, Emma thus moralized to herself:—

"I do not know whether it ought to be so, but certainly silly things do cease to be silly if they are done by sensible people in an impudent way. Wickedness is always wickedness, but folly is not always folly.—It depends upon the character of those who handle it. Mr. Knightley, he is *not* a trifling, silly young man. If he were, he would have done this differently. He would either have gloried in the achievement, or been ashamed of it. There would have been either the ostentation of a coxcomb, or the evasions of a mind too weak to defend its own vanities.—No, I am perfectly sure that he is not trifling or silly."

With Tuesday came the agreeable prospect of seeing him again, and for a longer time than hitherto; of judging of his general manners, and by inference, of the meaning of his manners towards herself; of guessing how soon it might be necessary for her to throw coldness into her air; and of fancying what the observations of all those might be, who were now seeing them together for the first time.

She meant to be very happy, in spite of the scene being laid at Mr. Cole's; and without being able to forget that among the failings of Mr. Elton, even in the days of his favour, none had disturbed her more than his propensity to dine with Mr. Cole.

Her father's comfort was amply secured, Mrs. Bates as well as Mrs. Goddard being able to come; and her last pleasing duty, before she left the house, was to pay her respects to them as they sat together after dinner; and while her father was fondly noticing the beauty of her dress, to make the two ladies all the amends in her power, by helping them to large slices of cake and full glasses of wine, for whatever unwilling self-denial his care of their constitution might have obliged them to practise during the meal.—She had provided a plentiful dinner for them; she wished she could know that they had been allowed to eat it.

She followed another carriage to Mr. Cole's door; and was pleased to see that it was Mr. Knightley's; for Mr. Knightley keeping no horses,[1] having little spare money and a great deal of health, activity, and independence, was too apt, in Emma's opinion, to get about as he could, and not use his carriage so often as became the owner of Donwell Abbey. She had an opportunity now of speaking her approbation while warm from her heart, for he stopped to hand her out.

"This is coming as you should do," said she, "like a gentleman.—I am quite glad to see you."

He thanked her, observing, "How lucky that we should arrive at the same moment! for, if we had met first in the drawing-room, I doubt whether you would have discerned me to be more of a gentleman than usual.—You might not have distinguished how I came, by my look or manner."

"Yes I should, I am sure I should. There is always a look of consciousness or bustle when people come in a way which they know to be beneath them. You think you carry it off very well, I dare say, but with you it is a sort of bravado, an air of affected unconcern; I always observe it whenever I meet you under those circumstances. *Now*

1 Having no dedicated carriage horses.

A Broadwood square piano, c. 1813; photograph courtesy of Lucy Coad. Square pianofortes were the most popular domestic instruments at the time, since they were considerably less expensive, and required less space, than grand pianos.

you have nothing to try for. You are not afraid of being supposed ashamed. You are not striving to look taller than any body else. *Now* I shall really be very happy to walk into the same room with you."

"Nonsensical girl!" was his reply, but not at all in anger.

Emma had as much reason to be satisfied with the rest of the party as with Mr. Knightley. She was received with a cordial respect which could not but please, and given all the consequence she could wish for. When the Westons arrived, the kindest looks of love, the strongest of admiration were for her, from both husband and wife; the son approached her with a cheerful eagerness which marked her as his peculiar object, and at dinner she found him seated by her[2]—and, as she firmly believed, not without some dexterity[3] on his side.

The party was rather large, as it included one other family, a proper unobjectionable country family, whom the Coles had the advantage of naming among their acquaintance, and the male part of Mr. Cox's family, the lawyer of Highbury. The less worthy females were to come

2 John Trusler offers the following summary of the etiquette of dinner seating:

> In all public companies precedence is attended to, and particularly at table. Women have here always taken place of men, and both men and women have sat above each other, according to the rank they bear in life. Where a company is equal in point of rank, married ladies take place of single ones, and older ones of younger ones.
>
> When dinner is announced, the mistress of the house requests the lady first in rank, in company, to shew the way to the rest, and walk first into the room where the table is served; she then asks the second in precedence to follow, and after all the ladies are passed, she brings up the rear herself. The master of the house does the same with the gentlemen . . .
>
> When they enter the dining-room, each takes his place in the same order; the mistress of the table sits at the upper-end, those of superior rank next her, right and left, those next in rank following, then the gentlemen, and the master at the lower-end, and nothing is considered as a greater mark of ill-breeding, than for a person to interrupt this order, or seat himself higher than he ought. Custom, however, has lately introduced a new mode of seating. A gentleman and a lady sitting alternately round the table, and this, for the better convenience of a lady's being attended to, and served by the gentleman next her. But notwithstanding this promiscuous seating, the ladies whether above or below, are to be served in order, according to their rank or age, and after them the gentlemen, in the same manner.

The Honours of the Table, or, Rules for Behaviour During Meals (Dublin: W. Sleater, 1791), pp. 4–5.

3 Artful contrivance.

in the evening, with Miss Bates, Miss Fairfax, and Miss Smith; but already, at dinner, they were too numerous for any subject of conversation to be general; and while politics and Mr. Elton were talked over, Emma could fairly surrender all her attention to the pleasantness of her neighbour. The first remote sound to which she felt herself obliged to attend, was the name of Jane Fairfax. Mrs. Cole seemed to be relating something of her that was expected to be very interesting. She listened, and found it well worth listening to. That very dear part of Emma, her fancy, received an amusing supply. Mrs. Cole was telling that she had been calling on Miss Bates, and as soon as she entered the room had been struck by the sight of a pianoforté—a very elegant looking instrument—not a grand, but a large-sized square pianoforté;[4] and the substance of the story, the end of all the dialogue which ensued of surprize, and inquiry, and congratulations on her side, and explanations on Miss Bates's, was, that this pianoforté had arrived from Broadwood's[5] the day before, to the great astonishment of both aunt and niece—entirely unexpected; that at first, by Miss Bates's account, Jane herself was quite at a loss, quite bewildered to think who could possibly have ordered it—but now, they were both perfectly satisfied that it could be from only one quarter;—of course it must be from Col. Campbell.

"One can suppose nothing else," added Mrs. Cole, "and I was only surprized that there could ever have been a doubt. But Jane, it seems, had a letter from them very lately, and not a word was said about it. She knows their ways best; but I should not consider their silence as any reason for their not meaning to make the present. They might chuse to surprize her."

Mrs. Cole had many to agree with her; every body who spoke on the subject was equally convinced that it must come from Col. Campbell, and equally rejoiced that such a present had been made; and there were enough ready to speak to allow Emma to think her own way, and still listen to Mrs. Cole.

"I declare, I do not know when I have heard any thing that has given me more satisfaction!—It always has quite hurt me that Jane Fairfax, who plays so delightfully, should not have an instrument. It seemed quite a shame, especially considering how many houses there

4 The square piano was the home piano of choice at the time.

5 A famous English piano company, dating in its original form from 1728, and still in business today. John Broadwood (1732–1812) was apprenticed to the firm of Burkat Shudi (1702–1773) in 1761, became a partner in 1769, and the company became John Broadwood & Son in 1795. Shudi had originally specialized in both harpsichords and pianos, but the company came to concentrate primarily on pianos as harpsichords fell out of fashion, becoming solely a piano manufacturer after 1793. Broadwood's made a significant contribution to the development of piano design—not least in improving and popularizing the square piano. Katalin Komlós discusses Broadwood's career in *Fortepianos and Their Music: Germany, Austria, and England, 1760–1800* (Oxford: Clarendon Press, 1995), pp. 3–16.

A Broadwood grand piano, 1801, from Temple Newsam House, Leeds; photograph courtesy of Lucy Coad. It is a measure of the Cole family's rising status that they not only can afford a grand but have the room to keep it.

are where fine instruments are absolutely thrown away. This is like giving ourselves a slap, to be sure! and it was but yesterday I was telling Mr. Cole, I really was ashamed to look at our new grand pianoforté[6] in the drawing-room, while I do not know one note from another, and our little girls, who are but just beginning, perhaps may never make any thing of it; and there is poor Jane Fairfax, who is mistress of music, has not any thing of the nature of an instrument, not even the pitifullest old spinnet[7] in the world, to amuse herself with. —I was saying this to Mr. Cole but yesterday, and he quite agreed with me; only he is so particularly fond of music that he could not help indulging himself in the purchase, hoping that some of our good neighbours might be so obliging occasionally to put it to a better use than we can; and that really is the reason why the instrument was bought—or else I am sure we ought to be ashamed of it.—We are in great hopes that Miss Woodhouse may be prevailed with to try it this evening."

Miss Woodhouse made the proper acquiescence; and finding that nothing more was to be entrapped from any communication of Mrs. Cole's, turned to Frank Churchill.

"Why do you smile?" said she.

"Nay, why do you?"

Me!—I suppose I smile for pleasure at Col. Campbell's being so rich and so liberal.—It is a handsome present."

"Very."

"I rather wonder that it was never made before."

"Perhaps Miss Fairfax has never been staying here so long before."

"Or that he did not give her the use of their own instrument—which must now be shut up in London, untouched by any body."

"That is a grand pianoforté, and he might think it too large for Mrs. Bates's house."

"You may *say* what you chuse—but your countenance testifies that your *thoughts* on this subject are very much like mine."

"I do not know. I rather believe you are giving me more credit for acuteness than I deserve. I smile because you smile, and shall proba-

6 That the Coles own a grand rather than a square piano indicates both the comfortable size of their rooms and the extent of their disposable income. As Komlós notes, "[s]quares were much more saleable than grands . . . their price being one-third of that of a grand piano" (*Fortepianos and Their Music,* p. 10).

7 A smaller relation of the harpsichord, especially popular in eighteenth-century Britain. Unlike the harpsichord, the spinet has only one string per note, making for a thinner timbre.

Mezzotint portrait of John Broadwood (1732–1812) by William Say after John Harrison, Jr., 1812. Broadwood was the pioneer of piano design and manufacture at the turn of the nineteenth century, and his company is still in business today.

Franz Xaver Wagenschön, *Marie-Antoinette at the Spinet,* 1768.

bly suspect whatever I find you suspect; but at present I do not see what there is to question. If Col. Campbell is not the person, who can be?"

"What do you say to Mrs. Dixon?"

"Mrs. Dixon! very true indeed. I had not thought of Mrs. Dixon. She must know as well as her father, how acceptable an instrument would be; and perhaps the mode of it, the mystery, the surprize, is more like a young woman's scheme than an elderly man's. It is Mrs. Dixon I dare say. I told you that your suspicions would guide mine."

"If so, you must extend your suspicions and comprehend *Mr.* Dixon in them."

"Mr. Dixon.—Very well. Yes, I immediately perceive that it must be the joint present of Mr. and Mrs. Dixon. We were speaking the other day, you know, of his being so warm an admirer of her performance."

"Yes, and what you told me on that head, confirmed an idea which I had entertained before.—I do not mean to reflect upon the good intentions of either Mr. Dixon or Miss Fairfax, but I cannot help suspecting either that, after making his proposals to her friend, he had the misfortune to fall in love with *her,* or that he became conscious of a little attachment on her side. One might guess twenty things without guessing exactly the right; but I am sure there must be a particular cause for her chusing to come to Highbury instead of going with the Campbells to Ireland. Here, she must be leading a life of privation and penance; there it would have been all enjoyment. As to the pretence of trying her native air, I look upon that as a mere excuse.—In the summer it might have passed; but what can any body's native air do for them in the months of January, February, and March? Good fires and carriages would be much more to the purpose in most cases of delicate health, and I dare say in her's. I do not require you to adopt all my suspicions, though you make so noble a profession of doing it, but I honestly tell you what they are."

"And, upon my word, they have an air of great probability. Mr. Dixon's preference of her music to her friend's, I can answer for being very decided."

"And then, he saved her life. Did you ever hear of that?—A water-party; and by some accident she was falling overboard. He caught her."

"He did. I was there—one of the party."

"Were you really?—Well!—But you observed nothing of course, for it seems to be a new idea to you.—If I had been there, I think I should have made some discoveries."

"I dare say you would; but I, simple I, saw nothing but the fact, that Miss Fairfax was nearly dashed from the vessel and that Mr Dixon caught her.—It was the work of a moment.[8] And though the consequent shock and alarm was very great and much more durable—indeed I believe it was half an hour before any of us were comfortable again—yet that was too general a sensation for any thing of peculiar anxiety to be observable. I do not mean to say, however, that you might not have made discoveries."

The conversation was here interrupted. They were called on to share in the awkwardness of a rather long interval between the courses,[9] and obliged to be as formal and as orderly as the others; but when the table was again safely covered, when every corner dish[10] was placed exactly right, and occupation and ease were generally restored, Emma said,

"The arrival of this pianoforté is decisive with me. I wanted to know a little more, and this tells me quite enough. Depend upon it, we shall soon hear that it is a present from Mr. and Mrs. Dixon."

"And if the Dixons should absolutely deny all knowledge of it, we must conclude it to come from the Campbells."

"No, I am sure it is not from the Campbells. Miss Fairfax knows it is not from the Campbells, or they would have been guessed at first. She would not have been puzzled, had she dared fix on them. I may not have convinced you perhaps, but I am perfectly convinced myself that Mr. Dixon is a principal in the business."

"Indeed you injure me if you suppose me unconvinced. Your reasonings carry my judgment along with them entirely. At first, while I supposed you satisfied that Col. Campbell was the giver, I saw it only as paternal kindness, and thought it the most natural thing in the

8 Compare the narratorial account of the aftermath of Louisa Musgrove's fall from the Cobb at Lyme Regis, in vol. I, chap. 12, of *Persuasion:*

> "A surgeon!" said Anne.
>
> He caught the word; it seemed to rouse him at once, and saying only "True, true, a surgeon this instant," was darting away, when Anne eagerly suggested,
>
> "Captain Benwick, would it not be better for Captain Benwick? He knows where a surgeon is to be found."
>
> Every one capable of thinking felt the advantage of the idea, and in a moment (it was all done in rapid moments) Captain Benwick had resigned the poor corpse-like figure to the brother's care, and was off to the town with the utmost rapidity.

9 Suggesting that the Coles's domestic staff have not yet fully mastered the timing of a large formal dinner.

10 Small dishes of accompaniments were often placed at the corners of the dining table during formal dinners; Hannah Glasse's suggestions for corner-dish recipes include forced (stuffed) hog's ears, pickled cock's combs, stewed cucumbers, and stewed red cabbage.

world. But when you mentioned Mrs. Dixon, I felt how much more probable that it should be the tribute of warm female friendship. And now I can see it in no other light than as an offering of love."

There was no occasion to press the matter farther. The conviction seemed real; he looked as if he felt it. She said no more, other subjects took their turn; and the rest of the dinner passed away; the dessert[11] succeeded, the children came in, and were talked to and admired amid the usual rate of conversation; a few clever things said, a few downright silly, but by much the larger proportion neither the one nor the other—nothing worse than every day remarks, dull repetitions, old news, and heavy[12] jokes.

The ladies had not been long in the drawing-room, before the other ladies, in their different divisions, arrived. Emma watched the entrée[13] of her own particular little friend; and if she could not exult in her dignity and grace, she could not only love the blooming sweetness and the artless manner, but could most heartily rejoice in that light, cheerful, unsentimental disposition which allowed her so many alleviations of pleasure, in the midst of the pangs of disappointed affection. There she sat—and who would have guessed how many tears she had been lately shedding? To be in company, nicely dressed herself and seeing others nicely dressed, to sit and smile and look pretty, and say nothing, was enough for the happiness of the present hour. Jane Fairfax did look and move superior; but Emma suspected she might have been glad to change feelings with Harriet, very glad to have purchased the mortification of having loved—yes, of having loved even Mr. Elton in vain—by the surrender of all the dangerous pleasure of knowing herself beloved by the husband of her friend.

In so large a party it was not necessary that Emma should approach her. She did not wish to speak of the pianoforté, she felt too much in the secret herself, to think the appearance of curiosity or interest fair, and therefore purposely kept at a distance; but by the others, the subject was almost immediately introduced, and she saw the blush of consciousness[14] with which congratulations were received, the blush of guilt which accompanied the name of "my excellent friend Col. Campbell."

11 Dessert followed the second course and would consist of dried fruits and other items that could be eaten by hand, the majority of the table having been cleared just beforehand. As the novel shows, the "cheese course" was also gaining in popularity. Maggie Lane points out that dessert often marked the first appearance of wine (*Jane Austen and Food* [London: The Hambledon Press, 1995], p. 45).

12 Labored.

13 As hinted at by the Gallic form, "entrée" in Austen's time denoted not only the simple act of entering a room but also the act of "making an entrance" at a fashionable social event. For example, in vol. I, chap. 4, of Edgeworth's novel *Patronage,* Commissioner Falconer compliments Miss Hauton by noting: "Such an entrée!—So much the air of a woman of fashion!"

14 Self-consciousness, but also with a strong connotation of having something to conceal.

Mrs. Weston, kind-hearted and musical, was particularly interested by the circumstance, and Emma could not help being amused at her perseverance in dwelling on the subject; and having so much to ask and to say as to tone, touch,[15] and pedal, totally unsuspicious of that wish of saying as little about it as possible, which she plainly read in the fair heroine's countenance.

They were soon joined by some of the gentlemen; and the very first of the early was Frank Churchill. In he walked, the first and the handsomest; and after paying his compliments en passant to Miss Bates and her niece, made his way directly to the opposite side of the circle, where sat Miss Woodhouse; and till he could find a seat by her, would not sit at all. Emma divined what every body present must be thinking. She was his object, and every body must perceive it. She introduced him to her friend, Miss Smith, and, at convenient moments afterwards, heard what each thought of the other. "He had never seen so lovely a face, and was delighted with her naïveté." And she,—"Only to be sure it was paying him too great a compliment, but she did think there were some looks a little like Mr. Elton." Emma restrained her indignation, and only turned from her in silence.

Smiles of intelligence passed between her and the gentleman on first glancing towards Miss Fairfax; but it was most prudent to avoid speech. He told her that he had been impatient to leave the dining-room—hated sitting long—was always the first to move when he could—that his father, Mr. Knightley, Mr. Cox, and Mr. Cole, were left very busy over parish business—that as long as he had staid, however, it had been pleasant enough, as he found them in general a set of gentlemen-like, sensible men; and spoke so handsomely of Highbury altogether—thought it so abundant in agreeable families—that Emma began to feel she had been used to despise the place rather too much. She questioned him as to the society in Yorkshire—the extent of the neighbourhood about Enscombe, and the sort; and could make out from his answers that, as far as Enscombe was concerned, there was very little going on; that their visitings were among a range of great families, none very near; and that even when days were fixed, and invitations accepted, it was an even chance that Mrs. Churchill were not in health or spirits for going; that they made a

15 The lightness or heaviness of the keyboard's action.

16 Effort.

point of visiting no fresh person; and that, though he had his separate engagements, it was not without difficulty, without considerable address[16] *at times,* that he could get away, or introduce an acquaintance for a night.

She saw that Enscombe could not satisfy, and that Highbury, taken in its best, might reasonably please a young man who had more retirement at home than he liked. His importance at Enscombe was very evident. He did not boast, but it naturally betrayed itself, that he had persuaded his aunt where his uncle could do nothing, and on her laughing and noticing it, he owned that he believed (excepting one or two points) he could *with time* persuade her to any thing. One of those points on which his influence failed, he then mentioned. He had wanted very much to go abroad—had been very eager indeed to be allowed to travel—but she would not hear of it. This had happened the year before. *Now,* he said, he was beginning to have no longer the same wish.

The unpersuadable point, which he did not mention, Emma guessed to be good behaviour to his father.

"I have made a most wretched discovery," said he, after a short pause.—"I have been here a week to-morrow—half my time. I never knew days fly so fast. A week to-morrow!—And I have hardly begun to enjoy myself. But just got acquainted with Mrs. Weston, and others!—I hate the recollection."

"Perhaps you may now begin to regret that you spent one whole day, out of so few, in having your hair cut."

"No," said he, smiling, "that is no subject of regret at all. I have no pleasure in seeing my friends, unless I can believe myself fit to be seen."

The rest of the gentlemen being now in the room, Emma found herself obliged to turn from him for a few minutes, and listen to Mr. Cole. When Mr. Cole had moved away, and her attention could be restored as before, she saw Frank Churchill looking intently across the room at Miss Fairfax, who was sitting exactly opposite.

"What is the matter?" said she.

He started. "Thank you for rousing me," he replied. "I believe I have been very rude; but really Miss Fairfax has done her hair in so odd a way—so very odd a way—that I cannot keep my eyes from her. I never saw any thing so outrée![17]—Those curls!—This must be a fancy of her own. I see nobody else looking like her!—I must go and ask her whether it is an Irish fashion. Shall I?—Yes, I will—I declare I will—and you shall see how she takes it;—whether she colours."

He was gone immediately; and Emma soon saw him standing before Miss Fairfax, and talking to her; but as to its effect on the young lady, as he had improvidently placed himself exactly between them, exactly in front of Miss Fairfax, she could absolutely distinguish nothing.

Before he could return to his chair, it was taken by Mrs. Weston.

"This is the luxury of a large party," said she:—"one can get near every body, and say every thing. My dear Emma, I am longing to talk to you. I have been making discoveries and forming plans, just like yourself, and I must tell them while the idea is fresh. Do you know how Miss Bates and her niece came here?"

"How!—They were invited, were not they?"

"Oh! yes—but how they were conveyed hither?—the manner of their coming?"

"They walked, I conclude. How else could they come?"

"Very true.—Well, a little while ago it occurred to me how very sad it would be to have Jane Fairfax walking home again, late at night, and cold as the nights are now. And as I looked at her, though I never saw her appear to more advantage, it struck me that she was heated, and would therefore be particularly liable to take cold. Poor girl! I could not bear the idea of it; so, as soon as Mr. Weston came into the room, and I could get at him, I spoke to him about the carriage. You may guess how readily he came into my wishes;[18] and having his approbation, I made my way directly to Miss Bates, to assure her that the carriage would be at her service before it took us home; for I thought it would be making her comfortable at once. Good soul! she was as grateful as possible, you may be sure. 'Nobody was ever so fortunate as herself!'—but with many, many thanks,—'there was no occasion to trouble us, for Mr. Knightley's carriage had brought, and was to take them home again.' I was quite surprized;—very glad, I am sure; but really quite surprized. Such a very kind attention—and

17 Excessive, bizarre. Frank Churchill's use of the Gallicism chimes with Knightley's assessment of him as modishly "aimable."

18 Concurred with my plans.

so thoughtful an attention!—the sort of thing that so few men would think of. And, in short, from knowing his usual ways, I am very much inclined to think that it was for their accommodation the carriage was used at all. I do suspect he would not have had a pair of horses for himself, and that it was only as an excuse for assisting them."

"Very likely," said Emma—"nothing more likely. I know no man more likely than Mr. Knightley to do the sort of thing—to do any thing really good-natured, useful, considerate, or benevolent. He is not a gallant man, but he is a very humane[19] one; and this, considering Jane Fairfax's ill health, would appear a case of humanity to him;—and for an act of un-ostentatious kindness, there is nobody whom I would fix on more than on Mr. Knightley. I know he had horses to-day—for we arrived together; and I laughed at him about it, but he said not a word that could betray."

"Well," said Mrs. Weston, smiling, "you give him credit for more simple, disinterested benevolence in this instance than I do; for while Miss Bates was speaking, a suspicion darted into my head, and I have never been able to get it out again. The more I think of it, the more probable it appears. In short, I have made a match between Mr. Knightley and Jane Fairfax. See the consequence of keeping you company!—What do you say to it?"

"Mr. Knightley and Jane Fairfax!" exclaimed Emma. "Dear Mrs. Weston, how could you think of such a thing?—Mr. Knightley!—Mr. Knightley must not marry!—You would not have little Henry cut out from Donwell?[20]—Oh! no, no, Henry must have Donwell. I cannot at all consent to Mr. Knightley's marrying; and I am sure it is not at all likely. I am amazed that you should think of such a thing."

"My dear Emma, I have told you what led me to think of it. I do not want the match—I do not want to injure dear little Henry—but the idea has been given me by circumstances; and if Mr. Knightley really wished to marry, you would not have him refrain on Henry's account, a boy of six years old, who knows nothing of the matter?"

"Yes, I would. I could not bear to have Henry supplanted.—Mr. Knightley marry!—No, I have never had such an idea, and I cannot adopt it now. And Jane Fairfax, too, of all women!"

19 "Kind; civil; benevolent; good-natured" (Johnson).

20 In the absence of any children from the elder brother, John Knightley's eldest son, Henry, would be the heir presumptive to the Donwell estate.

"Nay, she has always been a first favourite with him, as you very well know."

"But the imprudence of such a match!"

"I am not speaking of its prudence; merely its probability."

"I see no probability in it, unless you have any better foundation than what you mention. His good-nature, his humanity, as I tell you, would be quite enough to account for the horses. He has a great regard for the Bateses, you know, independent of Jane Fairfax—and is always glad to shew them attention. My dear Mrs. Weston, do not take to match-making. You do it very ill. Jane Fairfax mistress of the Abbey!—Oh! no, no;—every feeling revolts. For his own sake, I would not have him do so mad a thing."

"Imprudent, if you please—but not mad. Excepting inequality of fortune, and perhaps a little disparity of age, I can see nothing unsuitable."

"But Mr. Knightley does not want to marry. I am sure he has not the least idea of it. Do not put it into his head. Why should he marry?—He is as happy as possible by himself; with his farm, and his sheep, and his library, and all the parish to manage; and he is extremely fond of his brother's children. He has no occasion to marry, either to fill up his time or his heart."

"My dear Emma, as long as he thinks so, it is so; but if he really loves Jane Fairfax——"

"Nonsense! He does not care about Jane Fairfax. In the way of love, I am sure he does not. He would do any good to her, or her family; but——"

"Well," said Mrs. Weston, laughing, "perhaps the greatest good he could do them, would be to give Jane such a respectable home."

"If it would be good to her, I am sure it would be evil to himself; a very shameful and degrading connection. How would he bear to have Miss Bates belonging to him?—To have her haunting the Abbey, and thanking him all day long for his great kindness in marrying Jane?—'So very kind and obliging!—But he always had been such a very kind neighbour!'[21] And then fly off, through half a sentence, to her mother's old petticoat. 'Not that it was such a very old petticoat

21 Another example of Emma's ominous facility with Miss Bates's vocabulary and mannerisms.

either—for still it would last a great while—and, indeed, she must thankfully say that their petticoats were all very strong.'"

"For shame, Emma! Do not mimic her. You divert me against my conscience.[22] And, upon my word, I do not think Mr. Knightley would be much disturbed by Miss Bates. Little things do not irritate him. She might talk on; and if he wanted to say any thing himself, he would only talk louder, and drown her voice. But the question is not, whether it would be a bad connexion for him, but whether he wishes it; and I think he does. I have heard him speak, and so must you, so very highly of Jane Fairfax! The interest he takes in her—his anxiety about her health—his concern that she should have no happier prospect! I have heard him express himself so warmly on those points!—Such an admirer of her performance on the pianoforté, and of her voice! I have heard him say that he could listen to her for ever. Oh! and I had almost forgotten one idea that occurred to me—this pianoforté that has been sent her by somebody—though we have all been so well satisfied to consider it a present from the Campbells, may it not be from Mr. Knightley? I cannot help suspecting him. I think he is just the person to do it, even without being in love."

"Then it can be no argument to prove that he is in love. But I do not think it is at all a likely thing for him to do. Mr. Knightley does nothing mysteriously."

"I have heard him lamenting her having no instrument repeatedly; oftener than I should suppose such a circumstance would, in the common course of things, occur to him."

"Very well; and if he had intended to give her one, he would have told her so."

"There might be scruples of delicacy, my dear Emma. I have a very strong notion that it comes from him. I am sure he was particularly silent when Mrs. Cole told us of it at dinner."

"You take up an idea, Mrs. Weston, and run away with it; as you have many a time reproached me with doing. I see no sign of attachment—I believe nothing of the pianoforté—and proof only shall convince me that Mr. Knightley has any thought of marrying Jane Fairfax."

22 Amuse me against my better judgment.

They combated the point some time longer in the same way; Emma rather gaining ground over the mind of her friend; for Mrs. Weston was the most used of the two to yield; till a little bustle in the room shewed them that tea was over, and the instrument in preparation;—and at the same moment Mr. Cole approaching to entreat Miss Woodhouse would do them the honour of trying it. Frank Churchill, of whom, in the eagerness of her conversation with Mrs. Weston, she had been seeing nothing, except that he had found a seat by Miss Fairfax, followed Mr. Cole, to add his very pressing entreaties; and as, in every respect, it suited Emma best to lead, she gave a very proper compliance.

She knew the limitations of her own powers too well to attempt more than she could perform with credit; she wanted neither taste nor spirit in the little things which are generally acceptable, and could accompany her own voice well. One accompaniment to her song took her agreeably by surprize—a second, slightly but correctly taken by Frank Churchill.[23] Her pardon was duly begged at the close of the song, and every thing usual followed. He was accused of having a delightful voice, and a perfect knowledge of music; which was properly denied; and that he knew nothing of the matter, and had no voice at all, roundly asserted. They sang together once more; and Emma would then resign her place to Miss Fairfax, whose performance, both vocal and instrumental, she never could attempt to conceal from herself, was infinitely superior to her own.

With mixed feelings, she seated herself at a little distance from the numbers round the instrument, to listen. Frank Churchill sang again. They had sung together once or twice, it appeared, at Weymouth. But the sight of Mr. Knightley among the most attentive, soon drew away half Emma's mind; and she fell into a train of thinking on the subject of Mrs. Weston's suspicions, to which the sweet sounds of the united voices gave only momentary interruptions. Her objections to Mr. Knightley's marrying did not in the least subside. She could see nothing but evil in it. It would be a great disappointment to Mr. John Knightley; consequently to Isabella. A real injury to the children—a most mortifying change, and material loss to them

23 In other words, Frank has joined in with the vocal harmony, quietly but in tune. Another suggestive employment of vocal harmony for dramatic effect occurs in vol. I, chap. 11, of *Mansfield Park*. The wavering of Edmund Bertram's attentions and affections between Fanny Price and Mary Crawford is played out in space and sound, as his astronomical conversation with Fanny is curtailed by the three-part glee being performed across the room:

> "We must go out on the lawn for that. Should you be afraid?"
>
> "Not in the least. It is a great while since we have had any star-gazing."
>
> "Yes, I do not know how it has happened." The glee began. "We will stay till this is finished, Fanny," said he, turning his back on the window; and as it advanced, she had the mortification of seeing him advance too, moving forward by gentle degrees toward the instrument, and when it ceased, he was close by the singers, among the most urgent in requesting to hear the glee again.

all;—a very great deduction from her father's daily comfort—and, as to herself, she could not at all endure the idea of Jane Fairfax at Donwell Abbey. A Mrs. Knightley for them all to give way to![24]—No—Mr. Knightley must never marry. Little Henry must remain the heir of Donwell.

Presently Mr. Knightley looked back, and came and sat down by her. They talked at first only of the performance. His admiration was certainly very warm; yet she thought, but for Mrs. Weston, it would not have struck her. As a sort of touch-stone,[25] however, she began to speak of his kindness in conveying the aunt and niece; and though his answer was in the spirit of cutting the matter short, she believed it to indicate only his disinclination to dwell on any kindness of his own.

"I often feel concerned," said she, "that I dare not make *our* carriage more useful on such occasions. It is not that I am without the wish; but you know how impossible my father would deem it that James should put-to[26] for such a purpose."

"Quite out of the question, quite out of the question," he replied;—"but you must often wish it, I am sure." And he smiled with such seeming pleasure at the conviction, that she must proceed another step.

"This present from the Campbells," said she—"This pianoforté is very kindly given."

"Yes," he replied, and without the smallest apparent embarrassment.—"But they would have done better had they given her notice of it. Surprizes are foolish things. The pleasure is not enhanced, and the inconvenience is often considerable. I should have expected better judgment in Colonel Campbell."

From that moment, Emma could have taken her oath that Mr. Knightley had had no concern in giving the instrument. But whether he were entirely free from peculiar attachment—whether there were no actual preference—remained a little longer doubtful. Towards the end of Jane's second song, her voice grew thick.

"That will do," said he, when it was finished, thinking aloud—"You have sung quite enough for one evening—now, be quiet."

Another song, however, was soon begged for. "One more;—they

24 A married woman would take precedence over unmarried women at social functions, regardless of age; this is one of the many awkwardnesses occasioned by Lydia Bennet's precipitate marriage to Wickham in *Pride and Prejudice,* although this state of affairs does not persist for long, thanks to the betrothals of Bingley to Jane, and Darcy to Elizabeth.

25 Test.

26 Harness the horses.

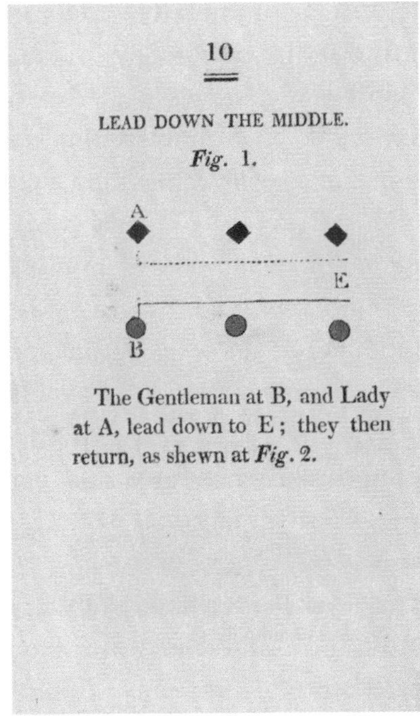

10

LEAD DOWN THE MIDDLE.

Fig. 1.

The Gentleman at B, and Lady at A, lead down to E; they then return, as shewn at *Fig.* 2.

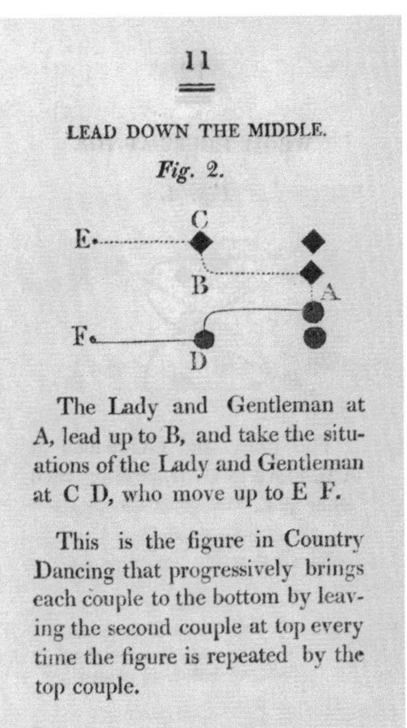

11

LEAD DOWN THE MIDDLE.

Fig. 2.

The Lady and Gentleman at A, lead up to B, and take the situations of the Lady and Gentleman at C D, who move up to E F.

This is the figure in Country Dancing that progressively brings each couple to the bottom by leaving the second couple at top every time the figure is repeated by the top couple.

Detail showing instructions for steps, from T. Wilson, *An Analysis of Country Dancing* (London: W. Calvert, 1808).

would not fatigue Miss Fairfax on any account, and would only ask for one more." And Frank Churchill was heard to say, "I think you could manage this without effort; the first part is so very trifling. The strength of the song falls on the second."

Mr. Knightley grew angry.

"That fellow," said he, indignantly, "thinks of nothing but shewing off his own voice. This must not be." And touching Miss Bates, who at that moment passed near—"Miss Bates, are you mad, to let your niece sing herself hoarse in this manner? Go, and interfere. They have no mercy on her."

Miss Bates, in her real anxiety for Jane, could hardly stay even to be grateful, before she stept forward and put an end to all further singing. Here ceased the concert part of the evening, for Miss Woodhouse and Miss Fairfax were the only young-lady-performers; but soon (within five minutes) the proposal of dancing—originating nobody exactly knew where—was so effectually promoted by Mr. and Mrs. Cole, that every thing was rapidly clearing away, to give proper space. Mrs. Weston, capital in her country-dances,[27] was seated, and beginning an irresistible waltz;[28] and Frank Churchill, coming up with most becoming gallantry to Emma, had secured her hand, and led her up to the top.

While waiting till the other young people could pair themselves off, Emma found time, in spite of the compliments she was receiving on her voice and her taste, to look about, and see what became of Mr. Knightley. This would be a trial. He was no dancer in general. If he were to be very alert in engaging Jane Fairfax now, it might augur something. There was no immediate appearance. No; he was talking to Mrs. Cole—he was looking on unconcerned; Jane was asked by somebody else, and he was still talking to Mrs. Cole.

Emma had no longer an alarm for Henry; his interest was yet safe; and she led off the dance with genuine spirit and enjoyment. Not more than five couple could be mustered; but the rarity and the suddenness of it made it very delightful, and she found herself well matched in a partner. They were a couple worth looking at.

Two dances, unfortunately, were all that could be allowed. It was growing late, and Miss Bates became anxious to get home, on her mother's account. After some attempts, therefore, to be permitted to begin again, they were obliged to thank Mrs. Weston, look sorrowful, and have done.

"Perhaps it is as well," said Frank Churchill, as he attended Emma to her carriage. "I must have asked Miss Fairfax, and her languid dancing would not have agreed with me, after your's."

27 English country dances were first collected and codified by John Playford in *The English Dancing Master* (1651). The fact that Mrs. Weston specializes in country dances may suggest the limitations of her musical skills, as opposed to Jane Fairfax's more sophisticated repertoire.

28 This reference may initially appear incongruous: after all, the waltz was a fashionable import from Germany and Austria of relatively recent vintage (it only became popular in Britain in the 1780s) and was still regarded with suspicion and derision in many quarters, owing to the potentially licentious bodily contact that its steps often demanded. In 1812 the waltz truly took over fashionable London society; although it did not convince Byron, that other fashionable sensation of 1812, who memorably depicted the craze in his poem "Waltz: An Apostrophic Hymn":

> Endearing Waltz—to thy more melting tune
> Bend Irish jig—and ancient rigadoon;
> Scotch reels avaunt!—and country-dance, forego
> Your future claims to each fantastic toe;
> Waltz—Waltz—alone both legs and arms demands,
> Liberal of feet—and lavish of her hands;
> Hands which may freely range in public sight,
> Where ne'er before—but—pray "put out the light."
> Methinks the glare of yonder chandelier
> Shines much too far—or I am much too near;
> And true, though strange—Waltz whispers this remark,
> "My slippery steps are safest in the dark."
> But here the Muse with due decorum halts,
> And lends her longest petticoat to "Waltz."

In fact, as Patrick Piggott has pointed out, what Mrs. Weston plays is a continental waltz air adapted to an English country dance; he cites Cecil Sharp and A. P. Oppé's book *The Dance: An Historical Survey of Dancing in Europe* (London & New York: Halton & Truscott Smith/Minton, Balch, 1924): "Although the dance did not reach us until 1812, numerous Collections of Waltz-airs had been published in England for twenty years or more before that date and used as Country Dance

Tunes, furnished with Country Dance figures and called Waltz Country Dances." Piggott concludes: "Obviously it was some of these tunes which Mrs Weston had ready at her finger tips for the amusement of her young friends, and the movements they performed to them were not the shocking gyrations (with couples closely 'engaged') of the recently imported waltz, but the familiar, old-fashioned figures of the English Country Dance" (*The Innocent Diversion: A Study of Music in the Life and Writings of Jane Austen* [London: D. Cleverdon, 1979], p. 93).

On literary responses to the mainstream "waltz craze," see William Childers, "Byron's *Waltz:* The Germans and their Georges," *Keats-Shelley Journal,* 18 (1969), pp. 81–95.

The English Dancing Mafter:

OR,

Plaine and eafie Rules for the Dancing of Country Dances, with the Tune to each Dance.

LONDON,

Printed by *Thomas Harper*, and are to be fold by *John Playford*, at his Shop in the Inner Temple neere the Church doore. 1651.

Frontispiece of John Playford, *The English Dancing Master* (London: Thomas Harper, 1651). Playford's work remained the standard guide to English country dancing well beyond the seventeenth century.

9

Emma did not repent her condescension[1] in going to the Coles. The visit afforded her many pleasant recollections the next day; and all that she might be supposed to have lost on the side of dignified seclusion, must be amply repaid in the splendour of popularity. She must have delighted the Coles—worthy people, who deserved to be made happy!—And left a name behind her that would not soon die away.

Perfect happiness,[2] even in memory, is not common; and there were two points on which she was not quite easy. She doubted whether she had not transgressed the duty of woman by woman, in betraying her suspicions of Jane Fairfax's feelings to Frank Churchill. It was hardly right; but it had been so strong an idea, that it would escape her, and his submission to all that she told, was a compliment to her penetration which made it difficult for her to be quite certain that she ought to have held her tongue.

The other circumstance of regret related also to Jane Fairfax; and there she had no doubt. She did unfeignedly and unequivocally regret the inferiority of her own playing and singing. She did most heartily grieve over the idleness of her childhood—and sat down and practised vigorously an hour and a half.

She was then interrupted by Harriet's coming in; and if Harriet's praise could have satisfied her, she might soon have been comforted.

"Oh! if I could but play as well as you and Miss Fairfax!"

1 "Condescend" and its cognates are terms whose semantic and social charges underwent significant change between the eighteenth and nineteenth centuries. "Condescension" initially had the relatively neutral sense of "[v]oluntary humiliation; descent from superiority; voluntary submission to equality with inferiours" (Johnson), which is largely the sense in which Austen uses it here, to indicate Emma's throwing off of class distinctions for the night. A notable Johnsonian example of this usage occurs in his "Life of Milton," in the description of the angels in *Paradise Lost:* "the virtue of Raphael is mild and placid, of easy condescension and free communication." It was only in the nineteenth century that terms like "condescend" and "condescending" acquired the more pejorative senses with which they are now more commonly associated, as in the *OED* definition of "condescending": "making a show, or assuming the air, of condescension; patronizing." For more on this word's history, and on eighteenth-century semantic change more generally, see Susie I. Tucker, *Protean Shape: A Study in Eighteenth-Century Vocabulary and Usage* (London: Athlone Press: 1967).

2 The first introduction in the novel of a phrase that will come to have great importance in vol. III, in particular at the very end of the story.

Two contemporary paintings of rural street scenes: J. M. W. Turner, *Frosty Morning* (exhibited 1813); and David Wilkie, *The Village Holiday* (1809–1811). One of the unusual features of Emma's viewing the main thoroughfare of Highbury in this chapter is that Austen narrates it almost as if it were a pictorial tableau.

"Don't class us together, Harriet. My playing is no more like her's, than a lamp is like sunshine."

"Oh! dear—I think you play the best of the two. I think you play quite as well as she does. I am sure I had much rather hear you. Every body last night said how well you played."

"Those who knew any thing about it, must have felt the difference. The truth is, Harriet, that my playing is just good enough to be praised, but Jane Fairfax's is much beyond it."

"Well, I always shall think that you play quite as well as she does, or that if there is any difference nobody would ever find it out. Mr. Cole said how much taste you had; and Mr. Frank Churchill talked a great deal about your taste, and that he valued taste much more than execution."

"Ah! but Jane Fairfax has them both, Harriet."

"Are you sure? I saw she had execution, but I did not know she had any taste. Nobody talked about it. And I hate Italian singing.[3]—There is no understanding a word of it. Besides, if she does play so very well, you know, it is no more than she is obliged to do, because she will have to teach. The Coxes were wondering last night whether she would get into any great family. How did you think the Coxes looked?"

"Just as they always do—very vulgar."

"They told me something," said Harriet rather hesitatingly, "but it is nothing of any consequence."

Emma was obliged to ask what they had told her, though fearful of its producing Mr. Elton.

"They told me—that Mr. Martin dined with them last Saturday."

"Oh!"

"He came to their father upon some business, and he asked him to stay dinner."[4]

"Oh!"

"They talked a great deal about him, especially Anne Cox. I do not know what she meant, but she asked me if I thought I should go and stay there again next summer."

"She meant to be impertinently curious, just as such an Anne Cox should be."

3 As Patrick Piggott points out, "if [Jane Fairfax's] songs *were* operatic arias, then Frank's musical attainments must have been even more considerable than one had supposed, since he sang with her, and presumably did so in Italian" (*The Innocent Diversion: A Study of Music in the Life and Writings of Jane Austen* [London: D. Cleverdon, 1979], p. 92).

4 In this construction, the preposition "to" was frequently dropped in the eighteenth and early nineteenth centuries. For example, in Letter 235 of *Clarissa* (1747–1748), Lovelace writes, "I presume Miss Rawlins had told her that she would not stay dinner" (ed. Angus Ross [Harmondsworth: Penguin, 1985], p. 799).

"She said he was very agreeable the day he dined there. He sat by her at dinner. Miss Nash thinks either of the Coxes would be very glad to marry him."

"Very likely.—I think they are, without exception, the most vulgar girls in Highbury."

Harriet had business at Ford's.—Emma thought it most prudent to go with her. Another accidental meeting with the Martins was possible, and, in her present state, would be dangerous.

Harriet, tempted by every thing and swayed by half a word, was always very long at a purchase; and while she was still hanging over muslins[5] and changing her mind, Emma went to the door for amusement.—Much could not be hoped from the traffic of even the busiest part of Highbury;—Mr. Perry walking hastily by, Mr. William Cox letting himself in at the office door, Mr. Cole's carriage horses returning from exercise, or a stray letter-boy on an obstinate mule, were the liveliest objects she could presume to expect; and when her eyes fell only on the butcher with his tray, a tidy old woman travelling homewards from shop with her full basket, two curs quarrelling over a dirty bone, and a string of dawdling children round the baker's little bow-window[6] eyeing the gingerbread,[7] she knew she had no reason to complain, and was amused enough; quite enough still to stand at the door. A mind lively and at ease, can do with seeing nothing, and can see nothing that does not answer.

She looked down the Randalls road. The scene enlarged; two persons appeared; Mrs. Weston and her son-in-law;[8] they were walking into Highbury;—to Hartfield of course. They were stopping, however, in the first place at Mrs. Bates's; whose house was a little nearer Randalls than Ford's; and had all but knocked, when Emma caught their eye.[9]—Immediately they crossed the road and came forward to her; and the agreeableness of yesterday's engagement seemed to give fresh pleasure to the present meeting. Mrs. Weston informed her that she was going to call on the Bateses, in order to hear the new instrument.

"For my companion tells me," said she, "that I absolutely promised Miss Bates last night, that I would come this morning. I was not

5 Muslin, a delicate woven cotton fabric, had been the material of choice for fashionable British women from the 1780s onward; the name derives either from "Maisolos" (the Greek name for the Indian port of Machilipatnam, where the fabric originated) or from the Iraqi city of Mosul, which was an important point on the trading route.

6 A curved bay window.

7 Hannah Glasse gives the following recipe: "Take three quarts of fine flour, two ounces of beaten ginger, a quarter of an ounce of nutmeg, cloves, and mace beat fine, but most of the last; mix all together, three quarters of a pound of fine sugar, two pounds of treacle, set it over the fire, but do not let it boil; three quarters of a pound of butter melted in the treacle, and some candied lemon and orange peel cut fine; mix all these together well: an hour will bake it in a quick oven" (*The Art of Cookery, Made Plain and Easy* [London: 1748; rev. ed., London: T. Longman, B. Law, et al., 1796], p. 312).

8 Stepson.

9 The precise sense of the phrase is ambiguous here. It might simply mean that Mrs. Weston and Frank suddenly noticed Emma's presence; however, Austen was also one of the earliest writers to use the phrase in its more intensive, intentional sense: as the *OED* puts it, "[a] person is said *to catch the eye of* another when their eyes meet, either fortuitously, or (more usually) when the one is purposely looking and thus arrests the glance of the other." The earliest *OED* citation for this sense is from Darcy's first encounter with Elizabeth in vol. I, chap. 3, of *Pride and Prejudice:* "turning round, he looked for a moment at Elizabeth, till catching her eye, he withdrew his own."

aware of it myself. I did not know that I had fixed a day, but as he says I did, I am going now."

"And while Mrs. Weston pays her visit, I may be allowed, I hope," said Frank Churchill, "to join your party and wait for her at Hartfield—if you are going home."

Mrs. Weston was disappointed.

"I thought you meant to go with me. They would be very much pleased."

"Me! I should be quite in the way. But, perhaps—I may be equally in the way here. Miss Woodhouse looks as if she did not want me. My aunt always sends me off when she is shopping. She says I fidget her to death; and Miss Woodhouse looks as if she could almost say the same. What am I to do?"

"I am here on no business of my own," said Emma, "I am only waiting for my friend. She will probably have soon done, and then we shall go home. But you had better go with Mrs. Weston and hear the instrument."

"Well—if you advise it.—But (with a smile) if Col. Campbell should have employed a careless friend, and if it should prove to have an indifferent tone—what shall I say? I shall be no support to Mrs. Weston. She might do very well by herself. A disagreeable truth would be palateable through her lips, but I am the wretchedest being in the world at a civil falsehood."[10]

"I do not believe any such thing," replied Emma.—"I am persuaded that you can be as insincere as your neighbours, when it is necessary; but there is no reason to suppose the instrument is indifferent. Quite otherwise indeed, if I understood Miss Fairfax's opinion last night."

"Do come with me," said Mrs. Weston, "if it be not very disagreeable to you. It need not detain us long. We will go to Hartfield afterwards. We will follow them to Hartfield. I really wish you to call with me. It will be felt so great an attention! and I always thought you meant it."

He could say no more; and with the hope of Hartfield to reward him, returned with Mrs. Weston to Mrs. Bates's door. Emma watched them in, and then joined Harriet at the interesting counter,

10 Another artful piece of double-talk on Frank's part, not least since it is itself a "civil falsehood." However, D. W. Harding has cogently pointed out that much of the social milieu of the whole novel is sustained by such "falsehoods": "what is the alternative," he suggests, "to some degree of polite insincerity and forbearance, making allowances, concealing boredom and irritation, in a small community where people have to go on meeting each other and minimizing the awkwardnesses created by differences in social standing and wealth, in intelligence, in education and cultural interests, in knowledge of the world; and sometimes in spite of serious quarrels?" ("Civil Falsehood in *Emma,*" in *Regulated Hatred and Other Essays on Jane Austen* [London: Athlone Press, 1998], p. 175).

—trying, with all the force of her own mind, to convince her that if she wanted plain muslin it was of no use to look at figured;[11] and that a blue ribbon, be it ever so beautiful, would still never match her yellow pattern. At last it was all settled, even to the destination of the parcel.

"Should I send it to Mrs. Goddard's, ma'am?" asked Mrs. Ford. "Yes—no—yes, to Mrs. Goddard's. Only my pattern gown[12] is at Hartfield. No, you shall send it to Hartfield, if you please. But then, Mrs. Goddard will want to see it.—And I could take the pattern gown home any day. But I shall want the ribbon directly—so it had better go to Hartfield—at least the ribbon. You could make it into two parcels, Mrs. Ford, could not you?"

"It is not worth while, Harriet, to give Mrs. Ford the trouble of two parcels."

"No more it is."

"No trouble in the world, ma'am," said the obliging Mrs. Ford.

"Oh! but indeed I would much rather have it only in one. Then, if you please, you shall send it all to Mrs. Goddard's—I do not know—No, I think, Miss Woodhouse, I may just as well have it sent to Hartfield, and take it home with me at night. What do you advise?"

"That you do not give another half-second to the subject. To Hartfield, if you please, Mrs. Ford."

"Aye, that will be much best," said Harriet, quite satisfied, "I should not at all like to have it sent to Mrs. Goddard's."

Voices approached the shop—or rather one voice and two ladies; Mrs. Weston and Miss Bates met them at the door.

"My dear Miss Woodhouse," said the latter, "I am just run across to entreat the favour of you to come and sit down with us a little while, and give us your opinion of our new instrument; you and Miss Smith. How do you do, Miss Smith?—Very well I thank you.—And I begged Mrs. Weston to come with me, that I might be sure of succeeding."

"I hope Mrs. Bates and Miss Fairfax are"——

"Very well, I am much obliged to you. My mother is delightfully well; and Jane caught no cold last night. How is Mr. Woodhouse?—I am so glad to hear such a good account. Mrs. Weston told me

11 Decorated.

12 The gown that Harriet's dressmaker would copy, or refer to as a size guide, using the material that Harriet has just bought.

you were here.—Oh! then, said I, I must run across, I am sure Miss Woodhouse will allow me just to run across and entreat her to come in; my mother will be so very happy to see her—and now we are such a nice party, she cannot refuse. 'Aye, pray do,' said Mr. Frank Churchill, 'Miss Woodhouse's opinion of the instrument will be worth having.'—But, said I, I shall be more sure of succeeding if one of you will go with me.—'Oh!' said he, 'wait half-a-minute till I have finished my job.'—For, would you believe it, Miss Woodhouse, there he is, in the most obliging manner in the world, fastening in the rivet of my mother's spectacles.—The rivet came out, you know, this morning.—So very obliging!—For my mother had no use of her spectacles—could not put them on. And, by the bye, every body ought to have two pair of spectacles; they should indeed. Jane said so. I meant to take them over to John Saunders the first thing I did, but something or other hindered me all the morning; first one thing, then another, there is no saying what, you know. At one time Patty came to say she thought the kitchen chimney wanted sweeping. Oh! said I, Patty do not come with your bad news to me. Here is the rivet of your mistress's spectacles out. Then the baked apples[13] came home,[14] Mrs. Wallis sent them by her boy; they are extremely civil and obliging to us, the Wallises, always—I have heard some people say that Mrs. Wallis can be uncivil and give a very rude answer, but we have never known any thing but the greatest attention from them. And it cannot be for the value of our custom now, for what is our consumption of bread, you know? Only three of us—besides dear Jane at present—and she really eats nothing—makes such a shocking breakfast, you would be quite frightened if you saw it. I dare not let my mother know how little she eats—so I say one thing and then I say another, and it passes off. But about the middle of the day she gets hungry, and there is nothing she likes so well as these baked apples, and they are extremely wholesome, for I took the opportunity the other day of asking Mr. Perry; I happened to meet him in the street. Not that I had any doubt before—I have so often heard Mr. Woodhouse recommend a baked apple. I believe it is the only way that Mr. Woodhouse thinks the fruit thoroughly wholesome. We have apple dumplings,[15] however, very often. Patty makes an ex-

13 Hannah Glasse's recipe suggests: "Put your apples into an earthen pan with a few cloves, a little lemon-peel, some coarse sugar, a glass of red wine; put them into a quick oven, and they will take an hour baking" (*The Art of Cookery,* p. 220).

14 In the days before all homes had ovens, it was customary for bakers to heat customers' own dishes in their ovens once the bread had been baked.

15 A much richer dish than baked apples (and therefore, presumably, not approved of by Mr. Woodhouse), made by coating pieces of apple in pastry and boiling them. Hannah Glasse provides detailed instructions:

> Make a good puff-paste, pare some large apples, cut them in quarters, and take out the cores very nicely; take a piece of crust, and roll it round enough for one apple; if they are big, they will not look pretty; so roll the crust around each apple, and make them round like a ball, with a little flour in your hand; have a pot of water boiling, take a clean cloth, dip it in the water and shake flour over it; tie each dumpling by itself, and put them in the water boiling, which keeps boiling all the time; and if your crust is light and good, and the apples not too large, half an hour will boil them; but if the apples be large, they will take an hour's boiling; when they are enough, take them up and lay them in a dish; throw fine sugar all over them, and send them to table; have good fresh butter melted in a cup, and fine beaten sugar in a saucer. (*The Art of Cookery,* pp. 256–257)

The Austens themselves were fond of apple dumplings; for example, Austen wrote to Cassandra on January 7, 1807: "When you receive this, our guests will be all gone or going; and I shall be left to the comfortable disposal of my time, to ease of mind from the torments of rice puddings and apple dumplings, and probably to regret that I did not take more pains to please them all" (*Letters,* p. 114).

cellent apple-dumpling. Well, Mrs. Weston, you have prevailed, I hope, and these ladies will oblige us."

Emma would be "very happy to wait on Mrs. Bates, &c." and they did at last move out of the shop, with no further delay from Miss Bates than,

"How do you do, Mrs. Ford? I beg your pardon. I did not see you before. I hear you have a charming collection of new ribbons from town. Jane came back delighted yesterday. Thank ye, the gloves do very well—only a little too large about the wrist; but Jane is taking them in."

"What was I talking of?" said she, beginning again when they were all in the street.

Emma wondered on what, of all the medley, she would fix.

"I declare I cannot recollect what I was talking of.—Oh! my mother's spectacles. So very obliging of Mr. Frank Churchill! 'Oh!' said he, 'I do think I can fasten the rivet; I like a job of this kind excessively.' —Which you know shewed him to be so very. . . . Indeed I must say that, much as I had heard of him before and much as I had expected, he very far exceeds any thing. . . . I do congratulate you, Mrs. Weston, most warmly. He seems every thing the fondest parent could. . . . 'Oh!' said he, 'I can fasten the rivet. I like a job of that sort excessively.' I never shall forget his manner. And when I brought out the baked apples from the closet, and hoped our friends would be so very obliging as to take some, 'Oh!' said he directly, 'there is nothing in the way of fruit half so good, and these are the finest looking home-baked apples I ever saw in my life.' That, you know, was so very. . . . And I am sure, by his manner, it was no compliment.[16] Indeed they are very delightful apples, and Mrs. Wallis does them full justice—only we do not have them baked more than twice, and Mr. Woodhouse made us promise to have them done three times[17]—but Miss Woodhouse will be so good as not to mention it. The apples themselves are the very finest sort for baking, beyond a doubt; all from Donwell—some of Mr. Knightley's most liberal supply. He sends us a sack every year; and certainly there never was such a keeping apple[18] any where as one of his trees—I believe there is two of them. My mother says the orchard was always famous in her younger days. But

16 Not said just for the sake of politeness.

17 A thrice-baked apple would be exceptionally soft, much like the texture of Mr. Woodhouse's beloved gruel.

18 A variety that keeps well during long storage.

Illustration of apples from George Brookshaw, *Pomona Britannica, or, A Collection of the Most Esteemed Fruits at Present Cultivated in Great Britain* (London: Bensley and Son, 1817). Some of these varieties of apple would keep until February or March.

I was really quite shocked the other day—for Mr. Knightley called one morning, and Jane was eating these apples, and we talked about them and said how much she enjoyed them, and he asked whether we were not got to the end of our stock. 'I am sure you must be,' said he, 'and I will send you another supply; for I have a great many more than I can ever use. William Larkins[19] let me keep a larger quantity than usual this year. I will send you some more, before they get good for nothing.' So I begged he would not—for really as to ours being gone, I could not absolutely say that we had a great many left—it was but half a dozen indeed; but they should be all kept for Jane; and I could not at all bear that he should be sending us more, so liberal as he had been already; and Jane said the same. And when he was gone, she almost quarrelled with me—No, I should not say quarrelled, for we never had a quarrel in our lives; but she was quite distressed that I had owned the apples were so nearly gone; she wished I had made him believe we had a great many left. Oh! said I, my dear, I did say as much as I could. However, the very same evening William Larkins came over with a large basket of apples, the same sort of apples, a bushel[20] at least, and I was very much obliged, and went down and spoke to William Larkins and said every thing, as you may suppose. William Larkins is such an old acquaintance! I am always glad to see him. But, however, I found afterwards from Patty, that William said it was all the apples of *that* sort his master had; he had brought them all—and now his master had not one left to bake or boil. William did not seem to mind it himself, he was so pleased to think his master had sold so many; for William, you know, thinks more of his master's profit than any thing; but Mrs. Hodges,[21] he said, was quite displeased at their being all sent away. She could not bear that her master should not be able to have another apple-tart[22] this spring. He told Patty this, but bid her not mind it, and be sure not to say any thing to us about it, for Mrs. Hodges *would* be cross sometimes, and as long as so many sacks were sold, it did not signify who ate the remainder. And so Patty told me, and I was excessively shocked indeed! I would not have Mr. Knightley know any thing about it for the world! He would be so very. . . . I wanted to keep it from Jane's knowledge; but unluckily, I had mentioned it before I was aware."

19 The steward of Knightley's Donwell Abbey estate.

20 It is uncertain precisely what quantity Miss Bates is referring to here, since, until 1826, when the Imperial Bushel was fixed as a measure of eight gallons' capacity, the term varied widely in its application.

21 The cook at Donwell.

22 Hannah Glasse suggests: "apples and pears, pare them, cut them into quarters, and core them; cut the quarters across again, set them on in a sauce-pan with just as much water as will barely cover them, let them simmer on a slow fire just till the fruit is tender; put a good piece of lemon-peel in the water with the fruit, then have your patties ready; lay fine sugar at bottom, then your fruit, and a little sugar at top; that you must put in at your discretion; pour over each tart a tea-spoonful of lemon-juice, and three tea-spoonfuls of the liquor they were boiled in; put on your lid, and bake them in a slack oven" (*The Art of Cookery,* p. 200).

Miss Bates had just done as Patty opened the door; and her visitors walked up stairs without having any regular narration to attend to, pursued only by the sounds of her desultory good-will.

"Pray take care, Mrs. Weston, there is a step at the turning. Pray take care, Miss Woodhouse, ours is rather a dark staircase—rather darker and narrower than one could wish. Miss Smith, pray take care. Miss Woodhouse, I am quite concerned, I am sure you hit your foot. Miss Smith, the step at the turning."

10

The appearance of the little sitting-room as they entered, was tranquillity itself; Mrs. Bates, deprived of her usual employment,[1] slumbering on one side of the fire, Frank Churchill, at a table near her, most deedily[2] occupied about her spectacles, and Jane Fairfax, standing with her back to them, intent on her pianoforté.

Busy as he was, however, the young man was yet able to shew a most happy countenance on seeing Emma again.

"This is a pleasure," said he, in rather a low voice, "coming at least ten minutes earlier than I had calculated. You find me trying to be useful; tell me if you think I shall succeed."

"What!" said Mrs. Weston, "have not you finished it yet? you would not earn a very good livelihood as a working-silversmith[3] at this rate."

"I have not been working uninterruptedly," he replied, "I have been assisting Miss Fairfax in trying to make her instrument stand steadily, it was not quite firm; an unevenness in the floor, I believe. You see we have been wedging one leg with paper. This was very kind of you to be persuaded to come. I was almost afraid you would be hurrying home."

He contrived that she should be seated by him; and was sufficiently employed in looking out the best baked apple for her, and trying to make her help or advise him in his work, till Jane Fairfax was quite ready to sit down to the pianoforté again. That she was not immediately ready, Emma did suspect to arise from the state of her nerves; she had not yet possessed the instrument long enough to

1 Without her glasses, Mrs. Bates can neither read nor sew.

2 A dialectal word for "actively." The *OED*'s two earliest citations for the adverbial form are this instance from *Emma* and Austen's letter to Cassandra of October 11–12, 1813, in which she writes of her nephews: "They amuse themselves very comfortably in the Even^{g}—by netting; they are each about a rabbit net, & sit as deedily to it, side by side, as any two Uncle Franks could do" (*Letters,* p. 234).

3 A jeweler who makes silverware rather than just selling it.

touch it without emotion; she must reason herself into the power of performance; and Emma could not but pity such feelings, whatever their origin, and could not but resolve never to expose them to her neighbour again.

At last Jane began, and though the first bars were feebly given, the powers of the instrument were gradually done full justice to. Mrs. Weston had been delighted before, and was delighted again; Emma joined her in all her praise; and the pianoforté, with every proper discrimination, was pronounced to be altogether of the highest promise.

"Whoever Col. Campbell might employ," said Frank Churchill, with a smile at Emma, "the person has not chosen ill. I heard a good deal of Col. Campbell's taste at Weymouth; and the softness of the upper notes I am sure is exactly what he and *all that party* would particularly prize. I dare say, Miss Fairfax, that he either gave his friend very minute directions, or wrote to Broadwood[4] himself. Do not you think so?"

Jane did not look round. She was not obliged to hear. Mrs. Weston had been speaking to her at the same moment.

"It is not fair," said Emma in a whisper, "mine was a random guess. Do not distress her."

He shook his head with a smile, and looked as if he had very little doubt and very little mercy. Soon afterwards he began again,

"How much your friends in Ireland must be enjoying your pleasure on this occasion, Miss Fairfax. I dare say they often think of you, and wonder which will be the day, the precise day of the instrument's coming to hand. Do you imagine Col. Campbell knows the business to be going forward just at this time?—Do you imagine it to be the consequence of an immediate commission from him, or that he may have sent only a general direction, an order indefinite as to time, to depend upon contingencies and conveniencies?"

He paused. She could not but hear; she could not avoid answering,

"Till I have a letter from Col. Campbell," said she, in a voice of forced calmness, "I can imagine nothing with any confidence. It must be all conjecture."

4 John Broadwood having died in 1812, Frank either means that Col. Campbell wrote to one of the piano-maker's sons (James or Thomas Broadwood), or he is using the surname to refer to the company in general.

"Conjecture—aye, sometimes one conjectures right, and sometimes one conjectures wrong. I wish I could conjecture how soon I shall make this rivet quite firm. What nonsense one talks, Miss Woodhouse, when hard at work, if one talks at all;—your real workmen, I suppose, hold their tongues; but we gentlemen labourers if we get hold of a word—Miss Fairfax said something about conjecturing. There, it is done. I have the pleasure, madam, (to Mrs. Bates,) of restoring your spectacles, healed for the present."

He was very warmly thanked both by mother and daughter; to escape a little from the latter, he went to the pianoforté, and begged Miss Fairfax, who was still sitting at it, to play something more.

"If you are very kind," said he, "it will be one of the waltzes we danced last night;—let me live them over again. You did not enjoy them as I did; you appeared tired the whole time. I believe you were glad we danced no longer; but I would have given worlds—all the worlds one ever has to give—for another half hour."

She played.

"What felicity it is to hear a tune again which *has* made one happy! —If I mistake not that was danced at Weymouth."

She looked up at him for a moment, coloured deeply, and played something else. He took some music from a chair near the pianoforté, and turning to Emma, said,

"Here is something quite new to me. Do you know it?—Cramer.[5] —And here are a new set of Irish melodies.[6] That, from such a quarter, one might expect. This was all sent with the instrument. Very thoughtful of Col. Campbell, was not it?—He knew Miss Fairfax could have no music here. I honour that part of the attention particularly; it shews it to have been so thoroughly from the heart. Nothing hastily done; nothing incomplete. True affection only could have prompted it."

5 Johann Baptist Cramer (1771–1858) was a famous pianist, composer, and sheet-music publisher. Born in Mannheim, Germany, he moved to London around 1774 and was established as a prodigious child performer by the age of twelve. He began composing piano sonatas and concertos in the 1790s, and his playing was praised by Beethoven. From 1805, he was also active and successful in the music publishing business; therefore Frank may be referring to a piece composed by Cramer, published by him, or both.

6 Patrick Piggott suggests that these "were almost certainly the fourth set of Thomas Moore's immensely popular collections (the third collection, published in 1813, could scarcely have been considered as still quite new)" (*The Innocent Diversion: A Study of Music in the Life and Writings of Jane Austen* [London: D. Cleverdon, 1979], p. 100).

Portrait of Johann Baptist Cramer (1771–1858) by George Lethbridge Saunders, 1827. Cramer was distinguished as a musician, composer, and music publisher.

Portrait of Thomas Moore (1779–1852), unknown artist, c. 1800–1805. Moore gained great public acclaim with the ten volumes of the *Irish Melodies,* published between 1808 and 1834, containing poems set to traditional Irish airs.

Emma wished he would be less pointed, yet could not help being amused; and when on glancing her eye towards Jane Fairfax she caught the remains of a smile, when she saw that with all the deep blush of consciousness, there had been a smile of secret delight, she had less scruple in the amusement, and much less compunction with respect to her.—This amiable, upright, perfect Jane Fairfax was apparently cherishing very reprehensible feelings.

He brought all the music to her, and they looked it over together. —Emma took the opportunity of whispering,

"You speak too plain. She must understand you."

"I hope she does. I would have her understand me. I am not in the least ashamed of my meaning."

"But really, I am half ashamed, and wish I had never taken up the idea."

"I am very glad you did, and that you communicated it to me. I have now a key to all her odd looks and ways. Leave shame to her. If she does wrong, she ought to feel it."

"She is not entirely without it, I think."

"I do not see much sign of it. She is playing *Robin Adair*[7] at this moment—*his* favourite."

Shortly afterwards Miss Bates, passing near the window, descried Mr. Knightley on horseback not far off.

"Mr. Knightley I declare!—I must speak to him if possible, just to thank him. I will not open the window here; it would give you all cold; but I can go into my mother's room you know. I dare say he will come in when he knows who is here. Quite delightful to have you all meet so!—Our little room so honoured!"

She was in the adjoining chamber while she still spoke, and opening the casement[8] there, immediately called Mr. Knightley's attention, and every syllable of their conversation was as distinctly heard by the others, as if it had passed within the same apartment.

"How d'ye do?—how d'ye do?—Very well, I thank you. So obliged to you for the carriage last night. We were just in time; my mother just ready for us. Pray come in; do come in. You will find some friends here."

So began Miss Bates; and Mr. Knightley seemed determined to be heard in his turn, for most resolutely and commandingly did he say,

"How is your niece, Miss Bates?—I want to inquire after you all, but particularly your niece. How is Miss Fairfax?—I hope she caught no cold last night. How is she to-day? Tell me how Miss Fairfax is."

And Miss Bates was obliged to give a direct answer before he would hear her in any thing else. The listeners were amused; and Mrs. Weston gave Emma a look of particular meaning. But Emma still shook her head in steady scepticism.

"So obliged to you!—so very much obliged to you for the carriage," resumed Miss Bates. He cut her short with,

"I am going to Kingston. Can I do any thing for you?"

"Oh! dear, Kingston—are you?—Mrs. Cole was saying the other day she wanted something from Kingston."

"Mrs. Cole has servants to send. Can I do any thing for *you?*"

7 An old Irish/Scottish air, which was reputed to have been given these words after Lady Caroline Keppel fell in love with and married the Irish surgeon Robert Adair in the 1750s:

What's this dull town to me:
  Robin's not near.
What was't I wished to see?
  What wish'd to hear?
Where's all the joy and mirth
Made this town a heaven on earth?
Oh! they're all fled with thee.
  Robin Adair.

What made th'assembly shine?
  Robin Adair.
What made the ball so fine?
  Robin was there.
What, when the play was o'er,
What made my heart so sore?
Oh! it was parting with
  Robin Adair.

But now thou'rt cold to me,
  Robin Adair,
But now thou'rt cold to me,
  Robin Adair.
Yet him I lov'd so well
Still in my heart shall dwell;
Oh! I can ne'er forget
  Robin Adair.

In his article "'Robin Adair' as a Musical Clue in Jane Austen's *Emma*" (*Review of English Studies*, n.s., XXXIX: 153 (1988), pp. 84–86), Peter F. Alexander notes how the words would carry an extra freight of significance for the secret lovers and suggests that "Emma understands the last pronoun to refer to Mr Dixon whereas Frank is almost certainly referring to himself" (p. 85).

8 Hinged window.

Portrait of Lady Caroline Keppel (c. 1734–1769) by Joshua Reynolds, 1755. Her romance with the surgeon Robin Adair in the 1750s is generally thought to have inspired the song that holds such meaning in this chapter.

"No, I thank you. But do come in. Who do you think is here?—Miss Woodhouse and Miss Smith; so kind as to call to hear the new pianoforté. Do put up your horse at the Crown, and come in."

"Well," said he in a deliberating manner, "for five minutes, perhaps."

"And here is Mrs. Weston and Mr. Frank Churchill too!—Quite delightful; so many friends!"

"No, not now, I thank you. I could not stay two minutes. I must get on to Kingston as fast as I can."

"Oh! do come in. They will be so very happy to see you."

"No, no, your room is full enough. I will call another day, and hear the pianoforté."

"Well, I am so sorry!—Oh! Mr. Knightley, what a delightful party last night; how extremely pleasant.—Did you ever see such dancing?

—Was not it delightful?—Miss Woodhouse and Mr. Frank Churchill; I never saw any thing equal to it."

"Oh! very delightful indeed; I can say nothing less, for I suppose Miss Woodhouse and Mr. Frank Churchill are hearing every thing that passes. And (raising his voice still more) I do not see why Miss Fairfax should not be mentioned too. I think Miss Fairfax dances very well; and Mrs. Weston is the very best country-dance player, without exception, in England. Now, if your friends have any gratitude, they will say something pretty loud about you and me in return; but I cannot stay to hear it."

"Oh! Mr. Knightley, one moment more; something of consequence—so shocked!—Jane and I are both so shocked about the apples!"

"What is the matter now?"

"To think of your sending us all your store apples. You said you had a great many, and now you have not one left. We really are so shocked! Mrs. Hodges may well be angry. William Larkins mentioned it here. You should not have done it, indeed you should not. Ah! he is off. He never can bear to be thanked. But I thought he would have staid now, and it would have been a pity not to have mentioned. . . . Well, (returning into the room,) I have not been able to succeed. Mr. Knightley cannot stop. He is going to Kingston. He asked me if he could do any thing. . . ."

"Yes," said Jane, "we heard his kind offers, we heard every thing."

"Oh! yes, my dear, I dare say you might, because you know the door was open, and the window was open, and Mr. Knightley spoke loud. You must have heard every thing to be sure. 'Can I do any thing for you at Kingston?' said he; so I just mentioned. . . . Oh! Miss Woodhouse, must you be going?—You seem but just come—so very obliging of you."

Emma found it really time to be at home; the visit had already lasted long; and on examining watches, so much of the morning was perceived to be gone, that Mrs. Weston and her companion taking leave also, could allow themselves only to walk with the two young ladies to Hartfield gates, before they set off for Randalls.

II

It may be possible to do without dancing entirely. Instances have been known of young people passing many, many months successively, without being at any ball of any description, and no material injury accrue either to body or mind;—but when a beginning is made—when the felicities of rapid motion have once been, though slightly, felt—it must be a very heavy[1] set that does not ask for more.

Frank Churchill had danced once at Highbury, and longed to dance again; and the last half hour of an evening which Mr. Woodhouse was persuaded to spend with his daughter at Randalls, was passed by the two young people in schemes on the subject. Frank's was the first idea; and his the greatest zeal in pursuing it; for the lady was the best judge of the difficulties, and the most solicitous for accommodation and appearance. But still she had inclination enough for shewing people again how delightfully Mr. Frank Churchill and Miss Woodhouse danced—for doing that in which she need not blush to compare herself with Jane Fairfax—and even for simple dancing itself, without any of the wicked aids of vanity—to assist him first in pacing out the room they were in to see what it could be made to hold—and then in taking the dimensions of the other parlour, in the hope of discovering, in spite of all that Mr. Weston could say of their exactly equal size, that it was a little the largest.

His first proposition and request, that the dance begun at Mr. Cole's should be finished there—that the same party should be collected, and the same musician engaged, met with the readiest acqui-

1 Dull, stolid.

2 Accommodated.

escence. Mr. Weston entered into the idea with thorough enjoyment, and Mrs. Weston most willingly undertook to play as long as they could wish to dance; and the interesting employment had followed, of reckoning up exactly who there would be, and portioning out the indispensable division of space to every couple.

"You and Miss Smith, and Miss Fairfax, will be three, and the two Miss Coxes five," had been repeated many times over. "And there will be the two Gilberts, young Cox, my father, and myself, besides Mr. Knightley. Yes, that will be quite enough for pleasure. You and Miss Smith, and Miss Fairfax, will be three, and the two Miss Coxes five; and for five couple there will be plenty of room."

But soon it came to be on one side,

"But will there be good room for five couple?—I really do not think there will."

On another,

"And after all, five couple are not enough to make it worth while to stand up. Five couple are nothing, when one thinks seriously about it. It will not do to *invite* five couple. It can be allowable only as the thought of the moment."

Somebody said that *Miss* Gilbert was expected at her brother's, and must be invited with the rest. Somebody else believed *Mrs.* Gilbert would have danced the other evening, if she had been asked. A word was put in for a second young Cox; and at last, Mr. Weston naming one family of cousins who must be included, and another of very old acquaintance who could not be left out, it became a certainty that the five couple would be at least ten, and a very interesting speculation in what possible manner they could be disposed of.[2]

The doors of the two rooms were just opposite each other. "Might not they use both rooms, and dance across the passage?" It seemed the best scheme; and yet it was not so good but that many of them wanted a better. Emma said it would be awkward; Mrs. Weston was in distress about the supper; and Mr. Woodhouse opposed it earnestly, on the score of health. It made him so very unhappy, indeed, that it could not be persevered in.

"Oh! no," said he; "it would be the extreme of imprudence. I could not bear it for Emma!—Emma is not strong. She would catch a dreadful cold. So would poor little Harriet. So you would all. Mrs. Weston, you would be quite laid up; do not let them talk of such a wild thing. Pray do not let them talk of it. That young man (speaking lower) is very thoughtless. Do not tell his father, but that young man is not quite the thing.[3] He has been opening the doors very often this evening, and keeping them open very inconsiderately. He does not think of the draught. I do not mean to set you against him, but indeed he is not quite the thing!"

Mrs. Weston was sorry for such a charge. She knew the importance of it, and said every thing in her power to do it away. Every door was now closed, the passage plan given up, and the first scheme of dancing only in the room they were in resorted to again; and with such good-will on Frank Churchill's part, that the space which a quarter of an hour before had been deemed barely sufficient for five couple, was now endeavoured to be made out quite enough for ten.

"We were too magnificent,"[4] said he. "We allowed unnecessary room. Ten couple may stand here very well."

Emma demurred. "It would be a crowd—a sad crowd; and what could be worse than dancing without space to turn in?"

"Very true," he gravely replied; "it was very bad." But still he went on measuring, and still he ended with,

"I think there will be very tolerable room for ten couple."

"No, no," said she, "you are quite unreasonable. It would be dreadful to be standing so close! Nothing can be farther from pleasure than to be dancing in a crowd—and a crowd in a little room!"

"There is no denying it," he replied. "I agree with you exactly. A crowd in a little room—Miss Woodhouse, you have the art of giving pictures in a few words. Exquisite, quite exquisite!—Still, however, having proceeded so far, one is unwilling to give the matter up. It would be a disappointment to my father—and altogether—I do not know that—I am rather of opinion that ten couple might stand here very well."

Emma perceived that the nature of his gallantry was a little self-willed, and that he would rather oppose than lose the pleasure of dancing with her; but she took the compliment, and forgave the rest. Had she intended ever to *marry* him, it might have been worth while

3 Does not behave as someone in his position ought to behave. Compare the idiomatic phrase "not the done thing."

4 Extravagant.

to pause and consider, and try to understand the value of his preference, and the character of his temper; but for all the purposes of their acquaintance, he was quite amiable enough.

Before the middle of the next day, he was at Hartfield; and he entered the room with such an agreeable smile as certified the continuance of the scheme. It soon appeared that he came to announce an improvement.

"Well, Miss Woodhouse," he almost immediately began, "your inclination for dancing has not been quite frightened away, I hope, by the terrors of my father's little rooms. I bring a new proposal on the subject:—a thought of my father's, which waits only your approbation to be acted upon. May I hope for the honour of your hand for the two first dances of this little projected ball, to be given, not at Randalls, but at the Crown Inn?"

"The Crown!"

"Yes; if you and Mr. Woodhouse see no objection, and I trust you cannot, my father hopes his friends will be so kind as to visit him there. Better accommodations, he can promise them, and not a less grateful welcome than at Randalls. It is his own idea. Mrs. Weston sees no objection to it, provided you are satisfied. This is what we all feel. Oh! you were perfectly right! Ten couple, in either of the Randalls rooms, would have been insufferable!—Dreadful!—I felt how right you were the whole time, but was too anxious for securing *any thing* to like to yield. Is not it a good exchange?—You consent—I hope you consent?"

"It appears to me a plan that nobody can object to, if Mr. and Mrs. Weston do not. I think it admirable; and as far as I can answer for myself, shall be most happy—— It seems the only improvement that could be. Papa, do you not think it an excellent improvement?"

She was obliged to repeat and explain it, before it was fully comprehended; and then, being quite new, further representations were necessary to make it acceptable.

"No; he thought it very far from an improvement—a very bad plan—much worse than the other. A room at an inn was always damp and dangerous; never properly aired, or fit to be inhabited. If they must dance, they had better dance at Randalls. He had never been in the room at the Crown in his life—did not know the people who kept it by sight.—Oh! no—a very bad plan. They would catch worse colds at the Crown than any where."

"I was going to observe, sir," said Frank Churchill, "that one of the great recommendations of this change would be the very little danger of any body's catching cold—so much less danger at the Crown than at Randalls! Mr. Perry might have reason to regret the alteration, but nobody else could."

"Sir," said Mr. Woodhouse, rather warmly, "you are very much mistaken if you suppose Mr. Perry to be that sort of character. Mr. Perry is extremely concerned when any of us are ill. But I do not understand how the room at the Crown can be safer for you than your father's house."

"From the very circumstance of its being larger, sir. We shall have no occasion to open the windows at all—not once the whole evening; and it is that dreadful habit of opening the windows, letting in cold air upon heated bodies,[5] which (as you well know, sir) does the mischief."

"Open the windows!—but surely, Mr. Churchill, nobody would think of opening the windows at Randalls. Nobody could be so imprudent! I never heard of such a thing. Dancing with open windows! —I am sure, neither your father nor Mrs. Weston (poor Miss Taylor that was) would suffer it."

"Ah! sir—but a thoughtless young person will sometimes step behind a window-curtain, and throw up a sash, without its being suspected. I have often known it done myself."

"Have you indeed, sir?—Bless me! I never could have supposed it. But I live out of the world, and am often astonished at what I hear. However, this does make a difference; and, perhaps, when we come to talk it over—but these sort of things require a good deal of consideration. One cannot resolve upon them in a hurry. If Mr. and Mrs. Weston will be so obliging as to call here one morning, we may talk it over, and see what can be done."

"But unfortunately, sir, my time is so limited—"

"Oh!" interrupted Emma, "there will be plenty of time for talking every thing over. There is no hurry at all. If it can be contrived to be

5 John Sinclair contends: "after hot bathing, or hard labour, when the body is in a sweat, by no means leave of any of your clothes, nor expose yourself to the fresh air; for this light refreshment may cost you dear. The cold air closes the pores, and thence comes a gathering of ill humours, which would have found vent this way, either by sensible sweat, or insensible perspiration, especially at the feet, the back, and belly, which should not feel the cold" (*The Code of Health and Longevity*, 1st ed., vol. III [Edinburgh: Printed for A. Constable, 1807], p. 232).

at the Crown, papa, it will be very convenient for the horses. They will be so near their own stable."

"So they will, my dear. That is a great thing. Not that James ever complains; but it is right to spare our horses when we can. If I could be sure of the rooms being thoroughly aired—but is Mrs. Stokes to be trusted? I doubt it. I do not know her, even by sight."

"I can answer for every thing of that nature, sir, because it will be under Mrs. Weston's care. Mrs. Weston undertakes to direct the whole."

"There, papa!—Now you must be satisfied—Our own dear Mrs. Weston, who is carefulness itself. Do not you remember what Mr. Perry said, so many years ago, when I had the measles?[6] 'If *Miss Taylor* undertakes to wrap Miss Emma up, you need not have any fears, sir.' How often have I heard you speak of it as such a compliment to her!"

"Aye, very true. Mr. Perry did say so. I shall never forget it. Poor little Emma! You were very bad with the measles; that is, you would have been very bad, but for Perry's great attention. He came four times a day for a week. He said, from the first, it was a very good sort[7]—which was our great comfort; but the measles are a dreadful complaint. I hope whenever poor Isabella's little ones have the measles, she will send for Perry."

"My father and Mrs. Weston are at the Crown at this moment," said Frank Churchill, "examining the capabilities of the house. I left them there and came on to Hartfield, impatient for your opinion, and hoping you might be persuaded to join them and give your advice on the spot. I was desired to say so from both. It would be the greatest pleasure to them, if you could allow me to attend you there. They can do nothing satisfactorily without you."

6 By the beginning of the nineteenth century, measles was a dangerous disease, but not a uniformly deadly one, and milder childhood strains were often left to run their course. In *Practical Illustrations of the Scarlet Fever, Measles, and Pulmonary Consumption* (London: Baldwin, Craddock, and Joy, 1818), John Armstrong remarked: "From an impartial consideration of the facts which have come before me, I am inclined to think, that our plan of treating the measles is too uniformly active, when the eruptive fever is developed; and that we should be more fortunate in the main run, if we interfered less with the operations of nature in cases of a mild or moderate character. Some children do well without the aid of medicine, and infants may be easily lost from an excess of applications" (p. 115).

7 A very mild strain.

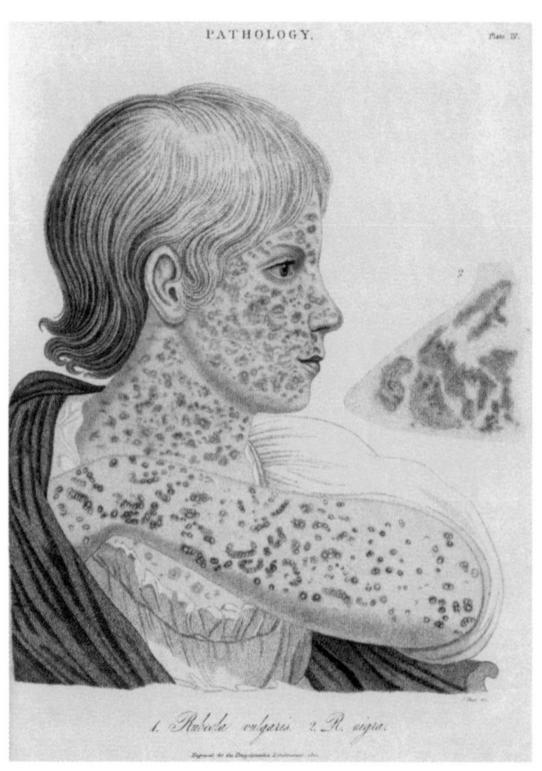

J. Pass, "Two Types of Measles," 1822. By Austen's time—as indicated by Mr. Perry's trusting in Mrs. Weston to look after Emma—milder strains of measles were no longer considered to be major causes for concern.

Emma was most happy to be called to such a council; and her father, engaging to think it all over while she was gone, the two young people set off together without delay for the Crown. There were Mr. and Mrs. Weston; delighted to see her and receive her approbation, very busy and very happy in their different way; she, in some little distress; and he, finding every thing perfect.

"Emma," said she, "this paper[8] is worse than I expected. Look! in places you see it is dreadfully dirty; and the wainscot is more yellow and forlorn[9] than any thing I could have imagined."

"My dear, you are too particular," said her husband. "What does all that signify? You will see nothing of it by candle-light. It will be as clean as Randalls by candle-light. We never see any thing of it on our club-nights."

The ladies here probably exchanged looks which meant, "Men never know when things are dirty or not;" and the gentlemen perhaps thought each to himself, "Women will have their little nonsenses and needless cares."

One perplexity, however, arose, which the gentlemen did not disdain. It regarded a supper-room. At the time of the ball-room's being built, suppers had not been in question;[10] and a small card-room[11] adjoining, was the only addition. What was to be done? This card-room would be wanted as a card-room now; or, if cards were conveniently voted unnecessary by their four selves, still was not it too small for any comfortable supper? Another room of much better size might be secured for the purpose; but it was at the other end of the house, and a long awkward passage must be gone through to get at it. This made a difficulty. Mrs. Weston was afraid of draughts for the young people in that passage; and neither Emma nor the gentlemen could tolerate the prospect of being miserably crowded at supper.

Mrs. Weston proposed having no regular supper; merely sandwiches, &c.[12] set out in the little room; but that was scouted[13] as a wretched suggestion. A private dance, without sitting down to supper, was pronounced an infamous fraud upon the rights of men and women;[14] and Mrs. Weston must not speak of it again. She then took another line of expediency, and looking into the doubtful room, observed,

8 Wallpaper.

9 Wretched.

10 Suppers at balls became widespread only at the end of the eighteenth century, which dates the time of the Crown's (and, by extension, Highbury's) more fashionable status to an earlier period—perhaps the time at which a younger Mr. Woodhouse became *au fait* with the licentious innuendo of Garrick's riddle "Kitty, a fair but frozen maid."

11 A card-room was required at a ball, for anyone not fit for or inclined to dancing.

12 The association of sandwiches and card-playing is proverbial. Indeed, although the combination of bread and fillings goes back to antiquity, the term "sandwich" itself has its origins in the eighteenth-century culture of late-night, gentlemanly card parties. The sandwich is named after John Montagu, the Fourth Earl of Sandwich (1718–1792), who was, legend has it, so addicted to gaming that he would not leave the table to eat, and instead had sliced beef brought to him between slices of bread. The *OED*'s earliest citation comes from Edward Gibbon's journal entry of November 24, 1762: "I dined at the Cocoa Tree . . . That respectable body affords every evening a sight truly English. Twenty or thirty of the first men in the kingdom . . . supping at little tables . . . upon a bit of cold meat, or a Sandwich."

13 Rejected, pooh-poohed.

14 Austen is alluding parodically to Mary Wollstonecraft's two famous works of radical political theory. *A Vindication of the Rights of Men* (1790) was one of the earliest major ripostes to Edmund Burke's *Reflections on the Revolution in France,* and *A Vindication of the Rights of Woman* (1792) is considered to be one of the founding texts of post-Enlightenment feminism. Despite their wide ideological differences, Wollstonecraft and Austen share a claustrophobic frustration with the limited options open to women and, in particular, with the culture of "female accomplishments," although Wollstonecraft tackles the issue with much greater discursive directness in the Introduction to *A Vindication of*

the Rights of Woman: "I wish to persuade women to endeavour to acquire strength, both of mind and body, and to convince them that the soft phrases, susceptibility of heart, delicacy of sentiment, and refinement of taste, are almost synonymous with epithets of weakness." For more on Austen and Wollstonecraft, see Claudia L. Johnson, *Equivocal Beings: Politics, Gender, and Sentimentality in the 1790s: Wollstonecraft, Radcliffe, Burney, Austen* (Chicago: University of Chicago Press, 1995).

15 Object lesson, type.

"I do not think it *is* so very small. We shall not be many, you know."

And Mr. Weston at the same time, walking briskly with long steps through the passage, was calling out,

"You talk a great deal of the length of this passage, my dear. It is a mere nothing after all; and not the least draught from the stairs."

"I wish," said Mrs. Weston, "one could know which arrangement our guests in general would like best. To do what would be most generally pleasing must be our object—if one could but tell what that would be."

"Yes, very true," cried Frank, "very true. You want your neighbours' opinions. I do not wonder at you. If one could ascertain what the chief of them—the Coles, for instance. They are not far off. Shall I call upon them? Or Miss Bates? She is still nearer.—And I do not know whether Miss Bates is not as likely to understand the inclinations of the rest of the people as any body. I think we do want a larger council. Suppose I go and invite Miss Bates to join us?"

"Well—if you please," said Mrs. Weston rather hesitating, if you think she will be of any use."

"You will get nothing to the purpose from Miss Bates," said Emma. "She will be all delight and gratitude, but she will tell you nothing. She will not even listen to your questions. I see no advantage in consulting Miss Bates."

"But she is so amusing, so extremely amusing! I am very fond of hearing Miss Bates talk. And I need not bring the whole family, you know."

Here Mr. Weston joined them, and on hearing what was proposed, gave it his decided approbation.

"Aye, do, Frank.—Go and fetch Miss Bates, and let us end the matter at once. She will enjoy the scheme, I am sure; and I do not know a properer person for shewing us how to do away difficulties. Fetch Miss Bates. We are growing a little too nice. She is a standing lesson[15] of how to be happy. But fetch them both. Invite them both."

"Both sir! Can the old lady?" . . .

"The old lady! No, the young lady, to be sure. I shall think you a great blockhead, Frank, if you bring the aunt without the niece."

"Oh! I beg your pardon, sir. I did not immediately recollect. Undoubtedly if you wish it, I will endeavour to persuade them both." And away he ran.

Long before he re-appeared, attending the short, neat, brisk-moving aunt, and her elegant niece,—Mrs. Weston, like a sweet-tempered woman and a good wife, had examined the passage again, and found the evils of it much less than she had supposed before—indeed very trifling; and here ended the difficulties of decision. All the rest, in speculation at least, was perfectly smooth. All the minor arrangements of table and chair, lights and music, tea and supper, made themselves; or were left as mere trifles to be settled at any time between Mrs. Weston and Mrs. Stokes.—Every body invited, was certainly to come; Frank had already written to Enscombe to propose staying a few days beyond his fortnight, which could not possibly be refused. And a delightful dance it was to be.

Most cordially, when Miss Bates arrived, did she agree that it must. As a counsellor she was not wanted; but as an approver, (a much safer character,) she was truly welcome. Her approbation, at once general and minute, warm and incessant, could not but please; and for another half-hour they were all walking to and fro, between the different rooms, some suggesting, some attending, and all in happy enjoyment of the future. The party did not break up without Emma's being positively secured for the two first dances by the hero of the evening, nor without her overhearing Mr. Weston whisper to his wife, "He has asked her, my dear. That's right. I knew he would!"

"Richmond-Bridge, Surrey," June 1801, by John Walker.

12

One thing only was wanting to make the prospect of the ball completely satisfactory to Emma—its being fixed for a day within the granted term of Frank Churchill's stay in Surry; for, in spite of Mr. Weston's confidence, she could not think it so very impossible that the Churchills might not allow their nephew to remain a day beyond his fortnight. But this was not judged feasible. The preparations must take their time, nothing could be properly ready till the third week were entered on, and for a few days they must be planning, proceeding and hoping in uncertainty—at the risk—in her opinion, the great risk, of its being all in vain.

Enscombe however was gracious, gracious in fact, if not in word. His wish of staying longer evidently did not please; but it was not opposed. All was safe and prosperous; and as the removal of one solicitude[1] generally makes way for another, Emma, being now certain of her ball, began to adopt as the next vexation Mr. Knightley's provoking indifference about it. Either because he did not dance himself, or because the plan had been formed without his being consulted, he seemed resolved that it should not interest him, determined against its exciting any present curiosity, or affording him any future amusement. To her voluntary communications Emma could get no more approving reply, than,

"Very well. If the Westons think it worth while to be at all this trouble for a few hours of noisy entertainment, I have nothing to say against it, but that they shall not choose pleasures for me.—Oh! yes, I must be there; I could not refuse; and I will keep as much awake as

1 Care, anxiety.

I can; but I would rather be at home, looking over William Larkins's week's account; much rather, I confess.—Pleasure in seeing dancing!—not I, indeed—I never look at it—I do not know who does.—Fine dancing, I believe, like virtue, must be its own reward.[2] Those who are standing by are usually thinking of something very different."

This Emma felt was aimed at her; and it made her quite angry. It was not in compliment to Jane Fairfax however that he was so indifferent, or so indignant; he was not guided by *her* feelings in reprobating the ball, for *she* enjoyed the thought of it to an extraordinary degree. It made her animated—open hearted—she voluntarily said;—

"Oh! Miss Woodhouse, I hope nothing may happen to prevent the ball. What a disappointment it would be! I do look forward to it, I own, with *very* great pleasure."

It was not to oblige Jane Fairfax therefore that he would have preferred the society of William Larkins. No!—she was more and more convinced that Mrs. Weston was quite mistaken in that surmise. There was a great deal of friendly and of compassionate attachment on his side—but no love.

Alas! there was soon no leisure for quarrelling with Mr. Knightley. Two days of joyful security were immediately followed by the overthrow of every thing. A letter arrived from Mr. Churchill to urge his nephew's instant return. Mrs. Churchill was unwell—far too unwell to do without him; she had been in a very suffering state (so said her husband) when writing to her nephew two days before, though from her usual unwillingness to give pain, and constant habit of never thinking of herself, she had not mentioned it; but now she was too ill to trifle, and must entreat him to set off for Enscombe without delay.

The substance of this letter was forwarded to Emma, in a note from Mrs. Weston, instantly. As to his going, it was inevitable. He must be gone within a few hours, though without feeling any real alarm for his aunt, to lessen his repugnance. He knew her illnesses; they never occurred but for her own convenience.

Mrs. Weston added, "that he could only allow himself time to hurry to Highbury, after breakfast, and take leave of the few friends

2 The phrase goes at least as far back as *"Ipsa virtus pretium sui"* in the *De vita beata* of Seneca (c. 4 BC–65 AD); a notable English version occurs in John Dryden's play *Tyrannick Love, or The Royal Martyr* (1669–1670): "To follow Vertue, as its own reward" (*The Works of John Dryden,* vol. X, ed. M. E. Novak and G. R. Guffey [Berkeley: University of California Press, 1970], p. 133).

there whom he could suppose to feel any interest in him; and that he might be expected at Hartfield very soon."

This wretched note was the finalé[3] of Emma's breakfast. When once it had been read, there was no doing any thing, but lament and exclaim. The loss of the ball—the loss of the young man—and all that the young man might be feeling!—It was too wretched!—Such a delightful evening as it would have been!—Every body so happy! and she and her partner the happiest!—"I said it would be so," was the only consolation.

Her father's feelings were quite distinct. He thought principally of Mrs. Churchill's illness, and wanted to know how she was treated; and as for the ball, it was shocking to have dear Emma disappointed; but they would all be safer at home.

Emma was ready for her visitor some time before he appeared; but if this reflected at all upon his impatience, his sorrowful look and total want of spirits when he did come might redeem him. He felt the going away almost too much to speak of it. His dejection was most evident. He sat really lost in thought for the first few minutes; and when rousing himself, it was only to say,

"Of all horrid things, leave-taking is the worst."

"But you will come again," said Emma. "This will not be your only visit to Randalls."

"Ah!—(shaking his head)—the uncertainty of when I may be able to return!—I shall try for it with a zeal!—It will be the object of all my thoughts and cares!—and if my uncle and aunt go to town this spring—but I am afraid—they did not stir last spring—I am afraid it is a custom gone for ever."

"Our poor ball must be quite given up."

"Ah! that ball!—why did we wait for any thing?—why not seize the pleasure at once?—How often is happiness destroyed by preparation, foolish preparation!—You told us it would be so.—Oh! Miss Woodhouse, why are you always so right?"

"Indeed, I am very sorry to be right in this instance. I would much rather have been merry than wise."

"If I can come again, we are still to have our ball. My father depends on it. Do not forget your engagement."[4]

3 The theatrical exaggeration of the term reflects Emma's melodramatic imagining of the ball and its loss.

4 A daring narratorial pun.

Black basalt bust of Seneca by Josiah Wedgwood & Sons, c. 1774–1820. Seneca is one possible source for the idiomatic maxim "Virtue is its own reward."

Emma looked graciously.

"Such a fortnight as it has been!" he continued; "every day more precious and more delightful than the day before!—every day making me less fit to bear any other place. Happy those, who can remain at Highbury!"

"As you do us such ample justice now," said Emma, laughing, "I will venture to ask, whether you did not come a little doubtingly at first? Do not we rather surpass your expectations? I am sure we do. I am sure you did not much expect to like us. You would not have been so long in coming, if you had had a pleasant idea of Highbury."

He laughed rather consciously; and though denying the sentiment, Emma was convinced that it had been so.

"And you must be off this very morning?"

"Yes; my father is to join me here: we shall walk back together, and I must be off immediately. I am almost afraid that every moment will bring him."

"Not five minutes to spare even for your friends Miss Fairfax and Miss Bates? How unlucky! Miss Bates's powerful, argumentative mind might have strengthened yours."

"Yes—I *have* called there; passing the door, I thought it better. It was a right thing to do. I went in for three minutes, and was detained by Miss Bates's being absent. She was out; and I felt it impossible not to wait till she came in. She is a woman that one may, that one *must* laugh at; but that one would not wish to slight. It was better to pay my visit, then"—

He hesitated, got up, walked to a window.

"In short," said he, "perhaps, Miss Woodhouse——I think you can hardly be quite without suspicion"—

He looked at her, as if wanting to read her thoughts. She hardly knew what to say. It seemed like the forerunner of something absolutely serious, which she did not wish. Forcing herself to speak, therefore, in the hope of putting it by, she calmly said,

"You were quite in the right; it was most natural to pay your visit, then"—

He was silent. She believed he was looking at her; probably reflecting on what she had said, and trying to understand the manner.

She heard him sigh. It was natural for him to feel that he had *cause* to sigh. He could not believe her to be encouraging him. A few awkward moments passed, and he sat down again; and in a more determined manner said,

"It was something to feel that all the rest of my time might be given to Hartfield. My regard for Hartfield is most warm"—

He stopt again, rose again, and seemed quite embarrassed.—He was more in love with her than Emma had supposed; and who can say how it might have ended, if his father had not made his appearance? Mr. Woodhouse soon followed; and the necessity of exertion made him composed.

A very few minutes more, however, completed the present trial. Mr. Weston, always alert when business was to be done, and as incapable of procrastinating any evil that was inevitable, as of foreseeing any that was doubtful, said, "It was time to go;" and the young man, though he might and did sigh, could not but agree, and rise to take leave.

"I shall hear about you all," said he; "that is my chief consolation. I shall hear of every thing that is going on among you. I have engaged Mrs. Weston to correspond with me. She has been so kind as to promise it. Oh! the blessing of a female correspondent, when one is really interested in the absent!—she will tell me every thing.[5] In her letters I shall be at dear Highbury again."

A very friendly shake of the hand, a very earnest "Good bye," closed the speech, and the door had soon shut out Frank Churchill. Short had been the notice—short their meeting; he was gone; and Emma felt so sorry to part, and foresaw so great a loss to their little society from his absence as to begin to be afraid of being too sorry, and feeling it too much.

It was a sad change. They had been meeting almost every day since his arrival. Certainly his being at Randalls had given great spirit to the last two weeks—indescribable spirit; the idea, the expectation of seeing him which every morning had brought, the assurance of his attentions, his liveliness, his manners! It had been a very happy fortnight, and forlorn must be the sinking from it into the common course of Hartfield days. To complete every other recommendation,

5 See note 5 to vol. I, chap. 7.

he had *almost* told her that he loved her. What strength, or what constancy of affection he might be subject to, was another point; but at present she could not doubt his having a decidedly warm admiration, a conscious preference of herself; and this persuasion, joined to all the rest, made her think that she *must* be a little in love with him, in spite of every previous determination against it.

"I certainly must," said she. "This sensation of listlessness, weariness, stupidity, this disinclination to sit down and employ myself, this feeling of every thing's being dull and insipid about the house!—I must be in love; I should be the oddest creature in the world if I were not—for a few weeks at least. Well! evil to some is always good to others. I shall have many fellow-mourners for the ball, if not for Frank Churchill; but Mr. Knightley will be happy. He may spend the evening with his dear William Larkins now if he likes."

Mr. Knightley, however, shewed no triumphant happiness. He could not say that he was sorry on his own account; his very cheerful look would have contradicted him if he had; but he said, and very steadily, that he was sorry for the disappointment of the others, and with considerable kindness added,

"You, Emma, who have so few opportunities of dancing, you are really out of luck; you are very much out of luck!"

It was some days before she saw Jane Fairfax, to judge of her honest regret in this woeful change; but when they did meet, her composure was odious. She had been particularly unwell, however, suffering from headache to a degree, which made her aunt declare, that had the ball taken place, she did not think Jane could have attended it; and it was charity to impute some of her unbecoming indifference to the languor of ill-health.

13

Emma continued to entertain no doubt of her being in love. Her ideas only varied as to the how much. At first, she thought it was a good deal; and afterwards, but little. She had great pleasure in hearing Frank Churchill talked of; and, for his sake, greater pleasure than ever in seeing Mr. and Mrs. Weston; she was very often thinking of him, and quite impatient for a letter, that she might know how he was, how were his spirits, how was his aunt, and what was the chance of his coming to Randalls again this spring. But, on the other hand, she could not admit herself to be unhappy, nor, after the first morning, to be less disposed for employment than usual; she was still busy and cheerful; and, pleasing as he was, she could yet imagine him to have faults; and farther, though thinking of him so much, and, as she sat drawing or working,[1] forming a thousand amusing schemes for the progress and close of their attachment, fancying interesting dialogues, and inventing elegant letters; the conclusion of every imaginary declaration on his side was that she *refused him.*[2] Their affection was always to subside into friendship. Every thing tender and charming was to mark their parting; but still they were to part. When she became sensible of this, it struck her that she could not be very much in love; for in spite of her previous and fixed determination never to quit her father, never to marry, a strong attachment certainly must produce more of a struggle than she could foresee in her own feelings.

"I do not find myself making any use of the word *sacrifice,*" said she.—"In not one of all my clever replies, my delicate negatives, is

1 Doing needlework.

2 This is the most explicit analogy made in the narrative between Emma's imaginative speculations and the activity of a novelist.

there any allusion to making a sacrifice. I do suspect that he is not really necessary to my happiness. So much the better. I certainly will not persuade myself to feel more than I do. I am quite enough in love. I should be sorry to be more."

Upon the whole, she was equally contented with her view of his feelings.

"*He* is undoubtedly very much in love—every thing denotes it—very much in love indeed!—and when he comes again, if his affection continue, I must be on my guard not to encourage it.—It would be most inexcusable to do otherwise, as my own mind is quite made up. Not that I imagine he can think I have been encouraging him hitherto. No, if he had believed me at all to share his feelings, he would not have been so wretched. Could he have thought himself encouraged, his looks and language at parting would have been different.—Still, however, I must be on my guard. This is in the supposition of his attachment continuing what it now is; but I do not know that I expect it will; I do not look upon him to be quite the sort of man—I do not altogether build upon his steadiness or constancy.—His feelings are warm, but I can imagine them rather changeable.—Every consideration of the subject, in short, makes me thankful that my happiness is not more deeply involved.—I shall do very well again after a little while—and then, it will be a good thing over; for they say every body is in love once in their lives,[3] and I shall have been let off easily."

When his letter to Mrs. Weston arrived, Emma had the perusal of it; and she read it with a degree of pleasure and admiration which made her at first shake her head over her own sensations, and think she had undervalued their strength. It was a long, well-written letter, giving the particulars of his journey and of his feelings, expressing all the affection, gratitude, and respect which was natural and honourable, and describing every thing exterior and local that could be supposed attractive, with spirit and precision. No suspicious flourishes now of apology or concern; it was the language of real feeling towards Mrs. Weston; and the transition from Highbury to Enscombe, the contrast between the places in some of the first blessings[4] of social life was just enough touched on to shew how keenly it was felt,

3 Austen's likely source here is book I, chap. 11, of *Tom Jones,* although Fielding's phrasing indicates that the idiom goes back much further: "It hath been observed by wise men or women, I forget which, that all men are doomed to be in love once in their lives." Regardless of that idea, writers like Samuel Johnson remained resolutely opposed to the notion that each person only ever had one ideal "soulmate." In *The Life of Samuel Johnson* (1790) Boswell records a famous exchange from March 1776:

> BOSWELL. "Pray, Sir, do you not suppose that there are fifty women in the world, with any one of whom a man may be as happy, as with any one woman in particular?" JOHNSON. "Ay, Sir, fifty thousand." BOSWELL. "Then, Sir, you are not of opinion with some who imagine that certain men and certain women are made for each other; and that they cannot be happy if they miss their counterparts?" JOHNSON. "To be sure not, Sir. I believe marriages would in general be as happy, and often more so, if they were all made by the Lord Chancellor, upon a due consideration of characters and circumstances, without the parties having any choice in the matter" (ed. R. W. Chapman [Oxford: Oxford University Press, 1904; rev. ed., 1970], p. 705).

4 Most important benefits.

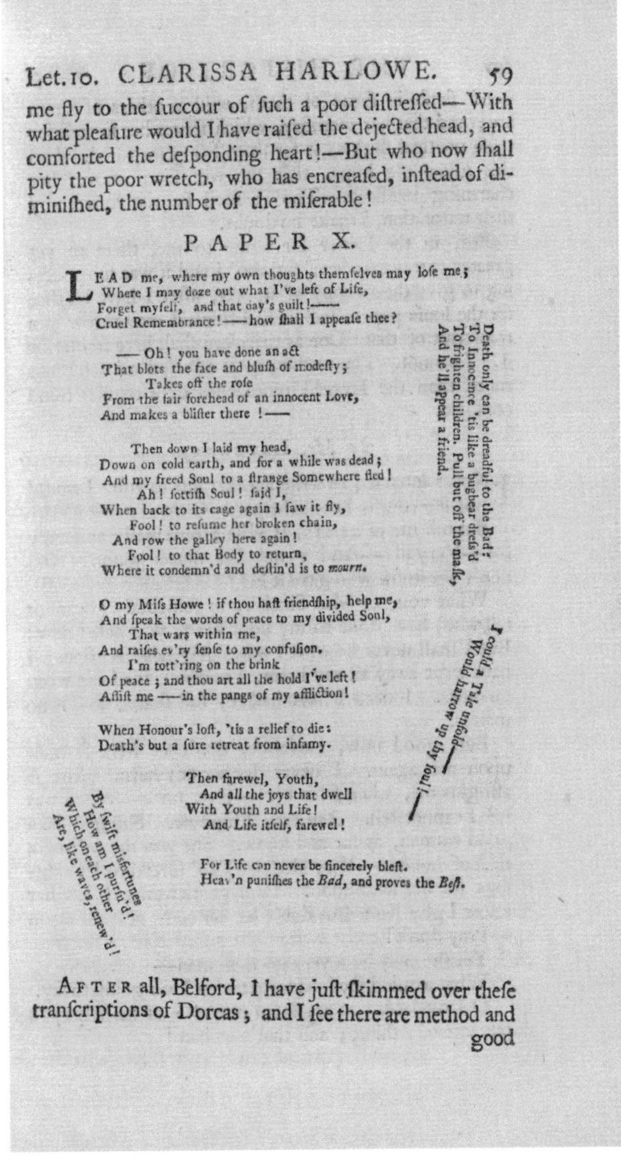

Let. 10. CLARISSA HARLOWE. 59

me fly to the ſuccour of ſuch a poor diſtreſſed—With what pleaſure would I have raiſed the dejected head, and comforted the deſponding heart!—But who now ſhall pity the poor wretch, who has encreaſed, inſtead of diminiſhed, the number of the miſerable!

PAPER X.

LEAD me, where my own thoughts themſelves may loſe me;
Where I may doze out what I've left of Life,
Forget myſelf, and that day's guilt!——
Cruel Remembrance!——how ſhall I appeaſe thee?

——Oh! you have done an act
That blots the face and bluſh of modeſty;
Takes off the roſe
From the fair forehead of an innocent Love,
And makes a bliſter there!——

Then down I laid my head,
Down on cold earth, and for a while was dead;
And my freed Soul to a ſtrange Somewhere fled!
Ah! ſottiſh Soul! ſaid I,
When back to its cage again I ſaw it fly,
Fool! to reſume her broken chain,
And row the galley here again!
Fool! to that Body to return,
Where it condemn'd and deſtin'd is to *mourn*.

O my Miſs Howe! if thou haſt friendſhip, help me,
And ſpeak the words of peace to my divided Soul,
That wars within me,
And raiſes ev'ry ſenſe to my confuſion.
I'm tott'ring on the brink
Of peace; and thou art all the hold I've left!
Aſſiſt me——in the pangs of my affliction!

When Honour's loſt, 'tis a relief to die:
Death's but a ſure retreat from infamy.

Then farewel, Youth,
And all the joys that dwell
With Youth and Life!
And Life itſelf, farewel!

For Life can never be ſincerely bleſt.
Heav'n puniſhes the *Bad*, and proves the *Beſt*.

Death only can be dreadful to the Bad:
To Innocence 'tis like a bugbear dreſs'd
To frighten children. Pull but off the maſk,
And he'll appear a friend.

I could a Tale unfold——
Would harrow up thy ſoul!——

By ſwift misfortunes
How am I purſu'd!
Which on each other
Are, like waves, renew'd!

AFTER all, Belford, I have juſt ſkimmed over theſe tranſcriptions of Dorcas; and I ſee there are method and good

Paper X from the so-called Mad Papers in Samuel Richardson, *Clarissa,* 3rd ed., 8 vols. (London: Samuel Richardson, 1751), vol. 5, letter 36. The disordered scraps of print are designed to suggest disparate jottings on a sheet of paper, and thereby the disordered state of the heroine's mind at this stage in the novel. In the mid-eighteenth century, novelists such as Richardson and Laurence Sterne achieved many creative effects through their ingenious and idiosyncratic employment of printed spacing and punctuation.

and how much more might have been said but for the restraints of propriety.—The charm of her own name was not wanting. *Miss Woodhouse* appeared more than once,[5] and never without a something of pleasing connection, either a compliment to her taste, or a remembrance of what she had said; and in the very last time of its meeting her eye, unadorned as it was by any such broad wreath of gallantry, she yet could discern the effect of her influence and acknowledge the greatest compliment perhaps of all conveyed. Compressed into the very lowest vacant corner[6] were these words—"I had not a spare moment on Tuesday, as you know, for Miss Woodhouse's beautiful little friend. Pray make my excuses and adieus to her." This, Emma could not doubt, was all for herself. Harriet was remembered only from being *her* friend. His information and prospects as to Enscombe were neither worse nor better than had been anticipated; Mrs. Churchill was recovering, and he dared not yet, even in his own imagination, fix a time for coming to Randalls again.

Gratifying, however, and stimulative[7] as was the letter in the material[8] part, its sentiments, she yet found, when it was folded up and returned to Mrs. Weston, that it had not added any lasting warmth, that she could still do without the writer, and that he must learn to do without her. Her intentions were unchanged. Her resolution of refusal only grew more interesting by the addition of a scheme for his subsequent consolation and happiness. His recollection of Harriet, and the words which clothed it, the "beautiful little friend," suggested to her the idea of Harriet's succeeding her in his affections. Was it impossible?—No.—Harriet undoubtedly was greatly his inferior in understanding; but he had been very much struck with the loveliness of her face and the warm simplicity of her manner; and all the probabilities of circumstance and connection were in her favour.—For Harriet, it would be advantageous and delightful indeed.

"I must not dwell upon it," said she.—"I must not think of it. I know the danger of indulging such speculations. But stranger things have happened; and when we cease to care for each other as we do now, it will be the means of confirming us in that sort of true disin-

5 Lingering on names was a permissible way of (consciously or unconsciously) registering attachment in the eighteenth-century epistolary tradition, especially in situations where direct allusion was impossible. For example, in vol. II, Letter XXI, of Fanny Burney's *Evelina, or the History of a Young Lady's Entrance into the World* (1778), the heroine's burgeoning fondness for Lord Orville is perceptible in her readiness to write down his name: "I fancy—that Lord Orville saw what passed, for scarcely was I at liberty, ere he returned. Methought, my dear Sir, the pleasure, the surprise of that moment, recompensed me for all the chagrin I had before felt: for do you not think, that this return, manifests, from a character so quiet, so reserved as Lord Orville's, something like solicitude in my concerns?"

6 This glancing reference, alerting a reader to the irregular, material presence of a handwritten letter beyond the impersonal uniformity of the printed text, also has affinities with the spatial and textual self-awareness of the eighteenth-century epistolary novel. Perhaps the most famous creative employment of irregular *mise-en-page* to suggest the contingencies of manuscript comes in the so-called Mad Papers composed by the heroine of *Clarissa* after her incarceration and rape at the hands of Lovelace. Michel Butor has also commented: "Reproducing a page, or even a line, within another page affords an optical partitioning whose properties are quite different from those of the usual partitioning of a quotation. It serves to introduce new tensions into the text" ("The Book as Object," in *Inventory*, trans. R. Howard [London: Jonathan Cape, 1970], p. 55).

7 Stimulating.

8 Relevant, crucial.

terested friendship which I can already look forward to with pleasure."

It was well to have a comfort in store on Harriet's behalf, though it might be wise to let the fancy touch it seldom; for evil in that quarter was at hand. As Frank Churchill's arrival had succeeded Mr. Elton's engagement in the conversation of Highbury, as the latest interest had entirely born down the first, so now upon Frank Churchill's disappearance, Mr. Elton's concerns were assuming the most irresistible form.—His wedding-day was named. He would soon be among them again; Mr. Elton and his bride. There was hardly time to talk over the first letter from Enscombe before "Mr. Elton and his bride" was in every body's mouth, and Frank Churchill was forgotten. Emma grew sick at the sound. She had had three weeks of happy exemption from Mr. Elton; and Harriet's mind, she had been willing to hope, had been lately gaining strength. With Mr. Weston's ball in view at least, there had been a great deal of insensibility to other things; but it was now too evident that she had not attained such a state of composure as could stand against the actual approach—new carriage, bell ringing and all.

Poor Harriet was in a flutter of spirits which required all the reasonings and soothings and attentions of every kind that Emma could give. Emma felt that she could not do too much for her, that Harriet had a right to all her ingenuity and all her patience; but it was heavy work to be for ever convincing without producing any effect, for ever agreed to, without being able to make their opinions the same. Harriet listened submissively, and said "it was very true—it was just as Miss Woodhouse described—it was not worth while to think about them—and she would not think about them any longer"—but no change of subject could avail, and the next half hour saw her as anxious and restless about the Eltons as before.—At last Emma attacked her on another ground.[9]

"Your allowing yourself to be so occupied and so unhappy about Mr. Elton's marrying, Harriet, is the strongest reproach you can make *me.* You could not give me a greater reproof for the mistake I fell into. It was all my doing, I know. I have not forgotten it, I assure

9 Front.

10 Reputation.

you.—Deceived myself, I did very miserably deceive you—and it will be a painful reflection to me for ever. Do not imagine me in danger of forgetting it."

Harriet felt this too much to utter more than a few words of eager exclamation. Emma continued,

"I have not said, exert yourself Harriet for my sake; think less, talk less of Mr. Elton for my sake; because for your own sake rather, I would wish it to be done, for the sake of what is more important than my comfort, a habit of self-command in you, a consideration of what is your duty, an attention to propriety, an endeavour to avoid the suspicions of others, to save your health and credit,[10] and restore your tranquillity. These are the motives which I have been pressing on you. They are very important—and sorry I am that you cannot feel them sufficiently to act upon them. My being saved from pain is a very secondary consideration. I want you to save yourself from greater pain. Perhaps I may sometimes have felt that Harriet would not forget what was due—or rather what would be kind by me."

This appeal to her affections did more than all the rest. The idea of wanting gratitude and consideration for Miss Woodhouse, whom she really loved extremely, made her wretched for a while, and when the violence of grief was comforted away, still remained powerful enough to prompt to what was right and support her in it very tolerably.

"You, who have been the best friend I ever had in my life—Want gratitude to you!—Nobody is equal to you!—I care for nobody as I do for you!—Oh! Miss Woodhouse, how ungrateful I have been!"

Such expressions, assisted as they were by every thing that look and manner could do, made Emma feel that she had never loved Harriet so well, nor valued her affection so highly before.

"There is no charm equal to tenderness of heart," said she afterwards to herself. "There is nothing to be compared to it. Warmth and tenderness of heart, with an affectionate, open manner, will beat all the clearness of head in the world, for attraction. I am sure it will. It is tenderness of heart which makes my dear father so generally beloved—which gives Isabella all her popularity.—I have it not—but I know how to prize and respect it.—Harriet is my superior in all the charm and all the felicity it gives. Dear Harriet!—I would not change you for the clearest-headed, longest-sighted, best-judging female breathing. Oh! the coldness of a Jane Fairfax!—Harriet is worth a hundred such.—And for a wife—a sensible man's wife—it is invaluable. I mention no names; but happy the man who changes Emma for Harriet!"

14

1 Formal visits paid to any new arrival in the community, but especially to new brides from another town.

2 In this context, *amour propre* or self-respect.

3 Figure.

Mrs. Elton was first seen at church: but though devotion might be interrupted, curiosity could not be satisfied by a bride in a pew, and it must be left for the visits in form[1] which were then to be paid, to settle whether she were very pretty indeed, or only rather pretty, or not pretty at all.

Emma had feelings, less of curiosity than of pride or propriety,[2] to make her resolve on not being the last to pay her respects; and she made a point of Harriet's going with her, that the worst of the business might be gone through as soon as possible.

She could not enter the house again, could not be in the same room to which she had with such vain artifice retreated three months ago, to lace up her boot, without *recollecting*. A thousand vexatious thoughts would recur. Compliments, charades, and horrible blunders; and it was not to be supposed that poor Harriet should not be recollecting too; but she behaved very well, and was only rather pale and silent. The visit was of course short; and there was so much embarrassment and occupation of mind to shorten it, that Emma would not allow herself entirely to form an opinion of the lady, and on no account to give one, beyond the nothing-meaning terms of being "elegantly dressed, and very pleasing."

She did not really like her. She would not be in a hurry to find fault, but she suspected that there was no elegance;—ease, but not elegance.—She was almost sure that for a young woman, a stranger, a bride, there was too much ease. Her person[3] was rather good; her face not unpretty; but neither feature, nor air, nor voice, nor manner, were elegant. Emma thought at least it would turn out so.

As for Mr. Elton, his manners did not appear—but no, she would not permit a hasty or a witty word from herself about his manners. It was an awkward ceremony at any time to be receiving wedding-visits, and a man had need be all grace to acquit himself well through it. The woman was better off; she might have the assistance of fine clothes, and the privilege of bashfulness, but the man had only his own good sense to depend on; and when she considered how peculiarly unlucky poor Mr. Elton was in being in the same room at once with the woman he had just married, the woman he had wanted to marry, and the woman whom he had been expected to marry, she must allow him to have the right to look as little wise, and to be as much affectedly, and as little really easy as could be.

"Well, Miss Woodhouse," said Harriet, when they had quitted the house, and after waiting in vain for her friend to begin; "Well, Miss Woodhouse, (with a gentle sigh,) what do you think of her?—Is not she very charming?"

There was a little hesitation in Emma's answer.

"Oh! yes—very—a very pleasing young woman."

"I think her beautiful, quite beautiful."

"Very nicely dressed, indeed; a remarkably elegant gown."

"I am not at all surprized that he should have fallen in love."

"Oh! no—there is nothing to surprize one at all.—A pretty fortune; and she came in his way."[4]

"I dare say," returned Harriet, sighing again, "I dare say she was very much attached to him."

"Perhaps she might; but it is not every man's fate to marry the woman who loves him best. Miss Hawkins perhaps wanted a home, and thought this the best offer she was likely to have."

"Yes," said Harriet earnestly, "and well she might, nobody could ever have a better. Well, I wish them happy with all my heart. And now, Miss Woodhouse, I do not think I shall mind seeing them again. He is just as superior as ever;—but being married, you know, it is quite a different thing. No, indeed, Miss Woodhouse, you need not

4 Emma's implication here is that Augusta Hawkins accepted Elton out of desperation, and that he was ready to marry anyone with enough money who came along.

be afraid; I can sit and admire him now without any great misery. To know that he has not thrown himself away, is such a comfort!—She does seem a charming young woman, just what he deserves. Happy creature! He called her 'Augusta.' How delightful!"

When the visit was returned, Emma made up her mind. She could then see more and judge better. From Harriet's happening not to be at Hartfield, and her father's being present to engage Mr. Elton, she had a quarter of an hour[5] of the lady's conversation to herself, and could composedly attend to her; and the quarter of an hour quite convinced her that Mrs. Elton was a vain woman, extremely well satisfied with herself, and thinking much of her own importance; that she meant to shine and be very superior, but with manners which had been formed in a bad school, pert and familiar; that all her notions were drawn from one set of people, and one style of living; that if not foolish she was ignorant, and that her society would certainly do Mr. Elton no good.

Harriet would have been a better match. If not wise or refined herself, she would have connected him with those who were;[6] but Miss Hawkins, it might be fairly supposed from her easy conceit, had been the best of her own set. The rich brother-in-law near Bristol was the pride of the alliance, and his place[7] and his carriages were the pride of him.

The very first subject after being seated was Maple Grove,[8] "My brother Mr. Suckling's seat"[9]—a comparison of Hartfield to Maple Grove. The grounds of Hartfield were small, but neat and pretty; and the house was modern and well-built. Mrs. Elton seemed most favourably impressed by the size of the room, the entrance, and all that she could see or imagine. "Very like Maple Grove indeed!—She was quite struck by the likeness!—That room was the very shape and size of the morning-room at Maple Grove; her sister's favourite room."—Mr. Elton was appealed to.—"Was not it astonishingly like?—She could really almost fancy herself at Maple Grove."

"And the staircase—You know, as I came in, I observed how very like the staircase was; placed exactly in the same part of the house. I really could not help exclaiming! I assure you, Miss Woodhouse, it is

5 Emma and Mrs. Elton are adhering to the conventions of form regarding the length of visits; see note 3 to vol. II, chap. 5, above.

6 Such as Emma herself.

7 Country seat.

8 The name suggests rural retreat, and it was the fashion for Bristol businessmen of a certain standing, like those in London, to move out of the urban bustle of the city itself.

9 Another of the novel's teasingly suggestive character names that hover between realism and allegory. As Frank Churchill may derive his surname from the eighteenth-century satirical poet Charles Churchill (1731–1764), Mrs. Elton's brother-in-law may owe his to the Cavalier poet Sir John Suckling (1609–1642). However, when presented in such proximity to other names such as Mrs. Partridge and Mrs. Bird, "Suckling" catches a flicker of the satirically animalistic; compare the diminishing effect of the generic names "Mr. Brown" and "Mrs. Green" in vol. II, chap. 4.

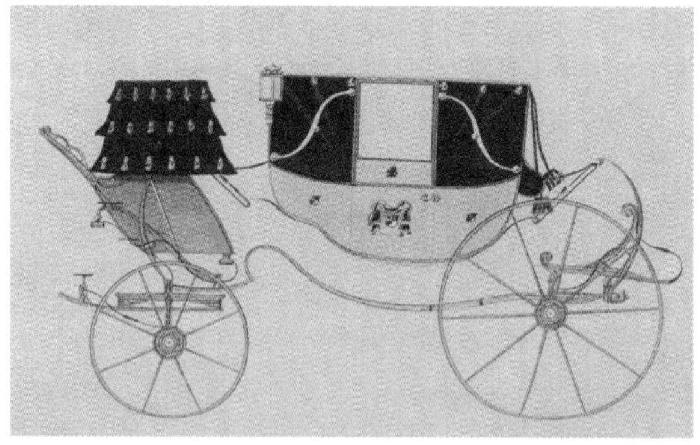

Illustration of a barouche-landau (the Sucklings' status-carriage of choice), from *Le Beau Monde, or Literary and Fashionable Magazine,* November 1806.

very delightful to me, to be reminded of a place I am so extremely partial to as Maple Grove. I have spent so many happy months there! (with a little sigh of sentiment). A charming place, undoubtedly. Every body who sees it is struck by its beauty; but to me, it has been quite a home. Whenever you are transplanted,[10] like me, Miss Woodhouse, you will understand how very delightful it is to meet with any thing at all like what one has left behind. I always say this is quite one of the evils of matrimony."

Emma made as slight a reply as she could; but it was fully sufficient for Mrs. Elton, who only wanted to be talking herself.

"So extremely like Maple Grove! And it is not merely the house—the grounds, I assure you, as far as I could observe, are strikingly like. The laurels at Maple Grove are in the same profusion as here, and stand very much in the same way—just across the lawn; and I had a glimpse of a fine large tree, with a bench round it, which put me so exactly in mind! My brother and sister will be enchanted[11] with this place. People who have extensive grounds themselves are always pleased with any thing in the same style."

Emma doubted the truth of this sentiment. She had a great idea that people who had extensive grounds themselves cared very little for the extensive grounds of any body else; but it was not worth while to attack an error so double-dyed,[12] and therefore only said in reply,

"When you have seen more of this country, I am afraid you will think you have over-rated Hartfield. Surry is full of beauties."

"Oh! yes, I am quite aware of that. It is the garden of England, you know. Surry is the garden of England."[13]

"Yes; but we must not rest our claims on that distinction. Many counties, I believe, are called the garden of England, as well as Surry."

"No, I fancy not," replied Mrs. Elton, with a most satisfied smile. "I never heard any county but Surry called so."

Emma was silenced.

"My brother and sister have promised us a visit in the spring, or summer at farthest," continued Mrs. Elton; "and that will be our time for exploring. While they are with us, we shall explore a great

10 Mrs. Elton is not the only character in the novel to have been "transplanted" from her original location or social station: Frank Churchill, Jane Fairfax, and, to some extent, Harriet Smith would also fall into this category.

11 A term that, like "charm" and "charming," had been worn into clichéd mobility by this time.

12 Fixed, as double-dyeing would fix and deepen the color of cloth.

13 In fact, the appellation "Garden of England" has been traditionally applied to the county of Kent.

deal, I dare say. They will have their barouche-landau,[14] of course, which holds four perfectly; and therefore, without saying any thing of *our* carriage, we should be able to explore the different beauties extremely well. They would hardly come in their chaise, I think, at that season of the year. Indeed, when the time draws on, I shall decidedly recommend their bringing the barouche-landau; it will be so very much preferable. When people come into a beautiful country of this sort, you know, Miss Woodhouse, one naturally wishes them to see as much as possible; and Mr. Suckling is extremely fond of exploring. We explored to King's-Weston[15] twice last summer, in that way, most delightfully, just after their first having the barouche-landau. You have many parties of that kind here, I suppose, Miss Woodhouse, every summer?"

"No; not immediately here. We are rather out of distance of the very striking beauties which attract the sort of parties you speak of; and we are a very quiet set of people, I believe; more disposed to stay at home than engage in schemes of pleasure."

"Ah! there is nothing like staying at home, for real comfort. Nobody can be more devoted to home than I am. I was quite a proverb for it at Maple Grove. Many a time has Selina said, when she has been going to Bristol, 'I really cannot get this girl to move from the house. I absolutely must go in by myself, though I hate being stuck up in the barouche-landau without a companion; but Augusta, I believe, with her own good will,[16] would never stir beyond the park paling.' Many a time has she said so; and yet I am no advocate for entire seclusion. I think, on the contrary, when people shut themselves up entirely from society, it is a very bad thing; and that it is much more advisable to mix in the world in a proper degree, without living in it either too much or too little. I perfectly understand your situation, however, Miss Woodhouse[17]—(looking towards Mr. Woodhouse)—Your father's state of health must be a great drawback. Why does not he try Bath?—Indeed he should. Let me recommend Bath to you. I assure you I have no doubt of its doing Mr. Woodhouse good."

"My father tried it more than once, formerly; but without receiving any benefit; and Mr. Perry, whose name, I dare say, is not un-

14 A fashionable hybrid form of carriage, invented in 1804. A barouche was a four-wheeled carriage holding up to four passengers, two facing forward, two facing backward, with two coachmen on the box; a landau had an adjustable, two-part cover, allowing it to be open, closed, or partially closed.

15 A grand house outside central Bristol, designed by Sir John Vanbrugh for Edward Southwell, secretary of state for Ireland, and built from 1710 to 1725.

16 If left to her own devices.

17 Mrs. Elton is implying here that Emma's life is *excessively* secluded and parochial.

known to you, does not conceive it would be at all more likely to be useful now."

"Ah! that's a great pity; for I assure you, Miss Woodhouse, where the waters do agree, it is quite wonderful the relief they give.[18] In my Bath life, I have seen such instances of it! And it is so cheerful a place, that it could not fail of being of use to Mr. Woodhouse's spirits, which, I understand, are sometimes much depressed. And as to its recommendations to *you,*[19] I fancy I need not take much pains to dwell on them. The advantages of Bath to the young are pretty generally understood. It would be a charming introduction for you, who have lived so secluded a life; and I could immediately secure you some of the best society in the place. A line from me would bring you a little host of acquaintance; and my particular friend, Mrs. Partridge,[20] the lady I have always resided with when in Bath, would be most happy to shew you any attentions, and would be the very person for you to go into public with."

It was as much as Emma could bear, without being impolite. The idea of her being indebted to Mrs. Elton for what was called an *introduction*[21]—of her going into public under the auspices of a friend of Mrs. Elton's, probably some vulgar, dashing[22] widow, who, with the help of a boarder, just made a shift to live![23]—The dignity of Miss Woodhouse, of Hartfield, was sunk indeed!

She restrained herself, however, from any of the reproofs she could have given, and only thanked Mrs. Elton coolly; "but their going to Bath was quite out of the question; and she was not perfectly convinced that the place might suit her better than her father." And then, to prevent further outrage and indignation, changed the subject directly:

"I do not ask whether you are musical, Mrs. Elton. Upon these occasions, a lady's character generally precedes her; and Highbury has long known that you are a superior performer."

"Oh! no, indeed; I must protest against any such idea. A superior performer!—very far from it, I assure you. Consider from how partial a quarter your information came. I am doatingly fond of music[24]—passionately fond;—and my friends say I am not entirely de-

18 The entire history of Bath is dependent on the reputed health benefits of its mineral springs. The founding myth of Bath, cemented by Geoffrey of Monmouth's *Historia Regum Britanniae* (c. 1136), was that King Bladud (father of King Leir or Lear) founded the city after being cured of leprosy by the waters. And the factual history is traceable as far back as 43 AD, when the Romans founded "Aquae Sulis."

19 Including, presumably, the chance to catch a husband, as Mrs. Elton has just done herself.

20 See note 9 above.

21 An introduction into polite society, usually the prerogative of the party higher up the social scale.

22 Ostentatious in manner or dress.

23 Just about scraped a living.

24 Passionately; Mrs. Elton is exaggerating affectedly.

void of taste; but as to any thing else, upon my honour my performance is *mediocre*[25] to the last degree. You, Miss Woodhouse, I well know, play delightfully. I assure you it has been the greatest satisfaction, comfort, and delight to me, to hear what a musical society I am got into. I absolutely cannot do without music. It is a necessary of life to me; and having always been used to a very musical society, both at Maple Grove and in Bath, it would have been a most serious sacrifice. I honestly said as much to Mr. E.[26] when he was speaking of my future home, and expressing his fears lest the retirement of it should be disagreeable; and the inferiority of the house too—knowing what I had been accustomed to—of course he was not wholly without apprehension. When he was speaking of it in that way, I honestly said that *the world* I could give up—parties, balls, plays,—for I had no fear of retirement. Blessed with so many resources[27] within myself, the world was not necessary to *me.* I could do very well without it. To those who had no resources it was a different thing; but my resources made me quite independent. And as to smaller-sized rooms than I had been used to, I really could not give it a thought. I hoped I was perfectly equal to any sacrifice of that description. Certainly I had been accustomed to every luxury at Maple Grove; but I did assure him that two carriages were not necessary to my happiness, nor were spacious apartments. 'But,' said I, 'to be quite honest, I do not think I can live without something of a musical society. I condition for[28] nothing else; but without music, life would be a blank to me.'"

"We cannot suppose," said Emma, smiling, "that Mr. Elton would hesitate to assure you of there being a *very* musical society in Highbury; and I hope you will not find he has outstepped the truth more than may be pardoned, in consideration of the motive."

"No, indeed, I have no doubts at all on that head. I am delighted to find myself in such a circle. I hope we shall have many sweet little concerts together. I think, Miss Woodhouse, you and I must establish a musical club, and have regular weekly meetings at your house, or ours. Will not it be a good plan? If *we* exert ourselves, I think we shall not be long in want of allies. Something of that nature would be

25 Although the adjective had crossed over from French to English as early as the sixteenth century, it became fashionable in the late eighteenth and early nineteenth centuries to italicize it in writing (sometimes even restoring the acute accent on the first "e"), to emphasize its continental sophistication. Indeed, the fact that Austen's narrative itself puts the word in italics may indicate that Mrs. Elton is affecting a foreign pronunciation; after all, it would not be her only "macaronic" affectation in this chapter.

26 A vulgarism, especially considering that Mrs. Elton is talking to a woman she barely knows.

27 Capabilities.

28 Stipulate.

particularly desirable for *me,* as an inducement to keep me in practice; for married women, you know—there is a sad story against them, in general. They are but too apt to give up music."

"But you, who are so extremely fond of it—there can be no danger, surely."

"I should hope not; but really when I look round among my acquaintance, I tremble. Selina has entirely given up music—never touches the instrument—though she played sweetly. And the same may be said of Mrs. Jeffereys—Clara Partridge, that was—and of the two Milmans, now Mrs. Bird[29] and Mrs. James Cooper; and of more than I can enumerate. Upon my word it is enough to put one in a fright. I used to be quite angry with Selina; but really I begin now to comprehend that a married woman has many things to call her attention. I believe I was half an hour this morning shut up with my housekeeper."

"But every thing of that kind," said Emma, "will soon be in so regular a train——"

"Well," said Mrs. Elton, laughing, "we shall see."

Emma, finding her so determined upon neglecting her music, had nothing more to say; and, after a moment's pause, Mrs. Elton chose another subject.

"We have been calling at Randalls," said she, "and found them both at home; and very pleasant people they seem to be. I like them extremely. Mr. Weston seems an excellent creature—quite a first-rate favourite with me already, I assure you. And *she* appears so truly good—there is something so motherly and kind-hearted about her, that it wins upon one directly. She was your governess, I think?"

Emma was almost too much astonished to answer; but Mrs. Elton hardly waited for the affirmative before she went on.

"Having understood as much, I was rather astonished to find her so very lady-like! But she is really quite the gentlewoman."

"Mrs. Weston's manners," said Emma, "were always particularly good. Their propriety, simplicity, and elegance, would make them the safest model for any young woman."

"And who do you think came in while we were there?"

29 See note 9 above.

Emma was quite at a loss. The tone implied some old acquaintance—and how could she possibly guess?

"Knightley!"[30] continued Mrs. Elton;—"Knightley himself!—Was not it lucky?—for, not being within when he called the other day, I had never seen him before; and of course, as so particular a friend of Mr. E.'s, I had a great curiosity. 'My friend Knightley' had been so often mentioned, that I was really impatient to see him; and I must do my cara sposo[31] the justice to say that he need not be ashamed of his friend. Knightley is quite the gentleman. I like him very much. Decidedly, I think, a very gentleman-like man."

Happily it was now time to be gone. They were off; and Emma could breathe.

"Insufferable woman!" was her immediate exclamation. "Worse than I had supposed. Absolutely insufferable! Knightley!—I could not have believed it. Knightley!—never seen him in her life before, and call him Knightley!—and discover that he is a gentleman! A little upstart, vulgar being, with her Mr. E., and her *cara sposo,* and her resources, and all her airs of pert pretension and under-bred finery. Actually to discover that Mr. Knightley is a gentleman! I doubt whether he will return the compliment, and discover her to be a lady. I could not have believed it! And to propose that she and I should unite to form a musical club! One would fancy we were bosom friends! And Mrs. Weston!—Astonished that the person who had brought me up should be a gentlewoman! Worse and worse. I never met with her equal. Much beyond my hopes. Harriet is disgraced by any comparison. Oh! what would Frank Churchill say to her, if he were here? How angry and how diverted he would be! Ah! there I am—thinking of him directly. Always the first person to be thought of! How I catch myself out! Frank Churchill comes as regularly into my mind!"——

All this ran so glibly[32] through her thoughts, that by the time her father had arranged himself, after the bustle of the Eltons' departure, and was ready to speak, she was very tolerably capable of attending.

"Well, my dear," he deliberately began, "considering we never saw her before, she seems a very pretty sort of young lady; and I dare say she was very much pleased with you. She speaks a little too quick. A little quickness of voice there is which rather hurts the ear. But I be-

30 To refer to a mere acquaintance without using his title is a considerable social *faux pas.*

31 Italian for "dear husband," a term that, as Pat Rogers has convincingly shown, had become almost unusably hackneyed by 1814 ("'Caro Sposo': Mrs Elton, Burneys, Thrales, and Noels," *Review of English Studies,* n.s., XLV: 177, 1994], pp. 70–75). However, someone who knew their Italian would also know that the adjective has to agree in gender with the noun, giving the correct form, "caro sposo." This error has become one of the most debated textual cruces in the novel, largely because critics and editors have been divided over whether the mistaken Italian belongs to Mrs. Elton the character or to Austen the author (or at least her printers). In his hugely influential 1923 Oxford edition of the novel, R. W. Chapman enshrined the latter view of the error in his orthography, correcting it to "caro sposo"—which he also substituted for the later misspellings of the phrase attributed to Mrs. Elton. Some more recent editions, such as the Cambridge edition, ed. Richard Cronin and Dorothy McMillan (2005), have returned to the 1816 text's variable spellings. John Sutherland's brilliant little discussion of this issue finally comes down in support of Chapman's emendations. "This is a very tiny puzzle," he concludes. "Its value is that it obliges readers to determine for themselves just how vulgar they think Mrs Elton is, and what kind of vulgar. Is she the kind of grossly uneducated woman who would mangle a well-known Italian phrase? Or is she merely someone who would use a once-fashionable phrase correctly, but long after it had ceased to be fashionable, and in provincial company where it would strike her listeners as disgustingly 'slangy'? Is she coarse; or merely egotistic and insensitive to social nuance? Readers will determine the issue for themselves; myself, I tend towards Chapman's view of Mrs Elton—she is vulgar, but not so ignorantly vulgar that she would say 'cara sposo'" (*Can Jane Eyre Be Happy? More Puzzles in Classic Fiction* [Oxford: Oxford University Press, 1987], p. 41). I concur with Sutherland's emphasis on the need for readers "to determine for themselves"; however, precisely for that reason, I have chosen to retain the original inconsistencies of

lieve I am nice;[33] I do not like strange voices; and nobody speaks like you and poor Miss Taylor. However, she seems a very obliging, pretty-behaved young lady, and no doubt will make him a very good wife. Though I think he had better not have married. I made the best excuses I could for not having been able to wait on[34] him and Mrs. Elton on this happy occasion; I said that I hoped I *should* in the course of the summer. But I ought to have gone before. Not to wait upon a bride is very remiss. Ah! it shews what a sad invalid I am! But I do not like the corner into Vicarage-lane."

"I dare say your apologies were accepted, sir. Mr. Elton knows you."

"Yes: but a young lady—a bride—I ought to have paid my respects to her if possible. It was being very deficient."[35]

"But, my dear papa, you are no friend to matrimony; and therefore why should you be so anxious to pay your respects to a *bride?* It ought to be no recommendation to *you.* It is encouraging people to marry if you make so much of them."

"No, my dear, I never encouraged any body to marry, but I would always wish to pay every proper attention to a lady—and a bride, especially, is never to be neglected. More is avowedly due to *her.* A bride, you know, my dear, is always the first in company, let the others be who they may."

"Well, papa, if this is not encouragement to marry, I do not know what is. And I should never have expected you to be lending your sanction to such vanity-baits[36] for poor young ladies."

"My dear, you do not understand me. This is a matter of mere common politeness and good-breeding, and has nothing to do with any encouragement to people to marry."

Emma had done. Her father was growing nervous, and could not understand *her.* Her mind returned to Mrs. Elton's offences, and long, very long, did they occupy her.

spelling, so that readers may choose to attribute them as they see fit.

32 Quickly and easily.

33 Too fussy.

34 Make the expected "visit in form" due to the new bride.

35 Negligent.

36 Incentives to vanity.

15

1 Overly familiar.

Emma was not required, by any subsequent discovery, to retract her ill opinion of Mrs. Elton. Her observation had been pretty correct. Such as Mrs. Elton appeared to her on this second interview, such she appeared whenever they met again,—self-important, presuming, familiar,[1] ignorant, and ill-bred. She had a little beauty and a little accomplishment, but so little judgment that she thought herself coming with superior knowledge of the world, to enliven and improve a country neighbourhood; and conceived Miss Hawkins to have held such a place in society as Mrs. Elton's consequence only could surpass.

There was no reason to suppose Mr. Elton thought at all differently from his wife. He seemed not merely happy with her, but proud. He had the air of congratulating himself on having brought such a woman to Highbury, as not even Miss Woodhouse could equal; and the greater part of her new acquaintance, disposed to commend, or not in the habit of judging, following the lead of Miss Bates's good-will or taking it for granted that the bride must be as clever and as agreeable as she professed herself, were very well satisfied; so that Mrs. Elton's praise passed from one mouth to another as it ought to do, unimpeded by Miss Woodhouse, who readily continued her first contribution and talked with a good grace of her being "very pleasant and very elegantly dressed."

In one respect Mrs. Elton grew even worse than she had appeared at first. Her feelings altered towards Emma.—Offended, probably, by the little encouragement which her proposals of intimacy met

with, she drew back in her turn and gradually became much more cold and distant; and though the effect was agreeable, the ill-will which produced it was necessarily increasing Emma's dislike. Her manners too—and Mr. Elton's, were unpleasant towards Harriet. They were sneering and negligent. Emma hoped it must rapidly work Harriet's cure; but the sensations which could prompt such behaviour sunk[2] them both very much.—It was not to be doubted that poor Harriet's attachment had been an offering to conjugal unreserve,[3] and her own share in the story, under a colouring the least favourable to her and the most soothing to him, had in all likelihood been given also. She was, of course, the object of their joint dislike.—

2 Diminished.

3 That Elton had made a point of discussing Harriet's attachment with his wife, as a proof of his candor and trustworthiness.

ELEGY

WRITTEN IN A

COUNTRY CHURCH-YARD.

THE Curfew tolls the knell of parting day,
The lowing herd wind ſlowly o'er the lea,
The plowman homeward plods his weary way,
And leaves the world to darkneſs, and to me.
Now fades the glimmering landſcape on the ſight,
And all the air a ſolemn ſtillneſs holds,
Save where the beetle wheels his droning flight,
And drowſy tinklings lull the diſtant folds;
Save

William Blake, illustration to the opening page of Gray's "Elegy Written in a Country Church-Yard" (c. 1797–1798).

When they had nothing else to say, it must be always easy to begin abusing Miss Woodhouse; and the enmity which they dared not shew in open disrespect to her, found a broader vent in contemptuous treatment of Harriet.

Mrs. Elton took a great fancy to Jane Fairfax; and from the first. Not merely when a state of warfare with one young lady might be supposed to recommend the other, but from the very first; and she was not satisfied with expressing a natural and reasonable admiration—but without solicitation, or plea, or privilege,[4] she must be wanting to assist and befriend her.—Before Emma had forfeited her confidence, and about the third time of their meeting, she heard all Mrs. Elton's knight-errantry[5] on the subject.—

"Jane Fairfax is absolutely charming, Miss Woodhouse.—I quite rave about[6] Jane Fairfax.[7]—A sweet, interesting creature. So mild and lady-like—and with such talents!—I assure you I think she has very extraordinary talents. I do not scruple to say that she plays extremely well. I know enough of music to speak decidedly on that point. Oh! she is absolutely charming! You will laugh at my warmth[8]—but upon my word, I talk of nothing but Jane Fairfax.—And her situation is so calculated to affect one!—Miss Woodhouse, we must exert ourselves and endeavour to do something for her. We must bring her forward. Such talents as her's must not be suffered to remain unknown.—I dare say you have heard those charming lines of the poet,

'Full many a flower is born to blush unseen,
'And waste its fragrance on the desert air.'[9]

We must not allow them to be verified in sweet Jane Fairfax."

"I cannot think there is any danger of it," was Emma's calm answer—"and when you are better acquainted with Miss Fairfax's situation and understand what her home has been, with Col. and Mrs. Campbell, I have no idea that you will suppose her talents can be unknown."

"Oh! but dear Miss Woodhouse, she is now in such retirement, such obscurity, so thrown away.—Whatever advantages she may have

4 Without being asked, and without any particular social right or obligation to do so.

5 A bitterly ironic implicature on Emma's part, since the keynote of true knight-errantry is selfless service.

6 The *OED* cites this as an early example of the prepositional form of "rave," meaning "to speak or write about something or someone with great enthusiasm or admiration."

7 Not only does Mrs. Elton employ the slangy "quite rave," she also presumes an indecorous degree of familiarity in using Jane's first name instead of her title in a polite conversation. This also allows her to implicate a much more friendly relationship with Jane than she has with Emma.

8 Enthusiasm.

9 Mrs. Elton is slightly misquoting two of the most famous lines of Thomas Gray's "Elegy Written in a Country Church-Yard," first published in 1751. The original stanzas run thus:

Full many a gem of purest ray serene
The dark unfathomed caves of ocean bear:
Full many a flower is born to blush unseen
And waste its sweetness on the desert air.

Some village-Hampden that with dauntless breast
The little tyrant of his fields withstood;
Some mute inglorious Milton here may rest,
Some Cromwell guiltless of his country's blood.

The (mis)quotation from Gray is suggestive on more than one level. Most simply, the precise nature of Mrs. Elton's error reflects back on her values, since "fragrance" has more resonances of artificial perfume than "sweetness": instances of this sense can be found as early as Alexander Pope's 1715 version of *The Iliad* ("Here first she bathes, and round her Body pours / Soft Oils of Fragrance, and ambrosial Show'rs"). In addition, by quoting the eighteenth century's most famous graveyard poem, she unwittingly contributes to the narrative's larger association of Jane Fairfax with mortality.

enjoyed with the Campbells are so palpably at an end! And I think she feels it. I am sure she does. She is very timid and silent. One can see that she feels the want of encouragement. I like her the better for it. I must confess it is a recommendation to me. I am a great advocate for timidity—and I am sure one does not often meet with it. —But in those who are at all inferior, it is extremely prepossessing. Oh! I assure you, Jane Fairfax is a very delightful character, and interests me more than I can express."

"You appear to feel a great deal—but I am not aware how you or any of Miss Fairfax's acquaintance here, any of those who have known her longer than yourself, can shew her any other attention than"——

"My dear Miss Woodhouse, a vast deal may be done by those who dare to act. You and I need not be afraid. If *we* set the example, many will follow it as far as they can; though all have not our situations. *We* have carriages to fetch and convey her home, and *we* live in a style which could not make the addition of Jane Fairfax, at any time, the least inconvenient.—I should be extremely displeased if Wright were to send us up such a dinner, as could make me regret having asked *more* than Jane Fairfax to partake of it. I have no idea of that sort of thing. It is not likely that I *should,* considering what I have been used to. My greatest danger, perhaps, in housekeeping, may be quite the other way, in doing too much, and being too careless of expense. Maple Grove will probably be my model more than it ought to be—for we do not at all affect to equal my brother, Mr. Suckling, in income. —However, my resolution is taken as to noticing Jane Fairfax.—I shall certainly have her very often at my house, shall introduce her wherever I can, shall have musical parties to draw out her talents, and shall be constantly on the watch for an eligible situation. My acquaintance is so very extensive, that I have little doubt of hearing of something to suit her shortly.—I shall introduce her, of course, very particularly to my brother and sister when they come to us. I am sure they will like her extremely; and when she gets a little acquainted with them, her fears will completely wear off, for there really is nothing in the manners of either but what is highly conciliating.[10]—I shall

10 Likeable, conducive to friendship.

have her very often indeed while they are with me, and I dare say we shall sometimes find a seat for her in the barouche-landau in some of our exploring parties."

"Poor Jane Fairfax!"—thought Emma.—"You have not deserved this. You may have done wrong with regard to Mr. Dixon, but this is a punishment beyond what you can have merited!—The kindness and protection of Mrs. Elton!—'Jane Fairfax and Jane Fairfax.' Heavens! Let me not suppose that she dares go about, Emma Woodhouse-ing[11] me!—But upon my honour, there seem no limits to the licentiousness of that woman's tongue!"

Emma had not to listen to such paradings again—to any so exclusively addressed to herself—so disgustingly decorated with a "dear Miss Woodhouse." The change on Mrs. Elton's side soon afterwards appeared, and she was left in peace—neither forced to be the very particular friend of Mrs. Elton, nor, under Mrs. Elton's guidance, the very active patroness of Jane Fairfax, and only sharing with others in a general way, in knowing what was felt, what was meditated, what was done.

She looked on with some amusement.—Miss Bates's gratitude for Mrs. Elton's attentions to Jane was in the first style of guileless simplicity and warmth. She was quite one of her worthies—the most amiable, affable,[12] delightful woman—just as accomplished and condescending as Mrs. Elton meant to be considered. Emma's only surprize was that Jane Fairfax should accept those attentions and tolerate Mrs. Elton as she seemed to do. She heard of her walking with the Eltons, sitting with the Eltons, spending a day with the Eltons! This was astonishing!—She could not have believed it possible that the taste or the pride of Miss Fairfax could endure such society and friendship as the Vicarage had to offer.

"She is a riddle, quite a riddle!" said she.—"To chuse to remain here month after month, under privations of every sort! And now to chuse the mortification of Mrs. Elton's notice and the penury of her conversation, rather than return to the superior companions who have always loved her with such real, generous affection."

Jane had come to Highbury professedly for three months; the Campbells were gone to Ireland for three months; but now the

11 As Emma's coinage implies, to speak of a formal acquaintance without their title is the equivalent of the French *tutoyer*—using an informal mode of address when etiquette requires a more respectful one.

12 "Easy of manners; accostable; courteous; complaisant" (Johnson).

Campbells had promised their daughter to stay at least till Midsummer,[13] and fresh invitations had arrived for her to join them there. According to Miss Bates—it all came from her—Mrs. Dixon had written most pressingly. Would Jane but go, means were to be found, servants sent, friends[14] contrived—no travelling difficulty allowed to exist; but still she had declined it!

"She must have some motive, more powerful than appears, for refusing this invitation," was Emma's conclusion. "She must be under some sort of penance, inflicted either by the Campbells or herself. There is great fear, great caution, great resolution somewhere.—She is *not* to be with the *Dixons*. The decree is issued by somebody. But why must she consent to be with the Eltons?—Here is quite a separate puzzle."

Upon her speaking her wonder aloud on that part of the subject, before the few who knew her opinion of Mrs. Elton, Mrs. Weston ventured this apology for Jane.

"We cannot suppose that she has any great enjoyment at the Vicarage, my dear Emma—but it is better than being always at home. Her aunt is a good creature, but, as a constant companion, must be very tiresome. We must consider what Miss Fairfax quits, before we condemn her taste for what she goes to."

"You are right, Mrs. Weston," said Mr. Knightley warmly, "Miss Fairfax is as capable as any of us of forming a just opinion of Mrs. Elton. Could she have chosen with whom to associate, she would not have chosen her. But (with a reproachful smile at Emma) she receives attentions from Mrs. Elton, which nobody else pays her."

Emma felt that Mrs. Weston was giving her a momentary glance; and she was herself struck by his warmth. With a faint blush, she presently replied,

"Such attentions as Mrs. Elton's, I should have imagined, would rather disgust than gratify Miss Fairfax. Mrs. Elton's invitations I should have imagined any thing but inviting."

"I should not wonder," said Mrs. Weston, "if Miss Fairfax were to have been drawn on beyond her own inclination, by her aunt's eagerness in accepting Mrs. Elton's civilities for her. Poor Miss Bates may very likely have committed her niece and hurried her into a greater

13 June 24.

14 Traveling companions.

appearance of intimacy than her own good sense would have dictated, in spite of the very natural wish of a little change."

Both felt rather anxious to hear him speak again; and after a few minutes silence, he said,

"Another thing must be taken into consideration too—Mrs. Elton does not talk *to* Miss Fairfax as she speaks *of* her. We all know the difference between the pronouns he or she and thou, the plainest-spoken amongst us; we all feel the influence of a something[15] beyond common civility in our personal intercourse with each other—a something more early implanted. We cannot give any body the disagreeable hints that we may have been very full of the hour before. We feel things differently. And besides the operation of this, as a general principle, you may be sure that Miss Fairfax awes Mrs. Elton by her superiority both of mind and manner; and that face to face Mrs. Elton treats her with all the respect which she has a claim to. Such a woman as Jane Fairfax probably never fell in Mrs. Elton's way before—and no degree of vanity can prevent her acknowledging her own comparative littleness in action, if not in consciousness."

"I know how highly you think of Jane Fairfax," said Emma. Little Henry was in her thoughts, and a mixture of alarm and delicacy made her irresolute what else to say.

"Yes," he replied, "any body may know how highly I think of her."

"And yet," said Emma, beginning hastily and with an arch look, but soon stopping—it was better, however, to know the worst at once—she hurried on—"And yet, perhaps, you may hardly be aware yourself how highly it is. The extent of your admiration may take you by surprize some day or other."

Mr. Knightley was hard at work upon the lower buttons of his thick leather gaiters,[16] and either the exertion of getting them together, or some other cause, brought the colour into his face, as he answered,

"Oh! are you there?—But you are miserably behind-hand. Mr. Cole gave me a hint of it six weeks ago."

He stopped.—Emma felt her foot pressed by Mrs. Weston, and did not herself know what to think. In a moment he went on—

15 For all the celebrated precision of her style, Austen also makes refined use of the resources of creative *im*-precision, as witnessed by the effects she derives from phrases such as "something" and "a something." For example, in vol. III, chap. 9, of *Sense and Sensibility*, Mrs. Dashwood claims, with the benefit of hindsight: "There was always a something,—if you remember,—in Willoughby's eyes at times, which I did not like." Perhaps the greatest poet of "something" at the time was Wordsworth, whose "Tintern Abbey" famously describes "a sense sublime/Of something far more deeply interfused."

16 Gaiters were worn by men to cover the ankle and the lower part of the leg.

"That will never be, however, I can assure you. Miss Fairfax, I dare say, would not have me if I were to ask her—and I am very sure I shall never ask her."

Emma returned her friend's pressure with interest; and was pleased enough to exclaim,

"You are not vain, Mr. Knightley. I will say that for you."

He seemed hardly to hear her; he was thoughtful—and in a manner which shewed him not pleased, soon afterwards said,

"So you have been settling that I should marry Jane Fairfax."

"No indeed I have not. You have scolded me too much for match-making, for me to presume to take such a liberty with you. What I said just now, meant nothing. One says those sort of things, of course, without any idea of a serious meaning. Oh! no, upon my word I have not the smallest wish for your marrying Jane Fairfax or Jane any body. You would not come in and sit with us in this comfortable way, if you were married."

Mr. Knightley was thoughtful again. The result of his reverie was, "No, Emma, I do not think the extent of my admiration for her will ever take me by surprize.—I never had a thought of her in that way, I assure you." And soon afterwards, "Jane Fairfax is a very charming young woman—but not even Jane Fairfax is perfect. She has a fault. She has not the open temper which a man would wish for in a wife."

Emma could not but rejoice to hear that she had a fault. "Well," said she, "and you soon silenced Mr. Cole, I suppose?"

"Yes, very soon. He gave me a quiet hint; I told him he was mistaken; he asked my pardon and said no more. Cole does not want to be wiser or wittier than his neighbours."

"In that respect how unlike dear Mrs. Elton, who wants to be wiser and wittier than all the world! I wonder how she speaks of the Coles—what she calls them! How can she find any appellation for them, deep enough in familiar vulgarity? She calls you, Knightley—what can she do for Mr. Cole? And so I am not to be surprized that Jane Fairfax accepts her civilities and consents to be with her. Mrs. Weston, your argument weighs most with me. I can much more readily enter into the temptation of getting away from Miss Bates, than I can believe in the triumph of Miss Fairfax's mind over Mrs. Elton. I have no faith in Mrs. Elton's acknowledging herself the inferior in thought, word, or deed;[17] or in her being under any restraint beyond her own scanty rule of good-breeding. I cannot imagine that she will not be continually insulting her visitor with praise, encouragement, and offers of service; that she will not be continually detailing her magnificent intentions, from the procuring her a permanent situation to the including her in those delightful exploring parties which are to take place in the barouche-landau."

"Jane Fairfax has feeling," said Mr. Knightley—"I do not accuse her of want of feeling. Her sensibilities, I suspect, are strong—and her temper excellent in its power of forbearance, patience, self-controul; but it wants openness. She is reserved, more reserved, I think, than she used to be—And I love an open temper. No—till Cole alluded to my supposed attachment, it had never entered my head. I saw Jane Fairfax and conversed with her, with admiration and pleasure always—but with no thought beyond."

"Well, Mrs. Weston," said Emma triumphantly when he left them, "what do you say now to Mr. Knightley's marrying Jane Fairfax?"

"Why really, dear Emma, I say that he is so very much occupied by the idea of *not* being in love with her, that I should not wonder if it were to end in his being so at last. Do not beat me."

17 A phrase from the Holy Communion service in the Book of Common Prayer: "Almighty God, Father of our Lord Jesus Christ, Maker of all things, Judge of all men: We acknowledge and bewail our manifold sins and wickedness, Which we from time to time most grievously have committed, By thought, word, and deed, Against thy Divine Majesty, Provoking most justly thy wrath and indignation against us."

16

Every body in and about Highbury who had ever visited Mr. Elton, was disposed to pay him attention on his marriage. Dinner-parties and evening-parties were made for him and his lady; and invitations flowed in so fast that she had soon the pleasure of apprehending they were never to have a disengaged day.

"I see how it is," said she. "I see what a life I am to lead among you. Upon my word we shall be absolutely dissipated.[1] We really seem quite the fashion. If this is living in the country, it is nothing very formidable. From Monday next to Saturday, I assure you we have not a disengaged day!—A woman with fewer resources than I have, need not have been at a loss."

No invitation came amiss to her. Her Bath habits made evening-parties perfectly natural to her, and Maple Grove had given her a taste for dinners. She was a little shocked at the want of two drawing rooms, at the poor attempt at rout-cakes,[2] and there being no ice in the Highbury card parties.[3] Mrs. Bates, Mrs. Perry, Mrs. Goddard and others, were a good deal behind hand in knowledge of the world, but *she* would soon shew them how every thing ought to be arranged. In the course of the spring she must return their civilities by one very superior party—in which her card tables should be set out with their separate candles and unbroken packs in the true style—and more waiters engaged for the evening than their own establishment could furnish, to carry round the refreshments at exactly the proper hour, and in the proper order.

1 In this context, distracted by variety.

2 As the name implies, cakes served at routs or sophisticated soirées. Maria Rundell offers this recipe for *"Rout Drop Cakes"*: "Mix two pounds of flour, one ditto butter, one ditto sugar, one ditto currants, clean and dry; then wet into a stiff paste, with two eggs, a large spoon of orange-flower water, ditto rose-water, ditto sweet wine, ditto brandy, drop on a tin-plate floured; a very short time bakes them" (*A New System of Domestic Cookery; formed Upon Principles of Economy* [London: John Murray, 1807; rev. ed., 1808], p. 234).

3 Mrs. Elton is tilting here both at Highbury's distance from London fashions and at the economic status of its inhabitants. Water ice and ice-cream (or "cream ices") were firmly established as fashionable dishes in the urban centers of Britain by the end of the eighteenth century, largely promoted by the enterprise of confectioners such as James Gunter and Frederick Nutt. Elizabeth David remarks on the range of recipes offered by Nutt in his book *The Complete Confectioner* (1789):

> There were thirty-one different ice-creams—called so, unusually for the period—many made with fresh fruit, others with jams or fruit jelly, some with a basis of fruit syrups and a flavouring of some potent essence such as bergamot orange. Ginger, chocolate, coffee, pistachio were other flavourings used by Nutt, and he had a good mixture of Naples and ratafia biscuits with

Emma, in the meanwhile, could not be satisfied without a dinner at Hartfield for the Eltons. They must not do less than others, or she should be exposed to odious suspicions,[4] and imagined capable of pitiful resentment. A dinner there must be. After Emma had talked about it for ten minutes, Mr. Woodhouse felt no unwillingness, and only made the usual stipulation of not sitting at the bottom of the table himself,[5] with the usual regular difficulty of deciding who should do it for him.

The persons to be invited, required little thought. Besides the Eltons, it must be the Westons and Mr. Knightley; so far it was all of course[6]—and it was hardly less inevitable that poor little Harriet must be asked to make the eighth:—but this invitation was not given with equal satisfaction, and on many accounts Emma was particularly pleased by Harriet's begging to be allowed to decline it. "She would rather not be in *his* company more than she could help. She was not yet quite able to see him and his charming happy wife together, without feeling uncomfortable. If Miss Woodhouse would not be displeased, she would rather stay at home." It was precisely what Emma would have wished, had she deemed it possible enough for wishing. She was delighted with the fortitude of her little friend—for fortitude she knew it was in her to give up being in company and stay at home; and she could now invite the very person whom she really wanted to make the eighth, Jane Fairfax.—Since her last conversation with Mrs. Weston and Mr. Knightley, she was more conscience-stricken about Jane Fairfax than she had often been.—Mr. Knightley's words dwelt with her. He had said that Jane Fairfax received attentions from Mrs. Elton which nobody else paid her.

"This is very true," said she, "at least as far as relates to me, which was all that was meant—and it is very shameful.—Of the same age—and always knowing her—I ought to have been more her friend.—She will never like me now. I have neglected her too long. But I will shew her greater attention than I have done."

Every invitation was successful. They were all disengaged and all happy.—The preparatory interest of this dinner, however, was not yet over. A circumstance rather unlucky occurred. The two eldest little Knightleys were engaged to pay their grandpapa and aunt a visit

cream and a sugar syrup, another with brown breadcrumbs—an ice-cream which later became a much-loved Gunter speciality—one consisting of perfectly plain cream very lightly sweetened, and a Royal ice-cream of dense richness in which 10 egg-yolks and 2 whole eggs were made into a custard with 1 pint of cream, the whole mixed with pistachios and three kinds of candied citrus peels. There was even an ice made with a cream custard and syrup and a strong flavouring of Parmesan cheese. In short, by 1800, the London confectioners were making, in somewhat primitive form, nearly all the ice-creams we still love today and some others which have disappeared, such as one called prunello ice-cream, an egg, cream, and syrup mixture flavoured with prunello spice, a mixture assumed by Nutt to be known to everyone (*Harvest of the Cold Months: The Social History of Ice and Ices* [London: Michael Joseph, 1994], p. 314). However, outside the cities, ices were the preserve of the wealthy, as ice would have to be stored in purpose-built underground ice-houses; hence Mrs. Elton's complaint about the parochial entertainments of Highbury.

4 That is, people might begin to suspect some previous history of affection (whether requited or not) between Emma and Mr. Elton.

5 Normally, the gentleman of the household would sit at the bottom of the table and carve the meat, something for which Mr. Woodhouse has neither the inclination nor the constitution.

6 A matter of course.

of some weeks in the spring, and their papa now proposed bringing them, and staying one whole day at Hartfield—which one day would be the very day of this party.—His professional engagements did not allow of his being put off, but both father and daughter were disturbed by its happening so. Mr. Woodhouse considered eight persons at dinner together as the utmost that his nerves could bear—and here would be a ninth—and Emma apprehended that it would be a ninth very much out of humour at not being able to come even to Hartfield for forty-eight hours without falling in with a dinner-party.

She comforted her father better than she could comfort herself, by representing that though he certainly would make them nine, yet he always said so little, that the increase of noise would be very immaterial. She thought it in reality a sad exchange for herself, to have him with his grave looks and reluctant conversation opposed to her instead of his brother.

The event was more favourable to Mr. Woodhouse than to Emma. John Knightley came; but Mr. Weston was unexpectedly summoned to town and must be absent on the very day. He might be able to join them in the evening, but certainly not to dinner. Mr. Woodhouse was quite at ease; and the seeing him so, with the arrival of the little boys and the philosophic[7] composure of her brother on hearing his fate, removed the chief of even Emma's vexation.

The day came, the party were punctually assembled, and Mr. John Knightley seemed early to devote himself to the business of being agreeable. Instead of drawing his brother off to a window while they waited for dinner, he was talking to Miss Fairfax. Mrs. Elton, as elegant as lace and pearls could make her, he looked at in silence—wanting only to observe enough for Isabella's information—but Miss Fairfax was an old acquaintance and a quiet girl, and he could talk to her. He had met her before breakfast as he was returning from a walk with his little boys, when it had been just beginning to rain. It was natural to have some civil hopes on the subject, and he said,

"I hope you did not venture far, Miss Fairfax, this morning, or I am sure you must have been wet.—*We* scarcely got home in time. I hope you turned directly."

7 Stoical. This loose idiomatic application of "philosophical" to describe a particular school of philosophy dates from the seventeenth century, and is one from which eighteenth-century writers, including Fielding, drew much comedy. In book V, chap. 7, of *Tom Jones* (1749), Squire Allworthy, on what he believes to be his deathbed, describes the bequest he has left to the philosopher Square: "But the little I have been able to leave you, will extricate you from those Difficulties with which you have formerly struggled, and then I doubt not but you will meet with sufficient Prosperity to supply what a Man of your Philosophical Temper will require." More recently, in Edward St. Aubyn's novel *Never Mind* (1992), the American Anne Moore quips: "But that's what the English mean, isn't it, when they say, 'He was very philosophical about it'? They mean that someone stopped thinking about something."

"I went only to the post-office," said she, "and reached home before the rain was much. It is my daily errand. I always fetch the letters when I am here.[8] It saves trouble, and is a something to get me out. A walk before breakfast does me good."

"Not a walk in the rain, I should imagine."

"No, but it did not absolutely rain when I set out."

Mr. John Knightley smiled, and replied,

"That is to say, you chose to have your walk, for you were not six yards from your own door when I had the pleasure of meeting you; and Henry and John had seen more drops than they could count long before. The post-office has a great charm at one period of our lives. When you have lived to my age, you will begin to think letters are never worth going through the rain for."

There was a little blush, and then this answer,

"I must not hope to be ever situated as you are, in the midst of every dearest connection, and therefore I cannot expect that simply growing older should make me indifferent about letters."

8 Postal deliveries were uncommon until after Rowland Hill's postal reforms at the beginning of the 1840s; recipients would have to collect their post from the local post office in person, or send a servant to do so.

W. H. Pyne, "Worcester and London Royal Mail," from *The Costume of Great Britain* (London: William Miller, 1808).

"Indifferent! Oh! no—I never conceived you could become indifferent. Letters are no matter of indifference; they are generally a very positive curse."

"You are speaking of letters of business; mine are letters of friendship."

"I have often thought them the worst of the two," replied he coolly. "Business, you know, may bring money, but friendship hardly ever does."

"Ah! you are not serious now. I know Mr. John Knightley too well—I am very sure he understands the value of friendship as well as any body. I can easily believe that letters are very little to you, much less than to me, but it is not your being ten years older than myself which makes the difference, it is not age, but situation. You have every body dearest to you always at hand, I, probably, never shall again; and therefore till I have outlived all my affections, a post-office, I think, must always have power to draw me out, in worse weather than to-day."

"When I talked of your being altered by time, by the progress of years," said John Knightley, "I meant to imply the change of situation which time usually brings. I consider one as including the other. Time will generally lessen the interest of every attachment not within the daily circle—but that is not the change I had in view for you. As an old friend, you will allow me to hope, Miss Fairfax, that ten years hence you may have as many concentrated objects[9] as I have."

It was kindly said, and very far from giving offence. A pleasant "thank you" seemed meant to laugh it off, but a blush, a quivering lip, a tear in the eye, shewed that it was felt beyond a laugh. Her attention was now claimed by Mr. Woodhouse, who being, according to his custom on such occasions, making the circle of his guests, and paying his particular compliments to the ladies, was ending with her—and with all his mildest urbanity, said,

"I am very sorry to hear, Miss Fairfax, of your being out this morning in the rain. Young ladies should take care of themselves.—Young ladies are delicate plants.[10] They should take care of their health and their complexion. My dear, did you change your stockings?"

9 Particular objects of affection.

10 This is exactly the kind of sentiment against which Wollstonecraft rages in *A Vindication of the Rights of Woman;* indeed, feminine "delicacy" is a repeated target for her. "I once knew a weak woman of fashion," she recounts, "who was more than commonly proud of her delicacy and sensibility. She thought a distinguishing taste and puny appetite the height of all human perfection, and acted accordingly.—I have seen this weak sophisticated being neglect all the duties of life, yet recline with self-complacency on a sofa, and boast of her want of appetite as a proof of delicacy that extended to, or, perhaps, arose from, her exquisite sensibility: for it is difficult to render intelligible such ridiculous jargon" (p. 156).

"Yes, sir, I did indeed; and I am very much obliged by your kind solicitude about me."

"My dear Miss Fairfax, young ladies are very sure to be cared for.—I hope your good grandmamma and aunt are well. They are some of my very old friends. I wish my health allowed me to be a better neighbour. You do us a great deal of honour to-day, I am sure. My daughter and I are both highly sensible of your goodness, and have the greatest satisfaction in seeing you at Hartfield."

The kind-hearted, polite old man might then sit down and feel that he had done his duty, and made every fair lady welcome and easy.

By this time, the walk in the rain had reached Mrs. Elton, and her remonstrances now opened upon Jane.

"My dear Jane, what is this I hear?—Going to the post-office in the rain!—This must not be, I assure you.—You sad girl, how could you do such a thing?—It is a sign I was not there to take care of you."

Jane very patiently assured her that she had not caught any cold.

"Oh! do not tell *me.* You really are a very sad girl, and do not know how to take care of yourself.—To the post-office indeed! Mrs. Weston, did you ever hear the like? You and I must positively exert our authority."

"My advice," said Mrs. Weston kindly and persuasively, "I certainly do feel tempted to give. Miss Fairfax, you must not run such risks.—Liable as you have been to severe colds, indeed you ought to be particularly careful, especially at this time of year. The spring I always think requires more than common care. Better wait an hour or two, or even half a day for your letters, than run the risk of bringing on your cough again. Now do not you feel that you had? Yes, I am sure you are much too reasonable. You look as if you would not do such a thing again."

"Oh! she *shall not* do such a thing again," eagerly rejoined Mrs. Elton. "We will not allow her to do such a thing again:"—and nodding significantly—"there must be some arrangement made, there must indeed. I shall speak to Mr. E. The man who fetches our letters every morning (one of our men, I forget his name) shall inquire for your's too and bring them to you. That will obviate all difficulties you know; and from *us* I really think, my dear Jane, you can have no scruple to accept such an accommodation."

"You are extremely kind," said Jane; "but I cannot give up my early walk. I am advised to be out of doors as much as I can, I must walk somewhere, and the post-office is an object; and upon my word, I have scarcely ever had a bad morning before."

"My dear Jane, say no more about it. The thing is determined, that is (laughing affectedly) as far as I can presume to determine any thing without the concurrence of my lord and master. You know, Mrs. Weston, you and I must be cautious how we express ourselves. But I do flatter my self, my dear Jane, that my influence is not entirely worn out. If I meet with no insuperable difficulties therefore, consider that point as settled."

"Excuse me," said Jane earnestly, "I cannot by any means consent to such an arrangement, so needlessly troublesome to your servant. If the errand were not a pleasure to me, it could be done, as it always is when I am not here, by my grandmamma's."

"Oh! my dear; but so much as Patty has to do!—And it is a kindness to employ our men."

Jane looked as if she did not mean to be conquered; but instead of answering, she began speaking again to Mr. John Knightley.

"The post-office is a wonderful establishment!" said she.—"The regularity and dispatch[11] of it! If one thinks of all that it has to do, and all that it does so well, it is really astonishing!"

"It is certainly very well regulated."

"So seldom that any negligence or blunder appears! So seldom that a letter, among the thousands that are constantly passing about the kingdom, is even carried wrong—and not one in a million, I suppose, actually lost! And when one considers the variety of hands,[12] and of bad hands too, that are to be deciphered, it increases the wonder!"

"The clerks grow expert from habit.—They must begin with some quickness of sight and hand, and exercise improves them. If you want any further explanation," continued he, smiling, "they are paid for it.[13] That is the key to a great deal of capacity. The public pays and must be served well."

11 Promptness.

12 Types of handwriting.

13 John Knightley has a point, as the Napoleonic Wars had a noticeable effect on the price of postage; as Howard Robinson notes, "by 1812 a single letter from London to Edinburgh—the cost in 1765 had been but 6d—had increased to 1s 2d. War had made the Post Office an instrument of taxation" (*The British Post Office: A History* [Princeton: Princeton University Press, 1948], p. 157).

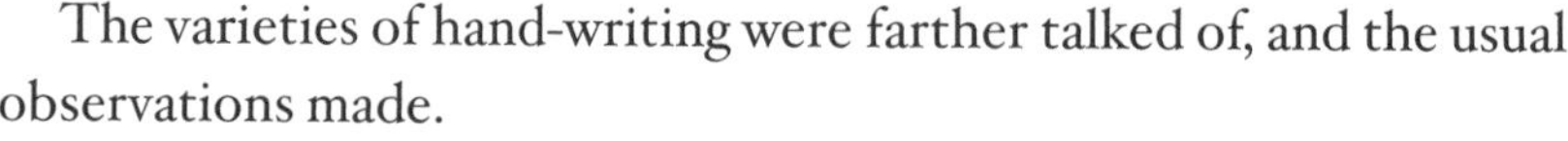

The varieties of hand-writing were farther talked of, and the usual observations made.

"I have heard it asserted," said John Knightley, "that the same sort of hand-writing often prevails in a family; and where the same master teaches, it is natural enough. But for that reason, I should imagine the likeness must be chiefly confined to the females, for boys have very little teaching after an early age, and scramble into any hand they can get. Isabella and Emma, I think, do write very much alike. I have not always known their writing apart."

"Yes," said his brother hesitatingly, "there is a likeness. I know what you mean—but Emma's hand is the strongest."

"Isabella and Emma both write beautifully," said Mr. Woodhouse; "and always did. And so does poor Mrs. Weston"—with half a sigh and half a smile at her.

"I never saw any gentleman's handwriting"—Emma began, looking also at Mrs. Weston; but stopped, on perceiving that Mrs. Weston was attending to some one else—and the pause gave her time to reflect, "Now, how am I going to introduce him?—Am I unequal to speaking his name at once before all these people? Is it necessary for me to use any roundabout phrase?—Your Yorkshire friend[14]—your correspondent in Yorkshire;—that would be the way, I suppose, if I were very bad.—No, I can pronounce his name without the smallest distress. I certainly get better and better.—Now for it."

Mrs. Weston was disengaged and Emma began again—"Mr. Frank Churchill writes one of the best gentlemen's hands I ever saw."

14 Austen herself uses a comparably arch circumlocution to refer to her flirtation with her neighbors' relative Tom Lefroy, in her earliest surviving letter to Cassandra, written on January 9–10, 1796. "You scold me so much," she writes, "in the nice long letter which I have this moment received from you, that I am almost afraid to tell you how my Irish friend and I behaved. Imagine to yourself everything most profligate and shocking in the way of dancing and sitting down together" (*Letters,* p. 1).

Miniature of Tom Lefroy (1776–1869) by G. Engleheart, 1799. An object of the young Austen's flirtatious affections, he has more recently been mythologized as her great lost love, in Julian Jarrold's 2007 movie *Becoming Jane,* starring Anne Hathaway as Austen and James McAvoy as Lefroy.

"I do not admire it," said Mr. Knightley. "It is too small—wants strength. It is like a woman's writing."

This was not submitted to by either lady. They vindicated him against the base aspersion. "No, it by no means wanted strength—it was not a large hand, but very clear and certainly strong. Had not Mrs. Weston any letter about her to produce?" No, she had heard from him very lately, but having answered the letter, had put it away.

"If we were in the other room," said Emma, if I had my writing-desk, I am sure I could produce a specimen. I have a note of his.—Do not you remember, Mrs. Weston, employing him to write for you one day?"

"He chose to say he was employed"——

"Well, well, I have that note; and can shew it after dinner to convince Mr. Knightley."

"Oh! when a gallant young man, like Mr. Frank Churchill," said Mr. Knightley drily, "writes to a fair lady like Miss Woodhouse, he will, of course, put forth his best."

Dinner was on table.—Mrs. Elton, before she could be spoken to, was ready; and before Mr. Woodhouse had reached her with his request to be allowed to hand her into the dining-parlour, was saying—

"Must I go first? I really am ashamed of always leading the way."

Jane's solicitude about fetching her own letters had not escaped Emma. She had heard and seen it all; and felt some curiosity to know whether the wet walk of this morning had produced any. She suspected that it *had;* that it would not have been so resolutely encountered but in full expectation of hearing from some one very dear, and that it had not been in vain. She thought there was an air of greater happiness than usual—a glow both of complexion and spirits.

She could have made an inquiry or two, as to the expedition[15] and the expense of the Irish mails;[16]—it was at her tongue's end—but she abstained. She was quite determined not to utter a word that should hurt Jane Fairfax's feelings; and they followed the other ladies out of the room, arm in arm, with an appearance of good-will highly becoming to the beauty and grace of each.

15 Speed.

16 Although England and Ireland had been joined by the 1800 Acts of Union, their postal services remained independent (and occasionally in conflict) at this period. The "expedition" of mail from Ireland may also have been materially affected by the treacherous nature of the Holyhead road; see Robinson's chapter on Irish Mails (*The British Post Office,* pp. 176–191).

17

1 Occupy completely. This usage dates from the early eighteenth century.

2 Subdued.

When the ladies returned to the drawing-room after dinner, Emma found it hardly possible to prevent their making two distinct parties;—with so much perseverance in judging and behaving ill did Mrs. Elton engross[1] Jane Fairfax and slight herself. She and Mrs. Weston were obliged to be almost always either talking together or silent together. Mrs. Elton left them no choice. If Jane repressed[2] her for a little time, she soon began again; and though much that passed between them was in a half-whisper, especially on Mrs. Elton's side, there was no avoiding a knowledge of their principal subjects:—The post-office—catching cold—fetching letters—and friendship, were long under discussion; and to them succeeded one, which must be at least equally unpleasant to Jane—inquiries whether she had yet heard of any situation likely to suit her, and professions of Mrs. Elton's meditated activity.

"Here is April come!" said she, "I get quite anxious about you. June will soon be here."

"But I have never fixed on June or any other month—merely looked forward to the summer in general."

"But have you really heard of nothing?"

"I have not even made any inquiry; I do not wish to make any yet."

"Oh! my dear, we cannot begin too early; you are not aware of the difficulty of procuring exactly the desirable thing."

"I not aware!" said Jane, shaking her head; "dear Mrs. Elton, who can have thought of it as I have done?"

"But you have not seen so much of the world as I have. You do not know how many candidates there always are for the *first* situations. I saw a vast deal of that in the neighbourhood round Maple Grove. A cousin of Mr. Suckling, Mrs. Bragge, had such an infinity of applications; every body was anxious to be in her family, for she moves in the first circle. Wax-candles in the school-room![3] You may imagine how desirable! Of all houses in the kingdom Mrs. Bragge's is the one I would most wish to see you in."

"Col. and Mrs. Campbell are to be in town again by midsummer," said Jane. "I must spend some time with them; I am sure they will want it;—afterwards I may probably be glad to dispose of myself. But I would not wish you to take the trouble of making any inquiries at present."

"Trouble! aye, I know your scruples. You are afraid of giving me trouble; but I assure you, my dear Jane, the Campbells can hardly be more interested about you than I am. I shall write to Mrs. Partridge in a day or two, and shall give her a strict charge to be on the look-out for any thing eligible."

"Thank you, but I would rather you did not mention the subject to her; till the time draws nearer, I do not wish to be giving any body trouble."

"But, my dear child, the time *is* drawing near; here is April, and June, or say even July, is very near, with such business to accomplish before us. Your inexperience really amuses me! A situation such as you deserve, and your friends would require for you, is no every day occurrence, is not obtained at a moment's notice; indeed, indeed, we must begin inquiring directly."

"Excuse me, ma'am, but this is by no means my intention; I make no inquiry myself, and should be sorry to have any made by my friends. When I am quite determined as to the time, I am not at all afraid of being long unemployed. There are places in town, offices, where inquiry would soon produce something—Offices for the sale—not quite of human flesh—but of human intellect."[4]

"Oh! my dear, human flesh! You quite shock me; if you mean a fling at the slave-trade, I assure you Mr. Suckling was always rather a friend to the abolition."[5]

3 A signifier of great wealth, as a schoolroom would normally be lit by cheaper (and much smellier) tallow candles.

4 If Austen's narratorial metaphors in vol. II, chap. 1, liken the governess trade to nunship, Jane Fairfax goes even further here, comparing employment agencies for governesses to procurers or human traffickers.

5 Mrs. Elton's touchy reply clearly shows a heightened awareness that her Bristol origins and connections might summon up undesirable associations (see vol. II, chap. 4). The abolitionist campaign began in the early 1780s and was cemented by the foundation in 1787 of the Society for Effecting the Abolition of the Slave Trade.

Thomas Sully, *Lady with a Harp: Eliza Ridgely,* 1818. Unlike pianists, who often faced away from their listeners, harpists could use their more open bodily stance to their social (and, perhaps, erotic) advantage.

"I did not mean, I was not thinking of the slave-trade," replied Jane; "governess-trade, I assure you, was all that I had in view; widely different certainly as to the guilt of those who carry it on; but as to the greater misery of the victims, I do not know where it lies. But I only mean to say that there are advertising offices,[6] and that by applying to them I should have no doubt of very soon meeting with something that would do."

"Something that would do!" repeated Mrs. Elton. "Aye, *that* may suit your humble ideas of yourself;—I know what a modest creature you are; but it will not satisfy your friends to have you taking up with any thing that may offer, any inferior, common-place situation, in a family not moving in a certain circle, or able to command the elegancies of life."

"You are very obliging; but as to all that, I am very indifferent; it would be no object to me to be with the rich; my mortifications, I think, would only be the greater; I should suffer more from comparison. A gentleman's family is all that I should condition for."[7]

"I know you, I know you; you would take up with any thing; but I shall be a little more nice,[8] and I am sure the good Campbells will be quite on my side; with your superior talents, you have a right to move in the first circle. Your musical knowledge alone would entitle you to name your own terms, have as many rooms as you like, and mix in the family as much as you chose;—that is—I do not know—if you knew the harp,[9] you might do all that, I am very sure; but you sing as well as play;—yes, I really believe you might, even without the harp, stipulate for what you chose;—and you must and shall be delightfully, honourably and comfortably settled before the Campbells or I have any rest."

"You may well class the delight, the honour, and the comfort of such a situation together," said Jane, "they are pretty sure to be equal; however, I am very serious in not wishing any thing to be attempted at present for me. I am exceedingly obliged to you, Mrs. Elton, I am obliged to any body who feels for me, but I am quite serious in wishing nothing to be done till the summer. For two or three months longer I shall remain where I am, and as I am."

6 Employment agencies. Alice Renton suggests that the dignity of these businesses may well have justified Jane's anxieties: "They appealed," she notes, "to 'the nobility and gentry' to scan their lists of English and Foreign governesses—'letters the only expense to principals'; it was the governesses who had to pay the fees. Few of these agencies were well or honestly run and the fact that none of them seems to have survived for very long is a reflection not only on their efficiency but also on the fact that many of the women trying to get jobs as governesses were less than honest about their abilities. The agencies could not live up to their promises of providing 'highly qualified ladies', for very few such ladies existed" (*Tyrant or Victim?: A History of the British Governess* [London: Weidenfeld and Nicolson, 1981], pp. 62–63).

7 Demand.

8 Particular.

9 As Mrs. Elton rightly points out, harpists were rarer and therefore even more valuable than pianists at the time. In addition, as David Selwyn has noted, a female harpist had an advantage over a female pianist in terms of decent bodily display, a fact not lost on Mary Crawford in *Mansfield Park:* "The 'elegant' harp, reflecting in its graceful curves the shape and posture of the female form, becomes an extension of the body itself; and it is a body at which it is now legitimate to look closely, as the eye is drawn by the seductive sounds emanating from it. Mary Crawford chooses her instrument carefully: a pianoforte, particularly a square, could never offer the same visual appeal. If anything, its solid rectangular shape would cause it to act as a barrier, since it half conceals its player, unless she is to be seen only from behind; and certainly the rather mechanical movements it requires have nothing of the sensuality afforded by the caressing indulged in by the harpist, in which the male listener might be said almost to enjoy a vicarious embrace" (*Jane Austen and Leisure* [London: The Hambledon Press, 1999], p. 126).

"And I am quite serious too, I assure you," replied Mrs. Elton gaily, "in resolving to be always on the watch, and employing my friends to watch also, that nothing really unexceptionable may pass us."

In this style she ran on; never thoroughly stopped by any thing till Mr. Woodhouse came into the room; her vanity had then a change of object, and Emma heard her saying in the same half-whisper to Jane,

"Here comes this dear old beau of mine, I protest!—Only think of his gallantry in coming away before the other men!—what a dear creature he is;—I assure you I like him excessively.[10] I admire all that quaint, old-fashioned politeness; it is much more to my taste than modern ease; modern ease often disgusts me.[11] But this good old Mr. Woodhouse, I wish you had heard his gallant speeches to me at dinner. Oh! I assure you I began to think my cara sposa[12] would be absolutely jealous. I fancy I am rather a favourite; he took notice of my gown. How do you like it?—Selina's choice—handsome, I think, but I do not know whether it is not over-trimmed; I have the greatest dislike to the idea of being over-trimmed—quite a horror of finery. I must put on a few ornaments *now,* because it is expected of me. A bride, you know, must appear like a bride, but my natural taste is all for simplicity; a simple style of dress is so infinitely preferable to finery. But I am quite in the minority, I believe; few people seem to value simplicity of dress,—shew and finery are every thing. I have some notion of putting such a trimming as this to my white and silver poplin.[13] Do you think it will look well?"

The whole party were but just re-assembled in the drawing-room when Mr. Weston made his appearance among them. He had returned to a late dinner, and walked to Hartfield as soon as it was over. He had been too much expected by the best judges, for surprize—but there was great joy. Mr. Woodhouse was almost as glad to see him now, as he would have been sorry to see him before. John Knightley only was in mute astonishment.—That a man who might have spent his evening quietly at home after a day of business in London, should set off again, and walk half-a-mile to another man's house, for the sake of being in mixed company till bed-time, of finishing his day in the efforts of civility and the noise of numbers, was a circumstance to strike him deeply. A man who had been in motion since eight

10 Mrs. Elton's slangy exaggeration for "enormously."

11 Regency manners prided themselves on their ease and openness, but the very same antiquated, late-Augustan mannerisms that Mrs. Elton prizes in Mr. Woodhouse were themselves once celebrated for being so much more relaxed than the affectations of earlier periods. For example, Joseph Addison's *Spectator* essays at the beginning of the eighteenth century frequently berate the stultifying manners of the previous generation, yet a century later, it is the legacy of Addison's social aesthetic that is being displaced by the "modern ease" of contemporary behavior. For more on Austen's response to late-Augustan manners, see the introduction to my book *Jane Austen and the Morality of Conversation* (London: Anthem Press, 2003).

12 The feminine, rather than the masculine, inflections of the Italian phrase.

13 A plain dress fabric, with a fine horizontal ribbing.

o'clock in the morning, and might now have been still, who had been long talking, and might have been silent, who had been in more than one crowd, and might have been alone!—Such a man, to quit the tranquillity and independence of his own fire-side, and on the evening of a cold sleety April day rush out again into the world!—Could he by a touch of his finger have instantly taken back his wife, there would have been a motive; but his coming would probably prolong rather than break up the party. John Knightley looked at him with amazement, then shrugged his shoulders, and said, "I could not have believed it even of *him.*"

Mr. Weston meanwhile, perfectly unsuspicious of the indignation he was exciting, happy and cheerful as usual, and with all the right of being principal talker, which a day spent any where from home confers, was making himself agreeable among the rest; and having satisfied the inquiries of his wife as to his dinner, convincing her that none of all her careful directions to the servants had been forgotten, and spread abroad what public news he had heard, was proceeding to a family communication, which, though principally addressed to Mrs. Weston, he had not the smallest doubt of being highly interesting to every body in the room. He gave her a letter, it was from Frank, and to herself; he had met with it in his way, and had taken the liberty of opening it.

"Read it, read it," said he, "it will give you pleasure; only a few lines—will not take you long; read it to Emma."

The two ladies looked over it together; and he sat smiling and talking to them the whole time, in a voice a little subdued, but very audible to every body.

"Well, he is coming, you see; good news, I think. Well, what do you say to it?—I always told you he would be here again soon, did not I?—Anne, my dear, did not I always tell you so, and you would not believe me?—In town next week, you see—at the latest, I dare say; for *she* is as impatient as the black gentleman[14] when any thing is to be done; most likely they will be there to-morrow or Saturday. As to her illness, all nothing of course. But it is an excellent thing to have Frank among us again, so near as town. They will stay a good while when they do come, and he will be half his time with us. This is pre-

14 A popular euphemism for the Devil, dating back at least as far as the seventeenth century. In Colley Cibber's 1728 comedy *The Provok'd Husband,* Myrtilla declares: "may the Black Gentleman tuck me under his Arm at the same time, if I shall not think myself oblig'd to you, as long as I live" ([London: J. Watts, 1728], p. 71).

15 Put it away.

cisely what I wanted. Well, pretty good news, is not it? Have you finished it? Has Emma read it all? Put it up, put it up;[15] we will have a good talk about it some other time, but it will not do now. I shall only just mention the circumstance to the others in a common way."

Mrs. Weston was most comfortably pleased on the occasion. Her looks and words had nothing to restrain them. She was happy, she knew she was happy, and knew she ought to be happy. Her congratulations were warm and open; but Emma could not speak so fluently. *She* was a little occupied in weighing her own feelings, and trying to understand the degree of her agitation, which she rather thought was considerable.

Mr. Weston, however, too eager to be very observant, too communicative to want others to talk, was very well satisfied with what she did say, and soon moved away to make the rest of his friends happy by a partial communication of what the whole room must have overheard already.

It was well that he took every body's joy for granted, or he might not have thought either Mr. Woodhouse or Mr. Knightley particularly delighted. They were the first entitled, after Mrs. Weston and Emma, to be made happy;—from them he would have proceeded to Miss Fairfax, but she was so deep in conversation with John Knightley, that it would have been too positive an interruption; and finding himself close to Mrs. Elton, and her attention disengaged, he necessarily began on the subject with her.

18

"I HOPE I SHALL SOON HAVE THE PLEASURE of introducing my son to you," said Mr. Weston.

Mrs. Elton, very willing to suppose a particular compliment intended her by such a hope, smiled most graciously.

"You have heard of a certain Frank Churchill, I presume," he continued—"and know him to be my son, though he does not bear my name."

"Oh! yes, and I shall be very happy in his acquaintance. I am sure Mr. Elton will lose no time in calling on him; and we shall both have great pleasure in seeing him at the Vicarage."

"You are very obliging.—Frank will be extremely happy, I am sure. —He is to be in town next week, if not sooner. We have notice of it in a letter to-day. I met the letters in my way this morning, and seeing my son's hand, presumed to open it—though it was not directed to me—it was to Mrs. Weston. She is his principal correspondent, I assure you. I hardly ever get a letter."

"And so you absolutely opened what was directed to her! oh! Mr. Weston—(laughing affectedly) I must protest against that.—A most dangerous precedent indeed!—I beg you will not let your neighbours follow your example.—Upon my word, if this is what I am to expect, we married women must begin to exert ourselves!—Oh! Mr. Weston, I could not have believed it of you!"

"Aye, we men are sad fellows. You must take care of yourself, Mrs. Elton.—This letter tells us—it is a short letter—written in a hurry, merely to give us notice—it tells us that they are all coming up to town directly, on Mrs. Churchill's account—she has not been well the whole winter, and thinks Enscombe too cold for her—so they are all to move southward without loss of time."

"Indeed!—from Yorkshire, I think. Enscombe is in Yorkshire?"

"Yes, they are about 190 miles from London.[1] A considerable journey."

"Yes, upon my word, very considerable. Sixty-five miles farther than from Maple Grove to London. But what is distance, Mr. Weston, to people of large fortune?—You would be amazed to hear how my brother, Mr. Suckling, sometimes flies about. You will hardly believe me—but twice in one week he and Mr. Bragge went to London and back again with four horses."

"The evil of the distance from Enscombe," said Mr. Weston, "is, that Mrs. Churchill, *as we understand,* has not been able to leave the sopha for a week together. In Frank's last letter she complained, he said, of being too weak to get into her conservatory without having both his arm and his uncle's! This, you know, speaks a great degree of weakness—but now she is so impatient to be in town, that she means to sleep only two nights on the road.—So Frank writes word. Certainly, delicate ladies have very extraordinary constitutions,[2] Mrs. Elton. You must grant me that."

"No, indeed, I shall grant you no thing. I always take the part of my own sex. I do indeed. I give you notice—You will find me a formidable antagonist on that point. I always stand up for women—and I assure you, if you knew how Selina feels with respect to sleeping at an inn, you would not wonder at Mrs. Churchill's making incredible exertions to avoid it. Selina says it is quite horror to her—and I believe I have caught a little of her nicety.[3] She always travels with her own sheets; an excellent precaution. Does Mrs. Churchill do the same?"

"Depend upon it, Mrs. Churchill does every thing that any other fine lady ever did. Mrs. Churchill will not be second to any lady in the land for"—

Mrs. Elton eagerly interposed with,

"Oh! Mr. Weston, do not mistake me. Selina is no fine lady, I assure you. Do not run away with such an idea."

1 This would place Enscombe somewhere near Ripon in Yorkshire.

2 Compare the Parker sisters in *Sanditon,* who expend so much energy in being ill that Charlotte Heywood is led to remark in chapter 10: "It should seem that they must either be very busy for the Good of others, or else extremely ill themselves. Some natural delicacy of Constitution in fact, with an unfortunate turn for Medecine, especially quack Medecine, had given them at various times, to various Disorders;—the rest of their sufferings was from Fancy, the love of Distinction & the love of the Wonderful."

3 Discernment.

"Is not she? Then she is no rule for Mrs. Churchill, who is as thorough a fine lady as any body ever beheld."

Mrs. Elton began to think she had been wrong in disclaiming so warmly. It was by no means her object to have it believed that her sister was *not* a fine lady; perhaps there was want of spirit in the pretence of it;—and she was considering in what way she had best retract, when Mr. Weston went on.

"Mrs. Churchill is not much in my good graces, as you may suspect—but this is quite between ourselves.[4] She is very fond of Frank, and therefore I would not speak ill of her. Besides, she is out of health now; but *that* indeed, by her own account, she has always been. I would not say so to every body, Mrs. Elton, but I have not much faith in Mrs. Churchill's illness."

"If she is really ill, why not go to Bath, Mr. Weston?—To Bath, or to Clifton?"[5]

"She has taken it into her head that Enscombe is too cold for her. The fact is, I suppose, that she is tired of Enscombe. She has now been a longer time stationary there, than she ever was before, and

4 Another of Mr. Weston's unconfidential "confidences"; see note 3 to vol. I, chap. 14.

5 An affluent town to the west of central Bristol, bordering on the Avon Gorge at one end, which was officially incorporated into the city in the 1830s; like Bath, it was famous as a spa town in the early nineteenth century. What Mrs. Elton pointedly doesn't mention is that much of Clifton's wealth was built on the spoils of the slave trade.

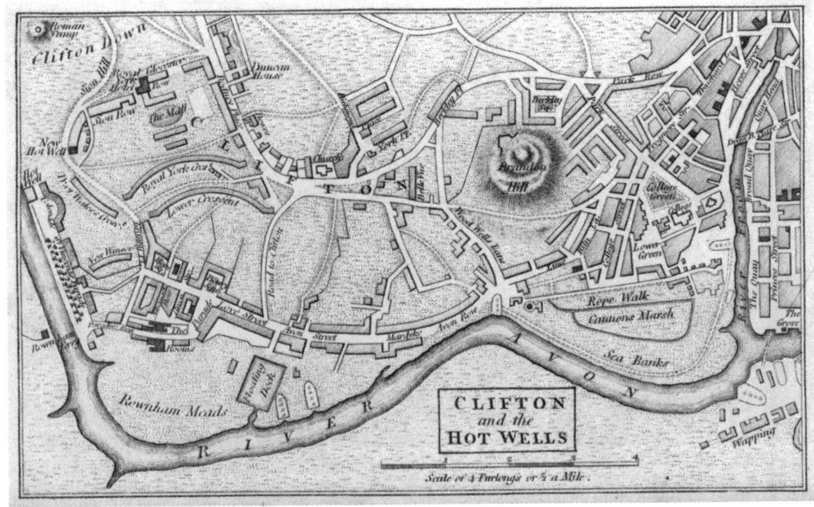

"Clifton and the Hot Wells" from *A Guide to All the Watering and Sea-Bathing Places* (London: Richard Phillips, 1803).

Two images of Hymen, the ancient Greek god of marriage: (above) Nicolas Poussin, *Hymenaeus Disguised as a Woman During an Offering to Priapus,* 1634–1638; (at right) Edward Burne-Jones, *Hymenaeus,* 1868. Burne-Jones's lush colors emphasize the "saffron robe" that Mrs. Elton mentions here.

6 Wooded park.

she begins to want change. It is a retired place. A fine place, but very retired."

"Aye—like Maple Grove, I dare say. Nothing can stand more retired from the road than Maple Grove. Such an immense plantation[6] all round it! You seem shut out from every thing—in the most complete retirement.—And Mrs. Churchill probably has not health or spirits like Selina to enjoy that sort of seclusion. Or, perhaps she may not have resources enough in herself to be qualified for a country life. I always say a woman cannot have too many resources—and I feel very thankful that I have so many myself as to be quite independent of society."

"Frank was here in February for a fortnight."

"So I remember to have heard. He will find an *addition* to the society of Highbury when he comes again; that is, if I may presume to call myself an addition. But perhaps he may never have heard of there being such a creature in the world."

This was too loud a call for a compliment to be passed by, and Mr. Weston, with a very good grace, immediately exclaimed,

"My dear madam! Nobody but yourself could imagine such a thing possible. Not heard of you!—I believe Mrs. Weston's letters lately have been full of very little else than Mrs. Elton."

He had done his duty and could return to his son.

"When Frank left us," continued he, "it was quite uncertain when we might see him again, which makes this day's news doubly welcome. It has been completely unexpected. That is, *I* always had a strong persuasion he would be here again soon, I was sure something favourable would turn up—but nobody believed me. He and Mrs. Weston were both dreadfully desponding. 'How could he contrive to come? And how could it be supposed that his uncle and aunt would spare him again?' and so forth—I always felt that something would happen in our favour; and so it has, you see. I have observed, Mrs. Elton, in the course of my life, that if things are going untowardly one month, they are sure to mend the next."

"Very true, Mr. Weston, perfectly true. It is just what I used to say to a certain gentleman in company in the days of courtship, when, because things did not go quite right, did not proceed with all the rapidity which suited his feelings, he was apt to be in despair, and exclaim that he was sure at this rate it would be *May* before Hymen's saffron robe[7] would be put on for us! Oh! the pains I have been at to dispel those gloomy ideas and give him cheerfuller views! The carriage—we had disappointments about the carriage;—one morning, I remember, he came to me quite in despair."

She was stopped by a slight fit of coughing, and Mr. Weston instantly seized the opportunity of going on.

"You were mentioning May. May is the very month which Mrs. Churchill is ordered, or has ordered herself, to spend in some warmer place than Enscombe—in short, to spend in London; so that we have the agreeable prospect of frequent visits from Frank the whole spring—precisely the season of the year which one should have chosen for it: days almost at the longest; weather genial[8] and pleasant, always inviting one out, and never too hot for exercise. When he was here before, we made the best of it; but there was a good deal of wet, damp, cheerless weather; there always is in February, you know, and we could not do half that we intended. Now will be the time. This will be complete enjoyment; and I do not know, Mrs. Elton, whether the uncertainty of our meetings, the sort of constant expectation there will be of his coming in to-day or to-morrow, and at any hour, may not be more friendly to happiness than having him actually in the house. I think it is so. I think it is the state of mind which gives most spirit and delight. I hope you will be pleased with my son; but you must not expect a prodigy. He is generally thought a fine young man, but do not expect a prodigy.[9] Mrs. Weston's partiality for him is very great, and, as you may suppose, most gratifying to me. She thinks nobody equal to him."

"And I assure you, Mr. Weston, I have very little doubt that my opinion will be decidedly in his favour. I have heard so much in praise of Mr. Frank Churchill.—At the same time it is fair to observe, that I am one of those who always judge for themselves, and are by no means implicitly guided by others. I give you notice that as I find your son, so I shall judge of him.—I am no flatterer."

7 A poetically clichéd description of marriage. Mr. Elton is possibly recalling Milton's "L'Allegro," first published in 1645 ("There let *Hymen* oft appear/In Saffron robe, with Taper clear"); however, there were more recent instances, such as Erasmus Darwin's work *The Temple of Nature* (1803) ("Onward with march sublime in saffron robe/Young Hymen steps, and traverses the globe"), and particularly the line spoken by Lady Jane Granville in vol. I, chap. 14, of Maria Edgeworth's novel *Patronage* (1814): "young ladies, nevertheless, usually think, that the saffron robe of Hymen would not be the most unbecoming dress in the world, and whether it be in compliance with their daughters' taste, or their own convenience, most parents are in a hurry to purchase it."

8 Comfortably warm.

9 This sense of the word, to refer to an exceptionally talented or accomplished person, developed during the eighteenth century.

10 See vol. II, chap. 4.

Mr. Weston was musing.

"I hope," said he presently, "I have not been severe upon poor Mrs. Churchill. If she is ill I should be sorry to do her injustice; but there are some traits in her character which make it difficult for me to speak of her with the forbearance I could wish. You cannot be ignorant, Mrs. Elton, of my connection with the family, nor of the treatment I have met with; and, between ourselves, the whole blame of it is to be laid to her. She was the instigator. Frank's mother would never have been slighted as she was but for her. Mr. Churchill has pride; but his pride is nothing to his wife's: his is a quiet, indolent, gentlemanlike sort of pride that would harm nobody, and only make himself a little helpless and tiresome; but her pride is arrogance and insolence! And what inclines one less to bear, she has no fair pretence of family or blood. She was nobody when he married her, barely the daughter of a gentleman; but ever since her being turned into a Churchill she has out-Churchill'd them all in high and mighty claims: but in herself, I assure you, she is an upstart."

"Only think! well, that must be infinitely provoking! I have quite a horror of upstarts. Maple Grove has given me a thorough disgust to people of that sort; for there is a family in that neighbourhood who are such an annoyance to my brother and sister from the airs they give themselves! Your description of Mrs. Churchill made me think of them directly. People of the name of Tupman, very lately settled there, and encumbered with many low connections, but giving themselves immense airs, and expecting to be on a footing with the old established families. A year and a half is the very utmost that they can have lived at West Hall; and how they got their fortune nobody knows. They came from Birmingham,[10] which is not a place to promise much, you know, Mr. Weston. One has not great hopes from Birmingham. I always say there is something direful in the sound: but nothing more is positively known of the Tupmans, though a good many things I assure you are suspected; and yet by their manners they evidently think themselves equal even to my brother, Mr. Suckling, who happens to be one of their nearest neighbours. It is infinitely too bad. Mr. Suckling, who has been eleven years a resident at Maple Grove, and whose father had it before him—I believe, at least

—I am almost sure that old Mr. Suckling had completed the purchase before his death."[11]

They were interrupted. Tea was carrying round,[12] and Mr. Weston, having said all that he wanted, soon took the opportunity of walking way.

After tea, Mr. and Mrs. Weston, and Mr. Elton sat down with Mr. Woodhouse to cards. The remaining five were left to their own powers, and Emma doubted their getting on very well; for Mr. Knightley seemed little disposed for conversation; Mrs. Elton was wanting notice, which nobody had inclination to pay, and she was herself in a worry of spirits which would have made her prefer being silent.

Mr. John Knightley proved more talkative than his brother. He was to leave them early the next day; and he soon began with—

"Well, Emma, I do not believe I have any thing more to say about the boys; but you have your sister's letter, and every thing is down at full length there we may be sure. My charge would be much more concise than her's, and probably not much in the same spirit; all that I have to recommend being comprised in, do not spoil them, and do not physic them."[13]

"I rather hope to satisfy you both," said Emma, "for I shall do all in my power to make them happy, which will be enough for Isabella; and happiness must preclude false indulgence and physic."

"And if you find them troublesome, you must send them home again."

"That is very likely. You think so, do not you?"

"I hope I am aware that they may be too noisy for your father—or even may be some incumbrance to you, if your visiting-engagements continue to increase as much as they have done lately."

"Increase!"

"Certainly; you must be sensible that the last half year has made a great difference in your way of life."

"Difference! No indeed I am not."

"There can be no doubt of your being much more engaged with company than you used to be. Witness this very time. Here am I come down for only one day, and you are engaged with a dinner-party!—When did it happen before, or any thing like it? Your neigh-

11 Even if this were definitely the case, it would hardly say much for the antiquity of the Sucklings.

12 Being carried; Austen's use of this particular grammatical voice may be a subliminal pointer at the invisible agency of the servants who are in fact doing much of the work.

13 Give them medicine. Elements of John Knightley's educational philosophy echo John Locke's massively influential treatise *Some Thoughts Concerning Education* (London: A. & J. Churchill, 1693), which was the standard English reference work on educational theory for most of the eighteenth century. In particular, Locke warns of the dangers of needless medication: "perhaps it will be expected from me, that I should give some Directions of *Physick* to prevent Diseases. For which I have only this one very sacredly to be observed: Never to give Children any *Physick* for prevention. The observation of what I have already advised, will, I suppose, do that better than Apothecarie's Drugs and Medicines. Have a great care of tampering that way, least, instead of preventing, you draw on Diseases. Nor even upon every little Indisposition is *Physick* to be given, or the Physician called to Children, especially if he be a Busy-man, that will presently fill their Windows with Gally-pots [small medicine-pots], and their Stomachs with Drugs. It is safer to leave them wholly to Nature, than to put them into the hands of one, forward to tamper, or that thinks Children are to be cured in ordinary Distempers, by any thing but Diet, or by a method very little distant from it" (pp. 30–31).

bourhood is increasing, and you mix more with it. A little while ago, every letter to Isabella brought an account of fresh gaieties; dinners at Mr. Cole's, or balls at the Crown. The difference which Randalls, Randalls alone makes in your goings-on, is very great."

"Yes," said his brother quickly, "it is Randalls that does it all."

"Very well—and as Randalls, I suppose, is not likely to have less influence than heretofore, it strikes me as a possible thing, Emma, that Henry and John may be sometimes in the way. And if they are, I only beg you to send them home."

"No," cried Mr. Knightley, "that need not be the consequence. Let them be sent to Donwell. I shall certainly be at leisure."

"Upon my word," exclaimed Emma, "you amuse me! I should like to know how many of all my numerous engagements take place without your being of the party; and why I am to be supposed in danger of wanting leisure to attend to the little boys. These amazing engagements of mine—what have they been? Dining once with the Coles—and having a ball talked of, which never took place. I can understand you—(nodding at Mr. John Knightley)—your good fortune in meeting with so many of your friends at once here, delights you too much to pass unnoticed. But you, (turning to Mr. Knightley,) who know how very, very seldom I am ever two hours from Hartfield, why you should foresee such a series of dissipation[14] for me, I cannot imagine. And as to my dear little boys, I must say, that if aunt Emma has not time for them, I do not think they would fare much better with uncle Knightley, who is absent from home about five hours where she is absent one—and who, when he is at home, is either reading to himself or settling his accounts."

Mr. Knightley seemed to be trying not to smile; and succeeded without difficulty, upon Mrs. Elton's beginning to talk to him.

14 Emma is parodying melodramatic "novel slang" here; indeed, "dissipation" was one of the terms Austen specifically singled out in the famous letter she wrote to her niece Anna on September 28, 1814, in which she commented on the fictional writing that Anna had sent her: "Devereux Forester's being ruined by his Vanity is extremely good; but I wish you would not let him plunge into a 'Vortex of Dissipation'. I do not object to the Thing, but I cannot bear the expression;—it is such thorough novel slang—and so old, that I dare say Adam met with it in the first novel he opened" (*Letters,* p. 277).

Portrait of John Locke (1632–1704) by Godfrey Kneller, 1697.

Volume III

I

A VERY LITTLE QUIET REFLECTION was enough to satisfy Emma as to the nature of her agitation on hearing this news of Frank Churchill. She was soon convinced that it was not for herself she was feeling at all apprehensive or embarrassed; it was for him. Her own attachment had really subsided into a mere nothing; it was not worth thinking of;—but if he, who had undoubtedly been always so much the most in love of the two,[1] were to be returning with the same warmth of sentiment which he had taken away, it would be very distressing. If a separation of two months should not have cooled him, there were dangers and evils before her:—caution for him and for herself would be necessary. She did not mean to have her own affections entangled again; and it would be incumbent on her to avoid any encouragement of his.

She wished she might be able to keep him from an absolute declaration. That would be so very painful a conclusion of their present acquaintance!—and yet, she could not help rather anticipating something decisive. She felt as if the spring would not pass without bringing a crisis, an event, a something to alter her present composed and tranquil state.

It was not very long, though rather longer than Mr. Weston had foreseen, before she had the power of forming some opinion of Frank Churchill's feelings. The Enscombe family were not in town quite so soon as had been imagined, but he was at Highbury very soon afterwards. He rode down for a couple of hours; he could not yet do more; but as he came from Randall's immediately to Hartfield, she could

1 As with so many of Emma's surmises about Frank Churchill, this is true, but not in the way she thinks.

then exercise all her quick observation, and speedily determine how he was influenced, and how she must act. They met with the utmost friendliness. There could be no doubt of his great pleasure in seeing her. But she had an almost instant doubt of his caring for her as he had done, of his feeling the same tenderness in the same degree. She watched him well. It was a clear thing he was less in love than he had been. Absence, with the conviction probably of her indifference, had produced this very natural and very desirable effect.

He was in high spirits; as ready to talk and laugh as ever, and seemed delighted to speak of his former visit, and recur to old stories: and he was not without agitation. It was not in his calmness that she read his comparative indifference. He was not calm; his spirits were evidently fluttered; there was restlessness about him. Lively as he was, it seemed a liveliness that did not satisfy himself: but what decided her belief on the subject, was his staying only a quarter of an hour,[2] and hurrying away to make other calls in Highbury. "He had seen a group of old acquaintance in the street as he passed—he had not stopped, he would not stop for more than a word—but he had the vanity to think they would be disappointed if he did not call, and much as he wished to stay longer at Hartfield, he must hurry off."

She had no doubt as to his being less in love—but neither his agitated spirits, nor his hurrying away, seemed like a perfect cure; and she was rather inclined to think it implied a dread of her returning power, and a discreet resolution of not trusting himself with her long.

This was the only visit from Frank Churchill in the course of ten days. He was often hoping, intending to come—but was always prevented. His aunt could not bear to have him leave her. Such was his own account at Randall's. If he were quite sincere, if he really tried to come, it was to be inferred that Mrs. Churchill's removal to London had been of no service to the wilful or nervous part of her disorder. That she was really ill was very certain; he had declared himself convinced of it, at Randall's. Though much might be fancy, he could not doubt, when he looked back, that she was in a weaker state of health than she had been half a year ago. He did not believe it to proceed from any thing that care and medicine might not remove, or at least

2 The minimum length of time for a polite formal visit, implying to Emma that Frank Churchill has no desire to linger in her presence.

that she might not have many years of existence before her; but he could not be prevailed on by all his father's doubts, to say that her complaints were merely imaginary, or that she was as strong as ever.

It soon appeared that London was not the place for her. She could not endure its noise. Her nerves were under continual irritation and suffering; and by the ten days' end, her nephew's letter to Randall's communicated a change of plan. They were going to remove immediately to Richmond.[3] Mrs. Churchill had been recommended to the medical skill of an eminent person there, and had otherwise a fancy for the place. A ready-furnished house in a favourite spot was engaged, and much benefit expected from the change.

Emma heard that Frank wrote in the highest spirits of this arrangement, and seemed most fully to appreciate the blessing of having two months before him of such near neighbourhood to many dear friends—for the house was taken for May and June. She was told that now he wrote with the greatest confidence of being often with them, almost as often as he could even wish.

Emma saw how Mr. Weston understood these joyous prospects. He was considering her as the source of all the happiness they offered. She hoped it was not so. Two months must bring it to the proof.

Mr. Weston's own happiness was indisputable. He was quite delighted. It was the very circumstance he could have wished for. Now, it would be really having Frank in their neighbourhood. What were nine miles[4] to a young man?—An hour's ride. He would be always coming over. The difference in that respect of Richmond and London was enough to make the whole difference of seeing him always and seeing him never. Sixteen miles—nay, eighteen—it must be full eighteen to Manchester-street[5]—was a serious obstacle. Were he ever able to get away, the day would be spent in coming and returning. There was no comfort in having him in London; he might as well be at Enscombe; but Richmond was the very distance for easy intercourse. Better than nearer![6]

One good thing was immediately brought to a certainty by this removal—the ball at the Crown. It had not been forgotten before, but it had been soon acknowledged vain to attempt to fix a day. Now,

3 A town in Surrey, some eight miles from London, founded when Henry VII built Richmond Palace there in 1501. Mrs. Churchill might well have "a fancy for the place" because of its large number of open green spaces, not least the royal park enclosed by Charles I in 1637.

4 The second element of Highbury's impossible triangulation.

5 A fashionable street in Marylebone that leads to Manchester Square, site of the Duke of Manchester's London residence (now the home of the Wallace Collection).

6 Presumably because this way, Mr. Weston has his son close enough to visit him, while simultaneously keeping the dreaded Mrs. Churchill at a safe distance.

however, it was absolutely to be; every preparation was resumed, and very soon after the Churchills had removed to Richmond, a few lines from Frank, to say that his aunt felt already much better for the change, and that he had no doubt of being able to join them for twenty-four hours at any given time, induced them to name as early a day as possible.

Mr. Weston's ball was to be a real thing. A very few to-morrows stood between the young people of Highbury and happiness.

Mr. Woodhouse was resigned. The time of year lightened the evil to him. May was better for every thing than February. Mrs. Bates was engaged to spend the evening at Hartfield, James had due notice, and he sanguinely hoped that neither dear little Henry nor dear little John would have any thing the matter with them, while dear Emma were gone.

Anon., "View of Manchester Square's north side," 1813.

2

No misfortune occurred, again to prevent the ball. The day approached, the day arrived; and, after a morning of some anxious watching, Frank Churchill, in all the certainty of his own self, reached Randall's before dinner, and every thing was safe.

No second meeting had there yet been between him and Emma. The room at the Crown was to witness it;—but it would be better than a common meeting in a crowd. Mr. Weston had been so very earnest in his entreaties for her early attendance, for her arriving there as soon as possible after themselves, for the purpose of taking her opinion as to the propriety[1] and comfort of the rooms before any other persons came, that she could not refuse him, and must therefore spend some quiet interval in the young man's company. She was to convey Harriet, and they drove to the Crown in good time, the Randalls' party just sufficiently before them.

Frank Churchill seemed to have been on the watch; and though he did not say much, his eyes declared that he meant to have a delightful evening. They all walked about together, to see that every thing was as it should be; and within a few minutes were joined by the contents of another carriage, which Emma could not hear the sound of at first, without great surprise. "So unreasonably early!" she was going to exclaim; but she presently found that it was a family of old friends, who were coming, like herself, by particular desire, to help Mr. Weston's judgement; and they were so very closely followed by another carriage of cousins, who had been entreated to come early with the same distinguishing earnestness, on the same errand, that it

1 In this context, the word denotes the rooms' suitability for their intended purpose. See note 4 to vol. I, chap. 7.

seemed as if half the company might soon be collected together for the purpose of preparatory inspection.

Emma perceived that her taste was not the only taste on which Mr. Weston depended, and felt, that to be the favourite and intimate of a man who had so many intimates and confidantes, was not the very first distinction in the scale of vanity. She liked his open manners, but a little less of open-heartedness would have made him a higher character.—General benevolence, but not general friendship, made a man what he ought to be.[2]—She could fancy such a man.

The whole party walked about, and looked, and praised again; and then, having nothing else to do, formed a sort of half circle round the fire, to observe in their various modes, till other subjects were started, that though *May,* a fire in the evening was still very pleasant.

Emma found that it was not Mr. Weston's fault that the number of privy counsellors was not yet larger. They had stopped at Mrs. Bates's door to offer the use of their carriage, but the aunt and niece were to be brought by the Eltons.

Frank was standing by her, but not steadily;[3] there was a restlessness, which showed a mind not at ease. He was looking about, he was going to the door, he was watching for the sound of other carriages, —impatient to begin, or afraid of being always near her.

Mrs. Elton was spoken of. "I think she must be here soon," said he. "I have a great curiosity to see Mrs. Elton, I have heard so much of her. It cannot be long, I think, before she comes."

A carriage was heard. He was on the move immediately; but coming back, said,

"I am forgetting that I am not acquainted with her. I have never seen either Mr. or Mrs. Elton. I have no business to put myself forward."

Mr. and Mrs. Elton appeared; and all the smiles and the proprieties passed.

"But Miss Bates and Miss Fairfax!" said Mr. Weston, looking about. "We thought you were to bring them."

The mistake had been slight. The carriage was sent for them now. Emma longed to know what Frank's first opinion of Mrs. Elton might be; how he was affected by the studied elegance of her dress,

2 Emma appears here, like her author, to have inherited some of her moral vocabulary (and some of her moral prose-rhythm) from Samuel Johnson. In the "Life of Pope," for example, Johnson voices an influential skepticism about the popular view of Pope's correspondence as a model of genial openness: "Of his social qualities, if an estimate be made from his Letters, an opinion too favourable cannot easily be formed; they exhibit a perpetual and unclouded effulgence of general benevolence and particular fondness. There is nothing but liberality, gratitude, constancy, and tenderness."

3 Constantly.

Portrait of Samuel Johnson (1709–1784) by Joshua Reynolds, 1756–1757. In the "Biographical Notice of the Author" appended to the first publication of *Northanger Abbey* and *Persuasion* in December 1817, Henry Austen noted of his late sister's tastes: "Her favourite moral writers were Johnson in prose, and Cowper in verse."

and her smiles of graciousness. He was immediately qualifying himself to form an opinion, by giving her very proper attention, after the introduction had passed.

In a few minutes the carriage returned.—Somebody talked of rain.—"I will see that there are umbrellas, sir," said Frank to his father: "Miss Bates must not be forgotten:" and away he went. Mr. Weston was following; but Mrs. Elton detained him, to gratify him by her opinion of his son; and so briskly did she begin, that the young man himself, though by no means moving slowly, could hardly be out of hearing.

"A very fine young man indeed, Mr. Weston. You know I candidly told you I should form my own opinion; and I am happy to say that I

4 Flatter.

5 Arrogance (see vol. I, chap. 8).

6 The legendary lamp that released a magic genie when rubbed. Another example of the phrase's idiomatic currency occurs in chap. 5 of "Ennui" in Maria Edgeworth's *Tales from Fashionable Life* (1809), as the Earl of Glenthorn reflects: "Money, I thought, had the power of Aladdin's lamp, to procure with magical celerity the gratification of my wishes. I expected that a cottage for Ellinor should rise out of the earth at my command. But the slaves of Aladdin's lamp were not Irishmen." Robert Irwin offers a valuable overview of the influence of the *Arabian Nights* on Romanticism in *The Arabian Nights: A Companion* (London: Allen Lane, 1994), pp. 237–292.

am extremely pleased with him.—You may believe me. I never compliment.[4] I think him a very handsome young man, and his manners are precisely what I like and approve—so truly the gentleman, without the least conceit or puppyism.[5] You must know I have a vast dislike to puppies—quite a horror of them. They were never tolerated at Maple Grove. Neither Mr. Suckling nor me had ever any patience with them; and we used sometimes to say very cutting things! Selina, who is mild almost to a fault, bore with them much better."

While she talked of his son, Mr. Weston's attention was chained; but when she got to Maple Grove, he could recollect that there were ladies just arriving to be attended to, and with happy smiles must hurry away.

Mrs. Elton turned to Mrs. Weston. "I have no doubt of its being our carriage with Miss Bates and Jane. Our coachman and horses are so extremely expeditious!—I believe we drive faster than anybody.—What a pleasure it is to send one's carriage for a friend!—I understand you were so kind as to offer, but another time it will be quite unnecessary. You may be very sure I shall always take care of *them*."

Miss Bates and Miss Fairfax, escorted by the two gentlemen, walked into the room; and Mrs. Elton seemed to think it as much her duty as Mrs. Weston's to receive them. Her gestures and movements might be understood by any one who looked on like Emma, but her words, every body's words, were soon lost under the incessant flow of Miss Bates, who came in talking, and had not finished her speech under many minutes after her being admitted into the circle at the fire. As the door opened she was heard,

"So very obliging of you!—No rain at all. Nothing to signify. I do not care for myself. Quite thick shoes. And Jane declares—Well!—(as soon as she was within the door) Well! This is brilliant indeed!—This is admirable!—Excellently contrived, upon my word. Nothing wanting. Could not have imagined it.—So well lighted up.—Jane, Jane, look—did you ever see any thing? Oh! Mr. Weston, you must really have had Aladdin's lamp.[6] Good Mrs. Stokes would not know her own room again. I saw her as I came in; she was standing in the entrance. 'Oh! Mrs. Stokes,' said I—but I had not time for more."—She was now met by Mrs. Weston.—"Very well, I thank you, ma'am.

I hope you are quite well. Very happy to hear it. So afraid you might have a headach!—seeing you pass by so often, and knowing how much trouble you must have. Delighted to hear it indeed. Ah! dear Mrs. Elton, so obliged to you for the carriage!—excellent time.—Jane and I quite ready. Did not keep the horses a moment. Most comfortable carriage—Oh! and I am sure our thanks are due to you, Mrs. Weston, on that score.—Mrs. Elton had most kindly sent Jane a note, or we should have been.—But two such offers in one day!—Never were such neighbours. I said to my mother, 'Upon my word, ma'am——.' Thank you, my mother is remarkably well. Gone to Mr. Woodhouse's. I made her take her shawl—for the evenings are not warm—her large new shawl—Mrs. Dixon's wedding present.[7]—So kind of her to think of my mother! Bought at Weymouth, you know—Mr. Dixon's choice. There were three others, Jane says, which they hesitated about some time. Colonel Campbell rather preferred an olive. My dear Jane, are you sure you did not wet your feet?—It was but a drop or two, but I am so afraid:—but Mr. Frank Churchill was so extremely—and there was a mat to step upon—I shall never forget his extreme politeness.—Oh! Mr. Frank Churchill, I must tell you my mother's spectacles have never been in fault since; the rivet never came out again. My mother often talks of your goodnature. Does not she, Jane?—Do not we often talk of Mr. Frank Churchill?—Ah! here's Miss Woodhouse.—Dear Miss Woodhouse, how do you do?—Very well I thank you, quite well. This is meeting quite in fairy-land!—Such a transformation!—Must not compliment, I know—(eyeing Emma most complacently)—that would be rude—but upon my word, Miss Woodhouse, you do look—how do you like Jane's hair?—You are a judge.—She did it all herself. Quite wonderful how she does her hair!—No hairdresser from London I think could.—Ah! Dr. Hughes I declare—and Mrs. Hughes. Must go and speak to Dr. and Mrs. Hughes for a moment.—How do you do? How do you do?—Very well, I thank you. This is delightful, is not it?—Where's dear Mr. Richard?—Oh! there he is. Don't disturb him. Much better employed talking to the young ladies. How do you do, Mr. Richard?—I saw you the other day as you rode through the town——Mrs. Otway, I protest!—and good Mr. Otway, and Miss Otway and Miss Caroline.

7 That is, a present given to Mrs. Bates by the Campbells to commemorate their daughter's wedding.

8 Complement each other.

—Such a host of friends!—and Mr. George and Mr. Arthur!—How do you do? How do you all do?—Quite well, I am much obliged to you. Never better.—Don't I hear another carriage?—Who can this be?—very likely the worthy Coles.—Upon my word, this is charming to be standing about among such friends!—And such a noble fire!—I am quite roasted. No coffee, I thank you, for me—never take coffee. —A little tea if you please, sir, by and bye,—no hurry—Oh! here it comes. Every thing so good!"

Frank Churchill returned to his station by Emma; and as soon as Miss Bates was quiet, she found herself necessarily overhearing the discourse of Mrs. Elton and Miss Fairfax, who were standing a little way behind her.—He was thoughtful. Whether he were overhearing too, she could not determine. After a good many compliments to Jane on her dress and look, compliments very quietly and properly taken, Mrs. Elton was evidently wanting to be complimented herself—and it was, "How do you like my gown?—How do you like my trimming?—How has Wright done my hair?"—with many other relative questions, all answered with patient politeness. Mrs. Elton then said,

"Nobody can think less of dress in general than I do—but upon such an occasion as this, when everybody's eyes are so much upon me, and in compliment to the Westons—who I have no doubt are giving this ball chiefly to do me honour—I would not wish to be inferior to others. And I see very few pearls in the room except mine.—So Frank Churchill is a capital dancer, I understand.—We shall see if our styles suit.[8]—A fine young man certainly is Frank Churchill. I like him very well."

At this moment Frank began talking so vigorously, that Emma could not but imagine he had overheard his own praises, and did not want to hear more;—and the voices of the ladies were drowned for awhile, till another suspension brought Mrs. Elton's tones again distinctly forward.—Mr. Elton had just joined them, and his wife was exclaiming,

"Oh! you have found us out at last, have you, in our seclusion?—I was this moment telling Jane, I thought you would begin to be impatient for tidings of us."

"Jane!"—repeated Frank Churchill, with a look of surprise and displeasure.—"That is easy[9]—but Miss Fairfax does not disapprove it, I suppose."

"How do you like Mrs. Elton?" said Emma in a whisper.

"Not at all."

"You are ungrateful."

"Ungrateful!—What do you mean?" Then changing from a frown to a smile—"No, do not tell me—I do not want to know what you mean.—Where is my father?—When are we to begin dancing?"

9 Meaning familiar, with an implication of excessive familiarity.

Robert Smirke, illustration of Aladdin and the genie or "Genius," from Edward Forster, trans., *The Arabian Nights,* 4 vols. (London: William Miller, 1802).

Emma could hardly understand him; he seemed in an odd humour. He walked off to find his father, but was quickly back again with both Mr. and Mrs. Weston. He had met with them in a little perplexity, which must be laid before Emma. It had just occurred to Mrs. Weston that Mrs. Elton must be asked to begin the ball;[10] that she would expect it; which interfered with all their wishes of giving Emma that distinction.—Emma heard the sad truth with fortitude.

"And what are we to do for a proper partner for her?" said Mr. Weston. "She will think Frank ought to ask her."

Frank turned instantly to Emma, to claim her former promise; and boasted himself an engaged man, which his father looked his most perfect approbation of—and it then appeared that Mrs. Weston was wanting *him* to dance with Mrs. Elton himself, and that their business was to help to persuade him into it, which was done pretty soon. —Mr. Weston and Mrs. Elton led the way, Mr. Frank Churchill and Miss Woodhouse followed. Emma must submit to stand second to Mrs. Elton, though she had always considered the ball as peculiarly for her. It was almost enough to make her think of marrying.

Mrs. Elton had undoubtedly the advantage, at this time, in vanity completely gratified; for though she had intended to begin with Frank Churchill, she could not lose by the change. Mr. Weston might be his son's superior.—In spite of this little rub,[11] however, Emma was smiling with enjoyment, delighted to see the respectable length of the set as it was forming,[12] and to feel that she had so many hours of unusual festivity before her.—She was more disturbed by Mr. Knightley's not dancing, than by any thing else.—There he was, among the standers-by, where he ought not to be; he ought to be dancing,—not classing himself with the husbands, and fathers, and whist-players, who were pretending to feel an interest in the dance till their rubbers were made up,[13]—so young as he looked!—He could not have appeared to greater advantage perhaps any where, than where he had placed himself. His tall, firm, upright figure, among the bulky forms and stooping shoulders of the elderly men, was such as Emma felt must draw every body's eyes; and, excepting her own partner, there was not one among the whole row of young men who could be compared with him.—He moved a few steps nearer, and those

10 As the new bride, Mrs. Elton would be *de facto* the guest of honor at the ball, and would therefore be given the honor of leading the dancing.

11 Minor setback.

12 The basic starting formation for English country dancing was one of long parallel lines, with partners facing each other; hence Frank and Emma's anxieties about finding a room large enough to dance in comfortably. Couples farther down the line would have to wait for the leading couple at the top to start the dance; therefore a "respectable" length of set would guarantee a long dance.

13 Till their games were set up.

few steps were enough to prove in how gentlemanlike a manner, with what natural grace, he must have danced, would he but take the trouble.—Whenever she caught his eye,[14] she forced him to smile; but in general he was looking grave. She wished he could love a ball-room better, and could like Frank Churchill better.—He seemed often observing her. She must not flatter herself that he thought of her dancing, but if he were criticising her behaviour, she did not feel afraid. There was nothing like flirtation between her and her partner. They seemed more like cheerful, easy friends, than lovers. That Frank Churchill thought less of her than he had done, was indubitable.

14 See vol. II, chap. 9.

The ball proceeded pleasantly. The anxious cares, the incessant attentions of Mrs. Weston, were not thrown away. Every body seemed happy; and the praise of being a delightful ball, which is seldom bestowed till after a ball has ceased to be, was repeatedly given in the very beginning of the existence of this. Of very important, very recordable events, it was not more productive than such meetings usually are. There was one, however, which Emma thought something of.—The two last dances before supper were begun, and Harriet had no partner;—the only young lady sitting down;—and so equal had been hitherto the number of dancers, that how there could be anyone disengaged was the wonder!—But Emma's wonder lessened soon afterwards, on seeing Mr. Elton sauntering about. He would not ask Harriet to dance if it were possible to be avoided: she was sure he would not—and she was expecting him every moment to escape into the card-room.

Escape, however, was not his plan. He came to the part of the room where the sitters-by were collected, spoke to some, and walked about in front of them, as if to show his liberty, and his resolution of maintaining it. He did not omit being sometimes directly before Miss Smith, or speaking to those who were close to her.—Emma saw it. She was not yet dancing; she was working her way up from the bottom, and had therefore leisure to look around, and by only turning her head a little she saw it all. When she was half way up the set, the whole group were exactly behind her, and she would no longer allow her eyes to watch; but Mr. Elton was so near, that she heard every syllable of a dialogue which just then took place between him and Mrs. Weston; and she perceived that his wife, who was standing immediately above her, was not only listening also, but even encouraging him by significant glances.—The kind-hearted, gentle Mrs. Weston had left her seat to join him and say, "Do not you dance, Mr. Elton?" to which his prompt reply was, "Most readily, Mrs. Weston, if you will dance with me."

"Me!—oh! no—I would get you a better partner than myself. I am no dancer."

"If Mrs. Gilbert wishes to dance," said he, "I shall have great pleasure, I am sure—for, though beginning to feel myself rather an old married man, and that my dancing days are over,[15] it would give me very great pleasure at any time to stand up with an old friend like Mrs. Gilbert."

"Mrs. Gilbert does not mean to dance, but there is a young lady disengaged whom I should be very glad to see dancing—Miss Smith."

"Miss Smith!—oh!—I had not observed.—You are extremely obliging—and if I were not an old married man.—But my dancing days are over, Mrs. Weston. You will excuse me. Any thing else I should be most happy to do, at your command—but my dancing days are over."

Mrs. Weston said no more; and Emma could imagine with what surprise and mortification she must be returning to her seat. This was Mr. Elton! the amiable, obliging, gentle Mr. Elton.—She looked round for a moment; he had joined Mr. Knightley at a little distance, and was arranging[16] himself for settled conversation, while smiles of high glee passed between him and his wife.

She would not look again. Her heart was in a glow, and she feared her face might be as hot.

In another moment a happier sight caught her;—Mr. Knightley leading Harriet to the set!—Never had she been more surprised, seldom more delighted, than at that instant. She was all pleasure and gratitude, both for Harriet and herself, and longed to be thanking him; and though too distant for speech, her countenance said much, as soon as she could catch his eye again.

15 The phrase derives from old Capulet's lines in Act I, Scene 5, of *Romeo and Juliet* ("Nay sit, nay sit, good Cozin *Capulet,*/For you and I are past our dauncing daies"), but it is one that had long passed into common idiomatic usage. Compare Cleopatra's words "My Sallad dayes,/When I was greene in iudgement" in Act I, Scene 5, of *Antony and Cleopatra.*

16 Compare Mr. Bennet's sardonic remark about his daughter Mary in vol. I, chap. 2, of *Pride and Prejudice:* "'While Mary is adjusting her ideas,' he continued, 'let us return to Mr. Bingley.'"

His dancing proved to be just what she had believed it, extremely good; and Harriet would have seemed almost too lucky, if it had not been for the cruel state of things before, and for the very complete enjoyment and very high sense of the distinction which her happy features announced. It was not thrown away on her, she bounded higher than ever, flew farther down the middle, and was in a continual course of smiles.

Mr. Elton had retreated into the card-room, looking (Emma trusted) very foolish. She did not think he was quite so hardened[17] as his wife, though growing very like her;—*she* spoke some of her feelings, by observing audibly to her partner,

"Knightley has taken pity on poor little Miss Smith!—Very good-natured, I declare."

Supper was announced. The move began; and Miss Bates might be heard from that moment, without interruption, till her being seated at table and taking up her spoon.

"Jane, Jane, my dear Jane, where are you?—Here is your tippet.[18] Mrs. Weston begs you to put on your tippet. She says she is afraid there will be draughts in the passage, though every thing has been done—One door nailed up—Quantities of matting—My dear Jane, indeed you must. Mr. Churchill, oh! you are too obliging!—How well you put it on!—so gratified! Excellent dancing indeed!—Yes, my dear, I ran home, as I said I should, to help grandmamma to bed, and got back again, and nobody missed me.—I set off without saying a word, just as I told you. Grandmamma was quite well, had a charming evening with Mr. Woodhouse, a vast deal of chat, and backgammon.—Tea was made down stairs, biscuits and baked apples and wine before she came away: amazing luck in some of her throws: and she inquired a great deal about you, how you were amused, and who were your partners. 'Oh!' said I, 'I shall not forestall Jane; I left her dancing with Mr. George Otway; she will love to tell you all about it herself to-morrow: her first partner was Mr. Elton, I do not know who will ask her next, perhaps Mr. William Cox.' My dear sir, you are too obliging.—Is there nobody you would not rather?—I am not helpless. Sir, you are most kind. Upon my word, Jane on one arm, and me

17 Grown so unfeeling.

18 A short cape or cloak, often made of wool or fur, worn by a woman to cover the neck and shoulders.

on the other!—Stop, stop, let us stand a little back, Mrs. Elton is going; dear Mrs. Elton, how elegant she looks! Beautiful lace!—Now we all follow in her train. Quite the queen of the evening!—Well, here we are at the passage. Two steps, Jane, take care of the two steps. Oh! no, there is but one. Well, I was persuaded there were two. How very odd! I was convinced there were two, and there is but one. I never saw any thing equal to the comfort and style—Candles every where.—I was telling you of your grandmamma, Jane,—There was a little disappointment.—The baked apples and biscuits, excellent in their way, you know; but there was a delicate fricassee of sweetbread[19] and some asparagus brought in at first, and good Mr. Woodhouse, not thinking the asparagus quite boiled enough, sent it all out again. Now there is nothing grandmamma loves better than sweetbread and asparagus—so she was rather disappointed, but we agreed we would not speak of it to any body, for fear of its getting round to dear Miss Woodhouse, who would be so very much concerned!—Well, this is brilliant! I am all amazement! could not have supposed any thing!—Such elegance and profusion!—I have seen nothing like it since—Well, where shall we sit? where shall we sit? Any where, so that Jane is not in a draught. Where *I* sit is of no consequence. Oh! do you recommend this side?—Well, I am sure, Mr. Churchill—only it seems too good—but just as you please. What you direct in this house cannot be wrong. Dear Jane, how shall we ever recollect half the dishes for grandmamma. Soup too! Bless me! I should not be helped so soon, but it smells most excellent, and I cannot help beginning."

Emma had no opportunity of speaking to Mr. Knightley till after supper; but when they were all in the ball-room again, her eyes invited him irresistibly to come to her and be thanked. He was warm in his reprobation of Mr. Elton's conduct; it had been unpardonable rudeness; and Mrs. Elton's looks also received the due share of censure.

"They aimed at wounding more than Harriet," said he. "Emma, why is it that they are your enemies?"

He looked with smiling penetration; and, on receiving no answer, added, "*She* ought not to be angry with you, I suspect, whatever he

19 Sweetbreads are an animal's thymus or pancreas, in this context probably those of a lamb. Lamb's sweetbreads, along with lambstones (lamb's testicles), were often served with asparagus; Hannah Glasse's recipe for *"A fricasey of lamb-stones and sweetbreads"* runs thus:

> Have ready some lamb-stones blanched, parboiled, and sliced, and flour two or three sweetbreads; if very thick, cut them in two; the yolks of six hard eggs whole, a few pistacho-nut kernels, and a few large oysters: fry these all of a fine brown, then pour out all the butter, and add a pint of drawn gravy, the lamb-stones, some asparagus tops about an inch long, some grated nutmeg, a little pepper and salt, two shalots shred small, and a glass of white wine. Stew all these together for ten minutes, then add the yolks of three eggs beat very fine, with a little cream, and a little beaten mace; stir altogether till it is of a fine thickness, and then dish it up. Garnish with lemon.

The Art of Cookery: Made Plain and Easy (London, 1748; rev. ed., London: T. Longman, B. Law, et al., 1796), p. 45.

may be.—To that surmise, you say nothing, of course; but confess, Emma, that you did want him to marry Harriet."

"I did," replied Emma, "and they cannot forgive me."

He shook his head; but there was a smile of indulgence with it, and he only said,

"I shall not scold you. I leave you to your own reflections."

"Can you trust me with such flatterers?—Does my vain spirit ever tell me I am wrong?"

"Not your vain spirit, but your serious spirit.—If one leads you wrong, I am sure the other tells you of it."

"I do own myself to have been completely mistaken in Mr. Elton. There is a littleness[20] about him which you discovered, and which I did not: and I was fully convinced of his being in love with Harriet. It was through a series of strange blunders!"

"And, in return for your acknowledging so much, I will do you the justice to say, that you would have chosen for him better than he has chosen for himself.—Harriet Smith has some first-rate qualities, which Mrs. Elton is totally without. An unpretending, single-minded, artless girl—infinitely to be preferred by any man of sense and taste to such a woman as Mrs. Elton. I found Harriet more conversable than I expected."

Emma was extremely gratified.—They were interrupted by the bustle of Mr. Weston calling on every body to begin dancing again.

"Come Miss Woodhouse, Miss Otway, Miss Fairfax, what are you all doing?—Come Emma, set your companions the example. Every body is lazy! Every body is asleep!"

"I am ready," said Emma, "whenever I am wanted."

"Whom are you going to dance with?" asked Mr. Knightley.

She hesitated a moment, and then replied, "With you, if you will ask me."

"Will you?" said he, offering his hand.

"Indeed I will. You have shown that you can dance, and you know we are not really so much brother and sister as to make it at all improper."[21]

"Brother and sister! no, indeed."

20 Meanness of spirit.

21 Emma and Knightley's relationship via Isabella's marriage does not make their dancing together inappropriate; neither, of course, does it prevent them from marrying, as confirmed by the Book of Common Prayer's "Table of Kindred and Affinity."

3

1 That is, Harriet will be educated harshly by witnessing the Eltons' deliberate slights to her.

This little explanation with Mr. Knightley gave Emma considerable pleasure. It was one of the agreeable recollections of the ball, which she walked about the lawn the next morning to enjoy.—She was extremely glad that they had come to so good an understanding respecting the Eltons, and that their opinions of both husband and wife were so much alike; and his praise of Harriet, his concession in her favour, was peculiarly gratifying. The impertinence of the Eltons, which for a few minutes had threatened to ruin the rest of her evening, had been the occasion of some of its highest satisfactions; and she looked forward to another happy result—the cure of Harriet's infatuation.—From Harriet's manner of speaking of the circumstance before they quitted the ball-room, she had strong hopes. It seemed as if her eyes were suddenly opened, and she were enabled to see that Mr. Elton was not the superior creature she had believed him. The fever was over, and Emma could harbour little fear of the pulse being quickened again by injurious courtesy. She depended on the evil feelings of the Eltons for supplying all the discipline of pointed neglect[1] that could be further requisite.—Harriet rational, Frank Churchill not too much in love, and Mr. Knightley not wanting to quarrel with her, how very happy a summer must be before her!

She was not to see Frank Churchill this morning. He had told her that he could not allow himself the pleasure of stopping at Hartfield, as he was to be at home by the middle of the day. She did not regret it.

Having arranged all these matters, looked them through, and put them all to rights, she was just turning to the house with spirits freshened up for the demands of the two little boys, as well as of their grandpapa, when the great iron sweep-gate opened, and two persons entered whom she had never less expected to see together—Frank Churchill, with Harriet leaning on his arm—actually Harriet!—A moment sufficed to convince her that something extraordinary had happened. Harriet looked white and frightened, and he was trying to cheer her.—The iron gates and the front door were not twenty yards asunder;—they were all three soon in the hall, and Harriet immediately sinking into a chair fainted away.

A young lady who faints, must be recovered; questions must be answered, and surprises be explained. Such events are very interesting, but the suspense of them cannot last long. A few minutes made Emma acquainted with the whole.

Miss Smith, and Miss Bickerton, another parlour boarder at Mrs. Goddard's, who had been also at the ball, had walked out together, and taken a road, the Richmond road, which, though apparently public enough for safety, had led them into alarm.—About half a mile beyond Highbury, making a sudden turn, and deeply shaded by elms on each side, it became for a considerable stretch very retired; and when the young ladies had advanced some way into it, they had suddenly perceived at a small distance before them, on a broader patch of greensward[2] by the side, a party of gipsies.[3] A child on the watch, came towards them to beg; and Miss Bickerton, excessively frightened, gave a great scream, and calling on Harriet to follow her, ran up a steep bank, cleared a slight hedge at the top, and made the best of her way by a short cut back to Highbury. But poor Harriet could not follow. She had suffered very much from cramp after dancing, and her first attempt to mount the bank brought on such a return of it as made her absolutely powerless—and in this state, and exceedingly terrified, she had been obliged to remain.

How the trampers[4] might have behaved, had the young ladies been more courageous, must be doubtful; but such an invitation for attack could not be resisted; and Harriet was soon assailed by half a dozen children, headed by a stout woman and a great boy, all clamor-

2 Turf.

3 Gypsies occupied a complex position in early nineteenth-century imaginations, since they figured both as symbols of wildness and otherness and as traditional elements of the English landscape. Deborah Epstein Nord catches this paradoxical circumstance well, when she notes, "Unlike colonial subjects . . . Gypsies were a domestic or an internal other, and their proximity and visibility were crucial features in their deployment as literary or symbolic figures. Their familiarity lent them an exoticism that was, at the same time, indigenous and homely" (*Gypsies and the British Imagination, 1807–1930* [New York: Columbia University Press, 2006], p. 3).

4 Vagrants.

Thomas Gainsborough, *Gypsy Encampment, Sunset,* c. 1778–1780. In the early nineteenth century, the marginal status of gypsies allowed them to be used both as social scapegoats and as romanticized figures of folk wisdom.

ous, and impertinent in look, though not absolutely in word.—More and more frightened, she immediately promised them money, and taking out her purse, gave them a shilling, and begged them not to want more, or to use her ill.—She was then able to walk, though but slowly, and was moving away—but her terror and her purse were too tempting, and she was followed, or rather surrounded, by the whole gang, demanding more.

In this state Frank Churchill had found her, she trembling and conditioning,[5] they loud and insolent. By a most fortunate chance his leaving Highbury had been delayed so as to bring him to her assistance at this critical moment. The pleasantness of the morning had induced him to walk forward, and leave his horses to meet him by another road, a mile or two beyond Highbury—and happening to have borrowed a pair of scissars the night before of Miss Bates, and to have forgotten to restore them, he had been obliged to stop at her door, and go in for a few minutes: he was therefore later than he had intended; and being on foot, was unseen by the whole party till almost close to them. The terror which the woman and boy had been creating in Harriet was then their own portion. He had left them completely frightened; and Harriet eagerly clinging to him, and hardly able to speak, had just strength enough to reach Hartfield, before her spirits were quite overcome. It was his idea to bring her to Hartfield: he had thought of no other place.

This was the amount of the whole story,—of his communication and of Harriet's as soon as she had recovered her senses and speech.—He dared not stay longer than to see her well; these several delays left him not another minute to lose; and Emma engaging to give assurance of her safety to Mrs. Goddard, and notice of there being such a set of people in the neighbourhood to Mr. Knightley,[6] he set off, with all the grateful blessings that she could utter for her friend and herself.

Such an adventure as this,—a fine young man and a lovely young woman thrown together in such a way,[7] could hardly fail of suggesting certain ideas to the coldest heart and the steadiest brain. So Emma thought, at least. Could a linguist, could a grammarian, could even a mathematician have seen what she did, have witnessed their

5 Bargaining.

6 As the local magistrate, Knightley would be responsible for dealing with the gypsies legally, and moving them on or charging them if necessary.

7 Emma Thompson's adaptation of *Sense and Sensibility* contrives a suggestive "adventure" of this nature by having Colonel Brandon rescue Marianne Dashwood from the pouring rain at Cleveland, whereas in vol III, chap. 6, of the novel, she catches her near-fatal cold from sitting in wet grass by herself: "Two delightful twilight walks on the third and fourth evenings of her being there, not merely on the dry gravel of the shrubbery, but all over the grounds, and especially in the most distant parts of them, where there was something more of wildness than in the rest, where the trees were the oldest, and the grass was the longest and wettest, had—assisted by the still greater imprudence of sitting in her wet shoes and stockings—given Marianne a cold so violent, as, though for a day or two trifled with or denied, would force itself by increasing ailments, on the concern of every body, and the notice of herself." For more on Austen adaptations, see Linda Troost and Sayre Greenfield, eds., *Jane Austen in Hollywood* (Lexington: University of Kentucky Press, 1988); Gina McDonald and Andrew McDonald, eds., *Jane Austen on Screen* (Cambridge: Cambridge University Press, 2003); Suzanne J. Pucci and James Thompson, eds., *Jane Austen and Co.: Remaking the Past in Contemporary Culture* (Albany: State University of New York Press, 2003); and Kathryn Sutherland, *Jane Austen's Textual Lives: From Aeschylus to Bollywood* (Oxford: Oxford University Press, 2005).

appearance together, and heard their history of it, without feeling that circumstances had been at work to make them peculiarly interesting[8] to each other?—How much more must an imaginist,[9] like herself, be on fire with speculation and foresight!—especially with such a ground-work of anticipation as her mind had already made.

It was a very extraordinary thing! Nothing of the sort had ever occurred before to any young ladies in the place, within her memory; no rencontre,[10] no alarm of the kind;—and now it had happened to the very person, and at the very hour, when the other very person was chancing to pass by to rescue her!—It certainly was very extraordinary!—And knowing, as she did, the favourable state of mind of each at this period, it struck her the more. He was wishing to get the better of his attachment to herself, she just recovering from her mania for Mr. Elton. It seemed as if every thing united to promise the most interesting consequences. It was not possible that the occurrence should not be strongly recommending each to the other.

In the few minutes' conversation which she had yet had with him, while Harriet had been partially insensible, he had spoken of her terror, her naïveté, her fervor as she seized and clung to his arm, with a sensibility amused and delighted; and just at last, after Harriet's own account had been given, he had expressed his indignation at the abominable folly of Miss Bickerton in the warmest terms. Every thing was to take its natural course, however, neither impelled nor assisted. She would not stir a step, nor drop a hint. No, she had had enough of interference. There could be no harm in a scheme, a mere passive scheme. It was no more than a wish. Beyond it she would on no account proceed.

Emma's first resolution was to keep her father from the knowledge of what had passed,—aware of the anxiety and alarm it would occasion: but she soon felt that concealment must be impossible. Within half an hour it was known all over Highbury. It was the very event to engage those who talk most, the young and the low; and all the youth and servants in the place were soon in the happiness of frightful news. The last night's ball seemed lost in the gipsies. Poor Mr. Woodhouse trembled as he sat, and, as Emma had foreseen, would scarcely be satisfied without their promising never to go be-

8 See note 5 to vol. I, chap. 6.

9 An Austenian coinage, which presumably denotes someone so expert in imaginative speculation that she ranks alongside grammarians and mathematicians.

10 Dispute, conflict.

yond the shrubbery again. It was some comfort to him that many inquiries after himself and Miss Woodhouse (for his neighbours knew that he loved to be inquired after), as well as Miss Smith, were coming in during the rest of the day; and he had the pleasure of returning for answer, that they were all very indifferent—which, though not exactly true, for she was perfectly well, and Harriet not much otherwise, Emma would not interfere with. She had an unhappy state of health in general for the child of such a man, for she hardly knew what indisposition was; and if he did not invent illnesses for her, she could make no figure in a message.

The gipsies did not wait for the operations of justice; they took themselves off in a hurry. The young ladies of Highbury might have walked again in safety before their panic began, and the whole history dwindled soon into a matter of little importance but to Emma and her nephews:—in her imagination it maintained its ground, and Henry and John were still asking every day for the story of Harriet and the gipsies,[11] and still tenaciously setting her right if she varied in the slightest particular from the original recital.

11 It is typical of the world of Highbury that the story of the gypsies should so quickly be converted into a narrative "keepsake," to be gone over again and again.

Another dramatic, romantic "adventure," albeit one not in Austen's original text: Colonel Brandon (Alan Rickman) rescues Marianne Dashwood (Kate Winslet) from the pouring rain in Ang Lee's 1995 film version of *Sense and Sensibility.*

4

A very few days had passed after this adventure, when Harriet came one morning to Emma with a small parcel in her hand, and after sitting down and hesitating, thus began:

"Miss Woodhouse—if you are at leisure—I have something that I should like to tell you—a sort of confession to make—and then, you know, it will be over."

Emma was a good deal surprised; but begged her to speak. There was a seriousness in Harriet's manner which prepared her, quite as much as her words, for something more than ordinary.

"It is my duty, and I am sure it is my wish," she continued, "to have no reserves with you on this subject. As I am happily quite an altered creature in *one respect,* it is very fit that you should have the satisfaction of knowing it. I do not want to say more than is necessary—I am too much ashamed of having given way as I have done, and I dare say you understand me."

"Yes," said Emma, "I hope I do."

"How I could so long a time be fancying myself! . . ." cried Harriet, warmly. "It seems like madness! I can see nothing at all extraordinary in him now.—I do not care whether I meet him or not—except that of the two I had rather not see him—and indeed I would go any distance round to avoid him—but I do not envy his wife in the least; I neither admire her nor envy her, as I have done: she is very charming, I dare say, and all that, but I think her very ill-tempered and disagreeable—I shall never forget her look the other night!—However, I assure you, Miss Woodhouse, I wish her no evil.—No, let them be ever

Tunbridge-ware box by T. Barton, Tunbridge Wells, 1800–1840. This photograph shows the contrasting patterns of inlaid wood so characteristic of the local style.

so happy together, it will not give me another moment's pang: and to convince you that I have been speaking truth, I am now going to destroy—what I ought to have destroyed long ago—what I ought never to have kept—I know that very well (blushing as she spoke).—However, now I will destroy it all—and it is my particular wish to do it in your presence, that you may see how rational I am grown. Cannot you guess what this parcel holds?" said she, with a conscious look.

"Not the least in the world.—Did he ever give you any thing?"

"No—I cannot call them gifts; but they are things that I have valued very much."

She held the parcel towards her, and Emma read the words *Most precious treasures* on the top. Her curiosity was greatly excited. Harriet unfolded the parcel, and she looked on with impatience. Within abundance of silver paper was a pretty little Tunbridge-ware[1] box, which Harriet opened: it was well lined with the softest cotton; but, excepting the cotton, Emma saw only a small piece of court plaister.[2]

"Now," said Harriet, "you *must* recollect."

"No, indeed I do not."

1 Decorative woodwork associated with the towns of Tunbridge and Tonbridge Wells since the seventeenth century. Tunbridge ware boxes featured delicate inlaid marquetry and were often sold as souvenirs to people visiting the town's mineral springs.

2 A sticking-plaster made of fabric (usually silk) coated in insinglass (fish gelatin).

3 A term that still survives today, although the practices to which the term refers are obsolete. A penknife and quill would originally have been used to cut and recut quill pens, and later to sharpen lead pencils.

4 Although the primary sense here is that Harriet's plaster is a memento or keepsake, Emma may also be glancing ironically at the original use of "relic" to denote an object that once belonged to a saint and was therefore sanctified—especially since the plaster does become interchangeable with Elton for Harriet ("There it goes, and there is an end, thank Heaven! of Mr. Elton"). In Amy Heckerling's film *Clueless,* the Harriet character Tai (Brittany Murphy) attempts to burn a towel touched by Elton and a cassette recording of Coolio's "Rollin' with My Homies," to which they danced at a party.

5 In 1802, A. F. M. Willich offered the following description of and recipe for spruce beer, a form of what is now familiarly known as root beer: "Spruce-Beer, a kind of diet-drink, which is prepared in the following manner: Eight gallons of water are first poured into a cask, or other vessel; and a similar quantity of boiling water is added: 16 pounds of molasses are then mixed, together with a few table-spoonsful of the *essence of spruce* (which is obtained from the cones of the *spruce-fir*). Half a pint of sweet yeast must now be put in; and the whole, after being well stirred, should be placed in a temperate room, for a few days, until the fermentation ceases. The liquor may then be bottled; and, in the course of a fortnight, it will be fit for use" (*The Domestic Encyclopaedia; or, A Dictionary of Facts, and Useful Knowledge,* 4 vols. [London: Murray & Highley, 1802], vol. IV, p. 123).

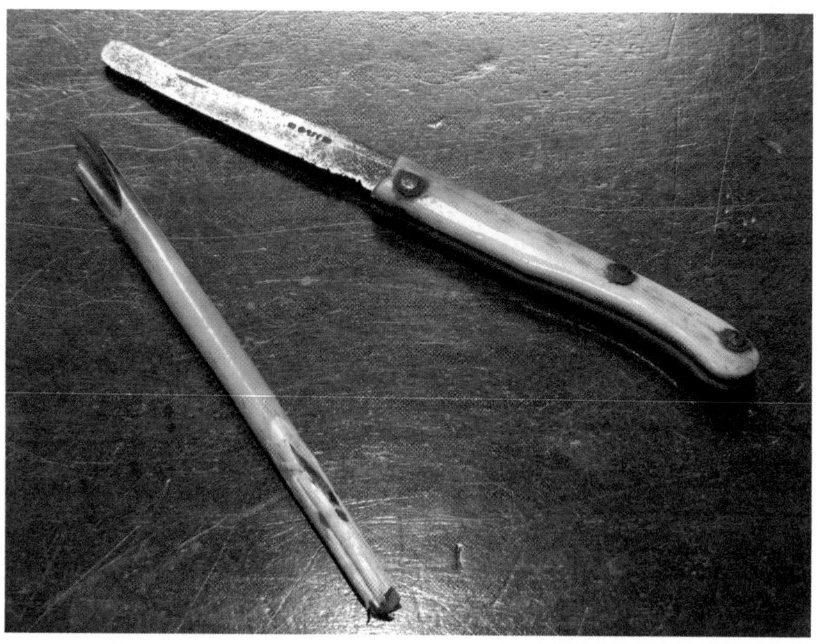

Photograph of Austen family pen-knives from Chawton Cottage.

"Dear me! I should not have thought it possible you could forget what passed in this very room about court plaister, one of the very last times we ever met in it!—It was but a very few days before I had my sore throat—just before Mr. and Mrs. John Knightley came—I think the very evening.—Do not you remember his cutting his finger with your new penknife,[3] and your recommending court plaister?—But as you had none about you, and knew I had, you desired me to supply him; and so I took mine out and cut him a piece; but it was a great deal too large, and he cut it smaller, and kept playing some time with what was left, before he gave it back to me. And so then, in my nonsense, I could not help making a treasure of it—so I put it by never to be used, and looked at it now and then as a great treat."

"My dearest Harriet!" cried Emma, putting her hand before her face, and jumping up, "you make me more ashamed of myself than I can bear. Remember it? Ay, I remember it all now; all, except your saving this relick[4]—I knew nothing of that till this moment—but the cutting the finger, and my recommending court plaister, and saying I had none about me!—Oh! my sins, my sins!—And I had plenty all the while in my pocket!—One of my senseless tricks!—I deserve to be under a continual blush all the rest of my life.—Well—(sitting down again) go on—what else?"

"And had you really some at hand yourself?—I am sure I never suspected it, you did it so naturally."

"And so you actually put this piece of court plaister by for his sake!" said Emma, recovering from her state of shame and feeling, divided between wonder and amusement. And secretly she added to herself, "Lord bless me! when should I ever have thought of putting by in cotton a piece of court plaister that Frank Churchill had been pulling about!—I never was equal to this."

"Here," resumed Harriet, turning to her box again, "here is something still more valuable, I mean that *has been* more valuable, because this is what did really once belong to him, which the court plaister never did."

Emma was quite eager to see this superior treasure. It was the end of an old pencil,—the part without any lead.

"This was really his," said Harriet.—"Do not you remember one morning?—no, I dare say you do not. But one morning—I forget exactly the day—but perhaps it was the Tuesday or Wednesday before *that evening*, he wanted to make a memorandum in his pocket-book; it was about spruce beer.[5] Mr. Knightley had been telling him something about brewing spruce beer, and he wanted to put it down; but when he took out his pencil, there was so little lead that he soon cut it all away, and it would not do, so you lent him another, and this was left upon the table as good for nothing. But I kept my eye on it; and, as soon as I dared, caught it up, and never parted with it again from that moment."

"I do remember it," cried Emma; "I perfectly remember it.—Talking about spruce beer.—Oh! yes—Mr. Knightley and I both saying we liked it, and Mr. Elton's seeming resolved to learn to like it too.[6] I perfectly remember it.—Stop; Mr. Knightley was standing just here, was not he?—I have an idea he was standing just here."[7]

6 In *A Practical Treatise on Diet* (London: R. Phillips, 1801), William Nisbet noted that spruce beer was something of an acquired taste: "Spruce beer is an article powerfully diuretic and antiscorbutic. It contains a large quantity of fixed air, is highly refreshing in summer, and sits easy on the most debilitated stomach; but, from its peculiar flavor, it is disagreeable to the taste of many" (p. 309). In this light, Elton's willingness to learn to like spruce beer can be read as yet another attempt to curry favor with Emma.

7 It is telling that it is Knightley's position that Emma recalls precisely.

Photograph of the cone buds and needles of a spruce tree, the main flavoring ingredient in spruce beer.

"Ah! I do not know. I cannot recollect.—It is very odd, but I cannot recollect.—Mr. Elton was sitting here, I remember, much about where I am now."—

"Well, go on."

"Oh! that's all. I have nothing more to show you, or to say—except that I am now going to throw them both behind the fire, and I wish you to see me do it."

"My poor dear Harriet! and have you actually found happiness in treasuring up these things?"

"Yes, simpleton as I was!—but I am quite ashamed of it now, and wish I could forget as easily as I can burn them. It was very wrong of me, you know, to keep any remembrances, after he was married. I knew it was—but had not resolution enough to part with them."

"But, Harriet, is it necessary to burn the court plaister?—I have not a word to say for the bit of old pencil, but the court plaister might be useful."

"I shall be happier to burn it," replied Harriet. "It has a disagreeable look to me. I must get rid of every thing.—There it goes, and there is an end, thank Heaven! of Mr. Elton."

"And when," thought Emma, "will there be a beginning of Mr. Churchill?"

She had soon afterwards reason to believe that the beginning was already made, and could not but hope that the gipsy, though she had *told* no fortune,[8] might be proved to have made Harriet's.—About a fortnight after the alarm, they came to a sufficient explanation, and quite undesignedly. Emma was not thinking of it at the moment, which made the information she received more valuable. She merely said, in the course of some trivial chat, "Well, Harriet, whenever you marry I would advise you to do so and so"—and thought no more of it, till after a minute's silence she heard Harriet say in a very serious tone, "I shall never marry."

Emma then looked up, and immediately saw how it was; and after a moment's debate, as to whether it should pass unnoticed or not, replied,

"Never marry!—This is a new resolution."

8 The association of gypsies with fortune-telling was proverbial; for example, in vol. I, chap. 4, of Walter Scott's novel *Guy Mannering, or The Astrologer* (1815), the gypsy Meg Merrilies casts a fortune by spinning thread.

"It is one that I shall never change, however."

After another short hesitation, "I hope it does not proceed from —I hope it is not in compliment to Mr. Elton?"

"Mr. Elton indeed!" cried Harriet indignantly.—"Oh! no"—and Emma could just catch the words, "so superior to Mr. Elton!"

She then took a longer time for consideration. Should she proceed no farther?—should she let it pass, and seem to suspect nothing?—Perhaps Harriet might think her cold or angry if she did; or perhaps if she were totally silent, it might only drive Harriet into asking her to hear too much; and against any thing like such an unreserve as had been, such an open and frequent discussion of hopes and chances, she was perfectly resolved.—She believed it would be wiser for her to say and know at once, all that she meant to say and know. Plain dealing was always best. She had previously determined how far she would proceed, on any application of the sort; and it would be safer for both, to have the judicious law of her own brain laid down with speed.—She was decided, and thus spoke—

"Harriet, I will not affect to be in doubt of your meaning. Your resolution, or rather your expectation of never marrying, results from an idea that the person whom you might prefer, would be too greatly your superior in situation to think of you. Is not it so?"

"Oh! Miss Woodhouse, believe me I have not the presumption to suppose—Indeed I am not so mad.—But it is a pleasure to me to admire him at a distance—and to think of his infinite superiority to all the rest of the world, with the gratitude, wonder, and veneration, which are so proper, in me especially."

"I am not at all surprised at you, Harriet. The service he rendered you was enough to warm your heart."

"Service! oh! it was such an inexpressible obligation!—The very recollection of it, and all that I felt at the time—when I saw him coming—his noble look—and my wretchedness before. Such a change! In one moment such a change! From perfect misery to perfect happiness."[9]

"It is very natural. It is natural, and it is honourable.—Yes, honourable, I think, to choose so well and so gratefully.—But that it will be a

9 Another occurrence of the phrase that plays such an important role in the novel's final sentence.

10 Lowering her social standing.

fortunate preference is more than I can promise. I do not advise you to give way to it, Harriet. I do not by any means engage for its being returned. Consider what you are about. Perhaps it will be wisest in you to check your feelings while you can: at any rate do not let them carry you far, unless you are persuaded of his liking you. Be observant of him. Let his behaviour be the guide of your sensations. I give you this caution now, because I shall never speak to you again on the subject. I am determined against all interference. Henceforward I know nothing of the matter. Let no name ever pass our lips. We were very wrong before; we will be cautious now.—He is your superior, no doubt, and there do seem objections and obstacles of a very serious nature; but yet, Harriet, more wonderful things have taken place, there have been matches of greater disparity. But take care of yourself. I would not have you too sanguine; though, however it may end, be assured that your raising your thoughts to *him,* is a mark of good taste which I shall always know how to value."

Harriet kissed her hand in silent and submissive gratitude. Emma was very decided in thinking such an attachment no bad thing for her friend. It's tendency would be to raise and refine her mind—and it must be saving her from the danger of degradation.[10]

5

In this state of schemes, and hopes, and connivance, June opened upon Hartfield. To Highbury in general it brought no material change. The Eltons were still talking of a visit from the Sucklings, and of the use to be made of their barouche-landau; and Jane Fairfax was still at her grandmother's; and as the return of the Campbells from Ireland was again delayed, and August, instead of Midsummer, fixed for it, she was likely to remain there full two months longer, provided at least she were able to defeat Mrs. Elton's activity in her service, and save herself from being hurried into a delightful situation against her will.

Mr. Knightley, who, for some reason best known to himself, had certainly taken an early dislike to Frank Churchill, was only growing to dislike him more. He began to suspect him of some double dealing[1] in his pursuit of Emma. That Emma was his object appeared indisputable. Every thing declared it; his own attentions, his father's hints, his mother-in-law's[2] guarded silence; it was all in unison; words, conduct, discretion, and indiscretion, told the same story. But while so many were devoting him to Emma, and Emma herself making him over to Harriet, Mr. Knightley began to suspect him of some inclination to trifle with Jane Fairfax. He could not understand it; but there were symptoms of intelligence[3] between them—he thought so at least—symptoms of admiration on his side, which, having once observed, he could not persuade himself to think entirely void of meaning, however he might wish to escape any of Emma's errors of imagination. *She* was not present when the suspicion first arose. He was

1 This focalization of the narrative through Knightley's perspective at the opening of the chapter marks the first time in the novel that Emma's consciousness is not the dominant presence alongside the narrator.

2 Stepmother's.

3 Signs of mutual understanding.

dining with the Randalls' family, and Jane at the Eltons'; and he had seen a look, more than a single look, at Miss Fairfax, which, from the admirer of Miss Woodhouse, seemed somewhat out of place. When he was again in their company, he could not help remembering what he had seen; nor could he avoid observations which, unless it were like Cowper and his fire at twilight,

> "Myself creating what I saw,"[4]

brought him yet stronger suspicion of there being a something[5] of private liking, of private understanding even, between Frank Churchill and Jane.

He had walked up one day after dinner, as he very often did, to spend his evening at Hartfield. Emma and Harriet were going to walk; he joined them; and, on returning, they fell in with a larger party, who, like themselves, judged it wisest to take their exercise early, as the weather threatened rain; Mr. and Mrs. Weston and their son, Miss Bates and her niece, who had accidentally met. They all united; and, on reaching Hartfield gates, Emma, who knew it was exactly the sort of visiting that would be welcome to her father, pressed them all to go in and drink tea with him. The Randalls' party agreed to it immediately; and after a pretty long speech from Miss Bates, which few persons listened to, she also found it possible to accept dear Miss Woodhouse's most obliging invitation.

As they were turning into the grounds, Mr. Perry passed by on horseback. The gentlemen spoke of his horse.

"By the bye," said Frank Churchill to Mrs. Weston presently, "what became of Mr. Perry's plan of setting up his carriage?"[6]

Mrs. Weston looked surprised, and said, "I did not know that he ever had any such plan."

"Nay, I had it from you. You wrote me word of it three months ago."

"Me! impossible!"

"Indeed you did. I remember it perfectly. You mentioned it as what was certainly to be very soon. Mrs. Perry had told somebody,

4 In book IV of *The Task,* "The Winter Evening," Cowper describes the act of imagining shapes while staring at the domestic fire:

> Me oft has fantasy ludicrous and wild
> Sooth'd with a waking dream of houses, tow'rs,
> Trees, churches, and strange visages express'd
> In the red cinders, while with poring eye
> I gazed, myself creating what I saw.

5 See note 15 to vol. II, chap. 15.

6 Even to be planning to acquire and equip a carriage and carriage-horses is a sign that Mr. Perry is coming up in the world, as one would have required an income of somewhere around £1,000 for it to be a viable proposition.

Pastel portrait of William Cowper (1731–1800) by George Romney, 1792. Cowper was fixed in the public imagination as one of Austen's favorite poets by Henry Austen's "Biographical Notice" in 1818, and by James Edward Austen-Leigh's *Memoir of Jane Austen* in 1871. Although Cowper's form and style may, on the surface, be quite distinct from Austen's, both authors share a talent for sudden, unexpected shifts of scale and focus, and an ability to modulate from seemingly trivial domestic details to much larger moral and spiritual levels of implication.

and was extremely happy about it. It was owing to *her* persuasion, as she thought his being out in bad weather did him a great deal of harm. You must remember it now?"

"Upon my word I never heard of it till this moment."

"Never! really, never!—Bless me! how could it be?—Then I must have dreamt it—but I was completely persuaded—Miss Smith, you walk as if you were tired. You will not be sorry to find yourself at home."

"What is this?—What is this?" cried Mr. Weston, about Perry and a carriage? Is Perry going to set up his carriage, Frank? I am glad he can afford it. You had it from himself, had you?"

7 The turn of the nineteenth century witnessed a great and varied interest in the origin and significance of dreaming. Some writers still held to the strictly materialist interpretations propounded by earlier authors such as Thomas Hobbes in book I, chap. 2, of *Leviathan:*

> The imaginations of them that sleep, are those we call *Dreams.* And these also (as all other Imaginations) have been before, either totally, or by parcells in the Sense. And because in sense, the Brain, and Nerves, which are the necessary Organs of sense, are so benummed in sleep, as not easily to be moved by the action of Externall Objects, there can happen in sleep, no Imagination; and therefore no Dreame, but what proceeds from the agitation of the inward parts of mans body; which inward parts, for the connexion they have with the Brayn, and other Organs, when they be distempered, do keep the same in motion; whereby the Imaginations there formerly made, appeare as if a man were waking; saving that the Organs of Sense being now benummed, so as there is no new object, which can master and obscure them with a more vigorous impression, a Dreame must needs be more cleare, in this silence of sense, than are our waking thoughts. (ed. R. Tuck [Cambridge: Cambridge University Press, 1991], p. 17)

Nevertheless, many early nineteenth-century poets were willing to grant a greater creative license to dreams; famous instances include Coleridge's prefatory note to "Kubla Khan" (first published in 1816): "The author continued for about three hours in a profound sleep, at least of the external senses, during which time he has the most vivid confidence, that he could not have composed less than from two to three hundred lines; if that indeed can be called composition in which all the images rose up before him as things, with a parallel production of the correspondent expressions, without any sensation or consciousness of effort."

Likewise, Keats wrote to Benjamin Bailey on November 22, 1817: "The Imagination may be compared

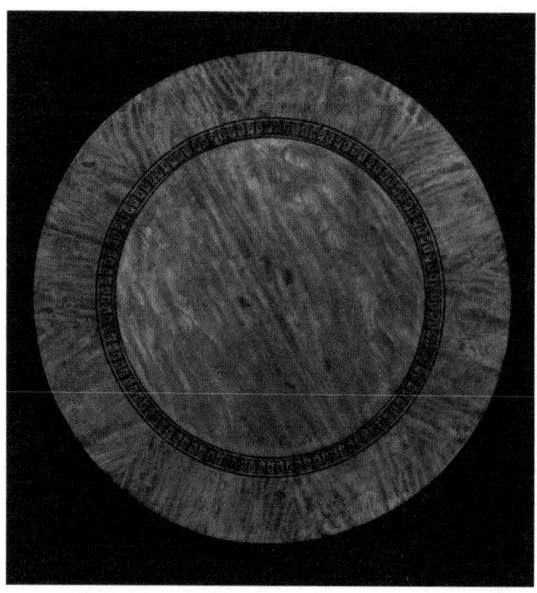

Circular table, c. 1820; courtesy of Mallett Antiques, London.

Pembroke table, satinwood inlaid with ebony, c. 1810. By the time of *Emma,* folding Pembroke tables were not nearly as fashionable as circular ones.

"No, sir," replied his son, laughing, "I seem to have had it from nobody.—Very odd!—I really was persuaded of Mrs. Weston's having mentioned it in one of her letters to Enscombe, many weeks ago, with all these particulars—but as she declares she never heard a syllable of it before, of course it must have been a dream. I am a great dreamer. I dream of every body at Highbury when I am away—and when I have gone through my particular friends, then I begin dreaming of Mr. and Mrs. Perry."

"It is odd though," observed his father, "that you should have had such a regular connected dream about people whom it was not very likely you should be thinking of at Enscombe.[7] Perry's setting up his carriage! and his wife's persuading him to it, out of care for his health—just what will happen, I have no doubt, some time or other; only a little premature. What an air of probability sometimes runs through a dream! And at others, what a heap of absurdities it is! Well, Frank, your dream certainly shows that Highbury is in your thoughts when you are absent. Emma, you are a great dreamer, I think?"

Emma was out of hearing. She had hurried on before her guests to prepare her father for their appearance, and was beyond the reach of Mr. Weston's hint.

"Why, to own the truth," cried Miss Bates, who had been trying in vain to be heard the last two minutes, "if I must speak on this subject, there is no denying that Mr. Frank Churchill might have—I do not mean to say that he did not dream it—I am sure I have sometimes the oddest dreams in the world—but if I am questioned about it, I must acknowledge that there was such an idea last spring; for Mrs. Perry herself mentioned it to my mother, and the Coles knew of it as well as ourselves—but it was quite a secret, known to nobody else, and only thought of about three days. Mrs. Perry was very anxious that he should have a carriage, and came to my mother in great spirits one morning because she thought she had prevailed. Jane, don't you remember grandmamma's telling us of it when we got home?—I forget where we had been walking to—very likely to Randall's; yes, I think it was to Randall's. Mrs. Perry was always particularly fond of my mother—indeed I do not know who is not—and she had mentioned it to her in confidence; she had no objection to her

to Adam's dream—he awoke and found it truth" (*The Letters of John Keats,* ed. M. Buxton Forman [London: Oxford University Press, 1931; 4th ed., 1952] p. 67). Jennifer Ford provides a valuable overview of the range of contemporary views of dreams in *Coleridge on Dreaming: Romanticism, Dreams, and the Medical Imagination* (Cambridge: Cambridge University Press, 1998), pp. 9–32.

telling us, of course, but it was not to go beyond: and, from that day to this, I never mentioned it to a soul that I know of. At the same time, I will not positively answer for my having never dropt a hint, because I know I do sometimes pop out a thing before I am aware. I am a talker, you know; I am rather a talker; and now and then I have let a thing escape me which I should not. I am not like Jane; I wish I were. I will answer for it *she* never betrayed the least thing in the world. Where is she?—Oh! just behind. Perfectly remember Mrs. Perry's coming.—Extraordinary dream indeed!"

They were entering the hall. Mr. Knightley's eyes had preceded Miss Bates's in a glance at Jane. From Frank Churchill's face, where he thought he saw confusion suppressed or laughed away, he had involuntarily turned to her's; but she was indeed behind, and too busy with her shawl. Mr. Weston had walked in. The two other gentlemen waited at the door to let her pass. Mr. Knightley suspected in Frank Churchill the determination of catching her eye—he seemed watching her intently—in vain, however, if it were so—Jane passed between them into the hall, and looked at neither.

There was no time for farther remark or explanation. The dream must be borne with, and Mr. Knightley must take his seat with the rest round the large modern circular table[8] which Emma had introduced at Hartfield, and which none but Emma could have had power to place there and persuade her father to use, instead of the small-sized Pembroke,[9] on which two of his daily meals had, for forty years, been crowded. Tea passed pleasantly, and nobody seemed in a hurry to move.

"Miss Woodhouse," said Frank Churchill, after examining a table behind him, which he could reach as he sat, "have your nephews taken away their alphabets—their box of letters?[10] It used to stand here. Where is it? This is a sort of dull-looking evening, that ought to be treated rather as winter than summer. We had great amusement with those letters one morning. I want to puzzle you again."

Emma was pleased with the thought; and producing the box, the table was quickly scattered over with alphabets, which no one seemed so much disposed to employ as their two selves. They were

8 Frederick S. Robinson suggests that the early nineteenth-century popularity of circular tables can be attributed to the famous designer Thomas Sheraton (1751–1806); see *English Furniture* (London: Methuen and Co., 1905), p. 315.

9 A small, folding-leaf table whose popularity dated from the middle of the eighteenth century. As Austen's reference indicates, a Pembroke would have been too small to use as a proper family dining-table, even for a family as small as the Woodhouses. Austen's own letter to Cassandra of November 8–9, 1800, expresses delight that the family need no longer rely on the Pembroke: "The Tables are come, & give general contentment. I had not expected that they would so perfectly suit the fancy of us all three, or that we should so well agree in the disposition of them; but nothing except their own surface can have been smoother;—The two ends put together form our constant Table for everything, & the centre peice stands exceedingly well under the glass; holds a great deal most commodiously, without looking awkwardly. They are both covered with green baize & send their best Love.—The Pembroke has got its destination by the sideboard, & my mother has great delight in keeping her Money & papers locked up" (*Letters,* p. 55).

10 Handwritten or commercially printed letters of the alphabet were used for anagrammatic games (precursors of Scrabble) to improve children's spelling. David Selwyn offers some cogent observations on this and other games in the "Toys and Games" chapter of *Jane Austen and Leisure* (London: The Hambledon Press, 1999), pp. 261–275.

rapidly forming words for each other, or for any body else who would be puzzled. The quietness of the game made it particularly eligible for Mr. Woodhouse, who had often been distressed by the more animated sort, which Mr. Weston had occasionally introduced, and who now sat happily occupied in lamenting, with tender melancholy, over the departure of the "poor little boys," or in fondly pointing out, as he took up any stray letter near him, how beautifully Emma had written it.

Frank Churchill placed a word before Miss Fairfax. She gave a slight glance round the table, and applied herself to it. Frank was next to Emma, Jane opposite to them—and Mr. Knightley so placed as to see them all; and it was his object to see as much as he could, with as little apparent observation. The word was discovered, and with a faint smile pushed away. If meant to be immediately mixed with the others, and buried from sight, she should have looked on the table instead of looking just across, for it was not mixed; and Harriet, eager after every fresh word, and finding out none, directly took it up, and fell to work. She was sitting by Mr. Knightley, and turned to him for help. The word was *blunder;* and as Harriet exultingly proclaimed it, there was a blush on Jane's cheek which gave it a meaning not otherwise ostensible. Mr. Knightley connected it with the dream; but how it could all be, was beyond his comprehension. How the delicacy, the discretion of his favourite could have been so lain asleep! He feared there must be some decided involvement. Disingenuousness and double-dealing seemed to meet him at every turn. These letters were but the vehicle for gallantry[11] and trick. It was a child's play, chosen to conceal a deeper game on Frank Churchill's part.

With great indignation did he continue to observe him; with great alarm and distrust, to observe also his two blinded companions. He saw a short word prepared for Emma, and given to her with a look sly and demure.[12] He saw that Emma had soon made it out, and found it highly entertaining, though it was something which she judged it proper to appear to censure; for she said, "Nonsense! for shame!" He heard Frank Churchill next say, with a glance towards Jane, "I will

11 In this context, the term carries its negative connotation of illicit intrigue. Compare canto I, stanza 63, of Byron's *Don Juan* (1819): "What men call gallantry, and gods adultery,/Is much more common where the climate's sultry."

12 "Affectedly modest" (Johnson); compare the later nineteenth-century American coinage of the "poker face."

Bone spelling alphabets, 1800–1840. The letters pictured here offer a more professional counterpart to Emma's homemade efforts at Hartfield.

give it to her—shall I?"—and as clearly heard Emma opposing it with eager laughing warmth. "No, no, you must not; you shall not, indeed."

It was done however. This gallant young man, who seemed to love without feeling, and to recommend himself without complaisance, directly handed over the word to Miss Fairfax, and with a particular degree of sedate civility entreated her to study it. Mr. Knightley's excessive curiosity to know what this word might be, made him seize every possible moment for darting his eye towards it, and it was not long before he saw it to be *Dixon.* Jane Fairfax's perception seemed to accompany his; her comprehension was certainly more equal to the covert meaning, the superior intelligence, of those five letters so arranged. She was evidently displeased; looked up, and seeing herself watched, blushed more deeply than he had ever perceived her, and saying only, "I did not know that proper names were allowed," pushed away the letters with even an angry spirit, and looked resolved to be engaged by no other word that could be offered. Her face was averted from those who had made the attack, and turned towards her aunt.

"Ay, very true, my dear," cried the latter, though Jane had not spoken a word—"I was just going to say the same thing. It is time for us to be going indeed. The evening is closing in, and grandmamma will be looking for us. My dear sir, you are too obliging. We really must wish you good night."

Jane's alertness in moving, proved her as ready as her aunt had preconceived. She was immediately up, and wanting to quit the table; but so many were also moving, that she could not get away; and Mr. Knightley thought he saw another collection of letters anxiously pushed towards her, and resolutely swept away by her unexamined. She was afterwards looking for her shawl—Frank Churchill was looking also—it was growing dusk, and the room was in confusion; and how they parted, Mr. Knightley could not tell.

He remained at Hartfield after all the rest, his thoughts full of what he had seen; so full, that when the candles came to assist his observations, he must—yes, he certainly must, as a friend—an anxious friend—give Emma some hint, ask her some question. He could not see her in a situation of such danger, without trying to preserve her. It was his duty.

"Pray, Emma," said he, "may I ask in what lay the great amusement, the poignant sting of the last word given to you and Miss Fairfax? I saw the word, and am curious to know how it could be so very entertaining to the one, and so very distressing to the other."

Emma was extremely confused. She could not endure to give him the true explanation; for though her suspicions were by no means removed, she was really ashamed of having ever imparted them.

"Oh!" she cried in evident embarrassment, "it all meant nothing; a mere joke among ourselves."

"The joke," he replied gravely, "seemed confined to you and Mr. Churchill."

He had hoped she would speak again, but she did not. She would rather busy herself about any thing than speak. He sat a little while in doubt. A variety of evils crossed his mind. Interference—fruitless interference. Emma's confusion, and the acknowledged intimacy, seemed to declare her affection engaged. Yet he would speak. He owed it to her, to risk any thing that might be involved in an unwelcome interference, rather than her welfare; to encounter any thing, rather than the remembrance of neglect in such a cause.

"My dear Emma," said he at last, with earnest kindness, "do you think you perfectly understand the degree of acquaintance between the gentleman and lady we have been speaking of?"

"Between Mr. Frank Churchill and Miss Fairfax! Oh! yes, perfectly.—Why do you make a doubt of it?"

"Have you never at any time had reason to think that he admired her, or that she admired him?"

"Never, never!"—she cried with a most open eagerness—"Never, for the twentieth part of a moment, did such an idea occur to me. And how could it possibly come into your head?"

"I have lately imagined that I saw symptoms of attachment between them—certain expressive looks, which I did not believe meant to be public."

"Oh! you amuse me excessively. I am delighted to find that you can vouchsafe to let your imagination wander—but it will not do—very sorry to check you in your first essay—but indeed it will not do. There is no admiration between them, I do assure you; and the appearances which have caught you, have arisen from some peculiar circumstances—feelings rather of a totally different nature:—it is impossible exactly to explain:—there is a good deal of nonsense in it—but the part which is capable of being communicated, which is sense, is, that they are as far from any attachment or admiration for one another, as any two beings in the world can be. That is, I *presume* it to be so on her side, and I can *answer* for its being so on his. I will answer for the gentleman's indifference."

She spoke with a confidence which staggered, with a satisfaction which silenced, Mr. Knightley. She was in gay spirits, and would have prolonged the conversation, wanting to hear the particulars of his suspicions, every look described, and all the wheres and hows of a circumstance which highly entertained her: but his gaiety did not meet[13] her's. He found he could not be useful, and his feelings were too much irritated for talking. That he might not be irritated into an absolute fever, by the fire which Mr. Woodhouse's tender habits required almost every evening throughout the year, he soon afterwards took a hasty leave, and walked home to the coolness and solitude of Donwell Abbey.

13 Match.

6

After being long fed with hopes of a speedy visit from Mr. and Mrs. Suckling, the Highbury world were obliged to endure the mortification of hearing that they could not possibly come till the autumn. No such importation of novelties could enrich their intellectual stores at present. In the daily interchange of news, they must be again restricted to the other topics with which for a while the Sucklings' coming had been united, such as the last accounts of Mrs. Churchill, whose health seemed every day to supply a different report, and the situation of Mrs. Weston, whose happiness it was to be hoped might eventually be as much increased by the arrival of a child, as that of all her neighbours was by the approach of it.

Mrs. Elton was very much disappointed. It was the delay of a great deal of pleasure and parade. Her introductions and recommendations must all wait, and every projected party be still only talked of. So she thought at first;—but a little consideration convinced her that every thing need not be put off. Why should not they explore to Box Hill[1] though the Sucklings did not come? They could go there again with them in the autumn. It was settled that they should go to Box Hill. That there was to be such a party had been long generally known: it had even given the idea of another. Emma had never been to Box Hill; she wished to see what every body found so well worth seeing, and she and Mr. Weston had agreed to choose some fine morning and drive thither. Two or three more of the chosen only were to be admitted to join them, and it was to be done in a quiet, unpretending, elegant way, infinitely superior to the bustle and prep-

1 A famous hill and scenic spot in the North Downs, near Dorking and Leatherhead in Surrey, rising to some 224 meters (735 feet) at its highest point. It has long been an attraction for visitors, not least because of the extensive views it offers over Dorking, and toward the Sussex Downs. John Keats also wrote some lines of the latter part of *Endymion* on Box Hill on November 22, 1817.

Photograph of Box Hill, near Dorking in Surrey. The hill commands some of the finest prospects in southern England, although at this point, it also forms the backdrop to one of the most miserable scenes in the whole of *Emma*.

aration, the regular eating and drinking, and pic-nic[2] parade of the Eltons and the Sucklings.

This was so very well understood between them, that Emma could not but feel some surprise, and a little displeasure, on hearing from Mr. Weston that he had been proposing to Mrs. Elton, as her brother and sister had failed her, that the two parties should unite, and go together; and that as Mrs. Elton had very readily acceded to it, so it was to be, if she had no objection. Now, as her objection was nothing but her very great dislike of Mrs. Elton, of which Mr. Weston must already be perfectly aware, it was not worth bringing forward again: —it could not be done without a reproof to him, which would be giving pain to his wife; and she found herself therefore obliged to consent to an arrangement which she would have done a great deal to avoid; an arrangement which would probably expose her even to the degradation of being said to be of Mrs. Elton's party! Every feeling was offended; and the forbearance of her outward submission left a heavy arrear due of secret severity in her reflections on the unmanageable good-will of Mr. Weston's temper.

"I am glad you approve of what I have done," said he very comfortably. "But I thought you would. Such schemes as these are nothing without numbers. One cannot have too large a party. A large party secures its own amusement. And she is a good-natured woman after all. One could not leave her out."

Emma denied none of it aloud, and agreed to none of it in private.

It was now the middle of June, and the weather fine; and Mrs. Elton was growing impatient to name the day, and settle with Mr. Weston as to pigeon-pies[3] and cold lamb, when a lame carriage-horse threw every thing into sad uncertainty. It might be weeks, it might be only a few days, before the horse were useable, but no preparations could be ventured on, and it was all melancholy stagnation. Mrs. Elton's resources were inadequate to such an attack.

"Is not this most vexatious, Knightley?"[4] she cried.—"And such weather for exploring!—These delays and disappointments are quite odious. What are we to do?—The year will wear away at this rate, and nothing done. Before this time last year I assure you we had had a delightful exploring party from Maple Grove to Kings Weston."

2 The term had been current since the eighteenth century.

3 Hannah Glasse gives this recipe for pigeon pie: "Make a puff-paste crust, cover your dish, let your pigeons be very nicely picked and cleaned, season them with pepper and salt, and put a good piece of fine fresh butter, with pepper and salt in their bellies; lay them in your pans, the necks, gizzards, livers, pinions, and hearts, lay between, with the yolk of a hard egg and beef-steak in the middle; put as much water as will almost fill the dish, lay on the top-crust and bake it well; this is the best way to make a pigeon-pie; but the French fill the pigeons with a very high force-meat, and lay force-meat balls round the inside, with asparagus-tops, artichoke-bottoms, mushrooms, truffles, and morels, and season high; but that is according to different palates" (*The Art of Cookery Made Plain and Easy* [London: 1748; rev. ed., London: T. Longman, B. Law, et al., 1796], p. 194).

4 Another excessively familiar address.

Portrait of Princess Dorothea von Lieven (1785–1857) by Sir Thomas Lawrence, c. 1812–1820. A German aristocrat and the wife of the Russian ambassador to London, she was also one of the feared and respected "Lady Patronesses" of Almack's.

"You had better explore to Donwell," replied Mr. Knightley. "That may be done without horses. Come, and eat my strawberries. They are ripening fast."

If Mr. Knightley did not begin seriously, he was obliged to proceed so, for his proposal was caught at with delight; and the "Oh! I should like it of all things," was not plainer in words than manner. Donwell was famous for its strawberry-beds, which seemed a plea for the invitation: but no plea was necessary; cabbage-beds[5] would have been enough to tempt the lady, who only wanted to be going somewhere.

5 Cabbages here may be chosen not only for their relative dowdiness but also for their not smelling as sweet as strawberries; compare Mr. Parker's worry about autumnal smells in chap. 4 of *Sanditon:* "we have in fact all the comfort of an excellent Kitchen Garden, without the constant Eyesore of its formalities; or the yearly nuisance of its decaying vegetation.—Who can endure a Cabbage Bed in October?"

Robert and George Cruikshank, "Tom & Jerry 'Sporting a Toe' among the Corinthians at Almacks in the West," 1821. Originally created as an illustration to *Life in London* (1821–1828), a saga of louche metropolitan life by Pierce Egan (1772–1849), the picture captures the claustrophobic glamor of the Almack's circle.

She promised him again and again to come—much oftener than he doubted—and was extremely gratified by such a proof of intimacy, such a distinguishing compliment as she chose to consider it.

"You may depend upon me," said she. "I certainly will come. Name your day, and I will come. You will allow me to bring Jane Fairfax?"

"I cannot name a day," said he, "till I have spoken to some others whom I would wish to meet you."

"Oh! leave all that to me. Only give me a carte-blanche.[6]—I am Lady Patroness,[7] you know. It is my party. I will bring friends with me."

"I hope you will bring Elton," said he:—"but I will not trouble you to give any other invitations."

"Oh! now you are looking very sly. But consider;—you need not be afraid of delegating power to *me.* I am no young lady on her preferment.[8] Married women, you know, may be safely authorized. It is my party. Leave it all to me. I will invite your guests."

"No,"—he calmly replied,—"there is but one married woman in the world whom I can ever allow to invite what guests she pleases to Donwell, and that one is——"

"—Mrs. Weston, I suppose," interrupted Mrs. Elton, rather mortified.

"No—Mrs. Knightley;—and, till she is in being, I will manage such matters myself."

"Ah! you are an odd creature!" she cried, satisfied to have no one preferred to herself.—"You are a humourist,[9] and may say what you like. Quite a humourist. Well, I shall bring Jane with me—Jane and her aunt.—The rest I leave to you. I have no objections at all to meeting the Hartfield family. Don't scruple. I know you are attached to them."

"You certainly will meet them if I can prevail; and I shall call on Miss Bates in my way home."

"That's quite unnecessary; I see Jane every day:—but as you like. It is to be a morning scheme, you know, Knightley; quite a simple thing. I shall wear a large bonnet, and bring one of my little baskets hanging on my arm. Here,—probably this basket with pink ribbon.

6 Free rein; a *carte blanche,* literally, is a blank piece of paper or card on which a person can write his or her own terms and conditions.

7 Mrs. Elton is alluding to Almack's, opened on King Street, St. James's, in 1765 by William Almack, originally Macall (d. 1781), and later the most exclusive and fashionable social club in Regency London. One distinctive feature of Almack's was that matters of membership and admittance were handled and enforced zealously (even ruthlessly) by a committee of "Lady Patronesses": in 1814, these were Lady Castlereagh, Princess Esterhazy, Lady Cowper, Lady Jersey, Mrs. Drummond Burrell, Lady Sefton, and the Princess Lieven. See E. Beresford Chancellor, *Memorials of St James's Street, together with The Annals of Almack's* (London: Grant Richards, 1922).

8 Looking to make an advantageous marriage.

9 "One who conducts himself by his own fancy" (Johnson).

10 The most famous (and probably the most disproportionate) precedent for Mrs. Elton's design was the Hameau de la Reine at Versailles, built for Marie Antoinette between 1783 and 1787, in which the queen and her entourage would play at being rustic shepherdesses and milkmaids.

The Hameau de la Reine, built on the grounds of Versailles for Marie Antoinette (1755–1793). At the Hameau, the queen and her entourage could play at being milkmaids—one precedent for the camp rusticity that Mrs. Elton is affecting.

Nothing can be more simple, you see. And Jane will have such another. There is to be no form or parade—a sort of gipsy party.[10]—We are to walk about your gardens, and gather the strawberries ourselves, and sit under trees;—and whatever else you may like to provide, it is to be all out of doors—a table spread in the shade, you know. Every thing as natural and simple as possible. Is not that your idea?"

"Not quite. My idea of the simple and the natural will be to have the table spread in the dining-room. The nature and the simplicity of gentlemen and ladies, with their servants and furniture, I think is best observed by meals within doors. When you are tired of eating strawberries in the garden, there shall be cold meat in the house."

"Well—as you please; only don't have a great set out. And, by the bye, can I or my housekeeper be of any use to you with our opinion? —Pray be sincere, Knightley. If you wish me to talk to Mrs. Hodges, or to inspect anything——"

"I have not the least wish for it, I thank you."

"Well—but if any difficulties should arise, my housekeeper is extremely clever."

"I will answer for it, that mine thinks herself full as clever, and would spurn anybody's assistance."

"I wish we had a donkey.[11] The thing would be for us all to come on donkies, Jane, Miss Bates, and me—and my caro sposo[12] walking by. I really must talk to him about purchasing a donkey. In a country life I conceive it to be a sort of necessary;[13] for, let a woman have ever so many resources, it is not possible for her to be always shut up at home;—and very long walks, you know——in summer there is dust, and in winter there is dirt."

"You will not find either, between Donwell and Highbury. Donwell-lane is never dusty, and now it is perfectly dry. Come on a donkey, however, if you prefer it. You can borrow Mrs. Cole's. I would wish every thing to be as much to your taste as possible."

"That I am sure you would. Indeed I do you justice, my good friend. Under that peculiar sort of dry, blunt manner, I know you have the warmest heart. As I tell Mr. E., you are a thorough humourist.—Yes, believe me, Knightley, I am fully sensible of your attention to me in the whole of this scheme. You have hit upon the very thing to please me."

Mr. Knightley had another reason for avoiding a table in the shade. He wished to persuade Mr. Woodhouse, as well as Emma, to join the party; and he knew that to have any of them sitting down out of doors to eat would inevitably make him ill. Mr. Woodhouse must not, under the specious pretence of a morning drive, and an hour or two spent at Donwell, be tempted away to his misery.

He was invited on good faith. No lurking horrors were to upbraid him for his easy credulity. He did consent. He had not been at Donwell for two years. "Some very fine morning, he, and Emma, and Harriet, could go very well; and he could sit still with Mrs. Weston, while

11 The Austens' donkey cart is still preserved at Chawton Cottage.

12 Mrs. Elton manages here to get the phrase right for once.

13 Necessity.

Photograph of Valle Crucis Abbey, Llantysilio, Wales. The fish pond that provided food for the monks is clearly visible in the foreground.

the dear girls walked about the gardens. He did not suppose they could be damp now, in the middle of the day. He should like to see the old house again exceedingly, and should be very happy to meet Mr. and Mrs. Elton, and any other of his neighbours.—He could not see any objection at all to his, and Emma's, and Harriet's, going there some very fine morning. He thought it very well done of Mr. Knightley to invite them—very kind and sensible—much cleverer than dining out.—He was not fond of dining out."

Mr. Knightley was fortunate in every body's most ready concurrence. The invitation was every where so well received, that it seemed as if, like Mrs. Elton, they were all taking the scheme as a particular compliment to themselves.—Emma and Harriet professed very high expectations of pleasure from it; and Mr. Weston, unasked, promised to get Frank over to join them, if possible; a proof of approbation and gratitude which could have been dispensed with.—Mr. Knightley was then obliged to say that he should be glad to see him; and Mr. Weston engaged to lose no time in writing, and spare no arguments to induce him to come.

In the meanwhile the lame horse recovered so fast, that the party to Box Hill was again under happy consideration; and at last Donwell was settled for one day, and Box Hill for the next,—the weather appearing exactly right.

Under a bright mid-day sun, at almost Midsummer, Mr. Woodhouse was safely conveyed in his carriage, with one window down,[14] to partake of this al-fresco[15] party; and in one of the most comfortable rooms in the abbey, especially prepared for him by a fire all the morning, he was happily placed, quite at his ease, ready to talk with pleasure of what had been atchieved, and advise every body to come and sit down, and not to heat themselves.—Mrs. Weston, who seemed to have walked there on purpose to be tired, and sit all the time with him, remained, when all the others were invited or persuaded out, his patient listener and sympathizer.

It was so long since Emma had been at the Abbey, that as soon as she was satisfied of her father's comfort, she was glad to leave him, and look around her; eager to refresh and correct her memory

14 An extremely small concession to the midsummer weather, which would make the carriage uncomfortable for anyone other than Mr. Woodhouse.

15 Open-air. This Italian idiom had been fashionable since the middle of the eighteenth century.

16 Compare the way in which Elizabeth Bennet's warming feelings toward Darcy in *Pride and Prejudice* are focused and crystallized by her viewing of the house and grounds of Pemberley, in vol. III, chap. 1:

> They were all of them warm in their admiration; and at that moment she felt, that to be mistress of Pemberley might be something! . . . They followed her into the dining-parlour. It was a large, well-proportioned room, handsomely fitted up. Elizabeth, after slightly surveying it, went to a window to enjoy its prospect. The hill, crowned with wood, from which they had descended, receiving increased abruptness from the distance, was a beautiful object. Every disposition of the ground was good; and she looked on the whole scene, the river, the trees scattered on its banks, and the winding of the valley, as far as she could trace it, with delight. As they passed into other rooms, these objects were taking different positions; but from every window there were beauties to be seen. The rooms were lofty and handsome, and their furniture suitable to the fortune of their proprietor; but Elizabeth saw, with admiration of his taste, that it was neither gaudy nor uselessly fine; with less of splendor, and more real elegance, than the furniture of Rosings.

Photograph of the Austen's donkey cart at Chawton Cottage.

with more particular observation, more exact understanding of a house and grounds which must ever be so interesting to her and all her family.[16]

She felt all the honest pride and complacency[17] which her alliance with the present and future proprietor could fairly warrant, as she viewed the respectable size and style of the building, its suitable, becoming characteristic situation, low and sheltered—its ample gardens stretching down to meadows washed by a stream, of which the Abbey, with all the old neglect of prospect,[18] had scarcely a sight—and its abundance of timber in rows and avenues, which neither fashion nor extravagance had rooted up.[19]—The house was larger than Hartfield, and totally unlike it, covering a good deal of ground, rambling and irregular, with many comfortable and one or two handsome rooms.[20]—It was just what it ought to be, and it looked what it was—and Emma felt an increasing respect for it, as the residence of a family of such true gentility, untainted in blood and understanding.

17 Contentment.

18 This "neglect of prospect" indicates that Knightley has, characteristically, resisted the temptation to have the grounds of Donwell "improved" according to the rules of picturesque landscape gardening, as typified by Lancelot "Capability" Brown (1716–1783) and Humphry Repton (1752–1818). The possibility of Mr. Rushworth's "improving" the landscape of Sotherton becomes a thematic concern in *Mansfield Park* from vol. I, chap. 6, onward, and forms the basis of Alistair M. Duckworth's thought-provoking study *The Improvement of the Estate: A Study of Jane Austen's Novels* (Baltimore: Johns Hopkins University Press, 1971).

19 Rows are single lines of trees, avenues double lines forming natural walkways. In *Mansfield Park,* it is the threat to the avenue at Sotherton that most troubles Fanny Price as she addresses Edmund Bertram in vol. I, chap. 6:

> "Cut down an avenue! What a pity! Does not it make you think of Cowper? 'Ye fallen avenues, once more I mourn your fate unmerited.'"
>
> He smiled as he answered, "I am afraid the avenue stands a bad chance, Fanny."

20 As was the case with so many "Abbey" houses, Donwell presumably passed into private ownership following Henry VIII's dissolution of the monasteries in England, Wales, and Ireland, which took place from 1536 to 1541. Austen's description of the irregularity of the house's rooms suggests that the present Donwell has grown piecemeal over two and a half centuries; such houses sometimes incorporated parts of the old religious buildings as well, and it is notable that the Knightleys have retained the old abbey's fishponds.

—Some faults of temper John Knightley had; but Isabella had connected herself unexceptionably. She had given them neither men, nor names, nor places, that could raise a blush. These were pleasant feelings, and she walked about and indulged them till it was necessary to do as the others did, and collect round the strawberry beds.—The whole party were assembled, excepting Frank Churchill, who was expected every moment from Richmond; and Mrs. Elton, in all her apparatus of happiness,[21] her large bonnet and her basket, was very ready to lead the way in gathering, accepting, or talking—strawberries, and only strawberries, could now be thought or spoken of.—"The best fruit in England—every body's favourite—always wholesome.—These the finest beds and finest sorts.—Delightful to gather for one's self—the only way of really enjoying them.—Morning decidedly the best time—never tired—every sort good—hautboy infinitely superior—no comparison—the others hardly eatable—hautboys very scarce—Chili preferred—white wood finest flavour of all[22]—price of strawberries in London—abundance about Bristol—Maple Grove—cultivation—beds when to be renewed—gardeners thinking exactly different—no general rule—gardeners never to be put out of their way—delicious fruit—only too rich to be eaten much of—inferior to cherries—currants more refreshing—only objection to gathering strawberries the stooping—glaring sun—tired to death—could bear it no longer—must go and sit in the shade."

Such, for half an hour, was the conversation—interrupted only once by Mrs. Weston, who came out, in her solicitude after her son-in-law, to inquire if he were come—and she was a little uneasy.—She had some fears of his horse.

Seats tolerably in the shade were found; and now Emma was obliged to overhear what Mrs. Elton and Jane Fairfax were talking of.—A situation, a most desirable situation, was in question. Mrs. Elton had received notice of it that morning, and was in raptures. It was not with Mrs. Suckling, it was not with Mrs. Bragge, but in felicity and splendour it fell short only of them: it was with a cousin of Mrs. Bragge, an acquaintance of Mrs. Suckling, a lady known at Maple Grove. Delightful, charming, superior, first circles, spheres, lines, ranks, every thing—and Mrs. Elton was wild to have the offer closed

21 The forced nature of Mrs. Elton's festivity is suggested by the overly technical connotations of "apparatus," as caught in the *OED*'s definition ("equipments, material, mechanism, machinery; material appendages or arrangements").

22 In *The Strawberry; Its Culture, Uses, and History* (London: R. Baldwin, 1847), George W. Johnson and Robert Reid record the following histories for the "Hautbois" and "Chili" strains of strawberry:

> The *Hautbois* is said by Miller to have been brought hither from America; but in this, we think, he was mistaken. It is not found native on that side of the Atlantic, but it is found wild in Germany; and Parkinson . . . calls it the Polonian or Bohemian, and says it was but lately introduced. Its very name seems to be a corruption of its German designation, *Haarbeer* . . . The *Chili Strawberry.*—The Spaniards conveyed the strawberry with them to South America, and at the foot of the Cordillera mountains, near Quito, our present Chili variety was raised. It was seen there by M. Frezier during his "Voyage in the South Sea," and brought to France by him on his return to Marseilles in 1716. It was called by the South American Spaniards *Frutilla,* or Little Fruit, a singularly inappropriate name if the comparison was with other strawberries, for it was then the largest of the known varieties. (pp. 6–7)

The "white wood" is, its name suggests, a common white form of the wood strawberry, one of the oldest native British strawberries; Johnson and Reid note: "The *Wood Strawberry* . . . was known to the Romans, and being a native of our own woods, it is the earliest, also, that is mentioned by authors as an inhabitant of our gardens." They list ten varieties of Hautbois, eight varieties of Chili, and ten varieties of wood strawberries.

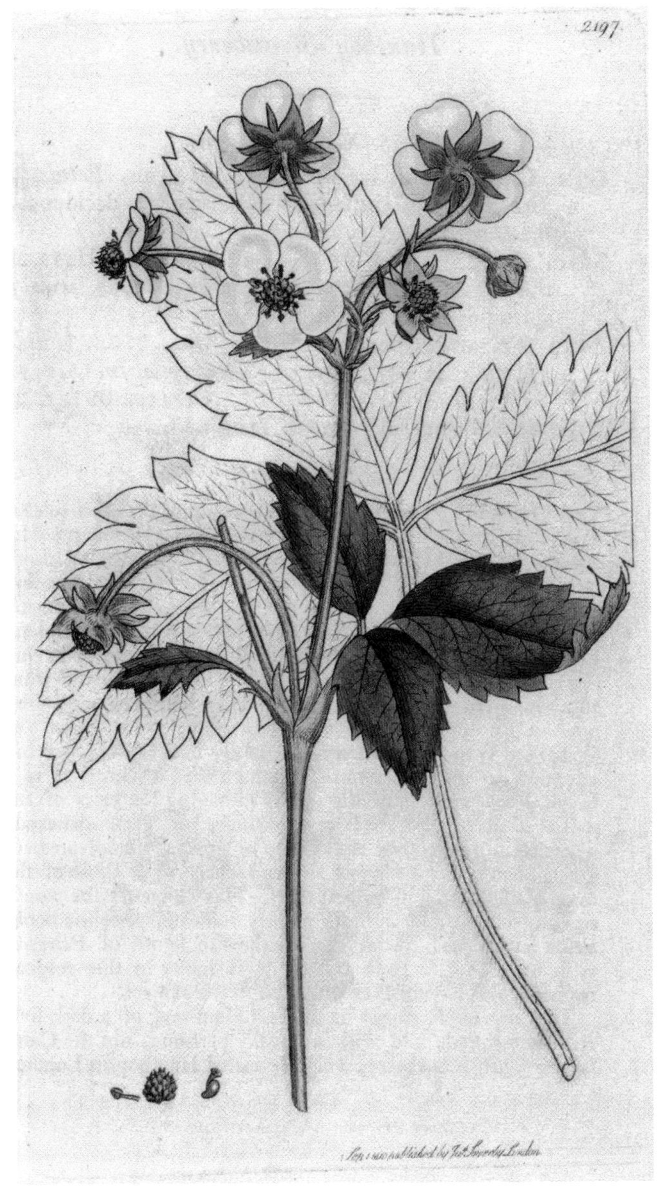

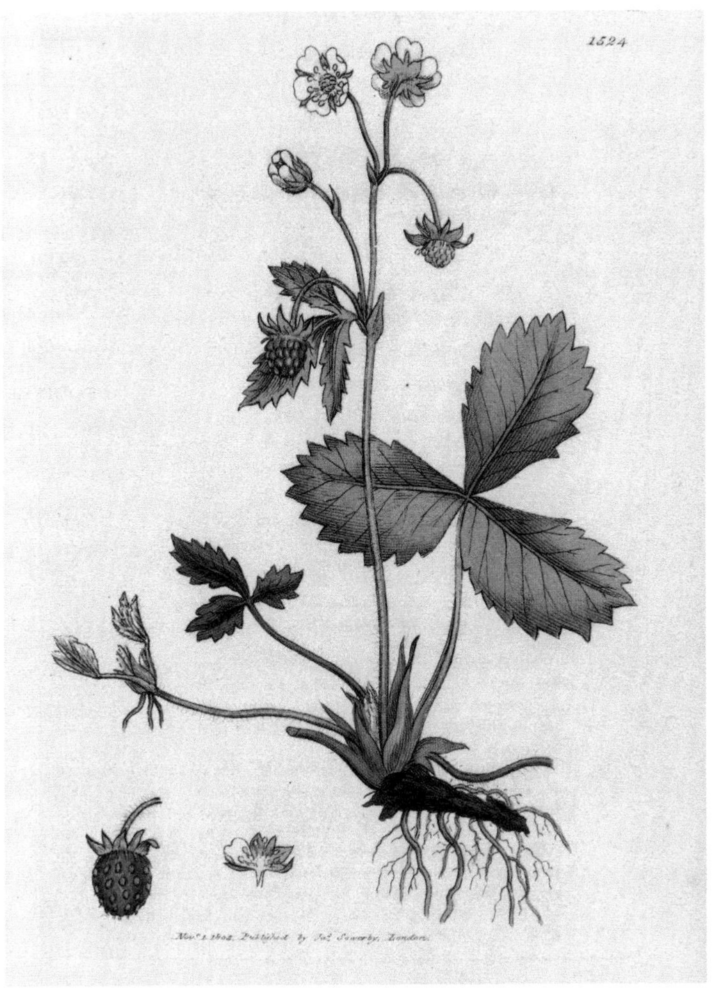

(left) James Sowerby, "*Fragaria elatior:* hautboy strawberry," from *English Botany,* 40 vols. (London: R. Taylor & Co., 1790–1814), vol. 31.

(right) James Sowerby, "*Fragaria vesca:* wood strawberry," from *English Botany,* vol. 22.

with immediately.—On her side, all was warmth, energy, and triumph—and she positively refused to take her friend's negative, though Miss Fairfax continued to assure her that she would not at present engage in any thing, repeating the same motives which she had been heard to urge before.—Still Mrs. Elton insisted on being authorized to write an acquiescence by the morrow's post.—How Jane could bear it at all, was astonishing to Emma.—She did look vexed, she did speak pointedly—and at last, with a decision of action unusual to her, proposed a removal.—"Should not they walk?—Would not Mr. Knightley show them the gardens—all the gardens?—She wished to see the whole extent."—The pertinacity of her friend seemed more than she could bear.

It was hot; and after walking some time over the gardens in a scattered, dispersed way, scarcely any three together, they insensibly followed one another to the delicious shade of a broad short avenue of limes,[23] which stretching beyond the garden at an equal distance from the river, seemed the finish of the pleasure grounds.—It led to nothing; nothing but a view at the end over a low stone wall with high pillars, which seemed intended, in their erection, to give the appearance of an approach to the house, which never had been there. Disputable, however, as might be the taste of such a termination, it was in itself a charming walk, and the view which closed it extremely pretty.—The considerable slope, at nearly the foot of which the Abbey stood, gradually acquired a steeper form beyond its grounds; and at half a mile distant was a bank of considerable abruptness and grandeur, well clothed with wood;—and at the bottom of this bank, favourably placed and sheltered, rose the Abbey-Mill Farm, with meadows in front, and the river making a close and handsome curve around it.

It was a sweet view—sweet to the eye and the mind. English verdure, English culture, English comfort, seen under a sun bright, without being oppressive.

In this walk Emma and Mr. Weston found all the others assembled; and towards this view she immediately perceived Mr. Knightley and Harriet distinct from the rest, quietly leading the way. Mr.

23 Trees of the genus *Tilia,* known as limes in Britain, and as lindens in America. Given that limes are very long-lived trees, they may also present a subliminal testimony to the longevity of the Knightleys' estate.

George Brookshaw, *Pomona Britannica, or, A Collection of the Most Esteemed Fruits at Present Cultivated in Great Britain,* 2 vols. (London: Bensley and Son, 1817), vol. 1, plate 1. The Chili strawberry is depicted in the middle of the arrangement.

Humphry Repton, "unimproved" image of West Wycombe, Buckinghamshire, with "improved" view concealed underneath, from *Observations on the Theory and Practice of Landscape Gardening* (London: J. Taylor, 1803). Repton's famous "Red Books" allowed potential clients to lift a flap and flip between what their properties currently looked like and what Repton's landscaping would make of them. This is exactly the kind of "improvement" that the Knightley family has resisted at Donwell Abbey.

Knightley and Harriet!—It was an odd tête-à-tête; but she was glad to see it.—There had been a time when he would have scorned her as a companion, and turned from her with little ceremony. Now they seemed in pleasant conversation. There had been a time also when Emma would have been sorry to see Harriet in a spot so favourable for the Abbey-Mill Farm; but now she feared it not. It might be safely viewed with all its appendages of prosperity and beauty, its rich pastures, spreading flocks, orchard in blossom,[24] and light column of smoke ascending.[25]—She joined them at the wall, and found them more engaged in talking than in looking around. He was giving Harriet information as to modes of agriculture, &c. and Emma received a smile which seemed to say, "These are my own concerns. I have a right to talk on such subjects, without being suspected of introducing Robert Martin."—She did not suspect him. It was too old a story.

24 One of the most famous apparent "continuity errors" in Austen's fiction. Apple trees are normally in blossom in the month of May, and their late appearance in *Emma* did not pass unnoticed by, among others, Austen's brother Edward Knight, who remarked: "Jane, I wish you could tell me where you get those apple-trees of yours that come into bloom in July" (quoted in *Jane Austen: A Family Record* [1913], revised and enlarged by Deirdre Le Faye [London, The British Library, 1989], p. 207). More recently, however, John Sutherland has argued that the description, if read closely, may not even be an error at all:

> In order to make this second case, one should note that there is not one "error" in the description (blossom in June), but two, and possibly three. Surely, on a sweltering afternoon in June, there would not be smoke rising from the chimney of Abbey-Mill Farm? Why have a fire? And if one were needed for the baking of bread, or the heating of water in a copper for the weekly wash, the boiler would surely be lit before dawn, and extinguished by mid-morning, so as not to make the kitchen (which would also be the family's dining-room) unbearably hot. The reference to the ascending smoke would seem to be more appropriate to late autumn. And the reference to "spreading flocks" would more plausibly refer to the lambing season, in early spring, when flocks enlarge dramatically . . . What this would seem to mean is that now Harriet is so effectively separated from Mr Robert Martin, the occupant of Abbey-Mill Farm, she is immune to its varying attractions over the course of the year—whether in spring, early summer, midsummer, or autumn. What Austen offers us in this sentence is not Radcliffian haze, but a precise depiction in the form of a miniature montage, of the turning seasons. (*Is Heathcliff a Murderer?: Puzzles in Nineteenth-Century Fiction* [Oxford: Oxford University Press, 1996], pp. 18–19)

Sutherland also addresses criticisms of his interpretation in *Who Betrays Elizabeth Bennet? Further Puzzles in Classic Fiction* (Oxford: Oxford University Press, 1999), pp. 28–33.

25 Austen's narrative here stages the movement of the eye through the plane of the landscape, in a manner reminiscent of eighteenth- and early nineteenth-century landscape painting. Compare the description of the River Ouse in book I of Cowper, *The Task:*

> How oft upon yon eminence, our pace
> Has slacken'd to a pause, and we have borne
> The ruffling wind scarce conscious that it blew,
> While admiration feeding at the eye,
> And still unsated, dwelt upon the scene.
> Thence with what pleasure have we just discern'd
> The distant plough slow-moving, and beside
> His lab'ring team that swerv'd not from the track,
> The sturdy swain diminish'd to a boy!
> Here Ouse, slow winding through a level plain
> Of spacious meads with cattle sprinkled o'er,
> Conducts the eye along his sinuous course
> Delighted. There, fast rooted in his bank
> Stand, never overlook'd, our fav'rite elms
> That screen the herdsman's solitary hut;
> While far beyond and overthwart the stream
> That as with molten glass inlays the vale,
> The sloping land recedes into the clouds;
> Displaying on its varied side, the grace
> Of hedge-row beauties numberless, square tow'r,
> Tall spire, from which the sound of chearful bells
> Just undulates upon the list'ning ear;
> Groves, heaths, and smoking villages remote.
> Scenes must be beautiful which daily view'd
> Please daily, and whose novelty survives
> Long knowledge and the scrutiny of years.

This mode of landscape depiction became an object of some critical scrutiny in the late twentieth century. In his pioneering study *The Dark Side of the Landscape: The Rural Poor in English Painting, 1730–1840* (Cambridge: Cambridge University Press, 1980), John Barrell draws attention to the selective vision that allowed such pictures to cohere:

> For the most part the art of rural life offers us the image of a stable, unified, almost egalitarian society; so that my concern . . . is to suggest that it is possible to look beneath the surface of the painting, and to discover there evidence of the very conflict it seems to deny. The painting, then, offers us a mythical unity and—in its increasing concern to present an apparently more and more actualised image of rural life—attempts to pass itself off as an image of the actual unity of an English countryside innocent of division. But by examining the process by which that illusion is achieved—by studying the imagery of the paintings, the constraints upon it, and upon its organisation in the picture-space—we may come to see that unity as artifice, as something made out of the actuality of division. (p. 5)

This line of inquiry has been extended more explicitly into the sphere of literary representation by many critics, notably Marjorie Levinson in *Wordsworth's Great Period Poems: Four Essays* (Cambridge: Cambridge University Press, 1986); commenting on Wordsworth's "Lines Written a Few Miles above Tintern Abbey, on Revisiting the Banks of the Wye During a Tour, July 13, 1798," she remarks: "The success or failure of the visionary poem turns on its ability to hide its omission of the historical. It must present culture as Nature and Nature as a landscape framed but not altered. And of course, the framing itself must figure as an innocent, inert procedure. Consider in this light the narrator's randomly descriptive musings—sylvan historiography, as it were, that tells no story but that of its own unfolding. The definition of objects and of a representational style must proceed continuously and impersonally so as to remain imperceptible. In this way, the figure appears to exclude nothing of the real. By these remarks, we might guess that the near seamlessness of 'Tintern Abbey' is proportional to the number and strength of the spirits it must suppress" (p. 39). For an alternative perspective, see Thomas McFarland's detailed response to Levinson in *William Wordsworth: Intensity and Achievement* (Oxford: Clarendon Press, 1992), pp. 1–33.

—Robert Martin had probably ceased to think of Harriet.—They took a few turns together along the walk.—The shade was most refreshing, and Emma found it the pleasantest part of the day.

The next remove was to the house; they must all go in and eat;—and they were all seated and busy, and still Frank Churchill did not come. Mrs. Weston looked, and looked in vain. His father would not own himself uneasy, and laughed at her fears; but she could not be cured of wishing that he would part with his black mare. He had expressed himself as to coming, with more than common certainty. "His aunt was so much better, that he had not a doubt of getting over to them."—Mrs. Churchill's state, however, as many were ready to remind her, was liable to such sudden variation as might disappoint her nephew in the most reasonable dependence—and Mrs. Weston was at last persuaded to believe, or to say, that it must be by some attack of Mrs. Churchill that he was prevented coming.—Emma looked at Harriet while the point was under consideration; she behaved very well, and betrayed no emotion.

The cold repast was over, and the party were to go out once more to see what had not yet been seen, the old Abbey fish-ponds;[26] perhaps get as far as the clover,[27] which was to be begun cutting on the morrow, or, at any rate, have the pleasure of being hot, and growing cool again.—Mr. Woodhouse, who had already taken his little round in the highest part of the gardens, where no damps from the river were imagined even by him, stirred no more; and his daughter resolved to remain with him, that Mrs. Weston might be persuaded away by her husband to the exercise and variety which her spirits seemed to need.

Mr. Knightley had done all in his power for Mr. Woodhouse's entertainment. Books of engravings, drawers of medals,[28] cameos,[29] corals, shells, and every other family collection within his cabinets, had been prepared for his old friend, to while away the morning; and the kindness had perfectly answered. Mr. Woodhouse had been exceedingly well amused. Mrs. Weston had been showing them all to him, and now he would show them all to Emma;—fortunate in having no other resemblance to a child, than in a total want of taste for what he saw, for he was slow, constant, and methodical.—Before this

26 Monasteries played a role in the history of freshwater fish cultivation, as the Rule of St. Benedict proscribed the flesh of four-footed animals, except for the very weak and sick. Species of fish included pike, bream, roach, perch, eels, and, from the sixteenth century onward, carp. However, modern historians have cast doubt on the centrality of monastic fishponds to the medieval economy. C. K. Currie notes: "fishponds played an important role in the monastic economy. This is demonstrated by the desire of lay benefactors to ensure that newly founded houses should have access to ponds. At the same time the large numbers of fishponds available in lay hands shows that the introduction of such features into this country had not been accomplished solely under monastic initiative. The evidence shows that it was royal and aristocratic directions that caused the majority of early fishponds to be built in England" ("The Role of Fishponds in the Monastic Economy," in Roberta Gilchrist and Harold Mytum, eds., *The Archaeology of Rural Monasteries* [Oxford: BAR British Series, 203, 1989], p. 159). See also C. J. Bond, "Monastic Fisheries," in Michael Aston, ed., *Medieval Fish, Fisheries and Fishponds in England,* part 1 (Oxford: BAR British Series, 182: 1, 1988), pp. 69–112.

27 An element of crop rotation; see note 8 to vol. I, chap. 12.

28 In this context, decorative coins rather than military decorations.

29 Small precious or semi-precious stones, carved with designs in relief. By Austen's time, however, cameos were also often commercially manufactured out of paste.

second looking over was begun, however, Emma walked into the hall for the sake of a few moments' free observation of the entrance and ground-plot[30] of the house—and was hardly there, when Jane Fairfax appeared, coming quickly in from the garden, and with a look of escape.—Little expecting to meet Miss Woodhouse so soon, there was a start at first; but Miss Woodhouse was the very person she was in quest of.

"Will you be so kind," said she, "when I am missed, as to say that I am gone home?—I am going this moment.—My aunt is not aware how late it is, nor how long we have been absent—but I am sure we shall be wanted, and I am determined to go directly.—I have said

30 Enclosed garden; the term could also denote the plan view of a property.

John Constable, *Dedham Vale* (1802). In the description of Donwell Abbey and its surroundings, Austen invites a reader's imagined eye to move toward the "vanishing point" in much the same manner as this kind of landscape does.

nothing about it to any body. It would only be giving trouble and distress. Some are gone to the ponds, and some to the lime walk. Till they all come in I shall not be missed; and when they do, will you have the goodness to say that I am gone?"

"Certainly, if you wish it;—but you are not going to walk to Highbury alone?"

"Yes—what should hurt me?—I walk fast. I shall be at home in twenty minutes."

"But it is too far, indeed it is, to be walking quite alone. Let my father's servant go with you.—Let me order the carriage. It can be round in five minutes."

"Thank you, thank you—but on no account.—I would rather walk.—And for *me* to be afraid of walking alone!—I, who may so soon have to guard others!"

She spoke with great agitation; and Emma very feelingly replied, "That can be no reason for your being exposed to danger now. I must order the carriage. The heat even would be danger.—You are fatigued already."

"I am"—she answered—"I am fatigued; but it is not the sort of fatigue—quick walking will refresh me.—Miss Woodhouse, we all know at times what it is to be wearied in spirits. Mine, I confess, are exhausted. The greatest kindness you can show me, will be to let me have my own way, and only say that I am gone when it is necessary."

Emma had not another word to oppose. She saw it all; and entering into her feelings, promoted her quitting the house immediately, and watched her safely off with the zeal of a friend. Her parting look was grateful—and her parting words, "Oh! Miss Woodhouse, the comfort of being sometimes alone!"—seemed to burst from an overcharged heart, and to describe somewhat of the continual endurance to be practised by her, even towards some of those who loved her best.

"Such a home, indeed! such an aunt!" said Emma, as she turned back into the hall again. "I do pity you. And the more sensibility you betray of their just horrors, the more I shall like you."

Jane had not been gone a quarter of an hour, and they had only accomplished some views of St. Mark's Place, Venice, when Frank

Portrait of Lord Byron (1788–1824) by Richard Westall, 1813.

Double-faced cameo pendant of King George III and Queen Charlotte, from the second half of the eighteenth century; obverse side, showing King George III.

Churchill entered the room. Emma had not been thinking of him, she had forgotten to think of him—but she was very glad to see him. Mrs. Weston would be at ease. The black mare was blameless; *they* were right who had named Mrs. Churchill as the cause. He had been detained by a temporary increase of illness in her; a nervous seizure, which had lasted some hours—and he had quite given up every thought of coming, till very late;—and had he known how hot a ride he should have, and how late, with all his hurry, he must be, he believed he should not have come at all. The heat was excessive; he had never suffered any thing like it—almost wished he had staid at home—nothing killed him like heat—he could bear any degree of cold, &c. but heat was intolerable—and he sat down, at the greatest possible distance from the slight remains of Mr. Woodhouse's fire, looking very deplorable.

"You will soon be cooler, if you sit still," said Emma.

"As soon as I am cooler I shall go back again. I could very ill be spared—but such a point had been made of my coming! You will all be going soon I suppose; the whole party breaking up. I met *one* as I came—Madness in such weather!—absolute madness!"

Emma listened, and looked, and soon perceived that Frank Churchill's state might be best defined by the expressive phrase of being out of humour. Some people were always cross when they were hot. Such might be his constitution; and as she knew that eating and drinking were often the cure of such incidental complaints, she recommended his taking some refreshment; he would find abundance of every thing in the dining-room—and she humanely pointed out the door.

"No—he should not eat. He was not hungry; it would only make him hotter." In two minutes, however, he relented in his own favour; and muttering something about spruce beer, walked off. Emma returned all her attention to her father, saying in secret—

"I am glad I have done being in love with him. I should not like a man who is so soon discomposed by a hot morning. Harriet's sweet easy temper will not mind it."

He was gone long enough to have had a very comfortable meal, and came back all the better—grown quite cool—and, with good manners, like himself—able to draw a chair close to them, take an interest in their employment; and regret, in a reasonable way, that he should be so late. He was not in his best spirits, but seemed trying to improve them; and, at last, made himself talk nonsense very agreeably. They were looking over views in Swisserland.[31]

"As soon as my aunt gets well, I shall go abroad," said he. "I shall never be easy till I have seen some of these places. You will have my sketches, some time or other, to look at—or my tour to read—or my poem. I shall do something to expose myself."

"That may be—but not by sketches in Swisserland. You will never go to Swisserland. Your uncle and aunt will never allow you to leave England."

"They may be induced to go too. A warm climate may be prescribed for her. I have more than half an expectation of our all going abroad. I assure you I have. I feel a strong persuasion, this morning, that I shall soon be abroad. I ought to travel. I am tired of doing nothing. I want a change. I am serious, Miss Woodhouse, whatever your penetrating eyes may fancy—I am sick of England[32]—and would leave it to-morrow, if I could."

"You are sick of prosperity and indulgences. Cannot you invent a few hardships for yourself, and be contented to stay?"

"*I* sick of prosperity and indulgence!—You are quite mistaken. I do not look upon myself as either prosperous or indulged. I am thwarted in every thing material.[33] I do not consider myself at all a fortunate person."

"You are not quite so miserable, though, as when you first came. Go and eat and drink a little more, and you will do very well. Another slice of cold meat, another draught of Madeira[34] and water, will make you nearly on a par with the rest of us."

"No—I shall not stir. I shall sit by you. You are my best cure."

"We are going to Box Hill to-morrow;—you will join us. It is not Swisserland, but it will be something for a young man so much in want of a change. You will stay, and go with us?"

"No, certainly not; I shall go home in the cool of the evening."

"But you may come again in the cool of to-morrow morning."

"No—It will not be worth while. If I come, I shall be cross."

31 A variant spelling for "Switzerland," also used, for example, by Maria Edgeworth in *Patronage.*

32 As witnessed by the reference to his putative "poem," Frank Churchill is affecting a fashionably "Byronic" discontent with his native land, which was popularized with the publication in 1812 of the first two cantos of *Childe Harold's Pilgrimage.* In stanza VI of canto I, for instance, Byron strikes an influential note:

> And now Childe Harold was sore sick at heart,
> And from his fellow bacchanals would flee;
> 'Tis said, at times the sullen tear would start,
> But Pride congeal'd the drop within his ee:
> Apart he stalk'd in joyless reverie,
> And from his native land resolv'd to go,
> And visit scorching climes beyond the sea;
> With pleasure drugg'd, he almost long'd for woe,
> And e'en for change of scene would seek the shades below.

See also Samuel C. Chew, *Byron in England: His Fame and After-Fame* (London: John Murray, 1924); Peter Larsen Thorslev, *The Byronic Hero: Types and Prototypes* (Minneapolis: University of Minnesota Press, 1962); and Tom Mole, *Byron's Romantic Celebrity: Industrial Culture and the Hermeneutic of Intimacy* (Basingstoke: Palgrave Macmillan, 2007).

33 Most important to me.

34 A fortified wine (usually sweet), made in the Portuguese Madeira archipelago. It became massively popular in the eighteenth century, owing to Madeira's position on the trade routes, and the fact that the means of production meant that the wine did not oxidize like other varieties. The presence of Madeira may also be another, almost subliminal glance at an economy built on the spoils of slavery.

"Then pray stay at Richmond."

"But if I do, I shall be crosser still. I can never bear to think of you all there without me."

"These are difficulties which you must settle for yourself. Choose your own degree of crossness. I shall press you no more."

The rest of the party were now returning, and all were soon collected. With some there was great joy at the sight of Frank Churchill; others took it very composedly; but there was a very general distress and disturbance on Miss Fairfax's disappearance being explained. That it was time for every body to go, concluded the subject; and with a short final arrangement for the next day's scheme, they parted. Frank Churchill's little inclination to exclude himself increased so much, that his last words to Emma were,

"Well;—if *you* wish me to stay, and join the party, I will."

She smiled her acceptance; and nothing less than a summons from Richmond was to take him back before the following evening.

J. M. W. Turner, *Childe Harold's Pilgrimage: Italy,* exhibited 1832. Frank Churchill's weariness with England and longing for Europe chime with the fashionable sentiment fired by the publication of the first two cantos of Byron's poem *Childe Harold's Pilgrimage* in 1812.

7

They had a very fine day for Box Hill; and all the other outward circumstances of arrangement, accommodation, and punctuality, were in favour of a pleasant party. Mr. Weston directed the whole, officiating safely between Hartfield and the vicarage, and every body was in good time. Emma and Harriet went together; Miss Bates and her niece, with the Eltons; the gentlemen on horseback. Mrs. Weston remained with Mr. Woodhouse. Nothing was wanting but to be happy when they got there. Seven miles[1] were travelled in expectation of enjoyment, and every body had a burst of admiration on first arriving; but in the general amount[2] of the day there was deficiency. There was a languor, a want of spirits, a want of union,[3] which could not be got over. They separated too much into parties. The Eltons walked together; Mr. Knightley took charge of Miss Bates and Jane; and Emma and Harriet belonged to Frank Churchill. And Mr. Weston tried, in vain, to make them harmonize better. It seemed at first an accidental division, but it never materially varied. Mr. and Mrs. Elton, indeed, showed no unwillingness to mix, and be as agreeable as they could: but during the two whole hours that were spent on the hill, there seemed a principle of separation, between the other parties, too strong for any fine prospects, or any cold collation,[4] or any cheerful Mr. Weston, to remove.

At first it was downright dulness to Emma. She had never seen Frank Churchill so silent and stupid.[5] He said nothing worth hearing—looked without seeing—admired without intelligence—listened without knowing what she said. While he was so dull, it was no

1 The final element in the impossible triangulation of Highbury.

2 Overall reckoning.

3 Togetherness.

4 Repast.

5 Dumbfounded.

wonder that Harriet should be dull likewise, and they were both insufferable.

When they all sat down it was better; to her taste a great deal better, for Frank Churchill grew talkative and gay, making her his first object. Every distinguishing attention that could be paid, was paid to her. To amuse her, and be agreeable in her eyes, seemed all that he cared for—and Emma, glad to be enlivened, not sorry to be flattered, was gay and easy too, and gave him all the friendly encouragement, the admission to be gallant,[6] which she had ever given in the first and most animating period of their acquaintance; but which now, in her own estimation, meant nothing, though in the judgment of most people looking on it must have had such an appearance as no English word but flirtation could very well describe. "Mr. Frank Churchill and Miss Woodhouse flirted together excessively." They were laying themselves open to that very phrase—and to having it sent off in a letter to Maple Grove by one lady, to Ireland by another. Not that Emma was gay and thoughtless from any real felicity; it was rather because she felt less happy than she had expected. She laughed because she was disappointed; and though she liked him for his attentions, and thought them all, whether in friendship, admiration, or playfulness, extremely judicious, they were not winning back her heart. She still intended him for her friend.

"How much I am obliged to you," said he, "for telling me to come to day!—If it had not been for you, I should certainly have lost all the happiness of this party. I had quite determined to go away again."

"Yes, you were very cross; and I do not know what about, except that you were too late for the best strawberries. I was a kinder friend than you deserved. But you were humble. You begged hard to be commanded to come."

"Don't say I was cross. I was fatigued. The heat overcame me."

"It is hotter to-day."

"Not to my feelings. I am perfectly comfortable to-day."

"You are comfortable because you are under command."

"Your command?—Yes."

"Perhaps I intended you to say so, but I meant self-command. You had, somehow or other, broken bounds yesterday, and run away from

6 To pay her romantic attentions.

7 Mickleham lies to the northwest of Box Hill, Dorking to the southwest.

8 Dumbstruck, torpid.

9 Grew indignant.

your own management; but to-day you are got back again—and as I cannot be always with you, it is best to believe your temper under your own command rather than mine."

"It comes to the same thing. I can have no self-command without a motive. You order me, whether you speak or not. And you can be always with me. You are always with me."

"Dating from three o'clock yesterday. My perpetual influence could not begin earlier, or you would not have been so much out of humour before."

"Three o'clock yesterday! That is your date. I thought I had seen you first in February."

"Your gallantry is really unanswerable. But (lowering her voice)—nobody speaks except ourselves, and it is rather too much to be talking nonsense for the entertainment of seven silent people."

"I say nothing of which I am ashamed," replied he, with lively impudence. "I saw you first in February. Let every body on the Hill hear me if they can. Let my accents swell to Mickleham on one side, and Dorking on the other.[7] I saw you first in February." And then whispering—"Our companions are excessively stupid.[8] What shall we do to rouse them? Any nonsense will serve. They *shall* talk. Ladies and gentlemen, I am ordered by Miss Woodhouse (who, wherever she is, presides,) to say, that she desires to know what you are all thinking of."

Some laughed, and answered good-humouredly. Miss Bates said a great deal; Mrs. Elton swelled[9] at the idea of Miss Woodhouse's presiding; Mr. Knightley's answer was the most distinct.

"Is Miss Woodhouse sure that she would like to hear what we are all thinking of?"

"Oh! no, no"—cried Emma, laughing as carelessly as she could—"Upon no account in the world. It is the very last thing I would stand the brunt of just now. Let me hear any thing rather than what you are all thinking of. I will not say quite all. There are one or two, perhaps, (glancing at Mr. Weston and Harriet,) whose thoughts I might not be afraid of knowing."

"It is a sort of thing," cried Mrs. Elton emphatically, "which *I* should not have thought myself privileged to inquire into. Though, perhaps, as the *Chaperon*[10] of the party—*I* never was in any circle—exploring parties—young ladies—married women—"

Her mutterings were chiefly to her husband; and he murmured, in reply,

"Very true, my love, very true. Exactly so, indeed—quite unheard of—but some ladies say any thing. Better pass it off as a joke. Every body knows what is due to *you*."

"It will not do," whispered Frank to Emma, "they are most of them affronted. I will attack them with more address.[11] Ladies and gentlemen—I am ordered by Miss Woodhouse to say, that she waves[12] her right of knowing exactly what you may all be thinking of, and only requires something very entertaining from each of you, in a general way. Here are seven of you, besides myself, (who, she is pleased to say, am very entertaining already,) and she only demands from each of you either one thing very clever, be it prose or verse, original or repeated—or two things moderately clever—or three things very dull indeed, and she engages to laugh heartily at them all."

"Oh! very well," exclaimed Miss Bates, "then I need not be uneasy. 'Three things very dull indeed.' That will just do for me, you know. I shall be sure to say three dull things as soon as ever I open my mouth, shan't I?—(looking round with the most good-humoured dependence on every body's assent)—Do not you all think I shall?"

Emma could not resist.

"Ah! ma'am, but there may be a difficulty. Pardon me—but you will be limited as to number—only three at once."

Miss Bates, deceived by the mock ceremony of her manner, did not immediately catch her meaning; but, when it burst on her, it could not anger, though a slight blush showed that it could pain her.

"Ah!—well—to be sure. Yes, I see what she means, (turning to Mr. Knightley,) and I will try to hold my tongue. I must make myself very disagreeable, or she would not have said such a thing to an old friend."

"I like your plan," cried Mr. Weston. "Agreed, agreed. I will do my best. I am making a conundrum. How will a conundrum reckon?"

"Low, I am afraid, sir, very low," answered his son;—"but we shall be indulgent—especially to any one who leads the way."

10 Unmarried women without their parents were not allowed to attend a social function unless accompanied by a married woman; and in the absence of Mrs. Weston, Mrs. Elton is indeed the *Chaperon*.

11 Dexterity.

12 An alternative spelling for "waives."

"No, no," said Emma, "it will not reckon low. A conundrum of Mr. Weston's shall clear him and his next neighbour. Come, sir, pray let me hear it."

"I doubt it's being very clever myself," said Mr. Weston. "It is too much a matter of fact, but here it is.—What two letters of the alphabet are there, that express perfection?"

"What two letters!—express perfection! I am sure I do not know."

"Ah! you will never guess. You, (to Emma), I am certain, will never guess.—I will tell you.—M. and A.—Em—ma.—Do you understand?"[13]

Understanding and gratification came together. It might be a very indifferent piece of wit; but Emma found a great deal to laugh at and enjoy in it—and so did Frank and Harriet.—It did not seem to touch[14] the rest of the party equally; some looked very stupid[15] about it, and Mr. Knightley gravely said,

"This explains the sort of clever thing that is wanted, and Mr. Weston has done very well for himself; but he must have knocked up every body else. *Perfection* should not have come quite so soon."

"Oh! for myself, I protest I must be excused," said Mrs. Elton; "*I* really cannot attempt—I am not at all fond of the sort of thing. I had an acrostic[16] once sent to me upon my own name, which I was not at all pleased with. I knew who it came from. An abominable puppy!—You know who I mean—(nodding to her husband). These kind of things are very well at Christmas, when one is sitting round the fire; but quite out of place, in my opinion, when one is exploring about the country in summer. Miss Woodhouse must excuse me. I am not one of those who have witty things at every body's service. I do not pretend to be a wit. I have a great deal of vivacity in my own way, but I really must be allowed to judge when to speak and when to hold my tongue. Pass us, if you please, Mr. Churchill. Pass Mr. E., Knightley, Jane, and myself. We have nothing clever to say—not one of us."

"Yes, yes, pray pass *me*," added her husband, with a sort of sneering consciousness; "*I* have nothing to say that can entertain Miss Woodhouse, or any other young lady. An old married man—quite good for nothing. Shall we walk, Augusta?"

13 Mr. Weston's conundrum is at once ham-fisted and allusively resonant. On one level, it simply doesn't work, since the letters *M* and *A*, whether spoken traditionally or "phonically," cannot be identical with the phonemes of "Emma" [ɛmə]. However, Mark Loveridge ("Francis Hutcheson and Mr Weston's Conundrum in *Emma*," *Notes and Queries*, 30: 3, n.s. [1983], pp. 214–216) has pointed out that Austen may also win a clever philosophical in-joke with her readers out of Mr. Weston's "indifferent piece of wit," since the Scottish Enlightenment philosopher Francis Hutcheson (1694–1746) offered the following moral formula in *An Inquiry into the Original of our Ideas of Beauty and Virtue* (1725), with *M* standing for "Moment of Good" and *A* standing for "Ability":

> Since then *Benevolence* or *Virtue* in any *Agent*, is as $\frac{M}{A}$, or $\frac{M+1}{A}$, and no *Being* can act above his *natural Ability;* that must be the Perfection of *Virtue* where M = A, or when the Being acts to the utmost of his power for the *publick Good;* and hence the Perfection of *Virtue* in this case, or $\frac{M}{A}$, is as Unity.

Loveridge remarks, comparing this instance with Knightley's possible echo of Shaftesbury in vol. III, chap. 15: "in terms of technique, such examples take their place in Jane Austen's habit or method of filling the novel with small jokes and party-games to do with words and phrases. These two, though, seem to be jokes made for the author and the reader (or those readers in the know) to share, at the expense of the characters. Mr Weston's conundrum in particular seems rather a private joke" (p. 215). In addition to this, Austen's private joke, despite its metatextual wit, may nevertheless suggest aspects of Mr. Weston's character and function in the plot itself: when this passage is considered in conjunction with the reference to "general benevolence" in vol. III, chap. 2, it appears that Austen, by alluding glancingly to Hutcheson, is offering Mr. Weston as a lineal descendant of the eighteenth-century culture of polite sociability, for which Hutcheson and Shaftesbury (along with Adam Smith) were the most erudite philosophical apologists (see Mullan, *Sentiment and Sociability: The Language of Feel-*

"With all my heart. I am really tired of exploring so long on one spot. Come, Jane, take my other arm."

Jane declined it, however, and the husband and wife walked off. "Happy couple!" said Frank Churchill, as soon as they were out of hearing:—"How well they suit one another!—Very lucky—marrying as they did, upon an acquaintance formed only in a public place!—They only knew each other, I think, a few weeks in Bath! Peculiarly lucky!—for as to any real knowledge of a person's disposition that Bath, or any public place, can give—it is all nothing; there can be no

(56)

The firſt Acroſtic.

A Deſcription of the Morning.

F rom the dull earth the muſty vapours fly,
A nd morn appears to paint the eaſtern ſky,
N ight's ſhades diſpers'd, the duſky clouds retire,
N octurnal orbs now ſhine with fainter fire,
Y et dimly ſeen, now fade, and now expire.

C onſpir'd to hail the half enlighten'd ſphere,
A general chorus riſes thro' the air;
R eſponſive echoes anſwering to the ſound,
R epeat the murm'ring muſic round and round.
O n the vaſt earth the morning breeze invades,
L eaves, flowers and trees, and dries the dewy ſhades,
L ifts the green herbs, and fans the fragrant meads.

This my firſt name, alas! my ſex is frail,
Elſe I had never chang'd it for *O'Neill.*

A Song. To B---ty Mulloy.

Sing, ſing her praiſes ſhrill and loud,
To thee I pay my vows,
Since even a monarch might be proud
To claim her for a ſpouſe.

Her tongue exceeds a ſharp edg'd tool,
A razor, ſword or knife,
Vers'd in cenſorious ridicule,
In miſchief, lies, and ſtrife.

She's dull and heavy as a log,
When'er ſhe moves ſhe falls,
Her body's bloated like a frog,
And like a toad ſhe crawls.

Mrs. Frances O'Neill, "The First Acrostic. A Description of the Morning," from *Poetical Essays* (London: A. Young, 1802). Read downward, the initial letters of the first twelve lines spell out "FANNY CARROLL."

ing in the Eighteenth Century [Oxford: Clarendon Press, 1988], pp. 18–56). This portrayal, of course, is not wholly to his credit, since it marks him out, not only as a worthy and generous man, but also, inescapably, as the father of Frank Churchill. For more on these issues, see Peter Knox-Shaw, *Jane Austen and the Enlightenment* (Cambridge: Cambridge University Press, 2004).

14 Affect.

15 Clueless.

16 Usually a poem in which the initial letters of each line spell out another word or set of words (often the name of the addressee) when read vertically downward. Since the name "Augusta Hawkins" contains fourteen letters, the poem may even have been an acrostic sonnet.

17 Emma is deliberately straining the facts to make Frank Churchill's words apply to Harriet, since, as a reader has already been informed, she herself is the only one of the three young ladies present with hazel eyes. The reference is, of course, designed to be covertly painful to the gray-eyed Jane Fairfax.

knowledge. It is only by seeing women in their own homes, among their own set, just as they always are, that you can form any just judgment. Short of that, it is all guess and luck—and will generally be ill-luck. How many a man has committed himself on a short acquaintance, and rued it all the rest of his life!"

Miss Fairfax, who had seldom spoken before, except among her own confederates, spoke now.

"Such things do occur, undoubtedly."—She was stopped by a cough. Frank Churchill turned towards her to listen.

"You were speaking," said he, gravely. She recovered her voice.

"I was only going to observe, that though such unfortunate circumstances do sometimes occur both to men and women, I cannot imagine them to be very frequent. A hasty and imprudent attachment may arise—but there is generally time to recover from it afterwards. I would be understood to mean, that it can be only weak, irresolute characters, (whose happiness must be always at the mercy of chance,) who will suffer an unfortunate acquaintance to be an inconvenience, an oppression for ever."

He made no answer; merely looked, and bowed in submission; and soon afterwards said, in a lively tone,

"Well, I have so little confidence in my own judgment, that whenever I marry, I hope somebody will choose my wife for me. Will you? (turning to Emma.) Will you choose a wife for me?—I am sure I should like any body fixed on by you. You provide for the family, you know, (with a smile at his father). Find somebody for me. I am in no hurry. Adopt her, educate her."

"And make her like myself."

"By all means, if you can."

"Very well. I undertake the commission. You shall have a charming wife."

"She must be very lively, and have hazle eyes.[17] I care for nothing else. I shall go abroad for a couple of years—and when I return, I shall come to you for my wife. Remember."

Emma was in no danger of forgetting. It was a commission to touch every favourite feeling. Would not Harriet be the very creature described?—Hazle eyes excepted, two years more might make her all that he wished. He might even have Harriet in his thoughts at the moment; who could say? Referring the education to her seemed to imply it.

"Now ma'am," said Jane to her aunt, "shall we join Mrs. Elton?"

"If you please, my dear. With all my heart. I am quite ready. I was ready to have gone with her, but this will do just as well. We shall soon overtake her. There she is—no, that's somebody else. That's one of the ladies in the Irish car party, not at all like her.—Well, I declare—"

They walked off, followed in half a minute by Mr. Knightley. Mr. Weston, his son, Emma, and Harriet, only remained; and the young man's spirits now rose to a pitch almost unpleasant. Even Emma grew tired at last of flattery and merriment, and wished herself rather walking quietly about with any of the others, or sitting almost alone, and quite unattended to, in tranquil observation of the beautiful views beneath her. The appearance of the servants looking out for them to give notice of the carriages was a joyful sight; and even the bustle of collecting and preparing to depart, and the solicitude of Mrs. Elton to have *her* carriage first, were gladly endured, in the prospect of the quiet drive home which was to close the very questionable enjoyments of this day of pleasure. Such another scheme, composed of so many ill-assorted people, she hoped never to be betrayed into again.

While waiting for the carriage, she found Mr. Knightley by her side. He looked around, as if to see that no one were near, and then said,

"Emma, I must once more speak to you as I have been used to do: a privilege rather endured than allowed, perhaps, but I must still use it. I cannot see you acting wrong, without a remonstrance. How could you be so unfeeling to Miss Bates? How could you be so insolent in your wit to a woman of her character, age, and situation?—Emma, I had not thought it possible."

Emma recollected, blushed, was sorry, but tried to laugh it off.

"Nay, how could I help saying what I did?—Nobody could have helped it. It was not so very bad. I dare say she did not understand me."

Portrait of Francis Hutcheson (1694–1746) by Allan Ramsay, c. 1740–1745. Along with Shaftesbury, Hutcheson was one of the major philosophers of "benevolence" in the first half of the eighteenth century.

"I assure you she did. She felt your full meaning. She has talked of it since. I wish you could have heard how she talked of it—with what candour and generosity. I wish you could have heard her honouring your forbearance, in being able to pay her such attentions, as she was for ever receiving from yourself and your father, when her society must be so irksome."

"Oh!" cried Emma, "I know there is not a better creature in the world: but you must allow, that what is good and what is ridiculous are most unfortunately blended in her."

"They are blended," said he, "I acknowledge; and, were she prosperous, I could allow much for the occasional prevalence of the ridiculous over the good. Were she a woman of fortune, I would leave every harmless absurdity to take its chance, I would not quarrel with you for any liberties of manner. Were she your equal in situation—but, Emma, consider how far this is from being the case. She is poor; she has sunk from the comforts she was born to; and, if she live to old age, must probably sink more. Her situation should secure your compassion. It was badly done, indeed!—You, whom she had known from an infant, whom she had seen grow up from a period when her notice was an honour, to have you now, in thoughtless spirits, and the pride of the moment, laugh at her, humble her—and before her niece, too—and before others, many of whom (certainly *some,*) would be entirely guided by *your* treatment of her.—This is not pleasant to you, Emma—and it is very far from pleasant to me; but I must, I will,—I will tell you truths while I can, satisfied with proving myself your friend by very faithful counsel, and trusting that you will some time or other do me greater justice than you can do now."

While they talked, they were advancing towards the carriage; it was ready; and, before she could speak again, he had handed her in. He had misinterpreted the feelings which had kept her face averted, and her tongue motionless. They were combined only of anger against herself, mortification, and deep concern. She had not been able to speak; and, on entering the carriage, sunk back for a moment overcome—then reproaching herself for having taken no leave, making no acknowledgement, parting in apparent sullenness, she looked out with voice and hand eager to show a difference; but it was just too late. He had turned away, and the horses were in motion. She continued to look back, but in vain; and soon, with what appeared unusual speed, they were half way down the hill, and every thing left far behind. She was vexed beyond what could have been expressed—almost beyond what she could conceal. Never had she felt so agitated, mortified, grieved, at any circumstance in her life. She was most forcibly struck. The truth of his representation there was no denying. She felt it at her heart. How could she have been so brutal, so cruel to Miss Bates!—How could she have exposed herself to such ill opinion in any one she valued! And how suffer him to leave her without saying one word of gratitude, of concurrence, of common kindness!

Time did not compose her. As she reflected more, she seemed but to feel it more. She never had been so depressed. Happily it was not necessary to speak. There was only Harriet, who seemed not in spirits herself, fagged,[18] and very willing to be silent; and Emma felt the tears running down her cheeks almost all the way home, without being at any trouble to check[19] them, extraordinary as they were.

18 Tired out.

19 Suppress.

8

The wretchedness of a scheme to Box Hill was in Emma's thoughts all the evening. How it might be considered by the rest of the party, she could not tell. They, in their different homes, and their different ways, might be looking back on it with pleasure; but in her view it was a morning more completely mispent, more totally bare of rational satisfaction at the time, and more to be abhorred in recollection, than any she had ever passed. A whole evening of backgammon with her father, was felicity to it. *There,* indeed, lay real pleasure, for there she was giving up the sweetest hours of the twenty-four to his comfort; and feeling that, unmerited as might be the degree of his fond affection and confiding esteem, she could not, in her general conduct, be open to any severe reproach. As a daughter, she hoped she was not without a heart. She hoped no one could have said to her, "How could you be so unfeeling to your father?—I must, I will tell you truths while I can." Miss Bates should never again—no, never! If attention, in future, could do away the past, she might hope to be forgiven. She had been often remiss, her conscience told her so; remiss, perhaps, more in thought than fact; scornful, ungracious. But it should be so no more. In the warmth of true contrition, she would call upon her the very next morning, and it should be the beginning, on her side, of a regular, equal, kindly intercourse.

She was just as determined when the morrow came, and went early, that nothing might prevent her. It was not unlikely, she thought, that she might see Mr. Knightley in her way; or, perhaps, he might come in while she were paying her visit. She had no objection. She would not be ashamed of the appearance of the penitence, so justly and truly hers. Her eyes were towards Donwell as she walked, but she saw him not.

"The ladies were all at home." She had never rejoiced at the sound before, nor ever before entered the passage, nor walked up the stairs, with any wish of giving pleasure, but in conferring obligation,[1] or of deriving it, except in subsequent ridicule.

There was a bustle on her approach; a good deal of moving and talking. She heard Miss Bates's voice, something was to be done in a hurry; the maid looked frightened and awkward; hoped she would be pleased to wait a moment, and then ushered her in too soon. The aunt and niece seemed both escaping into the adjoining room. Jane she had a distinct glimpse of, looking extremely ill; and, before the door had shut them out, she heard Miss Bates saying, "Well, my dear, I shall *say* you are laid down upon the bed, and I am sure you are ill enough."

Poor old Mrs. Bates, civil and humble as usual, looked as if she did not quite understand what was going on.

"I am afraid Jane is not very well," said she, "but I do not know; they *tell* me she is well. I dare say my daughter will be here presently, Miss Woodhouse. I hope you find a chair. I wish Hetty had not gone. I am very little able—Have you a chair, ma'am? Do you sit where you like? I am sure she will be here presently."

Emma seriously hoped she would. She had a moment's fear of Miss Bates keeping away from her. But Miss Bates soon came—"Very happy and obliged"—but Emma's conscience told her that there was not the same cheerful volubility as before—less ease of look and manner. A very friendly inquiry after Miss Fairfax, she hoped, might lead the way to a return of old feelings. The touch[2] seemed immediate.

"Ah! Miss Woodhouse, how kind you are!—I suppose you have heard—and are come to give us joy.[3] This does not seem much like joy, indeed, in me—(twinkling away a tear or two)—but it will be very trying for us to part with her, after having had her so long, and she has

1 Paying her dues.

2 "An impression upon the mind or soul; a feeling, sense (*of* some emotion, etc.)" *(OED)*.

3 Congratulate us.

a dreadful headach just now, writing all the morning:—such long letters, you know, to be written to Colonel Campbell, and Mrs. Dixon. 'My dear,' said I, 'you will blind yourself'—for tears were in her eyes perpetually. One cannot wonder, one cannot wonder. It is a great change; and though she is amazingly fortunate—such a situation, I suppose, as no young woman before ever met with on first going out—do not think us ungrateful, Miss Woodhouse, for such surprising good fortune—(again dispersing her tears)—but, poor dear soul! if you were to see what a headach she has. When one is in great pain, you know one cannot feel any blessing quite as it may deserve. She is as low as possible. To look at her, nobody would think how delighted and happy she is to have secured such a situation. You will excuse her not coming to you—she is not able—she is gone into her own room—I want her to lie down upon the bed. 'My dear,' said I, 'I shall say you are laid down upon the bed:' but, however, she is not; she is walking about the room. But, now that she has written her letters, she says she shall soon be well. She will be extremely sorry to miss seeing you, Miss Woodhouse, but your kindness will excuse her. You were kept waiting at the door—I was quite ashamed—but somehow there was a little bustle—for it so happened that we had not heard the knock, and till you were on the stairs, we did not know any body was coming. 'It is only Mrs. Cole,' said I, 'depend upon it. Nobody else would come so early.' 'Well,' said she, 'it must be borne some time or other, and it may as well be now.' But then Patty came in, and said it was you. 'Oh!' said I, 'it is Miss Woodhouse: I am sure you will like to see her.'—'I can see nobody,' said she; and up she got, and would go away; and that was what made us keep you waiting—and extremely sorry and ashamed we were. 'If you must go, my dear,' said I, 'you must, and I will say you are laid down upon the bed.'"

Emma was most sincerely interested. Her heart had been long growing kinder towards Jane; and this picture of her present sufferings acted as a cure of every former ungenerous suspicion, and left her nothing but pity; and the remembrance of the less just and less gentle sensations of the past, obliged her to admit that

Jane might very naturally resolve on seeing Mrs. Cole or any other steady friend, when she might not bear to see herself. She spoke as she felt, with earnest regret and solicitude—sincerely wishing that the circumstances which she collected from Miss Bates to be now actually determined on, might be as much for Miss Fairfax's advantage and comfort as possible. "It must be a severe trial to them all. She had understood it was to be delayed till Colonel Campbell's return."

"So very kind!" replied Miss Bates. "But you are always kind."

There was no bearing such an "always;" and to break through her dreadful gratitude, Emma made the direct inquiry of—

"Where—may I ask?—is Miss Fairfax going?"

"To a Mrs. Smallridge—charming woman—most superior—to have the charge of her three little girls—delightful children. Impossible that any situation could be more replete with comfort; if we except, perhaps, Mrs. Suckling's own family, and Mrs. Bragge's; but Mrs. Smallridge is intimate with both, and in the very same neighbourhood:—lives only four miles from Maple Grove. Jane will be only four miles from Maple Grove."

"Mrs. Elton, I suppose, has been the person to whom Miss Fairfax owes——"

"Yes, our good Mrs. Elton. The most indefatigable, true friend. She would not take a denial. She would not let Jane say 'No;' for when Jane first heard of it, (it was the day before yesterday, the very morning we were at Donwell,) when Jane first heard of it, she was quite decided against accepting the offer, and for the reasons you mention; exactly as you say, she had made up her mind to close with nothing till Colonel Campbell's return, and nothing should induce her to enter into any engagement at present—and so she told Mrs. Elton over and over again—and I am sure I had no more idea that she would change her mind!—but that good Mrs. Elton, whose judgement never fails her, saw farther than I did. It is not every body that would have stood out in such a kind way as she did, and refuse to take Jane's answer; but she positively declared she would *not* write any such denial yesterday, as Jane wished her; she would wait—and, sure enough, yesterday evening it was all settled that Jane should go. Quite a surprise to me! I had not the least idea!—Jane took Mrs. Elton aside, and told her at once, that upon thinking over the advantages of Mrs. Suckling's[4] situation, she had come to the resolution of accepting it.—I did not know a word of it till it was all settled."

"You spent the evening with Mrs. Elton?"

"Yes, all of us; Mrs. Elton would have us come. It was settled so, upon the hill, while we were walking about with Mr. Knightley. 'You *must all* spend your evening with us,' said she—'I positively must have you *all* come.'"

"Mr. Knightley was there too, was he?"

"No, not Mr. Knightley; he declined it from the first; and though I thought he would come, because Mrs. Elton declared she would not let him off, he did not;—but my mother, and Jane, and I, were all there, and a very agreeable evening we had. Such kind friends, you know, Miss Woodhouse, one must always find agreeable, though every body seemed rather fagged[5] after the morning's party. Even pleasure, you know, is fatiguing—and I cannot say that any of them seemed very much to have enjoyed it. However, *I* shall always think it a very pleasant party, and feel extremely obliged to the kind friends who included me in it."

"Miss Fairfax, I suppose, though you were not aware of it, had been making up her mind the whole day."

"I dare say she had."

"Whenever the time may come, it must be unwelcome to her and all her friends—but I hope her engagement will have every alleviation that is possible—I mean, as to the character and manners of the family."

"Thank you, dear Miss Woodhouse. Yes, indeed, there is every thing in the world that can make her happy in it. Except the Sucklings and Bragges, there is not such another nursery establishment, so liberal and elegant, in all Mrs. Elton's acquaintance. Mrs. Smallridge, a most delightful woman!—A style of living almost equal to Maple Grove—and as to the children, except the little Sucklings and little Bragges, there are not such elegant sweet children any where.

4 Miss Bates is presumably just getting Mrs. Suckling mixed up with Mrs. Smallridge, although she may be alluding to the fact that it was Mrs. Suckling who procured the offer in the first place.

5 Tired out.

Jane will be treated with such regard and kindness!—It will be nothing but pleasure, a life of pleasure.—And her salary![6]—I really cannot venture to name her salary to you, Miss Woodhouse. Even you, used as you are to great sums, would hardly believe that so much could be given to a young person like Jane."

"Ah! madam," cried Emma, "if other children are at all like what I remember to have been myself, I should think five times the amount of what I have ever yet heard named as a salary on such occasions, dearly earned."

"You are so noble in your ideas!"

"And when is Miss Fairfax to leave you?"

"Very soon, very soon indeed; that's the worst of it. Within a fortnight. Mrs. Smallridge is in a great hurry. My poor mother does not know how to bear it. So then, I try to put it out of her thoughts, and say, Come ma'am, do not let us think about it any more."

"Her friends must all be sorry to lose her; and will not Colonel and Mrs. Campbell be sorry to find that she has engaged herself before their return?"

"Yes; Jane says she is sure they will; but yet, this is such a situation as she cannot feel herself justified in declining. I was so astonished when she first told me what she had been saying to Mrs. Elton, and when Mrs. Elton at the same moment came congratulating me upon it! It was before tea—stay—no, it could not be before tea, because we were just going to cards—and yet it was before tea, because I remember thinking—Oh! no, now I recollect, now I have it; something happened before tea, but not that. Mr. Elton was called out of the room before tea, old John Abdy's son wanted to speak with him. Poor old John, I have a great regard for him; he was clerk to my poor father twenty-seven years; and now, poor old man, he is bed-ridden, and very poorly with the rheumatic gout[7] in his joints—I must go and see him to-day; and so will Jane, I am sure, if she gets out at all. And poor John's son came to talk to Mr. Elton about relief from the parish:[8] he is very well to do himself, you know, being head man at the Crown, ostler,[9] and every thing of that sort, but still he cannot keep his father without some help; and so, when Mr. Elton came

6 Miss Bates's delight is understandable, as governesses were generally very poorly recompensed, often making only twenty or thirty pounds a year.

7 In *Modern Domestic Medicine* (London: n.p., 1827), Thomas John Graham remarks: "*Rheumatic Gout* is a term frequently made use of in conversation; but it appears to me to have had its origin in ignorance, as I am not acquainted with any such complaint. Whatever difference of opinion there may be among discerning professional men on this subject, it is certain, that rheumatic gout is a malady whose symptoms cannot be clearly described, and that what is so called by the vulgar and uninformed is, generally speaking, acute or inflammatory rheumatism" (p. 499).

8 Following the conditions of the 1601 Poor Law, poor relief was administered locally, parish by parish, by the vicar and magistrate. See J. R. Poynter, *Society and Pauperism: English Ideas on Poor Relief, 1795–1834* (London: Routledge & Kegan Paul, 1969), and Alan Kidd, *State, Society, and the Poor in Nineteenth-Century England* (Basingstoke: Macmillan, 1999).

9 The keeper and groom of an inn's stables.

back, he told us what John ostler had been telling him, and then it came out about the chaise having been sent to Randall's to take Mr. Frank Churchill to Richmond. That was what happened before tea. It was after tea that Jane spoke to Mrs. Elton."

Miss Bates would hardly give Emma time to say how perfectly new this circumstance was to her; but as without supposing it possible that she could be ignorant of any of the particulars of Mr. Frank Churchill's going, she proceeded to give them all, it was of no consequence.

What Mr. Elton had learnt from the ostler on the subject, being the accumulation of the ostler's own knowledge, and the knowledge of the servants at Randall's, was, that a messenger had come over from Richmond soon after the return of the party from Box Hill—which messenger, however, had been no more than was expected; and that Mr. Churchill had sent his nephew a few lines, containing, upon the whole, a tolerable account of Mrs. Churchill, and only wishing him not to delay coming back beyond the next morning early; but that Mr. Frank Churchill having resolved to go home directly, without waiting at all, and his horse seeming to have got a cold, Tom had been sent off immediately for the Crown chaise, and the ostler had stood out and seen it pass by, the boy going a good pace, and driving very steady.

There was nothing in all this either to astonish or interest, and it caught Emma's attention only as it united with the subject which already engaged her mind. The contrast between Mrs. Churchill's importance in the world, and Jane Fairfax's, struck her; one was every thing, the other nothing—and she sat musing on the difference of woman's destiny, and quite unconscious on what her eyes were fixed, till roused by Miss Bates's saying,

"Ay, I see what you are thinking of, the piano forté. What is to become of that?—Very true. Poor dear Jane was talking of it just now.—'You must go,' said she. 'You and I must part. You will have no business here.—Let it stay, however,' said she; 'give it house-room till Colonel Campbell comes back. I shall talk about it to him; he will settle for me; he will help me out of all my difficulties.'—And to this day, I do believe, she knows not whether it was his present or his daughter's."

Now Emma was obliged to think of the piano forté; and the remembrance of all her former fanciful and unfair conjectures was so little pleasing, that she soon allowed herself to believe her visit had been long enough; and, with a repetition of every thing that she could venture to say of the good wishes which she really felt, took leave.

"Kings-Weston, Gloucestershire," engraving by John Walker after Francis Nicholson, 1799.

9

Emma's pensive meditations, as she walked home, were not interrupted; but on entering the parlour, she found those who must rouse her. Mr. Knightley and Harriet had arrived during her absence, and were sitting with her father.—Mr. Knightley immediately got up, and in a manner decidedly graver than usual, said,

"I would not go away without seeing you, but I have no time to spare, and therefore must now be gone directly. I am going to London, to spend a few days with John and Isabella. Have you any thing to send or say, besides the 'love,' which nobody carries?"

"Nothing at all. But is not this a sudden scheme?"

"Yes—rather—I have been thinking of it some little time."

Emma was sure he had not forgiven her; he looked unlike himself. Time, however, she thought, would tell him that they ought to be friends again. While he stood, as if meaning to go, but not going—her father began his inquiries.

"Well, my dear, and did you get there safely?—And how did you find my worthy old friend and her daughter?—I dare say they must have been very much obliged to you for coming. Dear Emma has been to call on Mrs. and Miss Bates, Mr. Knightley, as I told you before. She is always so attentive to them!"

Emma's colour was heightened by this unjust praise; and with a smile, and shake of the head, which spoke much, she looked at Mr. Knightley.—It seemed as if there were an instantaneous impression in her favour, as if his eyes received the truth from her's, and all that had passed of good in her feelings were at once caught and honoured.

—He looked at her with a glow of regard. She was warmly gratified —and in another moment still more so, by a little movement of more than common friendliness on his part.—He took her hand;—whether she had not herself made the first motion, she could not say—she might, perhaps, have rather offered it—but he took her hand, pressed it, and certainly was on the point of carrying it to his lips—when, from some fancy or other, he suddenly let it go.—Why he should feel such a scruple, why he should change his mind when it was all but done, she could not perceive.—He would have judged better, she thought, if he had not stopped.—The intention, however, was indubitable; and whether it was that his manners had in general so little gallantry, or however else it happened, but she thought nothing became him more.—It was with him, of so simple, yet so dignified a nature.—She could not but recall the attempt with great satisfaction. It spoke such perfect amity.—He left them immediately afterwards—gone in a moment. He always moved with the alertness of a mind which could neither be undecided nor dilatory, but now he seemed more sudden than usual in his disappearance.

Emma could not regret her having gone to Miss Bates, but she wished she had left her ten minutes earlier;—it would have been a great pleasure to talk over Jane Fairfax's situation with Mr. Knightley.—Neither would she regret that he should be going to Brunswick Square, for she knew how much his visit would be enjoyed—but it might have happened at a better time—and to have had longer notice of it, would have been pleasanter.—They parted thorough friends, however; she could not be deceived as to the meaning of his countenance, and his unfinished gallantry;—it was all done to assure her that she had fully recovered his good opinion.—He had been sitting with them half an hour,[1] she found. It was a pity that she had not come back earlier!

In the hope of diverting her father's thoughts from the disagreeableness of Mr. Knightley's going to London; and going so suddenly; and going on horseback, which she knew would be all very bad; Emma communicated her news of Jane Fairfax, and her dependence on the effect was justified; it supplied a very useful check,—interested, without disturbing him. He had long made up his mind to Jane

1 Twice the minimum length of a merely "formal" visit.

Fairfax's going out as governess, and could talk of it cheerfully, but Mr. Knightley's going to London had been an unexpected blow.

"I am very glad indeed, my dear, to hear she is to be so comfortably settled. Mrs. Elton is very good-natured and agreeable, and I dare say her acquaintance are just what they ought to be. I hope it is a dry situation,[2] and that her health will be taken good care of. It ought to be a first object, as I am sure poor Miss Taylor's always was with me. You know, my dear, she is going to be to this new lady what Miss Taylor was to us. And I hope she will be better off in one respect, and not be induced to go away after it has been her home so long."

The following day brought news from Richmond to throw every thing else into the back-ground. An express[3] arrived at Randall's to announce the death of Mrs. Churchill! Though her nephew had had no particular reason to hasten back on her account, she had not lived above six-and-thirty hours after his return. A sudden seizure of a different nature from any thing foreboded by her general state, had carried her off after a short struggle. The great Mrs. Churchill was no more.

It was felt as such things must be felt. Every body had a degree of gravity and sorrow; tenderness towards the departed, solicitude for the surviving friends; and, in a reasonable time, curiosity to know where she would be buried. Goldsmith tells us, that when lovely woman stoops to folly, she has nothing to do but to die;[4] and when she stoops to be disagreeable, it is equally to be recommended as a clearer of ill-fame. Mrs. Churchill, after being disliked at least twenty-five years, was now spoken of with compassionate allowances. In one point she was fully justified. She had never been admitted before to be seriously ill.[5] The event acquitted her of all the fancifulness, and all the selfishness of imaginary complaints.

"Poor Mrs. Churchill! no doubt she had been suffering a great deal: more than any body had ever supposed—and continual pain would try the temper. It was a sad event—a great shock—with all her faults, what would Mr. Churchill do without her? Mr. Churchill's loss would be dreadful indeed. Mr. Churchill would never get over it."—

2 Location.

3 An urgent postal message, the forerunner of the modern telegram.

4 The novel's second allusion to Goldsmith's famous song; see note 23 to vol. I, chap. 9.

5 Compare the epitaph "I told you I was ill," composed for himself by the Irish comedian and writer Spike Milligan (1918–2002).

An example of contemporary mourning costume, from *Ackermann's Repository of the Arts,* December 1817.

Even Mr. Weston shook his head, and looked solemn, and said, "Ah! poor woman, who would have thought it!" and resolved, that his mourning should be as handsome as possible; and his wife sat sighing and moralizing over her broad hems[6] with a commiseration and good sense, true and steady. How it would affect Frank was among the earliest thoughts of both. It was also a very early speculation with Emma. The character of Mrs. Churchill, the grief of her husband—her mind glanced over them both with awe and compassion—and then rested with lightened feelings on how Frank might be affected by the event, how benefited, how freed. She saw in a moment all the possible good. Now, an attachment to Harriet Smith would have nothing to encounter. Mr. Churchill, independent of his wife, was feared by nobody; an easy, guidable man, to be persuaded into any thing by his nephew. All that remained to be wished was, that the nephew should form the attachment, as, with all her good will in the cause, Emma could feel no certainty of its being already formed.

Harriet behaved extremely well on the occasion, with great self-command. Whatever she might feel of brighter hope, she betrayed nothing. Emma was gratified, to observe such a proof in her of strengthened character, and refrained from any allusion that might endanger its maintenance. They spoke, therefore, of Mrs. Churchill's death with mutual forbearance.

Short letters from Frank were received at Randall's, communicating all that was immediately important of their state and plans. Mr. Churchill was better than could be expected; and their first removal, on the departure of the funeral for Yorkshire, was to be to the house of a very old friend in Windsor, to whom Mr. Churchill had been promising a visit the last ten years. At present, there was nothing to be done for Harriet; good wishes for the future were all that could yet be possible on Emma's side.

It was a more pressing concern to show attention to Jane Fairfax, whose prospects were closing, while Harriet's opened, and whose engagements now allowed of no delay[7] in any one at Highbury, who wished to show her kindness—and with Emma it was grown into a first wish. She had scarcely a stronger regret than for her past cold-

6 Broad hems traditionally denoted mourning clothes—and, often, the opportunities for ostentation that mourning also offered. For example, in vol. II, chap. 3, of Susan Ferrier's novel *Marriage* (1818), the mourning family of Glenfern are described as follows: "after the first burst of sorrow, their ideas fastened with avidity on all the paraphernalia of affliction . . . The elder ladies began to calculate how many yards of broad hemming would be required, and to form a muster-roll of the company; with this improvement, that it was to be ten times as numerous as the one that had assembled at the christening; while the young ones busied their imaginations as to the effect of new mournings—a luxury to them hitherto unknown."

7 A brazen narratorial pun, given the revelations that are about to be made.

ness; and the person, whom she had been so many months neglecting, was now the very one on whom she would have lavished every distinction of regard or sympathy. She wanted to be of use to her; wanted to show a value for her society, and testify respect and consideration. She resolved to prevail on her to spend a day at Hartfield. A note was written to urge it. The invitation was refused, and by a verbal message. "Miss Fairfax was not well enough to write;" and when Mr. Perry called at Hartfield, the same morning, it appeared that she was so much indisposed as to have been visited, though against her own consent, by himself, and that she was suffering under severe headachs, and a nervous fever[8] to a degree, which made him doubt the possibility of her going to Mrs. Smallridge's at the time proposed. Her health seemed for the moment completely deranged—appetite quite gone—and though there were no absolutely alarming symptoms, nothing touching the pulmonary complaint, which was the standing apprehension of the family,[9] Mr. Perry was uneasy about her. He thought she had undertaken more than she was equal to, and that she felt it so herself, though she would not own it. Her spirits seemed overcome. Her present home, he could not but observe, was unfavourable to a nervous disorder:—confined always to one room;—he could have wished it otherwise—and her good aunt, though his very old friend, he must acknowledge to be not the best companion for an invalid of that description. Her care and attention could not be questioned; they were, in fact, only too great. He very much feared that Miss Fairfax derived more evil than good from them. Emma listened with the warmest concern; grieved for her more and more, and looked around eager to discover some way of being useful. To take her—be it only an hour or two—from her aunt, to give her change of air and scene, and quiet rational conversation, even for an hour or two, might do her good; and the following morning she wrote again to say, in the most feeling language she could command, that she would call for her in the carriage at any hour that Jane would name—mentioning that she had Mr. Perry's decided opinion, in favour of such exercise for his patient. The answer was only in this short note:

8 Although the term "nervous fever" could sometimes denote typhoid, the context here makes it clear that Jane is suffering from the more nebulously defined form of "nervous fever" as described in contemporary accounts. In *Observations on Epidemic Disorders, with Remarks on Nervous and Epidemic Fevers* (London: J. Johnson, 1773), James Sims observes: "The nervous fever generally attacks persons of a lax habit of body, who have been long confined or undergone great evacuations, fatigue, long dejection of spirits, salivations, too frequent purging, excessive venery, immoderate watchings or study; every one of which is known to weaken the stomach and digestion" (pp. 238–239); and in *The Domestic Physician, or Guardian of Health* (London: J. Murray, J. Bew, L. Davis, 1787), Bryan Cornwell suggests that "[t]he presaging symptoms of a nervous fever are low spirits, want of appetite, lassitude, watchfulness, sighing, and dejection of mind; these are succeeded by a low, quick, and unequal pulse; a dry tongue, without any considerable thirst; alternate chilness and flushing; giddiness and pain in the head; nausea and vomiting; pale urine, resembling dead small beer; difficult respiration, and slight alienations of mind" (p. 134).

9 The most overt reference in the novel to the possibility of Jane Fairfax's contracting tuberculosis.

"Miss Fairfax's compliments and thanks, but is quite unequal to any exercise."

Emma felt that her own note had deserved something better; but it was impossible to quarrel with words, whose tremulous inequality[10] showed indisposition so plainly, and she thought only of how she might best counteract this unwillingness to be seen or assisted. In spite of the answer, therefore, she ordered the carriage, and drove to Mrs. Bates's, in the hope that Jane would be induced to join her—but it would not do;—Miss Bates came to the carriage door, all gratitude, and agreeing with her most earnestly in thinking an airing might be of the greatest service—and every thing that message could do was tried—but all in vain. Miss Bates was obliged to return without success; Jane was quite unpersuadable; the mere proposal of going out seemed to make her worse.—Emma wished she could have seen her, and tried her own powers; but almost before she could hint the wish, Miss Bates made it appear that she had promised her niece on no account to let Miss Woodhouse in. "Indeed, the truth was, that poor dear Jane could not bear to see anybody—anybody at all—Mrs. Elton, indeed, could not be denied—and Mrs. Cole had made such a point—and Mrs. Perry had said so much—but, except them, Jane would really see nobody."

Emma did not want to be classed with the Mrs. Eltons, the Mrs. Perrys, and the Mrs. Coles, who would force themselves anywhere; neither could she feel any right of preference herself—she submitted, therefore, and only questioned Miss Bates farther as to her niece's appetite and diet, which she longed to be able to assist. On that subject poor Miss Bates was very unhappy, and very communicative; Jane would hardly eat any thing:—Mr. Perry recommended nourishing food; but every thing they could command (and never had anybody such good neighbours) was distasteful.

Emma, on reaching home, called the housekeeper directly, to an examination of her stores; and some arrow-root of very superior quality[11] was speedily despatched to Miss Bates with a most friendly note. In half an hour the arrow-root was returned, with a thousand thanks from Miss Bates, but "dear Jane would not be satisfied with-

10 Shaky orthography.

11 A starch derived from the tubers of the genus *Maranta,* native to the West Indies, popular in the eighteenth and nineteenth centuries as an easily digestible ingredient for invalids. Arrow-root was used to make, among other dishes, jellies and biscuits, the latter of which are often still made today. In James Joyce's short story "A Painful Case," published in *Dubliners* (1914), Mr. Duffy's unvaryingly frugal lunch consists of "a bottle of lager beer and a small trayful of arrowroot biscuits."

out its being sent back; it was a thing she could not take—and, moreover, she insisted on her saying, that she was not at all in want of any thing."

When Emma afterwards heard that Jane Fairfax had been seen wandering about the meadows, at some distance from Highbury, on the afternoon of the very day on which she had, under the plea of being unequal to any exercise, so peremptorily refused to go out with her in the carriage, she could have no doubt—putting every thing together—that Jane was resolved to receive no kindness from *her.* She was sorry, very sorry. Her heart was grieved for a state which seemed but the more pitiable from this sort of irritation of spirits, inconsistency of action, and inequality of powers; and it mortified her that she was given so little credit for proper feeling, or esteemed so little worthy as a friend: but she had the consolation of knowing that her intentions were good, and of being able to say to herself, that could Mr. Knightley have been privy to all her attempts of assisting Jane Fairfax, could he even have seen into her heart,[12] he would not, on this occasion, have found any thing to reprove.

12 Austen may be recalling here the famous moment in vol. I, chap. 23, of *Tristram Shandy,* in which Tristram declares:

> If the fixture of *Momus'* glass, in the human breast, according to the proposed emendation of that arch-critick, had taken place . . . nothing more would have been wanting, in order to have taken a man's character, but to have taken a chair and gone softly, as you would to a dioptrical beehive, and look'd in . . . But this . . . is not the case of the inhabitants of this earth;—our minds shine not through the body, but are wrapt up here in a dark covering of uncrystalized flesh and blood; so that if we would come to the specifick characters of them, we must go some other way to work.

In Greek mythology, Momus was the god of mockery and satire; in *Hermotimus,* attributed to the Roman writer Lucian (c. 25 AD–c. 80 AD), he mocked the god Hephaestus for having created man without a window in his breast.

Martin Rowson, detail from *The Life and Opinions of Tristram Shandy, Gentleman,* 1996; by kind permission of the artist. Throughout her writing, Austen gains much comic and serious energy from the fact that human beings have no window that enables them to see directly into the hearts and minds of others—a deficiency the Greek god Momus famously bemoaned.

10

One morning, about ten days after Mrs. Churchill's decease, Emma was called down stairs to Mr. Weston, who "could not stay five minutes, and wanted particularly to speak with her."—He met her at the parlour door, and hardly asking her how she did, in the natural key of his voice, sunk it immediately, to say, unheard by her father,

"Can you come to Randall's at any time this morning?—Do, if it be possible. Mrs. Weston wants to see you. She must see you."

"Is she unwell?"

"No, no, not at all—only a little agitated. She would have ordered the carriage, and come to you, but she must see you *alone,* and that you know—(nodding towards her father)—Humph!—Can you come?"

"Certainly. This moment, if you please. It is impossible to refuse what you ask in such a way. But what can be the matter?—Is she really not ill?"

"Depend upon me—but ask no more questions. You will know it all in time. The most unaccountable business! But hush, hush!"

To guess what all this meant, was impossible even for Emma. Something really important seemed announced by his looks; but, as her friend was well, she endeavoured not to be uneasy, and settling it with her father, that she would take her walk now, she and Mr. Weston were soon out of the house together, and on their way at a quick pace for Randall's.

"Now,"—said Emma, when they were fairly beyond the sweep gates,—"now Mr. Weston, do let me know what has happened."

"No, no,"—he gravely replied.—"Don't ask me. I promised my wife to leave it all to her. She will break it to you better than I can. Do not be impatient, Emma; it will all come out too soon."

"Break it to me," cried Emma, standing still with terror.—"Good God!—Mr. Weston, tell me at once.—Something has happened in Brunswick Square. I know it has. Tell me, I charge you tell me this moment what it is."

"No, indeed you are mistaken."—

"Mr. Weston do not trifle with me.—Consider how many of my dearest friends are now in Brunswick Square. Which of them is it?—I charge you by all that is sacred, not to attempt concealment."

"Upon my word, Emma."—

"Your word!—why not your honour!—why not say upon your honour, that it has nothing to do with any of them? Good Heavens!—What can be to be *broke* to me, that does not relate to one of that family?"

"Upon my honour," said he very seriously, "it does not. It is not in the smallest degree connected with any human being of the name of Knightley."

Emma's courage returned, and she walked on.

"I was wrong," he continued, "in talking of its being *broke* to you. I should not have used the expression. In fact, it does not concern you—it concerns only myself,—that is, we hope.—Humph!—In short, my dear Emma, there is no occasion to be so uneasy about it. I don't say that it is not a disagreeable business—but things might be much worse.—If we walk fast, we shall soon be at Randall's."

Emma found that she must wait; and now it required little effort. She asked no more questions, therefore, merely employed her own fancy, and that soon pointed out to her the probability of its being some money concern—something just come to light, of a disagreeable nature in the circumstances of the family,—something which the late event at Richmond had brought forward.[1] Her fancy was very active. Half a dozen natural children, perhaps—and poor Frank

1 Wills and their unexpected consequences had long been a staple of fictional plots, as witnessed, for example, by the opening of *Sense and Sensibility,* in which the Norland estate is settled on John Dashwood and his descendants by the "old gentleman," at the expense of Mrs. Dashwood and her daughters.

cut off![2]—This, though very undesirable, would be no matter of agony to her. It inspired little more than an animating curiosity.

"Who is that gentleman on horseback?" said she, as they proceeded—speaking more to assist Mr. Weston in keeping his secret, than with any other view.

"I do not know.—One of the Otways.—Not Frank;—it is not Frank, I assure you. You will not see him. He is half way to Windsor by this time."

"Has your son been with you, then?"

"Oh! yes—did not you know?—Well, well, never mind."

For a moment he was silent; and then added, in a tone much more guarded and demure,

"Yes, Frank came over this morning, just to ask us how we did."

They hurried on, and were speedily at Randall's.—"Well, my dear," said he, as they entered the room—"I have brought her, and now I hope you will soon be better. I shall leave you together. There is no use in delay. I shall not be far off, if you want me."—And Emma distinctly heard him add, in a lower tone, before he quitted the room,—"I have been as good as my word. She has not the least idea."

Mrs. Weston was looking so ill, and had an air of so much perturbation, that Emma's uneasiness increased; and the moment they were alone, she eagerly said,

"What is it my dear friend? Something of a very unpleasant nature, I find, has occurred;—do let me know directly what it is. I have been walking all this way in complete suspense. We both abhor suspense. Do not let mine continue longer. It will do you good to speak of your distress, whatever it may be."

"Have you indeed no idea?" said Mrs. Weston in a trembling voice. "Cannot you, my dear Emma—cannot you form a guess as to what you are to hear?"

"So far as that it relates to Mr. Frank Churchill, I do guess."

"You are right. It does relate to him, and I will tell you directly;" (resuming her work,[3] and seeming resolved against looking up.) "He has been here this very morning, on a most extraordinary errand. It

2 Disinherited.

3 Needlework.

is impossible to express our surprise. He came to speak to his father on a subject,—to announce an attachment—"

She stopped to breathe. Emma thought first of herself, and then of Harriet.

"More than an attachment, indeed," resumed Mrs. Weston; "an engagement—a positive engagement.—What will you say, Emma—what will anybody say, when it is known that Frank Churchill and Miss Fairfax are engaged;—nay, that they have been long engaged!"

Emma even jumped with surprise;—and, horror-struck, exclaimed,

"Jane Fairfax!—Good God! You are not serious? You do not mean it?"

"You may well be amazed," returned Mrs. Weston, still averting her eyes, and talking on with eagerness, that Emma might have time to recover—"You may well be amazed. But it is even so. There has been a solemn engagement between them ever since October—formed at Weymouth, and kept a secret from everybody. Not a creature knowing it but themselves—neither the Campbells, nor her family, nor his.—It is so wonderful,[4] that though perfectly convinced of the fact, it is yet almost incredible to myself. I can hardly believe it.—I thought I knew him."

Emma scarcely heard what was said.—Her mind was divided between two ideas—her own former conversations with him about Miss Fairfax; and poor Harriet;—and for some time she could only exclaim, and require confirmation, repeated confirmation.

"Well," said she at last, trying to recover herself; "this is a circumstance which I must think of at least half a day, before I can at all comprehend it. What!—engaged to her all the winter—before either of them came to Highbury?"

"Engaged since October,—secretly engaged.—It has hurt me, Emma, very much. It has hurt his father equally. *Some part* of his conduct we cannot excuse."

Emma pondered a moment, and then replied, "I will not pretend *not* to understand you; and to give you all the relief in my power, be assured that no such effect has followed his attentions to me, as you are apprehensive of."[5]

4 Astonishing; it was only later in the nineteenth century that the adjective came to be used in an almost exclusively positive sense.

5 Worried about.

Mrs. Weston looked up, afraid to believe; but Emma's countenance was as steady as her words.

"That you may have less difficulty in believing this boast, of my present perfect indifference," she continued, "I will farther tell you, that there was a period in the early part of our acquaintance, when I did like him, when I was very much disposed to be attached to him—nay, was attached—and how it came to cease, is perhaps the wonder. Fortunately, however, it did cease. I have really for some time past, for at least these three months, cared nothing about him. You may believe me, Mrs. Weston. This is the simple truth."

Mrs. Weston kissed her with tears of joy; and when she could find utterance, assured her, that this protestation had done her more good than any thing else in the world could do.

"Mr. Weston will be almost as much relieved as myself," said she. "On this point we have been wretched. It was our darling wish that you might be attached to each other—and we were persuaded that it was so.—Imagine what we have been feeling on your account."

"I have escaped; and that I should escape, may be a matter of grateful wonder to you and myself. But this does not acquit *him,* Mrs. Weston; and I must say, that I think him greatly to blame. What right had he to come among us with affection and faith engaged, and with manners so *very* disengaged? What right had he to endeavour to please, as he certainly did—to distinguish any one young woman with persevering attention, as he certainly did—while he really belonged to another?[6]—How could he tell what mischief he might be doing?—How could he tell that he might not be making me in love with him?—very wrong, very wrong indeed."

"From something that he said, my dear Emma, I rather imagine—"

"And how could *she* bear such behaviour? Composure with a witness! to look on, while repeated attentions were offering[7] to another woman, before her face, and not resent it.—That is a degree of placidity, which I can neither comprehend nor respect."

"There were misunderstandings between them, Emma; he said so expressly. He had not time to enter into much explanation. He was here only a quarter of an hour, and in a state of agitation which did

6 Trusler exhorts any young man "to steer clear of giving any particular lady to understand, that you are more attached to her than others; unless the case be really so, and you mean to pursue it up with honour. Such misrepresentation on your part, and misconception on hers, may lead to entanglements, attended with ruinous consequences" (*A System of Etiquette* [Bath, 1804; 2nd ed., 1819], p. 47).

7 Being offered.

not allow the full use even of the time he could stay—but that there had been misunderstandings he decidedly said. The present crisis, indeed, seemed to be brought on by them; and those misunderstandings might very possibly arise from the impropriety of his conduct."

"Impropriety![8] Oh! Mrs. Weston—it is too calm a censure. Much, much beyond impropriety!—It has sunk him, I cannot say how it has sunk him in my opinion. So unlike what a man should be!—None of that upright integrity, that strict adherence to truth and principle, that disdain of trick and littleness, which a man should display in every transaction of his life."

"Nay, dear Emma, now I must take his part; for though he has been wrong in this instance, I have known him long enough to answer for his having many, very many, good qualities; and—"

"Good God!" cried Emma, not attending to her.—"Mrs. Smallridge, too! Jane actually on the point of going as governess! What could he mean by such horrible indelicacy? To suffer her to engage herself—to suffer her even to think of such a measure!"

"He knew nothing about it, Emma. On this article I can fully acquit him. It was a private resolution of her's, not communicated to him—or at least not communicated in a way to carry conviction.—Till yesterday, I know he said he was in the dark as to her plans. They burst on him, I do not know how, but by some letter or message—and it was the discovery of what she was doing, of this very project of her's, which determined him to come forward at once, own it all to his uncle, throw himself on his kindness, and, in short, put an end to the miserable state of concealment that had been carrying on so long."

Emma began to listen better.

"I am to hear from him soon," continued Mrs. Weston. "He told me at parting, that he should soon write; and he spoke in a manner which seemed to promise me many particulars that could not be given now. Let us wait, therefore, for this letter. It may bring many extenuations. It may make many things intelligible and excusable which now are not to be understood. Don't let us be severe, don't let us be in a hurry to condemn him. Let us have patience. I must love him; and now that I am satisfied on one point, the one material

8 Johnson's definition of "impropriety" is the relatively mild "unfitness; unsuitableness; inaccuracy; want of justness."

point, I am sincerely anxious for its all turning out well, and ready to hope that it may. They must both have suffered a great deal under such a system of secresy and concealment."

"*His* sufferings," replied Emma drily, "do not appear to have done him much harm. Well, and how did Mr. Churchill take it?"

"Most favourably for his nephew—gave his consent with scarcely a difficulty. Conceive what the events of a week have done in that family! While poor Mrs. Churchill lived, I suppose there could not have been a hope, a chance, a possibility;—but scarcely are her remains at rest in the family vault, than her husband is persuaded to act exactly opposite to what she would have required. What a blessing it is, when undue influence does not survive the grave![9]—He gave his consent with very little persuasion."

"Ah!" thought Emma, "he would have done as much for Harriet."

"This was settled last night, and Frank was off with the light this morning. He stopped at Highbury, at the Bates's, I fancy, some time—and then came on hither; but was in such a hurry to get back to his uncle, to whom he is just now more necessary than ever, that, as I tell you, he could stay with us but a quarter of an hour.—He was very much agitated—very much, indeed—to a degree that made him appear quite a different creature from any thing I had ever seen him before.—In addition to all the rest, there had been the shock of finding her so very unwell, which he had had no previous suspicion of—and there was every appearance of his having been feeling a great deal."

"And do you really believe the affair to have been carrying on with such perfect secrecy?—The Campbells, the Dixons, did none of them know of the engagement?"

Emma could not speak the name of Dixon without a little blush.

"None, not one. He positively said that it had been known to no being in the world but their two selves."

"Well," said Emma, "I suppose we shall gradually grow reconciled to the idea, and I wish them very happy. But I shall always think it a very abominable sort of proceeding. What has it been but a system of hypocrisy and deceit,—espionage, and treachery?—To come among us with professions of openness and simplicity; and such a

9 Possibly an ironic inversion of Mark Antony's funeral oration in Act III, Scene 1, of *Julius Caesar:* "The euill that men do, liues after them,/The good is oft enterred with their bones."

Robert Home (1752–1834), *Portrait of the Irwin Sisters.*

league in secret to judge us all!—Here have we been, the whole winter and spring, completely duped, fancying ourselves all on an equal footing of truth and honour, with two people in the midst of us who may have been carrying round, comparing and sitting in judgment on sentiments and words that were never meant for both to hear.—They must take the consequence, if they have heard each other spoken of in a way not perfectly agreeable!"

"I am quite easy on that head," replied Mrs. Weston. "I am very sure that I never said any thing of either to the other, which both might not have heard."

"You are in luck.—Your only blunder was confined to my ear, when you imagined a certain friend of our's in love with the lady."

"True. But as I have always had a thoroughly good opinion of Miss Fairfax, I never could, under any blunder, have spoken ill of her; and as to speaking ill of him, there I must have been safe."

At this moment Mr. Weston appeared at a little distance from the window, evidently on the watch. His wife gave him a look which invited him in; and, while he was coming round, added, "Now, dearest Emma, let me intreat you to say and look every thing that may set his heart at ease, and incline him to be satisfied with the match. Let us make the best of it—and, indeed, almost every thing may be fairly said in her favour. It is not a connexion to gratify; but if Mr. Churchill does not feel that, why should we? and it may be a very fortunate circumstance for him, for Frank, I mean, that he should have attached himself to a girl of such steadiness of character and good judgment as I have always given her credit for—and still am disposed to give her credit for, in spite of this one great deviation from the strict rule of right. And how much may be said in her situation for even that error!"

"Much, indeed!" cried Emma, feelingly. "If a woman can ever be excused for thinking only of herself, it is in a situation like Jane Fairfax's.—Of such, one may almost say, that 'the world is not their's, nor the world's law.'"[10]

She met Mr. Weston on his entrance, with a smiling countenance, exclaiming,

10 Emma alludes to Romeo's speech in *Romeo and Juliet,* Act V, Scene 1: "The world is not thy friend, nor the worlds law." In his pioneering edition of *Emma,* R. W. Chapman suggests that "Austen is quoting the adaptation of *Romeo and Juliet* v. i. 72 to the plight of friendless women in [Johnson's] *Rambler* 107: 'The world is not their friend, nor the world's law'" ([Oxford: Oxford University Press, 1923; 3rd ed., 1933], p. 493).

"A very pretty trick you have been playing me, upon my word! This was a device,[11] I suppose, to sport with my curiosity, and exercise my talent of guessing. But you really frightened me. I thought you had lost half your property, at least. And here, instead of its being a matter of condolence, it turns out to be one of congratulation.—I congratulate you, Mr. Weston, with all my heart, on the prospect of having one of the most lovely and accomplished young women in England for your daughter."

A glance or two between him and his wife, convinced him that all was as right as this speech proclaimed; and its happy effect on his spirits was immediate. His air and voice recovered their usual briskness: he shook her heartily and gratefully by the hand, and entered on the subject in a manner to prove, that he now only wanted time and persuasion to think the engagement no very bad thing. His companions suggested only what could palliate imprudence, or smooth objections; and by the time they had talked it all over together, and he had talked it all over again with Emma, in their walk back to Hartfield, he was become perfectly reconciled, and not far from thinking it the very best thing that Frank could possibly have done.

11 Invention, contrivance.

II

"Harriet, poor Harriet!"—Those were the words; in them lay the tormenting ideas which Emma could not get rid of, and which constituted the real misery of the business to her. Frank Churchill had behaved very ill by herself—very ill in many ways,—but it was not so much *his* behaviour as her *own,* which made her so angry with him. It was the scrape which he had drawn her into on Harriet's account, that gave the deepest hue to his offence.—Poor Harriet! to be a second time the dupe of her misconceptions and flattery. Mr. Knightley had spoken prophetically, when he once said, "Emma, you have been no friend to Harriet Smith."—She was afraid she had done her nothing but disservice.—It was true that she had not to charge herself, in this instance as in the former, with being the sole and original author of the mischief; with having suggested such feelings as might otherwise never have entered Harriet's imagination; for Harriet had acknowledged her admiration and preference of Frank Churchill before she had ever given her a hint on the subject; but she felt completely guilty of having encouraged what she might have repressed. She might have prevented the indulgence and increase of such sentiments. Her influence would have been enough. And now she was very conscious that she ought to have prevented them.—She felt that she had been risking her friend's happiness on most insufficient grounds. Common sense would have directed her to tell Harriet, that she must not allow herself to think of him, and that there were five hundred chances to one against his ever caring for her.—"But, with common sense," she added, "I am afraid I have had little to do."

She was extremely angry with herself. If she could not have been angry with Frank Churchill too, it would have been dreadful.—As for Jane Fairfax, she might at least relieve her feelings from any present solicitude on her account. Harriet would be anxiety enough; she need no longer be unhappy about Jane, whose troubles and whose ill health having, of course, the same origin,[1] must be equally under cure.—Her days of insignificance and evil[2] were over.—She would soon be well, and happy, and prosperous.—Emma could now imagine why her own attentions had been slighted. This discovery laid many smaller matters open. No doubt it had been from jealousy.—In Jane's eyes she had been a rival; and well might any thing she could offer of assistance or regard be repulsed. An airing in the Hartfield carriage would have been the rack, and arrow-root from the Hartfield store-room must have been poison. She understood it all; and as far as her mind could disengage itself from the injustice and selfishness of angry feelings, she acknowledged that Jane Fairfax would have neither elevation nor happiness beyond her desert. But poor Harriet was such an engrossing[3] charge! There was little sympathy to be spared for any body else. Emma was sadly fearful that this second disappointment would be more severe than the first. Considering the very superior claims of the object, it ought; and judging by its apparently stronger effect on Harriet's mind, producing reserve and self-command, it would.—She must communicate the painful truth, however, and as soon as possible. An injunction of secresy had been among Mr. Weston's parting words. "For the present, the whole affair was to be completely a secret. Mr. Churchill had made a point of it, as a token of respect to the wife he had so very recently lost; and everybody admitted it to be no more than due decorum."—Emma had promised; but still Harriet must be excepted. It was her superior duty.

In spite of her vexation, she could not help feeling it almost ridiculous, that she should have the very same distressing and delicate office to perform by Harriet, which Mrs. Weston had just gone through

1 Austen's narrative is, repeatedly, much less sure than Emma about this interpretation of events.

2 Suffering.

3 All-encompassing, surpassing all others.

4 End result.

5 Yet another example of Mr. Weston's "discreet" indiscretions.

6 See note 12 to vol. III, chap. 9.

by herself. The intelligence, which had been so anxiously announced to her, she was now to be anxiously announcing to another. Her heart beat quick on hearing Harriet's footstep and voice; so, she supposed, had poor Mrs. Weston felt when *she* was approaching Randall's. Could the event[4] of the disclosure bear an equal resemblance!—But of that, unfortunately, there could be no chance.

"Well, Miss Woodhouse!" cried Harriet, coming eagerly into the room—"is not this the oddest news that ever was?"

"What news do you mean?" replied Emma, unable to guess, by look or voice, whether Harriet could indeed have received any hint.

"About Jane Fairfax. Did you ever hear any thing so strange? Oh!—you need not be afraid of owning it to me, for Mr. Weston has told me himself. I met him just now. He told me it was to be a great secret;[5] and, therefore, I should not think of mentioning it to any body but you, but he said you knew it."

"What did Mr. Weston tell you?"—said Emma, still perplexed.

"Oh! he told me all about it; that Jane Fairfax and Mr. Frank Churchill are to be married, and that they have been privately engaged to one another this long while. How very odd!"

It was, indeed, so odd; Harriet's behaviour was so extremely odd, that Emma did not know how to understand it. Her character appeared absolutely changed. She seemed to propose showing no agitation, or disappointment, or peculiar concern in the discovery. Emma looked at her, quite unable to speak.

"Had you any idea," cried Harriet, "of his being in love with her?—You, perhaps, might.—You (blushing as she spoke) who can see into everybody's heart;[6] but nobody else——"

"Upon my word," said Emma, "I begin to doubt my having any such talent. Can you seriously ask me, Harriet, whether I imagined him attached to another woman at the very time that I was—tacitly, if not openly—encouraging you to give way to your own feelings?—I never had the slightest suspicion, till within the last hour, of Mr. Frank Churchill's having the least regard for Jane Fairfax. You may be very sure that if I had, I should have cautioned you accordingly."

"Me!" cried Harriet, colouring, and astonished. "Why should you caution me?—You do not think I care about Mr. Frank Churchill."

"I am delighted to hear you speak so stoutly on the subject," replied Emma, smiling; "but you do not mean to deny that there was a time—and not very distant either—when you gave me reason to understand that you did care about him?"

"Him!—never, never. Dear Miss Woodhouse, how could you so mistake me?" turning away distressed.

"Harriet!" cried Emma, after a moment's pause—"What do you mean?—Good Heaven! what do you mean?—Mistake you!—Am I to suppose then?——"

She could not speak another word.—Her voice was lost; and she sat down, waiting in great terror till Harriet should answer.

Harriet, who was standing at some distance, and with face turned from her, did not immediately say any thing; and when she did speak, it was in a voice nearly as agitated as Emma's.

"I should not have thought it possible," she began, "that you could have misunderstood me! I know we agreed never to name him—but considering how infinitely superior he is to every body else, I should not have thought it possible that I could be supposed to mean any other person. Mr. Frank Churchill, indeed! I do not know who would ever look at him in the company of the other. I hope I have a better taste than to think of Mr. Frank Churchill, who is like nobody by his side. And that you should have been so mistaken, is amazing!—I am sure, but for believing that you entirely approved and meant to encourage me in my attachment, I should have considered it at first too great a presumption almost, to dare to think of him. At first, if you had not told me that more wonderful things had happened; that there had been matches of greater disparity (those were your very words);—I should not have dared to give way to—I should not have thought it possible—But if *you,* who had been always acquainted with him——"

"Harriet!" cried Emma, collecting herself resolutely—"Let us understand each other now, without the possibility of farther mistake. Are you speaking of—Mr. Knightley?"

"To be sure I am. I never could have an idea of anybody else—and so I thought you knew. When we talked about him, it was clear as possible."

"Not quite," returned Emma, with forced calmness, "for all that you then said, appeared to me to relate to a different person. I could almost assert that you had *named* Mr. Frank Churchill. I am sure the service Mr. Frank Churchill had rendered you, in protecting you from the gipsies, was spoken of."

"Oh! Miss Woodhouse, how you do forget!"

"My dear Harriet, I perfectly remember the substance of what I said on the occasion. I told you that I did not wonder at your attachment; that considering the service he had rendered you, it was extremely natural:—and you agreed to it, expressing yourself very warmly as to your sense of that service, and mentioning even what your sensations had been in seeing him come forward to your rescue. —The impression of it is strong on my memory."

"Oh, dear," cried Harriet, "now I recollect what you mean; but I was thinking of something very different at the time. It was not the gipsies—it was not Mr. Frank Churchill that I meant. No! (with some elevation) I was thinking of a much more precious circumstance—of Mr. Knightley's coming and asking me to dance, when Mr. Elton would not stand up with me; and when there was no other partner in the room. That was the kind action; that was the noble benevolence and generosity; that was the service which made me begin to feel how superior he was to every other being upon earth."

"Good God!" cried Emma, "this has been a most unfortunate—most deplorable mistake!—What is to be done?"

"You would not have encouraged me, then, if you had understood me. At least, however, I cannot be worse off than I should have been, if the other had been the person; and now—it *is* possible——."

She paused a few moments. Emma could not speak.

"I do not wonder, Miss Woodhouse," she resumed, "that you should feel a great difference between the two, as to me or as to anybody. You must think one five hundred million times more above me than the other. But I hope, Miss Woodhouse, that supposing—that if—strange as it may appear—. But you know they were your own words, that *more* wonderful things had happened, matches of *greater* disparity had taken place than between Mr. Frank Churchill and me; and, therefore, it seems as if such a thing even as this, may have occurred before—and if I should be so fortunate, beyond expression, as to—if Mr. Knightley should really—if *he* does not mind the disparity, I hope, dear Miss Woodhouse, you will not set yourself against it, and try to put difficulties in the way. But you are too good for that, I am sure."

Harriet was standing at one of the windows. Emma turned round to look at her in consternation, and hastily said,

"Have you any idea of Mr. Knightley's returning your affection?"

"Yes," replied Harriet modestly, but not fearfully—"I must say that I have."

Emma's eyes were instantly withdrawn; and she sat silently meditating, in a fixed attitude, for a few minutes. A few minutes were sufficient for making her acquainted with her own heart. A mind like her's, once opening to suspicion, made rapid progress. She touched—she admitted—she acknowledged the whole truth. Why was it so much worse that Harriet should be in love with Mr. Knightley, than with Frank Churchill? Why was the evil so dreadfully increased by Harriet's having some hope of a return? It darted through her, with the speed of an arrow, that Mr. Knightley must marry no one but herself![7]

Her own conduct, as well as her own heart, was before her in the same few minutes. She saw it all with a clearness which had never blessed her before. How improperly had she been acting by Harriet! How inconsiderate, how indelicate, how irrational, how unfeeling had been her conduct! What blindness, what madness, had led her on! It struck her with dreadful force, and she was ready to give it every bad name in the world. Some portion of respect for herself, however, in spite of all these demerits—some concern for her own appearance, and a strong sense of justice by Harriet—(there would be no need of *compassion* to the girl who believed herself loved by Mr. Knightley—but justice required that she should not be made unhappy by any coldness now,) gave Emma the resolution to sit and endure farther with calmness, with even apparent kindness.—For her own advantage indeed, it was fit that the utmost extent of Harriet's hopes should be enquired into; and Harriet had done nothing to forfeit the regard and interest which had been so voluntarily formed

7 This moment has been a point of focus in many adaptations of *Emma* into different media, not least because it represents one of the novel's few clear-cut, singular instances of decisive transition; however, the fact that it takes place within Emma's unspoken consciousness also presents challenges to media that depend on seeing and/or hearing things directly. Douglas McGrath's version, for example, gets around the problem by interpolating a scene in which Emma admits her love directly to Mrs. Weston. Amy Heckerling's *Clueless,* on the other hand, offers a brilliantly inventive visual analogue for this sudden realization, as the Emma character, Cher (Alicia Silverstone), pauses in front of a Los Angeles fountain that miraculously comes to life, just as her voiceover narrates: "Oh my God! I love Josh! I'm majorly, totally, butt crazy in love with Josh!"

A magnificently inventive cinematic analogue for Emma's realization of her love for Knightley, from Amy Heckerling's film *Clueless* (1995), as the inner voice of Cher (Alicia Silverstone) declares: "Oh my God! I love Josh! I'm majorly, totally, butt crazy in love with Josh!"

and maintained—or to deserve to be slighted by the person, whose counsels had never led her right.—Rousing from reflection, therefore, and subduing her emotion, she turned to Harriet again, and, in a more inviting accent, renewed the conversation; for as to the subject which had first introduced it, the wonderful story of Jane Fairfax, that was quite sunk and lost.—Neither of them thought but of Mr. Knightley and themselves.

Harriet, who had been standing in no unhappy reverie, was yet very glad to be called from it, by the now encouraging manner of such a judge, and such a friend as Miss Woodhouse, and only wanted invitation, to give the history of her hopes with great, though trembling delight.—Emma's tremblings as she asked, and as she listened, were better concealed than Harriet's, but they were not less. Her voice was not unsteady; but her mind was in all the perturbation that such a developement of self, such a burst of threatening evil, such a confusion of sudden and perplexing emotions, must create.—She listened with much inward suffering, but with great outward patience, to Harriet's detail.—Methodical, or well arranged, or very well delivered, it could not be expected to be; but it contained, when separated from all the feebleness and tautology of the narration, a substance to sink her spirit—especially with the corroborating circumstances, which her own memory brought in favour of Mr. Knightley's most improved opinion of Harriet.

Harriet had been conscious of a difference in his behaviour ever since those two decisive dances.—Emma knew that he had, on that occasion, found her much superior to his expectation. From that evening, or at least from the time of Miss Woodhouse's encouraging her to think of him, Harriet had begun to be sensible of his talking to her much more than he had been used to do, and of his having indeed quite a different manner towards her; a manner of kindness and sweetness!—Latterly she had been more and more aware of it. When they had been all walking together, he had so often come and walked by her, and talked so very delightfully!—He seemed to want to be acquainted with her. Emma knew it to have been very much the case. She had often observed the change, to almost the same extent.—

Harriet repeated expressions of approbation and praise from him—and Emma felt them to be in the closest agreement with what she had known of his opinion of Harriet. He praised her for being without art or affectation, for having simple, honest, generous, feelings.—She knew that he saw such recommendations in Harriet; he had dwelt on them to her more than once.—Much that lived in Harriet's memory, many little particulars of the notice she had received from him, a look, a speech, a removal from one chair to another,[8] a compliment implied, a preference inferred, had been unnoticed, because unsuspected by Emma. Circumstances that might swell to half an hour's relation, and contained multiplied proofs to her who had seen them, had passed undiscerned by her who now heard them; but the two latest occurrences to be mentioned, the two of strongest promise to Harriet, were not without some degree of witness from Emma herself.—The first, was his walking with her apart from the others, in the lime walk at Donwell, where they had been walking some time before Emma came, and he had taken pains (as she was convinced) to draw her from the rest to himself—and at first, he had talked to her in a more particular way than he had ever done before, in a very particular way indeed!—(Harriet could not recall it without a blush.) He seemed to be almost asking her, whether her affections were engaged.—But as soon as she (Miss Woodhouse) appeared likely to join them, he changed the subject, and began talking about farming:—The second, was his having sat talking with her nearly half an hour[9] before Emma came back from her visit, the very last morning of his being at Hartfield—though, when he first came in, he had said that he could not stay five minutes—and his having told her, during their conversation, that though he must go to London, it was very much against his inclination that he left home at all, which was much more (as Emma felt) than he had acknowledged to *her.* The superior degree of confidence towards Harriet, which this one article marked, gave her severe pain.

On the subject of the first of the two circumstances, she did, after a little reflection, venture the following question. "Might he not?—Is not it possible, that when enquiring, as you thought, into the state

8 Compare vol. I, chap. 15, of *Mansfield Park,* in which, after Mrs. Norris has slighted Fanny Price, Mary Crawford "moved away her chair to the opposite side of the table close to Fanny."

9 A length of time that would certainly suggest friendly interest.

of your affections, he might be alluding to Mr. Martin—he might have Mr. Martin's interest in view?"—But Harriet rejected the suspicion with spirit.

"Mr. Martin! No indeed!—There was not a hint of Mr. Martin. I hope I know better now, than to care for Mr. Martin, or to be suspected of it."

When Harriet had closed her evidence, she appealed to her dear Miss Woodhouse, to say whether she had not good ground for hope.

"I never should have presumed to think of it at first," said she, "but for you. You told me to observe him carefully, and let his behaviour be the rule of mine—and so I have. But now I seem to feel that I may deserve him; and that if he does choose me, it will not be any thing so very wonderful."

The bitter feelings occasioned by this speech, the many bitter feelings, made the utmost exertion necessary on Emma's side, to enable her to say on reply,

"Harriet, I will only venture to declare, that Mr. Knightley is the last man in the world, who would intentionally give any woman the idea of his feeling for her more than he really does."

Harriet seemed ready to worship her friend for a sentence so satisfactory; and Emma was only saved from raptures and fondness, which at that moment would have been dreadful penance, by the sound of her father's footsteps. He was coming through the hall. Harriet was too much agitated to encounter him. "She could not compose herself—Mr. Woodhouse would be alarmed—she had better go;"—with most ready encouragement from her friend, therefore, she passed off through another door—and the moment she was gone, this was the spontaneous burst of Emma's feelings: "Oh God! that I had never seen her!"

The rest of the day, the following night, were hardly enough for her thoughts.—She was bewildered amidst the confusion of all that had rushed on her within the last few hours. Every moment had brought a fresh surprise; and every surprise must be matter of humiliation to her.—How to understand it all! How to understand the deceptions she had been thus practising on herself, and living under!

—The blunders, the blindness of her own head and heart!—she sat still, she walked about, she tried her own room, she tried the shrubbery—in every place, every posture, she perceived that she had acted most weakly; that she had been imposed on by others in a most mortifying degree; that she had been imposing on herself in a degree yet more mortifying; that she was wretched, and should probably find this day but the beginning of wretchedness.

To understand, thoroughly understand her own heart, was the first endeavour. To that point went every leisure moment which her father's claims on her allowed, and every moment of involuntary absence of mind.

How long had Mr. Knightley been so dear to her, as every feeling declared him now to be? When had his influence, such influence begun?—When had he succeeded to that place in her affection, which Frank Churchill had once, for a short period, occupied?—She looked back; she compared the two—compared them, as they had always stood in her estimation, from the time of the latter's becoming known to her—and as they must at any time have been compared by her, had it—oh! had it, by any blessed felicity, occurred to her, to institute the comparison.—She saw that there never had been a time when she did not consider Mr. Knightley as infinitely the superior, or when his regard for her had not been infinitely the most dear. She saw, that in persuading herself, in fancying, in acting to the contrary, she had been entirely under a delusion, totally ignorant of her own heart—and, in short, that she had never really cared for Frank Churchill at all!

This was the conclusion of the first series of reflection. This was the knowledge of herself, on the first question of inquiry, which she reached; and without being long in reaching it.—She was most sorrowfully indignant; ashamed of every sensation but the one revealed to her—her affection for Mr. Knightley.—Every other part of her mind was disgusting.

With insufferable vanity had she believed herself in the secret of everybody's feelings; with unpardonable arrogance proposed to arrange everybody's destiny. She was proved to have been universally mistaken; and she had not quite done nothing—for she had done mischief. She had brought evil on Harriet, on herself, and she too much feared, on Mr. Knightley.—Were this most unequal of all connexions to take place, on her must rest all the reproach of having given it a beginning; for his attachment, she must believe to be produced only by a consciousness of Harriet's;—and even were this not the case, he would never have known Harriet at all but for her folly.

Mr. Knightley and Harriet Smith!—It was an union to distance every wonder of the kind.[10]—The attachment of Frank Churchill and Jane Fairfax became common-place, threadbare, stale in the comparison, exciting no surprise, presenting no disparity, affording nothing to be said or thought.—Mr. Knightley and Harriet Smith!—Such an elevation on her side! Such a debasement on his!—It was horrible to Emma to think how it must sink him in the general opinion, to foresee the smiles, the sneers, the merriment it would prompt at his expense; the mortification and disdain of his brother, the thousand inconveniences to himself.—Could it be?—No; it was impossible. And yet it was far, very far, from impossible.—Was it a new circumstance for a man of first-rate abilities to be captivated by very inferior powers? Was it new for one, perhaps too busy to seek, to be the prize of a girl who would seek him?—Was it new for any thing in this world to be unequal, inconsistent, incongruous—or for chance and circumstance (as second causes)[11] to direct the human fate?

Oh! had she never brought Harriet forward! Had she left her where she ought, and where he had told her she ought!—Had she not, with a folly which no tongue could express,[12] prevented her marrying the unexceptionable young man who would have made her happy and respectable in the line of life to which she ought to belong—all would have been safe; none of this dreadful sequel would have been.

How Harriet could ever have had the presumption to raise her thoughts to Mr. Knightley!—How she could dare to fancy herself the chosen of such a man till actually assured of it!—But Harriet was less humble, had fewer scruples than formerly.—Her inferiority, whether

10 To surpass even the most extraordinary instances of such unions.

11 Second causes were manifest agents in the world, as contrasted with God as the "first cause" of everything.

12 The phrase is more usually employed to describe the ineffability of God.

of mind or situation, seemed little felt.—She had seemed more sensible of Mr. Elton's being to stoop in marrying her, than she now seemed of Mr. Knightley's.—Alas! was not that her own doing too? Who had been at pains to give Harriet notions of self-consequence[13] but herself?—Who but herself had taught her, that she was to elevate herself if possible, and that her claims were great to a high worldly establishment?[14]—If Harriet, from being humble, were grown vain, it was her doing too.

13 Self-importance; the *OED* dates this sense from the late 1770s, tracing it back to Burney's novel *Evelina.*

14 A wealthy station in life.

John Hill, after John Claude Nattes, "A General View of Bath," from *Bath Illustrated by a Series of Views,* 1805.

12

1 "Contemptuous of others; haughty; overbearing" (Johnson).

Till now that she was threatened with its loss, Emma had never known how much of her happiness depended on being *first* with Mr. Knightley, first in interest and affection.—Satisfied that it was so, and feeling it her due, she had enjoyed it without reflection; and only in the dread of being supplanted, found how inexpressibly important it had been.—Long, very long, she felt she had been first; for, having no female connexions of his own, there had been only Isabella whose claims could be compared with hers, and she had always known exactly how far he loved and esteemed Isabella. She had herself been first with him for many years past. She had not deserved it; she had often been negligent or perverse, slighting his advice, or even wilfully opposing him, insensible of half his merits, and quarrelling with him because he would not acknowledge her false and insolent[1] estimate of her own—but still, from family attachment and habit, and thorough excellence of mind, he had loved her, and watched over her from a girl, with an endeavour to improve her, and an anxiety for her doing right, which no other creature had at all shared. In spite of all her faults, she knew she was dear to him; might she not say, very dear?—When the suggestions of hope, however, which must follow here, presented themselves, she could not presume to indulge them. Harriet Smith might think herself not unworthy of being peculiarly, exclusively, passionately loved by Mr. Knightley. *She* could not. She could not flatter herself with any idea of blindness in his attachment to *her*. She had received a very recent proof of its impartiality.—How shocked had he been by her behaviour to Miss Bates! How directly, how strongly had he expressed himself to her on the subject!—Not too strongly for the offence—but far, far too strongly to issue from any feeling softer than upright justice and clear-sighted good will.—She had no hope, nothing to deserve the name of hope, that he could have that sort of affection for herself which was now in question; but there was a hope (at times a slight one, at times much stronger,) that Harriet might have deceived herself, and be overrating his regard for *her.*—Wish it she must, for his sake—be the consequence nothing to herself, but his remaining single all his life. Could she be secure of that, indeed, of his never marrying at all, she believed she should be perfectly satisfied.—Let him but continue the same Mr. Knightley to her and her father, the same Mr. Knightley to all the world; let Donwell and Hartfield lose none of their precious intercourse of friendship and confidence, and her peace would be fully secured.—Marriage, in fact, would not do for her. It would be incompatible with what she owed to her father, and with what she felt for him. Nothing should separate her from her father. She would not marry, even if she were asked by Mr. Knightley.

It must be her ardent wish that Harriet might be disappointed; and she hoped, that when able to see them together again, she might at least be able to ascertain what the chances for it were.—She should see them henceforward with the closest observance; and wretchedly as she had hitherto misunderstood even those she was watching, she did not know how to admit that she could be blinded here.—He was expected back every day. The power of observation would be soon given—frightfully soon it appeared when her thoughts were in one course. In the meanwhile, she resolved against seeing Harriet.—It would do neither of them good, it would do the subject no good, to be talking of it farther.—She was resolved not to be convinced, as long as she could doubt, and yet had no authority for opposing Harriet's confidence. To talk would be only to irritate.—She wrote to her, therefore, kindly, but decisively, to beg that she would not, at present, come to Hartfield; acknowledging it to be her conviction, that all farther confidential discussion of *one* topic had better be avoided; and hoping, that if a few days were allowed to pass before they met again, except in the company of others—she objected only

Cassandra Austen, watercolor of Fanny Austen, later Knight (1805). The daughter of Austen's brother Edward, Fanny (1793–1882) was a favorite with her aunt Jane (perhaps because Austen perceived a kindred spirit in her articulate niece), and inherited Austen's extant letters to Cassandra on Cassandra's death in 1845. However, Fanny's memories of her aunts in later life were not so warm. In 1869, Lady Knatchbull, as she had been since her marriage in 1820, recalled: "They were not rich & the people around with whom they chiefly mixed, were not at all high bred, or in short anything more than *mediocre* & *they* of course tho' superior in *mental powers* & *cultivation* were on the same level as far as refinement goes—but I think in later life their intercourse with Mrs. Knight (who was very fond of & kind to them) improved them both & Aunt Jane was too clever not to put aside all possible signs of 'common-ness' (if such an expression is allowable) & teach herself to be more refined, at least in intercourse with people in general."

to a tête-à-tête—they might be able to act as if they had forgotten the conversation of yesterday.—Harriet submitted, and approved, and was grateful.

This point was just arranged, when a visitor arrived to tear Emma's thoughts a little from the one subject which had engrossed them, sleeping or waking, the last twenty-four hours—Mrs. Weston, who had been calling on her daughter-in-law elect, and took Hartfield in her way home, almost as much in duty to Emma as in pleasure to herself, to relate all the particulars of so interesting an interview.

Mr. Weston had accompanied her to Mrs. Bates's, and gone through his share of this essential attention most handsomely; but she having then induced Miss Fairfax to join her in an airing, was now returned with much more to say, and much more to say with satisfaction, than a quarter of an hour spent in Mrs. Bates's parlour, with all the incumbrance of awkward feelings, could have afforded.

A little curiosity Emma had; and she made the most of it while her friend related. Mrs. Weston had set off to pay the visit in a good deal of agitation herself; and in the first place had wished not to go at all at present, to be allowed merely to write to Miss Fairfax instead, and to defer this ceremonious call[2] till a little time had passed, and Mr. Churchill could be reconciled to the engagement's becoming known; as, considering every thing, she thought such a visit could not be paid without leading to reports:—but Mr. Weston had thought differently; he was extremely anxious to shew his approbation to Miss Fairfax and her family, and did not conceive that any suspicion could be excited by it; or if it were, that it would be of any consequence; for "such things," he observed, "always got about." Emma smiled, and felt that Mr. Weston had very good reason for saying so. They had gone, in short—and very great had been the evident distress and confusion of *the* lady. She had hardly been able to speak a word, and every look and action had shown how deeply she was suffering from consciousness. The quiet, heartfelt satisfaction of the old lady, and the rapturous delight of her daughter—who proved even too joyous to talk as usual, had been a gratifying, yet almost an affecting, scene. They were both so truly respectable in their happiness, so

2 It is a measure of the still awkward nature of the situation that the Westons restrict their "ceremonious" visit to the formal minimum of fifteen minutes.

disinterested in every sensation; thought so much of Jane; so much of everybody, and so little of themselves, that every kindly feeling was at work for them. Miss Fairfax's recent illness had offered a fair plea for Mrs. Weston to invite her to an airing; she had drawn back and declined at first, but on being pressed had yielded; and in the course of their drive, Mrs. Weston had, by gentle encouragement, overcome so much of her embarrassment, as to bring her to converse on the important subject. Apologies for her seemingly ungracious silence in their first reception, and the warmest expressions of the gratitude she was always feeling towards herself and Mr. Weston, must necessarily open the cause; but when these effusions were put by, they had talked a good deal of the present and of the future state of the engagement. Mrs. Weston was convinced that such conversation must be the greatest relief to her companion, pent up within her own mind as every thing had so long been, and was very much pleased with all that she had said on the subject.

"On the misery of what she had suffered, during the concealment of so many months," continued Mrs. Weston, "she was energetic. This was one of her expressions. 'I will not say, that since I entered into the engagement I have not had some happy moments; but I can say, that I have never known the blessing of one tranquil hour:'—and the quivering lip, Emma, which uttered it, was an attestation that I felt at my heart."

"Poor girl!" said Emma. "She thinks herself wrong, then, for having consented to a private engagement?"

"Wrong!—No one, I believe, can blame her more than she is disposed to blame herself. 'The consequence,' said she, 'has been a state of perpetual suffering to me; and so it ought. But after all the punishment that misconduct can bring, it is still not less misconduct. Pain is no expiation. I never can be blameless. I have been acting contrary to all my sense of right; and the fortunate turn that every thing has taken, and the kindness I am now receiving, is what my conscience tells me ought not to be. Do not imagine, madam,' she continued, 'that I was taught wrong. Do not let any reflection fall on the principles or the care of the friends who brought me up. The error has been all my own; and I do assure you that, with all the excuse that present circumstances may appear to give, I shall yet dread making the story known to Colonel Campbell.'"

"Poor girl!" said Emma again. "She loves him then excessively, I suppose. It must have been from attachment only, that she could be led to form the engagement. Her affection must have overpowered her judgment."

"Yes, I have no doubt of her being extremely attached to him."

"I am afraid," returned Emma, sighing, "that I must often have contributed to make her unhappy."

"On your side, my love, it was very innocently done. But she probably had something of that in her thoughts, when alluding to the misunderstandings which he had given us hints of before. One natural consequence of the evil she had involved herself in," she said, "was that of making her *unreasonable.* The consciousness of having done amiss, had exposed her to a thousand inquietudes,[3] and made her captious and irritable to a degree that must have been—that had been—hard for him to bear. 'I did not make the allowances,' said she, 'which I ought to have done, for his temper and spirits—his delightful spirits, and that gaiety, that playfulness of disposition, which, under any other circumstances, would, I am sure, have been as constantly bewitching to me, as they were at first.' She then began to speak of you, and of the great kindness you had shown her during her illness; and with a blush which showed me how it was all connected, desired me, whenever I had an opportunity, to thank you—I could not thank you too much—for every wish and every endeavour to do her good. She was sensible that you had never received any proper acknowledgment from herself."

"If I did not know her to be happy now," said Emma, seriously, "which, in spite of every little drawback from her scrupulous conscience, she must be, I could not bear these thanks;—for, oh! Mrs. Weston, if there were an account drawn up of the evil and the good I have done Miss Fairfax!—Well, (checking herself, and trying to be more lively), this is all to be forgotten. You are very kind to bring me these interesting particulars. They show her to the greatest advantage. I am sure she is very good—I hope she will be very happy. It is

3 Johnson defines "inquietude" as "disturbed state; want of quiet; attack on the quiet."

fit that the fortune should be on his side, for I think the merit will be all on her's."

Such a conclusion could not pass unanswered by Mrs. Weston. She thought well of Frank in almost every respect; and, what was more, she loved him very much, and her defence was, therefore, earnest. She talked with a great deal of reason, and at least equal affection—but she had too much to urge for Emma's attention; it was soon gone to Brunswick Square or to Donwell; she forgot to attempt to listen; and when Mrs. Weston ended with, "We have not yet had the letter we are so anxious for, you know, but I hope it will soon come," she was obliged to pause before she answered, and at last obliged to answer at random, before she could at all recollect what letter it was which they were so anxious for.

"Are you well, my Emma?" was Mrs. Weston's parting question.

"Oh! perfectly. I am always well, you know. Be sure to give me intelligence of the letter as soon as possible."

Mrs. Weston's communications furnished Emma with more food for unpleasant reflection, by increasing her esteem and compassion, and her sense of past injustice towards Miss Fairfax. She bitterly regretted not having sought a closer acquaintance with her, and blushed for the envious feelings which had certainly been, in some measure, the cause. Had she followed Mr. Knightley's known wishes, in paying that attention to Miss Fairfax, which was every way her due; had she tried to know her better; had she done her part towards intimacy; had she endeavoured to find a friend there instead of in Harriet Smith; she must, in all probability, have been spared from every pain which pressed on her now.—Birth, abilities, and education, had been equally marking one as an associate for her, to be received with gratitude; and the other—what was she?—Supposing even that they had never become intimate friends; that she had never been admitted into Miss Fairfax's confidence on this important matter—which was most probable—still, in knowing her as she ought, and as she might, she must have been preserved from the abominable suspicions of an improper attachment to Mr. Dixon, which she had not only so foolishly fashioned and harboured herself, but had so unpardonably imparted; an idea which she greatly feared had been made a subject of material distress to the delicacy of Jane's feelings, by the levity or carelessness of Frank Churchill's. Of all the sources of evil surrounding the former, since her coming to Highbury, she was persuaded that she must herself have been the worst. She must have been a perpetual enemy. They never could have been all three together, without her having stabbed Jane Fairfax's peace in a thousand instances; and on Box Hill, perhaps, it had been the agony of a mind that would bear no more.

The evening of this day was very long, and melancholy, at Hartfield. The weather added what it could of gloom. A cold stormy rain set in, and nothing of July appeared but in the trees and shrubs, which the wind was despoiling,[4] and the length of the day, which only made such cruel sights the longer visible.

The weather affected Mr. Woodhouse,[5] and he could only be kept tolerably comfortable by almost ceaseless attention on his daughter's side, and by exertions which had never cost her half so much before. It reminded her of their first forlorn tête-à-tête, on the evening of Mrs. Weston's wedding-day; but Mr. Knightley had walked in then, soon after tea, and dissipated every melancholy fancy. Alas! such delightful proofs of Hartfield's attraction, as those sort of visits conveyed, might shortly be over. The picture which she had then drawn of the privations of the approaching winter, had proved erroneous; no friends had deserted them, no pleasures had been lost.—But her present forebodings she feared would experience no similar contradiction. The prospect before her now, was threatening to a degree that could not be entirely dispelled—that might not be even partially brightened. If all took place that might take place among the circle of her friends, Hartfield must be comparatively deserted; and she left to cheer her father with the spirits only of ruined happiness.

The child to be born at Randall's must be a tie there even dearer than herself; and Mrs. Weston's heart and time would be occupied by it. They should lose her; and, probably, in great measure, her husband also;—Frank Churchill would return among them no more; and Miss Fairfax, it was reasonable to suppose, would soon cease to belong to Highbury. They would be married, and settled either at or near Enscombe. All that were good would be withdrawn; and if to these

4 Stripping bare.

5 In his susceptibility to the weather's influence, Mr. Woodhouse stands in sharp contrast to Johnson, who repeatedly denied any necessary connection between the elements and human moods. Whereas many eighteenth-century physicians, such as George Cheyne in *The English Malady; or, a Treatise of Nervous Diseases of All Kinds* (1733), emphasized the influence of bad weather on melancholy and sickness, Johnson's *Idler* no. 11 maintains: "This distinction of seasons is produced only by imagination operating upon luxury. To temperance every day is bright, and every hour is propitious to diligence. He that shall resolutely excite his faculties, or exert his virtues, will soon make himself superiour to the seasons, and may set at defiance the morning mist, and the evening damp, the blasts of the east, and the clouds of the south" (*The Works of Samuel Johnson*, vol. 2, ed. W. J. Bate, John M. Bullitt, and L. F. Powell [New Haven: Yale University Press, 1963], p. 39).

losses, the loss of Donwell were to be added, what would remain of cheerful or of rational society within their reach? Mr. Knightley to be no longer coming there for his evening comfort!—No longer walking in at all hours, as if ever willing to change his own home for their's!—How was it to be endured? And if he were to be lost to them for Harriet's sake; if he were to be thought of hereafter, as finding in Harriet's society all that he wanted; if Harriet were to be the chosen, the first, the dearest, the friend, the wife to whom he looked for all the best blessings of existence;[6] what could be increasing Emma's wretchedness but the reflection never far distant from her mind, that it had been all her own work?

When it came to such a pitch as this, she was not able to refrain from a start, or a heavy sigh, or even from walking about the room for a few seconds—and the only source whence any thing like consolation or composure could be drawn, was in the resolution of her own better conduct, and the hope that, however inferior in spirit and gaiety might be the following and every future winter of her life to the past, it would yet find her more rational, more acquainted with herself, and leave her less to regret when it were gone.

6 Whereas Emma herself, in the first sentence of the novel, only "seemed to unite some of the best blessings of existence."

13

The weather continued much the same all the following morning; and the same loneliness, and the same melancholy, seemed to reign at Hartfield—but in the afternoon it cleared; the wind changed into a softer quarter; the clouds were carried off; the sun appeared; it was summer again. With all the eagerness which such a transition gives, Emma resolved to be out of doors as soon as possible. Never had the exquisite sight, smell, sensation of nature, tranquil, warm, and brilliant after a storm, been more attractive to her. She longed for the serenity they might gradually introduce; and on Mr. Perry's coming in soon after dinner, with a disengaged hour to give her father, she lost no time in hurrying into the shrubbery.—There, with spirits freshened, and thoughts a little relieved, she had taken a few turns, when she saw Mr. Knightley passing through the garden door, and coming towards her.—It was the first intimation of his being returned from London. She had been thinking of him the moment before, as unquestionably sixteen miles distant.—There was time only for the quickest arrangement of mind. She must be collected and calm. In half a minute they were together. The "How d'ye do's," were quiet and constrained on each side. She asked after their mutual friends; they were all well.—When had he left them?—Only that morning. He must have had a wet ride.—Yes.—He meant to walk with her, she found. "He had just looked into the dining-room, and as he was not wanted there, preferred being out of doors." She thought he neither looked nor spoke cheerfully; and the first possible cause for it, suggested by her fears, was, that he had perhaps been communicating his plans to his brother, and was pained by the manner in which they had been received.

They walked together. He was silent. She thought he was often looking at her, and trying for a fuller view of her face than it suited her to give. And this belief produced another dread. Perhaps he wanted to speak to her, of his attachment to Harriet; he might be watching for encouragement to begin.—She did not, could not, feel equal to lead the way to any such subject. He must do it all himself. Yet she could not bear this silence. With him it was most unnatural. She considered—resolved—and, trying to smile, began—

"You have some news to hear, now you are come back, that will rather surprise you."

"Have I?" said he quietly, and looking at her; "of what nature?"

"Oh! the best nature in the world—a wedding."

After waiting a moment, as if to be sure she intended to say no more, he replied,

"If you mean Miss Fairfax and Frank Churchill, I have heard that already."

"How is it possible?" cried Emma, turning her glowing cheeks towards him; for while she spoke, it occurred to her that he might have called at Mrs. Goddard's in his way.

"I had a few lines on parish business from Mr. Weston this morning, and at the end of them he gave me a brief account of what had happened."

Emma was quite relieved, and could presently say, with a little more composure,

"*You* probably have been less surprised than any of us, for you have had your suspicions.—I have not forgotten that you once tried to give me a caution.—I wish I had attended to it—but—(with a sinking voice and a heavy sigh)[1] I seem to have been doomed to blindness."

For a moment or two nothing was said, and she was unsuspicious of having excited any particular interest, till she found her arm drawn within his, and pressed against his heart, and heard him thus saying, in a tone of great sensibility, speaking low,

1 Austen is usually abstemious in providing explicit vocal pointings and descriptions for her dialogue scenes, so the pointings and stage-directions that punctuate this chapter work to alert the reader to the emotional freight behind and beyond the spoken words. See Janis P. Stout, "Jane Austen's Proposal Scenes and the Limitations of Language," *Studies in the Novel,* 144 (1982), pp. 316–326.

"Time, my dearest Emma, time will heal the wound.—Your own excellent sense—your exertion for your father's sake—I know you will not allow yourself—." Her arm was pressed again, as he added, in a more broken and subdued accent, "The feelings of the warmest friendship—Indignation—Abominable scoundrel!"—And in a louder, steadier tone, he concluded with, "He will soon be gone. They will soon be in Yorkshire. I am sorry for *her.* She deserves a better fate."

Emma understood him; and as soon as she could recover from the flutter of pleasure, excited by such tender consideration, replied,

"You are very kind—but you are mistaken—and I must set you right.—I am not in want of that sort of compassion. My blindness to what was going on, led me to act by them in a way that I must always be ashamed of, and I was very foolishly tempted to say and do many things which may well lay me open to unpleasant conjectures, but I have no other reason to regret that I was not in the secret earlier."

"Emma!" cried he, looking eagerly at her, "are you, indeed?"—but checking himself—"No, no, I understand you—forgive me—I am pleased that you can say even so much.—He is no object of regret, indeed! and it will not be very long, I hope, before that becomes the acknowledgment of more than your reason.—Fortunate that your affections were not farther entangled!—I could never, I confess, from your manners, assure myself as to the degree of what you felt—I could only be certain that there was a preference—and a preference which I never believed him to deserve.—He is a disgrace to the name of man.[2]—And is he to be rewarded with that sweet young woman?—Jane, Jane, you will be a miserable creature."

"Mr. Knightley," said Emma, trying to be lively, but really confused—"I am in a very extraordinary situation. I cannot let you continue in your error; and yet, perhaps, since my manners gave such an impression, I have as much reason to be ashamed of confessing that I never have been at all attached to the person we are speaking of, as it might be natural for a woman to feel in confessing exactly the reverse.—But I never have."

He listened in perfect silence. She wished him to speak, but he would not. She supposed she must say more before she were entitled

2 A common locution in late eighteenth-century periodical writing.

to his clemency; but it was a hard case to be obliged still to lower herself in his opinion. She went on, however.

"I have very little to say for my own conduct.—I was tempted by his attentions, and allowed myself to appear pleased.—An old story, probably—a common case—and no more than has happened to hundreds of my sex before; and yet it may not be the more excusable in one who sets up as I do for Understanding.[3] Many circumstances assisted the temptation. He was the son of Mr. Weston—he was continually here—I always found him very pleasant—and, in short, for (with a sigh) let me swell out the causes ever so ingeniously, they all centre in this at last—my vanity was flattered, and I allowed his attentions. Latterly, however—for some time, indeed—I have had no idea of their meaning any thing.—I thought them a habit, a trick, nothing that called for seriousness on my side. He has imposed on[4] me, but he has not injured me. I have never been attached to him. And now I can tolerably comprehend his behaviour. He never wished to attach me. It was merely a blind[5] to conceal his real situation with another.—It was his object to blind all about him; and no one, I am sure, could be more effectually blinded than myself—except that I was *not* blinded—that it was my good fortune—that, in short, I was somehow or other safe from him."

She had hoped for an answer here—for a few words to say that her conduct was at least intelligible; but he was silent; and, as far as she could judge, deep in thought. At last, and tolerably in his usual tone, he said,

"I have never had a high opinion of Frank Churchill.—I can suppose, however, that I may have under-rated him. My acquaintance with him has been but trifling.—And even if I have not under-rated him hitherto, he may yet turn out well.—With such a woman he has a chance.—I have no motive for wishing him ill—and for her sake, whose happiness will be involved in his good character and conduct, I shall certainly wish him well."

"I have no doubt of their being happy together," said Emma; "I believe them to be very mutually and very sincerely attached."

"He is a most fortunate man!" returned Mr. Knightley, with energy. "So early in life—at three and twenty—a period when, if a man

3 Compare and contrast Emma in vol. I, chap. 5.

4 Deceived.

5 Decoy.

6 Knightley's optimistic prognosis does not sit entirely at ease with the manifold hints of mortality with which Austen's narrative has been surrounding Jane Fairfax.

7 Another variation on Emma's habitual description of Frank Churchill's character.

chooses a wife, he generally chooses ill. At three and twenty to have drawn such a prize!—What years of felicity that man, in all human calculation, has before him![6]—Assured of the love of such a woman—the disinterested love, for Jane Fairfax's character vouches for her disinterestedness; every thing in his favour,—equality of situation—I mean, as far as regards society, and all the habits and manners that are important; equality in every point but one—and that one, since the purity of her heart is not to be doubted, such as must increase his felicity, for it will be his to bestow the only advantages she wants.—A man would always wish to give a woman a better home than the one he takes her from; and he who can do it, where there is no doubt of *her* regard, must, I think, be the happiest of mortals.—Frank Churchill is, indeed, the favourite of fortune.[7] Every thing turns out for his good.—He meets with a young woman at a watering-place, gains her affection, cannot even weary her by negligent treatment—and had he and all his family sought round the world for a perfect wife for him, they could not have found her superior.—His aunt is in the way.—His aunt dies.—He has only to speak.—His friends are eager to promote his happiness.—He has used everybody ill—and they are all delighted to forgive him.—He is a fortunate man indeed!"

"You speak as if you envied him."

"And I do envy him, Emma. In one respect he is the object of my envy."

Emma could say no more. They seemed to be within half a sentence of Harriet, and her immediate feeling was to avert the subject, if possible. She made her plan; she would speak of something totally different—the children in Brunswick Square; and she only waited for breath to begin, when Mr. Knightley startled her, by saying,

"You will not ask me what is the point of envy.—You are determined, I see, to have no curiosity.—You are wise—but *I* cannot be wise. Emma, I must tell what you will not ask, though I may wish it unsaid the next moment."

"Oh! then, don't speak it, don't speak it," she eagerly cried. "Take a little time, consider, do not commit yourself."

"Thank you," said he, in an accent of deep mortification, and not another syllable followed.

Emma could not bear to give him pain. He was wishing to confide in her—perhaps to consult her;—cost her what it would, she would listen. She might assist his resolution, or reconcile him to it; she might give just praise to Harriet, or, by representing to him his own independence, relieve him from that state of indecision, which must be more intolerable than any alternative to such a mind as his.—They had reached the house.

"You are going in, I suppose," said he.

"No,"—replied Emma—quite confirmed by the depressed manner in which he still spoke—"I should like to take another turn. Mr. Perry is not gone." And, after proceeding a few steps, she added—"I stopped you ungraciously, just now, Mr. Knightley, and, I am afraid, gave you pain.—But if you have any wish to speak openly to me as a friend, or to ask my opinion of any thing that you may have in contemplation—as a friend, indeed, you may command me.—I will hear whatever you like. I will tell you exactly what I think."

"As a friend!"—repeated Mr. Knightley.—"Emma, that I fear is a word—No, I have no wish—Stay, yes, why should I hesitate?—I have gone too far already for concealment.—Emma, I accept your offer—Extraordinary as it may seem, I accept it, and refer myself to you as a friend.—Tell me, then, have I no chance of ever succeeding?"

He stopped in his earnestness to look the question, and the expression of his eyes overpowered her.

"My dearest Emma," said he, "for dearest you will always be, whatever the event of this hour's conversation, my dearest, most beloved Emma—tell me at once. Say 'No,' if it is to be said."—She could really say nothing.—"You are silent," he cried, with great animation; "absolutely silent! at present I ask no more."

Emma was almost ready to sink under the agitation of this moment. The dread of being awakened from the happiest dream, was perhaps the most prominent feeling.

"I cannot make speeches, Emma:"—he soon resumed; and in a tone of such sincere, decided, intelligible tenderness as was tolerably convincing.—"If I loved you less, I might be able to talk about it more. But you know what I am.—You hear nothing but truth from me.—I have blamed you, and lectured you, and you have borne it as

8 This sequence is a precociously experimental depiction of the potential distance between "real time" and the temporality of interior psychological experience. Austen here looks not only back to Sterne's *Tristram Shandy,* but also forward to the narratives of writers such as Henry James, James Joyce, and Virginia Woolf.

no other woman in England would have borne it.—Bear with the truths I would tell you now, dearest Emma, as well as you have borne with them. The manner, perhaps, may have as little to recommend them. God knows, I have been a very indifferent lover.—But you understand me.—Yes, you see, you understand my feelings—and will return them if you can. At present, I ask only to hear, once to hear your voice."

While he spoke, Emma's mind was most busy, and, with all the wonderful velocity of thought,[8] had been able—and yet without losing a word—to catch and comprehend the exact truth of the whole; to see that Harriet's hopes had been entirely groundless, a mistake, a delusion, as complete a delusion as any of her own—that Harriet was nothing; that she was every thing herself; that what she had been saying relative to Harriet had been all taken as the language of her own feelings; and that her agitation, her doubts, her reluctance, her discouragement, had been all received as discouragement from herself.—And not only was there time for these convictions, with all their glow of attendant happiness; there was time also to rejoice that Harriet's secret had not escaped her, and to resolve that it need not and should not.—It was all the service she could now render her poor friend; for as to any of that heroism of sentiment which might have prompted her to entreat him to transfer his affection from herself to Harriet, as infinitely the most worthy of the two—or even the more simple sublimity of resolving to refuse him at once and for ever, without vouchsafing any motive, because he could not marry them both, Emma had it not. She felt for Harriet, with pain and with contrition; but no flight of generosity run mad, opposing all that could be probable or reasonable, entered her brain. She had led her friend astray, and it would be a reproach to her for ever; but her judgment was as strong as her feelings, and as strong as it had ever been before, in reprobating any such alliance for him, as most unequal and degrading. Her way was clear, though not quite smooth.—She spoke then, on being so entreated.—What did she say?—Just what she ought, of course. A lady always does.—She said enough to show there need not be despair—and to invite him to say more himself. He *had* despaired at one period; he had received such an injunction to caution and si-

EMMA,
A NOVEL.
BY
JANE AUSTEN.

Tell me, then, have I no chance of succeeding?

LONDON:
RICHARD BENTLEY,
(SUCCESSOR TO H. COLBURN.)
CUMMING, DUBLIN.—BELL & BRADFUTE, EDINBURGH.
GALIGNANI, PARIS.
1833.

"Say 'No' if it is to be said." She could really say nothing

Two different illustrations of the proposal: from the 1833 edition (London: Richard Bentley), and from the 1898 edition (London: George Allen).

lence, as for the time crushed every hope;—she had begun by refusing to hear him.—The change had perhaps been somewhat sudden;—her proposal of taking another turn, her renewing the conversation which she had just put an end to, might be a little extraordinary!—She felt its inconsistency; but Mr. Knightley was so obliging as to put up with it, and seek no farther explanation.

Seldom, very seldom, does complete truth belong to any human disclosure; seldom can it happen that something is not a little disguised, or a little mistaken;[9] but where, as in this case, though the conduct is mistaken, the feelings are not, it may not be very material.—Mr. Knightley could not impute to Emma a more relenting heart than she possessed, or a heart more disposed to accept of his.

He had, in fact, been wholly unsuspicious of his own influence. He had followed her into the shrubbery with no idea of trying it. He had come, in his anxiety to see how she bore Frank Churchill's engagement, with no selfish view, no view at all, but of endeavouring, if she allowed him an opening, to soothe or to counsel her.—The rest had been the work of the moment, the immediate effect of what he heard, on his feelings. The delightful assurance of her total indifference towards Frank Churchill, of her having a heart completely disengaged from him, had given birth to the hope, that, in time, he might gain her affection himself;—but it had been no present hope—he had only, in the momentary conquest of eagerness over judgment, aspired to be told that she did not forbid his attempt to attach her.—The superior hopes which gradually opened were so much the more enchanting.—The affection, which he had been asking to be allowed to create if he could, was already his!—Within half an hour, he had passed from a thoroughly distressed state of mind, to something so like perfect happiness,[10] that it could bear no other name.

Her change was equal.—This one half hour had given to each the same precious certainty of being beloved, had cleared from each the same degree of ignorance, jealousy, or distrust.—On his side, there had been a long-standing jealousy, old as the arrival, or even the expectation, of Frank Churchill.—He had been in love with Emma, and jealous of Frank Churchill, from about the same period, one sentiment having probably enlightened him as to the other. It was his

9 This line of moral and epistemological skepticism once again echoes the thought and style of Samuel Johnson. Compare Johnson's remarks on human reasoning in his Preface to *The Plays of William Shakespeare* (1765): "because human judgment, though it be gradually gaining upon certainty, never becomes infallible; and approbation, though long continued, may yet be only the approbation of prejudice or fashion; it is proper to inquire, by what peculiarities of excellence Shakespeare has gained and kept the favour of his countrymen" (*The Works of Samuel Johnson,* vol. VII, ed. Arthur Sherbo [New Haven: Yale University Press, 1968], p. 61). See also George Butte, "Shame or Espousal? *Emma* and the New Intersubjectivity of Anxiety in Austen," in Juliet McMaster and Bruce Stovel, eds., *Jane Austen's Business: Her World and Her Profession* (Basingstoke: Macmillan, 1996), pp. 54–65.

10 This phrase both echoes vol. II, chap. 9, and anticipates the final words of the novel.

jealousy of Frank Churchill that had taken him from the country.—The Box-Hill party had decided him on going away. He would save himself from witnessing again such permitted, encouraged attentions.—He had gone to learn to be indifferent.—But he had gone to a wrong place. There was too much domestic happiness in his brother's house; woman wore too amiable a form in it; Isabella was too much like Emma—differing only in those striking inferiorities, which always brought the other in brilliancy before him, for much to have been done, even had his time been longer.—He had staid on, however, vigorously, day after day—till this very morning's post had conveyed the history of Jane Fairfax.—Then, with the gladness which must be felt, nay, which he did not scruple to feel, having never believed Frank Churchill to be at all deserving Emma, was there so much fond solicitude, so much keen anxiety for her, that he could stay no longer. He had ridden home through the rain; and had walked up directly after dinner, to see how this sweetest and best of all creatures, faultless in spite of all her faults, bore the discovery.

He had found her agitated and low.—Frank Churchill was a villain.—He heard her declare that she had never loved him. Frank Churchill's character was not desperate.—She was his own Emma, by hand and word, when they returned into the house; and if he could have thought of Frank Churchill then, he might have deemed him a very good sort of fellow.

14

What totally different feelings did Emma take back into the house from what she had brought out!—she had then been only daring to hope for a little respite of suffering;—she was now in an exquisite flutter of happiness,[1] and such happiness moreover as she believed must still be greater when the flutter should have passed away.

They sat down to tea—the same party round the same table—how often it had been collected!—and how often had her eyes fallen on the same shrubs in the lawn, and observed the same beautiful effect of the western sun!—But never in such a state of spirits, never in anything like it; and it was with difficulty that she could summon enough of her usual self to be the attentive lady of the house, or even the attentive daughter.

Poor Mr. Woodhouse little suspected what was plotting against him in the breast of that man whom he was so cordially welcoming, and so anxiously hoping might not have taken cold from his ride.—Could he have seen the heart,[2] he would have cared very little for the lungs; but without the most distant imagination of the impending evil, without the slightest perception of anything extraordinary in the looks or ways of either, he repeated to them very comfortably all the articles of news he had received from Mr. Perry, and talked on with much self-contentment, totally unsuspicious of what they could have told him in return.

As long as Mr. Knightley remained with them, Emma's fever continued; but when he was gone, she began to be a little tranquillized

1 "Flutter" is a favorite word of Austen's to denote a state of emotional agitation or disturbance. For example, Elizabeth Bennet's "spirits were in a high flutter" on approaching Pemberley in vol III, chap. 1, of *Pride and Prejudice;* likewise, Maria Bertram's "spirits were in as happy a flutter as vanity and pride could furnish" as she arrived at Sotherton in vol. I, chap. 8, of *Mansfield Park*. Austen may have inherited "flutter" from the sentimental vocabulary of Samuel Richardson (1689–1761): Clarissa Harlowe, for example, often employs the term to describe her feelings; see *Clarissa, or, the History of a Young Lady* (1748).

2 See note 12 to vol. III, chap. 9.

and subdued—and in the course of the sleepless night, which was the tax for such an evening, she found one or two such very serious points to consider, as made her feel, that even her happiness must have some alloy. Her father—and Harriet. She could not be alone without feeling the full weight of their separate claims; and how to guard the comfort of both to the utmost, was the question. With respect to her father, it was a question soon answered. She hardly knew yet what Mr. Knightley would ask; but a very short parley[3] with her own heart produced the most solemn resolution of never quitting her father.—She even wept over the idea of it, as a sin of thought. While he lived, it must be only an engagement; but she flattered herself, that if divested of the danger of drawing her away, it might become an increase of comfort to him.—How to do her best by Harriet, was of more difficult decision;—how to spare her from any unnecessary pain; how to make her any possible atonement; how to appear least her enemy?—On these subjects, her perplexity and distress were very great—and her mind had to pass again and again through every bitter reproach and sorrowful regret that had ever surrounded it.—She could only resolve at last, that she would still avoid a meeting with her, and communicate all that need be told by letter; that it would be inexpressibly desirable to have her removed just now for a time from Highbury, and—indulging in one scheme more—nearly resolve, that it might be practicable to get an invitation for her to Brunswick Square.—Isabella had been pleased with Harriet; and a few weeks spent in London must give her some amusement.—She did not think it in Harriet's nature to escape being benefited by novelty and variety, by the streets, the shops, and the children.—At any rate, it would be a proof of attention and kindness in herself, from whom every thing was due; a separation for the present; an averting of the evil day, when they must all be together again.

She rose early, and wrote her letter to Harriet; an employment which left her so very serious, so nearly sad, that Mr. Knightley, in walking up to Hartfield to breakfast, did not arrive at all too soon; and half an hour stolen afterwards to go over the same ground again with him, literally and figuratively, was quite necessary to reinstate her in a proper share of the happiness of the evening before.

3 Conversation.

Joseph Highmore, "Mr B. Finds Pamela Writing" (1743–1744). This image of a scene from Samuel Richardson's novel *Pamela; Or, Virtue Rewarded* (1740) registers the drama that the original novel derives from the immediate moment of letter-writing.

He had not left her long, by no means long enough for her to have the slightest inclination for thinking of anybody else, when a letter was brought her from Randall's—a very thick letter;—she guessed what it must contain, and deprecated the necessity of reading it.—She was now in perfect charity with Frank Churchill; she wanted no explanations, she wanted only to have her thoughts to herself—and as for understanding any thing he wrote, she was sure she was incapable of it.—It must be waded through, however. She opened the packet; it was too surely so;—a note from Mrs. Weston to herself, ushered in the letter from Frank to Mrs. Weston.

> "I have the greatest pleasure, my dear Emma, in forwarding to you the enclosed. I know what thorough justice you

will do it, and have scarcely a doubt of its happy effect.—I think we shall never materially disagree about the writer again; but I will not delay you by a long preface.—We are quite well.—This letter has been the cure of all the little nervousness I have been feeling lately.—I did not quite like your looks on Tuesday, but it was an ungenial morning; and though you will never own being affected by weather,[4] I think every body feels a north-east wind.—I felt for your dear father very much in the storm of Tuesday afternoon and yesterday morning, but had the comfort of hearing last night, by Mr. Perry, that it had not made him ill.

"Your's ever,

"A. W."

[To Mrs. Weston.]

My Dear Madam, Windsor—July.

"IF I made myself intelligible yesterday, this letter will be expected; but expected or not, I know it will be read with candour[5] and indulgence.—You are all goodness, and I believe there will be need of even all your goodness to allow for some parts of my past conduct.—But I have been forgiven by one who had still more to resent. My courage rises while I write.[6] It is very difficult for the prosperous to be humble. I have already met with such success in two applications for pardon, that I may be in danger of thinking myself too sure of your's, and of those among your friends who have had any ground of offence.—You must all endeavour to comprehend the exact nature of my situation when I first arrived at Randall's; you must consider me as having a secret which was to be kept at all hazards.[7] This was the fact. My right to place myself in a situation requiring such concealment, is another question. I shall not discuss it here. For my temptation to *think* it a right, I refer every caviller[8] to a brick house, sashed windows below, and casements above, in Highbury. I dared not address her openly; my difficulties in the then state of

4 Emma therefore has more in common with Samuel Johnson than with her father on this point; see note 5 to vol. III, chap. 12.

5 Fair-mindedness.

6 Emphasizing the real-time circumstances of the writing became a staple of eighteenth-century familiar correspondence; it also became a staple technique in epistolary fiction that imitated such letter writing, most notably in the novels of Samuel Richardson, who described it as "the new Manner of Writing—to the Moment" in a letter of October 9, 1756 (*Selected Letters of Samuel Richardson,* ed. John Carroll [Oxford: Clarendon Press, 1964], p. 329). The technique became so identified with Richardson's brand of sentimental immediacy that Fielding could parody the trope ruthlessly in letter VI of *Shamela* (1741): "Mrs Jervis and I are just in bed, and the door unlocked; if my master should come—Odsbobs! I hear him just coming in at the door. You see I write in the present tense, as Parson Williams says." In her letter to Cassandra of September 15, 1813, Austen also plays off the conventions of "writing to the moment": "Edward finds his quarters very snug & quiet.—I must get a softer pen.—This is harder. I am in agonies" (*Letters,* p. 218).

7 At all costs.

8 One who makes frivolous objections.

Enscombe must be too well known to require definition; and I was fortunate enough to prevail, before we parted at Weymouth, and to induce the most upright female mind in the creation to stoop in charity to a secret engagement.—Had she refused, I should have gone mad.—But you will be ready to say, what was your hope in doing this?—What did you look forward to?—To any thing, every thing—to time, chance, circumstance, slow effects, sudden bursts, perseverance and weariness, health and sickness.[9] Every possibility of good was before me, and the first of blessings secured, in obtaining her promises of faith and correspondence. If you need farther explanation, I have the honour, my dear madam, of being your husband's son, and the advantage of inheriting a disposition to hope for good,[10] which no inheritance of houses or lands can ever equal the value of.—See me, then, under these circumstances, arriving on my first visit to Randall's;—and here I am conscious of wrong, for that visit might have been sooner paid. You will look back and see that I did not come till Miss Fairfax was in Highbury; and as *you* were the person slighted, you will forgive me instantly; but I must work on my father's compassion, by reminding him, that so long as I absented myself from his house, so long I lost the blessing of knowing you. My behaviour, during the very happy fortnight which I spent with you, did not, I hope, lay me open to reprehension, excepting on one point. And now I come to the principal, the only important part of my conduct while belonging to you, which excites my own anxiety, or requires very solicitous explanation. With the greatest respect, and the warmest friendship, do I mention Miss Woodhouse; my father perhaps will think I ought to add, with the deepest humiliation.—A few words which dropped from him yesterday spoke his opinion, and some censure I acknowledge myself liable to.—My behaviour to Miss Woodhouse indicated, I believe, more than it ought.—In order to assist a concealment so essential to me, I was led on to make more than an allowable use of the sort of intimacy into which we were im-

9 Possibly a glancing echo of the Common Prayer marriage service: "for better for worse, for richer for poorer, in sickness and in health."

10 See vol. III, chap. 7, for more suggestions of Mr. Weston and Frank Churchill as descendants of the eighteenth-century culture of gentlemanly benevolence.

mediately thrown.—I cannot deny that Miss Woodhouse was my ostensible object—but I am sure you will believe the declaration, that had I not been convinced of her indifference, I would not have been induced by any selfish views to go on.—Amiable and delightful as Miss Woodhouse is, she never gave me the idea of a young woman likely to be attached; and that she was perfectly free from any tendency to being attached to me, was as much my conviction as my wish.—She received my attentions with an easy, friendly, goodhumoured playfulness, which exactly suited me. We seemed to understand each other. From our relative situation, those attentions were her due, and were felt to be so.—Whether Miss Woodhouse began really to understand me before the expiration of that fortnight, I cannot say;—when I called to take leave of her, I remember that I was within a moment of confessing the truth, and I then fancied she was not without suspicion; but I have no doubt of her having since detected me, at least in some degree.—She may not have surmised the whole, but her quickness must have penetrated a part. I cannot doubt it.[11] You will find, whenever the subject becomes freed from its present restraints, that it did not take her wholly by surprise. She frequently gave me hints of it. I remember her telling me at the ball, that I owed Mrs. Elton gratitude for her attentions to Miss Fairfax.—I hope this history of my conduct towards her will be admitted by you and my father as great extenuation of what you saw amiss. While you considered me as having sinned against Emma Woodhouse, I could deserve nothing from either. Acquit me here, and procure for me, when it is allowable, the acquittal and good wishes of that said Emma Woodhouse, whom I regard with so much brotherly affection, as to long to have her as deeply and as happily in love as myself.—Whatever strange things I said or did during that fortnight, you have now a key to. My heart was in Highbury, and my business was to get my body thither as often as might be, and with the least suspicion. If you remember any queernesses,[12]

11 Frank Churchill is overestimating Emma's detective capabilities.

12 Peculiar pieces of behavior.

set them all to the right account.—Of the pianoforté so much talked of, I feel it only necessary to say, that its being ordered was absolutely unknown to Miss F—, who would never have allowed me to send it, had any choice been given her.—The delicacy of her mind throughout the whole engagement, my dear madam, is much beyond my power of doing justice to. You will soon, I earnestly hope, know her thoroughly yourself.—No description can describe her. She must tell you herself what she is—yet not by word, for never was there a human creature who would so designedly suppress her own merit.—Since I began this letter, which will be longer than I foresaw, I have heard from her.[13]—She gives a good account of her own health; but as she never complains, I dare not depend. I want to have your opinion of her looks. I know you will soon call on her; she is living in dread of the visit. Perhaps it is paid already. Let me hear from you without delay; I am impatient for a thousand particulars. Remember how few minutes I was at Randall's, and in how bewildered, how mad a state: and I am not much better yet; still insane either from happiness or misery. When I think of the kindness and favour I have met with, of her excellence and patience, and my uncle's generosity, I am mad with joy: but when I recollect all the uneasiness I occasioned her, and how little I deserve to be forgiven, I am mad with anger. If I could but see her again!—But I must not propose it yet. My uncle has been too good for me to encroach.—I must still add to this long letter. You have not heard all that you ought to hear. I could not give any connected detail yesterday; but the suddenness, and, in one light, the unseasonableness, with which the affair burst out, needs explanation; for though the event of the 26th ult.,[14] as you will conclude, immediately opened to me the happiest prospects, I should not have presumed on such early measures, but from the very particular circumstances, which left me not an hour to lose. I should myself have shrunk from any thing so hasty, and she would have felt every scruple of mine with multiplied strength and re-

13 Another acknowledged trope of epistolary "writing to the moment." Compare Austen's letter to Cassandra of November 1, 1800: "Your letter is come; it came indeed twelve lines ago, but I could not stop to acknowledge it before, & I am glad it did not arrive till I had composed my first sentence, because the sentence had been made ever since yesterday, & I think forms a very good beginning" (*Letters,* p. 52). For further discussion on the vocabulary of emotional immediacy in eighteenth-century epistolary writing, see Bruce Redford, *The Converse of the Pen: Acts of Intimacy in the Familiar Letter* (Chicago: University of Chicago Press, 1986), and Janet Gurkin Altman, *Epistolarity: Approaches to a Form* (Columbus: Ohio State University Press, 1982).

14 The twenty-sixth of last month, an abbreviation of the Latin *ultimo mense.* In epistolary convention, "ult." denotes the previous month, "inst." (short for "instant" or *instante mense*), the present month.

finement.—But I had no choice. The hasty engagement she had entered into with that woman—— Here, my dear madam, I was obliged to leave off abruptly, to recollect and compose myself.—I have been walking over the country, and am now, I hope, rational enough to make the rest of my letter what it ought to be.[15]—It is, in fact, a most mortifying retrospect for me. I behaved shamefully. And here I can admit, that my manners to Miss W., in being unpleasant to Miss F., were highly blamable. *She* disapproved them, which ought to have been enough.—My plea of concealing the truth she did not think sufficient.—She was displeased; I thought unreasonably so: I thought her, on a thousand occasions, unnecessarily scrupulous and cautious: I thought her even cold. But she was always right. If I had followed her judgment, and subdued my spirits to the level of what she deemed proper, I should have escaped the greatest unhappiness I have ever known.—We quarreled.—Do you remember the morning spent at Donwell?—*There* every little dissatisfaction that had occurred before came to a crisis. I was late; I met her walking home by herself, and wanted to walk with her, but she would not suffer it. She absolutely refused to allow me, which I then thought most unreasonable. Now, however, I see nothing in it but a very natural and consistent degree of discretion. While I, to blind the world to our engagement, was behaving one hour with objectionable particularity to another woman, was she to be consenting the next to a proposal which might have made every previous caution useless?—Had we been met walking together between Donwell and Highbury, the truth must have been suspected.—I was mad enough, however, to resent.—I doubted her affection. I doubted it more the next day on Box-Hill; when, provoked by such conduct on my side, such shameful, insolent neglect of her, and such apparent devotion to Miss W., as it would have been impossible for any woman of sense to endure, she spoke her resentment in a form of words perfectly intelligible to me.—In short, my dear madam, it was a quarrel blameless on her side,

15 Compare Austen's letter of September 15, 1813: "I am going to write nothing but short Sentences. There shall be two full stops in every Line. Layton and Shear's *is* Bedford House. We mean to get there before breakfast if it's possible . . . Let me be rational & return to my two full stops" (*Letters*, p. 218).

16 "Importunely forward" (Johnson).

abominable on mine; and I returned the same evening to Richmond, though I might have staid with you till the next morning, merely because I would be as angry with her as possible. Even then, I was not such a fool as not to mean to be reconciled in time; but I was the injured person, injured by her coldness, and I went away determined that she should make the first advances.—I shall always congratulate myself that you were not of the Box-Hill party. Had you witnessed my behaviour there, I can hardly suppose you would ever have thought well of me again. Its effect upon her appears in the immediate resolution it produced: as soon as she found I was really gone from Randall's, she closed with the offer of that officious[16] Mrs. Elton; the whole system of whose treatment of her, by the bye, has ever filled me with indignation and hatred. I must not quarrel with a spirit of forbearance which has been so richly extended towards myself; but, otherwise, I should loudly protest against the share of it which that woman has known.—"Jane," indeed!—You will observe that I have not yet indulged myself in calling her by that name, even to you. Think, then, what I must have endured in hearing it bandied between the Eltons with all the vulgarity of needless repetition, and all the insolence of imaginary superiority. Have patience with me, I shall soon have done.—She closed with this offer, resolving to break with me entirely, and wrote the next day to tell me that we never were to meet again.—*She felt the engagement to be a source of repentance and misery to each: she dissolved it.*—This letter reached me on the very morning of my poor aunt's death. I answered it within an hour; but from the confusion of my mind, and the multiplicity of business falling on me at once, my answer, instead of being sent with all the many other letters of that day, was locked up in my writing-desk; and I, trusting that I had written enough, though but a few lines, to satisfy her, remained without any uneasiness.—I was rather disappointed that I did not hear from her again speedily; but I made excuses for her, and was too busy, and—may I add?—too cheerful in my views to be captious.—We removed to Windsor; and two days afterwards I received a parcel from her, my own letters all returned!—and a few lines at the same time by the post, stating her extreme surprise at not having had the smallest reply to her last; and adding, that as silence on such a point could not be misconstrued, and as it must be equally desirable to both to have every subordinate arrangement concluded as soon as possible, she now sent me, by a safe conveyance, all my letters, and requested, that if I could not directly command her's, so as to send them to Highbury within a week, I would forward them after that period to her at——: in short, the full direction to Mr. Smallridge's, near Bristol, stared me in the face. I knew the name, the place, I knew all about it, and instantly saw what she had been doing. It was perfectly accordant with that resolution of character which I knew her to possess; and the secrecy she had maintained, as to any such design in her former letter, was equally descriptive of its anxious delicacy. For the world would not she have seemed to threaten me.—Imagine the shock; imagine how, till I had actually detected my own blunder, I raved at the blunders of the post.[17]—What was to be done?—One thing only.—I must speak to my uncle. Without his sanction I could not hope to be listened to again.—I spoke; circumstances were in my favour; the late event had softened away his pride, and he was, earlier than I could have anticipated, wholly reconciled and complying; and could say at last, poor man! with a deep sigh, that he wished I might find as much happiness in the marriage state as he had done.—I felt that it would be of a different sort.—Are you disposed to pity me for what I must have suffered in opening the cause to him, for my suspense while all was at stake?—No; do not pity me till I reached Highbury, and saw how ill I had made her. Do not pity me till I saw her wan, sick looks.—I reached Highbury at the time of day when, from my knowledge of their late breakfast hour, I was certain of a good chance of finding her alone.—I was not disappointed; and at last I was not dis-

17 A particularly pointed narrative irony at Frank Churchill's expense, since it was Jane Fairfax's use of the post to inform him about the Perrys' carriage that occasioned the "blunder" in the letter-game in vol. III, chap. 5.

appointed either in the object of my journey. A great deal of very reasonable, very just displeasure I had to persuade away. But it is done; we are reconciled, dearer, much dearer, than ever, and no moment's uneasiness can ever occur between us again. Now, my dear madam, I will release you; but I could not conclude before. A thousand and a thousand thanks for all the kindness you have ever shown me, and ten thousand for the attentions your heart will dictate towards her.—If you think me in a way to be happier than I deserve,[18] I am quite of your opinion.—Miss W. calls me the child of good fortune.[19] I hope she is right.—In one respect, my good fortune is undoubted, that of being able to subscribe myself,

Your obliged and affectionate Son,

F. C. Weston Churchill.

18 Compare Captain Wentworth's words after his reconciliation with Anne Elliot, at the end of vol. II, chap. 11, of *Persuasion:* "'Like other great men under reverses,' he added with a smile, 'I must endeavour to subdue my mind to my fortune. I must learn to brook being happier than I deserve.'"

19 See note 17 to vol. II, chap. 6.

15

THIS LETTER MUST MAKE its way to Emma's feelings. She was obliged, in spite of her previous determination to the contrary, to do it all the justice that Mrs. Weston foretold. As soon as she came to her own name, it was irresistible; every line relating to herself was interesting, and almost every line agreeable; and when this charm ceased, the subject could still maintain itself, by the natural return of her former regard for the writer, and the very strong attraction which any picture of love must have for her at that moment. She never stopt till she had gone through the whole; and though it was impossible not to feel that he had been wrong, yet he had been less wrong than she had supposed—and he had suffered, and was very sorry—and he was so grateful to Mrs. Weston, and so much in love with Miss Fairfax, and she was so happy herself, that there was no being severe; and could he have entered the room, she must have shaken hands with him as heartily as ever.

She thought so well of the letter, that when Mr. Knightley came again, she desired him to read it. She was sure of Mrs. Weston's wishing it to be communicated; especially to one, who, like Mr. Knightley, had seen so much to blame in his conduct.

"I shall be very glad to look it over," said he, "but it seems long. I will take it home with me at night."

But that would not do. Mr. Weston was to call in the evening, and she must return it by him.

"I would rather be talking to you," he replied; "but as it seems a matter of justice, it shall be done."

Portrait engraving of Anthony Ashley Cooper, third earl of Shaftesbury (1671–1713), by Simon Gribelin after John Closterman, 1723.

He began—stopping, however, almost directly to say "Had I been offered the sight of one of this gentleman's letters to his mother-in-law a few months ago, Emma, it would not have been taken with such indifference."

He proceeded a little farther, reading to himself; and then, with a smile, observed, "Humph!—a fine complimentary opening:—But it is his way. One man's style must not be the rule of another's. We will not be severe."

"It will be natural for me," he added shortly afterwards, "to speak my opinion aloud as I read. By doing it, I shall feel that I am near you. It will not be so great a loss of time: but if you dislike it——"

"Not at all. I should wish it."

Mr. Knightley returned to his reading with greater alacrity.

"He trifles here," said he, "as to the temptation. He knows he is wrong, and has nothing rational to urge.—Bad.—He ought not to have formed the engagement.—'His father's disposition:'—he is unjust, however, to his father. Mr. Weston's sanguine temper was a blessing on all his upright and honourable exertions; but Mr. Weston earned every present comfort before he endeavoured to gain it.—Very true; he did not come till Miss Fairfax was here."

"And I have not forgotten," said Emma, "how sure you were that he might have come sooner if he would. You pass it over very handsomely—but you were perfectly right."

"I was not quite impartial in my judgment, Emma:—but yet, I think—had *you* not been in the case—I should still have distrusted him."

When he came to Miss Woodhouse, he was obliged to read the whole of it aloud—all that related to her, with a smile; a look; a shake of the head; a word or two of assent, or disapprobation; or merely of love, as the subject required; concluding, however, seriously, and, after steady reflection, thus—

"Very bad—though it might have been worse.—Playing a most dangerous game. Too much indebted to the event for his acquittal.—No judge of his own manners by you.—Always deceived in fact by his own wishes, and regardless of little besides his own convenience.—

Fancying you to have fathomed his secret. Natural enough!—his own mind full of intrigue, that he should suspect it in others.—Mystery; Finesse[1]—how they pervert the understanding! My Emma, does not every thing serve to prove more and more the beauty of truth and sincerity[2] in all our dealings with each other?"

Emma agreed to it, and with a blush of sensibility on Harriet's account, which she could not give any sincere explanation of.

"You had better go on," said she.

He did so, but very soon stopt again to say, "the piano-forté! Ah! That was the act of a very, very young man, one too young to consider whether the inconvenience of it might not very much exceed the pleasure. A boyish scheme, indeed!—I cannot comprehend a man's wishing to give a woman any proof of affection which he knows she would rather dispense with; and he did know that she would have prevented the instrument's coming if she could."

After this, he made some progress without any pause. Frank Churchill's confession of having behaved shamefully was the first thing to call for more than a word in passing.

"I perfectly agree with you, sir,"—was then his remark. "You did behave very shamefully. You never wrote a truer line." And having gone through what immediately followed of the basis of their disagreement, and his persisting to act in direct opposition to Jane Fairfax's sense of right, he made a fuller pause to say, "This is very bad.—He had induced her to place herself, for his sake, in a situation of extreme difficulty and uneasiness, and it should have been his first object to prevent her from suffering unnecessarily.—She must have had much more to contend with, in carrying on the correspondence, than he could. He should have respected even unreasonable scruples, had there been such; but her's were all reasonable. We must look to her one fault, and remember that she had done a wrong thing in consenting to the engagement, to bear that she should have been in such a state of punishment."

Emma knew that he was now getting to the Box-Hill party, and grew uncomfortable. Her own behaviour had been so very improper! She was deeply ashamed, and a little afraid of his next look. It was all

1 Cunning.

2 The philosopher Gilbert Ryle famously, and controversially, paralleled Austen's moral and aesthetic vocabulary with that of Shaftesbury in his 1966 essay "Jane Austen and the Moralists" (reprinted in B. C. Southam, ed., *Critical Essays on Jane Austen* [London: Routledge & Kegan Paul, 1968], pp. 106–122). "Jane Austen's moral system," Ryle suggests, "was a secular, Aristotelian ethic-cum-aesthetic. But to say all this is to say that her moral *Weltanschauung* was akin to that of Lord Shaftesbury . . . So I now put forward the historical hypothesis that Jane Austen's specific moral ideas derived, directly or indirectly, knowingly or unknowingly, from Shaftesbury" (p. 118). Whether or not one accepts such a direct or uncomplicated line of philosophical influence, it is true that Knightley's words bear comparison with a notable phrase from Shaftesbury's *Sensus Communis, and Essay on the Freedom of Wit and Humour in a Letter to a Friend* [1709]: "And thus, after all, the most natural beauty in the world is honesty and moral truth. For all beauty is truth" (*Characteristics of Men, Manners, Opinions, Times,* ed. L. E. Klein [Cambridge: Cambridge University Press, 1999], p. 65). Another, even more famous echo of Shaftesbury's words occurs at the end of Keats's "Ode on a Grecian Urn" [1820]:

> Thou shalt remain, in midst of other woe
> Than ours, a friend to man, to whom thou say'st,
> "Beauty is truth, truth beauty,"—that is all
> Ye know on earth, and all ye need to know.

See Harry M. Solomon, "Shaftesbury's *Characteristics* and the Conclusion to 'Ode on a Grecian Urn,'" *Keats-Shelley Journal,* 24 (1975), pp. 89–101.

read, however, steadily, attentively, and without the smallest remark; and, excepting one momentary glance at her, instantly withdrawn, in the fear of giving pain—no remembrance of Box-Hill seemed to exist.

"There is no saying much for the delicacy of our good friends, the Eltons," was his next observation.—"His feelings are natural.—What! actually resolve to break with him entirely!—She felt the engagement to be a source of repentance and misery to each—she dissolved it.—What a view this gives of her sense of his behaviour! —Well, he must be a most extraordinary——"

"Nay, nay, read on.—You will find how very much he suffers."

"I hope he does," replied Mr. Knightley coolly, and resuming the letter.—"'Smallridge!'—What does this mean? What is all this?"

"She had engaged to go as governess to Mrs. Smallridge's children—a dear friend of Mrs. Elton's—a neighbour of Maple Grove; and, by the bye, I wonder how Mrs. Elton bears the disappointment."

"Say nothing, my dear Emma, while you oblige me to read—not even of Mrs. Elton. Only one page more. I shall soon have done. What a letter the man writes!"

"I wish you would read it with a kinder spirit towards him."

"Well, there *is* feeling here.—He does seem to have suffered in finding her ill.—Certainly, I can have no doubt of his being fond of her. 'Dearer, much dearer than ever.' I hope he may long continue to feel all the value of such a reconciliation.—He is a very liberal thanker, with his thousands and tens of thousands.—'Happier than I deserve.' Come, he knows himself there. 'Miss Woodhouse calls me the child of good fortune.'—Those were Miss Woodhouse's words, were they?—And a fine ending—and there is the letter. The child of good fortune! That was your name for him, was it?"

"You do not appear so well satisfied with his letter as I am; but still you must, at least I hope you must, think the better of him for it. I hope it does him some service with you."

"Yes, certainly it does. He has had great faults, faults of inconsideration and thoughtlessness; and I am very much of his opinion in thinking him likely to be happier than he deserves: but still as he is, beyond a doubt, really attached to Miss Fairfax, and will soon, it may be hoped, have the advantage of being constantly with her, I am very ready to believe his character will improve, and acquire from her's the steadiness and delicacy of principle that it wants. And now, let me talk to you of something else. I have another person's interest at present so much at heart, that I cannot think any longer about Frank Churchill. Ever since I left you this morning, Emma, my mind has been hard at work on one subject."

The subject followed; it was in plain, unaffected, gentleman-like English, such as Mr. Knightley used even to the woman he was in love with, how to be able to ask her to marry him, without attacking the happiness of her father. Emma's answer was ready at the first word. "While her dear father lived, any change of condition must be impossible for her. She could never quit him." Part only of this answer, however, was admitted. The impossibility of her quitting her father, Mr. Knightley felt as strongly as herself; but the inadmissibility of any other change, he could not agree to. He had been thinking it over most deeply, most intently; he had at first hoped to induce Mr. Woodhouse to remove with her to Donwell; he had wanted to believe it feasible, but his knowledge of Mr. Woodhouse would not suffer him to deceive himself long; and now he confessed his persuasion, that such a transplantation[3] would be a risk of her father's comfort, perhaps even of his life, which must not be hazarded. Mr. Woodhouse taken from Hartfield!—No, he felt that it ought not to be attempted. But the plan which had arisen on the sacrifice of this, he trusted his dearest Emma would not find in any respect objectionable; it was, that he should be received at Hartfield; that so long as her father's happiness—in other words his life—required Hartfield to continue her home, it should be his likewise.

Of their all removing to Donwell, Emma had already had her own passing thoughts. Like him, she had tried the scheme and rejected it; but such an alternative as this had not occurred to her. She was sensible of all the affection it evinced. She felt that in quitting Donwell, he must be sacrificing a great deal of independence of hours and hab-

3 Austen's apt choice of metaphor emphasizes the ways in which Mr. Woodhouse himself is like a "delicate plant."

its; that in living constantly with her father, and in no house of his own, there would be much, very much, to be borne with. She promised to think of it, and advised him to think of it more; but he was fully convinced, that no reflection could alter his wishes or his opinion on the subject. He had given it, he could assure her, very long and calm consideration; he had been walking away from William Larkins the whole morning, to have his thoughts to himself.

"Ah! there is one difficulty unprovided for," cried Emma. "I am sure William Larkins will not like it. You must get his consent before you ask mine."

She promised, however, to think of it; and pretty nearly promised, moreover, to think of it, with the intention of finding it a very good scheme.

It is remarkable, that Emma, in the many, very many, points of view in which she was now beginning to consider Donwell Abbey, was never struck with any sense of injury to her nephew Henry, whose rights as heir expectant had formerly been so tenaciously regarded. Think she must of the possible difference to the poor little boy; and yet she only gave herself a saucy[4] conscious smile about it, and found amusement in detecting the real cause of that violent dislike of Mr. Knightley's marrying Jane Fairfax, or any body else, which at the time she had wholly imputed to the amiable solicitude of the sister and the aunt.

This proposal of his, this plan of marrying and continuing at Hartfield—the more she contemplated it, the more pleasing it became. His evils seemed to lessen, her own advantages to increase, their mutual good to outweigh every drawback. Such a companion for herself in the periods of anxiety and cheerlessness before her!—Such a partner in all those duties and cares to which time must be giving increase of melancholy!

She would have been too happy but for poor Harriet; but every blessing of her own seemed to involve and advance the sufferings of her friend, who must now be even excluded from Hartfield. The delightful family-party which Emma was securing for herself, poor Harriet must, in mere charitable caution, be kept at a distance from. She would be a loser in every way. Emma could not deplore her future

4 Johnson offers only the pejorative definition "pert; petulant; contemptuous of superiors; insolent; impudent; impertinent"; however, by the end of the century, the word's senses had expanded, and partially softened, to encompass something much closer to "cheeky," as witnessed by Edward Ferrars's chaffing of Marianne Dashwood in vol. I, chap. 17, of *Sense and Sensibility:*

> "What magnificent orders would travel from this family to London," said Edward, "in such an event! What a happy day for booksellers, music-sellers, and print-shops! You, Miss Dashwood, would give a general commission for every new print of merit to be sent you—and as for Marianne, I know her greatness of soul, there would not be music enough in London to content her. And books!—Thomson, Cowper, Scott—she would buy them all over and over again; she would buy up every copy, I believe, to prevent their falling into unworthy hands; and she would have every book that tells her how to admire an old twisted tree. Should not you, Marianne? Forgive me, if I am very saucy. But I was willing to shew you that I had not forgot our old disputes."

absence as any deduction from her own enjoyment. In such a party, Harriet would be rather a dead weight than otherwise; but for the poor girl herself, it seemed a peculiarly cruel necessity that was to be placing her in such a state of unmerited punishment.

In time, of course, Mr. Knightley would be forgotten, that is, supplanted; but this could not be expected to happen very early. Mr. Knightley himself would be doing nothing to assist the cure;—not like Mr. Elton. Mr. Knightley, always so kind, so feeling, so truly considerate for every body, would never deserve to be less worshipped than now; and it really was too much to hope even of Harriet, that she could be in love with more than *three* men in one year.

16

It was a very great relief to Emma to find Harriet as desirous as herself to avoid a meeting. Their intercourse was painful enough by letter. How much worse, had they been obliged to meet!

Harriet expressed herself very much, as might be supposed, without reproaches, or apparent sense of ill usage; and yet Emma fancied there was a something of resentment, a something bordering on it in her style,[1] which increased the desirableness of their being separate.—It might be only her own consciousness; but it seemed as if an angel only could have been quite without resentment under such a stroke.

She had no difficulty in procuring Isabella's invitation; and she was fortunate in having a sufficient reason for asking it, without resorting to invention.—There was a tooth amiss.[2] Harriet really wished, and had wished some time, to consult a dentist. Mrs. John Knightley was delighted to be of use; any thing of ill-health was a recommendation to her[3]—and though not so fond of a dentist as of a Mr. Wingfield, she was quite eager to have Harriet under her care.—When it was thus settled on her sister's side, Emma proposed it to her friend, and found her very persuadable.—Harriet was to go; she was invited for at least a fortnight; she was to be conveyed in Mr. Woodhouse's carriage.—It was all arranged, it was all completed, and Harriet was safe in Brunswick Square.

Now Emma could, indeed, enjoy Mr. Knightley's visits; now she could talk, and she could listen with true happiness, unchecked by that sense of injustice, of guilt, of something most painful, which had

1 See note 15 to vol. II, chap. 15.

2 Considered in one light, Harriet's desire to have her teeth treated in London rather than in Surrey may be understandable, as professional dental surgery as we would understand it was still in its infancy at the beginning of the nineteenth century. As Christine Hillam notes:

> Before about 1840, most British dentists acquired their techniques in a somewhat haphazard and pragmatic manner, either in imitation of claims made in other dentists' advertising pamphlets or from their preceptor during apprenticeship. There appear to have been no contemporary translations of major works by foreign writers and the few books of worth in English on the anatomy, physiology and treatment of the teeth comment only very generally on restorative and prosthetic techniques . . . Dentists jealously kept their trade secrets to themselves and there must have been a wide variation in the treatments offered to the patient, for each of which some theory could be called upon for support. Whether the average provincial dentist, with his frequently inadequate training and limited access to dental literature, was able to execute the available techniques proficiently, or even safely, depended very much on the level of his skill, experience and willingness to exercise his powers of observation rather than to per-

haunted her when remembering how disappointed a heart was near her, how much might at that moment, and at a little distance, be enduring[4] by the feelings which she had led astray herself.

The difference of Harriet at Mrs. Goddard's, or in London, made perhaps an unreasonable difference in Emma's sensations; but she could not think of her in London without objects of curiosity and employment, which must be averting the past, and carrying her out of herself.

She would not allow any other anxiety to succeed directly to the place in her mind which Harriet had occupied. There was a communication before her, one which *she* only could be competent to make—the confession of her engagement to her father; but she would have nothing to do with it at present.—She had resolved to defer the disclosure till Mrs. Weston were safe and well. No additional agitation should be thrown at this period among those she loved—and the evil should not act on herself by anticipation before

One view of what happens to a "tooth amiss": "Fellow Feeling" (London: Edward Orme, 1810).

petuate ill-founded procedures. (*Brass Plate and Brazen Impudence: Dental Practice in the Provinces, 1755–1855* ([Liverpool: Liverpool University Press, 1991], pp. 97–98)

However, this tells only part of the story: as Hillam points out, there was also a manifest link between cosmetic dentistry and the other forms of fashionable consumerism in which provincial visitors to the capital would indulge. "One comes away from the writers and advertisers of this early period," she notes, "with the distinct impression that the reader is being invited to make an association between repair of tooth loss and genteel living, between care of the mouth and the emulation of his social superiors. This would seem to reinforce the evidence . . . that, in the early years at least, fashion played a not inconsiderable part in stimulating the growing demand for the 'decency' of dental treatment, over and above the occasional necessity of extraction" (ibid., p. 116). Therefore, Harriet's trip to the dentist may have more in common with Frank Churchill's capricious foray to the hairdresser in London than first appears. For more on this polyvalent incident, and on the wider metaphorical and literal significances of teeth in Austen, see Mark Blackwell's discussion in "Harriet's 'Tooth Amiss' and Transplantation in *Emma*," *Modern Philology,* 103: 4 (2006), pp. 474–497; see also Christine Hillam, ed., *The Roots of Dentistry* (London: British Dental Association, 1990); A. S. Hargreaves, *White as Whales Bone: Dental Services in Early Modern England* (Leeds: Northern Universities Press, 1998).

3 Compare Diana Parker in *Sanditon.*

4 Being endured.

A woman with a reticule or "ridicule": "Half Dress," from *Ackermann's Repository of the Arts,* first series, January 1812.

the appointed time.—A fortnight, at least, of leisure and peace of mind, to crown every warmer, but more agitating, delight, should be her's.

She soon resolved, equally as a duty and a pleasure, to employ half an hour of this holiday of spirits in calling on Miss Fairfax.—She ought to go—and she was longing to see her; the resemblance of their present situations increasing every other motive of good will. It would be a *secret* satisfaction; but the consciousness of a similarity of prospect would certainly add to the interest with which she should attend to any thing Jane might communicate.

She went—she had driven once unsuccessfully to the door, but had not been into the house since the morning after Box-Hill, when poor Jane had been in such distress as had filled her with compassion, though all the worst of her sufferings had been unsuspected.—The fear of being still unwelcome, determined her, though assured of their being at home, to wait in the passage, and send up her name.—She heard Patty announcing it; but no such bustle succeeded as poor Miss Bates had before made so happily intelligible.—No; she heard nothing but the instant reply of, "Beg her to walk up;"—and a moment afterwards she was met on the stairs by Jane herself, coming eagerly forward, as if no other reception of her were felt sufficient.—Emma had never seen her look so well, so lovely, so engaging. There was consciousness, animation, and warmth; there was every thing which her countenance or manner could ever have wanted.—She came forward with an offered hand; and said, in a low, but very feeling tone,

"This is most kind, indeed!—Miss Woodhouse, it is impossible for me to express——I hope you will believe——Excuse me for being so entirely without words."

Emma was gratified, and would soon have shown no want of words, if the sound of Mrs. Elton's voice from the sitting-room had not checked her, and made it expedient to compress all her friendly and all her congratulatory sensations into a very, very earnest shake of the hand.

Mrs. Bates and Mrs. Elton were together. Miss Bates was out, which accounted for the previous tranquillity. Emma could have wished Mrs. Elton elsewhere; but she was in a humour to have patience with every body; and as Mrs. Elton met her with unusual graciousness, she hoped the rencontre[5] would do them no harm.

She soon believed herself to penetrate Mrs. Elton's thoughts, and understand why she was, like herself, in happy spirits; it was being in Miss Fairfax's confidence, and fancying herself acquainted with what was still a secret to other people. Emma saw symptoms of it immediately in the expression of her face; and while paying her own compliments to Mrs. Bates, and appearing to attend to the good old lady's replies, she saw her with a sort of anxious parade of mystery fold up a letter which she had apparently been reading aloud to Miss Fairfax, and return it into the purple and gold ridicule[6] by her side, saying, with significant nods,

"We can finish this some other time, you know. You and I shall not want opportunities. And, in fact, you have heard all the essential already. I only wanted to prove to you that Mrs. S. admits our apology, and is not offended. You see how delightfully she writes. Oh! she is a sweet creature! You would have doated on her, had you gone.—But not a word more. Let us be discreet—quite on our good behaviour.—Hush!—You remember those lines—I forget the poem at this moment:

"For when a lady's in the case,
"You know all other things give place."[7]

Now I say, my dear, in *our* case, for *lady,* read—— mum![8] a word to the wise.[9]—I am in a fine flow of spirits, an't I? But I want to set your heart at ease as to Mrs. S.—*My* representation, you see, has quite appeased her."

And again, on Emma's merely turning her head to look at Mrs. Bates's knitting, she added, in a half whisper,

"I mentioned no *names,* you will observe.—Oh! no; cautious as a minister of state. I managed it extremely well."

Emma could not doubt. It was a palpable display, repeated on ev-

5 In this context, the word carries the undertow of a hostile encounter.

6 An alternative spelling for "reticule," a small handbag, usually fastened by means of a drawstring. Reticules became popular at the end of the eighteenth century, replacing the older style of women's pockets, which did not suit the new, higher-waisted style of dress. For more on the creative and material possibilities of pockets, see Lucy Razzall, "The Pockets of Henry Fielding's Writing," *Cambridge Quarterly,* 35: 4 (2006), pp. 361–377.

7 A singularly inappropriate allusion on Mrs. Elton's part. The lines, in a slightly different form, originally come from John Gay's fable "The Hare and Many Friends," first published in 1727. In the poem, a hare who makes a virtue of superficial sociability ("Her care was, never to offend,/And ev'ry creature was her friend") finds all the animals to be fair-weather friends when she is being chased by the hunt. The bull's excuse is as follows:

Since ev'ry beast alive can tell
That I sincerely wish you well,
I may, without offence, pretend
To take the freedom of a friend;
Love calls me hence; a fav'rite cow
Expects me near yon barley mow:
And when a lady's in the case,
You know, all other things give place.
To leave you thus might seem unkind;
But see, the goat is just behind.

As with the possible echo of Hutcheson in vol. III, chap. 7, Austen creates a comic implicature for the reader "over the head" of the character herself: on one level, for Mrs. Elton to be comparing Frank Churchill and Jane Fairfax to a pair of cattle in heat is an unfortunate analogy; however, Gay's fable does consort well at the metatextual level with the novel's larger concerns with true and false friendship ("Friendship, like love, is but a name,/Unless to one you stint the flame").

8 Hush.

9 The proverb "a word to the wise is sufficient" goes back at least as far as the Roman comic dramatist Plautus (c. 254 BC–184 BC).

ery possible occasion. When they had all talked a little while in harmony of the weather and Mrs. Weston, she found herself abruptly addressed with,

"Do not you think, Miss Woodhouse, our saucy little friend here is charmingly recovered?—Do not you think her cure does Perry the highest credit?—(here was a side-glance of great meaning at Jane.) Upon my word, Perry has restored her in a wonderful short time!—Oh! if you had seen her, as I did, when she was at the worst!"—And when Mrs. Bates was saying something to Emma, whispered farther, "We do not say a word of any *assistance* that Perry might have; not a word of a certain young physician from Windsor.—Oh! no; Perry shall have all the credit."

"I have scarce had the pleasure of seeing you, Miss Woodhouse," she shortly afterwards began, "since the party to Box-Hill. Very pleasant party. But yet I think there was something wanting. Things did not seem—that is, there seemed a little cloud upon the spirits of some.—So it appeared to me at least, but I might be mistaken. However, I think it answered so far as to tempt one to go again. What say you both to our collecting the same party, and exploring to Box-Hill again, while the fine weather lasts?—It must be the same party, you know, quite the same party, not *one* exception."

Soon after this Miss Bates came in, and Emma could not help being diverted by the perplexity of her first answer to herself, resulting, she supposed, from doubt of what might be said, and impatience to say every thing.

"Thank you, dear Miss Woodhouse, you are all kindness.—It is impossible to say—Yes, indeed, I quite understand—dearest Jane's prospects—that is, I do not mean.—But she is charmingly recovered.—How is Mr. Woodhouse?—I am so glad.—Quite out of my power.—Such a happy little circle as you find us here.—Yes, indeed.—Charming young man!—that is—so very friendly; I mean good Mr. Perry!—such attention to Jane!"—And from her great, her more than commonly thankful delight towards Mrs. Elton for being there, Emma guessed that there had been a little show of resentment towards Jane, from the vicarage quarter, which was now graciously overcome.—After a few whispers, indeed, which placed it beyond a guess, Mrs. Elton, speaking louder, said,

"Yes, here I am, my good friend; and here I have been so long, that anywhere else I should think it necessary to apologize: but the truth is, that I am waiting for my lord and master. He promised to join me here, and pay his respects to you."

"What! are we to have the pleasure of a call from Mr. Elton?—That will be a favour indeed! for I know gentlemen do not like morning visits, and Mr. Elton's time is so engaged."

"Upon my word it is, Miss Bates.—He really is engaged from morning to night.—There is no end of people's coming to him, on some pretence or other.—The magistrates, and overseers, and churchwardens,[10] are always wanting his opinion. They seem not able to do any thing without him.—'Upon my word, Mr. E., I often say, rather you than I.—I do not know what would become of my crayons[11] and my instrument, if I had half so many applicants.'—Bad enough as it is, for I absolutely neglect them both to an unpardonable degree.—I believe I have not played a bar this fortnight.—However, he is coming, I assure you: yes, indeed, on purpose to wait on you all."—And putting up her hand to screen her words from Emma—"A congratulatory visit, you know.—Oh! yes, quite indispensable."

Miss Bates looked about her, so happily!—

"He promised to come to me as soon as he could disengage himself from Knightley; but he and Knightley are shut up together in deep consultation.—Mr. E. is Knightley's right hand."[12]

Emma would not have smiled for the world, and only said, "Is Mr. Elton gone on foot to Donwell?—He will have a hot walk."

"Oh! no, it is a meeting at the Crown, a regular meeting. Weston and Cole[13] will be there too; but one is apt to speak only of those who lead.—I fancy Mr. E. and Knightley have every thing their own way."

"Have not you mistaken the day?" said Emma. "I am almost certain that the meeting at the Crown is not till tomorrow.—Mr. Knightley was at Hartfield yesterday, and spoke of it as for Saturday."

"Oh! no; the meeting is certainly to-day," was the abrupt answer,

10 Magistrates, overseers (officers charged with the administration of poor relief), and churchwardens (lay assistants to the clergy) all came under the jurisdiction of local Church of England parishes.

11 Chalks.

12 Indispensible assistant, second in command. The phrase may ultimately derive from biblical iconography, as, for example, in Mark 16:19: "So then after the Lord had spoken vnto them, he was receiued vp into heauen, and sate on the right hand of God."

13 Mrs. Elton, typically, omits the gentlemen's titles.

14 Thoughtful mind (although the phrase also has an awkwardly tautological ring to it).

which denoted the impossibility of any blunder on Mrs. Elton's side. —"I do believe," she continued, "this is the most troublesome parish that ever was. We never heard of such things at Maple Grove."

"Your parish there was small," said Jane.

"Upon my word, my dear, I do not know, for I never heard the subject talked of."

"But it is proved by the smallness of the school, which I have heard you speak of, as under the patronage of your sister and Mrs. Bragge; the only school, and not more than five-and-twenty children."

"Ah! you clever creature, that's very true. What a thinking brain[14] you have! I say, Jane, what a perfect character you and I should make, if we could be shaken together. My liveliness and your solidity would produce perfection.—Not that I presume to insinuate, however, that *some* people may not think *you* perfection already.—But hush!—not a word, if you please."

It seemed an unnecessary caution; Jane was wanting to give her words, not to Mrs. Elton, but to Miss Woodhouse, as the latter plainly saw. The wish of distinguishing her, as far as civility permitted, was very evident, though it could not often proceed beyond a look.

Mr. Elton made his appearance. His lady greeted him with some of her sparkling vivacity.

"Very pretty, sir, upon my word; to send me on here, to be an encumbrance to my friends, so long before you vouchsafe to come!—But you knew what a dutiful creature you had to deal with. You knew I should not stir till my lord and master appeared.—Here have I been sitting this hour, giving these young ladies a sample of true conjugal obedience—for who can say, you know, how soon it may be wanted?"

Mr. Elton was so hot and tired, that all this wit seemed thrown away. His civilities to the other ladies must be paid; but his subsequent object was to lament over himself for the heat he was suffering, and the walk he had had for nothing.

"When I got to Donwell," said he, "Knightley could not be found. Very odd! very unaccountable! after the note I sent him this morning, and the message he returned, that he should certainly be at home till one."

Samuel Howitt, "Hare and Many Friends," from *A New Work of Animals: principally designed from the fables of Aesop, Gay, and Phaedrus* (London: Edward Orme, 1809–1811). The superficially genial hare is deserted by her fair-weather friends.

"Donwell!" cried his wife—"My dear Mr. E., you have not been to Donwell!—You mean the Crown; you come from the meeting at the Crown."

"No, no, that's to-morrow; and I particularly wanted to see Knightley to-day on that very account.—Such a dreadful broiling morning!—I went over the fields too—(speaking in a tone of great ill usage,) which made it so much the worse. And then not to find him at home! I assure you I am not at all pleased. And no apology left, no message for me. The housekeeper declared she knew nothing of my being expected.—Very extraordinary!—And nobody knew at all which way he was gone. Perhaps to Hartfield, perhaps to the Abbey Mill, perhaps into his woods.—Miss Woodhouse, this is not like our friend Knightley.—Can you explain it?"

Emma amused herself by protesting that it was very extraordinary indeed, and that she had not a syllable to say for him.

"I cannot imagine," cried Mrs. Elton, (feeling the indignity as a

15 Recipe.

16 Engage him in conversation.

17 Needs.

wife ought to do,) "I cannot imagine how he could do such a thing by you, of all people in the world! The very last person whom one should expect to be forgotten!—My dear Mr. E., he must have left a message for you, I am sure he must.—Not even Knightley could be so very eccentric;—and his servants forgot it. Depend upon it, that was the case: and very likely to happen with the Donwell servants, who are all, I have often observed, extremely awkward and remiss.—I am sure I would not have such a creature as his Harry stand at our sideboard for any consideration. And as for Mrs. Hodges, Wright holds her very cheap indeed.—She promised Wright a receipt,[15] and never sent it."

"I met William Larkins," continued Mr. Elton, "as I got near the house, and he told me I should not find his master at home, but I did not believe him.—William seemed rather out of humour. He did not know what was come to his master lately, he said, but he could hardly ever get the speech of him.[16] I have nothing to do with William's wants,[17] but it really is of very great importance that *I* should see Knightley to day; and it becomes a matter, therefore, of very serious inconvenience that I should have had this hot walk to no purpose."

Emma felt that she could not do better than go home directly. In all probability she was at this very time waited for there; and Mr. Knightley might be preserved from sinking deeper in aggression towards Mr. Elton, if not towards William Larkins.

She was pleased, on taking leave, to find Miss Fairfax determined to attend her out of the room, to go with her even down stairs; it gave her an opportunity which she immediately made use of, to say,

"It is as well, perhaps, that I have not had the possibility. Had you not been surrounded by other friends, I might have been tempted to introduce a subject, to ask questions, to speak more openly than might have been strictly correct.—I feel that I should certainly have been impertinent."

"Oh!" cried Jane, with a blush and an hesitation which Emma thought infinitely more becoming to her than all the elegance of all her usual composure—"there would have been no danger. The danger would have been of my wearying you. You could not have gratified me more than by expressing an interest——. Indeed, Miss

Woodhouse, (speaking more collectedly,) with the consciousness which I have of misconduct, very great misconduct, it is particularly consoling to me to know that those of my friends, whose good opinion is most worth preserving, are not disgusted to such a degree as to—I have not time for half that I could wish to say. I long to make apologies, excuses, to urge something for myself. I feel it so very due. But unfortunately—in short, if your compassion does not stand my friend——"

"Oh! you are too scrupulous, indeed you are," cried Emma, warmly, and taking her hand. "You owe me no apologies; and every body to whom you might be supposed to owe them, is so perfectly satisfied, so delighted even—"

"You are very kind, but I know what my manners were to you.—So cold and artificial!—I had always a part to act.—It was a life of deceit!—I know that I must have disgusted you."

"Pray say no more. I feel that all the apologies should be on my side. Let us forgive each other at once. We must do whatever is to be done quickest, and I think our feelings will lose no time there. I hope you have pleasant accounts from Windsor?"

"Very."

"And the next news, I suppose, will be, that we are to lose you—just as I begin to know you."

"Oh! as to all that, of course nothing can be thought of yet. I am here till claimed by Colonel and Mrs. Campbell."

"Nothing can be actually settled yet, perhaps," replied Emma, smiling—"but, excuse me, it must be thought of."

The smile was returned as Jane answered,

"You are very right; it has been thought of. And I will own to you, (I am sure it will be safe), that so far as our living with Mr. Churchill at Enscombe, it is settled. There must be three months, at least, of deep mourning;[18] but when they are over, I imagine there will be nothing more to wait for."

"Thank you, thank you.—This is just what I wanted to be assured of.—Oh! if you knew how much I love every thing that is decided and open!—Good bye, good bye."

18 Although Regency mourning customs were quite flexible, three months would have been a decent period of mourning for an aunt.

17

Mrs. Weston's friends were all made happy by her safety;[1] and if the satisfaction of her well-doing could be increased to Emma, it was by knowing her to be the mother of a little girl. She had been decided in wishing for a Miss Weston. She would not acknowledge that it was with any view of making a match for her, hereafter, with either of Isabella's sons; but she was convinced that a daughter would suit both father and mother best. It would be a great comfort to Mr. Weston as he grew older—and even Mr. Weston might be growing older ten years hence—to have his fireside enlivened by the sports and the nonsense, the freaks and the fancies[2] of a child never banished from home;[3] and Mrs. Weston—no one could doubt that a daughter would be most to her; and it would be quite a pity that any one who so well knew how to teach, should not have their powers in exercise again.

"She has had the advantage, you know, of practising on me," she continued—"like La Baronne d'Almane on La Comtesse d'Ostalis, in Madame de Genlis' Adelaide and Theodore,[4] and we shall now see her own little Adelaide educated on a more perfect plan."

"That is," replied Mr. Knightley, "she will indulge her even more than she did you, and believe that she does not indulge her at all. It will be the only difference."

"Poor child!" cried Emma; "at that rate, what will become of her?"

"Nothing very bad.—The fate of thousands. She will be disagreeable in infancy, and correct herself as she grows older. I am losing all

1 Safe delivery.

2 Whims.

3 Since Mr. Weston did not get the chance constantly to observe his son growing up.

4 *Adelaide and Theodore; or, Letters on Education,* 3 vols. (Dublin: Luke White, 1783) was an English translation of the 1782 novel *Adèle et Théodore, ou Lettres Sur L'Éducation* by the writer and educator Stéphanie Félicité du Crest de St-Aubin, Comtesse de Genlis (1746–1830). In the novel, the Baronne uses her successful education of her niece, the Comtesse, as the template for educating her daughter Adelaide. Susan Allen Ford has made a fascinating study of *Emma* as an extended critical dialogue with, and rewriting of, *Adelaide and Theodore;* see "Romance, Pedagogy and Power: Jane Austen Re-writes Madame de Genlis," *Persuasions,* 21 (1999), pp. 172–187.

Portrait of Madame de Genlis by Labille-Guiard, 1790.

my bitterness against spoilt children, my dearest Emma. I, who am owing all my happiness to *you,* would not it be horrible ingratitude in me to be severe on them?"

Emma laughed, and replied: "But I had the assistance of all your endeavours to counteract the indulgence of other people. I doubt whether my own sense would have corrected me without it."

"Do you?—I have no doubt. Nature gave you understanding:—Miss Taylor gave you principles. You must have done well. My interference was quite as likely to do harm as good. It was very natural for you to say, what right has he to lecture me?—and I am afraid very natural for you to feel that it was done in a disagreeable manner. I do not believe I did you any good. The good was all to myself, by making you an object of the tenderest affection to me. I could not think about you so much without doating on you, faults and all; and by dint of fancying so many errors, have been in love with you ever since you were thirteen at least."

"I am sure you were of use to me," cried Emma. "I was very often influenced rightly by you—oftener than I would own at the time. I am very sure you did me good. And if poor little Anna Weston[5] is to be spoiled, it will be the greatest humanity in you to do as much for her as you have done for me, except falling in love with her when she is thirteen."

"How often, when you were a girl, have you said to me, with one of your saucy looks—'Mr. Knightley, I am going to do so and so; papa says I may, or, I have Miss Taylor's leave'—something which, you knew, I did not approve. In such cases my interference was giving you two bad feelings instead of one."

"What an amiable creature I was!—No wonder you should hold my speeches in such affectionate remembrance."

"'Mr. Knightley.'—You always called me, 'Mr. Knightley;' and, from habit, it has not so very formal a sound.—And yet it is formal. I want you to call me something else, but I do not know what."

"I remember once calling you 'George,' in one of my amiable fits, about ten years ago.[6] I did it because I thought it would offend you; but, as you made no objection, I never did it again."

"And cannot you call me 'George' now?"

5 Barbara Everett offers a suggestive discussion of Anna Weston as a counterpoint to Jane Fairfax at the end of the novel: "Non-existent at the beginning," she notes, "the child becomes an almost thrusting, bustling presence before the close . . . Just as the infant Anna heads unreckoned-with towards the daylight, so Jane like some Eurydice moves through the novel darkwards ("Hard Romance," *London Review of Books,* February 8, 1996, p. 14).

6 Another of the novel's moments of precise recall.

"Impossible!—I never can call you any thing but 'Mr. Knightley.' I will not promise even to equal the elegant terseness of Mrs. Elton, by calling you Mr. K.—But I will promise," she added presently, laughing and blushing—"I will promise to call you once by your Christian name. I do not say when, but perhaps you may guess where;—in the building in which N. takes M. for better, for worse."[7]

Emma grieved that she could not be more openly just to one important service which his better sense would have rendered her, to the advice which would have saved her from the worst of all her womanly follies—her wilful intimacy with Harriet Smith; but it was too tender a subject.—She could not enter on it.—Harriet was very seldom mentioned between them. This, on his side, might merely proceed from her not being thought of; but Emma was rather inclined to attribute it to delicacy, and a suspicion, from some appearances, that their friendship were declining. She was aware herself, that, parting under any other circumstances, they certainly should have corresponded more, and that her intelligence would not have rested, as it now almost wholly did, on Isabella's letters. He might observe that it was so. The pain of being obliged to practise concealment towards him, was very little inferior to the pain of having made Harriet unhappy.

Isabella sent quite as good an account of her visitor as could be expected; on her first arrival she had thought her out of spirits, which appeared perfectly natural, as there was a dentist to be consulted; but, since that business had been over, she did not appear to find Harriet different from what she had known her before.—Isabella, to be sure, was no very quick observer; yet if Harriet had not been equal to playing with the children, it would not have escaped her. Emma's comforts and hopes were most agreeably carried on, by Harriet's being to stay longer; her fortnight was likely to be a month at least. Mr. and Mrs. John Knightley were to come down in August, and she was invited to remain till they could bring her back.

"John does not even mention your friend," said Mr. Knightley. "Here is his answer, if you like to see it."

It was the answer to the communication of his intended marriage. Emma accepted it with a very eager hand, with an impatience all

7 Emma is alluding comically to the order of service for the Solemnization of Matrimony in the Book of Common Prayer, in which the groom and bride are referred to as M and N respectively; she may also be punning phonetically on the sounds of the letters, as Mr. Weston does on Box Hill. For more on the Common Prayer marriage service in the novel, see Bharat Tandon, *Jane Austen and the Morality of the Conversation* (London: Anthem Press, 2003), pp. 160–175.

alive to know what he would say about it, and not at all checked by hearing that her friend was unmentioned.

"John enters like a brother into my happiness,"[8] continued Mr. Knightley, "but he is no complimenter;[9] and though I well know him to have, likewise, a most brotherly affection for you, he is so far from making flourishes, that any other young woman might think him rather cool in her praise. But I am not afraid of your seeing what he writes."

"He writes like a sensible man," replied Emma, when she had read the letter. "I honour his sincerity. It is very plain that he considers the good fortune of the engagement as all on my side, but that he is not without hope of my growing, in time, as worthy of your affection, as you think me already. Had he said any thing to bear a different construction, I should not have believed him."

"My Emma, he means no such thing. He only means——"

"He and I should differ very little in our estimation of the two,"—interrupted she, with a sort of serious smile—"much less, perhaps, than he is aware of, if we could enter without ceremony or reserve on the subject."

"Emma, my dear Emma—"

"Oh!" she cried with more thorough gaiety, "if you fancy your brother does not do me justice, only wait till my dear father is in the secret, and hear his opinion. Depend upon it, he will be much farther from doing *you* justice. He will think all the happiness, all the advantage, on your side of the question; all the merit on mine. I wish I may not sink into 'poor Emma' with him at once.—His tender compassion towards oppressed worth can go no farther."

"Ah!" he cried, "I wish your father might be half as easily convinced as John will be, of our having every right that equal worth can give, to be happy together. I am amused by one part of John's letter—did you notice it?—where he says that my information did not take him wholly by surprise, that he was rather in expectation of hearing something of the kind."

"If I understand your brother, he only means so far as your having some thoughts of marrying. He had no idea of me. He seems perfectly unprepared for that."

8 Shares my happiness as a brother should.

9 Flatterer.

"Yes, yes—but I am amused that he should have seen so far into my feelings. What has he been judging by?—I am not conscious of any difference in my spirits or conversation that could prepare him at this time for my marrying any more than at another.—But it was so, I suppose. I dare say there was a difference when I was staying with them the other day. I believe I did not play with the children quite so much as usual. I remember one evening the poor boys saying, 'Uncle seems always tired now.'"

The time was coming when the news must spread farther, and other persons' reception of it tried. As soon as Mrs. Weston was sufficiently recovered to admit Mr. Woodhouse's visits, Emma having it in view that her gentle reasonings should be employed in the cause, resolved first to announce it at home, and then at Randall's.—But how to break it to her father at last!—She had bound herself to do it, in such an hour of Mr. Knightley's absence, or when it came to the point her heart would have failed her, and she must have put it off; but Mr. Knightley was to come at such a time, and follow up the beginning she was to make.—She was forced to speak, and to speak cheerfully too. She must not make it a more decided subject of misery to him, by a melancholy tone herself. She must not appear to think it a misfortune.—With all the spirits she could command, she prepared him first for something strange, and then, in few words, said, that if his consent and approbation could be obtained—which, she trusted, would be attended with no difficulty, since it was a plan to promote the happiness of all—she and Mr. Knightley meant to marry; by which means Hartfield would receive the constant addition of that person's company whom she knew he loved, next to his daughters and Mrs. Weston, best in the world.

Poor man!—it was at first a considerable shock to him, and he tried earnestly to dissuade her from it. She was reminded, more than once, of her having always said she would never marry, and assured that it would be a great deal better for her to remain single; and told of poor Isabella, and poor Miss Taylor.—But it would not do. Emma hung about[10] him affectionately, and smiled, and said it must be so; and that he must not class her with Isabella and Mrs. Weston, whose marriages taking them from Hartfield had indeed made a melan-

10 Embraced. Compare Camillo's narration of the miraculously revived Hermione in Act V, Scene 3, of Shakespeare's play *The Winter's Tale:* "She hangs about his necke."

11 Practically useful.

choly change: but she was not going from Hartfield; she should be always there; she was introducing no change in their numbers or their comforts but for the better; and she was very sure that he would be a great deal the happier for having Mr. Knightley always at hand, when he were once got used to the idea.—Did not he love Mr. Knightley very much?—He would not deny that he did, she was sure.—Whom did he ever want to consult on business but Mr. Knightley?—Who was so useful to him, who so ready to write his letters, who so glad to assist him?—Who so cheerful, so attentive, so attached to him?—Would not he like to have him always on the spot? —Yes. That was all very true. Mr. Knightley could not be there too often; he should be glad to see him every day;—but they did see him every day as it was.—Why could not they go on as they had done?

Mr. Woodhouse could not be soon reconciled; but the worst was overcome, the idea was given; time and continual repetition must do the rest.—To Emma's entreaties and assurances succeeded Mr. Knightley's, whose fond praise of her gave the subject even a kind of welcome; and he was soon used to be talked to by each, on every fair occasion.—They had all the assistance which Isabella could give, by letters of the strongest approbation; and Mrs. Weston was ready, on the first meeting, to consider the subject in the most serviceable[11] light—first, as a settled, and secondly, as a good one—well aware of the nearly equal importance of the two recommendations to Mr. Woodhouse's mind.—It was agreed upon, as what was to be; and every body by whom he was used to be guided assuring him that it would be for his happiness; and having some feelings himself which almost admitted it, he began to think that some time or other—in another year or two, perhaps—it might not be so very bad if the marriage did take place.

Mrs. Weston was acting no part, feigning no feelings in all that she said to him in favour of the event.—She had been extremely surprised, never more so, than when Emma first opened the affair to her; but she saw in it only increase of happiness to all, and had no scruple in urging him to the utmost.—She had such a regard for Mr. Knightley, as to think he deserved even her dearest Emma; and it was in every respect so proper, suitable, and unexceptionable a connexion, and in one respect, one point of the highest importance, so peculiarly eligible, so singularly fortunate, that now it seemed as if Emma could not safely have attached herself to any other creature, and that she had herself been the stupidest of beings in not having thought of it, and wished it long ago.—How very few of those men in a rank of life to address Emma would have renounced their own home for Hartfield! And who but Mr. Knightley could know and bear with Mr. Woodhouse, so as to make such an arrangement desirable!—The difficulty of disposing of[12] poor Mr. Woodhouse had been always felt in her husband's plans and her own, for a marriage between Frank and Emma. How to settle[13] the claims of Enscombe and Hartfield had been a continual impediment—less acknowledged by Mr. Weston than by herself—but even he had never been able to finish the subject better than by saying—"Those matters will take care of themselves; the young people will find a way."—But here there was nothing to be shifted off in a wild speculation on the future. It was all right, all open, all equal. No sacrifice on any side worth the name. It was a union of the highest promise of felicity in itself, and without one real, rational difficulty to oppose or delay it.

Mrs. Weston, with her baby on her knee, indulging in such reflections as these, was one of the happiest women in the world. If any thing could increase her delight, it was perceiving that the baby would soon have outgrown its first set of caps.[14]

The news was universally a surprise wherever it spread; and Mr. Weston had his five minutes share of it; but five minutes were enough to familiarize the idea to his quickness of mind.—He saw the advantages of the match, and rejoiced in them with all the constancy of his wife; but the wonder of it was very soon nothing; and by the end of an hour he was not far from believing that he had always foreseen it.

"It is to be a secret, I conclude," said he. "These matters are always a secret, till it is found out that every body knows them. Only let me be told when I may speak out.—I wonder whether Jane has any suspicion."

He went to Highbury the next morning, and satisfied himself on that point. He told her the news. Was not she like a daughter, his eldest daughter?—he must tell her; and Miss Bates being present, it

12 Dealing with, accommodating, but probably with an added pun on "getting rid of."

13 Balance, arbitrate between.

14 Not only a charming domestic detail, but an indication that Anna Weston has made it safely through the dangerous first weeks of life, although these weeks were not quite as fraught by Austen's time as they had once been, given that infant mortality rates had been declining since the late eighteenth century. See Lawrence Stone, *The Family, Sex and Marriage in England, 1500–1800* (London: Weidenfeld and Nicolson, 1997; rev. ed. Harmondsworth: Pelican, 1979).

passed, of course, to Mrs. Cole, Mrs. Perry, and Mrs. Elton, immediately afterwards. It was no more than the principals were prepared for; they had calculated from the time of its being known at Randall's, how soon it would be over Highbury; and were thinking of themselves, as the evening wonder[15] in many a family circle, with great sagacity.[16]

In general, it was a very well approved match. Some might think him, and others might think her, the most in luck. One set might recommend their all removing to Donwell, and leaving Hartfield for the John Knightleys; and another might predict disagreements among their servants; but yet, upon the whole, there was no serious objection raised, except in one habitation, the vicarage.—There, the surprise was not softened by any satisfaction. Mr. Elton cared little about it, compared with his wife; he only hoped "the young lady's pride would now be contented," and supposed "she had always meant to catch Knightley if she could;" and, on the point of living at Hartfield, could daringly exclaim, "Rather he than I!"—But Mrs. Elton was very much discomposed indeed.—"Poor Knightley! poor fellow! —sad business for him."—She was extremely concerned; for, though very eccentric, he had a thousand good qualities.—How could he be so taken in?—Did not think him at all in love—not in the least.—Poor Knightley!—There would be an end of all pleasant intercourse with him.—How happy he had been to come and dine with them whenever they asked him! But that would be all over now.—Poor fellow!—No more exploring parties to Donwell made for *her*. Oh! no; there would be a Mrs. Knightley to throw cold water on every thing. —Extremely disagreeable! But she was not at all sorry that she had abused the housekeeper the other day.—Shocking plan, living together. It would never do. She knew a family near Maple Grove who had tried it, and been obliged to separate before the end of the first quarter.[17]

15 That evening's most popular topic of conversation and gossip.

16 Accuracy.

17 Within three months.

18

Time passed on. A few more to-morrows, and the party from London would be arriving. It was an alarming change; and Emma was thinking of it one morning as what must bring a great deal to agitate and grieve her, when Mr. Knightley came in, and distressing thoughts were put by. After the first chat of pleasure he was silent; and then, in a graver tone, began with,

"I have something to tell you, Emma; some news."

"Good or bad?" said she, quickly, looking up in his face.

"I do not know which it ought to be called."

"Oh! good I am sure.—I see it in your countenance. You are trying not to smile."

"I am afraid," said he, composing his features, "I am very much afraid, my dear Emma, that you will not smile when you hear it."

"Indeed! but why so?—I can hardly imagine that any thing which pleases or amuses you, should not please and amuse me too."

"There is one subject," he replied, "I hope but one, on which we do not think alike." He paused a moment, again smiling, with his eyes fixed on her face. "Does nothing occur to you?—Do not you recollect?—Harriet Smith."

Her cheeks flushed at the name, and she felt afraid of something, though she knew not what.

"Have you heard from her yourself this morning?" cried he. "You have, I believe, and know the whole."

"No, I have not; I know nothing; pray tell me."

"You are prepared for the worst, I see—and very bad it is. Harriet Smith marries Robert Martin."

Emma gave a start, which did not seem like being prepared—and her eyes, in eager gaze, said, "No, this is impossible!" but her lips were closed.

"It is so, indeed," continued Mr. Knightley; "I have it from Robert Martin himself. He left me not half an hour ago."

She was still looking at him with the most speaking amazement.[1]

"You like it, my Emma, as little as I feared.—I wish our opinions were the same. But in time they will. Time, you may be very sure, will make one or the other of us think differently; and in the meanwhile, we need not talk much on the subject."

"You mistake me, you quite mistake me," she replied, exerting herself. "It is not that such a circumstance would now make me unhappy, but I cannot believe it. It seems an impossibility!—You cannot mean to say, that Harriet Smith has accepted Robert Martin. You cannot mean that he has even proposed to her again—yet. You only mean, that he intends it."

"I mean that he has done it," answered Mr. Knightley, with smiling but determined decision, "and been accepted."

"Good God!" she cried.—"Well!"—Then having recourse to her work-basket, in excuse for leaning down her face, and concealing all the exquisite feelings of delight and entertainment which she knew she must be expressing, she added, "Well, now tell me every thing; make this intelligible to me. How, where, when?—Let me know it all. I never was more surprised—but it does not make me unhappy, I assure you.—How—how has it been possible?"

"It is a very simple story. He went to town on business three days ago, and I got him to take charge of some papers which I was wanting to send to John.—He delivered these papers to John, at his chambers, and was asked by him to join their party the same evening to Astley's.[2] They were going to take the two eldest boys to Astley's. The party was to be our brother and sister, Henry, John—— and Miss Smith. My friend Robert could not resist. They called for him in their way; were all extremely amused; and my brother asked him to dine with them the next day—which he did—and in the course of

1 The metaphorical transference of eloquent faculties to the eyes is a long-standing poetic trope; the rhetorician Gilbert Austin remarked in his treatise *Chironomia; or, a Treatise on Rhetorical Delivery: Comprehending Many Precepts, both Ancient and Modern, for the Proper Regulation of the Voice, the Countenance and Gesture. Together with an Investigation of the Elements of Gesture, and a New Method for the Notation Thereof; Illustrated by Many Figures* (London: T. Cadell & W. Davies, 1806): "We seem to have the power, as it were, of touching each other by the sense of sight" (p. 102). Austen, likewise, is sensitive to the eye's metaphorically expressive capacities—particularly in *Persuasion,* where, for example, Captain Wentworth's "bright, proud, eye spoke" (vol. I, chap. 7).

2 Astley's Amphitheatre was a popular venue for theatrical, equestrian, and circus presentations, opened by Philip Astley in Lambeth in 1773. By the time of *Emma,* the amphitheater was into its third incarnation, having already burned down twice. Charles Dickens writes fondly of the democratic appeal of Astley's in *Sketches By Boz* (1836): "We like to watch a regular Astley's party in the Easter or Midsummer holidays—pa and ma, and nine or ten children, varying from five foot six to two foot eleven: from fourteen years of age to four" (*Sketches by Boz and Other Early Papers, 1833–39,* ed. M. Slater [London: J. M. Dent, 1994], p. 107), and Dickens's fictional characters visit Astley's in chap. 39 of *The Old Curiosity Shop* (1840–1841) and in chap. 21 of *Bleak House* (1852–1853).

Recently, Paula Byrne has pointed out that it is not absolutely certain *which* "Astley's" the party visits, since "following the success of his amphitheatre, which only operated on a summer licence, Astley opened a new theatre on Wych Street in the Strand in 1806. He called his new theatre the Olympic Pavilion, but it was also known as Astley's Pavilion, the Pavilion Theatre, the Olympic Saloon, and sometimes simply Astley's. . . . Jane Austen was not absolutely precise about dates in *Emma:* the theatre visit takes place some time in late summer and Harriet marries Martin shortly afterwards, in late September. This opens up the possibility of the Astley's reference being to either the sum-that visit (as I understand) he found an opportunity of speaking to Harriet; and certainly did not speak in vain.—She made him, by her acceptance, as happy even as he is deserving. He came down by yesterday's coach, and was with me this morning immediately after breakfast, to report his proceedings, first on my affairs, and then on his own. This is all that I can relate of the how, where, and when. Your friend Harriet will make a much longer history when you see her.—She will give you all the minute particulars, which only woman's language can make interesting.—In our communications we deal only in the great.[3]—However, I must say that Robert Martin's heart seemed for *him,* and to *me,* very overflowing; and that he did mention, without its being much to the purpose, that on quitting their box at Astley's, my brother took charge of Mrs. John Knightley and little John, and he followed with Miss Smith and Henry; and that at one time they were in such a crowd, as to make Miss Smith rather uneasy."

He stopped.—Emma dared not attempt any immediate reply. To speak, she was sure would be to betray a most unreasonable degree of happiness. She must wait a moment, or he would think her mad. Her silence disturbed him; and after observing her a little while, he added,

"Emma, my love, you said that this circumstance would not now make you unhappy; but I am afraid it gives you more pain than you expected. His situation is an evil—but you must consider it as what satisfies your friend; and I will answer for your thinking better and better of him as you know him more. His good sense and good principles would delight you.—As far as the man is concerned, you could not wish your friend in better hands. His rank in society I would alter if I could; which is saying a great deal I assure you, Emma.—You laugh at me about William Larkins; but I could quite as ill spare Robert Martin."

He wanted her to look up and smile; and having now brought herself not to smile too broadly—she did—cheerfully answering,

"You need not be at any pains to reconcile me to the match. I think Harriet is doing extremely well. *Her* connexions may be worse than *his.* In respectability of character, there can be no doubt that

mer amphitheatre in Lambeth or the winter Olympic house off Drury Lane" (*Jane Austen and the Theatre* [London and New York: Hambledon and London, 2002], pp. 32–34).

3 Compare Walter Scott's famous comparison of himself to Austen in his journal entry from March 14, 1826: "Also read again and for the third time at least Miss Austen's very finely written novel of *Pride and Prejudice.* That young lady had a talent for describing the involvement and feelings and characters of ordinary life which is to me the most wonderful I ever met with. The Big Bow-wow strain I can do myself like any now going, but the exquisite touch which renders ordinary commonplace characters and things interesting from the truth of the description and sentiment is denied to me" (*Jane Austen: The Critical Heritage,* vol. 1, p. 106).

they are. I have been silent from surprise merely, excessive surprise. You cannot imagine how suddenly it has come on me! how peculiarly unprepared I was!—for I had reason to believe her very lately more determined against him,[4] much more, than she was before."

"You ought to know your friend best," replied Mr. Knightley; "but I should say she was a good-tempered, soft-hearted girl, not likely to be very, very determined against any young man who told her he loved her."

Emma could not help laughing as she answered, "Upon my word, I believe you know her quite as well as I do.—But, Mr. Knightley, are you perfectly sure that she has absolutely and downright *accepted* him.—I could suppose she might in time—but can she already?—Did not you misunderstand him?—You were both talking of other things; of business, shows of cattle, or new drills[5]—and might not you, in the confusion of so many subjects, mistake him?—It was not Harriet's hand that he was certain of—it was the dimensions of some famous ox."[6]

The contrast between the countenance and air of Mr. Knightley and Robert Martin was, at this moment, so strong to Emma's feelings, and so strong was the recollection of all that had so recently passed on Harriet's side, so fresh the sound of those words, spoken with such emphasis, "No, I hope I know better than to think of Robert Martin," that she was really expecting the intelligence to prove, in some measure, premature. It could not be otherwise.

"Do you dare say this?" cried Mr. Knightley. "Do you dare to suppose me so great a blockhead, as not to know what a man is talking of?—What do you deserve?"

"Oh! I always deserve the best treatment, because I never put up with any other; and, therefore, you must give me a plain, direct answer. Are you quite sure that you understand the terms on which Mr. Martin and Harriet now are?"

"I am quite sure," he replied, speaking very distinctly, "that he told me she had accepted him; and that there was no obscurity, nothing doubtful, in the words he used; and I think I can give you a proof that it must be so. He asked my opinion as to what he was now to do.

4 A "civil falsehood" on Emma's part, given that her "reason" was Harriet's declared attachment to Knightley; it is only later in the chapter that she can look forward to the point at which "all necessity of concealment from Mr. Knightley would soon be over."

5 The seed drill, a horse-drawn mechanism for delivering seeds at a steady rate along a ploughed row, was invented in 1701 by Jethro Tull (1674–1741), and is generally credited as one of the most important inventions in the Agricultural Revolution.

6 Advancements in cattle-breeding techniques at the end of the eighteenth century led to a rise in prodigiously sized specimens, most notably the "Durham Ox," which allegedly weighed some 2,646 pounds at its death in 1807.

He knew of no one but Mrs. Goddard to whom he could apply for information of her relations or friends. Could I mention any thing more fit to be done, than to go to Mrs. Goddard? I assured him that I could not. Then, he said, he would endeavour to see her in the course of this day."

"I am perfectly satisfied," replied Emma, with the brightest smiles, "and most sincerely wish them happy."

"You are materially changed since we talked on this subject before."

"I hope so—for at that time I was a fool."

"And I am changed also; for I am now very willing to grant you all Harriet's good qualities. I have taken some pains for your sake, and for Robert Martin's sake, (whom I have always had reason to believe

Engraving of the "Durham Ox" by J. Wessel, after John Boultbee, 1802. The Durham Ox was the most famous product of the craze for breeding monster cattle in the early nineteenth century. The fact that someone as deliberately indifferent to farming and farmers as Emma Woodhouse can make this joke indicates just how far the giant-ox trend had made its way into the popular imagination.

as much in love with her as ever,) to get acquainted with her. I have often talked to her a good deal. You must have seen that I did. Sometimes, indeed, I have thought you were half suspecting me of pleading poor Martin's cause, which was never the case: but, from all my observations, I am convinced of her being an artless, amiable girl, with very good notions, very seriously good principles, and placing her happiness in the affections and utility of domestic life.—Much of this, I have no doubt, she may thank you for."

"Me!" cried Emma, shaking her head.—"Ah! poor Harriet!"

She checked herself, however, and submitted quietly to a little more praise than she deserved.

Their conversation was soon afterwards closed by the entrance of her father. She was not sorry. She wanted to be alone. Her mind was in a state of flutter and wonder, which made it impossible for her to be collected. She was in dancing, singing, exclaiming spirits; and till she had moved about, and talked to herself, and laughed and reflected, she could be fit for nothing rational.

Her father's business was to announce James's being gone out to put the horses to, preparatory to their now daily drive to Randall's; and she had, therefore, an immediate excuse for disappearing.

Scale model of Jethro Tull's 1701 seed drill. Tull's invention was the most important early breakthrough in the eighteenth-century "Agricultural Revolution" in England.

The joy, the gratitude, the exquisite delight of her sensations may be imagined. The sole grievance and alloy thus removed in the prospect of Harriet's welfare, she was really in danger of becoming too happy for security.—What had she to wish for? Nothing, but to grow more worthy of him, whose intentions and judgment had been ever so superior to her own. Nothing, but that the lessons of her past folly might teach her humility and circumspection in future.

Serious she was, very serious in her thankfulness, and in her resolutions; and yet there was no preventing a laugh, sometimes in the very midst of them. She must laugh at such a close! Such an end of the doleful disappointment of five weeks back! Such a heart—such a Harriet!

Now there would be pleasure in her returning.—Every thing would be a pleasure. It would be a great pleasure to know Robert Martin.

High in the rank of her most serious and heartfelt felicities, was the reflection that all necessity of concealment from Mr. Knightley would soon be over. The disguise, equivocation, mystery, so hateful to her to practise, might soon be over. She could now look forward to giving him that full and perfect confidence which her disposition was most ready to welcome as a duty.

In the gayest and happiest spirits she set forward with her father; not always listening, but always agreeing to what he said; and, whether in speech or silence, conniving at the comfortable persuasion of his being obliged to go to Randall's every day, or poor Mrs. Weston would be disappointed.

They arrived.—Mrs. Weston was alone in the drawing-room:—but hardly had they been told of the baby, and Mr. Woodhouse received the thanks for coming, which he asked for, when a glimpse was caught through the blind,[7] of two figures passing near the window.

"It is Frank and Miss Fairfax," said Mrs. Weston. "I was just going to tell you of our agreeable surprise in seeing him arrive this morning. He stays till to-morrow, and Miss Fairfax has been persuaded to spend the day with us.—They are coming in, I hope."

In half a minute they were in the room. Emma was extremely glad

7 A brilliantly resonant narratorial pun: whereas in vol. III, chap. 13, Emma complains that Frank Churchill's interest was "merely a blind to conceal his real situation," now that the truth is out, Frank and Jane are visible together through the other sort of "blind."

8 Silence.

9 Expected amount.

to see him—but there was a degree of confusion—a number of embarrassing recollections on each side. They met readily and smiling, but with a consciousness which at first allowed little to be said; and having all sat down again, there was for some time such a blank[8] in the circle, that Emma began to doubt whether the wish now indulged, which she had long felt, of seeing Frank Churchill once more, and of seeing him with Jane, would yield its proportion[9] of pleasure. When Mr. Weston joined the party, however, and when the baby was fetched, there was no longer a want of subject or animation—or of courage and opportunity for Frank Churchill to draw near her and say,

"I have to thank you, Miss Woodhouse, for a very kind forgiving message in one of Mrs. Weston's letters. I hope time has not made you less willing to pardon. I hope you do not retract what you then said."

"No, indeed," cried Emma, most happy to begin, "not in the least. I am particularly glad to see and shake hands with you—and to give you joy in person."

He thanked her with all his heart, and continued some time to speak with serious feeling of his gratitude and happiness.

"Is not she looking well?" said he, turning his eyes towards Jane. "Better than she ever used to do?—You see how my father and Mrs. Weston doat upon her."

But his spirits were soon rising again, and with laughing eyes, after mentioning the expected return of the Campbells, he named the name of Dixon.—Emma blushed, and forbad its being pronounced in her hearing.

"I can never think of it," she cried, "without extreme shame."

"The shame," he answered, "is all mine, or ought to be. But is it possible that you had no suspicion?—I mean of late. Early, I know you had none."

"I never had the smallest, I assure you."

"That appears quite wonderful. I was once very near—and I wish I had—it would have been better. But though I was always doing wrong things, they were very *bad* wrong things, and such as did me no service.—It would have been a much better transgression had I broken the bond of secrecy and told you every thing."

"It is not now worth a regret," said Emma.

"I have some hope," resumed he, "of my uncle's being persuaded to pay a visit at Randall's; he wants to be introduced to her. When the Campbells are returned, we shall meet them in London, and continue there, I trust, till we may carry her northward.—But now, I am at such a distance from her—is not it hard, Miss Woodhouse?—Till this morning, we have not once met since the day of reconciliation. Do not you pity me?"

Emma spoke her pity so very kindly, that, with a sudden accession of gay thought, he cried,

"Ah! by the bye,"—then sinking his voice, and looking demure for the moment—"I hope Mr. Knightley is well?" He paused.—She coloured and laughed.—"I know you saw my letter, and think you may remember my wish in your favour. Let me return your congratulations.—I assure you that I have heard the news with the warmest interest and satisfaction.—He is a man whom I cannot presume to praise."

Emma was delighted, and only wanted him to go on in the same style; but his mind was the next moment in his own concerns and with his own Jane, and his next words were,

"Did you ever see such a skin?—such smoothness! such delicacy!—and yet without being actually fair.—One cannot call her fair. It is a most uncommon complexion, with her dark eyelashes and hair—a most distinguishing complexion!—So peculiarly the lady in it.—Just colour enough for beauty."

"I have always admired her complexion," replied Emma, archly; "but do not I remember the time when you found fault with her for being so pale?—When we first began to talk of her.—Have you quite forgotten?"

"Oh! no—what an impudent dog I was!—How could I dare—"

But he laughed so heartily at the recollection, that Emma could not help saying,

"I do suspect that in the midst of your perplexities at that time, you had very great amusement in tricking us all.—I am sure you had.—I am sure it was a consolation to you."

"Oh! no, no, no—how can you suspect me of such a thing?—I was the most miserable wretch!"

"Not quite so miserable as to be insensible to mirth. I am sure it was a source of high entertainment to you, to feel that you were taking us all in.—Perhaps I am the readier to suspect, because, to tell you the truth, I think it might have been some amusement to myself in the same situation. I think there is a little likeness between us."

He bowed.

"If not in our dispositions," she presently added, with a look of true sensibility, "there is a likeness in our destiny; the destiny which bids fair to connect us with two characters so much superior to our own."

"True, true," he answered, warmly. "No, not true on your side. You can have no superior, but most true on mine.—She is a complete angel. Look at her. Is not she an angel in every gesture? Observe the turn of her throat. Observe her eyes, as she is looking up at my father.—You will be glad to hear (inclining his head, and whispering seriously) that my uncle means to give her all my aunt's jewels. They are to be new set. I am resolved to have some in an ornament for the head. Will not it be beautiful in her dark hair?"

"Very beautiful indeed," replied Emma: and she spoke so kindly, that he gratefully burst out,

"How delighted I am to see you again! and to see you in such excellent looks!—I would not have missed this meeting for the world. I should certainly have called at Hartfield, had you failed to come."

The others had been talking of the child, Mrs. Weston giving an account of a little alarm she had been under, the evening before, from the infant's appearing not quite well. She believed she had been foolish, but it had alarmed her, and she had been within half a minute of sending for Mr. Perry. Perhaps she ought to be ashamed, but Mr. Weston had been almost as uneasy as herself.—In ten minutes, however, the child had been perfectly well again. This was her history; and particularly interesting it was to Mr. Woodhouse, who commended her very much for thinking of sending for Perry, and only regretted that she had not done it. "She should always send for Perry, if the child appeared in the slightest degree disordered, were it only for a moment. She could not be too soon alarmed, nor send for Perry too often. It was a pity, perhaps, that he had not come last night; for, though the child seemed well now, very well considering, it would probably have been better if Perry had seen it."

Frank Churchill caught the name.

"Perry!" said he to Emma, and trying, as he spoke, to catch Miss Fairfax's eye. "My friend Mr. Perry! What are they saying about Mr. Perry?—Has he been here this morning?—And how does he travel now?—Has he set up his carriage?"

Emma soon recollected, and understood him; and while she joined in the laugh, it was evident from Jane's countenance that she too was really hearing him, though trying to seem deaf.

"Such an extraordinary dream of mine!" he cried. "I can never think of it without laughing.—She hears us, she hears us, Miss Woodhouse. I see it in her cheek, her smile, her vain attempt to frown. Look at her. Do not you see that, at this instant, the very passage of her own letter, which sent me the report, is passing under her eye—that the whole blunder is spread before her[10]—that she can attend to nothing else, though pretending to listen to the others?"

Jane was forced to smile completely, for a moment; and the smile partly remained as she turned towards him, and said in a conscious, low, yet steady voice,

"How you can bear such recollections, is astonishing to me!—They *will* sometimes obtrude—but how you can *court* them!"

He had a great deal to say in return, and very entertainingly; but Emma's feelings were chiefly with Jane, in the argument; and on leaving Randall's, and falling naturally into a comparison of the two men, she felt, that pleased as she had been to see Frank Churchill, and really regarding him as she did with friendship, she had never been more sensible of Mr. Knightley's high superiority of character. The happiness of this most happy day, received its completion, in the animated contemplation of his worth which this comparison produced.

10 A cheeky allusion to the letter game in vol. III, chap. 5.

A. C. Pugin and Thomas Rowlandson, "Astley's Amphitheatre" from Rudolph Ackermann, *The Microcosm of London* (London: R. Ackermann, 1808).

19

If Emma had still, at intervals, an anxious feeling for Harriet, a momentary doubt of its being possible for her to be really cured of her attachment to Mr. Knightley, and really able to accept another man from unbiassed inclination, it was not long that she had to suffer from the recurrence of any such uncertainty. A very few days brought the party from London, and she had no sooner an opportunity of being one hour alone with Harriet, than she became perfectly satisfied—unaccountable as it was!—that Robert Martin had thoroughly supplanted Mr. Knightley, and was now forming all her views of happiness.

Harriet was a little distressed—did look a little foolish at first; but having once owned that she had been presumptuous and silly, and self-deceived, before, her pain and confusion seemed to die away with the words, and leave her without a care for the past, and with the fullest exultation in the present and future; for, as to her friend's approbation, Emma had instantly removed every fear of that nature, by meeting her with the most unqualified congratulations.—Harriet was most happy to give every particular of the evening at Astley's, and the dinner the next day; she could dwell on it all with the utmost delight. But what did such particulars explain?—The fact was, as Emma could now acknowledge, that Harriet had always liked Robert Martin; and that his continuing to love her had been irresistible.—Beyond this, it must ever be unintelligible to Emma.

The event, however, was most joyful, and every day was giving her fresh reason for thinking so.—Harriet's parentage became known.

She proved to be the daughter of a tradesman,[1] rich enough to afford her the comfortable maintenance which had ever been her's, and decent enough to have always wished for concealment.—Such was the blood of gentility which Emma had formerly been so ready to vouch for!—It was likely to be as untainted, perhaps, as the blood of many a gentleman: but what a connexion had she been preparing for Mr. Knightley—or for the Churchills—or even for Mr. Elton!—The stain of illegitimacy, unbleached by nobility or wealth, would have been a stain indeed.

No objection was raised on the father's side; the young man was treated liberally; it was all as it should be: and as Emma became acquainted with Robert Martin, who was now introduced at Hartfield, she fully acknowledged in him all the appearance of sense and worth which could bid fairest for her little friend. She had no doubt of Harriet's happiness with any good tempered man; but with him, and in the home he offered, there would be the hope of more, of security, stability, and improvement. She would be placed in the midst of those who loved her, and who had better sense than herself; retired enough for safety, and occupied enough for cheerfulness. She would be never led into temptation,[2] nor left for it to find her out. She would be respectable and happy; and Emma admitted her to be the

Emma (Gwyneth Paltrow) and Knightley (Jeremy Northam) at the end of Douglas McGrath's film of *Emma*.

1 This revelation finally gives the lie to the mythology of aristocratic intrigue that Emma has been building around Harriet's status as a parlor-boarder.

2 An allusion to the Lord's Prayer, as in the Authorized Version translation of Matthew 6:13 ("And lead vs not into temptation, but deliuer vs from euill").

Cher and Josh at the end of *Clueless.*

luckiest creature in the world, to have created so steady and persevering an affection in such a man;—or, if not quite the luckiest, to yield only to herself.

Harriet, necessarily drawn away by her engagements with the Martins, was less and less at Hartfield; which was not to be regretted. —The intimacy between her and Emma must sink; their friendship must change into a calmer sort of goodwill; and, fortunately, what ought to be, and must be, seemed already beginning, and in the most gradual, natural manner.

Before the end of September, Emma attended Harriet to church, and saw her hand bestowed on Robert Martin with so complete a satisfaction, as no remembrances, even connected with Mr. Elton as he stood before them, could impair.—Perhaps, indeed, at that time she scarcely saw Mr. Elton, but as the clergyman whose blessing at the altar might next fall on herself.—Robert Martin and Harriet Smith, the latest couple engaged of the three, were the first to be married.

Jane Fairfax had already quitted Highbury, and was restored to the comforts of her beloved home with the Campbells.—The Mr. Churchills were also in town; and they were only waiting for November.

3 See note 3 to vol. I, chap. 11.

4 Compare vol. III, chaps. 15–17, of *Mansfield Park,* in which Austen similarly disrupts the causality of her romantic *dénouement* by suggesting that it might depend, at least in part, upon accident and contingency rather than directly on merit.

5 Although the robberies take place at night, housebreaking is, strictly speaking, robbery of property during the daytime.

6 See note 2 to vol. 1, chap. 11.

The intermediate month was the one fixed on, as far as they dared, by Emma and Mr. Knightley.—They had determined that their marriage ought to be concluded while John and Isabella were still at Hartfield, to allow them the fortnight's absence in a tour to the seaside,[3] which was the plan.—John and Isabella, and every other friend, were agreed in approving it. But Mr. Woodhouse—how was Mr. Woodhouse to be induced to consent?—he, who had never yet alluded to their marriage but as a distant event.

When first sounded on the subject, he was so miserable, that they were almost hopeless.—A second allusion, indeed, gave less pain.—He began to think it was to be, and that he could not prevent it—a very promising step of the mind on its way to resignation. Still, however, he was not happy. Nay, he appeared so much otherwise, that his daughter's courage failed. She could not bear to see him suffering, to know him fancying himself neglected; and though her understanding almost acquiesced in the assurance of both the Mr. Knightleys, that when once the event were over, his distress would be soon over too, she hesitated—she could not proceed.

In this state of suspense they were befriended, not by any sudden illumination of Mr. Woodhouse's mind, or any wonderful change of his nervous system, but by the operation of the same system in another way.—Mrs. Weston's poultry-house was robbed one night of all her turkies—evidently by the ingenuity of man.[4] Other poultry-yards in the neighbourhood also suffered.—Pilfering was *housebreaking*[5] to Mr. Woodhouse's fears.—He was very uneasy; and but for the sense of his son-in-law's protection, would have been under wretched alarm every night of his life. The strength, resolution, and presence of mind of the Mr. Knightleys, commanded his fullest dependance. While either of them protected him and his, Hartfield was safe.—But Mr. John Knightley must be in London again by the end of the first week in November.[6]

The result of this distress was, that, with a much more voluntary, cheerful consent than his daughter had ever presumed to hope for at the moment, she was able to fix her wedding-day—and Mr. Elton was called on, within a month from the marriage of Mr. and

Mrs. Robert Martin, to join the hands of Mr. Knightley and Miss Woodhouse.

The wedding was very much like other weddings, where the parties have no taste for finery or parade; and Mrs. Elton, from the particulars detailed by her husband,[7] thought it all extremely shabby, and very inferior to her own.—"Very little white satin, very few lace veils; a most pitiful business!—Selina would stare when she heard of it."—But, in spite of these deficiencies, the wishes, the hopes, the confidence, the predictions of the small band of true friends who witnessed the ceremony, were fully answered in the perfect happiness of the union.[8]

FINIS.

7 A glancing reference to the fact that Mrs. Elton is *persona non grata* at Emma and Knightley's wedding ceremony.

8 The tantalizing fact of Austen's closing the narrative precisely at this point, with no definitive information as to how the marriage turns out in the "ever after," has both frustrated and inspired Austen's critics, with one of the central debates revolving around whether the ending is to be read "straight" or as savagely ironic. Edmund Wilson, writing in 1945, had little doubt that Emma would be up to her old tricks in the future: "Emma, who was relatively indifferent to men, was inclined to infatuations with women; and what reason is there to believe that her marriage with Knightley would prevent her from going on as she had done before: from discovering a new young lady as appealing as Harriet Smith, dominating her personality and situating her in a dream-world of Emma's own in which Emma would be able to confer on her all kinds of imaginary benefits but which would have no connection whatever with her condition or her real possibilities?" ("A Long Talk about Jane Austen," reprinted in Ian Watt, ed., *Jane Austen: A Collection of Critical Essays* [Englewood Cliffs, NJ: Prentice-Hall, 1963], p. 39). Marvin Mudrick influentially called attention to what he perceived as a double valency in the ending: "Of course," he argues, "the denouement brushes aside confusion and unhappiness, and brings Emma and Churchill into ostensibly happy marriages. *Emma* can be read as the story of a spoiled rich girl who is corrected by defeat and love, and who lives happily ever after. This is a limited vision, but it is not a false one; for JA does succeed on her primary levels in achieving her 'ripest and kindliest,' her most perfect love comedy . . . *Emma* can be read so; but it has more to give, and not easily" (*Jane Austen: Irony as Defense and Discovery* (Princeton: Princeton University Press, 1952; repr. Berkeley: University of California Press, 1974), pp. 201–202. Against such readings, Wayne C. Booth's book *The Rhetoric of Fiction* insists on the imaginative reality of Emma and Knightley's happiness:

> But it is precisely because this ending is neither life itself nor a simple bit of literary irony that it can serve so well to heighten our sense of a complete and indeed perfect resolution to all that has gone before. If we look at the values that have been realized in this marriage and compare them with those realized in conventional marriage plots, we see that Jane Austen means what she says: this will be a happy marriage because there is simply nothing left to make it anything less than perfectly happy. ([Chicago and London: University of Chicago Press, 1961; 2nd ed., 1983], p. 259)

However, he himself felt constrained to revisit and partially to revise this assessment in *The Company We Keep: An Ethics of Fiction* (Berkeley: University of California Press, 1988): "On the one hand, we must see the ending as indeed a happy one, not in the least ironic, given the world of the conventional plot, a world that we are to enter with absolute whole-heartedness. And yet, simultaneously, we are asked to embrace standards according to which the ending can only be viewed as a fairy tale or fantasy" (p. 435). Booth's later formulation of the question seems to echo one of the most penetrating analyses of the ending, made in 1957 by Lionel Trilling: "This England, especially as it is represented in *Emma,* is an idyll. The error of identifying it with the actual England ought always to be remarked. Yet the same sense of actuality that corrects the error should not fail to recognize the remarkable force of the ideal that leads many to make the error" ("*Emma* and the Legend of Jane Austen," in *Beyond Culture* [London: Martin Secker & Warburg, 1966; repr. Oxford: Oxford University Press, 1980], p. 49). For an incisive reading of the narrative psychology of the novel's ending, see also D. A. Miller, *Narrative and Its Discontents: Problems of Closure in the Traditional Novel* (Princeton: Princeton University Press, 1981), pp. 3–106.

Chris Hammond, "The wedding was very much like other weddings" from *Emma* (London: George Allen, 1898).

List of Emendations

VOLUME I

		The 1816 Text	*Emended to*
Chapter 4	page 60, lines 5–6	he is below it..	he is below it.
	page 64, line 17	the more valuable The older	the more valuable. The older
Chapter 6	page 74, line 31	drawing-room, at Randalls?	drawing-room, at Randalls?”
	page 77, line 4	“Yes, it was	‘Yes, it was
	page 77, line 5	do him justice.”	do him justice.’
	page 78, line 19	We shall be mos happy	We shall be most happy
Chapter 7	page 81, lines 13–14	direct proposal of marriage	direct proposal of marriage.
Chapter 8	page 93, line 22	think this a good match.”	think this a good match.’”
	page 94, lines 13–14	she i left in Mrs. Goddard’s	she is left in Mrs. Goddard’s hands
Chapter 9	page 102, line 32	destin’d to feel	destin’d to feel;
	page 115, line 24	replied Mr. Elton,” though	replied Mr. Elton, though
Chapter 10	page 119, line 2	when you grow old?	when you grow old?”
Chapter 12	page 135, line 3	South End is probibited	South End is prohibited
	page 140, line 10	my dear,” as Perry says, “where	my dear, as Perry says, where
Chapter 13	page 144, lines 23–24	having extricated himself	having extricated him
Chapter 14	page 155, lines 30–31	great wish on the Churchills	great wish on the Churchills’
Chapter 15	page 157, lines 17–18	any thing about er	any thing about her
	page 160, lines 5–6	I admired you spirit	I admired your spirit
	page 163, line 34	truggles for politenes	struggles for politeness

VOLUME II

		The 1816 Text	*Emended to*
Chapter 3	page 209, line 13	"Oh! my dear, said I	Oh! my dear, said I
	page 215, line 18	how it went one	how it went on
Chapter 6	page 237, line 17	yes—he replied	yes—" he replied
	page 237, line 17	I was just going	"I was just going
Chapter 7	page 244, lines 14–15	liable to all these changes	liable to all these charges
	page 246, line 12	in fortuue and style	in fortune and style
Chapter 10	page 286, line 28	at Kingston? said he	at Kingston?' said he
Chapter 11	page 287	Chapter XIII	Chapter 11
Chapter 11	page 293, line 9	any thing could have imagined	any thing I could have imagined
Chapter 12	page 299, lines 4–5	lament and exclain	lament and exclaim
	page 300, line 8	you expectations?	your expectations?
Chapter 14	page 313, line 3	a little sign	a little sigh
Chapter 15	page 327, line 24	Mr. Cole, I supposed?	Mr. Cole, I suppose?
Chapter 16	page 334, line 23	Mrs. Waston kindly	Mrs. Weston kindly

VOLUME III

		The 1816 Text	*Emended to*
Chapter 2	page 368, line 21	could notlose	could not lose
	page 369, lines 32–33	up fron the bottom	up from the bottom
	page 371, line 30	"Oh!" said I, "I shall not	'Oh!' said I, 'I shall not
	page 371, line 33	perhaps Mr. William Cox."	perhaps Mr. William Cox.'
Chapter 4	page 385, line 4	—Oh! no"—	—"Oh! no"—
Chapter 6	page 398, lines 32–33	—And such weather	—"And such weather
	page 401, line 11	—but I will not trouble you	—"but I will not trouble you
	page 415, lines 6–7	I shall never be easy	"I shall never be easy
Chapter 8	page 431, line 10	such an 'always;'	such an "always;"
Chapter 10	page 444, line 17	that does relate to one	that does not relate to one
	page 446, line 3	Shestopped to breathe	She stopped to breathe
	page 446, lines 11–12	do not mean it?	do not mean it?"
Chapter 11	page 454, line 34	cautioned you accordingly.	cautioned you accordingly."
	page 458, line 29	she had been used to do	he had been used to do
	page 461, lines 2–3	tried the sbrubbery	tried the shrubbery

	page 462, line 24	the human fate?"	the human fate?
Chapter 13	page 472, line 21	wet side	wet ride
	page 481, line 15	stay no longer?	stay no longer.
Chapter 16	page 506, lines 31–32	said Emma. I am almost certain	said Emma. "I am almost certain
Chapter 17	page 518, line 19	sad business for him.—	sad business for him."—
Chapter 18	page 528, line 23	"and she spoke so kindly	and she spoke so kindly

Further Reading

This list contains only full-length books; references for chapters and articles can be found in the notes to the novel.

Bradbrook, Frank W. *Jane Austen and Her Predecessors.* Cambridge: Cambridge University Press, 1966.

Butler, Marilyn. *Jane Austen and the War of Ideas.* Oxford: Clarendon Press, 1975; 2nd ed., 1987.

Byrne, Paula. *Jane Austen and the Theatre.* London: Hambledon and London, 2002.

Chapman, R. W. *Jane Austen: Facts and Problems.* Oxford: Clarendon Press, 1948.

Copeland, Edward, and Juliet McMaster, eds. *The Cambridge Companion to Jane Austen.* Cambridge: Cambridge University Press, 1997; 2nd ed., 2011.

Deresiewicz, William. *Jane Austen and the Romantic Poets.* New York: Columbia University Press, 2004.

Duckworth, Alistair M. *The Improvement of the Estate.* Baltimore: Johns Hopkins University Press, 1971.

Dussinger, John A. *In the Pride of the Moment: Encounters in Jane Austen's World.* Columbus: Ohio State University Press, 1990.

Ehrenpreis, Irvin. *Acts of Implication: Suggestion and Covert Meaning in the Works of Dryden, Swift, Pope, and Austen.* Berkeley: University of California Press, 1980.

Galperin, William H. *The Historical Austen.* Philadelphia: University of Pennsylvania Press, 2003.

Gard, Roger. *Jane Austen's Novels: The Art of Clarity.* New Haven: Yale University Press, 1992.

Harding, D. W. *Regulated Hatred and Other Essays on Jane Austen.* London: Athlone Press, 1998.

Hardy, Barbara. *A Reading of Jane Austen.* London: Athlone Press, 1975; 2nd ed., 1979.

Harris, Jocelyn. *Jane Austen's Art of Memory.* Cambridge: Cambridge University Press, 1989.

Iser, Wolfgang. *The Implied Reader: Patterns of Communication in Prose Fiction from Bunyan to Beckett.* Baltimore: Johns Hopkins University Press, 1974.

Johnson, Claudia L. *Jane Austen: Women, Politics, and the Novel.* Chicago: University of Chicago Press, 1988.

Kaplan, Deborah. *Jane Austen among Women.* Baltimore: Johns Hopkins University Press, 1992.

Kermode, Frank. *The Sense of an Ending: Studies in the Theory of Fiction.* New York: Oxford University Press, 1967.

Knox-Shaw, Peter. *Jane Austen and the Enlightenment.* Cambridge: Cambridge University Press, 2004.

Lane, Maggie. *Jane Austen and Food.* London: Hambledon Press, 1995.

Le Faye, Deirdre. *Jane Austen: The World of Her Novels.* London: Frances Lincoln, 2002.

MacDonagh, Oliver. *Jane Austen: Real and Imagined Worlds.* New Haven: Yale University Press, 1991.

McMaster, Juliet, and Bruce Stovel, eds. *Jane Austen's Business: Her World and Her Profession.* Basingstoke, UK: Macmillan/St. Martin's Press, 1996.

Miller, D. A. *Jane Austen, or The Secret of Style.* Princeton: Princeton University Press, 2003.

Monaghan, David, ed. *Jane Austen in a Social Context.* London: Macmillan, 1981.

Morgan, Susan. *In the Meantime: Character and Perception in Jane Austen's Fiction.* Chicago: University of Chicago Press, 1980.

Mudrick, Marvin K. *Jane Austen: Irony as Defense and Discovery.* Princeton: Princeton University Press, 1952.

Nokes, David. *Jane Austen: A Life.* London: Fourth Estate, 1997.

Page, Norman. *The Language of Jane Austen.* Oxford: Oxford University Press, 1972.

Sales, Roger. *Jane Austen and Representations of Regency England.* London: Routledge, 1994.

Selwyn, David. *Jane Austen and Leisure.* London: Hambledon Press, 1999.

Southam, B. C., ed. *Jane Austen: The Critical Heritage,* 2 vols. London: Routledge and Kegan Paul, 1968–87.

Sutherland, Kathryn. *Jane Austen's Textual Lives: From Aeschylus to Bollywood.* Oxford: Oxford University Press, 2005.

Tandon, Bharat. *Jane Austen and the Morality of Conversation.* London: Anthem Press, 2003.

Tanner, Tony. *Jane Austen.* Basingstoke, UK: Macmillan, 1986.

Thompson, James. *Between Self and World: The Novels of Jane Austen.* University Park: Pennsylvania State University Press, 1988.

Todd, Janet, ed. *Jane Austen in Context.* Cambridge: Cambridge University Press, 2005.

Troost, Linda, and Sayre Greenfield, eds. *Jane Austen in Hollywood.* Lexington: University of Kentucky Press, 1998.

Tuite, Clara. *Romantic Austen: Sexual Politics and the Literary Canon.* Cambridge: Cambridge University Press, 2002.

Waldron, Mary. *Jane Austen and the Fiction of Her Time.* Cambridge: Cambridge University Press, 1999.

Wiltshire, John. *Jane Austen and the Body: "The Picture of Health."* Cambridge: Cambridge University Press, 1992.

Illustration Credits

M. Darly (after R. St. G. Mansergh), "Matthew Manna, a country apothecary outside his shop," 1783. Wellcome Library, London, 16094i. *48*

"The Village Doctor Besieg'd," c. 1800. Wellcome Library, London, 10978i. *48*

Engraving after Francis Hayman, "Playing the Game at Quadrille, after an Original Painting in Vauxhall Gardens," c. 1750. Courtesy of The Lewis Walpole Library, Yale University, image ID lwlpr01405. *50*

Alderney cow, from George Vassey, *A Monograph of the Genus Bos* (London: J. R. Smith, 1857), p. 189. From the collections of the Ernst Mayr Library, Museum of Comparative Zoology, Harvard University. *57*

Portrait of Oliver Goldsmith after Joshua Reynolds, 1769–1770. National Portrait Gallery, NPG 828. Copyright National Portrait Gallery. *58*

Title page of first edition of Vicesimus Knox, *Elegant Extracts* (London: C. Dilly, 1770). Courtesy of Houghton Library, Harvard University. *63*

Cassandra Austen, watercolor and pencil portrait of Jane Austen, c. 1810. Copyright National Portrait Gallery. *66*

Portrait of Samuel Taylor Coleridge by Peter Vandyke, 1795. National Portrait Gallery, NPG 192. Copyright National Portrait Gallery. *69*

Miniature of Jane Austen's cousin Eliza Hancock (de Feuillide), c. 1780. By kind permission of Tibbie Adams. *76*

Image of a page from Austen's music MSS at Jane Austen's House Museum, Chawton Cottage. Jane Austen's House Museum, Jane Austen Memorial Trust. *83*

James Gillray, "High Change in Bond Street," 1796. Library of Congress, LC-USZC4-8766. *86*

Portrait of Mary Wollstonecraft by John Opie, 1790–1791. Tate Collection, NO1167. Copyright Tate, London, 2012. *97*

James Gillray, "A pig in a poke. Whist, whist," 1788. National Portrait Gallery, NPG D12392. Copyright National Portrait Gallery. *99*

Title page from contemporary collection of riddles, perhaps "Peter Puzzlewell," *A Choice Collection of Riddles, Charades, Rebusses*, &c. (London: E. Newbery, 1792). Courtesy of Houghton Library, Harvard University. *103*

Engraving of Steventon Rectory from J. E. Austen-Leigh, *A Memoir of Jane Austen* (London: R. Bentley, 1870). Courtesy of Houghton Library, Harvard University. *117*

Photograph of Chawton Cottage, showing proximity to main road. Photograph by Bharat Tandon. *118*

Vincent Van Gogh, "Small House on a Road with Pollard Willows," 1881. Collection Kröller-Müller Museum, Otterlo, The Netherlands. *123*

John Hassell, "Payne's Hill [Painshill, Cobham], the seat of Lady Carhampton," 1822. Copyright of Surrey History Centre, 6985/6. Reproduced by permission of Surrey History Centre. *128*

C. C. Coventry, *Royal Terrace from the Sea,* 1807. Courtesy of the Southend Museum. *134*

Temple West, "An address of thanks from the faculty to the Right Hon. Mr Influenzy for his kind visit to the country," 1803. Wellcome Library, London, 41. *137*

"View of Cromer from the West Cliff in the very early 1800s; ships in the offing, lighthouse and signal station on the hill and characters in the foreground," from Edmund Bartell, *Cromer Considered as a Watering Place* (1806). Cromer Museum, Norfolk, CRRMU: CP3162. Cromer Museum, Norfolk Museums. *139*

Watercolor of Jane Austen by her sister, Cassandra, painted about 1802. Private collection. *141*

Photograph of three volumes of *Emma* (London: John Murray, 1815). Courtesy of Houghton Library, Harvard University. *153*

Title page of John Clark, *Observations on Fevers* (London: T. Cadell, 1780). Courtesy of Houghton Library, Harvard University. *159*

View of Weymouth from the Look-out, taken May 1812, published June 25, 1813, by I. W. Upham, Weymouth. British Library, shelfmark: Maps K. Top. 12.12.b . Copyright The British Library Board. *179*

Robert Cruikshank, "Comparative Anatomy or The Dandy Tribe," 1818. British Museum, BM 13068. Copyright The Trustees of the British Museum. *183*

W. H. Pyne, "Worcester and London Royal Mail," from *The Costume of Great Britain* (London: William Miller, 1808), plate 54. Courtesy of Houghton Library, Harvard University. *187* and *332*

Thomas Rowlandson, *The Comforts of Bath*, plate 10: "The Ball" (London, 1798). Courtesy of Houghton Library, Harvard University. *191*

Facsimile of an Austen family letter, showing crossing. Jane Austen's House Museum, Jane Austen Memorial Trust. *192*

William Daniell, *The Harbour Lighthouse at Holyhead Port,* 1813. British Library digital image, filename c13872-76, source G.7043, plate 23. Copyright The British Library Board. *197*

William Redmore Bigg (1755–1828), *The Romps* (oil on canvas). Copyright Leeds Museums and Art Galleries (Temple Newsam House) UK / The Bridgeman Art Library. *205*

Portrait of Charles Lamb by William Hazlitt, 1804. National Portrait Gallery, NPG 507. Copyright National Portrait Gallery. *209*

Illustration of a spencer, c. 1807. Copyright Victoria and Albert Museum, London. *210*

"The Great Roman Bath, Bath," nineteenth-century photograph, English photographer. Private collection/Stapleton Collection/Bridgeman Art Library International. *213*

"The Linen Draper," from *The Book of English Trades; and Library of the Useful Arts* (London: Richard Phillips, 1818), opp. p. 226. Science, Industry, and Business Library, The New York Public Library, Astor, Lenox, and Tilden Foundations. *217*

Chromo/litho of "The White Hart, Bath, in the Old Coaching Time," c. 1870. Bath Central Library, 10822. *225*

Photograph of espalier fruit trees at Temple Newsam Park, Yorkshire, by Humphrey Bolton, licensed for reuse through Creative Commons. *227*

Photograph of The Wheatsheaf, North Waltham, by Bharat Tandon. *236*

"Modifications of the Beaver Hat," from Horace T. Martin, *Castorologia, or the History and Traditions of the Canadian Beaver* (London: Edward Stanford, 1892), opp. p. 124. Harvard University, Widener Library, KF 27957. *239*

Regency period folding screen with foliate cresting, c. 1815, mahogany, English School. Private collection/photo © Christie's Images/Bridgeman Art Library International. *247*

Title page from Edmund Hoyle, *A Short Treatise on the Game of Piquet* (London: F. Cogan, 1744). Courtesy of Houghton Library, Harvard University. *249*

Illustration of a Broadwood square piano, c. 1813. Photograph kindly supplied by Lucy Coad. *252*

Illustration of a Broadwood grand piano, 1801. Photograph kindly supplied by Lucy Coad. *253*

Mezzotint portrait of John Broadwood by William Say after John Harrison, Jr., 1812. National Portrait Gallery, NPG D32157. Copyright National Portrait Gallery. *254*

Franz Xaver Wagenschön, *Marie-Antoinette at the Spinet,* 1768. Courtesy of Kunsthistorisches Museum, Vienna. *255*

Instructions for steps, from T. Wilson, *An Analysis of Country Dancing* (London: W. Calvert, 1808), pp. 10–11. Courtesy of Houghton Library, Harvard University. *267*

Title / frontispiece of John Playford, *The English Dancing Master* (London: Thomas Harper, 1651). Courtesy of Houghton Library, Harvard University. *269*

J. M. W. Turner, *Frosty Morning,* exhibited 1813. Tate Collection, N00492. Copyright Tate, London, 2012. *271*

David Wilkie, *The Village Holiday,* 1809–1811. Tate Collection, N00122. Copyright Tate, London, 2012. *271*

Illustration of apples from George Brookshaw, *Pomona Britannica, or, A Collection of the Most Esteemed Fruits at Present Cultivated in Great Britain*, 2 vols. (London: Bensley and Son, 1817), vol. 2, plate LV. Courtesy of Houghton Library, Harvard University. *277*

Portrait of Johann Baptist Cramer by George Lethbridge Saunders, 1827. National Portrait Gallery, NPG 5190. Copyright National Portrait Gallery. *282*

Portrait of Thomas Moore, unknown artist, c. 1800–1805. National Portrait Gallery, NPG 1340. Copyright National Portrait Gallery. *283*

Portrait of Lady Caroline Keppel by Joshua Reynolds, 1755. Reproduced by kind permission of His Grace the Duke of Bedford and the Trustees of the Bedford Estates. *285*

J. Pass, "Two Types of Measles," 1822. Science and Society Picture Library, image 10436470. Courtesy of Science and Society Picture Library, Science Museum, London. *292*

"Richmond-Bridge, Surrey," June 1801, by John Walker. Harvard Art Museums/Fogg Museum, John Witt Randall Fund, R76NA. *296*

Black basalt bust of Seneca by Josiah Wedgwood and Sons, c. 1774–1820. Victoria and Albert Museum, 291-1866. Copyright Victoria and Albert Museum, London. *299*

Facsimile of Paper X from the "Mad Papers," in Samuel Richardson, *Clarissa*, 3rd ed., 8 vols. (London: Samuel Richardson, 1751), vol. 5, letter 36, p. 308. Courtesy of Houghton Library, Harvard University. *305*

Illustration of a barouche-landau, from *Le Beau Monde, or Literary and Fashionable Magazine*, vol. 1, November 1806. Copyright Victoria and Albert Museum, London. *312*

The Poems of Thomas Gray, Design 107, "Elegy Written in a Country Church-Yard," illustration by William Blake. Yale Center for British Art, Paul Mellon Collection. *321*

Miniature of Tom Lefroy by G. Engleheart, 1799. Private collection, UK. *336*

Thomas Sully, *Lady with a Harp: Eliza Ridgely,* oil on canvas, 1818. NGA, 1945.9.1. Gift of Maude Monell Vetlesen. Image courtesy of the National Gallery of Art, Washington, D.C. *340*

"Clifton and the Hot Wells," from *A Guide to All the Watering and Sea-Bathing Places* (London: Richard Phillips, 1803), opp. p. 93. Courtesy of Harvard University Library, Widener Library, KC 11549. *347*

Hymenaus Disguised as a Woman during an Offering to Priapus by Nicolas Poussin, 1634–1638. São Paolo Museum of Art. Óleo sobre tela, 167 X 376 cm. Coleção MASP, Museu de Arte de São Paulo Assis Chateaubriand. Fotografia: João L. Musa. *348*

Hymenaeus by Sir Edward Burne-Jones, oil and gold leaf on panel. Delaware Art Museum, DAM 1935-2. Delaware Art Museum, Wilmington / Samuel and Mary R. Bancroft Memorial / Bridgeman Art Library International. *349*

Portrait of John Locke by Godfrey Kneller, 1697. The State Hermitage Museum, St Petersburg. Photograph copyright The State Hermitage Museum / photo by Vladimir Terebenin, Leonard Kheifets, Yuri Molodkovets. *354*

Illustrations of the proposal scene, *Emma* (London: Richard Bentley, 1833), frontispiece. Courtesy of Houghton Library, Harvard University. *355* and *479*

Anonymous, "View of Manchester Square's north side," 1813. City of London, London Metropolitan Archives, Pr.M / MAN. *360*

Portrait of Samuel Johnson by Joshua Reynolds, 1756–1757. National Portrait Gallery, NPG 1597. Copyright National Portrait Gallery. 363

Robert Smirke, illustration of Aladdin and the genie from *The Arabian Nights*, trans. Edward Forster, 4 vols. (London: William Miller, 1802), vol. 4, p. 338. Courtesy of Houghton Library, Harvard University. *367*

Thomas Gainsborough, *Gypsy Encampment, Sunset,* c. 1778–1780. Tate Collection, N05803. Copyright Tate, London, 2012. *376*

James Sowerby, "*Fragaria vesca*: wood strawberry," from *English Botany*, vol. 22, plate 1524. Harvard University, Widener Library, KF 28122. *407*

George Brookshaw, *Pomona Britannica, or, A Collection of the Most Esteemed Fruits at Present Cultivated in Great Britain*, 2 vols. (London: Bensley and Son, 1817), vol. 1, plate 1. Courtesy of Houghton Library, Harvard University. *408*

Humphry Repton, images of "unimproved" and "improved" designs for West Wycombe, from *Observations on the Theory and Practice of Landscape Gardening* (London: J. Taylor, 1803), opp. p. 34. Courtesy of Houghton Library, Harvard University. *409*

John Constable, *Dedham Vale* (1802). Victoria and Albert Museum, 124-1888. Copyright Victoria and Albert Museum, London. *412*

Portrait of Byron by Richard Westall, 1813. National Portrait Gallery, NPG 4243. Copyright National Portrait Gallery. *413*

Photograph of late eighteenth- / early nineteenth-century cameo. Copyright Victoria and Albert Museum, London. *414*

J. M. W. Turner, *Childe Harold's Pilgrimage: Italy*, exhibited 1832. Tate Gallery, N00516. Copyright Tate, London, 2012. *417*

Mr.s Frances O'Neill, "The First Acrostic. A Description of the Morning," from *Poetical Essays* (London: A. Young, 1802), p. 56. *423*

Portrait of Francis Hutcheson by Allan Ramsay, c. 1740–1745; Copyright © The Hunterian, University of Glasgow, 2012. GLAHA 44025. *426*

"Kings-Weston, Gloucestershire," engraving by John Walker after Francis Nicholson, May 1799; *The Copper-Plate Magazine*, vol. 4; no. LXXXVIII, plate CLXXVI. Harvard Art Museums/Fogg Museum, John Witt Randall Fund, R720NA. Photo: Imaging Department © President and Fellows of Harvard College. *435*

Walking dress (color litho), English School, nineteenth century / Fashion Museum, Bath and North East Somerset Council / The Bridgeman Art Library. *438*

Martin Rowson, detail: "If the fixture of Momus' glass . . . every day of our lives," from *The Life and Opinions of Tristram Shandy, Gentleman* (London and Basingstoke: Picador, 1996), vol. 1. Copyright Martin Rowson, used by permission. *442*

Robert Home (1752–1834), *Portrait of the Irwin Sisters* (oil on canvas). Copyright Royal Hospital Chelsea, London, UK / The Bridgeman Art Library. *449*

Alicia Silverstone as Cher from Amy Heckerling's film *Clueless* (1995). *457*

"A General View of Bath," from *Bath Illustrated by a Series of Views,* engraved by John Hill (1770–1850) after John Claude Nattes (c. 1765–1822). Private Collection / The Stapleton Collection / The Bridgeman Art Library. *463*

Fanny Austen-Knight (1793–1882), watercolor on paper of Cassandra Austen (c. 1772–1845) / Private Collection / The Bridgeman Art Library. *465*

From *Emma* (1898), opp. p. 444. Courtesy of Houghton Library, Harvard University. *479*

Joseph Highmore, "Mr B. Finds Pamela Writing" (1743–1744). Tate Collection, N03573. Copyright Tate, London, 2012. *484*

Portrait engraving of Anthony Ashley Cooper, Third Earl of Shaftesbury (1671–1713) by Simon Gribelin after John Closterman, 1723. National Portrait Gallery, NPG 16247. Copyright National Portrait Gallery. *494*

"Fellow Feeling" (London: Edward Orme, 1810). Wellcome Library, London, L0015067. *501*

Contemporary illustration of a woman with a reticule, "Half Dress" from *Ackermann's Repository of Arts*, first series, January 1812. Photograph © 2012 Museum of Fine Arts, Boston. *502*

Samuel Howitt, "The Hare and Many Friends," from *A New Work of Animals: principally designed from the fables of Aesop, Gay, and Phaedrus* (London: Edward Orme, 1809–1811). Courtesy of Houghton Library, Harvard University. *507*

Portrait of Madame de Genlis by Labille-Guiard, 1790. LA County Museum of Art. Digital Image © Museum Associates / LACMA. Licensed by Art Resource, NY. *511*

The "Durham Ox," color engraving by J. Wessel, after John Boultbee, 1802. Private collection / Bridgeman Art Library International. *523*

Photograph of scale model of Jethro Tull's 1701 seed drill. Science Museum, London, image 10301394. Courtesy of Science and Society Picture Library, Science Museum, London. *524*

A. C. Pugin and Thomas Rowlandson, "Astley's Amphitheatre," from *Rudolph Ackermann, The Microcosm of London* (London: R. Ackermann, 1808), vol. 1, between pp. 22 and 23. Courtesy of Houghton Library, Harvard University. *530*

Gwyneth Paltrow as Emma and Jeremy Northam as Knightley in Douglas McGrath's film *Emma* (1996). *532*

Acknowledgments

I am grateful to the students with whom I have studied Austen over the years at Cambridge and Oxford, who have continually proven with great aplomb that there is always something new to be said about the novels, and always something new for teachers of Austen to learn.

St. Anne's College and Lady Margaret Hall, Oxford, provided stimulating environments in which to prepare this edition and its annotations, and the staff at the Bodleian and British Libraries offered valuable assistance as I compiled and corrected the copy-text and sourced the illustrations.

My editor at Harvard University Press, John Kulka, has been exemplary in his support for and encouragement of the project, as well as in his advice on the final revisions. I also owe a debt of gratitude to my readers at HUP, whose cogent suggestions sharpened both my introduction and the commentary.

In addition, I would like to thank the following individuals for their contributions; whether in terms of direct assistance or more general encouragement, this edition would not exist as it does without them: Tibbie Adams, Helen Barr, Lucy Coad, Karen Collis, Robert Douglas-Fairhurst, Lindsay Duguid, Christine Foard, Kendal Gaw, Christine Gerrard, Vincent Gillespie, Erin Goeres, Siân Grønlie, Katie Halsey, Judith Hibbert, Natalie Hudson, Heather Hughes, Kevin Jackson, Angie Johnson, Freya Johnston, Deirdre Le Faye, Matthew Leigh, Ruth Maclennan, Thomas Marks, John McTague, Elio Messimeris, Tassia Messimeris, Lauren Monaghan-Pisano, Marley Monteiro, Ann Pasternak Slater, Ian Patterson, Seamus Perry, Adrian Poole, James Purdon, Sophie Ratcliffe, Lucy Razzall, Noam Reisner, Matthew Reynolds, Helen Small, Keith Stretten, Kathryn Sutherland, Asha Tandon, Bipin Tandon, Felix Tandon, Mini Tandon, Leela Tandon-Stretten, Max Tandon-Stretten, Julie Taylor, Christine Thorsteinsson, Janet Todd, David Trotter, Christopher Vilmar, Freydis Welland, Philip West, and James Wood.